THE COZY CORGI COZY MYSTERIES

COLLECTION FOUR: BOOKS 10-12

MILDRED ABBOTT

Cover, Logo, Chapter Heading Designer: A.J. Corza - SeeingStatic.com

Main Editor: Desi Chapman

2nd Editor: Ann Attwood

3rd Editor: Corrine Harris

Recipe and photo provided by: Rolling Pin Bakery, Denver, Co. - RollingPinBakeshop.com

Recipe and photo (Killer Keys only) provided by: Baldpate Inn, Estes Park, Co. - The Baldpate Inn

Visit Mildred's Webpage: MildredAbbott.com

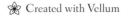 Created with Vellum

COZY CORGI COZY MYSTERIES BOOKS 10-12

Killer Keys
Perilous Pottery
Ghastly Gadgets

CONTENTS

KILLER KEYS

PERILOUS POTTERY

GHASTLY GADGETS

for
Nancy Drew
Phryne Fisher
and
Julia South

A Cozy Corgi Mystery

Killer Keys

MILDRED ABBOTT

KILLER KEYS

Mildred Abbott

for
Lois Smith
&
the Baldpate Inn

A knot began to form in my shoulders from gripping the steering wheel so tightly as I focused on Saint Vrain's twisting path, taking us ever higher into the mountains. Though it was only midafternoon, with the heavy clouds and the snowfall, the sun was little more than a hint of a glow behind the clouds that continued to grow heavier and heavier throughout the day. The town of Estes Park below us was nothing more than mist.

Even with the tension and concentration required for the treacherous roads, a sense of relaxed happiness washed over me. A weekend away! Though I was living my dream life, owning a perfect little bookshop in a gorgeously charming Colorado town, it had been forever since I'd had anything resembling a vacation. Maybe staying at an inn less than ten miles from my bookshop didn't technically qualify as a vacation, but I was going to count it nevertheless.

And I'd be surrounded by the people I loved the most. Life was good. So, so good.

The wintry scene of rugged peaks and jagged valleys filled with forests of pine and aspen covered in a thick blanket of snow was nothing short of spectacular. Despite the growing winter storm adding an ominous layer over the scene, I let out a long, contented sigh.

A pained grunt answered from the back seat of the Mini Cooper. I dared a glance from the winding, snow-covered mountain road to inspect the rearview mirror.

"Everything okay back there?"

Katie attempted a smile. "I'm regretting every single tr —" Her eyes went wide barely catching herself. "*T. R. E. A. T.* that I've made for our furry friend here. I never thought this sentence would leave my mouth, but I think it's diet time."

My overly *fluffy* corgi, Watson, paid the insult no mind and continued to shove his weight against Katie's lap in his attempt to wedge himself between the front seats of the car.

"I know you're excited to see me, little man, but we've got two whole nights together! There'll be plenty of bonding time." Beside me, Leo Lopez twisted around, simultaneously patting Watson and helping nudge his hearty backside off Katie's lap. "But if you crush our favorite baker, that's going to put a damper on the weekend."

Katie took a relieved breath, freed from Watson's... fluff... and swatted at Leo. "And if our favorite park ranger didn't have obnoxiously long legs, *he* could've squeezed himself in the back of the Mini Cooper and this whole situation would be avoided."

"Can't help how the good Lord made me." Stretching farther, Leo ruffled the fur between Watson's ears and then did the same to Katie's brown curls, earning himself another swat. "Plus, did I mention that I have claustrophobia issues?"

"Really?" Katie's tone held a glower. "Did I imagine sitting through a twenty-minute slideshow of your spelunking trip in New Zealand from a few years ago?"

Leo turned back around, chuckling. "That was different. I wasn't going to pass up my chance to see the *arachnocampa luminosa*."

Katie grunted again as Watson made yet another attempt to get to Leo. "Just because you know the fancy word for glowworm doesn't mean you're not riding in the back seat on the way home."

Overpowering a claustrophobic wave of my own at the idea of wedging through a tight dark cave miles below the surface of the earth, my contentment grew at my friends' bickering.

Leo had been gone during the first two weeks of January, visiting his family since he'd worked in the national park during Christmas. I'd missed him, maybe not with Watson's frantic enthusiasm, but... I cast another quick glance away from the road, taking in Leo's handsome features as he twisted back, making some comment to Katie once more. Before the holidays, I could've convinced myself I'd only missed him as a friend. Or at least enough that I would have been able to avoid looking much deeper. I couldn't do that anymore. And the awareness of his presence made my skin tingle to such a degree I marveled the two of them didn't pick up on it. Or knowing Katie and Leo, they probably did.

"Slow down." That time, it was Katie leaning up between the front seats, ducking her head so she could have a better view through the windshield. "I haven't driven up here very often, but I think this is one of my favorite formations in Estes Park."

Though I was already going slowly due to the ice on the road, I eased off the gas a little more, and the three of us stared at the rocky cliffs surrounding the road, towering at least fifty feet above our heads. Directly in front of us, a tall, narrow opening cut through the rock like the eye of a needle, allowing us passage. It truly was breathtaking. "The last time I drove through it, I couldn't help but think that Watson and I were traveling into Narnia. I almost expected Aslan to be on the other side."

Katie snorted. "Instead you went to the home of the White Witch, and you weren't even turned to stone. It was a Christmas miracle."

"Oh, come on now." Though Leo clearly meant it as a reprimand, there was still humor in his tone. "Susan's not *that* bad."

"Surprisingly no, she isn't." I still couldn't believe the abrasive police officer lived in what almost equated to a storybook cottage. "However, ten to one, if she has trouble sleeping this weekend, she'll blame us for being so close to her house." As I spoke, we passed through the opening, and even though we hadn't actually entered a magical realm on the other side, the snowstorm did seem to increase instantly, the flurries making it harder to see through the windshield.

"They said it was going to be bad. Looks like they weren't wrong."

At the sound of concern in Leo's voice, I glanced his way. "Are you worried about the park?"

"No. Nadiya and the others have it under control, and it's not like there's anything I can do about the weather anyway. The animals take care of themselves." He studied the swirling mass of silver and gray in front of us. "Although, this is the longest I've been gone from the park since I moved to Estes. Feels a little strange. But when Percival and Gary asked me to attend, and it lined up so perfectly with the end of my trip, I wasn't about to say no."

And there was that tingling sensation over my skin once more. Every person taking part in the weekend anniversary celebration for my uncles was either family or longtime friends of Percival and Gary. Leo was the exception. They cared about him, but it wasn't like Gary and Percival ever hung out with Leo on their own. And he wasn't exactly considered family the way Katie was, either. He was something in the middle, something… different. The fact that my uncles had invited him to the anniversary party was a kind gesture, but it also lacked any subtlety, which was exactly what I would expect from Percival.

"There it is. On the left." Katie nudged my shoulder. "That's it, isn't it?"

Thankful for the distraction, I shoved thoughts of Leo and the obvious "setup" aside and followed where Katie pointed. "Good catch. I would've driven right past it." The carved wooden sign that read *Baldpate Inn* over the image of an old-fashioned key was nearly buried in the snow, as was the sharp turn from the highway into the trees.

"Good thing this baby does so good with winter weather." I patted the Mini Cooper's dashboard as I turned left. "But hold on, nevertheless."

Despite the snow tires, we fishtailed slightly over the ice as we rounded the corner and entered the lane cut between the tall trees.

Katie let out a little cry of surprise, and Watson took advantage of her distraction, gave a giant leap, and proved that despite his added padding, he could still claim moments of athleticism as he flung himself over the console between the front seats. His head banged my elbow, causing me to twist the wheel and send the car into a spin.

Gasping, I gripped tighter and used all my willpower to turn into the spin instead of the opposite way, as the trees blurred around us. After the first revolution, we'd slowed enough that I cranked the wheel slightly and hit the gas once more, and we shot off in our original direction.

Almost disbelieving, I glanced around, then sent Watson a glare. "If you kill your mama and her baker best friend, that's greatly going to impact the amount of treats you get."

Despite being wedged between the seats and grunting while Leo pulled him through and onto his lap, Watson issued a pleading whimper at the sound of his favorite word.

"Don't even think about it, buddy." I didn't bother looking at him, and only then realized my hands were trembling from the adrenaline.

Leo locked his arms around my corgi, not that he needed to bother. Now that Watson was on his lap, there was nowhere else he wanted to be. "That was impressive, Fred. If the whole bookselling and sleuthing thing doesn't work out, you can always be a racecar driver."

"No kidding." Though Katie sounded impressed, there was a waver in her voice that matched the shaking of my hands. "Don't take this the wrong way, but despite your skill, I think I'm never going to ride with you again. This is the second time we've almost died in one of your Mini Coopers."

Before I could comment on that, Baldpate Inn emerged, towering over us like a mirage in the snow.

"Wow!" Awe filled Leo's voice as he leaned over Watson to get a better view. "That is stunning."

"You've not been here before?"

He didn't look at me as he shook his head, completely focused on the old hotel. "No. I've heard about it, just haven't ever made my way up here."

"I haven't been here since I was a kid. We'd always come up here to eat when we'd visit my grandparents. It was one of my grandmother's favorite places." I slowed to a crawl, both because of the winter weather and simply to enjoy the sight.

"I've been reading about it," Katie piped up happily from the back.

Leo and I exchanged a quick, knowing glance. Katie was notorious for her Google binges.

"It's a century old and was named after a book. There's been a couple of plays and a movie based off it." Katie continued, either not noticing or not caring about Leo's smirk. "There's a tradition of hiring international students to staff the place, giving it a cosmopolitan kind of feel. And there's a collection of thousands and thousands of keys. In fact..." Katie's words trailed away to a wistful sigh as we drew nearer.

The century-old Baldpate Inn looked like a massive combination between a log cabin and a Swiss chalet. It had been built on the slope of the mountain, and nestled back into the trees. Its covered front porch jutted over the driveway, supported by massive logs. Smoke billowed from the chimneys, giving the large mansion structure a cozy, welcoming feel—a literal safe haven from the blizzard.

"Looks like we're the last ones here." I parked the Mini Cooper at the end of a long row of cars, each one belonging to a different member of my family.

"Sorry about that. I think after driving across the country the past couple days, my Jeep just decided it'd had enough."

"I didn't mean it like that. We're not late or anything. I'm glad you caught Katie and me before we left, so we were able to pick you up." Unbuckling my seat belt, I turned to Leo, hating the guilt I heard in his voice. "More, I meant it as a warning. We should all take a couple deep breaths now, because the minute we walk in there, we've got my whole crazy family to deal with. There's not going to be a moment's rest until the weekend is over."

He grinned, honey-brown eyes twinkling as he looked over at me, even as Watson lathered the underside of his jaw with kisses. "Knowing your uncles, it will be unforgettable."

"Don't let Percival hear you say that. Unforgettable doesn't cover it. Fabulous. He's been very adamant that the weekend is going to be *fabulous*," Katie piped up with a laugh, then shoved against the back of my seat. "Now, no more chitchat. Get out of this car. I feel like *I'm* the one who's been spelunking in New Zealand." She reached over and shoved Leo for good measure. "And if my leg cramps when I try to unfold from this pretzel shape I've had to be in, you're going to carry me, Smokey Bear. Put those muscles and long legs to some use."

Despite the building blizzard, I couldn't help but feel like I was slipping back nearly thirty years into my past as we made our way up the log staircase that opened to the expansive deck running along the front of Baldpate Inn. Though I barely spared a glance due to the cold, I could easily recall sitting at the edge of the railing with my grandmother, looking out over the panorama of mountains and the ant-sized version of Estes Park far below while scores of hummingbirds swarmed around us. Strange that I hadn't returned to the place since I moved. Even though the hummingbird feeders were empty and the birds themselves were surely tucked away in hibernation—or had flown south for the winter, I wasn't sure; I'd have to ask Leo—the place felt magical, just like when I'd been a child. No wonder Percival and Gary had wanted to have their anniversary here.

Leo barely cracked open the front door of the inn before Watson darted inside as if he was on the verge of turning into an ice sculpture.

Katie followed him, chuckling. "The only one of us wearing an actual fur coat, and you'd think the poor thing was a hairless cat on an iceberg."

"Not to mention"—I smiled in thanks at Leo as I

stepped past him into the warmth—"the added layers of insulation he's accumulated over the past year, *not* that I'm in any place to judge."

Leo closed the door, ushering in a last flurry of snow, and the three of us paused in the entryway. The magical feeling evaporated in the sense of tension that filled the space.

In front of us was an old-time check-in counter, complete with little cubicles on the back wall for each room. To the left, were the two rooms that made up the dining space, and on the right, seated in the overstuffed sofas arranged in front of the roaring river rock fireplace, was the source of the negative energy.

I nearly chuckled at the thought. *Negative energy.* Living close to my mother once more must've been having an effect.

My twin stepsisters, Verona and Zelda, bookended their four children on the couches, their husbands, Jonah and Noah standing nearby, looking uncomfortable. Beyond them, standing in the doorway that led to two other rooms of the inn was my mother, stepfather, and Carl and Anna Hanson, who owned a high-end home furnishings store across from my bookshop.

The negative energy—I couldn't think of a more apt descriptor—radiated from my nieces and nephews. Ocean and Brittany, both fifteen, sat sullen-faced with their arms crossed. Leaf, who was nine, was red-faced, and from the streaks running down his' cheeks, it appeared we'd just missed a breakdown of epic proportions. Beside him, Christina, who was also nine, glanced up, and though she looked equally as devastated as Leaf, she cracked a small smile and twinkled her fingers toward Watson.

For his part, Watson didn't notice, instead giving a

forlorn look up at Leo, as if apologizing for what he was about to do, and then issued a happy bark as he tore off across the space to collide into my stepfather's shins.

Barry's laugh broke the tension, at least somewhat, and he knelt to accept Watson's worshipful greeting. "Perfect timing, my furry little friend. We needed to be reminded of what matters."

Mom smiled at the sight of us and began to cross the room, but Leaf's wail cut her short. "Can't we just go home and get the—"

"If you ask that one more time, you won't see electronics again until you're in high school." Verona's bark caused me to flinch. She was slightly more serious than her sister, Zelda, but I'd never heard her snap like that toward any of the children. She careened around, offering a similar expression to her husband. "This is *your* fault, your obsession with electronics and gadgets and gizmos. I said I didn't want any of that stuff in my house, and now look at us. Five minutes being unplugged and it's a complete meltdown, making the entire family miserable."

Jonah blushed and stuffed his hands into his pockets, but didn't offer any more of a reply.

"Verona, let's just—" Zelda attempted a soothing tone, but didn't finish the thought when Verona's gaze flashed back her way.

The gorgeous room fell back into awkward silence, save for Watson's happy whimpering at Barry's ministrations.

Verona continued to glare at the children and finally looked toward Katie, Leo, and me. After a second, she sighed, and her shoulders slumped. "Hi, you guys. Sorry you had to walk in on this."

The rest of the room relaxed as one, sensing the worst had passed.

"It's okay. We all have our moments." I gave what I hoped was a carefree shrug. "Not even half an hour ago, Watson threw a fit when he was relegated to the back seat of the Mini Cooper, so we understand."

Verona attempted a tight smile, and I noticed Zelda wince.

Sometimes I forgot parents didn't appreciate a comparison between child-rearing and pet-ownership. Well... whatever. They were just jealous. A corgi never threw a fit that held an entire room hostage.

"In all fairness, I threw a similar one when *I* was *relegated* to the back seat as well," Katie chimed in, nonplussed. She shoved Leo, clearly trying to lighten the mood. "*This one* claimed it's because of his long legs, but I say it's pure and blatant misogyny."

Playing along, Leo raised his hand. "Guilty as charged."

Verona finally cracked a smile, but sent another glare toward Leaf. "One more word about any of it, and I promise you, *anything* requiring electricity gets donated or recycled the second we get home." She glared for a few seconds, then turned back to us. "We warned the kids that we wouldn't have any cell reception here, so we were prepared. However—"

"There's no Wi-Fi or computer access at all," Zelda jumped in. "*That* we weren't prepared for."

"Wait a minute..." All humor left Katie's tone. "You're telling me there's *no* internet? *At all?*"

Ocean, Leaf's older brother, smirked, clearly recognizing a kindred spirit.

I laid a hand on Katie's shoulder, lest whatever she said next caused my nephews and nieces to revolt. "I'm sure you'll survive two nights without Google."

She didn't reply, but her expression said she wasn't so certain of that.

"I am sorry." A voice pulled our attention back to the check-in counter, where a middle-aged woman with soft blonde hair emerged from the door behind the counter. "With it being slow season, it was the perfect time. We decided to have the inn rewired for high-speed internet, wireless"—she fluttered a hand—"the whole nine yards. With the building as old as this, we knew it wouldn't be a simple process, but it's been a nightmare. It was supposed to be done before Christmas, but..." She shrugged. "Here we are. I'm even having to run credit cards manually. Had to dig out that old swipey-machine thing." She walked around the counter and extended a hand, eyes twinkling. "I'm Lisa Bloomberg, owner of Baldpate, and destroyer of online entertainment, it seems."

I liked her instantly. "Well, I understand how that goes. Katie and I have closed the bookshop and bakery while we have an elevator installed to the second floor. There haven't been any huge glitches, but it's not exactly over yet." We'd given our employees a skiing trip during the time off as a late Christmas present.

"Speaking of which..." Katie gave me a meaningful look. "We need to call the contractor and give him the hotel's number in case there're problems, since our cell phones don't have reception here. I didn't even think before we left." She turned back to Lisa. "Do you have a landline phone?"

"We do." Lisa's eyes twinkled. "Not everything is a hundred years old here at Baldpate." She glanced at the few bags Katie, Leo, and I carried. "You have more luggage in your car? I can send Luca and Beau out to get it."

"Oh no. This is all we brought. But thank you." Leo

glanced around, peering past the space into the room behind the glass French doors, the walls and beamed ceiling completely covered with keys. "I've never been here. This place is amazing."

"It is. Thank you." She grinned, pleased. "And I can say that with all humility since I'm not the one who built it, as I'm not a hundred years old either. I was actually getting ready to give a tour when..." She cast a hesitant glance toward the sofas, as if expecting another outburst. "Well, I can do that now as I show you three to your rooms."

"I would love that. I'm curious about the history of this place." Though Leo wasn't a native, his devotion to the national park had created a love of everything Estes Park.

"In a second." Mom finished her path across the room and pulled me down into a hug. "Good to see you, darling. It's beautifully bittersweet to be here again, isn't it?"

"It is. I think it'd make Grandma happy, everyone being together here again."

She patted my cheek before giving Katie and Leo welcoming embraces, as well.

The next minute or two was caught up in everyone greeting everyone. It was a beautiful aspect of living in a small town that I hadn't anticipated. We saw one another constantly, yet somehow, through all the events, celebrations, and bumping into one another, each and every time seemed special. Though sullen, even my nieces' and nephews' greetings were warm and sincere.

"We're missing some people. Where are the stars of the show?" I scanned the room again, realizing who else was missing besides my uncles. "And Gerald and Angus, they're supposed be here too, correct?"

Anna gave a long-suffering sigh. "Angus called Carl this morning. He and Gerald are driving up together, but of course..." She sighed again and judgment filled her voice. "They'll be running late because Gerald was finishing up his latest batch of kombucha. I swear that man ought to lose his license to practice law, considering—"

"Now, Anna," Carl broke in, "Gerald's a fine lawyer, and it's a free country. Just because..." His objection withered away under his wife's glare.

"And you know your uncles." Mom grabbed my hand as she lifted her voice, clearly jumping in before Anna could go on a tirade about all the reasons Gerald Jackson shouldn't be allowed to be a lawyer. And even though I was certain I'd agree with every item on the list, I was glad to avoid it. "They want to make an entrance." Mom chuckled. "Well... *Percival* anyway. They're staying in one of the separate cabins on the property—" She glanced toward Lisa.

"The Pinetop Sweetheart Cabin." Lisa waggled her eyebrows playfully. "It's like a little honeymoon suite, complete with a fireplace and a whirlpool."

"Oh..." Katie clucked, then continued in a swooning voice, "That's adorable, like a second honeymoon for Percival and Gary."

"Yes. Although, in this case, Percival is using it more as a cabin-sized closet. Never mind that we're only going to be here two nights. He brought enough clothes to have an outfit change every hour on the hour." Mom shook her head, grinning. "Which is exactly why they're not here yet. I'm sure Percival is primping for his grand arrival. Gary's probably watching football."

"No..." Lisa sounded hesitant. "The televisions are out of service as well."

One of the kids groaned in forlorn despondency, followed by Verona issuing a swift shushing sound.

"Don't you worry about it for a second." Mom patted

Lisa's arm. "I think it worked out wonderfully. Three days and two nights of nothing but family time and bonding. It's perfect."

"And if anyone gets bored, we have plenty to entertain us." Barry gave me a quick hug as Watson pranced happily back and forth between him and Leo. "Not to mention more wonderful food than we can possibly eat. Not that we aren't already used to that." He gave Katie a hug as well before offering one to Leo.

Within another five minutes, Lisa led Katie, Leo, and me on the tour. Mom, Barry, Anna, and Carl joined in. Zelda, Verona, and their families retired to their rooms, deciding to regroup before Percival and Gary made their entrance. Lisa directed us to a staircase that ran up along the far wall of the main room, and we headed upstairs, the old wooden steps creaking comfortingly under our weight. "Let's drop off your bags first." She motioned down the hallway to her left, and we all followed. She gestured toward a small room. "Mr. Lopez, this is you."

"We're right across the hall, dear." Mom tapped the old-fashioned doorknob of hers and Barry's room.

Barry chuckled. "Yes, in case you get scared in the middle of the night and have a bad dream, you can have Mom and Dad soothe you back to sleep."

Mom swatted at him. "You know what I mean. I know Leo's not a child."

Though Leo grinned, his gaze flicked to me, just for a second, and my heart... well... I didn't give my heart long enough to decide what it did exactly.

Lisa didn't pause as Leo dropped off his bag, and she headed to the end of the hallway to unlock the last door on the right. "Ms. Page, Ms. Pizzolato, this is your room."

"And we're right across the hall from you." Anna

sounded excited, as if she was envisioning late-night gossip sessions.

As we entered the room, Katie and I both paused. It hadn't been updated. It wasn't sleek-or-shiny modern. The walls were log, the floor was old planks, the ceiling exposed log beams. Between the two beds in the center of the long narrow room was an old porcelain sink.

"Oh, I love it." Katie sighed. "It's like we're staying in a Colorado version of *Little House on the Prairie*."

Lisa laughed, almost sounding relieved. "That's a new description; I like it. I'm glad you're pleased. Sometimes people are irritated when the rooms don't look like they just stepped into the Ritz."

Barry scoffed. "That would ruin the whole thing."

"I quite agree." Taking a cue from Watson, though I didn't follow his example of sniffing around the floor as he wandered around, I walked through the room, pausing by the bed to touch the beautiful patchwork quilts, tracing my finger over the golden key stitched in the center. "This is wonderful."

"Thank you. I made one for each bed in the inn." Pride filled Lisa's voice. "Keys are very important. Baldpate was inspired by the 1913 novel *Seven—*"

"*Seven Keys to Baldpate*." Katie, true to form, sounded like the girl in class jumping up and down in her seat while she raised her hand and answered the question before the teacher could even finish. "Seven strangers were given the keys to an old mountain hotel. It didn't end well for them. It's also been made into a couple of plays and a movie from the 1940s."

Lisa looked impressed. "You've read it?"

Katie flushed and I answered for her. "No, but Katie is a master of trivia." I slid my bag off my shoulder and placed it on the bed. "I started reading when Percival and Gary decided to have their anniversary here. It's kind of like an old-fashioned cozy murder mystery, though I must confess I have to keep reminding myself not to judge how women are described since the book was written over a hundred years ago."

"Yes, times change, thankfully." Lisa smiled again. "But I find it a lovely part of our history."

At that moment, the windows rattled, and the wind howled. Watson whimpered and scurried over to take his place beside me, a low growl emanating from his chest.

I moved across the room, Watson at my heels, and peered out. Though it was still before sunset, it was nearly dark outside, the scene little more than a grayish-white blur through the windows.

"Typically you'd have one of the best views from this room." Lisa moved beside me and peered out. "The way it sounds, you won't have much of a better view tomorrow. Maybe on the day you leave."

With our bags deposited, Lisa continued the tour, Leo joining us as we passed back in front of his room. She gestured down the hall that ran behind the stairs. "That's the staff wing. You may know this, but Baldpate prides itself on hosting international students, some of them here for college, others simply here to have an American experience for a year or so. Right now we have young adults from Germany, France, Holland, Italy, and England." She snickered. "And one from Arkansas, of all places. They're good kids, and I promise you they won't be loud or disruptive during the night. Most of them are taking a break right now before the party this evening, and the rest are cooking away."

The inn was shaped like a broken cross—a long center

hallway and then two jutting off on either side, one sitting a little farther back than the other. When we passed the steps, Lisa pointed. "The east wing has our other guest rooms. That's where the twins and their families are staying as well as Mr. Witt and Mr. Jackson when they arrive."

Once back downstairs, Lisa led us through the larger dining room. Baldpate was unique in that it didn't offer a menu of normal food items. It was simply an all-you-can-eat salad bar that was situated in an old cast-iron bathtub. It also hosted several varieties of homemade bread, an assortment of stews and soups, and made-from-scratch pies placed near an old iron stove in the middle of the room. I could practically feel Katie's sensation that she'd died and gone to heaven. The second dining space was adjacent to the first but attached through two sets of French doors. The closed-in porch was filled with rustic log tables, and the wall of windows that curved around the space showed just how ominous the storm was becoming.

"Once more, typically you can see Estes Park snuggled into the valley, the whole mountain range, and beyond." Lisa leaned in close to one of the windows. "I can't even see the trees on the other side of the driveway. It's been years since we've had a storm this bad."

Leo moved beside her, concern etching his face. "It seems like they were off on their predictions. It's a lot worse than what they told us. Doesn't look like it's even considering slowing down."

"Are you worried? Do you feel like you need to leave?" Without thinking, I stepped to him and put my hand on the back of his shoulder.

Leo flinched slightly and glanced toward his shoulder, then at me. Some expression I couldn't read crossed behind his eyes, but whatever it was lightened the concern that had been there. "No. There's nothing I can do. It simply is what it is. I just hope no one is foolish enough to go out in it."

I dropped my hand, wondering if anyone else had noticed the gesture.

Lisa continued the tour before I could check. "Now, if you'll follow me, I'll show you the key room. It's my favorite place in Baldpate." She led us back past the check-in counter and paused by the roaring fireplace. "Remind me to show you this later. Right now I don't want to interrupt the dinner preparations, but the fireplace is double-sided. If you pass through the door, you'll enter the staff lounge surrounded by the kitchen. But the key room is where—"

At that moment, the front door of the lodge burst open, followed by a whirlwind of snow.

Watson yelped, dashed underneath my skirt, and then poked his head out to begin barking.

Leo chuckled affectionately. "So brave."

"We're heeeerrrreeee!" Percival emerged through the blizzard, long, lanky arms lifted above his head as if he were Marilyn Monroe arriving at a star-studded gala. He did a little twirl, which fanned out the nearly floor-length tails of his white, rhinestone-encrusted tux jacket. The rest of his outfit, from the shoes, to the slacks, to the shirt, tie, and vest, to his top hat, were a deep wine-red purple. "Let the festivities begin!"

Percival's eyes narrowed as he glanced around the main room and peered behind him into the dining spaces, before looking back at us in accusation. "Where is everyone?" He did a quick finger-count. "Over half the group is missing."

Gary shut the door behind them, cutting off the billows of snow, then dusted the piles of flakes from the shoulders of his tux. He'd gone classic elegance and looked more handsome than I'd ever seen him. "I told you we should've called over and said we were arriving if you really wanted to make an entrance."

Percival considered and then scowled. "Well, it is what it is. I'm not going out there just to come back in. The snow is ruining my suede shoes."

"I told you suede wasn't a good—" Gary shut his mouth with Percival's second glare, then caught my bemused look from across the room and winked.

I adored the two of them. So different and yet perfectly matched.

Before anyone could respond, there was a clatter down the steps and my four nephews and nieces arrived, followed by Verona, Zelda, Noah, and Jonah. Thankfully, the tension they'd carried with them earlier seemed to have dissipated. Zelda halted at the base of the steps when she caught sight of Percival and Gary. "You're here! Look at you, aren't you both smashing!"

"I believe the word is *fabulous*," Leo blurted out, then went scarlet.

"Exactly so! And yes, we do, yes. Thanks for noticing." Percival barked out a laugh, and pointed at Leo before narrowing his eyes at the twins. "Even if you did spoil the entrance." When Gary shoved his shoulder, Percival smiled. "But... not a big deal. I plan on making more than *one* entrance this weekend." He stepped forward, opening both arms wide. "Thank you all for being here. It means the world to us to be surrounded by those we love. Now... lavish us with your affections."

The next several minutes were lost to another round of greetings, hugs, and congratulating Gary and Percival on their anniversary. The cold outside was forgotten, as well as the drama over no connection to the outside world as we fell into step being together.

Lisa cleared her throat to get our attention. "Dinner is on schedule, but we can wait for the others if you want. That's a good thing about a salad bar, it's flexible, and the soups and stews aren't going to be spoiled by simmering. We can get to the key room later."

Barry, who was kneeling by Watson, spoke up decisively. "I say we go ahead. We love Gerald, but even without a blizzard the man would be late to his own funeral."

"Doubly true since he's messing around with his demon liquor," Anna mumbled under her breath, but nudged Leo with her elbow. "You're law enforcement. Can't you do something about that?"

"Anna!" Carl hissed. "Stop that. It's not illegal, and it's not liquor."

Leo simply chuckled. "And I'm not exactly law enforcement. Unless Gerald is somehow using his homemade kombucha to poach protected species of wildlife, I think he's a little bit out of my jurisdiction."

Anna looked unsatisfied with that answer, but then her eyes brightened, and she smacked Carl's arm. "Oh, I just remembered. We left the treats we brought for Watson in the car. Go get them."

Carl gaped at the door, then back at her. "Right now? We're just getting ready to sit down to dinner, and there's a blizzard."

"Well, then I guess you should have remembered to bring them in the first place, shouldn't you? Surely you don't expect sweet little Watson to sit there in forlorn depression while we have dinner and he has nothing special?"

"Anna, it's okay. Trust me, Watson's not going to starve. There'll be some things he can—"

She cut me off with another swat at her husband. "The quicker you go, the quicker you'll return."

"Fine. Let me go get my jacket," Carl grumbled as he turned and trudged back up the steps.

I studied Anna for a second. She was always rather bossy with Carl, but it seemed a little mean, even for her.

As if feeling my gaze, Anna clapped her hands and lifted her voice. "I agree with Barry. Let's eat!"

Lisa waved us forward. "All right then, follow me." She led us from the place in front of the fire to the buffet spread out over ice in the clawfoot bathtub. "We have the salad bar with all the fixings, of course, and down here we've got our world-famous cornbread, loaves of honey-wheat bread, apple-raisin spice muffins, green-onion cream cheese muffins, and our Swiss knots." She walked toward the center of the room where three black kettle warmers were arranged on a separate table. "Tonight we have the Baldpate cowboy buffalo stew, red chili, and a broccoli cheese soup." Finally Lisa moved to another table filled with pies. "For dessert, there's a selection of Keyroom lime, coconut angel cream, chocolate cream, Baldpate rhubarb, Key pecan, and Scandinavian apple."

Beside me, Katie whimpered, then turned her wide brown eyes up at me. "How have you never brought me here?"

"I was wondering the same thing myself." I patted my stomach, the memory of the cornbread drifting back from childhood. "I think the next time we take a weekend away from the bookshop we might need to attend one of those diet camps."

A look of genuine utter horror flitted over Katie's face. "I think that's the ugliest thing I've ever heard you say."

Laughing, I threw an arm over her shoulder and gave her a squeeze. "And this is why we work, you and me."

Before long, we were all spread out over the small log tables that filled the glassed-in porch. The dining room was beautiful, but there was something lovely about being clustered together with the blizzard blowing outside as we lost ourselves to the warmth and comfort of delicious soups and stews and the yeasty perfection of the assortment of breads. At times when the blizzard softened just a bit, the twinkling lights of Estes Park could be seen far below.

Watson was in corgi heaven as he wandered from table to table and followed people around while they made trips back and forth from the buffet line, scooping up any scraps that fell quicker than any Hoover could boast.

Anna returned from her second trip to the salad bar, her plate laden with cornbread and muffins, and paused before she took her seat at the table behind Katie, Leo, and me. "I just realized, Carl still hasn't returned." She stepped closer to the window, pressing her hand against the glass and trying to peer down. "Maybe I shouldn't have sent him outside."

"Is he a heavy man, miss?" Our adorably young German waiter appeared from nowhere. "Glasses, and with a fuzzy beard?"

Anna turned slowly from the window, her hand lowering from the glass to rest on her girth. "He's *big-boned*, yes."

The waiter nodded enthusiastically, pointing out the window where Anna had been looking. "I noticed him in the parking lot a few minutes ago with two other men."

"Two other—" Her voice lowered. "Oh really. Were they drinking something?"

He nodded again. "Yes, ma'am."

She growled. "I'm going to murder him." Then she piped up, "What was your name, young man?"

"Luca, ma'am."

She patted his hand. "Well, Luca, keep an eye on that one for me and report back, and I'll make sure you get a special tip at the end of the weekend."

Impossibly, Luca brightened even further. "Yes, ma'am!"

Katie leaned into the table so only Leo and I could hear her. "What's up with Anna and her tirade against the kombucha?"

"Don't you remember? Gerald makes his kombucha with cannabis-infused tea." I cast my glance over to where Mom and Barry were seated with my uncles. Mom was aware that Barry liked to partake in edibles from time to time, but I didn't want to bring up any sore subjects.

"From the looks of things, it appears Gerald might be starting a war with Anna." Leo chuckled. "Good luck with that, buddy."

As if on cue, the front door burst open as Carl and Gerald tumbled in laughing and accompanied by a fresh gust of wind and snow. The more subdued owner of the knitting store downtown, Angus Witt, followed behind them, shutting the door once more.

Carl's laughter faded as he noticed Anna standing between the tables, hands on her hips. He cleared his throat and then lifted a cardboard box. "I was... helping them bring in their luggage."

"Sure you were." Anna folded her arms. "Did you even remember Watson's treats?"

Watson scurried over at the word, and Carl's face fell even further.

"That's okay! Believe me, Watson's fine. We all are." I jumped up before Anna could tell him to go back out into the snow. "Why don't the three of you grab some food and join the celebration?"

Anna looked like she was about to argue, but Percival intervened. "And hurry it up, you three. It's about time for speeches, and I don't want any of you to be deprived of telling me how wonderful I am." Mom swatted at her brother, and he sighed good-naturedly before kissing Gary on the cheek. "How wonderful *we* are, I mean, of course."

"In high school, I was desperately in love with the star quarterback." Percival stood at the table, a glass of champagne in one hand, his other on Gary's shoulder, and the blizzard raging behind his back. "Of course, he didn't know I was alive. Which is a good thing as he would've beat me to a pulp."

He laughed, and most of the room chuckled with him. I did as well, though I couldn't help but marvel at the strength and bravery my flamboyant, and often flighty, uncle possessed. I could only imagine what it would have been like going through high school in a small town as a gay kid over sixty years before.

"I never would've guessed I'd end up spending my life with an ex-pro-football player." Percival ran his hand over Gary's broad shoulders in a rare tender gesture, then he bugged his eyes and returned to his typical showmanship. "Somebody should've warned me how many hours I'd be forced to watch sports on television! Let this be a lesson, kids." He held his champagne flute aloft, and everyone clinked their glasses together.

"Ever the romantic." Gary stood, his low rumble of a voice barely audible over the howls of the wind outside. "My dad wanted me to marry one of the cheerleaders." He winked at Percival. "I came pretty close."

Percival shimmied his narrow shoulders, causing the light to glisten off the rhinestone-encrusted jacket, sending rainbows around the room. "I have no idea what you mean."

Gary laughed, and the adoration he felt for his husband, even after their decades together, was on full display. Then he turned toward the rest of us, growing slightly serious, his dark eyes flitting over the tables and then pausing at me. "I think the real lesson is to find someone who causes you to laugh, helps you feel safe, and makes breathing just a little bit easier." Then his gaze moved on, and his tone brightened as he launched into the story of when he and Percival first met.

I only half listened, trying to get my racing heart under

control, making sure that no emotion or nerves played over my face. I dropped my hand beside my chair, and sure enough, my fingertips found Watson's pointy fox ears waiting, and I stroked his head. He always knew when I needed him. And like every time before, just his presence soothed.

I'd spent the past weeks since Christmas not thinking. I'd used a lot of energy to *not* think.

There'd been a moment between Leo and me late afternoon Christmas Day when my family had gone sledding at Hidden Valley. I thought he'd been about to kiss me, and if I'd been reading him correctly, I think he thought the same thing. But that wasn't the moment. Well... it was, but the perceived near-kiss was merely the catalyst. Something clicked in that moment. It had flitted around me since I'd met Leo. I'd kept it at bay—at times it was little more than an awareness, and at others I'd had to beat it back with a baseball bat.

There'd been a million reasons. I hadn't moved to Estes Park for a relationship, hadn't even wanted one. There was a life to reinvent, a bookstore to open, family to reconnect with, unexpected murders to solve. Leo was eight years younger than me, and prettier than I was. Both thoughts shallow and ultimately unimportant... but they'd been there. And then there'd been... *whatever* it had been with Sergeant Branson Wexler. Not quite a romance, but... kind of.

In that moment at the base of the sledding hills of Hidden Valley, after all the reasons to ignore or pretend it was something other than it was, my guard slipped, and some puzzle piece clicked into place. It snapped so loudly that I couldn't pretend I didn't feel it, and from the expression that crossed Leo's face, I could've sworn he heard it too.

But then Leaf's sled crashed into Christina's, and there

was much screaming and laughing. The moment passed, and we didn't mention it again.

After, Leo left to visit his family, and I threw myself into the bookshop, bringing in the New Year and helping Katie get the bakery ready to be shut down while the elevator was installed. I hadn't allowed myself to think of it, not the worries or the hopes. To the point that Katie was frequently asking me what was the matter. That I seemed distant, shut off. She hadn't been wrong. I'd felt a million miles away, even to myself.

But there, in the middle of family and friends, the snow-storm circling the inn, my uncles celebrating their love and the life they'd built together, with Watson's comforting presence at my fingertips, something cracked, and it all began to seep back in.

My heart thundering, I angled my head just slightly so I could study Leo's profile as he focused on Gary's speech.

Leo was handsome, breathtakingly so, but that didn't have anything to do with it, at least not much.

There'd been so much uncertainty, so much loss in my life, not just in the past year, though that had been enough. Being involved in solving murders and then being betrayed by a man I thought I could trust. But, before that, there'd been my ex-husband's affair, our divorce, the duplicity of my best friend and business partner as I was cut out from our publishing house.

My father's murder.

From the second I'd met Leo Lopez, even with my nerves and the ridiculous number of butterflies in my stomach that left me tongue-tied, I felt safe with him. And while Leo didn't make me laugh like he was some great comedian, he made the moments he was near brighter. And he definitely helped me breathe easier.

It happened again, as I studied him. That click. Well... that's not exactly right. It hadn't ever unclicked. I was simply forced to admit it again. Leo and I hadn't dated. Hadn't kissed. Nothing like that. We were friends, best friends. He, Katie, and I were the Three Amigos. It was one of the ways I'd been able to shove it aside. But even without any of the romantic buildup, dating—whatever the steps were supposed to be—I knew. Maybe he had known the whole time.

Probably feeling me studying him, Leo turned slightly, his honey-brown eyes catching my gaze, and he started to smile, then flinched ever so slightly, and his eyes widened.

He could see it. Even though I attempted to throw the walls back up, Leo could see it. The corners of his lips finished their curve into a smile, one more self-conscious than I was used to seeing from him, and I could feel the hum of energy build between us.

We both jumped when the front door of the inn burst open behind us, and for what felt like the millionth time that night, a torrent of wind and snow gushed in.

As one, everyone in the anniversary party turned and looked toward the door. A group of women, each loaded down with a suitcase or two, bumbled inside. It was like they wouldn't stop coming. Three, then four. By the time the sixth one entered, the first few had started taking off hats and scarves.

The one in front ran fingers through smashed stylish blonde hair, and her eyes widened when she saw all of us staring at them. "Sorry to interrupt! We're a little early."

An African-American woman beside her chuckled. "I think an entire day is a bit more than a *little* early."

As the squeak of the door opening and closing sounded, Lisa Bloomberg hurried out from behind the check-in counter. "We're in the middle of a private party, I'm sorry. May I help you?"

The blonde spoke again. "Yes. We're not supposed to check in until tomorrow. The plan was to spend the night in Denver, but the storm was getting so bad we decided to forge ahead. We tried to call, but it didn't ring through."

Confusion flitted over Lisa's face, then seemed to clear. "Oh. You're the um... knitting group?"

Before they could answer, a seventh woman entered, slamming the door shut behind her before ripping off her hood. She was gorgeous and a couple decades younger, from what I could tell of the group. She tossed a snow-covered bag on the floor. "You really need to get someone out there to clear your driveway. The snow was over my knees. Our vans practically slid all the way down the drive. You're just begging for a lawsuit."

At Katie's intake of breath, I glanced her way. Her brows knitted and an atypical hostile expression flitted over her face as she looked at me. "Alexandria Bell. I can't stand that woman."

After welcoming the women to take off their coats and warm up in front of the roaring fire, Lisa hurried through our party and headed directly to Percival and Gary. They were seated close enough she was easily overheard. "I'm so, so sorry. I know you wanted the inn all to yourselves this evening. This was the group that I told you would show up tomorrow night."

"Don't you stress. It's not a big deal." Gary didn't miss a beat before he reassured her. "There's enough room, more than enough food, and it's not like we don't see one another all the time. The more the merrier."

Relief flooded her features. "Are you sure you don't mind?" She glanced toward the larger dining room. "I imagine it will take us a little while to get settled. I can serve them dinner in about an hour, try to give your group time to wind down, or—"

"Whenever is totally fine. Including right now. Sounds like they've had a rough go of it." Gary cut her off with a friendly pat on the back. "No need to make them wait."

Percival, however, had narrowed his eyes and weaved his head as he tried get a better view of the group of women, then turned and looked at Angus, his eyes twinkling. "Your gal pal is early!"

"She's..." Angus's cheeks pinked, and he gave an exasperated huff. "I'm sorry." Without another word, he headed toward the group of women.

"Angus has a gal pal?" Beside me, Katie stood on tiptoe and leaned to get a better view around Leo's shoulder.

Leo chuckled. "People still use the term *gal pal*?"

"Oh, hush up." Katie angled farther around him. "That's adorable. I wonder who..." Her words faded away as a horrified expression washed over her face.

Angus beelined directly toward Alexandria, took her by the elbow, and led her toward the far corner.

"Well, that's just disgusting." Katie sounded revolted.

"Oh, come on now." Leo nudged her with his elbow. "So she's a little younger than Angus. It's not a big deal." He shot me a glance but looked away quickly, as if he knew the eight years between us gave me pause.

"A *little*? Try three decades." Katie elbowed him back. "But that's not the issue. Angus is a total sweetheart. Alexandria... isn't."

"You can say that again." Anna arrived at our table, causing Watson to look up in excited anticipation, equating her arrival with his favorite treats. For the second time that night, she let him down, and on this occasion didn't even notice him. "She's nothing but a highfalutin man-eater. I don't know what Angus sees in her." She sniffed. "Well... yes, I do. Just goes to show, even men who are as kind and classy as Angus Witt are still just *men*."

From what I could see, it *was* an odd pairing, but I took Anna's claim with a grain of salt. Alexandria wouldn't be the first woman Anna had labeled a man-eater. I put more stock in Katie's reaction; she got along with everyone.

The anniversary party settled back down, though Angus didn't return. As Lisa and the rest of the staff got accommodations sorted for the group of women, we refocused on Gary and Percival, listening as they shared memories of their life together and offering a few of our own.

By the time we'd started the dessert round, and our tables were laden with pies, the staff had refreshed the salad bar, breads, and soups, and the newly arrived group was gathered around the large circular table in the other room.

I was halfway through my piece of rhubarb pie when I realized Watson was no longer between Leo and me. I did a cursory glance toward Barry, certain that I'd see him. But he wasn't there. I started to rise, just a touch of panic flickering in me. It wasn't like Watson to wander away, but there'd been a lot of going in and out of the front door as the rest of the group's luggage had been brought in. There was a chance he'd darted outside and gotten trapped.

"Watson's over there." Leo's whisper was gentle, and he gestured with his head toward the other room. "He's making friends."

Of course Leo knew where Watson was. I looked to where he'd indicated, and found Watson plopped beside the chair of one of the women. Strange. Making friends wasn't one of Watson's typical activities. Then I did the math, which should have been obvious enough. Making friends might not be a motivator, but begging for food most definitely was.

I finished standing and excused myself. "I'll be right back."

I slowed as I approached the table. Unless I was reading the situation wrong, Watson wasn't begging. Instead he was sitting contentedly beside one of the older women as she scratched behind his ears and cooed sweetly to him.

There didn't appear to be any food motivation at all.

Maybe the snowstorm had thrown him off.

"I'm so sorry. I didn't realize my dog had wandered off." All six women looked up at me as I approached. There was an empty chair, which I assumed was for Alexandria. She and Angus still hadn't returned. "Watson will eat you out of house and home if you let him."

"Watson." The one who'd been petting him smiled down at him affectionately. "That suits you. You look like a Watson."

In response he shoved his nose against her palm, demanding more affection. She obliged, lowering her other hand to scratch Watson's side.

What in the world? "He really likes you."

Watson shot me a glance that clearly said, *Don't you dare ruin this for me, lady.*

"You must be a corgi whisperer." I knelt beside him so I was on level with the seated woman. "Watson hardly likes anybody."

Still petting him, she shrugged, lifted her blue eyes to mine, and smiled. "No, I'm just good with animals. I grew up on a farm." She chuckled. "Still live on that farm, so there's been a lot of animals through the years. And we always have at least one dog running around."

She could shrug it off all she wanted; there was one thing I'd learned—when Watson responded so powerfully to a person, they were someone to be trusted. The opposite wasn't always true, as he truly wasn't a people person. There were plenty of perfectly wonderful people who Watson wouldn't give the time of day, but he most definitely didn't fawn over someone who wasn't exceptional. Leo and my stepfather were proof of that. "Well, I appreciate you letting him interrupt your meal." I offered my hand. "I'm

Winifred Page, Watson's mama. But everyone calls me Fred."

Sure enough, the second she removed one of her hands from Watson to take mine, he shot me another glare.

"Nice to meet you, Fred. I'm—"

A sharp intake of breath cut her off, and I looked up to see the blonde with the perfectly coiffed hair I'd noticed earlier, gaping at me. "Winifred Page... and a corgi." Her blue eyes, which matched the other woman's, looked from me, down to Watson, then back up. "*You* own the Cozy Corgi Bookshop."

I was a little taken aback. "Yes. I do."

The woman's tone grew more excited. "Then you know Katie Pizzolato!"

"I... do." Caution bells went off in the back of my mind. If this was someone from Katie's past, she might not have the best of intentions. It wouldn't be the first time Katie's history had come calling. From the lady's tone, she sounded like Santa Claus had just come down the chimney as opposed to plotting some murderous revenge. "Do... *you* know Katie?"

"Oh no! But I'm dying to." The blonde went into cheer-leader hyperdrive. "She's the reason we're here. Well... kind of. I found out Alexandria was coming to Estes Park. And of course, we all know about Knit Witt's—we're a knitting club, you see. So we're dying to see his store—but really, it's Katie I wanted to meet. I've been dying to for months."

Again I didn't hear any hint of malevolence in her tone, more like a rabid boy band fan than anything, but it didn't make sense. I knew Katie was the object of many specula-tive conspiracy theories because of her parents' criminal pasts, but this lady didn't look like the type to be intrigued by that. Still, you never could tell. "Why do you want to meet Katie?"

"Oh my goodness, I got carried away. I'm sorry. You must think I'm insane." The woman fluttered her hands excitedly. "I'm a devout follower of *The Sybarite*, and ever since a review of the bakery came out, I've just been desperate to visit. This perfectly cozy little bakery on top of a perfectly cozy little bookshop nestled in a perfectly cozy little mountain town? Well... it just sounds... perfect."

"And cozy, apparently." The older woman with the matching blue eyes and the object of Watson's crush laughed indulgently.

I relaxed instantly. Our friend Athena Rose was the author of that particular food blog, though she wrote it under the pen name Maxine Maxwell. So the woman's adoration was based around pastries, not murder. That was a good sign.

The blonde continued, undeterred. "If the snow thins out tomorrow, I hope we can go down into town and visit the bakery. I plan on sampling every single thing there."

"Oh, I'm sorry." I patted Watson's head and stood, my knees refusing to remain in the hovering position any longer. "We're doing some renovations in the bookshop and bakery. It's closed for the next several days." The woman's face fell, and I hurried on. "But you can still meet Katie. We're up here for my uncles' anniversary, and Katie's with me. I know that doesn't help with sampling the baked items, but—"

"Oh no, that's wonderful! Thank you!" The woman clapped, pleased once more, and stuck out her hand. "I'm Pamela." She gestured toward the other woman. "This is my sister, Cordelia."

Once more, Cordelia lifted a hand from Watson and shook mine. "Pleasure to meet you. And I'm so sorry we interrupted your party." Before I could respond, she pointed around the table, each of the women nodding in turn. Most of the women appeared to be in their fifties and sixties, with a couple of notable exceptions. "The rest of our little knitting entourage are Wanda"—she indicated to the African-American woman I had noticed when they came in. "Betsy, Minnie, and Cassidy." Minnie and Cassidy seemed to be the outliers. Minnie looked to be in her eighties, while Cassidy appeared barely out of high school. Cordelia gestured toward the empty chair. "Alexandria is here... somewhere."

"She and an older gentleman are arguing in the back of the key room." We all turned to see the waiter, Luca, approach the table, water pitcher in his hand. "From the sound, it's finally winding down."

Pamela made a disapproving sound. "Well... I know it's been a long trip and she's irritated, but I wish she wouldn't take it out on—" She stopped abruptly, her eyes widening, and then she cleared her throat.

Alexandria appeared in the doorway, paused at the soup table to pour a small bowl of stew, and then continued over to take the empty chair. A glance in the other room revealed Angus joining the anniversary party. From up close, Alexandria was even more beautiful than I'd realized.

She sneered at Pamela. "Oh, please don't stop. I'd love to hear the gossip about me firsthand." With a sniff, she stared disapprovingly at Watson, then lifted her gaze to me. "What have they told you? That I'm insufferably selfish? That I made their trip miserable all the way across Kansas because I didn't want them to tag along to begin with?"

"Alexandria," Cordelia hissed reproachfully, while Pamela flinched. "No one said anything. We were just meeting the lovely—"

"Winifred Page, right?" Alexandria cocked a brow. "Can't imagine there're too many other Freds who tag along with a corgi."

"I... am..." I blanched, both from being recognized and for clearly being disdained. "I'm sorry, have we met?"

"No, but I know of you." Once more her tone made clear that whatever she knew about me didn't leave her feeling impressed. But she offered no further explanation and took a spoonful of her stew.

Luca paused with the water pitcher lifted in midair above Pamela's glass and darted his gaze back and forth between Alexandria and me, as if hoping for more drama.

I bit my tongue, refusing to give it to him, and not knowing what in the world I could've done to disgust a person I'd never met.

The rest of the group looked abashed, though none of them were guilty of the faux pas. Cordelia cast another reproachful glance at Alexandria, then refocused on me as she continued to pat Watson. "Well... it was lovely to meet you, and again I'm so sorry we interrupted your party. I promise you we won't be a disruption again."

I glanced back at Alexandria before addressing the kind older woman in front of me. "Not a problem at all. Thanks for being so sweet to my little man here. I'm certain we'll bump into each other again." I started to turn away, then addressed Pamela once more. "I'll make sure to introduce you and Katie."

As I settled back at the table with Katie and Leo, Watson by my side, I couldn't quite get back into the nostalgic, romantic mood I'd been in before. Alexandria had left me unnerved. I had no doubt she knew who I was. Though I'd never seen her, Katie and Anna had apparently, and she had a romantic involvement with Angus, so there were obvious ties to Estes Park. Even so... I couldn't imagine what I had done to cause such a reaction from Alexandria.

Outside the bedroom window, snow streaked by in a rage. There wasn't even a hint of the twinkling lights of Estes Park, not even a glimpse of the treetops surrounding us. "I think if we went outside right now, we wouldn't even be able to see our hands in front of our faces. Not to mention that we'd probably be instantly covered with a foot of—" I broke off abruptly as I turned to see a life-sized Cookie Monster on the other side of the room. "Oh... my...."

Katie's smile beamed as her face peered out from under two large googly eyes affixed to the fuzzy blue hood. Some of her brown curls sprang out, hindering the effect, or... maybe adding to it. "You like it?"

Watson growled and backed up, bumping his nub of a tail on the edge of the bed.

"Oh, come on now, it's just me, you big grump." Katie squatted and held out a fuzzy blue hand. "Smell, I'm still your favorite baker lady."

Watson cocked his head back and forth as if considering, took a step forward, sniffed, and then backed up once more, though he didn't growl again.

"He's probably afraid you're going to try to stuff him in something like that." Without meaning to, I realized I was copying Watson, cocking my own head to the side as I inspected Katie. "Although, you are adorable."

"Yes, I am." Katie straightened. "And I would never force an outfit on Watson. Mainly because I know I'd lose a hand. But I'm glad you approve, because..." She turned and began digging through one of her backpacks.

A sinking feeling arrived in my stomach.

Sure enough, when she turned back around, she held out an equally fuzzy monstrosity, this time in yellow. "I got you one as well."

I gestured down at my own nightgown. "I'm already prepared."

"Not hardly." She tossed it to me, and I caught it on instinct. "Percival and Gary wanted pajama night for the first night. It's their anniversary; we need to make it special."

Holding out the yellow material, I let it unfold, and a large orange beak protruded from the hood. "I'm *Big Bird?*"

"You're tall." She shrugged. "And yellow was as close as I could get to *mustard*. Be happy I remembered your coloring and didn't dress you up like Elmo."

She had a point there, about red not being my color and about Gary and Percival deserving us to go all out. I began to change into the yellow mess, then paused at a thought. "Oh, good grief. You mean Leo has to see me like this?"

Katie balked slightly, and that time she did an imitation of Watson's head tilt.

Realizing what I'd just unintentionally admitted, I did a quick one eighty as I continued to stuff myself into Big Bird's skin. "So... what's the deal with Alexandria? Granted, my own first impression of her wasn't great, to say the least, but why don't you like her?"

For a moment it looked like Katie wasn't going to allow

herself to be sidetracked, but then she plopped onto her bed as she waited for me to change. "She would come into Black Bear Roaster when I worked for Carla. She's good friends with the family. And she's just as condescending and elitist as the whole lot of them. She was almost as bad as Carla's father in treating me like I was dirt under her shoe."

"I can see that. That was how she treated me." I finished zipping up the front of the ridiculous pajamas. "Actually, she treated me a lot worse than dirt under her shoe. I don't think I've ever met her before, but clearly she hates me."

"Well... you and Carla weren't exactly on good terms either, and we know they partially blame you for Black Bear Roaster going out of business. Well... *us*, I suppose." She held up a hand before I could interject. "I'm not saying any of it's valid, but that's their perspective. I'm sure nothing Alexandria's heard from them has been good about you. Not that it would matter. From what I see, she's only friendly to people she thinks she can get something from. Now that I think about it, it's kind of strange that she's part of a knitting club. One, they don't exactly look like her kind of people, and two, the artsy type typically are friendlier."

"Friendly, she isn't." I slipped my hand under my long auburn hair so I could put on the hood without it being in the way. A large beak wobbled in front of my face, and I went a little cross-eyed.

Watson growled again.

I bent down in a flourish and wrapped my arms around him, pulling him to me. His growling increased, but more indignation at being treated in such an unsophisticated manner than fear of the beak. "Oh, you're fine. Just be glad you get to be pajama free."

· · ·

I halted at the base of the stairs on our way back down. Once again proving he was more agile than I typically gave him credit for, Watson swerved and darted directly toward the one who'd given me pause.

Leo knelt, and Watson hurtled into him as if they hadn't just seen each other ten minutes before. Then Leo looked up at me, tossed the fuzzy brown elephant trunk attached to his hood over his shoulder—to which Watson didn't even bother to rumble at, much less growl—and grinned.

I smiled back before twisting to glare at Katie. "You ordered Leo's pajamas too, didn't you?"

Katie tapped the side of my head. "Say, it's like you're a real detective. You knew instantly that Leo isn't wandering around dressed like Snuffleupagus of his own accord."

"Big Bird and Snuffleupagus?" I could feel my cheeks heat.

"What?" She simply shrugged and darted around me as if she wasn't in danger. "They go together."

The rest of our party was there, though everyone else had worn normal pajamas. Even the younger nieces and nephews weren't dressed up like Muppets or cartoon characters. It was only a matter of minutes before the blizzard-inducing front door opened once more, and Percival and Gary made their second entrance of the evening. The sight of them made all apprehension of Katie's choice disappear. Gary was clothed in pajamas that looked like Bert while Percival was a too-tall Ernie.

From Katie's gasp of surprise, it seemed she hadn't been aware they'd also been going for a Sesame Street motif.

As soon as they saw us, Percival and Gary erupted in laughter, then the five of us were swept up as everyone began taking photos. Watson, happy for the distraction, wandered over to the hearth of the main fireplace and curled up to sleep.

The waitstaff served steaming spiced cider and hot chocolate and premade s'mores. On the opposite end of the dining room was a long narrow room filled with couches and tables that operated as a library and game room. Most of our party had congregated there. The angst of no internet and wireless seemed long forgotten as my nephews and nieces got lost in a competitive, very loud game of Monopoly with my uncles and Anna and Carl. Leo, Gerald, Jonah, and Noah were at the other end of the room playing a game of cards.

In the dining room, most of the knitting group gathered around Angus, though Alexandria seemed missing. Pamela might've been excited to visit the Cozy Corgi, but the real purpose of their trip was to visit Angus's store, Knit Witt's. He was leading a demonstration of what apparently was an extremely advanced technique.

Katie had talked Lisa into sharing the cornbread recipe, and the two of them were baking away in the kitchen.

Mom, Barry, the twins, and I wandered around in the large room between the library and where Watson continued to sleep contentedly by the lobby fire.

"Look at this one." Mom pointed to an elaborately carved key in a glass case. "Its label says it's from Tibet and is over fourteen hundred years old."

"This one's from Buckingham Palace," Zelda called out from across the room.

Beside her, Verona chimed in, "And this one is from a castle in Ireland."

The entire room was covered in keys—the walls, the

beams overhead, splayed over different cases and stands. Keys of every age, shape, and size. Lisa had finally been able to give the tour of her favorite room when we'd all gathered for the faux slumber party. She'd said that at an official count in 1988 there had been over twelve thousand keys. Since then, several hundred had been added every year. Nearly all of them had tags explaining where they were from. They'd been sent from all over the world, by presidents, celebrities, royalty, and everyday folks who had visited Estes Park. As I wandered around, once more the years folded in and déjà vu washed over me from doing the exact same thing as a child.

"This one was your grandma's favorite." Mom smiled at me as if reading my mind and tapped a three-foot-long key with theatrical mask at one end and an elaborate *E* on the other making up the tines. "It's from the 1920s and was donated by Elitch Gardens, the amusement park in Denver. Mom said she and Dad would go there on dates when they were younger. Quite a drive down the mountain back then."

Barry slipped an arm over her shoulder. "Lotta history in this room. So many lives, so many stories."

It was palpable, a weightiness in the space, but not oppressive. More of a lovely, soft thing. I could easily see why it was Lisa's favorite space in the inn.

I traced one of the nearby letter openers with old-fashioned keys soldered onto the ends. "Maybe Katie and I should leave a key to the Cozy Corgi." I hurried on at Mom's wide-eyed expression. "One of the old ones, before we had the front door locks changed after the break-in."

She relaxed. "I think your grandma would like that." She glanced around, a soft smile playing on her lips as Percival's laugh rang out from the adjacent room before demanding an outrageous amount in rent. "She would like all of this. The family together, happy, safe."

"Oh!" Zelda let out a squeal and motioned for us to join her and Verona. "This is fun and creepy. It's the key to the Stanley Hotel room that inspired *The Shining*."

Mom shuddered and clutched the crystal dangling from her necklace. "I'm glad Percival and Gary wanted to have their anniversary here and not at the Stanley."

"I spent the night at the Stanley once; it's not haunted. Even did the ghost tour." Barry waggled his eyebrows. "Maybe it was a little haunted."

The Stanley was a huge sprawling hotel on the other side of Estes Park and was the inspiration for one of Stephen King's most beloved novels. "I'm with Mom. I'd rather spend the week surrounded by cornbread, pies, and thousands of keys than murdering ghosts. I've had enough murder for a while."

Zelda waggled her eyebrows in an exact, and probably unintentional, imitation of her father. "Well, the weekend is not over yet."

"Oh, stop it." Verona swatted at her twin, but smirked.

Barry's gaze flitted around the keys and then came to rest on the one from the Stanley once more before his tone grew ponderous. "Maybe that's what Jonah and Noah could do with their shop. One of those escape rooms that are so popular right now. They could design it like Baldpate. Perfect with all the keys."

"Don't you dare suggest anything else to them." All levity left Verona's expression. "I'm ready to murder them both." She shot a look at Zelda, then to me. "You know what? You're right. The weekend isn't over yet. Fred, if you wake up tomorrow and one of them is dead, you know exactly where to look." Without a moment's hesitation, she stormed off.

"Dad!" Zelda gave a reproachful hiss to her father before following Verona.

"I wasn't thinking." Barry looked abashed, and Mom slipped her hand into his.

"What's going on? I've never seen Verona snap at Jonah like she did earlier." I wasn't one to gossip about my stepsisters, even with family, but it was a little off-putting.

Barry shook his head as if in defeat, and Mom answered for them. "Jonah and Noah announced yesterday that they are going to remodel the store another time."

"*Again?*" I couldn't believe my ears. My stepsisters and their husbands had each taken over the two shops on either side of the Cozy Corgi. Verona and Zelda had opened their New Age store months ago. Their husbands seemed close on several occasions but still the windows were papered over. "What is that, the fourth time?"

"The sixth." Barry sighed. "Even I'm getting a little tired of it."

That was saying something. Barry was the most patient man I knew.

"I think I'd be a little frustrated by that myself. In fact, I'd probably..." We'd walked over to the doorway between the key room and the lobby as we spoke. I glanced over to check on Watson, still snoring away by the fire, but stopped talking as I caught a motion at the bend of the steps. Our server from dinner had been watching us, then darted away.

"What is it, dear?" Mom angled her head to follow my gaze.

"One of the waitstaff..." I had to dig back for his name. "Luca. I think... think he was recording us with his cell phone."

Mom studied the empty spot for a second, then looked back at me. "Why in the world would he do that? Talk about boring subject matter."

"Hey!" Barry reared back and slipped his thumbs into the straps of his fuzzy, oversized, tie-dyed hoodie. "Speak for yourself. I'm an extremely fascinating creature."

With a laugh, they appeared to have shoved the thought away, but I lingered on it for a second. There was a chance I hadn't seen correctly, but I was certain I wasn't mistaken. Maybe Luca hadn't been recording us, but he'd definitely been watching us, and *not* for refills on cider or hot chocolate.

SIX

The lobby fire roared, the crackling and popping competing with the raging blizzard outside the windows. Taking a slow breath, I closed my eyes and snuggled deeper into the cushions of the overstuffed sofa.

Everyone else had gone to bed less than ten minutes before, and Lisa had stoked the fire for me before she'd gone up. I had yet to open the book on my lap, relishing being alone, save for the warm weight of Watson as he napped on my feet. As much as I loved my family and friends, I'd discovered long before that I required time alone in order to recharge. If I'd simply gone upstairs and fallen asleep at the same time as Katie, I'd have woken the next morning exhausted, no matter how much sleep I might've gotten.

Letting the wind and the fire soothe, I opened my eyes, smiled lovingly at Watson, and finally cracked open the latest installment of Kelley Armstrong's *Rockton* series. It was a little bit mystery and a little lost in the wilderness, and it seemed perfect for the weekend. Despite the sensation that Luca had been observing us earlier, I settled in between the barely glowing lights of the key room and the glassed-in porch, and felt nearly as safe and cozy as I did in my own home, or in the mystery room at the bookshop.

Grabbing a piece of the cakelike cornbread I'd snagged

from the kitchen, I chewed happily and made it about halfway through the first chapter before a squeak at the stairs caused me to flinch.

Watson lifted his head, giving a sleepy growl. It faded quickly, as he was able to see into the dark stairwell more easily than me.

After a pause, there was another squeak, and Carl Hanson came into view. He gave a little self-conscious wave. "Well... Fred and ah... Watson." He glanced behind, clearly considering retreat. "I didn't realize anyone was awake."

"Just catching up on some reading." I knew it was horrible of me, but I so hoped Carl didn't decide to sit down and chat.

He didn't, instead rushing toward the kitchen. "Anna... wanted a snack."

Relieved, I gestured toward the plate of cornbread on the coffee table. "Help yourself to these. Katie and Lisa made it, so they're fresh, even a little warm still."

Another hesitation and then he came forward. "Sure, you don't mind?"

I held them out to him. "Honestly you'd be doing me a favor. If you don't take them, I'll eat every single piece."

"Perfect. Thank you." After taking them, he headed upstairs.

I turned back to the book, but before I reached the second chapter, the front door of the inn opened, ushering in snow and wind. That time Watson's growl didn't stop when the person came into view, though it wasn't overly aggressive.

Gerald shut the door and stamped the snow off his boots before noticing the two of us and giving a little jump. "Oh! I didn't expect anyone to be awake."

Déjà vu. Might as well go with it. "Just catching up on some reading."

"Good idea." Gerald cleared his throat and gestured back to the door. "I was just... I had... um..." With a flick of his hand, he appeared to give up and headed toward the stairs. "Well, have a good night, you two."

For the billionth time, I wondered how in the world the man experienced any success at all as a lawyer. "You too, Gerald."

I stared after Gerald though he'd disappeared, tracing Carl's footsteps into the dark. Both men had been acting strange, somewhat guilty. Carl often acted strange, but *guilty*? Not so much. Perhaps he hadn't been getting a snack for Anna after all. Seemed like a coincidence that he and Gerald would be up and about at the same time. Probably another kombucha run, though surely Gerald had that in his room, not in his car.

Letting it go, I turned back to the book, allowing myself to get lost in the comfort of the fire, and made it nearly to chapter five before the combination of Watson snoring and the white noise of the blizzard outside began to lull me to sleep.

Another creak at the steps shot me awake once more. Though it had the same effect on Watson, that time he didn't growl.

I was starting to feel like I was in the middle of Grand Central Station. Considering I'd just seen Carl and Gerald, chances were high it was Angus, the third of the kombucha buddies.

It wasn't. And by Watson's lack of a growl and the happy wagging of his nubbed tail, I should've figured it out instantly. That time, Leo emerged from the stairs. He smiled in surprise. "Hey, you're awake." There was no hesitation or guilt in his tone.

"Thought I'd just do a little reading." Third time's a charm. "But it was about to turn into napping."

"Well, I don't want to disturb you." Despite his words, he hesitated. "I was having trouble sleeping, so I thought I might peruse the little library, see if there was anything good."

His hesitation was clearer than Carl's and Gerald's, and my heart began to pound, a spike of adrenaline clearing out any notion of sleep. I gestured to the other side of Watson. "Go grab a book, and you can join us, if you want."

"Okay. Sounds nice." He smiled, but instead of heading toward the key room and the library behind it, he walked around the coffee table and joined us on the couch. Proving just how tired he was, Watson didn't do a happy dance, but whimpered contentedly as Leo's fingers sank into his fur, and pressed his head against Leo's thigh. Leo cooed something nonsensical to him and sighed. "This is nice—the fire, even the storm outside."

I couldn't help myself. "You didn't get a book."

He chuckled softly. "No, I suppose I didn't. But I can. We can just sit and read. We don't have to chat."

If it had been anyone else, even Katie, I would've taken that offer. But the idea of talking with Leo, though both exciting and uncomfortable in ways, was about as far from draining as I could imagine. "No, let's chat."

Another smile, and a nod. Leo opened his mouth and then closed it once more, apparently not sure what to say.

Neither was I, and I was suddenly aware I'd not taken off the Big Bird onesie Katie had stuffed me in, but at least I didn't have the hood on and a big beak sticking out over my face. Of course I'd find myself seated on the couch with

Leo, by a fire, and dressed in fuzzy yellow. I went with it. "I can't believe you changed out of your Snuffleupagus pajamas. That trunk looked unbelievably comfortable."

Leo snorted, and some of his ease returned. "I think now I know how people with long hair feel. I had to keep flipping it over my shoulder like it was the world's longest ponytail."

"True, but most of the time ponytails don't come out of the center of your forehead."

He graciously chuckled again at my poor attempt of a joke, then fell silent. I could see the awareness in his eyes, even from the flickering light of the fire. I'd been certain, but was even more so in that moment—he'd sensed the change in me, felt an unspoken awareness that we weren't just friends, not really.

I cleared my throat. "So... how was... um... time with family?" I grasped the lowest hanging fruit I could reach, and I regretted it instantly. Leo wasn't overly secretive, but he never said much about his childhood or provided any details that were too specific about his mother or siblings.

"Oh. Fine. It was... fine."

Sure enough, that had been a wet blanket. I tried to think of something else, but nothing was coming.

He twisted suddenly, angling more toward me while never losing contact with Watson, and his demeanor changed. "Actually, it was rough. Exhausting, really. It's good to be back."

The abrupt shift in his tone surprised me, and I realized that this too was a change, an opening up, a risk. "I think a lot of people experience that during the holidays. Even though my family is pretty wonderful, with so much time together and all the parties and events, it can leave me a little desperate for an opportunity to close the door and shut out the world." I started to leave it at that, but then decided to go a little further. "Want to share what made it stressful?"

Leo was silent for a while, but I got the sense he was debating *how* to say it, not *if*. Finally he sighed again, like he was giving up a little bit. "Without getting into all the details, as that's really not what I want to dwell on right now, let's just say I'm starting to realize I simply have to accept my family is who they are. I keep hoping for more growth, more progress, but..." He shrugged.

Once more unsure what to say, I decided to try to make him laugh. "You mean like all of us hoping that at some point Barry will wear something other than tie-dye?"

It worked. A soft bark of a laugh erupted from him. "Yes, exactly like that." And though his chuckle faded away, Leo seemed lighter again, even as he went deeper. "I wish it was that. My father was a pretty... despicable guy. To Mom, to us kids. And being the oldest"—another shrug—"it was my job to keep everybody safe, at least as much as I could. Mom included."

He had never spoken that clearly, but it matched the impression I'd formed from the few things he'd said, so I nodded in understanding. "Your dad's out of the picture, right?"

"Yeah. Since I was sixteen." He nodded and sighed again. "But in ways, it's like he never left. Or at least that everyone still fulfills the same roles they always did." He held my gaze. "Mom sees herself as a victim. Instead of my father, it's everyone. Her boss at work, the guy in front of her in the grocery store checkout line, the lady who delivers the mail. She's constantly waging war with everyone. Except... for the landlord who is horrible to her. Except for the pastor at her church who tells her she needs to work on the marriage with my father even though he's been gone for nearly two decades, because marriage is forever. Except with my little brother who lives two blocks away and has apparently decided he wants to fill in Dad's old shoes." He looked away, focusing on Watson. "To *those* people, Mom's still a victim. And she won't hear a word against any of them."

Once more I didn't know what to say, and after a moment's hesitation, I leaned forward and slid my hand on top of his where it had come to rest on Watson's hip.

His bright eyes lifted to mine once more, and when I didn't pull away, I saw things in the depths that he'd only allowed me to see flashes of now and again since the day we met—flashes I'd ignored or shoved off as something else.

When he spoke, his words were thick with emotion, but the corner of his lips curved into a soft smile. "One of the things I've loved..." He flinched as if he just shocked himself, then after a blink, shook his head and met my eyes again. "No, I'm just going to call it like it is. I could say one of the things I've admired about you, and that's true, but it doesn't really capture it." He moved his other hand, covering mine so it was sandwiched between both of his. As if he was giving me time to pull away, he didn't speak for a few seconds. When I didn't, his smile grew. "It's one of the things I've loved about you from the day we met. You're strong, Fred. You came barging into the national park with that owl feather, determined to find answers, and you haven't stopped since. It doesn't matter if you're in danger or if people tell you to mind your own business. You're nobody's victim. You're nobody's fool."

I could barely breathe from the sincerity and admiration in his gaze. I wanted to argue. After Branson, I'd very much felt like I'd played the fool. Just like I had with my ex-husband and my ex-business partner.

"You're just the opposite. You fight for people who are victims, for truth. I have seen you weather bump after bump over the past year... more than a year... that we've known each other. Bumps and betrayals, things that would flatten other people, and you... just keep going. And you don't get hard because of it, either."

"Leo... don't..." Even I could barely hear my whisper.

"Sorry. I said too much." He started to pull his hand back.

I gripped it, holding him in place so we were ridiculously stacked like a tower on top of Watson. "No, it's not too much, not like that."

When his gaze lifted once more, there was hope there.

Maybe we'd already crossed a line we couldn't go back from. Probably had. Maybe, for him, that had happened the night he'd given me the silver corgi earrings. Maybe, for me, that moment on Christmas Day at Hidden Valley.

"Not like that." As I repeated it, I moved my thumb over the back of his hand. "I just don't deserve the praise you're heaping on me. You're sugarcoating it all. I'm bullheaded, sometimes too aggressive. I demand too much from—"

"Don't do that." His voice was firm, but there was no unkindness in it. "That's exactly what I'm talking about. Those descriptors you're trying to put on yourself right now? They're from what everyone else says Winifred Page should or shouldn't be. But even so, you charge right ahead, and even when you're not entirely sure of yourself, you're always who you are."

I couldn't help but laugh at that. "Well, that's true. For better or worse."

"Exactly." He nodded. "Exactly. And it blows my mind every time I get to see it."

My eyes stung suddenly. I wanted to tell him everything

I admired about him. How I'd come to depend on his friendship, his strength, his goodness. How his stabilizing force had made the past few months bearable. Without him there were times I would've crumbled. But I didn't trust my voice to attempt to speak.

He didn't offer me the chance to, anyway. He took his top hand off mine and lifted it to my cheek, his thumb stroking it as I had the back of his hand, and he leaned nearer, his gaze refusing to let me look away.

We stayed like that for several moments. The light of the fire flickered over the right side of his face as his left was awash in the cool bluish gray from the snow whirling outside the window.

No, there was no coming back. Even if we stopped right there, right then, things would never be the same again, if they'd ever had any chance of it anyway.

If I'd planned it, I would've taken longer. Maybe weeks, maybe months, taking little bitty steps. Or knowing me, one step toward him and then five back. But I'd been doing that since the day I met him, hadn't I? Even though I'd not been aware of it.

Before I could second-guess, before I could list all the reasons we needed to slow down and not go from the pace of molasses to the speed of lightning, I covered his hand with mine and leaned nearer as well so we were mere inches apart. "Kiss me."

A laugh broke from Leo once more, one that sounded of happiness and relief. He cut off the sound as he pressed his lips to mine.

In the moments I'd let myself consider this possibility, I feared that when we finally gave in to what had slowly built between us, our lips would touch and we'd discover we really were just friends after all, that there would be no spark, just the cold affection of relatives, or something equally as horrible.

They'd been wasted worries.

A sigh escaped, but I wasn't sure if it was from me or him. Leo's hand slipped from my cheek and moved through my hair until he cupped the back of my head and deepened the kiss.

I didn't know. Maybe sparks flew, maybe the earth shook. Possibly, as there was a loud pop from the fire. Or... maybe none of those things happened.

Either way, my world shifted. Perhaps that had been part of why I'd refused to even consider the possibility for so long. Leo Lopez was dangerous. There would be no coming back from him, and some part of me had always known that. Things would never be the same.

Between us, Watson gave an irritated huff and hopped off the sofa, his hind legs sliding behind him like a seal's tail as he plopped to the floor.

Though we both chuckled, neither of us broke the kiss, and Leo drew himself nearer, his other arm slipping behind my back and pulling me to him until he was cradling me against him.

I didn't know how long the kiss lasted, nor how we shifted positions. But at some point his back was against the arm of the sofa and I was cradled between his legs, my head resting on his chest as his fingers played through my hair.

Watson sat below us on the floor, snoring softly.

Neither of us spoke for a long time, just settling into this new strange world. But that was the weird part—it didn't feel strange. It just felt... right. Natural.

After a while, I tilted my head slightly to kiss him again, right as there was a gasp from across the room.

Watson barked, and Leo and I jerked apart.

"Oh my goodness, I'm so sorry." Lisa Bloomberg stood at the base of the steps, her hand covering her mouth. "I didn't think anyone would be up."

I started to pull farther away, but Leo laid a hand on mine as he chuckled self-consciously. "It's okay."

Lisa pointed above her head. "I woke up and walked to the bathroom, but the lights wouldn't come on. I thought I'd check the breaker." She pointed again. "I can go back up and—"

"No. It's totally fine." It was my turn to laugh. I glanced toward the key room and the glassed-in front porch. "Huh, I didn't even notice the lights go out." Maybe the loud pop hadn't been from the fire after all.

Lisa hurried around the fireplace, flicked on the flashlight on her cell phone, and disappeared behind the counter. There was a metal scrape from what I assumed was the fuse box, then a few clicks. When she emerged, she was shaking her head. "No power at all." Without waiting, she crossed to the glassed-in front porch where we'd celebrated the anniversary only a few hours before and peered through. "It's hard to tell, given the blizzard, but I don't even see a faint flickering of a light from downtown. Looks like the power is out everywhere."

Over the next half hour, we helped Lisa retrieve lanterns, candles, and matches from a back room, lit our own, and then dispersed others in front of the bedroom doors so people would have them in case anyone else woke up in the middle of the night.

We said an awkward goodnight to Lisa, and then we were standing in front of Leo's door, Watson at our feet, only our two lit lanterns illuminating us.

Leo cupped my cheek as he had downstairs. For the first

time, there was a sliver of nervousness in his tone. "Are you okay? Freaking out a little bit?"

I started to shake my head, then paused, doing a quick self-assessment, wanting to be truthful. "Actually, I'm not freaking out. I know I should be."

"I'm not either." The nervousness left his voice. "And why should we? We're not teenagers. And while this aspect might be new, *we* are not. I know exactly who you are."

Save for a few details, like the ins and outs of his family, I knew who Leo was as well—at least the core of who the man was.

He kissed me again, long, sweet, with an undercurrent of fire. Finally, he pulled away.

There was that moment. We'd already darted across so many bridges, I could slip into his room and cross another.

For whatever reason, that felt too soon.

"See you in the morning?" Whether he'd read my feelings or was having the same himself, there was no sound of frustration or disappointment. Only happiness, and a contented quality that I'd never realized had been missing from Leo.

"Yeah." Maybe it was too soon, but I was disappointed, pleasantly so. "See you in the morning."

Another kiss, and then Watson and I walked a few feet to Katie's and our room, turned to give Leo a wave, and disappeared inside.

I shot up, sitting straight in my bed, trying to figure out my surroundings. There'd been a noise. Someone was in the kitchen.

Watson grunted as the bed squeaked. His scowl was barely visible in the dim light when I looked over the side of the bed. Then he rested his head over his forepaws once more with a grunt.

Only then did I realize we weren't at home. But I couldn't quite place it until I looked across the room and saw Katie sleeping soundly.

Right. Baldpate. The anniversary party.

Good Lord, I had to be completely exhausted if I was that out of it. A glance at my cell phone revealed it wasn't even four in the morning. No wonder.

I peered out the window. The storm was still blowing, nothing visible but gray streaks of snow, and even that was hard to see.

My head almost reached my pillow when I shot back up again, this time fully awake, my heart pounding. And *not* because of any sounds in the night.

The memory of Leo and me in front of the fire crashed back into view.

For a moment or two, there was nothing but pure, unadulterated terror.

What had we done?

What had *I* done?

Had we really jumped from being friends on the drive up to Baldpate Inn to... to... whatever this was, in a few short hours?

Another noise sounded from somewhere outside my room, distant and muffled. I barely noticed it. Probably just something from the wind outside, or someone going for another midnight snack.

Just as I began to struggle to catch my breath in my panic, I felt Leo's hand on my cheek, remembered the sincerity in his honey-brown eyes as he spoke of all the things he loved about me. My body relaxed as I exhaled, and my lips tingled with the ghost of our kiss.

I slid from the bed and sat beside Watson, put my arms around him where he lay, and folded over him.

He merely grunted once more, an annoyed indulgence.

His warmth, his constant presence, grounded me, lessening my panic the rest of the way.

Maybe Leo and I had skipped over several steps in one big leap, and sure, such recklessness wasn't like me, but that was all protocol. We'd been building up to this for over a year, even if I hadn't let myself realize it. And besides, every other thing in my life I'd planned methodically. Step by excruciating step. My degrees, my first marriage to Garrett, opening the publishing house with Charlotte. And look how they had all turned out. There'd been one other time where I'd simply closed my eyes, tossed caution to the wind, and leapt. That spur-of-the-moment decision had brought Watson and me to Estes Park to open the Cozy Corgi. And *that*, without a doubt, had been the best decision of my life.

Fear gave way to peace. And in a matter of a heartbeat, peace gave way to anticipatory excitement. Everything was going to change, but it was right. I could feel it, and just like on the snowy slopes of Hidden Valley, just like on the couch in front of the fire, further puzzle pieces snapped together, erasing all doubts. Things were falling into place, even if I couldn't quite see the final image.

I pressed a kiss between Watson's ears. "At least I know you approve." I nearly laughed at that thought. As if there was going to be anyone in my life who didn't approve of Leo and me. And like I'd change anything even if they didn't.

After a few more seconds of snuggling with Watson, I stood, intending to get back into bed, but couldn't make myself. I was wide-awake, despite barely any sleep. I was too excited, too happy, too... everything.

I'd go back down, grab another piece of cornbread, relight the fire in the hearth, and read. Or at least pretend to read. I'd probably just sit there and glow.

I snagged the lantern I'd left beside the bed, crossed to the door, and slowly turned the handle so it didn't squeak. I intended to let Watson sleep, but he popped up and followed me the second I moved into the hall, his nails clacking softly over the hardwood. After shutting the door once more, I lit the lantern, and then Watson and I made our way to the stairs, only pausing by Leo's door. I touched the old smooth wood, letting my hand rest there for a few moments.

Finally.

The thought surprised me. I hadn't realized I'd been waiting. I didn't think I had been. But the sensation was true enough. There was excitement, anticipation, butter-flies, but woven through everything was a sense of relief. Contentment.

Dropping my hand, we continued to the steps and made our way down, a few squeaks here and there.

There was another noise from somewhere in the dark. It sounded like it was over to my left, toward the key room. Goose bumps prickled on my arms, threatening the warm peace that had been cascading through me. I attempted to shove the unease aside.

Watson didn't help by issuing a low, warning growl.

"It's okay. The inn is over a hundred years old, and we are in the middle of one of the worst blizzards I've ever seen. There's going to be strange sounds," I whispered to Watson, but I might've been reassuring myself more than him. The lobby was notably colder than the few hours before, a frigid draft blew over my legs from under the nightgown I'd changed into before crawling into bed.

Instead of going to the kitchen first, I knelt in front of the fire and pulled logs from the stack on the hearth.

Watson growled again, and I looked over to see him with his ears pointed back and his head low to the ground as he crept toward the key room.

I stood instantly, clutching one of the pieces of firewood in my right hand, just in case I needed a weapon. There was no reason to try to reassure myself or Watson that it was the settling of the old hotel. By that point, I more than knew Watson's growl—I should've recognized it the first time, should've realized from the prickling of my flesh.

Lifting the lantern, I took a few steps forward, the candlelight only illuminating the first few steps into the key room.

Watson trailed beside me, his continuing growl low but steady.

I stopped a few feet into the key room and chastised myself. This was hardly our first rodeo. I might know what we were getting ready to find, but I had no idea what situation we were about to walk into. There was no reason to do it on my own.

However, just as I turned around, ready to go wake up Leo, Katie... everyone, that very thought forced all caution to the wind. My entire family was under this roof; it could be one of them.

I hurried forward, swinging the lamp from side to side, the candlelight casting bizarre and jagged shadows from the thousands of keys. It was hard to tell in the dimness, but nothing seemed out of place. The farther we went, the stronger the icy draft became. At the far end of the room, the door swung slightly on its hinges. It was the source of the cold, and it wasn't a draft—it was a breeze. Watson and I increased our pace and paused only when we reached the doorway into the library game room. I peered in. Sure enough, the other door at the opposite end of the long narrow room also swung on its hinges, ushering in the cold, wind, and snow from the outside.

Watson's growl transitioned from low rumble to full-on warning agitation, and he slunk farther into the room.

I nearly called him back, but fear over who I'd find pressed me onward as well.

From what the lantern light revealed, everything looked the same as it had earlier that night. We'd nearly reached the door to the outside before the shadowy figure came into view. It was male, clearly, but I couldn't tell much else in the flickering shadows. He lay partway behind an old armchair, sprawled on the floor. The pool of blood was inky black in the darkness, flecks of snow whipping in through the door and covering it, only to melt instantly.

Dropping the piece of firewood, I rushed toward the body, some part of my brain screaming that with that amount of blood there was no way the person could be alive. Even so, I didn't pause as I reached the prone form. With panic rushing through me, I grabbed an arm, experienced a bit of hope feeling the warmth of the skin, and rolled him over.

All hope vanished at the sight of the slit throat.

I had to hold the lantern right by the face before I realized who it was.

Luca. The handsome young German waiter.

Maybe it was horrible to admit, but relief so strong flooded through me that I nearly collapsed. So great, that I had to reach behind me and steady myself by gripping the back of the armchair. He wasn't family, wasn't a friend.

Watson's snarl pulled me back to the moment. He was standing in the doorway, growling out into the stormy night.

Moving around Luca, I hurried toward Watson and slipped my fingers into his collar, lest he decided to give chase. Holding my lantern out past the door revealed nothing. There was only darkness and swirling snow. The moonlight barely broke through the swirls. A glance down didn't even expose footprints. In whatever time had passed, though it couldn't have been much at all, snow was already piling in a heap through the doorway, covering any tracks. Only then did I notice an old-fashioned key partway between the growing mound of snow and the pool of blood. I repositioned the lantern once more, causing the key's tarnished pewter to glisten. Not just a key, but one of the letter openers I'd noticed earlier in the evening. Blood glistened over its sharp blade.

EIGHT

Tears brimmed in Lisa's eyes, but I was impressed at how well she pulled herself together. She bent, reaching lovingly toward Luca's soiled face, but she caught herself before I could tell her to stop. Standing, she wiped the tears from her eyes. "Guess I shouldn't disturb Luca's body."

"No, we need to leave the scene as close to how we found it as possible." Never mind that I had already turned over the body, but that couldn't be helped. My gaze flitted from Leo and Katie to my mom and Barry. All of their faces were tense and strained in the light of our lanterns. They were the only ones I'd woken up. "The first thing we need to do is alert the police. I tried dialing 911 before I got any of you. I'd forgotten the phones don't work."

"I can run out to my Jeep and see if I can get anyone on the..." Leo's words faded away, and he shook his head. "Right... I rode up with you and Katie. No CB in the Mini Cooper."

Katie's brows furrowed. "I can't believe I'm suggesting this, but doesn't Susan—?"

"I just don't understand who would do this to Luca." The words burst from Lisa, and fresh tears finally began to fall. "He is a..." She scrunched her eyes closed. "He *was* such a sweet boy. So full of life. I can't accept that anyone would..."

Mom moved closer and put her arm around Lisa. She didn't say anything, just held her supportively.

Watson paced the room, sniffing the path we'd taken over and over again, every once in a while disappearing into the key room and then returning again.

"Come here, buddy." Barry knelt, holding a hand out to him and then patting his head comfortingly when Watson came. To my surprise, Watson only indulged Barry for a moment or two before taking off once more, sniffing around as if his life depended on it. Barry's gaze traveled after him as Watson disappeared into the key room again. "Looks like Watson's already on the case. I'd wager he'll have it figured out in a matter of minutes." He chuckled as he stood once more.

"Barry," Mom whispered scoldingly.

Barry cleared his throat self-consciously and looked to Katie. "You were getting ready to suggest contacting Officer Green, I believe."

Watson's growl drew all our attention to the doorway before Katie could respond.

A soft muttering followed, only increasing Watson's irritation.

Before I could make it to the doorway, two women peered in, the lantern they held illuminating their faces in a ghostly uplight. They were from the knitting group. I couldn't remember their names, but one of them was the youngest member.

The older spoke. "I heard noises, so I woke Cassidy. I have trouble sleeping anyway because of the knee replacement I had last year. It aches something awful all the time. But this cold is making it worse." They entered the room, still not able to see Luca's body from that angle. "Goodness. You are quite the partying lot, aren't you? Have you even gone to bed yet?"

The younger woman, Cassidy, it seemed, yawned and then motioned upward. "We discovered the noise, Betsy. Are you satisfied? Can we go back to bed now?"

Watson was still sniffing around their feet, the rumble in his chest continuing, and then, giving a sharp bark, he darted back into the key room once more.

Leo shot me a glance and headed toward Cassidy and Betsy. "Why don't you come with me and we can—"

"Lisa!" a girl's voice sounded from somewhere in the shadows.

Watson let out another bark.

"Lisa?"

"Oh no." Lisa sucked in a gasp. "I didn't even think." She pulled away from Mom and headed across the room.

"Lisa?" The girl's voice sounded panicked.

"Lisa? Are you back there?" A male's voice, sounding more annoyed than worried.

"Hold on. I'm coming."

Though Lisa called out to them, the two hurried into the back room, joining our small crowd, Watson on their heels.

Two of the waitstaff, though I didn't remember their names either. As soon as he noticed the group gathered, the man halted, but the girl hurried forward when she saw Lisa. "We can't find Luca. He was supposed to stay with me last night, and I woke up and realized he wasn't there. I must've fallen asleep... but... I went to his and Beau's room, and he—"

Even as her eyes went wide and her words fell away,

Lisa took the girl by the shoulders, attempting to spin her around and lead her away, but it was too late.

The girl jerked free, stumbling toward Luca's body. Lisa was able to regain her grip and pulled the girl close, stopping her before she got any closer. For a few seconds, the girl stared in confusion, then horror washed over her face, and she began to scream.

Within a matter of minutes, nearly everyone was gathered in the lobby. Someone had lit the fire, but I wasn't sure who. The girl, whose name turned out to be Juliet, had screamed and screamed and screamed, waking the entire inn. Her screams had given way to sobs that wafted through from the other side of the fireplace where the staff lounge was hidden. Lisa had left her with Beau and the rest of the young staff who'd come downstairs at the commotion.

The rest of us, now joined by Zelda's and Verona's families, the Hansons, Angus and Gerald, and Minnie, the eldest member of the knitting group, gathered in a misshapen circle, some of us seated on the sofas, some standing, while others paced. The only ones not accounted for were Percival and Gary and four others of the knitting club, as they were all staying in the smaller cabins outside the inn.

I'd taken a seat on the floor, directly in front of the spot Leo and I had occupied on the sofa only a few hours before, making room for the others. Watson plopped at my side, sitting at attention, pointed ears twisting back and forth at every noise.

"So one of us is a murderer." With the roaring fire and all the lanterns lit, the wild expression over Anna's face was crystal clear. "And we're stuck in the middle of the forest, during a blizzard, without any contact to the outside world, without any electricity. We don't have any heat even. So not only are we at the mercy of the elements, but we've got a crazed killer among us."

"Anna." Noah was reproachful as he spared a glance toward his children, then glared back at Anna. "Let's not slip into dramatics. The fire is plenty warm, and we're not on the set of a horror movie."

"Aren't we?" Anna went shrill, gesturing toward the key room and library. "We've got a dead boy bleeding all over the floor. *That* would say otherwise."

"I have to agree with my wife." Though Carl's tone was icy serious, the flicker in his eyes revealed that he was enjoying the excitement. "It could be anybody. *Any* one of us."

Murmurs broke out among the group at that, while the members of the knitting club looked terrified, and Lisa appeared nearly sick to her stomach.

"Enough!" Leo's voice cut through the chatter. "This isn't helping. Noah's right. We're not in some slasher flick." He swung his gaze toward Anna, anticipating her interruption, and cut her off at the chase. "But you're right as well. Clearly *someone* killed Luca, but that doesn't mean it was someone within these walls. And even if it was, it hardly indicates a killing spree. There's no reason to believe anyone else is in danger. Either way, panicking isn't going to help."

While I hadn't even come close to slipping into a panic, my thoughts had been more along the lines of Anna's—instantly wondering who among us had killed Luca. I'd already taken out half the suspects. No one who'd come for the anniversary party would do such a thing. Of course. I couldn't imagine anyone from the knitting group doing it either. Once before I might've excluded the possibility simply because most of them were older women, although I'd learned the hard way that just because someone looked like a grandma didn't mean they weren't a murderer, but still. Why would one of them drive across the country, arrive in the middle of a snowstorm, and kill one of the employees of the hotel?

That left the owner, who looked grief-stricken as she stood by the fire. Or one of the other young people who were currently comforting the still-wailing girl.

"Susan Green lives pretty close, right, Fred?" Katie was finally able to finish her thought from before. "We might not have phone service or electricity or anything, but we could drive to Susan's house. She might have power, or at least a way to get in contact with the station."

"That's a good idea. I was preparing to suggest that myself." Gerald had been about to lift a bottle of kombucha to his lips but lowered it once more. "As a lawyer, I have to stress the importance of getting law enforcement involved as quickly as possible." His gaze flitted to me. "The murder scene has already been compromised."

"Oh, Gerald." Mom gave a similarly reproachful tone to the one she'd used with Barry earlier, though it was harsher. "What did you want Winifred to do? *Not* check to see if she could help the poor boy?"

"Now, Phyllis, don't get riled. Clearly, with his throat cut, the boy was beyond—"

Angus put a restraining hand on Gerald's shoulder from where he stood beside him, but didn't bother to address the sentiment, instead looking toward Katie. "Have you looked outside? There's not a car up here that will make it through the snow. It's up to my midthigh."

"I have two snowmobiles. They're in good working order." Lisa sounded exhausted, her voice faraway. "I need to call Luca's parents. I wonder what time it is in Germany. I've never had to..." Her words trailed off as she shook her head. "Oh... Right. No phones."

Mom went to Lisa again, attempting to comfort her.

"That will work. I'm good on a snowmobile. We use them in the park all the time," Leo spoke up, decisively.

"You're not going on your own." Katie gestured toward the window. "It's still storming, and if it's too dangerous to drive, then—"

"I'll go with him." I spoke up before I'd even thought it through.

Leo smiled knowingly at me. "Have you driven a snow-mobile before?"

I lifted my chin. "No, but... I can figure it out."

"This depth of snow isn't the time to try to learn, dear," Barry interjected. "I'll go with you, Leo."

I could see Mom start to object, but she stopped herself.

"Besides..." Leo crossed the space between us and knelt down to look me meaningfully in the eyes as he stroked Watson's head. "You've got a job to start, don't you?"

"A job...?" His meaning clarified instantly, and I couldn't help but chuckle. "I'm sure Susan will appreciate that when you bring her here."

He shrugged. "Maybe not, but don't you think she'd be disappointed if you didn't give her something to complain about?"

Gerald put down his kombucha bottle once more. "Now listen here. I know Winifred has solved more than her share of—"

"Good idea, Leo." Once more, Angus stopped his friend before he'd barely gotten started. I decided Gerald was a lot more palatable when Angus was around. He looked to me. "I'll help you any way I can, Fred. I'm sure we all will."

Most of our rather large group nodded along. I was a little taken aback both by the assumption that I was instantly going to start looking into who killed Luca and by the show of faith they had in me. For a split second, I started to deny that I was going to try to figure out what happened, then didn't see the point. Hadn't I already been crossing off suspects in my mind? And really, by this point, it was just what I did. And if there was ever a murder that justified me looking into it, it was this one—shut off from the rest of the world with no police involved.

I glanced out the window, then back to Leo. "It's probably still an hour and a half before sunrise. You should at least wait until then."

"We'll be fine." He paused for a couple of moments, his gaze holding mine. Even in the midst of what was going on and all the people around us, I could see the memory of the night before flicker behind his eyes, and I thought maybe a question as well, wondering if I was regretting, having second thoughts, or about to panic. Then it was gone. "Besides, by the time Barry and I bundle up and we get the snowmobiles running, it'll be that much closer to sunrise. And with how heavy the blizzard still is, the sun won't make that much difference anyway."

With that, it was decided. Leo and Barry went off to put on as many layers as possible. Jonah and Noah moved a sofa in front of the doors to the key room, marking it off-limits. And Lisa vanished behind the fireplace to comfort the rest of her brood of employees.

Watson was nearly beside himself watching Barry and Leo disappear into the dark swirl of snow, barking furiously from where he, Mom, and I stood on the deck overlooking the parking lot.

Mom glanced at him in concern and then toward the path Barry and Leo had taken. "You think Watson knows something? That they shouldn't go?"

Though I was worried as well, I couldn't help but chuckle. "No. That's not his warning bark. That's his offended *why are you leaving me when I want to play* demonstration."

Sure enough, Watson barked again, bounced up and down on his short stubby front legs, eliciting a small avalanche over the side of the porch.

"Never mind that half the time he puts one paw out in the snow when we're home and decides he's too delicate for such weather, but if it's Barry and Leo, he's ready to be strapped to a snowmobile and tear through a blizzard."

Mom studied him and finally gave a little chuckle of her own, looking relieved.

Unable to help myself, I stared off once more to where they'd disappeared. What little I could see of the forest was so dark and mostly obliterated by the whorls of snow whipping around. I had no doubt Leo knew what he was doing. As a park ranger, he'd done more than one rescue mission in bad weather conditions, but I didn't know if they had been as intense as this. Would it really have made that much difference to at least have waited until sunrise?

After a few moments, I felt Mom's gaze on me and looked over to her.

She cocked her head, and then a knowing look entered her eyes. "Oh. Something's changed, hasn't it?"

I flinched, feeling like I'd been caught red-handed at something. "What do you mean?"

She only smiled and patted my hand. "That makes me

happy." Another pat. "Don't worry. Our men will come back to us."

Juliet's sobs had lessened to sniffles and ragged breaths by the time Watson and I made our way to the other side of the fireplace. Beau remained by her side, holding her hand. Lisa had gotten the rest of the staff preparing breakfast. It would be mostly leftovers and cold items, but there was an old wood-burning stove they'd kept for appearances that they were attempting to put back into working order.

With one hand in the young man's beside her and her other stroking Watson's head, Juliet looked at me in sad confusion. "So... you're a detective or something? You going to question us?"

"No." I tried for a soothing smile. "I own a bookshop downtown. But I've helped solve a few murders in the past, and my father was a detective, so I'm aware of some of the protocols. But... you are, of course, under no legal obligation to speak to me at all. I simply wanted to ask a few questions about last night, about Luca." As I said his name, Juliet's tears increased. I decided to use her emotion over the boy to my advantage. "I hope I can help get justice for Luca as quickly as possible."

"Okay." Sniffing, she nodded and pulled her hand from Watson long enough to wipe her eyes, not that it did any good. "What do you want to know?"

"If I understood you correctly, it sounded like Luca was supposed to spend the night with you?"

Another nod.

I spared a glance toward Beau beside her and then back to Juliet. She'd said she wanted him to stay, so apparently there weren't any secrets between them. "Does that mean you and Luca were... romantically involved?"

She nodded again, and her tears increased.

Beau slid his free arm over her shoulder, pulling her close tenderly, and kissed the top of her head as he murmured gently. The familiarity of the gesture caught me off guard. It seemed more than what a friend would normally do.

Maybe...

I refocused on Juliet. "Were the two of you keeping your relationship a secret?"

"No." She spoke in a questioning way, as if unable to imagine why they would. "Luca didn't have secrets. He doesn't believe in them."

The memory of him videotaping Barry, Mom, and me the night before flickered in my mind. I highly doubted Luca didn't believe in secrets, but he most definitely didn't believe in privacy. "And you said he was supposed to spend the night with you last night?"

"Yeah. It was our night together. But I hadn't slept very well the night before." Juliet struggled to take a breath and then pushed on. "Maybe if I hadn't fallen asleep, I would've realized something was wrong."

"Juliet, it's not your fault." Beau pulled her closer once more. "I didn't notice Luca hadn't come back to our room either, like he normally does before he goes to you."

"Oh, you and Luca were roommates?"

"Kinda." Beau offered a partial shrug and met my gaze for the first time. His eyes were nearly as red and puffy as Juliet's. "We are roommates, but more than roommates."

"He and Luca were dating as well." Juliet squeezed Beau's hand, clearly trying to comfort him.

"You and..." My brain short-circuited as it tried to do

the math and couldn't. Then studying Beau's arm over Juliet's shoulder and where their hands were clasped, I thought I did. "So the *three* of you were dating?"

They both shook their heads. But it was Beau who answered, and Juliet's tears increased once more. "No. *We*"—he gestured with a nod toward Juliet—"were both dating *Luca*."

I thought I knew the answer but pushed ahead for clarification anyway. "Luca was dating both of you, and you both knew it?"

Once more that look of bafflement crossed Juliet's face. "Of course."

"And you were okay with that? Both of you?" I didn't have a problem with how people chose to live their lives, even so, this particular concept baffled me a little. "And were the two of you dating as well?"

"No." Exasperation filled Beau's voice, slipping into a quality as if he was explaining the obvious to a five-year-old. "*Juliet* was dating Luca, and *I* was dating Luca. Juliet and I are not dating. We're just good friends. Everyone knew; everyone was okay with it. It's just like Juliet said earlier. Luca didn't believe in secrets. None of this was secret, not from any of us."

Juliet scrunched up her nose, considering. "I don't think Lisa really caught on."

I knew I was pushing things, given Beau's irritation. However, I wasn't sure if he was growing short with me because he felt it should all be obvious, or because I was barging in on things he didn't want me to know. A little further push might answer that question. I leveled my gaze on his. "Do you *want* a romantic relationship with Juliet?"

The genuine grimace that crossed his expression left no

doubt about his sincerity. "No. She's my friend. That's it. I have *no* interest in girls. Not that way. I loved Luca."

"Oh, Beau." Juliet started sobbing again and wrapped herself fully in Beau's embrace.

I blinked, trying to sort it all out. Attempting to connect their relationship to Luca's murder. Perhaps Beau was done sharing Luca with anyone else. Although if that was the case, wouldn't he have killed Juliet? Something about that didn't sit right, and both Juliet's and Beau's affection felt genuine. But... complications in romantic relationships were frequent motives, so... maybe...

"Good morning! Hope you're all ready for day two, because we've got a bunch of..." Percival burst through the front door of the inn, Gary directly behind him. He scanned the lobby. His gaze flitted over our group, which was gathered around the sofas arranged in front of the fireplace, then traveled over to where most of the knitters clustered in another grouping of overstuffed chairs. Some were knitting, others simply looked shell-shocked, probably wondering what they'd gotten themselves into. Percival's cheerful expression fell. "Good Lord, this is a celebration, and you all look like you've gathered for a funeral. Who died?" He attempted to crack a smile but didn't quite make it.

"One of the young waiters." Mom spoke up from where she was braiding Christina's hair. "Luca."

Gary's eyes went wide, but Percival's narrowed. "Oh, don't be..." His words trailed away as his gaze landed on me. "Fred... really? This weekend of *all* weekends?" He flung open his boysenberry-colored fur coat, revealing a glittery T-shirt. "I ordered my Barbara and Judy outfit special."

Despite the heaviness that had settled over the hotel, I couldn't hold back a squawk of laugh. "Me? *I* didn't do it!"

Percival propped a bony hand on his hip. Before he could argue, Gary gave him a nudge, but addressed me.

"And we know you'll solve it as quick as that." He snapped his fingers.

"I think I'll go back to our cabin, sit in the whirlpool until this is over, even without the bubbles." Percival wheeled around. "Let me know when the party mood returns."

Gary rolled his eyes and put a hand on Percival's shoulder, holding him in place.

"Seriously, Percival. Don't you think you're being a little callous?" While she reprimanded her brother, Mom glanced over at the group of knitters, clearly embarrassed to imagine what they were thinking.

"After this happening so many times, it's hard to—" A fresh wail of sobbing filtered in from another room. Juliet would do well for a while and then launch into hysterics once more. Percival glanced toward the sound, then sighed as he blushed. "Good point. He was a handsome, charming kid, if I recall. The blond German young man, right?" When I nodded, Percival sighed again and took the empty place on the arm of the sofa. "Let us know how we can help."

Lisa emerged from the dining room, holding a large pot of coffee. "Breakfast is served. It's been a while since we've had to use the wood-fired stove, so it may not be quite up to snuff." She gestured with her head toward the dining room where two other members of her staff—neither of whom I recalled from dinner the night before—were carrying heaping trays. "But it's warm, and I'm sure we all could use it."

Watson had been napping by the fire, but at the scent of food, he perked up and barely spared me a glance before springing off the hearth, shooting like a bullet to the dining room.

Katie chuckled beside me. "I love that little guy. Good to know there's a few things in life you can always depend on."

"Yeah." Percival's mutter was barely audible. "A chubby dog who likes food, and a murderer to ruin every party."

"Percival!" Mom hissed at the exact same moment Gary elbowed him.

As our group and the knitters started to wander into the dining room, Lisa pulled me aside. Katie hung back with me. "Do you mind if Kelvin and I speak to you for a second? He's just informed me of some things I think you ought to know." She glanced at Katie, eyes narrowing in slight distrust. I was sure it was weird enough to be talking to a bookseller about a murder, let alone her baker friend.

Katie didn't seem the least bit offended and smiled at me. "I'll make sure Watson doesn't eat his weight in carbs, and I'll fix you a plate as well."

Lisa motioned toward one of the vacated sofas, and I followed her over. It'd been a little over an hour and half since Leo and Barry left. The sun was coming up, brightening the whirling snow outside the windows. We'd barely gotten seated before one of the servers who had been delivering breakfast came in.

"Winifred, this is Kelvin." Lisa gestured toward the young man, then prodded him gently. "It's okay. Just tell Ms. Page what you told me. It's better to get it all out in the open."

He gulped and met my gaze but then darted away quickly. "I... ah..." He shook his head.

I stayed silent, unsure what to say.

After a few moments, his dark eyes flashed at me. "I didn't hurt Luca." He had a thick British accent.

"Okay. That's good." I attempted an encouraging smile. "Anything you can tell me may help."

Kelvin fell silent again.

I heard the clacking of Watson's claws on the hardwood before I saw him waddling into view, peering around questioningly, and then his brown gaze landed on me, clearly wondering why I wasn't at breakfast. To my complete shock, instead of hurrying back to the food, he plodded over and plopped down at my feet with an annoyed sigh.

A partial smile flitted over Kelvin's lips as he watched Watson, and then he looked back up at me. "I couldn't stand the bugger, but I didn't hurt him. No matter what they say."

"Okay, I believe you." Maybe I did, maybe I didn't. He sounded genuine enough, or at least genuinely angry enough even in those few words. If he'd truly killed Luca, surely he'd try to do a better job covering his dislike. "And no one has told me anything about you yet."

"I know. I already asked Juliet and Beau what they told you, so I figure it's better for you to hear it from me, before one of the other snitches blabs." Kelvin glanced down at Watson again and then unleashed. "Luca was an obnoxious git. Constantly filming everybody on his stupid cell phone and then lording it against us. Last week he caught me..." His cheeks reddened, and he glanced at Lisa, who nodded. After considering for a moment, Kelvin continued again. "Well, let's just say Luca was threatening if I didn't do the things he told me to, he'd post it online."

"What did he tell you to do?"

Kelvin reached down and started stroking Watson, his gaze following the movement, and he seemed to become more at ease.

He shrugged. "Nothing horrible. To do more of his job

responsibilities while he napped or messed around with Beau or Juliet. Had me buy him cigarettes when we went into town. Junk like that, but I was already getting tired of it. We had a big blowup two days ago, so..." Another shrug.

"So you're worried people will think because of what he was doing, because of your fight, that I'll think you killed Luca."

He nodded.

Lisa jumped in. "I thought I'd put a stop to Luca's videoing months ago. He fancied himself a documentarian." Kelvin snorted at that, but Lisa kept going. "He was applying to some film schools. I knew he had been filming some of the staff without their permission, and I caught him filming me once, nothing incriminating or embarrassing, just going throughout the normal routine. He *never* did it to any guests. If he had, I would've had no choice but to let him go." She cringed. "Although, maybe I was wrong about that. I thought he'd stopped altogether. I shouldn't have trusted him."

"Nah. Not your fault. You're just good-hearted. You treat us all like you're our mum." The affection Kelvin felt for Lisa was clear, and matched the impression I had of her. "Luca was good at deceiving people."

I did believe Kelvin. He seemed forthcoming and open. And while I didn't think he'd been the one to murder Luca, he'd opened another possibility. Maybe Luca had caught another member of the staff in a moment serious enough they were willing to kill over it.

Watson perked up, gave a happy bark, and then bounced onto the sofa, standing on his hind legs so he could look over the back and see out the window. A second later, I heard the reason why. The faint sound of engines, then silence.

"Leo and Barry must be back." I stood and offered a hand to Kelvin. "Thank you. May I come to you if I have any more questions?"

He shrugged again. "'Course."

When footsteps sounded on the stairs outside, Watson hopped off the sofa with another happy yip, ran to the front door, and began spinning in circles in pure delight. I knew at the end of the day I was the one Watson loved, *his* human, but I never stopped marveling at the reaction Barry and Leo prompted in my cantankerous little corgi.

When the door opened and the first person stepped in, Watson stopped halfway through one of his happy spins and growled.

"Trust me, fleabag, you're not who I wanted to see either." Officer Green ripped off a wool cap, her brown hair loose and messy instead of in the typical short tight ponytail she normally wore. Her pale blue gaze found mine. "You just can't help yourself, can you?"

I let out an exasperated huff. "As I've already said, *I* didn't kill anyone."

She smirked. "Whatever you have to tell yourself to sleep at night, Angel of Death."

Leo and Barry followed behind her, reigniting Watson's joy to nearly astronomical levels as they both knelt and simultaneously lavished attention on him.

Within a few minutes, Barry, Leo, Katie, Lisa, and I were gathered at the far end of the library game room.

Susan had been asking questions as she snapped pictures of the scene and jotted notes. She'd finished a few close-ups of the key letter opener and turned to me. "So your primary theory right now is that our victim here spied on the wrong person. You're dismissing the love-triangle aspect?"

I waited for the punchline of Susan's question, she sounded as if she genuinely wanted my input. When it didn't come, and I was silent for an awkward amount of time, she prompted with a cocked eyebrow. "Yes. It doesn't make sense, and I don't think Juliet is capable of killing someone." From my peripheral, I noticed Lisa nod her agreement. "I'm leaning toward his spying and filming habit."

Susan considered, looking down at Luca's body once more. "You may be right. Whoever did this was most definitely not happy with him."

Again I waited for a punch line. But it didn't seem like one was coming. Maybe things really had changed between Susan and me. She was treating me like my theories held water. Not only that, but there hadn't been one comment about me sticking my nose anywhere it didn't belong.

"I suppose the good thing, at least for the moment, is that all of our suspects are contained." Susan opened the back door before looking at me. "Although, you said this was open when you came in?"

"Yes. But they could've easily circled around and come back in through another of the doors."

Lisa chimed in, "There are also four smaller cabins on the grounds, three of which are in use at the moment."

"There's always the possibility it's somebody who's not staying at Baldpate." Leo shrugged when Susan gave him a doubtful stare. "Maybe, it's not likely, especially considering the weather, but the way it appears, maybe this kid had romantic entanglements in town, or was attempting to blackmail someone else."

"During a blizzard?" Again Susan sounded skeptical. And once more threw me off. I was used to that tone with me, not directed at Leo. Though, there was none of the scorn that typically went along when she addressed me.

"I'm not saying it's likely, just that we need to consider all possibilities." Leo grimaced. "We also need to figure out what to do with Luca's body. He's stayed there too long as it is."

I glanced toward Susan, then back at Leo. "What do you mean? Now that Susan's here, the rest of the authorities can't be far behind."

Barry shook his head. "Turns out, things are worse than we realized."

Susan bugged her eyes out at me. "Maybe you haven't noticed, with your nose in a book and in other people's business, but there's the blizzard of the century going on outside." *There* was the annoyed, condescending tone I was used to. It was almost reassuring. "No one is going to be joining us here today, maybe not even tomorrow. It's almost like a disaster area out there. I shouldn't have come home last night. It took me hours. By the time I considered turning around, I'd already gone halfway. By this point it's a billion times worse." She studied Luca's body as she spoke. "There's no power in town at all. Last communication I had, they still weren't sure how many lines were down. Trust me, short of a tank, there's no car or vehicle that's going to be able to come up here anytime soon."

It was hard to imagine the whole town without power. "But we can't leave Luca like this. Surely helicopters could—"

"In case you didn't notice, Fred. He's as dead as he's going to get. It's not exactly an emergent situation." She sounded like she was enjoying herself. *Yes, still Susan.*

True to form, I felt my own tone take on a condescending quality. "In case *you* haven't noticed, the murdered body indicates a murderer. And while Leo's theory might be right, it's a very good possibility that whoever killed Luca is still here with us."

Susan groaned. "Great, so now you're going to turn this into a serial-killer type of situation? Who's the next victim?" She raised a finger. "Wait, wait, let me guess. It's the fat dog, with a knitting needle, in the kitchen."

"Breathe, Susan." Leo gave her a reproachful glance, then turned to me, his tone softening. "From what Susan's been told, there was a mass pileup late last night on Highway 34, and a rock-and-snow avalanche in the canyon as well. All available emergency crews, including helicopters, will be dealing with them for the foreseeable future, as those take precedence since there're lives that may need saving."

I was struck dumb for a moment at the thought of it all. Estes Park sounded as if it had transitioned from magical little village contained in a snow globe to disaster area. "That's horrible."

Susan looked over at Lisa. "Now there, we're all caught up. We do need to move our victim's body. I'm assuming your refrigerators would be large enough to..." She shook her head. "No electricity, but they should stay cold for quite awhile."

A look of horror crossed Lisa's face.

Susan didn't notice and kept going, talking to herself as she glanced out the window. "The snow would be better, but out in the open like that..."

"There's an old icehouse." Lisa sounded sick to her stomach, growing pale as a sheet. "It used to be..."

Katie put a steadying hand on Lisa's arm. "It's okay. This is awful, but you don't have to face it alone."

Susan nodded, moving along. "An icehouse will work. We'll just—"

"Hey!" A shout from the other room caused us all to turn. "Give that back."

As one, we all hurried from the room. As we entered the key room, I saw Beau chasing Watson, my little guy's eyes wide with fear, and something gripped in his mouth.

I rushed toward Beau and grabbed his arm. "What do you think you're doing?" I didn't bother to worry about how tightly I squeezed when I jerked him to a stop.

He flung out a hand toward Watson, who'd taken shelter behind a large showcase filled with key paraphernalia. "He's got Luca's phone."

"What?" I looked at him like he was crazy.

"His phone." Beau gestured again, but this time over to another case by the entrance to the key room. "He was snuffling behind that, then popped out with Luca's cell phone in his mouth. When I tried to get it, he tore off."

"Fred." Leo's voice drew my attention. He was kneeling beside Watson, comforting him with one hand and holding up an iPhone in a red case with his other.

I shot a glare at Beau before going to Leo and Watson. I knelt down and took Watson's face in my hands, pressing my forehead to his. "It's okay, buddy. You're a good boy. You're a good, good boy." He was trembling. Watson might not be the biggest people person, but he wasn't used to humans acting aggressively toward him, either.

Leo spoke again before I could give in to my own murderous thoughts. "There's something sticky all over it."

"Probably that dog's spit." Beau spoke up from behind me, and I whirled around just in time to see him snatch the phone from Leo's hands. I was about to launch into him, but the expression that crossed his face held me back

—a little jolt of surprise, followed by a quiet gasp that sounded part pain and part fondness. "I think it's cookie dough." A small smile turned the corner of his lips. "Luca was always sneaking into the refrigerator, stealing cookie dough."

As I continued to stroke Watson, I made a mental note to get him a piece of that cookie dough. Even if it wasn't good for dogs, or anyone else, for that matter. My poor little guy just thought he'd found a delicious snack and then got chased all over the room for it.

Not swayed by Beau's emotion, Susan stomped over and plucked the phone out of his hands. "Is this what Luca would spy on people with?"

Anger flitted over Beau's face, but he nodded.

Susan tapped the screen and let out a frustrated grunt. "Passcoded."

"I'm not giving it to you!" The angry words burst from Beau.

He tried to snatch the phone back, but Susan yanked it out of reach. "Calm down. I didn't even ask you to." She considered and looked at me though she spoke to Beau. "*I'm* not in the place to ask you that."

I caught on instantly. She couldn't demand anything without a warrant. With the final scratch on Watson's head, I stood, channeling my anger to something productive. "No one can make you give the password up, Beau, but the fact is, someone killed Luca. Probably someone within these walls right now. And unless you're the one who did it, I'd think you'd want to help solve his murder. You *claim* that you loved him."

He glared, fury radiating from his eyes. "I did love him. I *do*."

Maybe Leo was feeling the same as me because when

he gestured to the phone, his voice was hard. "Then prove it."

"Beau, please." Lisa came up, speaking in a motherly tone and attempting a reassuring touch.

He shrugged her off, sneering. "What do you expect to find on here anyway? You think he recorded his own murder?"

Susan looked at him with all the disdain she typically saved for me. "Are you afraid he did?"

Beau's face grew so red he looked like he would pop. Then with a curse, he yanked the cell from her grasp, punched his finger repeatedly against the screen, before thrusting it at me.

When she hesitated, I took it. "Good choice, Beau. This might help Luca."

He didn't reply, but a tear made its way down his cheek.

Before he could change his mind, or the lock-screen returned, I found the camera app and went into the photos and videos. Everyone except Beau gathered around, watching over my shoulders. I tapped the most recent video and felt my heart lurch.

It was nearly too dark to see, but from the angle, it looked like Luca had been spying from the corner of the glassed-in front porch to the strip of parking below. He was zoomed in on one of the vans the knitting club had driven—the back doors were open, and there were two figures unloading something.

Gusts of gray snow obliterated the entire scene for several moments, and Luca's whispered curses cut out the sound of the wind.

The figures returned to view and fluttered out again.

They came into view once more. One figure remained

shadowed in the back of the van, another moved a few feet away, holding something.

"Is that...?" Katie nudged closer, her whisper brushing against my neck.

Before she could finish the thought, the figure looked up, searching as if knowing someone was watching, then looked directly into the camera.

Luca cursed again before the figure took off, heading in the direction of the stairs up to the inn. The image vanished in a blur and a loud crash. It took a second to realize Luca must've dropped the phone. He picked it up with yet another curse and then, from the motion and sounds, ran.

The video stopped.

I turned to look at Katie. "Alexandria."

She nodded.

"Alexandria?" Susan snatched the cell out of my hand and reversed the video a few seconds, squinting at the screen. "Alexandria who?"

"Uhm..." I racked my brain, trying to recall if I'd heard her last name. "I'm not—"

"Bell," Katie piped up, but her tone wasn't bright, as it normally was when she answered a question.

Susan's eyes narrowed further, then widened. "You've got to be kidding." She glared at Katie, then me, as if it was our fault. "Alexandria Bell is here, seriously?"

I pointed toward the dining room, though from where we were, we couldn't see in. "She came with the group of knitters."

Without another word, Susan turned on her heel and stomped off across the lodge. As she moved, she dug a band out of the back pocket of her slacks and twisted her hair into her trademark short ponytail.

Katie and I, and the rest of the group, exchanged looks and followed her.

"Where is she?" Susan hadn't finished stepping up to the table full of knitters before barking out the question.

The six women looked over at her, startled. The one who'd bonded with Watson... Cordelia... gave a quick once-over at Susan's uniform, sat up a little straighter and lifted her chin. "Where is who, Officer?"

"Don't play games. And don't try to cover for her, or I'll—"

I hurried to the table, Watson by my side. It seemed Alexandria had the same effect on Susan as she had on Katie—more so, actually. "We're looking for Alexandria." I shot Susan a warning glance, for all the good it would do, and then addressed Cordelia. "We have a few questions about... what she might've seen last night."

The fancy blonde, Pamela, gasped and lifted her fingers to her throat. "You don't think Alexandria had anything to do with that poor boy, do you?" She cast a quick look around at the other women, then addressed me instead of Susan. "I mean, she can be harsh, judgmental, and a little... superior, I suppose, but surely she wouldn't murder someone."

"Of course not." Betsy shuddered and her weathered hand reached over to pat Cassidy's beside her. "We'll never get the image out of our heads. Alexandria might not be the most pleasant, but she couldn't do something like *that*."

"We're not at liberty to discuss any matters of the case at this time, and we're not asking for theories." Susan's impatience was palpable, but she did seem to attempt a more cordial tone. "I simply asked her whereabouts. Are others of your group absent this morning?"

"No, the rest of us are here." Cordelia spoke smoothly and more calmly than her sister. She also appeared more curious than anything else. "I'm afraid we wore out our welcome with Alexandria when we invited ourselves along on this little adventure. She—"

"I wouldn't put it like that." Pamela spoke up again. "We didn't *invite* ourselves. We merely—"

Cordelia silenced her with a look and then turned back to us. As she spoke, Watson padded over to her and received a scratch on his head for his efforts. "She needed some space from us and has her own cabin. I'm sure she's still sleeping."

"I placed her in the twin sisters' cabin." Lisa had joined us at the table and addressed Susan. "She requested lodging that was the farthest away."

"Typical." All attention turned to the oldest member of the group. She sniffed primly, though her eyes looked blood-shot and the tip of her nose a bulbous red. "She's a little snooty, that one."

"Minnie." Pamela gasped once more. "Really, she's not even here to defend herself. There's no need to—"

"I've met Alexandria on more than one occasion. Snooty is apt, I'd say." Pamela was cut off again, this time by Susan. "Not to mention, arrogant, entitled, rude, and down-right annoying."

The entire table, even Cordelia, looked somewhat shocked at Susan's declaration, all except for Minnie, who tapped the end of her red nose with one finger and pointed at Susan with another. "Good discernment is an honor to your badge." Minnie leaned forward, speaking directly to Susan. "Good thing you're here. I don't know what all happened last night, but every few seconds, there was the creaking and moaning of floorboards in the hallways, and every time I looked out, there was someone or other sneaking about. It was like everyone in the inn had some-where else to be than tucked in bed like proper people." Her bloodshot gaze flitted to me, held, and looked away. She sniffed once more. "Murder wasn't the only scandal occur-ring during the night."

I felt my cheeks heat. Maybe she'd heard Leo and me walking back up from our time at the fire. Had she seen us hesitating by his door? I hadn't felt anyone's eyes on us, not that it mattered. Although, she had a point. I'd noticed myself that it seemed there had been a lot of movement in the middle of the night.

Surprisingly, Susan didn't seem to notice Minnie's accusing stare and turned to Lisa. "Take me to her cabin."

Lisa only hesitated a moment before she nodded and started to turn away, but then Cordelia spoke up again. "Perhaps you'd like me to come with you. It might go easier if you have someone Alexandria knows."

"I'm more than capable of doing my job. Thank you." Susan barely spared Cordelia a glance before motioning Lisa onward.

I gave an apologetic wince toward the table, then followed Susan and Lisa, Watson hurrying to catch up when I was a few paces away.

We hesitated long enough by the check-in counter for Lisa to grab a jacket. Barry started to ask Susan something, but she shushed him. In surprise, I realized I knew Susan well enough by this time to recognize she was coming up with a plan. From her growing scowl, it appeared she wasn't overly fond of whatever scheme she was hatching. Finally she turned toward our group, pointing to Leo. "You, come." Her finger moved to me, and she hesitated a moment longer. "You as well. Go get your jacket." She turned to Katie and Barry. "You two stay here. I don't need the entire Scooby Gang. Besides, you can both keep your eyes on those knitting women. I don't trust anyone who has nothing better to do than sit around all day twisting fabric together."

Within a matter of minutes, Lisa led Susan down the steps of the inn and then toward a path that was nothing more than a gap in the trees, considering the depth of the snow that wound up the steep embankment. We passed a couple of other cabins, and Leo and I trailed behind. Watson, proving once more that as long as Leo was present he was in heaven, trundled through the snow without a complaint, one moment barreling along underneath the thick white blanket like a groundhog and the next bounding through it as much as his tiny legs could bound through the tracks we left behind.

Though I couldn't tell from the flakes, I got the sense that the blizzard was waning somewhat, more from the increasing brightness than a lessening of the snowfall. I was thankful I'd abandoned my broomstick skirt in the room as I grabbed my jacket, trading it for snow pants and winter boots, as the snow came up to midthigh in several places. The wind had died down, allowing the snow to fall in a way that didn't smack into our faces. Outside of the crunch of steps and the rustle of our clothes, the world was an oddly muffled silence. If I didn't know how destructive it had been in Estes Park and the canyon, not to mention walking in on a murder that morning, I would've found it beautiful, maybe the most beautiful winter landscape I'd ever seen, completely otherworldly in a way.

Even the sound of Susan pounding on the door seemed faraway. When there was no answer, she glanced at Lisa. "You brought your keys?"

Lisa nodded, suddenly looking nervous again. "I did, and I'm sure you're clearer on the laws than me, but I can't unlock her door unless you have a warrant."

Susan had already started to knock again and paused with her hand still raised. "I wasn't suggesting—"

The click of the deadbolt cut her off, and a second later, Alexandria's pretty face glared through a crack in the door. "What is it? I don't like to be..." Her words fell away as she noticed a small group outside her door.

"Alexandria Bell?" Susan's tone took on a distant professional quality.

Alexandria focused on Susan, studying her with an expression that suggested she recognized the police officer, but wasn't entirely sure who she was. "Yes?" The word came out questioningly, and then, as if not liking the sound of it, Alexandria straightened, opened the door a few more inches as her tone took on a defiant quality. "Yes, I am she. Who are *you*, and what do you want?"

"I'm Officer Green. A young man was murdered at the main lodge sometime in the night or early this morning." Susan delivered the line without a shred of emotion, then waited.

Alexandria barely missed a beat. "That's terrible." She spared a glance toward Baldpate, then at the rest of us before looking back at Susan. "What do you need?"

Her response surprised me, no emotion was evident in her voice or flooded over her face. She didn't even bother feigning concern.

"I need you to come back to the lodge. I have some questions for you." Susan gestured at the gap in the door. "Or you can invite us in."

Alexandria bristled. "As I said, that is terrible, but I don't appreciate my privacy being interrupted. Nor your implication that I might be involved in anything to do with such unsavory events."

"I wasn't implying anything." A slight enjoyment seeped into Susan's voice. "However, we do have a video shot by the deceased, which very clearly shows you and another person out in the middle of the night loitering at the back of one of the vans."

The twinge in her eyes was barely noticeable, if I hadn't been inspecting her, I would've missed it. "I'm sorry, is there a curfew in Colorado mountain towns that I'm not aware of? Is it illegal for me to be outside of my cabin after a certain time?"

The corner of Susan's lips curved slightly. "So you're not denying you were meeting with someone in the middle of the night during the worst blizzard we've seen in years?"

Alexandria's chin lifted even further, and she stood a little straighter, the door opening a little more at the motion. "Again, is there a curfew or some other Podunk law that I've unintentionally violated?"

"From the training I've received, Ms. Bell, murder is against the law, regardless if you find the locale to be Podunk or a metropolis."

Alexandria rolled her eyes, and instead of seeming offended, shifted to uninterested. "Really? I'm a suspect in a murder? What did I do? Kill someone, then saunter back here, light a fire, and curl up in bed?"

"That's what I'd like to ask you about." Susan took a step back, the heel of her boot bumping against Watson's leg. Though he chuffed in protest and moved out of the way, Susan didn't look down. "Would you like to invite us in or return to the inn?"

"Actually I didn't sleep very well last night. I'm going back to bed." She started to shut the door.

Susan moved again, bumping into Watson once more, that time with a touch more force. Her movement cutting off Watson from Leo and me.

Before I could protest, Watson, completely irritated and cut off by Susan's legs, took his only escape route and darted through the door of the cabin.

Alexandria let out a startled cry and then cursed angrily. "Get your nasty animal out of my room. He's dragging in snow and goodness knows what else."

Susan pushed open the door and gestured through. "You heard the woman, Fred. Go get your fleabag." Though I'd been about to reprimand Susan, there was a quality in the look she gave me that helped me realize she was up to something. "Leo, why don't you help her? The last time that dog did this, someone got bitten. I don't want to add that paperwork on top of what I already have to do."

Trying to control my irritation and confusion along with my expression, I walked in past Alexandria, Leo behind me. The entirety of the small cabin was visible from the doorway. Directly in front was a large restroom, to the left a bedroom, and to the right a large family room with a fireplace. Watson sat in front of the hearth, glaring.

I started to say something to Leo, then noticed Alexandria giving us a glare of her own.

Not sure what Susan was up to, I attempted my best guess. "You're making him uncomfortable. Would you mind giving us a little space? Watson has anxiety issues."

"*Anxiety issues*? For crying out loud," Alexandria practically hissed.

"They need a little room." Leo casually put his arm over Alexandria's shoulder, angling her away.

Alexandria twisted free, then whipped around to face Leo, venom and fury dripping. Not that I could blame her for a man she didn't know to be acting so familiar. "If you touch me again, I'll sue you for assault."

"Listen, lady." Leo held up his hands. "I'm not trying to assault you or anything. Just hoping to keep you from getting bitten by a dog. I only wanted to—"

Alexandria hissed out something else at him, but Susan's quick motion at the inside door handle behind Alexandria caught my attention. She pulled her hand back and her eyes met mine. "Hurry it up, Ms. Page. We don't need any more drama today. Can you get that dog out of here, or do I have to call the pound?"

Both somewhat impressed with what had just gone down and irritated that she'd used Watson in such a manner, I bent down and wrapped one arm around Watson while slipping the other under his chest and belly to give support, whispering by his ear before I lifted him up, "Sorry, buddy. I promise I'll make this up to you."

Watson hated being carried and played the part of crazed dog perfectly by thrashing in my arms. He was heavy enough, I nearly dropped him and had to hold tighter, which only made him writhe more. It was enough to pull Alexandria's attention away from Leo as Watson and I squeezed past them and out the door.

Susan pointed to the far side of the cabin. "Take him over there, keep him far away from Ms. Bell and the rest of us."

Through it all, Lisa stared wide-eyed at the display. From her expression, I got the sense that she too knew something was going on more than met the eyes but wasn't sure what. I didn't think she'd noticed Susan messing with the door.

Leo followed me out, sidestepping Alexandria and joining us in the deep drifts of snow by the cabin. As soon as I set him down, Watson darted a couple of feet away, clearly feeling betrayed, only to have a large embankment of snow crash down on him. Leo came to the rescue, shoving the snow away, then plopping down to cradle Watson in his lap.

Instantly soothed, Watson snuggled up to Leo while casting glares in my direction.

I refocused on the scene in the cabin doorway just in time to hear the end of Alexandria's accusation. "If it was some kind of ploy to get into my cabin, Officer, I promise you, I'll have your badge. I have connections to this town that will—"

"It's a dog, Ms. Bell," Susan interrupted, and though her voice was loud, her tone remained bored. "An ill-trained, annoying one at that. I can promise you, it has no association with the police department or me. If it did, I'd be the first one to toss the fleabag in a sack and launch it over the nearest bridge."

Even as my temper spiked hearing such words from Susan, despite knowing they were merely a means to an end, I couldn't help but be surprised at Alexandria's revolted expression. "You really are as awful as I'd heard."

To my further surprise, Susan flinched, as if stung. She gathered herself quickly enough. "Your personal opinions of me, or other people's for that matter, are of no consequence. If you don't want us to come in, then I invite you, once more, to join us at the main lodge."

Alexandria opened her mouth, her impending refusal clear, but Lisa broke in. "We have breakfast ready, and coffee. It's hot, and I think we could all use a little caffeine, don't you?" She actually smiled at the woman. "And I'm so sorry this is happening during your visit. Believe me, I'll make it up to you. How about a weekend, all-expenses-paid stay here, in the cabin of your choosing?" I was impressed with the innkeeper's quick thinking.

"You think I'd ever stay here again?" Alexandria sounded disgusted, but relaxed somewhat at Lisa's offer and her tone. Finally, with a glare at Susan, she nodded. "Fine. Coffee it is. Wait while I slip into something warm."

Before she could shut the door, Susan took a step forward, one foot in the doorjamb.

Though she glared, Alexandria disappeared from view, I assumed to get dressed. Within a minute or two, she was back, clothed in an expensive matching fur jacket-and-boot set. She shut the door, cast another glare toward Watson, Leo, and me, and then stormed off toward the main lodge, leading the way as if it had been her idea.

As soon as they were out of sight, Leo stood, Watson cradled in his arms, content as a baby. He grinned at me. "Come on, let's see what we can find."

ELEVEN

For a few moments, I stared dumbfounded at Leo's retreating back as he carried Watson toward the cabin, glancing from him to where the three women disappeared. It was almost like Susan and Leo had rehearsed.

Realizing I was playing the part of a fool by standing out in the snow, I hurried after them. Leo had already placed Watson on the floor of the cabin and held the door open for me, then closed it once I stepped inside. "Did you and Susan go over possible scenarios while driving over on the snowmobiles?"

Leo gave me a puzzled look, then gestured to the door. "You mean this?" He shook his head. "How could we? Alexandria wasn't a suspect in my mind. And I didn't even think about telling Susan she was here, although, I didn't know they knew of each other."

"It's like you two were reading each other's minds." Somewhere in there, I reprimanded myself. It didn't matter, at least not in the moment. I needed to search Alexandria's cabin, figure out the how and why of it all later.

Leo's puzzled expression shifted, growing darker somehow, and his tone became more concerned. "Remember, with all the poaching stuff and the rest of the police department and..."

I sighed when he paused and forced a smile. "It's okay. You can say his name. We have plenty of times before."

"True enough." He swallowed and nodded before charging ahead. "When Branson and the rest of the police wouldn't take my concerns about the poaching seriously, Susan did, or at least tried to. There were a couple times she looked into things with me behind their backs." He shrugged, then gestured to the door again. "As far as this, Susan couldn't search the cabin without a warrant, but you and I can. Well..." He gave a dark chuckle. "I guess not really, but more than Susan. I figured she needed to make sure the door wouldn't lock when it was closed. And it's not like you and I haven't done this kind of thing before."

As soon as he said it, things clicked, and I was able to label my ill-at-ease moment. Yes, we had done it before. Here we were again.

I heard more than felt the brush of Watson's fur on my snow pants and looked to see him staring up at me. He gave a questioning whimper and an expression that read, *What in the world is wrong with you? This is Leo. He's better than treats!*

Before I could reassure or even mentally answer my perceived question, Leo stepped nearer, gently taking me by both arms and holding me lightly until I met his gaze. "I'm not Branson, Fred. I don't have a secret life. I don't have a different name. I'm not involved in any criminal activity. As you know, I have a past, a past that has me mostly comfortable in situations like this. I figured we'd get to them over time, but if you need all the details, we can sit down right here and right now and go through every one."

He hadn't even finished his little speech before I was breathing easier. He'd labeled that too, but it had merely taken looking into his eyes for a few seconds for me to rest assured that while I may not know every in and out of Leo's life, I knew who the man was, the real man. And part of him knew how to break into a house, and another part of him both understood and was okay with searching someone's cabin while local law enforcement turned her back.

His thumb rubbed gently over my shoulder. "If you're not comfortable with this, we don't do it. That's not a problem."

I considered for another moment. I couldn't help but think about what my father would do in this situation. He'd been, like Susan, part of the law, and I couldn't imagine him doing this. Though I was certain there were things I didn't know about his career and choices he'd had to make on the job. And what was more, my father wasn't there in the cabin with us. I was definitely my father's daughter, but I was also my own woman. And maybe this had shades of gray, but we were in special circumstances; we needed to know who the murderer was. All signs indicated Alexandria had been the last to see Luca alive. Somehow it felt right, but we needed to be sure. "No, I'm okay with this. Let's see what we can find."

With a smile and a minuscule nod, Leo dropped his hands from my arms.

I grabbed one of them, catching his attention once more. "*And* I know you're *not* Branson. I trust you. And I don't want to hear everything in one big explanation like it's a confession or something. We'll get there when we get there."

Leo relaxed a little but stayed serious. "Okay. If you ever change your mind, let me know. There's nothing I won't tell you, even the shadowy stuff."

The urge to kiss him washed over me, it almost made me laugh. Such a strange new development, but I shook both impulses away. "All right, let's do this. Though I have no idea what we're looking for." I refocused on Watson again, who was now seated at our feet, looking back and forth between the two of us. "You found Luca's cell phone. Can you find anything tying his murder to Alexandria?"

Proving that whatever we were looking for wasn't covered in smudges of cookie dough, Watson didn't tear off to uncover all the answers in the corner of the room, merely sat there, tongue lolling happily as he basked in the presence of two people he adored.

The thought made me laugh, and I bent to pet him. "Looks like you've forgiven me, by the way. I really am sorry that I picked you up and—" Before I could touch him, Watson chuffed, scooted toward Leo, and pulled his tongue in, giving me a serious expression. "Spoke too soon it seems."

Leo chuckled and nudged my arm. "What do you think? Divide and conquer?"

"Sure." I scanned the tiny cabin. There were only a few things that seemed like her personal items scattered over the living area and the bathroom. The majority was in the bedroom. "I'll take here. You hit the other two?"

"Yes, ma'am." Leo gave a playful salute and then stepped into the living room, Watson right on his heels, casting me another accusatory glare over his shoulder before trotting out of view.

Sometimes Watson seemed unreasonably quick to be offended, but this time, I couldn't blame him. Knowing it was only a matter of time, and treats, I tried to decide where to begin. Not sure where to start or even what we were looking for, I went directly to the closet.

It seemed Alexandria and my uncle Percival were kindred spirits. She had more clothes than I would've taken on a two-week vacation, and all of them looked expensive and lush. Feeling a little silly, I patted them down, checking the pockets and feeling for any strange bulges within the material.

There was nothing. Next I moved to the drawers of the TV stand. Like the closet, they were full—undergarments, scarves, all sorts of various products and accessories. I didn't find anything there, either. I glanced at my cell; we'd been searching for almost ten minutes. "Any luck over there?"

"No. Nothing at all." As if they'd been waiting, Leo and Watson stepped into the bedroom. "What have you done? Where would you like me—" He grinned down at Watson. "—*us* to help."

"You're already done with both rooms?"

He shrugged one shoulder. "There wasn't much."

"I've done the closet and TV stand. We've got suitcases, that desk over there, and the bed itself." I headed toward the stack of suitcases. With all their pockets and zippers, they looked like the most work. "I'll start in on these."

"Okay, I'll get going on the desk." Though not needed, Leo tapped his thigh, inviting Watson to follow him.

Alexandria had brought five suitcases. She might actually be outdoing Percival. What solitary person owned *five* suitcases? I was working through the third one when I realized why they were striking me as strange. "There is not a solitary piece of scrap paper, abandoned string of dental floss, gum wrappers, or loose change in any of these. It's like they're brand-new." I started to look up at Leo but paused to inspect the ribbing stitched on the outside of the suitcases. Sure enough. "But there's a significant amount of wear and tear on the suitcases themselves. Not like they've been abused, just well used and well traveled."

Leo paused from flipping through one of the books from the stack on the desk. "Maybe she's just really neat."

"There's not even lint, Leo." I ran my hand inside the bottom crease of one of the pockets, then held up my fingers as if for inspection. "Nothing."

He considered for a second. "So... you're thinking they're spotless because they were recently cleaned free of evidence, more than Alexandria is a neat freak?"

"Maybe..." I gestured toward the closet and the TV stand. "Although everything's hung up and put away tidily, like she moved in here. But... still..."

"You've got great instincts. If your gut is telling you something's fishy about the suitcases, I bet money that you're right." He turned back to flipping through the pages. "If Alexandria did kill Luca, she would've had enough time to come back here and get rid of any evidence that might be incriminating."

"Maybe so, but where? It isn't like she could drive it away." I scanned the room, paused when I glanced toward the living room. "The fireplace could help get rid of all kinds of things."

"True. There's also about a gazillion tons of snow to cover up stuff for a while as well." Leo continued flipping as he responded, then set the book down, picked up another, and started flipping again. "As far as things that someone would be willing to kill for, it could be anything—weapons, drugs, cash, poached antlers, or..." He flinched, staring at whatever he'd found in the book, then went sheet white.

I stood. Likewise, Watson rose to attention, feeling the change in the air. "What did you find?"

Leo shook his head, closed the book, and looked toward me. "Nothing. I..." He blinked, then shook his head again, though this time it seemed in resignation rather than denial.

"You're not gonna like it, and it won't be easy. But..." He crossed the room, met me in the middle, handed me the book, his thumb holding the page. "Here."

I took it like it was a ticking bomb, a sense of dread growing as I turned to the page. It looked to be a sketchbook. It seemed Alexandria Bell was a skilled artist. Remarkably skilled artist, judging from the instant recognition of the face staring up at me. Knees suddenly feeling weak, I sank to the bed, gaping at the page.

"He's younger." Unable to stop myself, I smoothed a fingertip over his face, smearing the drawing slightly. "They both are."

Leo sat beside me, and feeling my mood, Watson did as well, pressing his warm flank to my shins and resting one of his paws on the top of my foot. "You okay?"

I nodded slowly, then realized how it must look to Leo, so I refocused on him, meeting his eyes so he could see the truth of my words. "I *am* okay. Shocked as it was rather unexpected. But I am okay. There are no feelings or anything like that."

"Fred, it's okay if there are. It's only natural that—"

I cut him off with a shake of my head. "There aren't." My words sounded harsher than I'd meant them, but they weren't really directed toward Leo. "There aren't." I softened my tone before looking back at the drawing of a much younger Alexandria with a much younger Branson Wexler standing beside her, one arm draped over her shoulders, pulling her in close.

TWELVE

"Wow. You really are something." Alexandria glared at me, looked back down at the sketchbook I'd tossed in front of her, then sneered at Susan by my side. "Kiss your badge goodbye, honey. It'll be too bad that you're losing the shine, though. It's the only piece of jewelry that looks good on a mannish frame like yours."

"Come on. There's no reason to—"

Susan cast a glare of her own at Leo, cutting him off, before addressing Alexandria, her tone professional and cold. "Insults aren't going to help you, Ms. Bell. Some explanations are in order."

"I'll say." Alexandria repositioned the wooden armchair, fully at ease. "You practically dragged me from my cabin and—"

"No one dragged you, Ms. Bell."

Alexandria cocked an eyebrow. "You practically *dragged* me from my cabin, and then proceed to allow it to be broken into by these two." She looked at me again. "And probably that mutt of yours. Not only will I have the cop's badge, but I'll sue you for every stray hair and stain on my property"—without a break she returned to Susan—"and to top it off, you're interrogating me without a warrant, right next to, judging from the bloodstains, where that boy was killed."

That had thrown me off as well when Leo and I had walked back into the main lodge, only to have Lisa tell us Susan had taken Alexandria to the library game room. I'd barely glanced to where Luca's body had been before I'd shown Susan what Leo and I had found.

"Don't forget to add this to your bevy of complaints." Susan picked up the key letter opener in an evidence bag she'd placed on a nearby table. Slight mocking entered Susan's voice when Alexandria merely rolled her eyes. "You're not even going to pretend to be disturbed by the sight of the murder weapon you used?"

"I'm hardly a fainting flower." Alexandria smiled. "So that's it, then, you're truly accusing me of murder?" She gestured toward the sketchpad. "Because of this? How in the world is an old drawing of me and an ex-boyfriend tied to some poor waiter or custodian, whatever he was, getting himself killed?"

I flinched, despite myself.

Alexandria noticed but didn't have time to say anything before Susan responded.

"Acting so nonchalant around murder doesn't exactly put any cards in your favor."

"Like I said, I'm not a fainting flower." Alexandria barely spared Susan a glance before studying me, her blue gaze dipping down to Watson, who hadn't left my side since finding the sketchbook. After a second, she blinked, then her gaze traveled up and down my body before she met my eyes. "I'm a little embarrassed that I've been so slow to catch on. In my defense, you are about as far from his type as I could imagine."

Leo stiffened and stepped closer.

Alexandria didn't miss a beat, though she didn't spare Leo a glance, a wicked smile growing as she addressed me. "But apparently *you* do have a type. Tall, dark, and handsome. Gotta say, I'm impressed, if not completely baffled. What's your secret? I don't think I've known any other frumpy, dog-hair-covered bookworms who have such good luck as you. Although... two in a row, that suggests something more than luck."

My cheeks burned, but I refused to let her get the better of me. "So you admit you dated Branson?"

She sneered. "Why wouldn't I admit that? The man's gorgeous and charming." She tapped the drawing again. "Plus, the proof is right here. We dated for quite a while. Though, as you can tell by the drawing, it was some time ago."

"Then how did you know about Winifred?" There was a growl in Leo's voice that nearly reminded me of Watson.

That time, she did look at him. "Excuse me?"

"You just implied that you somehow knew about the... relationship between Branson and Fred. If the two of you dated so long ago, how would you even know about her?"

I noticed Susan give Leo an approving nod, but any hope to snag Alexandria failed. Her cocky, entitled attitude didn't falter.

"I said we *dated* some time ago. Not that I hadn't seen him." She looked back at me, the challenge in her eyes. "We saw each other at Christmas. Just because we're not dating doesn't mean we can't... *see* each other from time to time. I'm not so small that I can't admit it hurt to see him upset about another woman. You really did a number on him. But still, it was me he ran to."

"You saw Branson... at Christmas?" Not long after he left Estes Park.

"Jealous?" She cocked her chin and gestured with a flick of her wrist toward the bloodstain. "Is this how you get your revenge?"

The bark of laughter that sounded was so unlike me it took a second to realize I was the one who'd made the sound. "Not hardly. And if you're the one carrying around the drawing you did years ago of the two of you, I'd say that's answer enough about who's jealous." Something about her demeanor helped snap me back into place, get over the unexpected shock of it all. When I spoke again, I was pleased to discover my voice sounded normal, strong, calm, and direct. "It's just more proof. Clearly your association with Branson Wexler, or whatever his real name is—" I paused for a heartbeat, seeing if there was any reaction, but there wasn't. "—is current. You saw him at Christmas, then show up here a couple weeks later, engage in suspicious activity at the back of a van during a blizzard, and then the young man who you caught recording you is murdered. I don't believe in coincidences."

She shrugged, unflappable and unconcerned. "I don't see how any association with Branson, past or present, would have anything to do with the murder. Especially the murder of a member of the service team at a hotel."

I tried again, partially to push, partially out of curiosity. "You called him Branson Wexler."

Her brows knitted. "Of course I did."

"If you dated him years ago, what did you call him back then?"

"Branson Wexler." Alexandria looked at me as if I was daft. "I'm not really sure where you're going with all of this."

"Branson Wexler was an alias, a fairly new one." Susan spoke up, sounding impatient. Knowing her, she'd had enough of Alexandria attempting to mark Branson as her territory. "As Winifred implied, if you knew him many years ago, you knew him under his real name, or another alias. What was it?"

Confusion flitted over Alexandria's features, and I couldn't get a read on whether it was genuine, or if she was just an exceptional actress. "I'm afraid you've had faulty information. Branson Wexler was most definitely not an alias. It was his real name. We dated long enough I would know. I saw his driver's license, credit cards"—she shrugged —"everything. He was and *is* Branson Wexler."

Susan squatted, propping her elbows on her knees to be at eye level with Alexandria. With her heavily muscled body, somehow she was even more intimidating, like a mountain lion ready to pounce. "You're only making this worse for yourself. We know that can't possibly be true. He admitted as much to Winifred in person. You sticking to this story only makes you look guiltier."

This time, Alexandria stared Susan in the eye, then her gaze traveled to Leo and stopped with me. "I'm afraid I have no idea what any of you are talking about."

Susan was right. Though Alexandria was unshakable, not revealing a solitary chink in her armor, it was only more proof. Not only had she known and dated Branson, but she worked with and was just as skilled at deception as he was, clearly. My heart sped up, pounding painfully in my chest in a way that had absolutely nothing to do with Sergeant Wexler. I lowered my voice to a whisper, just in case it started to shake. "What role do you play in the Irons family?" I wanted to go further, demand to know if she had anything to do with my father's murder.

"The Irons family?" The glint of humor in her eyes confirmed we were right. "Is that another of Branson's so-called aliases? Branson Irons doesn't have a very good ring, does it?"

Susan shocked us all by lurching forward and grabbing Alexandria by the shoulder. For the first time, Alexandria's unflappable demeanor broke. She let out a yelp and gave a wince of pain.

Moving at an impressive speed, with her other hand, Susan reached for handcuffs and had Alexandria's wrist secured to the arm of the chair before she could protest further. I started to reach for Susan, thinking she was about to do more to Alexandria than handcuff her, judging from the pure hatred covering Susan's face, but I pulled back as Susan stood. "You want to lie to us about last night as well? Tell us that *wasn't* you Luca recorded by the van?"

Seemingly unable to get her composure back, Alexandria gave a jerk of her wrist, rattling the handcuffs, and fury laced her words. "Not only will I have your badge, I'll see you behind bars. This is assault, harassment. You have absolutely no jurisdiction or right to—"

"Save it!" Susan nearly shouted, her fists trembling at her sides.

Watson whimpered and moved so he stood in between my legs.

At Watson's sound, Susan glanced down, and took a breath before looking back at Alexandria. "What were you doing at the van last night?"

"None of your business," Alexandria bit back, not a bit of her fury evaporating.

Susan tried again. "What was so important in that van that you were willing to kill over?"

"I didn't kill that snooping brat." Alexandria rattled the

handcuff again. "But the second I'm out of this chair, you're a dead woman."

Susan laughed. "Trust me, promising threats is only going to—"

"Let's take a break." Leo proved his bravery by putting a hand on the back of Susan's shoulder. She snarled, but he left it there. "Come on. All of us. This won't go anywhere good."

When Susan looked like she was going to argue, I chimed in. "I think it's a good idea. We could all use a breather." I turned, tapping my thigh for Watson to follow, and I hoped Susan and Leo would do the same. I'd been on the receiving end of Susan's disdain multiple times, but I'd never seen hate like that from her. I wasn't entirely sure what she was capable of.

"Come on." Leo spoke from behind me, sounding like he was attempting to soothe. "She's handcuffed. She's not going anywhere. Let's regroup."

I paused in the doorway until I heard their footsteps, and then continued. I nearly stopped once I was inside the key room, but from what I could see through the French doors, no one occupied the sofas in front of the fireplace. That would be better.

"She is so clearly lying it's disgusting," Susan bickered at Leo as we crossed the room. He started to reply, but she kept going.

Watson and I were nearly to the sofas before I noticed the small group of women clustered around the other set. They'd been out of view, hidden by the other side of the wall.

"Of course she's part of the Irons family." Susan was still going as she and Leo entered the lobby. "Which means she's also part of the stain over my police department. Which makes this a lot bigger than a solitary murder. We might not have Wexler here to interrogate, but this is as close as we've got. I'm not missing my chance for—"

"Susan." I had called her name twice before she stopped talking, and I nodded toward the group of knitters.

She followed the gesture and closed her mouth. She continued heading toward Watson and me, then paused and whirled on the women. "How many of you are part of the Irons family? Is this whole knitting group nonsense, some sort of cover? If I go out to the vans right now, will I find a whole bunch of drugs under your spools of yarn?"

"Susan!" My bark was sharp enough Susan flinched, and while she looked like she was going to argue for a moment, she didn't. Turning on her heels, she strode the rest of the way to me, then plopped down on the far side of the sofa.

Four of the knitters were present, and all four of them stared, wide-eyed and slack-jawed. The oldest, Minnie, and the youngest, whose name I couldn't recall, weren't present.

"Sorry." Leo attempted a smile. "It's been a stressful couple of hours. For everyone."

"That's okay. We understand." Cordelia recovered the quickest, though she glanced at Susan, then looked at me. "You really believe Alexandria had something to do with that boy's murder?"

I started to nod, then hesitated. I knew that information shouldn't be shared, but none of it was going according to protocol. It was a complete mess. Not the least of which was that Alexandria was right. She would be able to have Susan's badge over this and would doubtless bring charges against Leo and me for breaking into her cabin. Might as well go for broke—who knew, maybe Susan was onto something. If these women were part of the cover for the Irons family, perhaps seeing how they reacted would give us some answers. "We do. Yes."

"Alexandria..." Betsy blinked repeatedly, then looked toward her friends. "A murderer?"

All four of the women's expressions were mirror images of one another, their shock never fading. Cordelia shook her head. "That's... unsettling." She glanced toward the French doors as if trying to peer back to Alexandria, but there was no way she could see anything from her angle. "If we can help... in any way, please say."

I expected Susan to go off again, demanding they confess to being part of the crime ring that had so disrupted our lives and our town. She didn't.

"Thank you." I considered questioning them but wasn't even sure where to begin. Even if I did, I would only increase the odds of another outburst. "For now, would you mind giving us a little privacy?"

"Of course. No problem at all." Cordelia nodded seriously, and as she stood, the other three followed suit.

"Thank you so much. We appreciate it." The other women—Cordelia's sister, Pamela, Wanda, and Betsy nodded their agreement, though they still looked shell-shocked.

Cordelia gave a friendly nod toward Watson as they headed to the front door, but he stayed where he was.

Before I could sit, Katie and Anna passed the group of women on their way out of the dining room.

"You caught the murderer already, didn't you?" Anna hurried over, passing Katie, her hands fluttering. "I must say, Fred, this is record speed for you. It's only been a matter of hours." She bent toward Watson. "Of course you helped, didn't you, little angel?"

Watson slunk backward, staying out of reach of her hands.

"Poor dear." She straightened, looking partially offended. "He's clearly thrown off and beside himself."

I started to respond but noticed several other members of my family and the anniversary party heading our way from the dining room as well.

"Get back!" Susan's voice rose again, and she appeared beside me, pointing toward the dining room. "All of you. This is an official police investigation, and we don't need your intrusion."

"Well, I never!" Anna gasped in full-blown offense that time, her hand coming to rest on her bosom. "Of all the—"

"Oh, save it, Anna!" Susan gestured again, this time her pointed finger shaking. "Move it!"

Casting me a wide-eyed stare before coming to the rescue, Leo addressed the group. "Guys, sorry, things are a bit of a mess. You might give us a few minutes? We will fill you in when we can."

"No, we won't. It's none of your alls—"

"Susan!" Leo hissed at her, and she backed down, her cheeks growing redder. He turned back to the group once more. "If you don't mind."

There were a few murmurs of assent, and the group turned and headed back into the dining room, Anna practically sputtering as she left.

Before Katie turned to join them, I motioned her over.

Susan cast me a warning glare but didn't protest, surprisingly.

I took a couple of minutes and filled in Katie. Though she looked nearly as shocked as the group of knitters, she accepted it quickly and nodded. "You know, it doesn't mean much, but it's one more little puzzle piece, as you say." She held my gaze, as if treading lightly. "The knitting group is from Willow Lane, some little town in the Ozarks. That would be close to Kansas City, right? Where you grew up?"

Her gentle way of saying, *close to where your dad was killed.* I took a steadying breath and nodded. One more puzzle piece indeed. "Which means Alexandria lived close to the heart of the Irons family headquarters, at least from all we've figured out."

"That also means they could be involved. I'm tempted to arrest the whole lot of them." Susan's tone was quieter but just as brisk. "Although I only have one pair of handcuffs."

Leo petted Watson silently as I explained all the details to Katie. When he spoke, it sounded as if he was addressing himself as much as the rest of us. "Either way, whether we're just talking about Alexandria, all of them, or something in the middle, the bigger question is why are they here? Why now? That can't be a coincidence."

All three of us turned to look at him, and a cold dread settled in my gut. "You mean... they're meeting other members of the Irons family here."

"Here?" Katie looked around nervously. "As in Baldpate or Estes Park in general?"

He shrugged. "Either. Both."

From the other side, I stroked Watson as well, trying to push my fear away. The feeling was ridiculous. It wasn't like any of this was a surprise. "It makes sense. Branson said there were other members of the Irons family in Estes, even ones he didn't know about." I looked toward Susan. "Even Alexandria said as much, in her own way. When she was threatening your badge at the cabin. She said she had contacts here."

Susan's pale blue eyes widened, and she nodded. "You're right. Not exactly a confession, but... close." She looked around too, though not as nervously as Katie, nor like she was seeing spies everywhere. "From the research I've done, the Irons family also has ties internationally. Maybe one of the exchange kids is involved. Or..." She gave a little shake of her head, uncharacteristically looking embarrassed or something.

I finished the thought for her. "Or part of the anniversary celebration."

She nodded.

"No." Leo shook his head, looked over his shoulder into the dining room as if he could see everyone, then shook his head again. "No. None of us would do that."

"We would have said the same thing about Branson." Katie sounded heartbroken, as if it was a guarantee we had another betrayer in our midst.

"*I* wouldn't have," Susan snarled. "Maybe I didn't know exactly what it was, but I told everybody who would listen Branson was nothing more than a snake."

That was true, she had.

Several more minutes passed, each of us caught in our own mix of fear, suspicion, and worry. All except for Watson, who gave a happy grunt and twisted around so he could get a double-handed belly scratch from Leo and me.

He soothed me, just a bit. Enough to take the edge off so I could breathe a touch easier. I didn't want to consider that a member of my family or one of our friends could be involved in any of this. It was too much, and nothing that could be figured out at the moment. "Okay, that's out there now, and we'll have to deal with it at some point. But in this instance, let's focus on Alexandria."

Susan brightened, though her smile was dark. "Good point. But maybe you're wrong. She may hold the answers to all of it. She can point out the other snake among us."

She started to stand, but Leo reached out and grabbed her arm. "Don't act irrationally. We're already in deep water as it is."

"I'm not going to kill her or anything so ridiculous." Susan wrinkled her nose in disgust but stayed where she was. I couldn't help but marvel at the camaraderie she and Leo had. "But you make a good point. We're *already* in deep water, especially me. What's a bit more pushing going to hurt?"

To my surprise, Leo tilted his head as if acknowledging the idea. "Fine. But we don't hurt her. We don't become the bad guys in order to catch bad guys."

Katie and I exchanged glances, and as much as I wanted to disagree with Leo, I couldn't. "Okay, but before we go back in there, let's plan this thing out. What direction do we want to head? And we need some guidelines or rules. If—" I started to say Susan's name and barely caught myself. "If someone starts to get carried away or loses their temper to a dangerous degree, we all step in and stop it."

The next several minutes were lost in the debate of protocol and boundaries. To my relief, that part wasn't so hard. Then we started mapping out the plan, different angles to try to break Alexandria's reserve, coming up with questions and ways to ensnare.

Katie joined us as we walked back through the key room. As we approached the doorway, this time Watson didn't growl. His full attention was focused on Leo as he happily trotted between the two of us.

Susan halted after she stepped in and then let out an angry curse.

Behind her, the rest of us froze.

Across the room, still handcuffed to the chair, Alexandria sat, her head lolled back, the old-fashioned key handle of the letter opener, still wrapped in the clear evidence bag, protruding from her heart.

THIRTEEN

"I don't think it's legal for you to be able to keep us all in here." Minnie, the oldest member of the knitting group, glared at Katie, Leo, and me from her spot at the dining room table, her gnarled hands never ceasing to wield the knitting needles. "We came out here on vacation, to knit, to enjoy the mountains, not to be held prisoner."

"We're not holding you prisoner, and we're only doing what the local law enforcement asked." I addressed Minnie, then scanned the room. "Officer Green simply wants everyone together in one place."

Minnie wasn't finished. "That woman officer isn't here right now. So you really don't have any authority to—"

"Leo is a park ranger," Katie spoke up, pointing across me to Leo. "He's a federal employee and can step in for law enforcement when needed."

I wasn't sure about the accuracy of that statement.

Leo's eyes bugged slightly, but before he could respond, Watson chose that moment to rear up on his hind legs and bump Leo's thighs with his forepaws, demanding attention.

"We're fine. We'll help in any way we can." Cordelia sat across the table from Minnie and sounded like she was reprimanding a child, though the woman was a couple decades older than herself. "Besides, everyone is trapped in here, thanks to the snow. We've got tons of wonderful food, we're warm, and we're safe."

"Safe? Really?" Minnie seemed nonplussed. "Did you forget about that poor boy who had his throat slit this morning? I'd hardly call that safe." She reached for a slice of the cornbread, took a bite, and then spoke with her mouth full while holding a half-finished sweater away from crumbs. "You're right about the food, though."

A couple of the other knitters shook their heads in embarrassment, and Cordelia sent me apologetic grimace.

At that moment, their youngest member, Cassidy, hurried in and joined them at her spot at the table. If I was counting correctly, she was the final person missing out of everyone, except for Susan.

The two sets of French doors that led from the dining room to the glassed-in front porch were open, revealing the blizzard continuing to blow outside, though it seemed less ferocious as the sun was able to break through. No one was seated on the porch, however. The members of my family and the anniversary party were gathered around multiple tables closest to the French doors, all of them looking strained and concerned, but not offering any resistance, of course.

The knitting group sat at their normal spot in the center. Alexandria's chair was the only empty seat, but by that point, everyone knew she'd been taken in for questioning, so no one asked where she was.

The Baldpate staff made up a few tables on the far side of the room. Some of them had also been slow to wander in. Lisa sat with an arm around Juliet, who had yet to stop crying. The only member missing was Beau, as he was with Susan.

Had it really only been the night before that the space

had been filled with joy and revelry as we celebrated Percival and Gary? It was just as beautiful and cozy as then. If anything, more so with the lack of electricity. The room was lit from what filtered in through the windows and the countless candles and lanterns spread throughout the room. The wood in the old iron stove sitting in the middle of the room crackled and popped happily. Even so, it felt a little ominous, and a little claustrophobic, despite the massive size of the hotel. We were trapped, with a murderer. That feeling hadn't sunk in when we'd thought it was Alexandria —we'd had a name, and within a few moments, the woman herself. But now, there was another killer, at least one, within the walls of Baldpate Inn. The thought sent a shiver down my spine, which surprised me, considering all I'd seen over the past year or so. But this felt different somehow.

Once more I scanned the room, skimming over the members of my family and the anniversary party. Between the six remaining knitters, Lisa, and five remaining staff members, not counting Beau, that left too many possibilities for my liking. Though my gut instantly cut out both Lisa and Cordelia as possibilities. Even as the thought crossed my mind, I added them back in. With a sinking feeling, I glanced back at the tables filled with people I knew and loved, my mind filtering in Alexandria's "connections" and Branson's past confession that there were other members of the Irons family in Estes, even ones he didn't know about.

It was too awful to consider. No wonder this time felt different.

All eyes focused behind us, and at the sound of steps, Katie, Leo, and I all turned. Beau walked in, his expression like he'd been put through an emotional wringer. Susan followed not far behind. As Beau joined the staff, Susan stood beside Leo, casting a scowl down at Watson when he gave a little territorial growl for being too close to one of his idols.

Her expression didn't change as she looked up at the room, but she hesitated, just for a second. It was the first time I'd seen her uncertain—even when her own brother had been accused of murder, she'd been decisive. But the moment passed quickly, and she lifted her chin and raised her voice. "Alexandria Bell was killed about an hour ago."

The room went dead still for half a second and then chaos erupted. Anna let out a scream. One of the knitters, Pamela, I thought, did as well, though it didn't reach the volume or shrillness of Anna's. Angus stood, his face ghost-white and anger flaring in his eyes. Beside him Gerald flinched, knocking over a bottle of his kombucha, splashing it over Percival and my mom. Percival let out a screech as well, at that. The only table that didn't react in panic was the staff. Lisa covered her mouth, her eyes wide with horror. Her cluster of young employees looked startled, and, as one, turned toward Lisa as if she were their mother hen.

"That's it! I'm not staying here another minute." Minnie stood, lifting one of the knitting needles as if brandishing a sword and shooting a glare over the room. "Whichever one of you is going on a killing spree, just try me. I won't hesitate to shove this through your eye!"

Cordelia reached out, trying to calm her, but Minnie shook her off.

"Everyone, just hold—" Leo moved forward, raising his voice, but Susan shot out a hand, jerking him back.

She didn't even bother to glare at Watson when he growled threateningly.

One glance at her revealed what Susan was doing, her pale blue eyes shrewd as her gaze darted from person to person, table to table. I didn't know if it was the best plan as far as keeping order, but I had to admire her daring. Drop a bomb and observe the reactions.

"I'm with the old one!" Anna stood, pointing toward Minnie, then turned to Barry. "Can you drive us out of here on that snowmobile you used this morning?"

"Anna Hanson, get a grip!" Susan barked at her for the second time, seeming almost more annoyed that Anna had distracted her observation than for the outburst itself. "No one's going anywhere, even if it was a possibility."

"You can't keep us here!" Minnie shook her knitting needle again. "We're all in danger!"

"Yes. I can." Susan took a couple of steps forward and placed a hand on the grip of her holstered gun. Though her words had been firm and clear, she now raised her voice to a near shout. "Everyone sit down and shut up!"

They did. Anna plopped down instantly, looking offended. Minnie seemed to be judging her chances, and then she, too, sat, after another tug from Cordelia.

Once more, Susan studied the room, slowly, methodically, her hand never leaving her holster. It seemed she met every single gaze in the place. She wasn't handling things the way I would, but I couldn't help but be impressed with her control, her power. Finally, Susan's stance relaxed, but the authority in her tone didn't. "There have been two deaths in the past twelve hours. From what we could tell, we apprehended the first killer, but as she was also murdered, we clearly have another killer."

Still her eyes tracked the room, and I found myself following her example, watching the expressions flicker and change over people's faces. Noticed the kombucha bottle tremble in Gerald's hands as he chugged what remained. The looks of fear that Zelda and Verona exchanged before they turned their gazes to their children. The expression of nausea that rose over Pamela's face. The glare of defiance and hate Beau shot in Susan's direction.

Finally she spoke again. "Considering we're snowed in during a blizzard, that means someone in this room... maybe multiple someones in this room... is a murderer."

At that, people's gazes left Susan and the rest of us in the front of the room and turned on one another. Expressions altering from disbelief, to fear, to suspicion.

Once more Susan waited, once more I observed. And what I saw was telling. The knitters were the only group where not a single set of eyes looked at another member—every one of the women, whether in fear or suspicion looked toward the strangers around them. But there were those of the staff whose gazes flicked to someone sitting at their table, lingering a moment as if wondering, *Is it you?* My heart hurt when I noticed the same thing at the tables occupied by my family and friends. Noah turned narrowed eyes on Carl. Barry's gaze flicked to Angus. Even my own mother cast a suspicious glance toward Gerald, then, as if feeling me studying her, looked at me, a sad expression in her eyes.

Susan let the final ball drop. "Furthermore, one, or more of you, we believe, is involved with the crime ring known as the Irons family."

That time I kept my attention fully focused on the ones I knew best, praying and hoping I didn't see confirmation of my worst fears. Without exception, every single member of the anniversary party flinched—everyone, even Ocean and Britney, the oldest of my nephews and nieces. Nearly every resident of Estes Park knew of the Irons family by that point —for a couple of weeks after Branson left, the *Chipmunk Chronicles* ran a series of articles about the organization. Considering both the town's police chief and sergeant were members, that only made sense. Maybe I'd wasted the opportunity to discover some telltale reaction from someone at the other tables.

Without fail, every member of my group looked shocked as well. And that also made sense. Even though they all knew about the Irons family, like me, they hadn't expected it to show up here. Although... could some of those shocked expressions only be caused by Susan and the rest of us discovering that connection? Maybe... I couldn't tell.

When I met Mom's gaze, I recognized my own fear and hurt. It was almost more than I could take, knowing those remotely responsible for my father's death were near. I could only imagine how that knowledge cut through her.

What little murmuring had occurred died down. Susan spoke again, this time addressing the table of knitters. "Why are you all here again?"

The question surprised me, both that she began there and that she'd ask it in front of the whole group instead of splitting everyone up.

Minnie scowled, but the rest of the women all looked toward Cordelia. I wasn't sure if she was the leader of the knitting group or not, but clearly they all deferred to her.

If she was offended, she didn't let on, her voice calm and clear as she spoke to Susan. "We have a knitting club back home. My sister"—she motioned to Pamela—"found out that Alexandria was planning another trip to Estes Park. She'd heard about the Cozy Corgi bakery and wanted to visit. She—"

"What in the world does a knitting club have to do with baking?" Susan interrupted and cast an accusatory glance toward Katie.

Cordelia opened her mouth to respond, but Pamela beat her to it, sounding flustered. "That's why *I* wanted to come. Alexandria had talked a lot about the Knit Witt shop and how skilled Mr. Witt was... er... is. So I thought it would be a good excuse. Plus, some of us needed a..." Her eyes widened and her words trailed off, as she cast an apologetic glance at another one of the members.

"Needed a what?" Susan's impatient tone was almost soothing in its constancy.

"Needed a break, needed to get away." The only black woman of the group, Wanda, I believed, spoke up, her voice resigned. "My father passed away during the holidays. It's been an exhausting couple of months."

Pamela spoke up again, rushing forward as if she was trying to rescue Wanda. "It really is all my fault. Inasmuch as I don't want to admit it, I guess I did invite us along on Alexandria's trip. She wasn't overly happy about it, but..." Her cheeks pinked. "I suppose it's bad to speak ill of the dead, but Alexandria was irritated and short a lot of the time. So it didn't seem like anything unusual."

"The knitting club is not a cover for something else." Cordelia spoke up again, addressing Susan with a level stare. "The three of us"—she motioned at Wanda and Pamela—"also have a food delivery business, but that's the only other organization attached in any fashion to our knitting club. This was merely a vacation, a chance to grow as friends." She glanced across the room toward Angus. "And hopefully grow in our skills by meeting with a master knitter."

Susan studied the group for a second. "Any of you want to confess to nighttime wanderings last night?"

Confusion flitted over their faces as the women looked at one another, but I noticed Cassidy glanced down at the table, her cheeks pinking like Pamela's had moments before.

"Interesting." Susan surprisingly didn't push. She

turned toward the anniversary party. "Angus, from the rumor mill, I gather you had an ongoing sexual relationship with the deceased?"

He flinched and anger flashed in his eyes. "Please show some respect, Officer Green. Both for Alexandria and myself."

Susan rolled her eyes. "Fine. A *romantic* relationship. Is that better?"

Gerald shifted uncomfortably, casting a commiserating glance at his friend.

Angus bristled. "Not much, no. And I'll not be discussing such private matters in this setting. I will answer any questions you want to give in a more respectable manner and in private. Until then, I will say that, like many of us in town, I've known Alexandria for years. She was an exceptional artist, demanding, and a creative soul. I also knew that she and the knitting group were coming, though they were earlier than expected. I had plans to do a knitting demonstration with them the day after tomorrow. Once we were all back in town."

Susan looked like she was going to press the point, but then switched tactics. "What about the rest of you? Any nighttime adventures any of you need to get off your chests?"

And again, those suspicious gazes flitted about my family and friends, causing an ache.

For a second, I wondered where Susan was going with that questioning, then remembered she'd met with Beau on her own. I was willing to bet she'd gotten the password for Luca's cell phone once more. Goodness knows what he'd managed to capture in his spying, or documenting, as he would've described it. The thought caused me to give a flinch of my own, and I glanced at Susan. Had Luca captured the moment between Leo and me?

"No volunteers on that one either, I see." Susan shook her head in disgust and turned toward the staff table. "Which one of you is Darrell?"

A handsome redheaded man, who appeared slightly older than the rest of the staff, maybe twenty-two or twenty-three, raised a hand and looked terrified.

Susan narrowed in on him with a laser-focused stare. "Where are you from, Darrell?"

He swallowed. "Uhm. Eureka Springs."

"Arkansas, correct?"

He nodded.

"And Arkansas is in the Ozarks, correct?"

He nodded again.

Susan turned her attention toward the knitters. "And Willow Lane is in the Ozarks as well?"

Cordelia and a couple of the others nodded.

Susan turned to our group, focusing on my mother. "As is Kansas City, right?"

Mom shook her head. "Technically—"

"Is it close, Phyllis?" Susan snapped at my mom, reminding me that though things had improved between the Green family and my own, there was a long history of hard feelings.

"Comparatively, yes." Mom started to nod and froze, things clicking into place. She cast wide eyes on me, then turned in her seat, looking first at the knitting group, then to Darrell. After a second she looked back at me, her gaze knowing.

I glanced at Susan as I tried to catch my breath. She'd connected those dots quickly. Surely that was too much coincidence. The Irons family being centered from Kansas City, where my father had been killed. A knitting group from the nearby Ozarks with a newly deceased member with direct ties to the Irons family. And an employee of the inn also from the Ozarks, when all the rest of the staff were international.

Susan tried once more. "I'll ask one more time. Anyone want to come clean about their nighttime activities? There're only two people I trust in this room at the moment..." She glanced toward Leo and me, which in and of itself was startling, then her gaze settled on Katie, and her nose wrinkled in dislike. "Well... three of you, I suppose." She turned back to the group. "As far as I'm concerned, every single one of the rest of you is a suspect. Speaking up now might go a long way."

The room stayed silent.

I exchanged glances with Leo. I could tell he was also wondering if we were subjects of Susan's viewing.

"Fine, then," Susan spat. "We're done. You're all to stay in this room." Once more she looked at Katie. "Are you capable of keeping watch? From everything I've seen from you, you're the biggest teacher's pet there is. Surely you can tattle if someone tries to leave." She didn't give Katie a chance to answer before looking back at everyone. "It's going to be a long afternoon of questioning, so sit tight. And for all that's holy, please refrain from killing anyone else."

Lisa sucked in a quick gasp from across the room, drawing everyone's attention to her. She flinched before pointing toward the wall of windows. "The snow has stopped."

Again the entire room turned as one toward the opposite side. Sure enough, somewhere in the group interrogation, the blizzard had ceased. The sky was bright blue and filled with gray fluffy clouds. The sight was stunningly gorgeous. Under a few feet of snow, the world outside looked like the landscape of another planet. In the middle of it all, barely visible, lay Estes Park, glittering in a way that hid all the chaos Susan reported was going on in town. Which was fine; we had enough chaos of our own to deal with.

Susan clapped her hands, pulling all attention back to her. "While that's good news, it doesn't change anything. Even if the blizzard doesn't start again, we have no idea how long it will take for electricity to return, and for us to get any help up here. Until then, I'm in charge, and we're going to catch ourselves a murderer."

Angus sat on the opposite couch and bent slightly so he could lower his hand close to the floor. Watson left his spot between Leo's and my feet, crossed the short distance, and sniffed the offered palm. "Such a good, handsome little man." Genuine affection filled Angus's warm voice.

Watson gave the hand a lick, then nudged demandingly with his nose.

Following directives, Angus scratched Watson's head, eliciting a cloud of dog hair. A hint of a smile played on his lips before he laughed softly. "He is his own little blizzard, isn't he?"

"It's true." I studied the interaction between the two of them, trying to decide if I could read into Watson's behavior. "Thanks to corgis, the lint roller companies will never be in danger of going out of business."

Angus laughed again, though the humor didn't reach his eyes. "I did have to do a thorough vacuuming of the yarn shop after Watson's visit. Even so, a couple days later there were occasional fur balls floating across the hardwood floor."

"Are you two kidding me with this?" Susan sounded thoroughly disgusted and shot a glare between Angus and me. "If that dog is going to be a distraction, shut him outside.

You just proved he has enough fur for him to be warm and toasty."

Before I could give in to my temper and say something I probably wouldn't regret, Leo patted his knee. In response, Watson whirled and rushed back, smashing into Leo's shins, and looking utterly pleased at the impact.

"You're a good police officer, Officer Green. Intelligent and canny." Angus straightened and settled back into the sofa. "You'll be a *great* one when you learn that you catch more flies with honey."

"Save it, Angus. I'm hardly taking career advice from an old man who spends his days knitting and his nights wasting time on role-playing games with my brother." Susan shot me a warning glare from the other side of our couch but didn't make any more threats toward Watson.

We'd moved two of the sofas from the lobby into the key room, the French doors giving more privacy, but allowing us to be close enough to the dining room that if there was a revolt, we could hear. There'd been no debate about who to speak to first, not that Susan had given Leo or me a chance for input. As soon as we'd set the couches a few feet apart, facing each other in some sort of cozy interrogation-room resemblance, Susan demanded Angus join us.

"Interesting that your girlfriend was just murdered a hot second ago and you're in here laughing and playing with an overstuffed puppy." Susan refocused on Angus, leaning forward so her elbows rested on her knees, her muscular shoulders flexing beneath the fabric of her uniform. "Was there a recent lovers' spat?"

His green eyes flashed in anger, as they had before in the dining room. It was an unusual expression on Angus.

"Oh, sorry." Susan didn't sound sorry in the slightest. "That not have enough honey for you? Well then, you're really not going to like my next inquiry. How much older are you than Alexandria? Twenty, twenty-five years? I'm wondering if she decided to trade you in for someone younger? Maybe someone *much* younger."

I spared a quick glance at Susan and noticed Leo doing the same thing. She sounded like she had a theory, a specific one.

Angus's lips thinned, but when I decided he wasn't going to answer, he spoke, his voice tight and hard. "Alexandria was free to do as she wished. As was I."

Susan scoffed. "Really? You expect me to believe that? You're a little old for one of those newfangled open relationships, aren't you?"

Anger flashed once more, then faded to something else, something removed and distant as Angus shook his head. "I'm sorry you're so miserable, Susan. Life doesn't have to be this way." Her hands clenched, but he kept going. "Regardless, despite what you think you may know, we were not in a relationship. Alexandria was not my girlfriend."

When Susan didn't reply instantly, I looked over. She was nearly shaking in rage. It seemed Angus's arrow had struck its mark.

Leo jumped in, his tone softer. "Sorry to pry into your personal affairs, Angus, but from what I gathered, the gossip seems to be that you and Alexandria had more than a friendship. I think that's clouding the issue at the moment."

"We did have more than friendship. We were two consenting adults." His green eyes shot a challenge at Susan. "Even if I was a couple decades her senior, as you've so delicately pointed out. But it was one of... convenience and respect, nothing more."

I liked Angus, from what little I knew. His yarn shop

was one of the most beautiful stores in town, and his talent was awe-inspiring. Not to mention, while Watson didn't go bonkers with love over him, he clearly felt safe with the man, and that went a long way. At the same time, I couldn't disagree with Susan—something about his reaction was off. "Maybe it's my Midwest sensibilities, but you do seem rather... calm and collected about Alexandria's murder, considering you two were involved, even if in a nontraditional way."

He smiled and held out his hand to me as he addressed Susan. "You should take lessons. There wasn't even honey involved, yet I don't feel like I'm being taunted by a child." Then he focused on me. "I'm not one for hysterics, but no, even if I was, I don't think this would be a situation that would cut me as deeply as people would assume it should." He folded his hands in his lap, and for the first time his gaze drifted away, as if reliving a memory. "Alexandria wasn't a kind woman; she wasn't mean, either. In a lot of ways, she was distant and cold. However, she was intelligent, ardent, and insanely talented." Warmth crept into his smile then. "I think that's the biggest loss. Within a couple of years, her knitting skills would've surpassed mine. Who knows what she would've accomplished? I respected her, admired her, and we had a few deep and strong bonds. Outside of that, we were very different people. There were things about her I didn't like. She would've said the same about me." Another glance toward Susan. "There were times she found me just as insufferable as you're feeling about me right now, I'd wager. I'm sorry she's dead. I will miss her, but I'm not heartbroken. If anything, I'm angry. About how she was killed. And... how, it seems, I was deceived."

"Deceived?" Susan spoke again, finally. "Deceit and betrayal are excellent motives."

"Yes, I suppose they are." Angus sounded unconcerned. "If what you're saying is true, a woman I've known for years, one I've had a relationship with, not only killed the young man in the night, but was involved with an organization that's touched all of our lives recently."

"*If* what I'm saying is true?" Susan bit out the words. "Do you have a reason to believe I'm wrong?"

He nodded toward me. "I've become an admirer of Miss Page, of her intelligence, deductive reasoning, and tenacity. But this is quick, even for her. I can't imagine what evidence any of you have found that would link Alexandria to the Irons family. If it's such an extensive crime organization as we've been led to believe, that would be a massive slipup. It would seem to me, in our desperation to understand and tie things with the pretty little red bow, we've jumped to conclusions."

As he spoke, though I wasn't sure why, it was like I saw a ribbon weaving its way through the picture, indeed tying itself into a pretty little red bow. Alexandria's connection to the Irons family, the knitting group, to Kansas City, to Angus's yarn shop, all combusting at our time at the inn. It was too much coincidence, way too much. And Angus was a touch too controlled, almost... too perfect. Even as the puzzle pieces tried to fall together, I attempted to scatter them again. I liked the man, quite a lot. He was a lifelong friend of my stepfather. Every instinct I had said I could trust him, well, nearly every instinct. But hadn't that been true about Branson?

As if reading my mind, Susan took the sketchbook from where she'd laid it beside the couch, opened it to the saved page, and shoved it toward Angus. "Care to explain that?"

For the first time, Angus's composure slipped a bit, confusion crossing his expression as he stared at the drawing of the younger Alexandria and Branson in disbelief. "Where did you find this?"

"It was in her cabin, Angus." Still petting Watson with one hand, Leo leaned forward, and though there was respect and concern in his tone, I thought I caught something else, something that hinted he was thinking along the same lines as me. "It's hers. There's no doubt about it."

"No, there isn't." Angus didn't look up at Leo, keeping his focus on the drawing. "This is Alexandria's work. I'd know it anywhere. Like I said, she was talented. Even more so with a pair of knitting needles, which should tell you something." He studied it a bit longer and closed the sketchbook reverently, placing one hand on the cover, then looked at me. "Are you okay?"

There was such gentleness in his tone that it caught me off guard and somehow issued a quick stab of pain. I felt my lips move, but I couldn't make any words come out.

Angus shot Susan a glare, as if it was all her fault, then returned to me. "I can't help but feel somewhat responsible. From what I understand, in some ways you were closer to Sergeant Wexler than I was to Alexandria, and other ways, less so, but I think his betrayal probably hurt you more than Alexandria's does me. I'm so sorry they're connected. I'm sorry you have to face it again."

Angus had told me before that if I ever needed anything, I only needed to come to him. At the memory, the sincerity in his offer, I felt the tug of guilt over my thoughts about him only moments before.

"I take it your doubt has been cleared?"

Angus ignored her for a few moments, keeping a sympathetic gaze on me, then finally handed the sketchbook back to Susan with a sigh. "Yes. I don't see any other way to interpret that. Over all the years we've known each other, I had no clue about her connection to Sergeant Wexler. Clearly, he wasn't the only one with the double life." With that, he straightened again, and the walls returned, both in his eyes and in his tone. "I'll answer any more questions you want, but let me take care of a few for you right off. I didn't kill Alexandria. Or that boy. I didn't know she was involved with the Irons family, but yes, I do believe you that she was. And while I do not agree with your methods or your attitude, Officer Green, in this case, perhaps they are justified. Obviously we have a killer among us."

"I'm not asking for your approval, Angus. I only want answers." Though the anger left Susan's voice, she was clearly unimpressed.

"Like I said, I'll answer anything you want. Furthermore, I'll help in any way you deem appropriate. Estes Park is my town, its residents are my friends, my family. I'll help cut out the infection that's threatening to spread its darkness. Just let me know what to do and I'll do it."

True to his word, Angus answered the rest of Susan's questions without hesitation. She peppered them so fast that it was nearly hard to keep track. *Where were you at the time of Luca's murder? Where were you at the time of Alexandria's murder? Did you wander around in the middle of the night? Did you meet Alexandria at the van?* On and on and on. For each question, Angus had a quick, simple, clear answer. At the end, before he patted Watson goodbye, he requested that we keep the specific details of his relationship, as he called it, or his arrangement as Susan called it, with Alexandria private, but said that if for some reason it would help bring light to the dangerous connections, that he would understand.

"I detest that man." Susan slammed the French door as she returned from accompanying Angus back to Katie's supervision in the dining room. "He acts so intelligent, superior, and informed, though he's done nothing but play along in my brother's childish negative behavior over the years."

Susan's older brother, Mark, was a challenging personality, much like Susan herself, and I couldn't blame her for her strained relationship with him. He wasn't a bad guy, necessarily, but selfish and shortsighted. However, Susan was fiercely loyal to him, and so anyone who aided in his irresponsibility was nearly as guilty as Mark himself.

"But if you put that aside, do you believe him about Alexandria?" I asked.

She scowled at my question but didn't answer as she crossed the room and plopped down into the spot Angus had occupied opposite us. Then she surprised me. "Honestly, I don't think I can put it aside. Which means I can't be unbiased on the situation. What do you two think?"

It seemed Leo was more accustomed to that sort of response from Susan than me as he responded instantly. "I'm not sure. I've always liked Angus. He's an extremely respected and valued member of the community. But..." He looked toward the sketchbook, then cast me an apologetic look before continuing. "It seems like a lot of coincidences piling up right now. A lot."

"That's where I'm falling, too." Maybe it was hypocritical for me to doubt him when I'd fallen for Branson's lies, but could Alexandria really have deceived him? Alexandria *and* Branson? I turned to Susan. "Did Branson and Angus have a relationship that you know of?"

"Like I've told you a billion times, I was not that scumbag's keeper." She frowned, sounding irritated again. "You'd know more than me. For all I know, the two of you might've gone on a double date with Alexandria and Angus."

I could feel Leo tense beside me, ready to come to my defense, but I cut him off. "We didn't, as much as I'm sure that disappoints you, and unless I'm forgetting something, I don't recall Branson ever mentioning Angus." I switched tactics, both to avoid more conflict with Susan and to simply give my brain a break from the constant reminder of betrayal. "You seemed to have another theory besides the Irons family when you were questioning Angus. More like you suspected Alexandria was having an affair."

She shrugged. "I did, though if Angus's explanation of the relationship is to be believed, it doesn't really matter. And there's no reason to really doubt that part of the story."

"Maybe so, but at this point, we can't sweep aside anything." Watson had crawled onto the couch between Leo and me when Angus left. I stroked him absently as my gaze flitted around the key room, taking in the thousands of keys and their individual labels lining the ceilings above our heads—so many stories, each one representing a different person, a different life. Probably each one with their own secrets, maybe even some had their own double lives. "Who did you think she was having an affair with?"

"That redheaded kid... man... whatever. Darrell." She said it with a sigh. "The one from the Ozarks. Again, one more coincidence. I almost pulled him in first, but Angus seemed so angry when we were speaking to the group that I decided we should start with him."

That had been my first inclination as well, but I'd forgotten about the redhead as we'd spoken to Angus. "But why did you think the two of them were having an affair? Because of where they lived?"

"No. Luca's phone." Susan shuddered. "That little guy was a creep. There's well over a hundred videos on there of him spying on people. I watched them until the battery died."

"I have an external charger. If you need it."

Susan waved Leo's offer away. "No. I'd finished the ones he'd shot from last night. The rest were of other members of the staff here. Last night"—she leveled a knowing stare at Leo and me, making me think Luca had caught our time in front of the fire—"was pretty much Grand Central Station here. It seemed like everyone was out of bed and roaming around. There were ones of Carl and Gerald—inasmuch as I said I don't trust anyone earlier, and that's true, I can no more see Carl or Gerald having the gumption to murder someone than my brother growing up enough to quit dressing up like an overgrown wizard. There was an interesting one of that old knitter woman, whatever her name is. But despite her attitude in there, what Luca caught wasn't sinister. It just looks like the old bat has a covert drinking problem. The one of the redhead—"

"Darrell." I spoke his name without a second thought.

"Like I care." She waved me off as well. "There was nothing incriminating about it either, except the way he moved. It was clear he was trying not to get caught; he was up to something."

"You suspect he might've been wandering off for a romantic interlude with Alexandria?" Leo's tone suggested he was pondering the idea, but then he shook his head. "Or meeting with her at the van."

Susan nodded.

Maybe so. Perhaps he was her touch point in Estes Park, both being centrally located to the heart of the Irons family organization. They might've made a trade or an exchange or a drop off at the van. Either way, though I hadn't seen the recordings, Darrell definitely looked nervous about something. Maybe he was the other figure in the blurry video. Perhaps he helped Alexandria kill Luca, then decided he'd better turn on Alexandria before she turned on him. Another thought hit me, and I looked back to Susan. "The vans. Do you think you can get the knitters to open them, or do we need to do another break and enter?"

Watson proved to be unpredictable yet again as the small herd of us made our way to the vans. He frolicked like a puppy in the path made by those ahead of us, bouncing along happily, leaping ungracefully in the air, attempting to catch snowflakes carried in the breeze, only to shove his face into the wall of snow with a chuff, pull back out with a sneeze, and start all over again.

When he stumbled in one of his leaps and bumped into the back of Cordelia's legs, she turned around to smile at him. "You're one of the happiest dogs I've ever seen." She paused to scratch the top of his head with her gloved hands and looked up at me. "I've met a couple other corgis during my day. I must say, Watson's the most cheerful one. The others seem to be rather grumpy and stubborn, though I found that quality endearing as well."

"Oh, trust me, you're seeing Watson on a good day, or a good moment. He's typically so grumpy he reminds me of those two cantankerous old man Muppets that complain about everything from their theater box seats. And he's almost as stubborn as I am."

Watson paused in his frolic to glare at me over his shoulder in apparent reprimand, then returned to his fun, lunged forward and dumped his head again in the wall of snow bordering our path.

"I think he was getting a little cooped up inside, so he's feeling extra playful. Not to mention that he's got two of his favorite people here, my stepfather and Leo." I motioned toward the front of our little parade, where Leo was clearing a path to the vans.

"I'm glad he's here. With the... events that are going on, it's nice to have some innocence." Cordelia looked like she was about to say more but instead smiled sadly at Watson, then turned to catch up with the rest of the group.

Though we expected a protest, the knitters had been instantly accommodating when Susan asked to see inside the vans. Four of them even joined Susan, Leo, and me. Only Cassidy and Minnie stayed back. The younger one still seemed distraught, and the older didn't want to risk walking in the deep snow.

Though the vans were parked less than a hundred yards from the inn, with the depth of the snow, it was slow going. I couldn't help but feel a little like prancing myself. I wasn't exactly tempted to shove my face in the snow, but it was good to be outside. The calm after the storm was remarkably beautiful—here and there, the weight of snow would be too much for an upper branch of a tree and cascade down in tumbling avalanches, like sparkling waterfalls over a cliff.

I used the time to shift through the small amount of information we had. Luca's death made sense. Horrible and a waste, but he'd caught Alexandria in an incriminating moment. And if she was part of the same group as Branson, I'd seen firsthand how nonchalant killing another person could be. I couldn't quite envision how the murder went down, but was close. Luca, startled at being caught, fleeing from the window while Alexandria sprinted over the parking lot and up the front steps. I wasn't sure if Luca had hidden his cell phone in the key room so he could claim he didn't know what she was talking about, or if he'd stumbled and it had slid. Maybe it didn't matter, but I was certain whatever had happened did so before Alexandria found him. From the way he was killed, I was willing to bet she'd expected to find it on his body, stuffed in a pocket or something. A quick slice of his throat didn't imply taking time to try to pry information out of him.

Had she looked for the cell phone? It hadn't appeared like it, nothing else was disturbed. Though from all the people that were up and about in the middle of the night, perhaps she heard someone walking about and fled. Either way, the second Luca had turned his cell phone on the scene at the van, he'd signed his death warrant.

But why Alexandria? My first inclination suggested it was the mystery person with her at the van. Eliminating another witness. But something about that didn't feel right either. If they were both members of the Irons family, wasn't there more strength in numbers? If anything, killing her only drew more attention to the coincidences, to the connections of Estes Park, Kansas City, the Ozarks. To Angus, to Darrell, possibly.

I hadn't reached any conclusions, not even close, when we finally arrived at the vans. Susan, Wanda, Betsy, and Pamela took the nearest, the one in Luca's recording. Leo, Cordelia, and I took the other.

Leo and I both let out matching sounds of awe as we opened the back doors of the van. Beside us, Cordelia chuckled. "It's a little type A, isn't it?"

Type A didn't begin to cover it. I'd never seen a vehicle packed so neatly. In fact, it reminded me a little of Angus's shop. Semitransparent plastic containers with pink drawer pulls lined the space, skeins of wool, arranged in descending gradient colors showing through. Each container had its own label—not the handwritten kind but the sort that had been done with a professional label maker.

"Yarn from sheep's wool has white labels, alpaca is yellow, angora goats are green, angora rabbits are purple." Cordelia pointed to one side of the van, then moved on to the other. "Over here we have patterns, knitting needles, crochet hooks... well, I guess you can read." She chuckled again.

"You were planning on getting some serious knitting done during this vacation." Leo reached for one of the container drawers and hesitated. "I'm almost afraid I'm going to mess up all your hard work."

"Oh no!" Cordelia shuddered. "That's not my handi-work. That's *all* Wanda. A place for everything and everything in its place. That's her motto. And don't worry about messing it up. Getting to the bottom of this is much more important than keeping the different hues of yarn together. Plus, I think she finds it soothing to rearrange. You'd give her a good excuse to get lost in her methods of madness."

"No wonder you brought two vans. I thought it was because there were seven of you, but it's because you brought a few stores' worth of materials along." I debated where to start. "Does the other van have this much? How long were you planning on staying?"

"This one was a supply van. Pamela, Wanda, and I took turns driving." She gestured toward the other, where Susan was bossing the other women around. "That was our luggage van. Alexandria drove it."

I started to reach for a drawer of knitting needles, though unsure why I'd chosen it, but studied Cordelia. "As in, she's the only one who drove it?"

Cordelia nodded, communicating with a cocked eyebrow rather than words.

"Control issues?"

"To say the least." Cordelia gestured toward the beautiful array of knitting supplies once more. "The same is true for Wanda, clearly. But... manifested in a very different way, and demeanor, for that matter."

Once more I started to turn back to the drawer, but there was a whimper and a jab against my calf. I looked down to find Watson glaring up at me, lifting one of his paws as if he was suddenly too dainty to have it touch the white fluffy stuff. "I tried to get you to stay at the inn. I told you you'd be warmer by the fire."

He whimpered again.

I glanced back the way we'd come, hating to lose the time, but maybe Watson wasn't just being his persnickety self. His paws were probably genuinely getting cold.

Before I could decide what to do, Cordelia bent, swept him into her arms, lifted with a grunt, and placed him in one sure motion in the back of the van, speedily enough she didn't even give Watson a chance to squirm or protest.

He stood there, surrounded by the knitting supplies, looking perplexed on how his world had suddenly shifted.

Leo laughed and ruffled his fur, spreading a cloud of dog fur and melting snow.

"Goodness. He is heavier than he looks." Cordelia rubbed the small of her back. "And that's saying something."

I marveled at her. "You're tougher than *you* look."

She waved me off with her free hand. "Sixty-five years of living on a farm tends to do a body good. I've lifted more than one calf to the back of a truck in my day. I wouldn't dare try that now. Luckily, little Watson here's not quite as heavy as a calf, but close."

I hoped I'd be as spry as Cordelia when I was her age.

With Watson satisfied, we got to work, going through drawer after drawer and finding nothing of interest or out of place. Not even anything mislabeled. We were probably wasting our time. Since Alexandria had driven the other van, the one that was in the recording, if there was anything to be found, it would be there. Even so, we kept going. After a few minutes, we decided to spread out. Leo continued with the supplies, Cordelia moved to the middle, searching the crevices of the seats, under mats, and pockets, and I took the front, rifling through the contents of the glove compartment. Watson stayed with Leo.

"What's this thing?" After a minute or two, Leo held up a large purple plastic tool that resembled a mangled umbrella missing the fabric.

Cordelia and I both peered toward the back from our respective places.

"Oh! I actually know that one, which is rare. It's a..." Cordelia squeezed her eyes shut in concentration for a moment. "Strike that, I don't recall the name, but I know what it's for. You use it to hold the yarn in place as you wind it into a ball." She gave a halfhearted shrug. "I'm the least knitterish of the group. I enjoy it, mostly, but I'm not passionate about it like most of the others. I use it more as a social activity, a break from everything else. I frequently knit on my own, but nothing more elaborate than a scarf or hat every now and then. But I've seen them use it, so I can attest it's not a murder weapon or anything."

Watson reared up, propping his forepaws on Leo's shoulder so he could sniff the purple contraption, his attention focused on the rubber handle.

"No, buddy, not for you." Leo held it out of reach.

"Oh, let him have it. Looks like a good chew toy,

besides, Wanda was complaining about it anyway—it doesn't work as well as the metal kind. Plus, if Minnie sees him with it inside later, it'll give her something to gripe about." Cordelia smiled wickedly, her eyes twinkling. "Nothing makes her happier."

Lowering it once more, Leo offered it to Watson, who snapped it out of his hands, padded to the side of the van, and curled up and began to chew on the handle.

I wasn't finding anything of particular interest in the glove compartment, either. Mostly just forms from a rental company that showed that the group didn't own the vans themselves. "Speaking of Minnie, I couldn't help but notice that you're an interesting collection of women. Sounds like there are a lot of strong personalities, especially considering Alexandria."

"That's true. Part of what I enjoy." Cordelia pushed herself up from her kneeling place on the floorboards and plopped down on one of the seats, rubbing her knees. "Alexandria definitely had the most personality..." She shook her head, reconsidering. "No, she had the most *challenging* personality, that's a different thing. She didn't seem to like very many people, but she was talented, breathtakingly so."

That seemed to be the consensus about her and matched what I'd noticed. Even Angus, who'd had some sort of romantic relationship with her, considered her unlikable. "If Alexandria didn't care for people very much, why was she part of the knitting group?"

Cordelia cocked her head and narrowed her eyes. "In other words, is our knitting group a cover for this group? The... Irons family?"

Either she was very quick, or I hadn't been very covert. Or both.

She didn't give me a chance to answer. "If it is, I'd hardly tell you that, would I?" She chuckled again. Cordelia did that a lot—it was a soft, pleasing sound. Not at all fake or overdone. A sound that made me think she was content and at ease in her own skin.

My gut told me she was trustworthy, she wasn't a part of this. But she'd said herself that she was the least of the knitters, so maybe she wasn't aware of what the group truly was. Although... hadn't I noticed that the rest of them seemed to defer to her?

"I can't say Alexandria loved the group, but I think she was lonely, and she definitely enjoyed feeling superior with her skill. And while she was a frequent member, she missed a lot of our meetings and get-togethers. She was constantly going out of town at the drop of a hat, often without warning. You never knew if she was going to show up or not." Cordelia's tone was a little darker. "It was always easier, more relaxing at least, when she wasn't there."

I froze, staring at Cordelia.

She shifted uncomfortably. "What? Did I say something wrong?"

"No." I blinked, trying to shove the unease I felt away. "Just that she would come and go without warning. Without telling anyone." I felt Leo's gaze and looked past Cordelia to him. He offered an encouraging smile, one that said he was sorry, one that said he was there with me. With effort, I refocused on Cordelia. "The person I knew who was involved with the Irons family did the same thing. He was dependable and trustworthy to a fault, until he wasn't. He'd disappear instantly without warning and simply say it was personal business for a day or two and then show back up. It felt strange at the time, but..." I shrugged. "You know, you give excuses, decide things aren't your business or that you're being pushy or whatever. But now, looking back, it all seems so clear."

"I know what you mean." Cordelia sighed. "Wanda, Pamela, Betsy, and I were having the same conversation earlier, before Alexandria was killed. Even though none of it makes sense... it does. Things that we shrugged off as idiosyncrasies or just part of her abrasive personality suddenly are understandable, even if in an outlandish and unbelievable way. She wasn't pleasant, but I never would've thought she was a murderer."

"When did Alexandria move to...?" Suddenly I'd forgotten the name of the town.

"Willow Lane." Cordelia smiled encouragingly. "And she didn't. Alexandria was born there."

"Really?" That struck me as odd. "I guess my impression was that your town was small, a farming community."

"It is. At least partly. It's also got a decent influx of tourists during parts of the year. Nothing like here, I imagine, but we're located centrally enough between Kansas City, Branson, and Eureka Springs, which are all big destinations, that we catch some of the overflow. Especially during the spring and fall at the height of flowers and leaf changes."

I'd forgotten about the town Branson. We'd gone there once when I was a kid. It was like a different version of Nashville.

Leo spoke up from the back. "Do you know if Alexandria had any ties to Kansas City?"

She didn't hesitate. "Yes. Alexandria's parents divorced when she was young. I'm not sure how old, three or four maybe. Her dad moved to Kansas City. I wasn't close friends with her family, so I can't tell you the exact schedule or anything, but my impression was she would spend about a fourth of the time with him, during Christmas and summer breaks from school and such. That's not saying too much, though. A lot of us have connections to Kansas City. That's where we go when we have a large shopping trip to do or we want to see the lights. Branson and Eureka are bigger than Willow Lane, but they don't feel like going to a big city."

There it was again, that ribbon winding closer, pulling my father, Branson, and Estes closer together. Not to mention Alexandria, and maybe Angus and Darrell as well.

Cordelia leaned over, cracking open the side door of the van, letting in some fresh, cool air. "Did the person you knew have connections to Kansas City?" Her gaze was shrewd. "That seems to be important."

"He did. Yes. At least for a little while." My knees were starting to hurt as well, and I repositioned to the seat. For whatever reason, because some part of me already trusted the woman, or simply because I needed to release some of the tension and memories, I shared more than I normally would with Cordelia. "I grew up in Kansas City. My mother grew up in Estes, but I didn't move here until little over a year ago."

Cordelia hummed, as if in confirmation. "That explains it. I thought you felt like a Midwest girl."

"I am, at least in a lot of ways." I laughed. "But in nearly as many, I'm not. Even before I moved here, I think part of me had the Western sensibilities as well. Just a touch more liberal and... well, some of the expectations around women seem to be a little more... up to date here. But that could just be my relationship with my ex-husband talking." I forced a second laugh.

"You don't need to sugarcoat, honey." Cordelia cocked an eyebrow. "I'm a sixty-five-year-old woman who owns a farm. I've had more than my share of men telling me what I can or cannot do." She reached forward and smacked my arm. "And it gives me a lot of pleasure proving them wrong every time."

Leo's soft chuckle emanated from the back. When I looked at him, there was warmth and pride in his honey-brown eyes.

The sight made my breath catch. I'd seen that look before, but the eyes had been a different hue. Now that I'd seen it, I couldn't believe I hadn't caught on to the similarity before. Unlike my ex-husband, my father had instilled in me that there was nothing I couldn't do. That I was no weaker or less capable than any man in my life. And his eyes shone with pride and love every time they turned my way. Just like Leo. It was too much. Wonderful, but over-whelming and too much. I looked away, returning to Cordelia, but still needing to talk about my father. "My dad was a detective. He was killed several years ago, by the same group."

There was a gasp by the sliding door. "Page. You're Charles Page's girl?"

I looked over to see one of the other knitters, Betsy, standing there staring at me. Hearing his name took my breath away. "You knew my dad?"

She shook her head. "No. I didn't. But I had family there. I remember them talking about your father. It was a big deal. It even made the local news in Willow Lane. That bust in a warehouse gone wrong."

Cordelia gasped as well, looking from Betsy to me. "Oh. I do remember that." She reached forward to my arm once more, this time giving a soft squeeze. "I'm so, so sorry."

Betsy slid the door open farther and held a hand out toward Cordelia. "Help me up. I'm coming in." Once inside, she shut the door, shivering and rubbing her knee as well. "This cold is getting to me, and that officer woman has the whole van torn up over there and not letting anybody join her. I'd had enough."

"Have they found anything?"

"From the way that lady officer is reacting, you'd think so. Every little flick of lint is getting labeled and bagged." Betsy gave Leo a cursory glance. "But no, not a thing. I don't know what Alexandria hid in there, but..." Her eyes widened as she noticed Watson chewing away, and then she looked toward Cordelia. "You're trying to give Wanda a heart attack, aren't you? Although, it's a small price to pay. Looks like you guys are being pretty neat. Having that officer in here messing up all the labels and categories might be more than Wanda can handle."

I couldn't care less at that point about categories, labels, or knitting tools. I lasered in on Betsy. "Do you know who Alexandria was visiting in Kansas City?"

"Not a clue." She shook her head definitively. "Alexandria was part of our knitting group, but never really a *part* of our knitting group, if you know what I mean. And she always had a hardness about her. I kept my distance." She shivered. "I'll never get that boy's image out of my head. Lying there with his throat slit. I knew Alexandria was cold, but I never would've guessed that." She lifted her brows toward Cordelia. "And poor Cassidy. I don't think she'll ever be the same. Such a nervous wreck. Poor thing. These are harder on the young ones. Not that it's easy on us, but we've seen enough hardships over the years that we can take it in stride."

I'd forgotten that Betsy and Cassidy had walked in when we'd discovered the body. Those details had all gotten carried away when Juliet came in and started screaming.

I'd also forgotten Cassidy for the moment. She hadn't seemed to be handling things very well. "Does..." I nearly stopped myself from asking, unsure if I should trust Betsy with what I was thinking, but then didn't see the harm. "Does Cassidy have a connection to Kansas City?"

"Oh, yes," Betsy answered instantly. Beside her I saw Cordelia's eyes widen, an expression that made me think some of her puzzle pieces were clicking together. "She dated a young man up there for a couple of years. Handsome thing, Tanner or Brody..." She wrinkled her nose. "Can't quite remember that either. One of those newfangled names. It ended badly. Cassidy was a mess for months."

That red ribbon just kept tying tighter and tighter.

SIXTEEN

"I really was starting to feel like a jailer down there." Katie plopped on the bed on her side of the room, then as if not quite relaxed enough, fell back so she was lying all the way down. "Between that Minnie woman and Anna, I've had my hands full."

"*Anna* is causing you problems?" I paused, sliding out of my clothes. As I'd shut the van's sliding door, an avalanche of snow fell off the roof, covering my hair, and somehow managing both to fall down the back of my sweater and snow pants. As soon as we walked in, I headed to the room to change, and Katie took advantage of Susan wanting to lecture the group—not having found any evidence in either one of the vehicles had put her in a foul mood.

Watson had stayed with Barry, as if he'd missed him desperately during our short time outside.

"Not problems per se, just..." Katie sighed, "Well, you know Anna. She's got a million different theories about who killed Luca and Alexandria. She has no problem specu-lating aloud, even if the object of her current theory is sitting less than ten feet away. She's found some way to implicate every single staff member and each of the knitters. She even accused Gerald at one point."

I pulled a different sweater and a broomstick skirt out of my backpack, considering Anna's theories. She'd been right on other occasions—of course, given her high percentage of theories, she had to be correct sometimes. "Chances are she's on the right track with at least one of them. I can't see Gerald killing anyone, but he was up and about last night, and seemed a little jumpy when our paths crossed."

"Probably went out to his car to get more kombucha." Katie chuckled. "One of Anna's theories was that Gerald was having an affair with Alexandria. That was when you all were interviewing Angus, thankfully."

"Really? That's an interesting hypothesis. I suppose that could've happened. He might've been coming back from her cabin."

"You think?" Katie propped herself up on her elbows. "Alexandria didn't strike me as a very nice person, but did you see her? She was gorgeous. And Gerald is so much older."

"He's about the same age as Angus, and Alexandria and Angus had a..." I hesitated, trying to figure out a way to describe it, then gave up. "A thing."

"Yeah, but Angus is..." Katie hesitated that time, also seeming to search for words. "I don't know, intriguing a little bit, talented, kind of classy. Gerald..." She shuddered.

"That about sums it up." I agreed with her. I could see the allure of Angus, but Gerald was everything that drove me crazy about the good old boys club members all rolled into one. Yet... that ribbon seemed to be weaving around Angus, not Gerald. "Still, I'd say you were closer with the kombucha, especially since Carl was up and about last night as well. I don't suppose Anna threw his name out there?" As I looked in the mirror to fix my hair, I chuckled again. I couldn't imagine Anna tossing her husband's name in the ring as far as suspects, but I wouldn't entirely put it past her, either. "From the sounds of it, everybody and their dog were awake during the night last night. I saw several, and then according to Susan, Luca caught several more. She didn't mention Leo and me, so somehow we must've avoided Luca's spying camera, because I can't imagine Susan not rubbing it in our faces." Satisfied that my damp long hair wasn't going to turn into a frizzy mess, I turned to find Katie sitting straight up on the bed, gaping at me. I froze. "What?"

"You *and Leo* avoided Luca's camera?" Brown eyes narrowed suspiciously even as her lips began to curve into a smile. "You two were up in the middle of the night?"

"No. I..." *Crud!* I hadn't realized what I'd said. Somehow, I'd also managed to forget Katie didn't already know. "It wasn't the *middle* of the night."

Katie popped the rest of the way up, hurried across the room, grabbed my hands, and pulled me beside her as she plopped on my bed. "*Please* tell me you two have quit beating around the bush already. It's killing me."

I started to feign ignorance, or at least claim that we'd not been beating around the bush or anything else, but she wasn't wrong. Though it felt indulgent, considering there were two dead bodies within the past many hours, I allowed myself to have this moment with my best friend and angled toward her, feeling a touch like a giddy schoolgirl. "It's kind of unreal." Even as I spoke, my heart began to race pleasantly at the memory of us beside the fire.

"What is?" She smacked my arm impatiently. "What's unreal? What happened? Tell me everything."

Telling everything, all the minute details, wasn't my style, Katie knew that, but... "We kissed. And..." My cheeks began to burn. "I just... *we* just know. You know?"

When Katie didn't respond immediately, I looked back up at her, finding her gaping once more.

"What?"

"What!" Katie practically screeched. "How can you even ask that? The two of you have been slower than frozen molasses since the day you met, and now you've suddenly gone from driving up here like the best of friends with me *yesterday* to being a thing within a couple of hours?"

"Well..." Her reaction threw me off, maybe seeing it from an outside perspective, as right as it felt, I had to admit it was rather a massive leap. "I suppose it was a bit fast."

Katie groaned and grabbed my arm. "Fast? Did you hear me? Glaciers move faster. But leave it to you to finally go for it, *really* go for it, when you decide to go for it."

"I *think* I understood that sentence." Some of my giddiness returned. "So you approve?" As soon as the question left my lips, I wished I could pull it back. I wasn't a giddy schoolgirl. I didn't require anyone's approval.

"Dear Lord, yes!" Katie was too quick to pull it back, and I was glad. She grew hesitant instantly, though. "So... you two are... together? Officially?"

I opened my mouth to speak but was lost for words. Were we official? What did that even mean? "All I know is while maybe it'll seem crazy to everyone, kind of does to me, it just feels right, like when the puzzle pieces finally click and my gut just knows something—*that's* how this is. It's kind of tilting my world out of whack, but at the same time... I just know. And when we kissed—" I chuckled again, self-consciously that time "—I'd have thought it would have been weird, that we were too good of friends, that it would've felt like relatives or something, but... it didn't. It felt right too, it felt... wonderful."

When Katie was silent again, I discovered her eyes

brimming with unshed tears, her face shining, and then she launched across the space between us, wrapping her arms around my neck with such force that we fell over, causing the bed to squeak, and we got lost in happy laughter.

"Good grief! What took you so long?" Susan growled as we entered the dining room. "Katie, take over again. And this time there's no talking at all. None." Susan looked back at three different groups of people spread throughout the dining room, pointing at each one individually. "I mean it! If no one's going to come clean, then we'll go one by one, and then repeat the process as many times as we have to." She sounded close to becoming unhinged. "No, no, Percival. I *don't* care if it's your anniversary. Dead bodies trump wedding vows or whatever." With a final shake of her finger, she whirled back around and stormed off toward the key room. She was nearly to the fireplace in the lobby before she looked back at me. "Are you coming or not, Fred? Leo's already got Darrell and your fleabag in the key room. But if you're done playing detective for once, take a seat."

Okay... it seemed she'd well and truly jumped over the line of becoming unhinged. I exchanged a quick glance with Katie, then hurried after Susan.

Thankfully, Leo was seated in the middle of the sofa, so Susan and I took our spots on either side. Watson licked my hand, then settled his rump on my boot and lay so that his forepaws were crossed on Leo's shoe, content to touch both of us.

Leo started to smile at me, but when his eyes met mine, he paused as if seeing something in me. The corner of his lip turned up. "Everything good?"

I felt my own lip smile in return. "Very."

"Good grief, you two. Get a room." Susan scowled. "Actually, don't. That's a disgusting thought. But for crying out loud, tone it down. Today is horrible enough without having to deal with nausea issues." She whirled to Darrell, who was practically trembling in the hot seat. "Why were you sneaking around in the middle of the night last night?"

His eyes went wide, and he started to open his mouth.

"Nope!" Susan sliced her hand through the air. "Don't even try to deny it. I saw you on that weaselly Luca's phone. He caught you. Is that why you killed him? Tired of him snooping around, filming everyone behind their backs? Did he finally catch you in an incriminating situation? Were you the one with Alexandria at the van?"

Darrell flinched with every question Susan threw at him, and his fair complexion grew more flushed with each one as well. By the time she was done, his face was crimson. "I... no... I..." He shook his head violently. "No."

"No what?" Susan snarled, her top lip actually pulling up over her teeth. "No, you didn't kill him because of the video, or you weren't by the van with Alexandria? Or no, there's a different reason you killed Luca?"

Leo spoke, his voice calm and soft, as if soothing a wild animal. "Why don't we try one question at a time? Like Officer Green said, Luca caught you moving around in the middle the night. What were you doing?"

Darrell seemed to relax somewhat, but his voice was barely more than a squeak. "Nothing. I just got up to... get water. And I... had a bad dream."

Susan groaned, loud and exaggerated. "You had a bad dream? How old are you? Five?"

Darrell glanced at the French doors, as if hoping someone would come to save him.

Susan clapped her hands, making him jump and look back at her. "Answer the question!"

"No! I'm not five!"

Susan flinched, thrown off, then groaned again and began to rub her temples. "I'm surrounded by idiots."

I laughed, I couldn't help it. It started as a soft chuckle and then something got a hold of me, and I started to laugh. Just the ridiculousness of the whole situation, all of it. It was all so preposterous, topped off with this handsome redheaded man—clearly terrified by Susan, not that I could blame him—proclaiming that he was not a five-year-old.

After a second, Leo joined in.

At our feet, Watson sat up, looking back and forth between us, tongue lolling as if he was in on the joke.

Susan simply glared, while Darrell looked as if we were crazy.

After a minute or so, I managed to get myself under control. And ridiculous or not, the laughter had helped. "Why don't we try this?" I leaned forward, looking intensely at Darrell and using a tone that fell somewhere between Susan's and Leo's. "I'm going to cut to the chase. There're too many coincidences to be believable in this situation. The Irons family is based in Kansas City. It shows up here, where there are also ties. There appears to be some sort of exchange or secret event happening in the middle of the night. And *you're* here, the only employee of Baldpate Inn who's not international. Not only that, but you're from the Ozarks, near the heart of this whole thing. Don't you think that's a little too much to be..." My words fell away as I studied the pure confusion and alarm over his face, which, in a way, truly transformed him into an overgrown child. Too much coincidence or not, I suddenly knew, without a doubt, we were wasting our time with Darrell. He had no clue what the Irons family was. "You don't know anything, do you?"

He shook his head, wide-eyed.

Leo and Susan both turned to look at me, their expressions as different from each other's as possible. Leo appearing somewhat surprised, but instantly believing me. Susan seemed as if she was about ready to rip my head off.

At that exact moment, the French doors burst open. "Me! He was with me."

Watson let out a yelp of surprise and jumped to attention at the outburst, and all of us turned to stare at the beautiful blonde rushing into the room.

Cassidy hurried to Darrell's side, and placed a hand on his shoulder, but didn't sit down, as if she was the protector he'd been waiting on. "Darrell was with me last night. I made him promise not to say. I didn't want people to think..." Her cheeks went scarlet as well, but she didn't look away. "Nothing happened between us. He was innocent. I'm not that kind of girl. But people would think..." She shook her head.

"She's *not* that kind of girl." Darrell found his voice again. "We were just talking. Well... we might have kissed, but... that's all."

Though Cassidy seemed like even that much detail was humiliating, she nodded.

Beside me, Leo snickered, but then the sound cut off as if he'd bit his lip to stop it.

It took all I could do to not lose it.

"You mean..." Susan started, then let out a long angry breath before trying again. "You mean to tell me that Luca caught you heading to some midnight rendezvous with"— she fluttered her hand at Cassidy—"this Barbie doll knitter-wannabe?"

"Hey!" Darrell started to stand, apparently getting over his fear of Susan. "You can't—"

"That won't help." I stood, motioning for Darrell to sit, and focused on Cassidy. "You're dating Darrell?"

She hesitated. "Well... not exactly. We just met last night, but..."

I halted. "*Last* night?"

Darrel looked back up at her and took her hand. "But when you know, you know."

"Oh, good God." Susan truly did sound like she was battling nausea. "I don't know how much more of this I can take."

I ignored her, studying the two of them. "You just met yesterday? From my understanding, don't you both live pretty close to each other?"

They nodded as one, both looking excited, and it was Darrell who spoke again. "That's part of it, like fate. So close to each other all this time and yet we meet here, of all places. When I get back home, I'm going to move to Willow Lane so I can be—"

"You're going to move?" Susan interrupted again, gesturing toward Cassidy. "You're going to *move*? For a woman you just met..." She checked her watch then seemed to give up. "Ten seconds ago?"

"Yeah." Darrell repeated his earlier sentiment. "When you know, you know."

Hadn't I just been saying the equivalent about Leo and myself? Although it'd taken us over a year to get to that point, not less than a day.

Cassidy beamed down at Darrell, her eyes filled with happy tears.

"But, Cassidy, what about—" I cut off my words when she looked at me. I'd been going to ask her about Kansas

City. About the man she'd dated. Just like before, nothing clicked, my gut just knew. No matter the coincidence, no matter how the red ribbon seemed to be looping and tying, these two were the wrong pieces to the wrong puzzle. They weren't involved. They didn't know a thing.

Carl scooted his chair nearer to the fire in the staff lounge and balanced his heavily laden plate on his legs. Reconsidering, he glanced around, discovered a decorative pillow on another chair, grabbed it, and plopped it on his lap to use as a table.

As the two of us had walked through the kitchen, he'd snagged a plate and piled it high. Though it was the exact same food as what everyone else was snacking on in the dining room, from the pleased expression on his face, he clearly felt as if he'd gotten something special.

When Carl judged himself appropriately situated, he peered over his glasses and smiled at me, once more reminding me of the perpetual Santa Claus with his bald head, white cottony beard, and cheerful girth. "I'm glad you're the one interrogating me, Fred. I was afraid it would be Susan. Sometimes I get so flustered with her. I..." He shuddered, then propped his feet up on the hearth. "Well, who knows, I might just confess to a murder I didn't commit to get it over with."

I could almost see him doing that very thing. "I'm not interrogating you, Carl. There's no reason to be nervous."

Watson propped his forepaws up on the hearth as well, sniffing Carl's shoes, and whimpered.

"I don't think Watson knows that." Carl chuckled, started to lean forward to scratch Watson's head, but leaned back, as if it was too much effort. "Sorry, little man. I know Anna always has me get your favorite... food items..." He shot me a knowing wink, having successfully avoided Watson's favorite word. "But I'm all out at the moment."

Either understanding Carl's words, or not picking up any scent of the all-natural dog bone treat he so adored, Watson let out a huff, crashed back to the floor, and padded over to curl up under my chair.

After the rather disastrous interview with Darrell, Susan announced she'd had enough. She suggested the three of us split up to talk to the rest of the Estes Park crew. Susan had taken Gary into the key room, and Leo and Anna were on the far side of the kitchen.

As I watched Carl arranging chunks of cheese between two large slices of cornbread, crafting a makeshift sandwich, I couldn't help but feel like we were wasting our time. Carl wasn't entirely wrong. Interrogating was exactly what we were doing, but... it wasn't working, and I didn't think it was going to. The murders were connected to the Irons family. They had to be. Clearly, it wasn't like the three of us were going to be so intimidating to a member of the crime organization that they'd crack. Watson might be a little grumpy, but he was hardly threatening. I supposed there was a chance that someone outside of the Irons family might have incriminating information that they weren't aware of knowing, but I doubted it. From what I'd seen so far, they were too careful, and if someone had been privy to something so incriminating, they probably would've already been taken out of the picture.

Even so... I couldn't think of another approach.

"My goodness." Carl hummed happily, then spoke

with his mouth full. "I've always loved Baldpate's corn-bread. With all that I've eaten the past couple of days, you'd think I'd be sick of it, but I think I'm growing more obsessed by the moment." Still chewing, he lowered his partially eaten cornbread sandwich, opened it up and popped a few pepperoni slices from the salad bar on top of the cheese.

Might as well jump in. "Did Anna enjoy the cornbread for her midnight snack last night?"

"Anna?" He'd already had the sandwich raised partway to his lips, but jolted, looking at me wide-eyed. "Oh..." He looked away, toward Watson, then settled on the fire. "Right. Yes. The snack. Yes." He looked back to me. "Yes."

Carl was a world-class gossip, but not a good liar. I hadn't truly been attempting to catch him in a lie, I no more expected Carl being involved than I did Watson. But from the flush that crept over his already rosy cheeks, his nose might as well have grown a foot.

Obviously, Anna had *not* requested a midnight snack. Carl had seemed nervous and strange when he'd run across Watson and me reading in front of the fire—looked like Katie's theory was correct. "Were you sneaking out to get some of Gerald's kombucha? I know Anna doesn't approve."

"No! I have a bottle stashed in—" His eyes widened once more, and he snapped his mouth shut. The excuses flooding behind his eyes were so clear I nearly laughed. "I mean..."

"It's okay, Carl. I'm not going to tattle on you." I did laugh, a little, at his relieved expression, but pushed forward anyway. "So what were you doing? After you went back upstairs, Gerald came in from outside. You really weren't meeting for kombucha?"

His relief faded, and he tried for offense, though he

didn't quite succeed. "I thought you said this wasn't an interrogation."

I cocked my head at him, taken aback. Carl *did* have a secret. One that had nothing to do with kombucha, apparently. Maybe that shouldn't surprise me; everyone had secrets. It seemed Luca had a cell phone filled with other people's secrets. Suddenly, I wasn't sure I wanted to know what Carl's secret was. I liked him, considered him a friend. Considered Anna a friend. I didn't want there to be anything to jeopardize that. I knew that Carl hadn't killed anyone, but that didn't mean he was innocent.

"Don't look at me like that." Carl sounded hurt, guilty.

"Sorry." I could barely force myself to whisper. "I didn't mean to."

Though I hadn't even been trying, Carl cracked like an egg. "Fine. Fine. Just... don't tell Anna." He looked over my shoulder toward the closed door that was between the staff lounge and the kitchen as if she might be listening on the other side.

The sick knot in my stomach tightened. I didn't want to know this. Whatever it was, I didn't want to know this.

Even so, I nodded.

"I was meeting with Gerald. Or... was supposed to." Carl stopped again, peering over my shoulder once more, and then, for some odd reason, at the fire, before turning his earnest eyes back on me. "We were going to meet outside, under the deck, but when I found you and Watson, I... got the cornbread instead."

"You were meeting *Gerald*?" Relief flooded me. Though I hadn't even been aware of what I'd feared, I think some part of me expected him to say he was meeting up with Alexandria for some sort of tryst.

He nodded guiltily. "You can't tell Anna." I started to cut

him off, to keep him from sharing whatever it was. There was no way he'd been meeting with Gerald to plan murder, so it was better for me not to know, I didn't want to keep things from Anna. Before I could, Carl got going, as if relieving a weight on his soul to a priest. "I'm relocating some money, quite a bit of money, in an investment opportunity that Gerald presented me. He thinks it can quadruple its profits within a year."

"Investments?" Again a wave of relief. Not an affair, nothing I'd feel I'd have to tell Anna. The relief was short-lived. I'd heard more than one story of a spouse making financial decisions without the other's input only to ruin both of their futures. "Wait a minute, Carl, what kind of investment? How much are you talking about?"

He shrugged, again not meeting my gaze. "A good chunk of change. I'm only taking money out of my retirement, not accounts that Anna and I have together."

That was something, I supposed. Still... "This is an investment idea of Gerald's?"

Carl nodded, looking hopeful suddenly, misinterpreting the disbelief he'd heard in my tone. "Yeah. If you want to join in, you can."

Not in a million years would I throw a penny at any idea Gerald Jackson had. That was beside the point. Something didn't add up. There were a million ways he could speak to Gerald without Anna's knowledge. "Why were you two meeting outside in the middle of a blizzard? Doesn't Gerald have his own room?"

Again his cheeks pinked in embarrassment. "Yeah, but it's next to Angus's, and there's a door connecting the two. Gerald was afraid Angus would overhear."

It still didn't add up. "Why wouldn't Gerald want Angus to know?"

"Angus helps Gerald with everything." Relief flooded Carl's voice at finally being asked an easy question. "Angus... well, you know... he's smart, talented, handsome." The pink deepened yet again. "Has a gorgeous girlfriend, or... did." Carl offered an obligatory grimace.

I nodded for him to continue.

"Angus is Angus." He shrugged self-consciously. "We wanted to prove that we could do this on our own. Impress him, you know? It's not like he'd be missing out when it goes well. He already has a fortune."

"He does?" That was news to me, not that I was privy to people's financials.

Carl simply nodded as if that should've been common knowledge.

Maybe it was, perhaps I was just looking into things. Angus always appeared well dressed and cultured. Though I wouldn't have thought of it unprompted, I could see why his friends would feel a little intimidated about him. Still... a fortune? From a yarn store in Estes Park? However... Angus had mentioned in the past that some of his knitted artwork was in galleries, and the price tags of the ones he had for sale at his shop were staggering. Even so, that ribbon continued to wind a little tighter.

I leaned forward, the chair squeaking. "Did you run into Angus last night?"

"Uhm... no?" Carl flinched, looking puzzled. "That was the whole point. Gerald and I were meeting outside because Anna was in my room, of course, and Angus was too close to Gerald's."

Right... Angus had been asleep in his room. Or had he waited until Gerald fell asleep and met Alexandria by the vans? "I'm a little surprised you guys had to worry about him. You said yourself Angus had a beautiful girlfriend. Why wouldn't he be with Alexandria in her cabin?"

"You know, I wondered that too." All worry was forgotten in Carl's tone. "If *I* had a girl who looked like..." The worry-free Carl was short-lived. He balked at his own words, pulling his feet off the hearth and leaning toward me with panicked sincerity. "I am not jealous of Angus and Alexandria. I love Anna. I don't need a pretty girlfriend. Nor do I want one."

"Carl, I didn't—"

"I'm serious." Carl leaned closer, the decorative pillow falling to the floor as he discarded the plate of food on the hearth before grabbing my hands and locking his gaze on mine. "I *love* Anna. I've never betrayed her, and never will."

I tried again. "Carl, I really wasn't—"

"Sure, she's a little sharp at times, a little mean, but that's just her way." Carl squeezed my hands. "She's not as thin as when we got married, neither am I! She's the mother of my children. We spent decades building our business together. And when things happened with Billy at Christmas..." Emotion thickened his voice. "When we found out our son hurt..." He squeezed his eyes shut for a second, but then his hard gaze was back. "I wouldn't trade Anna for a billion Alexandrias. Not even for a second."

Carl's words were so heartfelt, so sincere, that it made my eyes sting. I squeezed his hands back. "I know." Even though I'd worried what I was about to hear around that very area only a few moments before. In a lot of ways they were a ridiculous mess, the two of them. But they couldn't be better matched. "I know you love Anna. And I know she loves you."

He studied me for a second, more intensely than Carl had looked at me before. Finally he relaxed, released me, and after getting his plate once more, sat back, satisfied. "Good. Because I do."

At the movement, Watson poked his head out from under my chair and peered up at us. Convinced nothing was amiss, Watson returned to his nap, letting out a contented snort.

When Carl had taken a couple more bites of the cornbread, cheese, and pepperoni sandwich, I tried again. "Do you have a theory on why Angus wasn't with Alexandria last night?"

"Yeah. Well, not a theory. I *know*." Carl finished swallowing. "They had a disagreement. Angus was irritated that she'd shown up with her knitting group and ruined our friends' anniversary party. He really cares about your uncles. We all do. It was supposed to be their special night, and then Alexandria and her knitting friends, half of which see Angus as a rock star, come blundering in and—" He sucked in a breath. "Fred! You cannot think that Angus would hurt her. Or that boy. He is *not* a murderer."

I didn't respond, trying to piece through things.

"I'm serious," Carl continued, filled with as much sincerity as when he'd spoken about Anna. "Why, Angus is one of the best people I've ever met. Anna and I were struggling with Cabin and Hearth after a really horrible tourist season a few years ago. He gave us a loan, interest-free. Told us we didn't even need to worry about paying him back if we couldn't. He's done similar for many people. He's a good man, a great friend, and a... better man than me." The hero worship was so evident, Carl might as well have been talking about Superman.

"I'm not saying he isn't, Carl." Angus never struck me as Superman, but the few interactions we'd had made me feel like he was a genuinely good guy. "But it's hard to ignore that a lot of these details are swirling around him. He—" When a look mixed with horror and denial crossed Carl's face, I changed tactics. "I'm sure you're right. I'm probably... just desperate to solve this case."

Carl's eyes narrowed, and then he seemed satisfied. "Can't blame you for that, but you're wasting your time looking at Angus. He's a good man, Fred. Ask anybody. A good, good man."

"I know." That time, I leaned toward Carl. "It's my turn to ask for a favor. Don't mention my suspicions to Angus, okay?" Even as the words left my lips, I knew they were pointless. Carl could swear up to high heaven, but it was a promise I knew he couldn't keep. The juicy tidbit, to him and his wife, was a morsel so delectable, that the only way to enjoy it was to share it. Even if he promised, my suspicions would get back to Angus, maybe today, maybe in a week, maybe in a month. I'd just have to hope whenever it was, I'd figure out if Angus was connected to the Irons family *before* that occurred.

Seemingly unaware of his own limitations, Carl barely had to consider. "Of course. I care about you, Fred. You know that. I'm not going to spread gossip and rumors about you. And I also know it's only part of why you're so good at all of this. You have to ask the hard questions."

"Thank you, Carl." Even though I knew he wouldn't be able to help himself, I appreciated it.

"Can I ask the same of you?" He didn't sit back. "Will you keep my secret from Anna? When the investment pays off, she'll be so happy."

I almost said yes instantly, both because it wasn't my business and in hopes that it would help him stay silent a bit longer. But my gut clenched at the thought. Maybe he was right, maybe the investment was sound, even with Gerald's involvement, and I didn't know his and Anna's financial situation, either. But... he'd just stated they'd needed help not too long before. I settled on a compromise. "How about this, Carl? If for some reason I feel inclined that I should let Anna know about Gerald's"—I nearly said scheme—"plan, I'll let you know first. Give you a chance to tell her yourself. Will that work?"

He seemed like he was about to argue, then nodded reluctantly. "I suppose. Thank you."

As Carl finished his strange sandwich, I tried to come up with some sort of scheme of my own that would help me reveal Angus's involvement one way or another.

EIGHTEEN

The sunset glowed pale purple over the landscape of rugged mountains and forests of trees blanketed in snow. The shadows extended over the valley, the darkness of where I knew Estes Park to be only confirming that no one had regained power yet.

Susan's loud, yet muffled, curse drifted from the dining room. Watson lifted his head from where he was curled up beside me, glaring in the noise's direction and then glowering up at me as if irritated that I had yet to fix the situation.

"I think she's starting to crack." I rubbed the pale pink spot on his nose earning a deeper scowl. "Not that I can blame her." I truly had been impressed with Susan for much of the day, but after hours of interviews with not a single insight or lead, we were all frazzled. When Susan suggested doing a second round with everyone, I told her I was finished, that I couldn't help but feel we were wasting our time.

The fireplace called to me from the lobby, but it was too close to Susan's group interrogation, so I'd taken refuge on the love seat by a window in the key room. I wasn't surprised that the interviews led nowhere. We were dealing with the Irons family, after all—why would they crack under a lowly small-town police officer, a park ranger, and a bookshop owner?

I looked out at the beautiful sunset once more, then scanned the thousands of keys hanging from the ceiling. They were a marvel. Keys from all over the world, from all sorts of people, from foreign royalty to a small child in Wisconsin. Thousands of strangers connected by this one room, this century-old log cabin resort. That had to be the answer—connection. There was some connection we were missing, one that wouldn't come out simply because the three of us lined up on a sofa with a corgi at our feet while we drilled question after question after question. The answer was here somewhere. It had to be.

Unless... like Leo's current theory... the murderer wasn't among us anymore. The other figure beside Alexandria at the van had come and gone. The notion still didn't sit right with me. If there was some outside person involved with Alexandria, they were probably part of the Irons family as well, so why kill her?

Watson stretched, pressing his back against my thigh as he groaned contentedly, already dreaming.

I'd brought Alexandria's sketchbook with me. After adjusting the lantern on the side table, I opened the pages. I'd already looked through it once, but decided to go through one more time. Inside the front cover was a list of twenty-three dates. No description, no explanation, just dates. Then a blank page, like in a published book, then the drawings.

Angus was right, Alexandria's skill was remarkable. Every single sketch was beautiful. Each had depth and texture. It didn't matter if the subject was animal, flora, or people—they were lifelike. It seemed offensive somehow, that someone with so much talent, who could create things of such beauty, would waste their life with crime. Would kill a young man who was barely more than a child.

The sketch of Alexandria and Branson was near the front of the book, so I came to it quickly, and I paused, studying him. Though the drawings were charcoal, or lead, I couldn't tell, even in absence of color, the details were so fine I could practically see the green of his eyes looking at me from the page. His lips so lifelike that I could hear his whisper to Watson that'd he'd always keep his mama safe. And he had. Though nearly everything said or done had been a lie, that was a promise he'd kept. He'd turned my world upside down, but he'd also saved my life.

Studying the younger version of his face, I realized I didn't hate him, that I was barely even angry at him. More than anything, I wished I could close the book and have him disappear. Have the whole Irons family and their effect on my life vanish.

I started to turn the page, but then noticed something at the end of Alexandria's swirling signature. A date. The third of June, fourteen years earlier. I flipped back to the inside cover. Sure enough, it matched the very first date on the top of the list. All thoughts and ponderings of Branson vanished as a shot of excitement coursed through me.

I began to flip the pages, discovering dates on every single drawing and matching some of them with the list.

"You doing okay in here?"

I looked up, startled. I hadn't heard the squeak of the French doors.

At the sound of Leo's voice, Watson sprang from sleep, leaped off the love seat, and bounded toward Leo.

He stepped in, closed the door behind him, and knelt to greet Watson, but kept his concerned gaze on me.

"Yeah, I'm..." I glanced around, realizing I'd lost track of time. The sunset was long gone, the dark sky filled with stars over the snow outside the window. The corners of the key room were pitch-black, and strange key-shaped shadows flickered over the ceiling and the walls. "I guess I was gone awhile."

With a final pat on Watson's head, Leo stood across the room. "Don't worry, you didn't miss much. Although I think we're about to have a rebellion if Susan makes everyone continue to stay in the dining room. It's a long time in one place." He started to sit beside me and paused halfway, noticing the sketchbook in my lap, then finished, looking at me with concern. "Are you okay?"

Before I could answer, Watson jumped up, filling the small space between us.

As one, we both lowered our hands to stroke him, and our fingers touched.

There was a jolt, a little shot of electricity that was both unnerving and pleasant. I remembered feeling it when Leo and I had touched months and months ago. I wondered at that... how had we not felt that every time? Before the question even finished forming I knew the answer. I'd avoided touching Leo as much as possible. Whether that choice had been intentional or unconscious, I wasn't entirely sure. I pulled my hand back at the contact, out of reflex, then lowered it again, covering his hand where it lay on top of Watson's side. The jolt happened again, though it was sharp and quick, giving way to a pleasant buzz. I lifted my gaze to Leo's, which glowed nearly yellow in the candlelight.

"Yes. I'm okay." I stroked my thumb over the back of his hand. "Very."

A relieved smile crossed his handsome face, and he kept his voice low. "Several times today I wondered if I'd imagined things last night. I know I didn't, but it's just hard to believe that we're finally..." He ended with a small shrug.

Finally. Like I'd kept him waiting. Which... I supposed, I had. "Did you know this would happen? It was just a matter of time?"

"No." He chuckled self-consciously. "I'm sure I'm supposed to say yes, that I did. It would be more romantic that way. If I could claim I knew we were fated to be together, that it was destiny, or written in the stars or something. But I didn't. In fact—" His gaze darted to the sketchbook, as if expecting to see Branson's face there. He didn't. It was opened to a drawing of a tractor in a field of sunflowers, framed on one side with a large tree, its branches stretching over the top. He looked back up. "I gave up for a while. When it looked like you'd made your choice, you *had* made your choice. I decided I'd have to be content with being your friend. Even so, it wasn't like I could move on." Another chuckle, followed by a grimace. "As I said, not the most romantic of answers."

"Actually, it is." The warmth inside burned brighter than any lantern ever could. "I don't know if I believe in destiny or fate anyway. But I..." My words caught, the weight of the sketchbook on my lap suddenly heavier, causing me to reevaluate what I was about to say, and in that moment, I realized just how true it actually was. "I trust this. Maybe because of the wait, because of our friendship. I trust... *us.*"

Smiling, he leaned closer and kissed me softly, tenderly.

Disrupted, Watson grunted, and hopped off the love seat, casting an irritated glare at Leo.

I laughed. "I didn't even know he could look at you that way."

Leo barely spared Watson a glance. "I'll survive." And then he kissed me again.

"See here…" I flipped back and forth from the inside cover of the sketchbook to various pages. "These dates correspond. Every single date goes with the drawing."

Leo had scooted closer, one of his arms over my shoulders. Watson had joined us and snored from his curled-up spot on the other side. Leo used his free hand to turn a few pages. "But not all the drawings have dates on the list."

"Right." I'd noticed that as well but hadn't been able to figure out the reasoning of it, but it was important. I could feel an answer there. Though if it had to do with the current murderers, the Irons family, or something else, I had no idea. "There has to be something significant about the pictures on that list. But I don't see any common theme through them. There's a few that are people's faces, but most are landscapes or still-life studies. Even those don't have a unifying theme either. Some are rural, others are cities or large buildings, there's even a couple that are landmarks from other countries."

"But the first one on the list is the drawing of Alexandria and Branson." Even though the way Leo said it wasn't a question, I nodded. He continued. "The most recent on the list was two weeks ago."

I flipped to it. "Yeah. This drawing of Niagara Falls. I don't want to start the interrogations again, but I'm going to see if any of the knitters know if Alexandria was there two weeks ago, or sometime recently. It wouldn't be definitive, but it would indicate that this was like a diary of some sort, places she's been, people she's with."

"Seems reasonable." Leo reached over once more, flipping through the pages, not stopping on any one in particular. "It's strange that this goes back fourteen years. It's not *that* big of a book. For an artist, why would she make this last so long?"

I hadn't thought of that, but an answer came quickly, right or wrong. "From what Angus says, it sounds like knitting was her first love, her medium of choice. Even though these are exceptional, maybe she didn't draw all that frequently."

The French doors burst open again, and Watson, as before, lunged off the chair, this time giving a growl and bark.

"Oh, calm down, drama queen." Percival entered with a flourish and halted a few steps into the room, gaping at Leo and me.

Leo scooted over and took his arm from my shoulders.

Cocking his head, his eyes shrewd, Percival perched a hand on his hip as a huge smile lit his face. "Well... it's *about* time. You two were so slow that Gary and I were considering having an intervention."

Embarrassment flooded me for a moment as I felt like a teenager being caught by their parent bursting into the room. Shoving it aside, I reached over, took Leo's hand, and looked at him for confirmation.

He merely smiled, gave a squeeze, and turned to Percival. "I think you and Gary should still do it. I've never had an intervention. Could be fun. And knowing you two, there'd be glitter."

Percival sucked in an exaggerated gasp. "Stereotype much?" He shook his head in mock disgust at Leo and looked at me, shaking his finger. "You better hold on to this one, my lovely niece. A handsome man with a smart mouth is a catch." He glared down at Watson. "Not to mention he's good with your furball of attitude."

Leo chuckled, and though it was quiet, at the end, I caught a sigh of contentment. Happily, I realized that underneath the buzz of nerves and excitement around it all, that was how I felt as well—content, at peace. I most definitely had never felt that with Branson, and… looking back, I didn't think I'd ever experienced it with my ex-husband, either.

Fate, destiny, or whatever, that was a good sign.

"Hurry up!" Percival pulled my attention back, as he waved us onward. "Murders or not, it's still Gary's and my anniversary, and it's time to party." He grimaced. "Maybe not party, since there's no electricity, no music, and we'll be eating the same food we've had for two days, delicious though it is, but it's a party nonetheless."

"Really?" Leo stared, disbelieving. "Susan gave her permission?"

"*Permission?*" Percival practically shrieked. "Honey, I don't need her permission. I've had enough. I stood up and said as much. Of course, she sputtered and threatened and whatnot…" He rolled his eyes exaggeratedly. "I told *her* that if she wanted to stop it, she'd have to shoot me."

"I'm kind of surprised she didn't."

Percival nodded at me sagely. "Honestly, I am too." He motioned for us to follow again. "So hurry up. Enough of this. If there really is a murderer in our midst, it's all the more reason we should grasp at living in the moment. And now, I have this wonderful juicy gossip of you two to share with the entire group. Talk about an anniversary present!" With a whirl, he headed back the way he came.

"Oh Lord. I'm so sorry." I started to rush after him, but Leo caught my hand. I turned to look at him.

He was hesitant, but the look in his eyes was sincere. "I don't care if everyone knows, if you don't."

Though it wasn't my style, I discovered I rather liked the idea of sharing my excitement.

"Announcing... Mr. and Mrs. Winifred Page!" Percival had barely stepped one foot into the lantern-lit dining room before trilling out his announcement, then swept aside and gestured toward Leo and me with the twirling gesture. "That's right, Leo, you're taking *her* name. It's time to turn the patriarchy on its head."

Both of us halted, as did the rest of the room, at least the Estes Park side. Watson trotted forward a few feet and looked back quizzically.

After a second, Anna screamed, stood, and clapped her hands. "You're married?"

"Oh, for crying out loud," Susan muttered, and leaned against the curling iron lip of the bathtub salad bar as she rubbed one of her temples.

"No..." Leo came to his senses before me and laughed nervously. "Not married. We're just..." At a loss for words, it seemed, he looked at me, then simply held out his hand. We'd only dropped our grip moments before as we passed the lobby fireplace.

I took it again.

Another wave of silence, and then the Estes Park crew began to cheer and clap and holler. After a few seconds, the knitters and the staff joined in, though they seemed more confused than anything.

Though it felt like my cheeks were about to burst into flames, I couldn't help but giggle at their response and feel completely wrapped in their love. I found Mom's gaze from where she'd been talking with Zelda. Tears were already streaming down her cheeks as she made her way across the dining room and wrapped me in a hug. Typically I would've found it a little overdramatic, but... I was happy, and so was she.

Before I knew it, Leo and I were swept up in a tidal wave of congratulations.

From just outside the group, Susan threw up her hands in exasperation. "Good grief! It's not like you two announced your engagement or that you're having a baby, or did something important like solving cancer... or a murder."

Barry had just finished kissing me on the cheek, and he dashed toward her, arms wide. "Come on now, we needed some good news, celebrate with us!"

One of her hands instantly went to the holster of her gun and the other shot out in front of her. "If you even *think* of hugging me, you crazy old man, there'll be another murder."

Nonplussed, Barry crashed into her, wrapping her sturdy frame in his long, lanky arms. At their feet, Watson pranced around, ready and willing to play any game Barry found entertaining.

Though Susan glowered at me over Barry's shoulder, I thought I caught a hint of a grin.

.   .   .

Within half an hour, Lisa and the staff had brought out more food. For the first time, maybe because of the celebratory spirit Percival had prompted, all three groups mingled together around the dining room. After the food was delivered, even some of the members of the staff dispersed among the rest of us.

Susan shared a table with Angus, Gerald, Barry, and my uncles. Probably sensing that Mom wanted some time with me, Leo joined them after a bit. From the intensity of their expressions, I assumed they were debating either the murders, or how we were going to get through the night safely when there might be a killer among us.

Not concerned about such issues, Watson lay on the floor between Barry's and Leo's chairs, looking back and forth at them in adoration, his little knob of a tail wagging happily.

Cordelia and Wanda had joined Katie, Mom, and me at our table. They'd seen us looking through Alexandria's sketchbook and were curious. Cordelia angled the drawing of Alexandria and Branson toward Wanda. "I'm certain I've never seen him. I think I'd remember. He'd stick out in Willow Lane."

Wanda cocked an eyebrow and tapped the page. "*He'd* stick out anywhere. He looks more like a movie star than a policeman."

It was an apt description. Leo and Branson were both handsome. But where Branson was more Hollywood perfection, almost uncomfortably so, Leo's beauty was more approachable, and maybe more alluring because of it.

"Well, we know for certain he was in Kansas City. He said as much to Fred." Mom glared at Branson's image, nowhere near being ready to forgive him for his deception.

"I don't know if it matters if he was ever in Willow Lane or not. He was close, and knew Alexandria, clearly."

"What a waste." Katie sighed in disgust beside me.

"I agree." Mom nodded fervently. "That man is nothing but a waste."

"No, not Branson." Katie faltered. "I mean... I'm not defending him, but I meant Alexandria." She gestured toward the sketchbook. "She was a remarkable artist. I know it's different from baking, but it kills me seeing an artist so talented waste it all."

"You should see what that girl could knit." Cordelia shook her head in disbelief. "It was almost aggravating. I'd be struggling to knit so that it resembled anything recognizable, and she'd come along and craft something in a matter of hours that would take your breath away. Unfortunately, she knew it. She was always superior to everyone."

"In addition to skill, she was structured." Wanda nodded sagely. "She was organized, scheduled, and disciplined." She flipped to the inside cover. "Just look at these dates. Handwritten, but they're perfectly neat and straight, as if formatted on a computer."

Cordelia shot a knowing look at her friend. "It was always your favorite aspect of her."

"It was *my only* favorite aspect of hers." Wanda tapped the list. "It was her only soothing quality."

I'd forgotten that Wanda was the one who'd labeled all the yarn supplies. It made sense she'd connect to that characteristic of Alexandria.

"And you think the pictures that correspond with the dates are the important ones?" Katie angled the sketchbook her way. "Like a diary or something?"

"Exactly. They must..." Katie's words replayed through my mind. *A diary*. I'd thought the same thing when I'd perused it earlier, but as I pulled the book back and began flipping through the pages, checking the drawings with a date list again, it clicked. "I think it's a kill list."

The entire table turned toward me.

I flinched at the attention but reiterated the sentiment. "The dates. I bet they correspond with the times she murdered someone."

"Why?" Katie looked from me to the sketchbook and back to me again.

"Mostly a feeling." I shrugged. "But, it would be a sort of diary. Like you said."

Katie's eyes widened, looking excited, then almost sounded apologetic when she spoke again. "That makes sense as the first date matches the drawing of her and Branson."

The thought made my blood run cold. "Why do you think that?"

"I kind of wonder if he trained her. Maybe that was the day of her first kill." Her eyes met mine. "It might've been part of their relationship."

I refocused on the picture and considered Katie's words, combining her theory with mine. Part of me wanted to dismiss it, knowing about some of the crimes Katie's parents had committed, slough it off as nothing more than her projecting. But... as I studied the drawing, I felt the truth of it. I couldn't say what, but as Katie said, some instinct suggested it was the right track. I began flicking through the sketchbook again, finding the drawings that corresponded with the dates. "So maybe the ones of places are where she killed. A farm with the tractor, a little cottage, Niagara Falls. And the still lifes..." I flipped through the pages again. "A stack of books, a sleeping dog, an antique lamp... They're what? Things that she observed during the murder? I don't know. That seems a little far-fetched."

Mom pulled the book toward her, studying it as she addressed me. "Your father always said most of the killers he went after, at least the ones who'd killed a few times, ones that required planning, always kept some sort of record or souvenir. This could have been Alexandria's." As she spoke, Mom's finger trailed down the list, stopping about three-fourths of the way down. "Goodness, if we're right, that means she killed someone on Valentine's Day. That seems especially cold."

It was such a comment my mother would make. Valentine's Day was nothing more than just another commercialized day to me. To her, it signified romance and gentility. "Mom, I doubt—"

"Valentine's Day?" Cordelia stiffened, and her voice dipped to a whisper. She leaned closer to my mother. "Does it have the year?"

Mom angled the sketchbook toward Cordelia. "Yes. Right here. It was—"

"Oh." Cordelia gasped and looked over at her friend. "Wanda. 2012."

Confusion flared in Wanda's expression, and then her face went slack with understanding. "No. She couldn't have."

Mom, Katie, and I exchanged glances, but before any of us could ask, Cordelia had pulled the sketchbook toward her and was flipping through the pages. "You said there was a drawing of a tractor?"

"Yes. It's in the middle of this big sunflower field." I leaned across the table, getting ready to help her get to it, but Cordelia found it and gaped.

Beside her, Wanda's eyes widened, and two of them

exchanged a look. As one, they both twisted in their chairs toward a table with a couple of the other knitters.

Overhead, the lights flickered, went out, flickered again.

The room went still.

Then the lights came on again, and this time stayed. The hum of electrical items began to purr in the distance.

"Oh, look!" Anna cried out from across the room and pointed through the French doors toward the glassed-in porch. Everyone followed her gesture, and there, glistening far away in the night, sheltered by the mountains, was the toy-sized Estes Park glittering and sparkling in the snow.

The entire room began to cheer. Everyone, except for our little table.

"The light is wonderful. Even so, I'm going to have to increase my prescription when we get home." Betsy adjusted her glasses and held up the blanket she was knitting. "Counting stitches by lantern light did irreparable damage. I don't know how they did it back in the days before electricity."

"We got up when the sun did and went to bed the same way. We had a natural rhythm to things." Minnie scowled across the small group. "It's you young ones who try to change the world to fit your whims, instead of going with the way the good Lord intended."

Betsy laughed. "I don't think anyone has called me young in thirty years." That time, she looked over the brim of her glasses. "And you're hardly older than electricity, Minnie."

Minnie grunted some comeback, but I didn't catch it. I was too captivated staring at Betsy from where Susan, Watson, and I sat across the lobby.

"Quit staring. It's like you're trying to give it away." Susan nudged me hard with her elbow and hissed. "I barely agreed to this harebrained scheme of yours. Don't make me regret it."

A warning growl rumbled in Watson's chest.

Susan leaned forward and hissed to him as well. "Hush up, fleabag. Your momma is safe with me."

I flinched at her words and stared at her. There'd been many hard exchanges between the two of us in the past, but that comment seemed low, even for her. Especially when our relationship had been improving.

At my expression, Susan flinched right back. "What?"

I studied her for half a second, then relaxed. She hadn't meant anything. It had just been a coincidence. There was no way she'd known Branson used to say those exact words to Watson. "Nothing."

She narrowed her eyes at me, but didn't say anything, and we returned to looking through the sketchbook while eavesdropping on the knitters.

"Now, Katie." Angus spoke up from his spot of honor in the group. "Try not to hold your knitting needles so tightly. It's like kneading. The more relaxed you are with it, the better the bread will turn out."

"This is *nothing* like baking bread." Though Katie was only taking part in Angus's impromptu knitting lesson in pretense, the frustration was clear in her voice. At any other time, I probably would've laughed at my best friend. She hated not being top of the class in anything, and it seemed knitting wasn't coming naturally.

"Try this, dear." Mom reached over and adjusted the knitting needles in Katie's fingers.

"You're a natural, Phyllis." Angus peered over at what Mom had been working on. "We might have a new master knitter in the making."

"No, I don't think so." Mom waved him off, though she flushed happily at the praise. She'd insisted on being part of the ruse, saying that Katie and I always had all the fun.

"Knitting is pretty and all, but I miss my crystals. I think I'll stick with jewelry making."

"Oh, Phyllis." Angus clucked affectionately. "There's many ways to incorporate crystals into knitting. We'll do a few private lessons when we get back. I'll open a whole new world to you."

Susan huffed out an impatient breath. "This is taking forever. Why did I listen to you again?"

Instead of answering, I nudged her with my elbow as she had me moments before.

In truth, the plan had only been partly mine. After Cordelia and Wanda had explained what the tractor drawing had revealed to them, my first inclination had been to have a confrontation then and there. Both of the women had negated that impulse, saying that if they were right, a direct accusation would be the last thing to prompt a confession.

Pamela issued a long, contented sigh. "I must say, there's nothing more soothing than knitting." She smiled graciously at Katie. "At least when you get the hang of it. Until then it's extremely frustrating. It took me a while. But once your brain can let go and allow your fingers to take over, it helps all the cares of the world fade away." She sighed again, dramatically. Too much so, she was too obvious. Beside me, I felt Susan stiffen, clearly having the same thought. Pamela shifted her focus from Katie to Betsy. "Not to mention that it helps get through the hard times in life, doesn't it, dear?"

Betsy looked to Pamela as she responded, her knitting needles not missing a beat. "It's true. It's a little like prayer. During the rough moments, or the rough years, you get lost in the stitches, each one healing your heart a little more than the last."

"I found the same thing to be true," Angus chimed in, his easy tone more natural than Pamela's. "Even now, I'm finding my heart a little more at ease, having the chance to return to this familiar comfort. It doesn't take away the loss, but it helps."

"She was important to you, wasn't she?" Cordelia delivered her prompt as naturally as Angus had set her up.

"She was." He hesitated for just the right amount of time, and when Angus spoke, he infused the perfect amount of anger into his sorrowful tone. "Alexandria wasn't who I thought she was, and I've not begun to grasp that fully, but her loss cuts me deeply. She was a—"

"I'm sorry." Minnie cut in, her tone harsh. "Are you actually lamenting that woman?"

Beside me, Susan started to stand. I gripped her knee, urging her to stay in place.

Angus didn't even flinch. "I am. Like I said, she might not have been who I thought she was, but the persona she presented to me was real. To me."

Minnie sniffed, unimpressed. "Seems to me you should be counting your lucky stars, not mourning someone like that." Her words were slightly slurred, bringing to mind whatever Susan had seen on the recordings that made her think Minnie might be hiding a drinking problem. "You could've ended up with your neck slit like that nosey young whippersnapper."

"That only increases my ache. To know that a woman I cared about so deeply not only had a double life but was so cold, so cruel. That she could so easily take a life." Though I'd been hesitant to include Angus, given my suspicions, he proved it had been the right call, not only hitting the exact right note in the emotion to his voice, but seamlessly leaping to the heart of our setup. "I can't help but think back on our time together. All the long evenings we spent knitting together. Talking about our lives, comparing stories and experiences."

Betsy leaned across Wanda to pat Angus's arm sympathetically.

For once, it looked like Angus was thrown off, but only for a moment. Holding the knitting needles and the piece he was working on with one hand, he patted Betsy's hand. "I shared my favorite spot in the world with her. This beautiful pool way back in the mountains that, during the spring snowmelt, has three different waterfalls flowing into it." He smiled at Betsy as she pulled her hand away. "I shared that with someone I thought was a kindred spirit, a trusted friend and... companion."

Betsy offered a tight smile in return.

"I'm sure some of the moments you two shared were real." Unlike her sister, Cordelia delivered her prompt flawlessly. "Even in the darkest of hearts, I'm sure there are some light areas. Some semblances of the innocent child they were. Maybe you were a symbol of goodness to Alexandria. Perhaps she let you see the light she tried to bury in her own heart."

"Good grief, Cordelia." Minnie sounded thoroughly disgusted. "When did you get to be such a sap? Carrying on about a murderess? For crying out loud, Alexandria was barely likable to begin with. Now that we know the truth, there's no need to sugarcoat what she really was."

"I hate to say it, but I rather agree." Betsy spoke quietly, but the determination in her voice was clear. "When someone reveals their true nature, we have to accept it, even if it hurts." She looked at Angus once more, a little sympathy returning in her tone. "I'm so sorry for your loss, Angus, but just as much, I'm sorry that you cared for someone who never existed. That you shared part of your heart with someone who couldn't truly share hers with you."

"But she did," Angus pressed on, guiding the conversation just as he'd sworn he'd be able to do. "You can see a person's soul in the things they create. There was goodness in her, darkness as well, but goodness too." His voice quavered. "She was going to show me a place that was dear to her. Later this summer she was going to introduce... well..." He gave a sad smile. "To all of you, actually. I was going to fly down and see her home, see where she grew up. Just like my little pool, she was going to share her favorite places with me. There was a little farm she always talked about. With a field of sunflowers and a large oak tree that blazed orange in the fall. We were going to carve our—"

I gasped, then worried that like Pamela, I might have overdone it. Watson reared up beside me, looking startled. "Angus... what did you say?"

He looked over at me as if confused.

I stood, lifting the sketchbook with me. "A field of sunflowers and an oak tree?" I began walking across the space, toward the group, Watson trailing along behind.

Angus nodded. "Yes. She talked about it often."

"Like this?" I laid the open sketchbook on the table in the center of the knitting circle and pushed it toward Angus, coming to a stop directly within the knitters' view.

Betsy gasped as well, but the intake of breath held pain.

On cue, Pamela, Wanda, and Cordelia all leaned in to study the drawing, as if for the first time. Cordelia slowly looked up toward her friend. "Betsy... isn't that...?"

Betsy's hand trembled as she stretched out to touch the sketch of the tractor in the sunflower field. "I can't believe it." Fury laced her whisper. "She drew it?"

"That is James's field, right?" Cordelia pushed on. "I'd know that tree anywhere."

Betsy didn't appear to hear Cordelia, didn't seem to remember that anyone else was even around her. She grabbed the book, glaring at the page as tears began to flow down her cheeks. "She drew James's field? His *tractor*?" Despite the tears, there wasn't sorrow in her voice, nothing but shock, rage, and hatred. "*She drew his tractor!*"

At her yell, Watson wedged himself in front of my legs, growling.

Betsy didn't notice. "She drew his tractor, the very thing she killed him with." With a savage jerk, she ripped out the page, shoved the sketchbook from her lap and stood shakily to her feet, one of her knees popping. She stormed toward the fireplace, carrying the page she'd torn to pieces as she walked and then began throwing them into the flames. "That evil demon. Like what she did wasn't bad enough. She had to gloat about it." More scraps went into the fire. "She probably looked back on this over and over again and laughed, remembered driving over..." She'd thrown the last bits in the fire and whirled back around, having to grip the mantle to keep from falling. "She deserved what she got. I wish I would've known she'd drawn this, that she reveled in it. Not that I'm surprised. She laughed when I confronted her. *She laughed.* It should've been worse, taken more time. I should have...." Her words fell away, and her eyes widened slightly as she realized what she was saying.

"What?" Susan had already been walking toward her. She held out a letter opener with an old-fashioned key at the end, another one of the set that had been used to kill Luca and Alexandria. "Used this in a different way? Not just a quick thrust to her heart? Made her suffer longer?"

Betsy stared at the letter opener, the tarnished metal of

the antique key glistening in the firelight. With her lips drawn back over her teeth, Betsy glared up at Susan defiantly. "Yes. I should've stabbed her over and over and over. Do you know what she put James through? How he must've suffered? And then she laughed." She looked back at the blade. "I wish I could do it again."

Susan lowered the letter opener, and with her other hand reach for the handcuffs she'd secured behind her back. "Betsy Whitaker, you're under arrest for the murder of Alexandria Bell."

Betsy was secured in the key room, a rotating shift of guards assigned by Susan posted at either entrance. With the phones working, she'd been able to call the station, but as there was no pending emergency, they hadn't been able to even give an estimate of when help would be on its way.

Leo, Watson, and I were on the couch by the fire in the lobby, Angus sitting across from us.

"Alexandria killed him with the tractor?" Leo had heard the story, been in on the plan from the beginning—though he hadn't taken part in the knitting circle—yet hadn't seemed able to shake that one detail. "Seems exceptionally cruel, and rather inefficient for an official killing."

That particular detail had been new. When she'd confessed, Betsy didn't hold back, feeling justified in what she'd done. Her nephew, James, had confided in her a few months before he died that he'd been involved with an organization called the Irons family. He told her that he'd left it, and that if anything happened to him, anything that looked like an accident, or if he went missing, the Irons family was responsible.

James's death had been ruled a freak accident, just a mishap on the family farm. Betsy admitted she'd believed differently, but she wasn't willing to let her nephew's name, or the family, be tarnished by his involvement in crime.

Angus blinked, and then spoke soberly. "From all we've learned about the Irons family since the truth of Sergeant Wexler came out, it only makes sense that they'd kill him. It's not a group you walk away from. And if Alexandria was a part of it, though it's hard for me to accept, *if* I look at it openly and honestly from the hindsight perspective, *if* I picture Alexandria taking part in such things, it makes a horrible sort of sense that she would do so in a cold yet personal way." His gaze flicked to me. "I imagine you experienced such thoughts as you've looked back on conversations and moments you shared with Branson."

I nodded. "Yes, I have. I know what you mean—though too horrible to even really consider, once you hear the truth, it's hard to fathom how you didn't see it the whole time. Certain aspects of their personalities seemed quirky, or a little difference could be twisted into something dark." I replayed part of my final conversation with Branson. With the warmth of the flames flickering over the left side of my face, I couldn't help but remember that conversation had also been in front of a fire. "You're also right about the Irons family not being something you can walk away from. Branson made it very clear that by making the choice he did, saving me..." I reached across Watson and took Leo's hand. "Saving *us*, he put a price on his head. The same was probably true for Betsy's nephew."

Leo squeezed my hand in response. Instead of letting go, we let our hands rest on top of Watson's flank.

Watson sighed happily and stretched from his place between Leo's and my thighs, mindless of the concerns of those around him, simply content to be warm, well fed, and touching two of those he loved the most.

"But Betsy's claiming she had nothing to do with Luca's death."

Angus gave Leo a puzzled expression. "Of course she didn't. Betsy says she put two and two together easily enough when she heard that Alexandria was part of the Irons family. Betsy was simply enacting revenge... or justice, if you look at it from her perspective. I don't believe Betsy is a serial killer or anything."

"No. I don't either." Leo glanced at me, though I knew he wasn't convinced of my suspicions, I was certain he was fishing for me. "But it still doesn't explain who the other person was with Alexandria that night in Luca's recording."

"No. It doesn't." Angus smiled at me affectionately. "But... I'm betting that will come out in time. And if there's another member of the Irons family among us, I'm certain our resident sleuth will uncover them."

Guilt bit at me for having suspected Angus of killing Alexandria. Even as it did, I couldn't stop from wondering if he'd been the figure beside her in the dark blizzard. He couldn't be. There wasn't a shadow of deception in Angus's eyes or in his voice. And the affection and fondness he'd always shown for me felt genuine, not the least bit forced. To cover both my doubts and my guilt, I made light of it. "Not sure I've earned that trust, Angus. I haven't outsmarted the Irons family yet. I didn't figure out about Branson until it was right in front of my face, and it turns out, the Irons family didn't have anything to do with Alexandria's murder after all."

"Trust me, Fred. If there's anything to figure out, you'll do it." He waved me off, the smile genuine. "And even if there's not, Estes Park is a better place with you in it, safer, and a whole lot more interesting."

. . .

Three days later, Katie, Leo, and I stood in front of the newly installed elevator tucked behind the sweeping staircase of the Cozy Corgi.

"You do it, Fred." Katie nudged my arm, urging me forward, excitement in her voice.

"Yeah. It should be you." Leo chimed in his encouragement.

Feeling self-conscious, I stepped forward and hit a little round button. It glowed yellow behind the decorative brass swirls. After a second, the two wood-paneled doors that stood where our old storage closet had been slid apart. Watson growled at the movement and shuffled backward several steps.

Katie oohed. "It's beautiful."

I'd never thought about an elevator being beautiful before, but it was. The small square cubicle was done in glowing wood and aged brass. "It blends with the bookshop and bakery perfectly, doesn't it?"

The doors started to slide shut, causing Watson to increase his growl and back up farther. Leo jumped forward, shoving his hand through the gap in the doors, and caused them to open once more. He stepped inside, then waved us in. "Come on. Let's ride it."

We'd spent two more days at Baldpate, until the roads had been plowed and it was deemed safe enough to leave. During that time, life had returned to normal in Estes, and the elevator had been finished. The bakery was now accessible to anyone, no matter their capabilities. It shouldn't have taken us a year to make that happen.

Katie hopped in and I followed her. When I turned around, Watson was clearly in the middle of a crisis, looking at Leo, to me, then back to Leo. He came forward a few steps, then growling, backed up once more.

Still holding the door open, Leo knelt and held out his hand. "Come on, buddy. It's safe."

I urged him on as well.

Once more, he came a few steps closer, growled, and stood where he was on short, trembling legs.

"I'll walk up the stairs with him." I stepped out. "It hadn't occurred to me, but I don't think Watson's ever seen an elevator."

Leo pulled me back in and stepped out, taking my place. "No. This is yours and Katie's moment. Enjoy it. Watson and I will meet you upstairs."

Watson pranced around Leo as if in a joyful reunion, but then paused, looking at me in concern as the doors slid closed.

Katie giggled. "I bet you Watson will love the elevator in no time. Something else to be grumpy about."

"You're probably right." Suddenly I realized we were just standing there. "I suppose I should hit the button."

"I think that's how these newfangled things work," Katie jibed. "You'll want to choose the button with a number *two* on it."

"Smart aleck." I grinned at her and hit the button.

The ride was smooth, and it took nearly less time to go up the one story than to take a breath. It was so quick that Leo and Watson were still walking up the stairs when there was a chime and the doors slid open. Katie and I stepped out.

"It is beautiful, but considering how expensive that thing was, the trip should have been a little longer."

"No kidding." Katie looked over her shoulder as if annoyed, then shrugged. "Well, I guess it just gets people to pastries faster, and that's never a bad thing." She turned and surveyed the bakery's kitchen. "It's going to be strange having people walk through the center of everything. We'll have to make an aisle somehow."

Watson and Leo joined us. "How was it?"

"Speedy." I grinned at him before kneeling to rub Watson's sides. "See? Everyone made it, safe as cucumbers."

At that moment, the door slid shut behind me. Watson flattened his ears, growled again, then trotted off to safety under his favorite table in the bakery.

"There you go." Katie nudged my arm once more. "Told you he'd enjoy being grumpy about it."

At that moment, a knock sounded from downstairs. Watson popped right back up, began to bark, ran across the bakery, passed us, and tore down the steps, as if thrilled for an excuse to get away from the new terrifying contraption.

As one, all three of us exchanged glances, considered the elevator, and walked down the steps.

When I unlocked the door, Cordelia and the other four remaining members of the knitting club bumbled inside. "We saw your lights on, so we thought we'd drop in." Watson approached, and she bent down, obligingly stroking his head.

"Angus was showing us the shop." Wanda motioned over her shoulder. "It was just as beautiful as..." She faltered, then let out a huff of breath as if she was diving in. "Just as beautiful as Alexandria had described."

"I don't know. It's a little too fancy for my liking. Knitting is supposed to be practical, good hard work, and purifying of soul." Minnie scrunched up her nose. "I'm surprised. I'd expect such things from millennials." She made a sweeping gesture toward Cassidy. "But not a man of Angus's age giving in to such frivolity."

Cassidy simply offered a long-suffering expression and gave the old woman a clearly unwelcomed squeeze over her shoulders.

"We're going to be leaving town soon." As Pamela spoke, her gaze traveled over the bookshop and settled on the stairs. "I couldn't leave without seeing the bakery." Her eyes widened, and she looked at me in apology. "And the bookshop too, of course."

"Well, come on," Katie piped up before I could respond, clearly excited to show off the place she loved the most. "I just hate that I don't have the cases filled with things for you to sample. But surely you've got a little time, don't you? I can do a quick lemon bar recipe—it's delicious—at least to be able to have something."

"Really?" Pamela beamed. "Typically, I'd insist you wouldn't go to such trouble, but..." She turned a longing gaze toward her sister.

Cordelia laughed and used one hand to push off her thigh as she straightened from petting Watson. "Wanda and I heard little else besides the anticipation of Katie's baking on the drive out here. I'd say we definitely can make time for that."

Minnie's scowl deepened more than I'd seen over the past several days as she glared at the stairs. "You've got to be kidding me. My knees are aching because of the godforsaken blizzard and snow, and now we have to *hike*?"

Katie practically trilled, and she clapped her hands. "No! Remember, we just had an elevator installed. You'll be our first patrons to try it."

"I hate elevators." Minnie grumbled as she walked by us, earning another squeeze from Cassidy. Minnie shooed her away. "Good grief, girl, let a woman breathe."

Leo and I watched them go. Watson started to follow, realized we weren't, and trotted back to us. Leo chuckled softly. "They're quite the little group, aren't they?"

"They are. I like them." I could still hear Minnie griping as the elevator chimed its arrival. "They're two members smaller than when they arrived. I hope they'll be okay."

"They seem like it. I have no doubt." Leo turned to me. "Susan called this afternoon. She told me she'd already called you."

I nodded, suddenly tired. I crossed the few steps to the main counter and leaned against it. "She did. What do you make of it?"

Leo and Watson joined me. "I'm more curious what *you* make of it. Are you still suspicious of Angus?"

"I don't know." I considered. "No. I guess I'm not. I say I don't believe in coincidence, at least not very much. And a vacation house being broken into less than a quarter of a mile away from Baldpate during the same blizzard would seem like a pretty large coincidence. Chances are it's Alexandria's mystery figure from that night. Susan thinks so. But still..." I shrugged. "It would be nice to be a little more certain. If they found something definitive."

Leo grinned. "Like some drugs stuffed into the center of a missing skein of yarn?"

"Actually, yes, that's exactly what I mean." I laughed at his expression and shook my head. "I know... if something like that had been found, I probably would've said it was too obvious and clearly planted there. The fact that it wasn't only indicates that the likelihood of the two events being connected has a higher probability."

His honey-brown eyes leveled on mine, growing serious. "What does your gut say?"

"I don't know." I had asked myself that countless times over the past couple of days as we'd finished Percival and Gary's snowed-in anniversary. Every time I looked Angus's way. "I just don't know."

Watson nudged my shin with his hip, demanding attention, or maybe sensing I needed his grounding presence. Either way, I knelt, started to pet, and received a quick lick on my cheek for the effort.

"Did Susan...?" I looked up at Leo, hesitant and suddenly a little embarrassed. "Was that the only update Susan gave you?"

His brows knitted as he knelt on the other side of Watson. "I think so. Why? Did she give you more details?"

I could tell he wasn't teasing or playing coy, and I was surprised. Susan and Leo had always gotten along, at least as well as anyone got along with Susan. "She didn't send you a video?"

He shook his head. "There's a video? Of the break-in?"

"No, not hardly." I shook my head, and my heart warmed a little more toward Susan. I wasn't sure if the gesture was another one of her goodwill offerings, or simply something she considered the right thing to do for another woman. "It seems..." My gaze darted away. I caught myself. Why was I embarrassed or shy around Leo, after everything? From the looks he'd given, the times he touched my hand since we came back down, he'd more than proven the page we'd turned was going to stay that way, that it hadn't been some fluke of the blizzard. I refocused on his beautiful eyes, even though my cheeks burned. "It seems Luca *did* catch the two of us that night by the fire."

His brows rose. "Oh really?"

I nodded.

"How much?"

"Nearly all. I still have no idea where he was or how we couldn't see him, but he was near enough that he even got our conversation." I hurried on, ridiculous or not, I was self-conscious. "We don't need to worry about the video. Susan said she deleted it before she turned the phone in to evidence. That way it would stay private."

"Really?" Leo looked genuinely surprised. "That doesn't sound like Susan."

I agreed. Which made it even more meaningful. "I told her she shouldn't have, that if they noticed something had been deleted after Luca's death that it could get her in trouble. She empathetically let me know that she didn't appreciate me questioning her skills with electronics."

Leo laughed. "Now *that* sounds like Susan." This time, Leo's blush grew, and his voice lowered. "Did... you watch it?"

I nodded. I had. Despite knowing that our privacy had been invaded by Luca, I couldn't help but be a touch grateful. I got to relive that conversation with Leo, saw the fear and wonder over my face, heard the tremble and hope in my voice. Saw the same reflected in Leo. Got to view and relive our first kiss.

"May... I watch it?" Leo sounded nervous.

"Of course." I couldn't hold back the butterflies from Leo's expression, then wondered why I would want to. "But first, maybe we should..." I motioned upstairs, and as if on cue, laughter floated down to us from the bakery.

"I suppose so." He grinned and then refocused on Watson, releasing a torrent of hair as he ruffled Watson's fur. "What do you say, little man? Want a snack?"

Watson hopped and gave a pitiful yet excited whimper. His wild, manic eyes rolled from Leo to me.

Laughing I pointed upward again. "Katie, buddy. Katie."

Leo's and my affection was cast off to the wind as Watson's nails scrambled in place over the hardwood floor before he shot off, tearing across the bookshop and up the staircase as if he hadn't eaten in a week.

I took Leo's hand and we followed.

A Cozy Corgi Mystery

Perilous Pottery

MILDRED ABBOTT

PERILOUS POTTERY

Mildred Abbott

Watson's reflection cocked its head, and one of his corgi eyebrows seemed to arch.

"Don't look at me like that." I met his warm brown gaze in the bedroom mirror. "You're only making me more nervous. And I shouldn't be nervous to begin with." I refocused on a smattering of freckles crossing over my bare shoulders and gave a matching head-cock of my own. "Maybe I'll use that fox fur wrap Percival gave me for Christmas a few years ago. I've been looking for a reason to wear it."

Another check of Watson's reflection revealed the second eyebrow arch.

"Okay, you're right. I've not been looking for a reason to wear it. I know it's faux fur, but still... Not to mention, the coloring is a little too close to your fur—it would be like I was wearing a corgi over my shoulders, which was probably Percival's intention anyway." I took a step back to get a better view in the log-trimmed full-length mirror. Even that small movement caused a cascade of sparkles from the gemstone-encrusted bodice I wore. I winced and turned to face Watson directly.

He took a wary step away, a concerned rumble rising from his chest.

"Oh, come on, I don't look that bad, do I?"

Watson took another step back in way of response. It looked like it took an effort for him to keep from flattening his pointed fox ears.

Sparkling caught my attention through the doorway from another reflection in the bathroom mirror. I was nervous enough I nearly jumped at the sight of the stranger. I looked back at Watson with a sigh. "I don't look bad, I just don't look like your mama, do I?" I gave a final glance at the full-length mirror—I hadn't scrutinized myself so much in decades—then chuckled. "Actually, I look like a nearly forty-year-old version of your mama trying to go to her high school senior prom." *Not* that I'd worn such a dress back then, either.

Without another thought, I wrenched my hand behind my back and jerked down the zipper. At least I could tell Katie I'd tried. I'd sworn that I'd never wear the gaudy seafoam gown when she forced me to buy it a couple of weeks earlier. Katie insisted I needed to trust her. That the coloring did amazing things to my skin tone, auburn hair, and blue eyes. She was right. It did. She'd sworn that the cut flattered my fuller figure, morphing me into some sort of voluptuous 1940s pinup girl, instead of a frumpy bookshop owner who took too many trips to her best friend's bakery upstairs. She was right about that too—it did, mostly. The gown worked miracles. So many miracles, that Winifred Page had ceased to exist. I wasn't sure who this other woman was, but she wasn't me.

Some of the anxiety dissipated as the gown pooled at my feet. I stepped free of it, leaving it where it lay. Watson padded over and gave the material a hesitant sniff before growling as I headed back to the closet. I'd wasted too much time trying to talk myself into wearing the monstrosity, and now I had less than ten minutes to get ready.

I had a couple more formal pieces, also forced on me by either Katie or my mother, but I rejected them. One I'd worn on another date—a date that seemed like a lifetime ago, a date that left a bitter taste in my mouth.

In a reaction to that, I pulled out my go-to—a long, crinkled broomstick skirt of soft turquoise blue and faded brown. In honor of the occasion, and as a compromise to Katie, I chose a newer, dusty-rose peasant blouse instead of the mustard yellow I favored.

After slipping into the normal clothes, instead of inspecting the mirror, I turned to my overly fluffy corgi and spread out my arms. "Well, what do you think?"

Watson barely spared me a glance before looking longingly through another doorway that led to the living room and into the kitchen. Clearly, serving as fashion consultant had made him ready for a snack. Things were back to normal.

"Perfect. I'll take that as a yes." I glanced at the clock. Five minutes. With another bit of hesitation, I made up my mind and hurried to the restroom. I might be wearing my typical Fred clothing, but I could at least show that I'd made some effort for the special occasion. With a couple of twists and bobby pins, my long hair was piled in a loose bun on top of my head, a few tendrils escaping here and there. Different than my standard, but... I still looked like me. And it showed off the dangling earrings of pounded silver shaped like corgis.

From the bedroom, Watson let out a sudden, frantic bark of pure excitement and tore off in a run. From the sound of his claws on the hardwood floor, I could tell he slipped a couple of times before he barreled toward the front door.

Only increasing Watson's frantic joy, a knock sounded.

Leo was early.

I started to leave the bedroom, then realized I hadn't put on shoes. After rushing to the closet, I reached for my standard cowboy boots, then noticed the rhinestone-and-gem-encrusted boots my stepsisters had made for me. They were garish and ridiculous and had only been worn once. Not to mention, they were heavy enough they could be used by the mob for weighting people down when they threw them into a river. I stuffed my feet into them on a whim and yanked them on. They'd be mostly covered by the broomstick skirt anyway.

Watson was practically in seizures, barking and doing a combination of dance and crazed frolic by the time I got to the front door. "Breathe, buddy. It's not like you don't see him every day." I twisted the deadbolt and opened the door to my little cabin. A gust of wind ushered in a wave of snow. Without a greeting, I reached out and grabbed Leo's arm. "Get in here. Sorry you had to wait, I'm still getting ready."

"That's all right, I'm early." Leo allowed himself to be pulled inside, then sank instantly to one knee to greet Watson's hero worship at eye level.

I shivered as I shut the door. Only more proof I was right not to wear the ridiculous gown. Who went bare-shouldered in the middle of February in the Colorado mountains?

Leo was giving Watson a final pat on his head and standing as I turned back around. "It's actually turning into quite the snow..." Though his mouth stayed open, Leo went wordless, and his honey-brown eyes widened as he looked at me.

I flinched and my heart sped up. For a second I thought I'd made a mistake, then recognized Leo's expression for what it was and felt my cheeks burn.

Leo lifted a hand toward my face, then paused, proving that the barely month-old transition from friends to something more was still new to us. After closing the distance, he touched a cold thumb to the lobe of my ear, causing the earring he'd given me so long ago to shimmy, and then trailed his finger over my jaw and down my neck. "I've never seen you with your hair up. You look beautiful." His cheeks pinked. "Of course, you always do."

I laughed self-consciously, both happy I hadn't opted for the gown and simultaneously wondering what he'd feel about it. "Thank you. Glad you think so. Katie's going to kill me when she finds out I wore a broomstick skirt on Valentine's Day." Maybe someday I'd get used to the way Leo looked at me, *maybe*. In the meantime, I distracted him by pulling up the hem of the skirt a little bit and shaking one of the boots, causing a kaleidoscope of rainbows to shoot around the room like a disco ball. "I do have these, just in case you didn't think I dressed up for the occasion."

He glanced down, chuckled, and a grin spread over his handsome face. "Verona and Zelda will be pleased." For a moment it looked like Leo was going to touch me again, but Watson reared up on his tiny back legs and shoved his forepaws into Leo's knee, earning him a scratch on his head. "Yes, yes, you look beautiful as well, little man."

The distraction gave me a chance to inspect Leo. From the brand-new dark brown boots he wore, it seemed he'd gone shopping as well. He'd traded in his park ranger uniform and the jeans and T-shirts he normally wore for a pink dress shirt under a casual suit jacket and form-fitting dress pants. "You look rather beautiful yourself." The words were out before I realized I'd spoken the thought aloud.

Leo's gaze flashed back up to me, and though clearly embarrassed, he also looked pleased. "I'm happy you approve."

Anyone with eyes would approve. And again, though the change in our dynamic was both natural and easy, at times it was still a little overwhelming. "We're going to be late. Let me grab Watson one of those dental chew bones, so he'll be distracted for a few minutes after we leave. They're supposed to last for days, but you know him. In about five minutes, he'll be finished and plotting our murder for leaving him behind."

"I expect no less." He gave Watson another scratch on his head.

I started to head toward the kitchen, but when Leo grabbed my arm, I paused.

"It's okay to be a little late." He stepped into me, his beautiful eyes heated and gentle. "Happy Valentine's Day, Fred."

With that, he kissed me, and my nerves faded away.

"Oh... my—" Leo cut off his words by clearing his throat as the two of us halted just inside the door of Habaneros.

I had a similar reaction and focused on closing my gaping jaw.

In front of us, Marcus Gonzales, the owner of the Mexican restaurant, stood in front of the welcome stand, a bright smile across his face and his arms spread wide in greeting. He wore a red patent-leather tuxedo, complete with a vibrant pink tie and matching loafers. "Winifred, Leo! Happy Valentine's Day!" He walked toward us as if getting ready to give us an embrace and glanced down at our feet, his expressive face shifting to clear disappointment. "Where's Watson? You know he is always welcome!"

"I figured he should stay home, considering it's a special occasion." I liked Marcus well enough, but took the opportunity of his distraction to pat him on the shoulder and avoid the impending hug.

Marcus's eyes narrowed. "How are you supposed to solve a murder in my establishment without your sidekick?"

I laughed. Marcus always wanted his restaurant to be the center of a murder. He seemed to view the whole thing as a soap opera drama with his restaurant as the stage, overlooking the implications of a dead body.

Leo chuckled as well. "Has there been a Valentine's Day murder, Marcus? If so, we can turn right back around and go get the little guy."

Excitement flared and then disappeared just as quickly. "No." Then he grinned and winked. "At least not yet. But now that you're here..."

"Oh, knock it off, Marcus." His wife arrived as if from thin air, dressed in a gown that matched the pink of Marcus's shoes and tie. It resembled the seafoam one I'd left on the bedroom floor. However, despite her being nearly a decade older than me, Hester Gonzales pulled it off flawlessly. She shoved Marcus aside playfully and focused on Leo and me. "The only person close to getting murdered here tonight is my husband. At least if he keeps saying ridiculous things like that." She took my hand. "Follow me, quickly, before Marcus decides he needs another picture with you." She motioned toward the framed photographs that lined the walls, Marcus the center of each one.

He gave a dismissive snort. "Why would I? There's no

murder, no dog, no fun." Grinning, he stood aside and let us pass.

I halted again as Hester led us into the main dining room. The restaurant was always over the top, with its cacophony of brightly painted Mexican colors and the large rainforest mural that spread across the far wall—it was beautiful, fun, celebratory. However, my eyes watered at the clashing pink and red spread everywhere. Every single chair had at least three heart-shaped balloons tied to its back. Streamers looped and twisted, covering the entirety of the ceiling, even hanging down in spirals to the floor here and there. A golden table had been placed in the center of the room, with a massive white plastic fountain large enough to be in someone's front yard placed on top. Chocolate sprayed from the utmost peak and cascaded down the sides.

Suddenly, I realized Hester had paused a few feet away, and she and Leo had both turned around to look at me. From Leo's expression, it appeared he was barely holding back laughter. Thankfully, Hester couldn't read my reaction as well as Leo. She beamed. "Marcus went *all* out. He did a wonderful job, didn't he? After this, we'll knock Pasta Thyme out of the top slot for the most romantic ambience of Estes Park."

I opened my lips but couldn't find the words, which—knowing my tendency to shove my foot into my mouth—was probably a blessing. I settled for a huge nod.

Satisfied, Hester turned and continued weaving through the crowded room until she came to a small table for two near the front window that overlooked the parking lot and the snow-covered mountains with stars twinkling overhead in the background. Once we were seated, Hester assured us that our server would be over shortly, then disappeared.

A ridiculous grin still spread over Leo's face as he gestured at the speaker above our heads. "At least they nailed the romantic music. The rest..."

I hadn't even noticed. But he was right. The Spanish music was soft and beautiful, in direct contrast to the harsh mishmashed color scheme. I peered around at the other diners crowding the space. It seemed I had been in the minority. Nearly all the women were dressed like they were at a formal affair. I turned back to Leo. "Katie tried to get me to wear a gown. Apparently she was right."

"A gown?" He winced, his expression reminding me of Watson. "The idea of you wearing..." His eyes grew wide, as if he'd made a mistake, before he rushed ahead. "Not that you wouldn't look gorgeous, you would... It's just that... well... that's not you."

"You're fine, and I agree." I reached my hand across the table and took his reassuringly. "Well... not that I would look gorgeous, but that it's not me. Not at all." Over his shoulder, another redhead caught my eye—Delilah Johnson. I hadn't noticed her when we'd walked in. She was seated with a man I didn't recognize. Delilah had poured herself into a skimpy black sequined gown, and she looked like every man's dream of the ideal woman.

"I'm glad of that." Leo's warm tone pulled my attention back to him. I wasn't sure if he'd seen my spark of insecurity or not, but either way, his sincerity couldn't be clearer. "All that flash would only take away from how beautiful you really are." I didn't know if I would ever get used to being called beautiful. At least not in the matter-of-fact way that Leo said it. Before I could figure out how to respond, he glanced around, and whatever insecurity I'd been feeling seemed to be contagious. "Even so... I should've gone with a more traditional Valentine's Day option—a place *without* a chocolate fountain."

At that, I reached my other hand across the table and enclosed his, waiting for his gaze to meet mine. I knew what he was thinking. Pasta Thyme was classic, elegant, and romantic at the best of times, and I was certain even more so on Valentine's Day. It was also about five times more expensive. "You have no idea how relieved I was when you suggested coming here. Pasta Thyme is delicious, but this is much more my style."

"Still, you deserve the..." He shook his head. "I wish there were more options up here."

Even more than his limited funds on a park ranger's salary, though unspoken, I knew the deciding factor in not eating at the exclusive Italian restaurant was the fact that I'd gone on more than one romantic date with Branson Wexler at the restaurant. I loved that Leo simply had known how much I would've hated having our dinner there. "This is perfect. Literally."

He smiled, seemingly convinced, and then a dreamy look entered his eyes. "Do you remember this time last year?"

I had to think for a second, and when it hit me, I couldn't believe I hadn't thought about it before. I barked out a laugh. "We were here. You, me, and Katie, protesting Valentine's Day as nothing more than a holiday to make single people feel inadequate."

Leo nodded. "We weren't wrong."

I laughed again. "No, we weren't."

"It helped that Habaneros didn't look like Cupid had thrown up all over it last year." He shrugged. "But... this is kind of fun."

"True." I hadn't celebrated Valentine's Day for at least fifteen years, not since the first year of my marriage. I'd worn a gown for that, come to think of it, at Garrett's insistence. I shoved the memory aside. "Next year, how about we go even more low-key and do something at home. Maybe invite Katie over and make heart-shaped dog snacks for Watson?"

Leo gave the smallest of flinches, then beamed. "It's a date. And it sounds perfect."

Only then did I realize I'd just insinuated we would be celebrating the next Valentine's Day together as if it was written in stone. For a moment, my nerves started to spike, but they gave less than a halfhearted attempt before fading away. Maybe it wasn't written in stone, but it was close. It'd taken Leo and me long enough to make the transition from friendship, but now that we had... well... it was about as close to stone as you could get.

"Marcus and Hester sent this over special." Our server arrived for the first time and plopped a bottle of champagne in an elegant silver ice bucket down on our table, causing me to have to release Leo's hands to pull my arms back in time. "It's *pink* champagne, of course."

"Of course it is." Leo chuckled again and smiled at our waitress. "Please tell them thank you."

She nodded with a little sniff and then pulled out a pad and a pen from her apron. "Are you two ordering from the menu or doing the five-course Valentine's special? It's only $32.95."

Still laughing, Leo grinned at me and waggled his eyebrows. "What do you say, Fred? Should we shoot the moon?"

Before I could reply, there was a screech from across the restaurant. All three of us turned to look, as did the rest of the diners. I might've groaned, or possibly cursed, who knew? My Uncle Percival, dressed in a tux equally as garish as Marcus Gonzales's raised both his hands in the air and hurried toward us. "Fred! Leo!"

From across the room, Delilah caught my eye and grinned conspiratorially.

Gary called after Percival, pulling my attention back, then with a shake of his head gave up and followed his husband.

To make matters even more beautifully awkward, my mother and stepfather were also in tow. Before I could think of what to say, Percival was upon us. "My, Leo, you clean up nicely. Even more handsome than usual, which I didn't think would be possible." He started to bend his tall lanky frame down to kiss me on the cheek, then halted and straightened once more, his brows furrowing as his voice lowered to a hiss. "*What* are you wearing, Fred? Katie showed me pictures of your dress over a week ago." Even as his brows creased further, his eyes somehow managed to widen. "You didn't even do special makeup! Really... *Fred!*"

Gary arrived just in time and finished the kiss to my cheek that Percival had abandoned. "What your uncle is trying to say is that you look gorgeous as always, my dear." As he pulled back, he glanced under the table. "No Watson?"

"Oh, thank goodness." Percival fluttered a hand at his chest. "At least there was some common sense going on."

Mom and Barry arrived, with another couple right behind them. Leo and I stood, and there was a flurry of hugs and greetings.

Barry, his pink and yellow tie-dyed tux shirt peeking out from under his winter coat, gestured to the two women.

"Fred, Leo, you've met Violet and Joan before, haven't you?"

"Of course they have. Joan and I have been into the bookshop many times." The statuesque woman clasped my hand graciously, her thick white hair done in a matching style to my own, but the resemblance stopped there. She, too, was dressed in a gorgeous gown, as was her wife, who was giving a quick hug to Leo.

"I figured you had." Barry nodded in approval and glanced over to where they'd abandoned Hester in the middle of the restaurant. "I wish I had known you two were dining here. I would have added you to our reservation. Doesn't look like you've gotten your dinner yet. I can see if they can squeeze two more chairs at our table."

"Don't you dare!" Mom swatted Barry away and gave me a meaningful look. "We are *not* going to intrude, I promise." She cast an apologetic expression toward Leo. "At least not any more than we already have. If I'd known you two were coming here, I would've insisted on us going somewhere else."

I could've sworn I'd mentioned it, but apparently not, although Mom tended to be forgetful. Before I could respond, Percival spoke again. "Well, who would ever guess you two would spend your first Valentine's Day *here*. Habaneros is wonderful, of course, but for a truly romantic experience, you should've gone to Pasta Thyme. It's where all—" The elbow from Gary came at the exact moment I saw the realization cross Percival's eyes. He'd been so excited when Branson had taken me on our first date to the Italian restaurant. "Oh... right."

Leo shifted uncomfortably.

Violet came to the rescue, though I wasn't certain if it was intentional or not. "As your mother said, we won't take more of your time, but any chance you two are coming to the Koffee Kiln after this? We're meeting my friend Rachel." She winced and lowered her voice. "She got divorced a couple of years ago and is a bit of a downer on romantic occasions, so we didn't invite her to this part."

"Oh, that's too bad, I hope she—" Before I could finish, the name of the shop clicked, stealing my words. It had taken me a second to place the name, though it shouldn't have. Perhaps I'd tried to shove it as far from my thoughts as I could.

She hurried on. "I didn't see you at Carla's grand opening yesterday, but they're having a special Valentine's event this evening. Very romantic." Concern crossed her features. "Oh, that won't be pleasant for Rachel." Violet shrugged after a second and excitement returned to her voice. "Each couple will get their own miniature potter's wheel. The two of you should come. We can all reenact that scene from *Ghost*."

Percival snickered. "Oh yes, Fred, do! *That* would make Carla's day."

That time, Mom swatted at her brother, ignoring Violet's perplexed expression, and then she gave me a brisk hug. "We're going to leave you two alone now. Have a good night, dear."

After another quick round of goodbyes, they returned to an exasperated-looking Hester.

I watched them go and sat down with a sigh. "At least they're seated on the far side of the restaurant, so the chocolate fountain pretty much blocks them from view."

Leo attempted a smile but still seemed a little thrown off by the Pasta Thyme reference, or maybe just from having my family descend on us in the middle of the date. "We both know there isn't a fountain, no matter if it's the size of a small mountain, that will keep Percival from spying if he gets it in his mind to do so."

"You're right about that." I attempted some levity. "Violet might've had a good idea, though. You think we should swing by Carla's new shop after this?"

Leo joined right in. "Oh, absolutely. Nothing would top off Valentine's Day like ending the night with poisoned coffee."

I laughed. "You know, I wouldn't put it past Carla to poison me."

Our waitress arrived once more. I hadn't even realized she'd disappeared in the chaos of my family. "I believe you two were about to order the Valentine's Day special, correct?"

I started to nod, but Leo spoke up, his voice hesitant. "Actually... how about we get the Valentine's Day special to go?" He looked at me questioningly. "What do you say, Fred? Take our Valentine's celebration to your house? Hang out with Watson on the sofa? Get a jumpstart on next year's plan?"

Relief flooded me. "I'd say that sounds perfect."

From our waitress's expression, she didn't agree. "I'll have to go check with Marcus and Hester."

The unusually warm March evening was accompanied by a spectacularly pink sunset washing over the picture-perfect shops that made up downtown. The mix of classic '60s mountain-style and log-cabin façades most of the buildings boasted were highlighted by the sunset, but I couldn't fully appreciate the beauty of it all due to my nerves being on edge.

Unbothered by my mood, Watson trotted along happily beside me, pausing momentarily to peer at the pair of corgis staring out the front door of the pet shop.

"Carla isn't going to kill us, you know." Katie gave me a teasing yet reproachful glance.

"Actually, I *don't* know that." I tugged lightly on Watson's leash, and he turned away from the yapping Flotsam and Jetsam without any more hesitation. "I can't say I blame her after all the drama between the Cozy Corgi and her old coffee shop, and then with everything that went down with her family." I eyed the embossed T-shirt peering through her jacket. "And I doubt she'll appreciate a hippo and bear having a tea party."

"First off"—Katie puffed up her chest—"they're having a *coffee* party, and it's a kind nod to the old Black Bear Roaster. If you'll notice, the mugs they're using look homemade, as if they'd made them out of *pottery*, like her new shop."

I merely cocked an eyebrow.

She sighed. "*Furthermore*, neither of us caused any of the drama around Carla having to close down the coffee shop. *She* was the one who insisted there was competition between my bakery and hers, *not* the other way." An unusual hardness seeped into Katie's tone. "And as far as her family, you didn't kill her father-in-law, and you didn't cause her grandfather to make the choices he did."

True enough, but knowing Carla Beaker, I was willing to bet she blamed me for every hardship that had come her way. I also knew without a doubt she held Katie responsible as well. "I don't see why we're doing this. I guarantee Carla doesn't want us there. And you can't convince me that you want to go any more than I do."

Katie paused on the sidewalk, scooting nearer to let a woman pushing a stroller pass. "No, I don't. But her new place has been open for a month now. It's the perfect moment to get it over with. She's had enough time to feel like we aren't barging in or spying, but if we wait much longer, then it will seem as if we wish her ill will or are avoiding her entirely."

"I *am* avoiding her entirely." I jerked a bit as Watson plodded ahead, tugging on his leash and looking back in annoyance.

"Exactly." Katie nodded as if I'd only proved her point. "Besides, I made a reservation just so Carla would be forewarned we're attending. She won't be caught unaware." Katie gestured toward Watson. "Carla even said Watson was welcome."

"That's only more proof she's planning to poison us. She'll take care of all three of us at once." I was aware I sounded ungracious, but I wasn't entirely certain I was exaggerating.

"You're ridiculous." Laughing, Katie slipped her arm through mine and led me onward. "Besides, it's a perfect night for us as well. The twins are watching the bookshop and bakery, and spring break starts tomorrow, so it's our last night for a week where we won't be overrun with tourists."

I made a grumbling noise in way of response.

Katie laughed again. "You know, you're starting to resemble Watson more every day."

At his name, my grumpy, overly fluffy corgi glanced back, a clear warning in his eyes that we'd better not be stopping again unless there was a treat involved.

Katie was right, and I knew it. It was the right time to offer a show of peace to Carla and her new business. I didn't truly hold any hard feelings toward her, not really, but I knew she did me. And I couldn't shake the sensation that the two of us were destined to be at odds—it seemed wiser to keep my distance. As we approached the end of the block where the Black Bear Roaster had sat empty for the past many months, I told myself I was being unreasonable, plastered a smile on my face, and the three of us walked in under the new sign over the door that read The Koffee Kiln.

I'd heard of the extensive renovations to the coffee shop through Estes Park's rich and flourishing grapevine but hadn't so much as snuck a peek through the windows. The gossip hadn't been exaggerated. Other than the two walls of windows, because the location was a corner lot, the old Black Bear Roaster was unrecognizable. Walls were covered with thick wood planks, the kind that looked as if they'd survived a fire, giving the space a deeply earthy feel. The fixtures were done in copper, and the metalwork of the tables and chairs that took up the center of the room were brass. Against the back wall was the barista station and a glass pastry case. Between the decor and the heavy scent of coffee, the effect was rich, elegant, and soothing. It also felt a touch romantic, somehow. Carla had been smart to have her opening during Valentine's week.

The place was packed, nearly every table filled with people drinking and painting pottery.

"Wow." At Katie's quiet whisper, I glanced toward her, and she turned wide eyes on me. It seemed she hadn't peeked through the windows either. "This is beautiful."

I started to verbalize my agreement, but a little rumble from Watson pulled my attention away.

Carla had spotted us and was making her way over. The petite blonde woman forced a tight smile onto her lips, one that didn't reach her eyes. "Katie, Fred." She glanced down at Watson and clearly struggled to suppress a grimace. "Kind of you three to drop by."

She was trying, I had to give her that. I'd practiced a couple of options in my mind of how to start a conversation with Carla after all this time. Asking about her year-old son, Maverick Espresso Beaker, inquiring about her grandfather's health, or diving right in and saying I hoped the two of us could start fresh. Now she was in front of me, I rejected all three options. "The Koffee Kiln is absolutely breathtaking. You've done a wonderful job."

Beside me, Katie nodded her agreement.

Carla's green eyes widened below the sharp line of her bangs, then softened somewhat. "Thank you. I'm quite proud of it. And it's turned out better than I even hoped." She turned, gesturing for us to follow. "Come on, let me show you the place and get you a table." She headed toward the barista station and spoke over her shoulder as she walked. "My original idea was to open one of those businesses that do paintings and serve alcohol, like Canvas and Cocktails. This is sort of a riff on that. We do have cocktails..." She reached the counter and pointed up at the large menu posted on the wall written in scrolling script. "Each one has our signature *Maverick* espresso in it, of course. But there're plenty of options without alcohol, every sort of coffee drink imaginable."

"Sounds like a smart business plan. Coffee is extremely popular. Did you know"—Katie began a strange, slow bounce, rising to the tips of her toes and then settling back down again—"that one third of all tap water in America is used to make coffee?"

Carla hesitated, then shook her head. "No... I can't say that I did."

"It's true." Katie nodded enthusiastically, still rocking. "In fact, behind crude oil, coffee is the world's most widely traded commodity."

I nearly laughed, both at Carla's expression and at Katie clearly resorting to her vast trivia knowledge base out of nerves.

Carla caught on. "Oh, I forgot about this particular idiosyncrasy of yours." She muttered as she grimaced. "Charming."

Katie seemed unable to stop herself. "All in all, coffee is mostly healthy for a person as well. One cup has more antioxidants than a cup of grape juice."

A bright laugh sounded behind the counter, drawing our attention to a stunning dark-skinned woman whose hair fell to her waist in thick dreads, some of them wrapped with copper coils. "You're quite the coffee connoisseur, clearly, but did you know that coffee was first discovered by shepherds when they wandered upon their goats dancing in a field one day?"

Katie both relaxed and grew excited instantly as she stopped rocking and leaned against the counter. "No! I've never heard that. Is that true? Because their goats were dancing?"

The woman shrugged. "Apparently the goats had wandered into a patch of coffee beans and had gotten into a java high."

"Great. Now there's two of you." Though Carla groaned exaggeratedly, the smile she cast at the woman was full of genuine affection. "Simone, this is Winifred Page and Katie Pizzolato. They own the Cozy Corgi Bookshop and Bakery. Ladies, this is Simone Pryce."

I waited for the punch line, some statement about how I'd stolen Katie away from Carla when she'd worked at the Black Bear Roaster. It didn't come.

Simone stuck out a graceful hand in greeting. "Nice to meet you both. I went into the bookshop when I moved here in November. It's charming." Her dark eyes turned to Katie. "And while your bakery smelled delicious, I didn't go up." Her hand patted her flat stomach. "I avoid carbs."

"Oh, I'm sorry." Katie sucked in a sympathetic breath, clearly horrified.

Simone just laughed again and peered over the counter. "And this must be the corgi in question."

"Yes, this is Watson."

Watson peered up, ignoring me and looking at Simone. He didn't growl, but he didn't wag his knob of a tail, either, putting Simone right into the neutral zone. A lock of her dreads fell forward, causing a growl to arrive.

"He's adorable." Simone readjusted her hair and straightened once more, but before she could say anything else, Carla launched into an explanation.

"Simone is the reason I didn't do a coffee and painting

shop like I originally intended. She's a potter and talked me into doing this. Kind of like the two of you. Two business partners with two different specialties." She waved a hand over the store. "A coffee and pottery combo. So far, it seems to be a hit."

I'd heard the details over the month as people talked about the Koffee Kiln, but took the opportunity to demonstrate interest with Carla. "So... how does it work? We order coffee and then paint pottery?"

Carla gave a look that said that much had been self-explanatory.

Simone didn't have the same reaction, excitement seeping into her voice. "That's one of the things, yes." She gestured toward the other wall, lined with shelves of unpainted ceramics, half of which were various incarnations of coffee mugs. "Most nights, like tonight, that's exactly what happens. You pick out whatever piece you want to paint, enjoy your coffee and coffee-themed pastries—"

"We bring them in from a bakery in Lyons," Carla interrupted, some of her old defensiveness surfacing. "They nearly won a James Beard award last year. And everything they send up is coffee-flavored, of course. You have to try the chocolate espresso scone. It's scrumptious."

I felt my jaw fall open, thinking she was kidding for a moment. The scones at the Black Bear Roaster had been some of the worst things ever baked, more cardboard than pastry. Not to mention the scones had been responsible for two deaths, one of which had been her father-in-law's. I followed her gesture toward the pastry case. Sure enough, a large platter of chocolaty triangle scones was piled high. And they did look scrumptious.

Simone continued, sounding as if she was attempting to

compensate for the growing tension. "A couple of nights a week we do pottery making. We pull out clay and potter's wheels, and you can make anything you like. Or you can follow along with the lessons I give."

Carla clapped her hands. "I'm afraid the two of us have to get back to work now." It seemed pleasant-time was over. "Why don't you each pick out a coffee mug to paint, or something else, on the house. I'll also bring you over a couple of coffee cocktails, decaf I'm assuming, based on your ages..." She rushed on, barely giving the dig time to settle, "And a couple of chocolate espresso scones."

I forced a smile, determined not to let her get the best of me. "That sounds perfect. Thank you."

Within a matter of minutes, Katie and I were seated at one of the tables. Watson curled up beneath my chair, gnawing happily on one of his favorite all-natural dog-bone treats I'd brought along with us.

Katie had chosen a mug, and I'd found a small dog bowl. Simone helped arrange our paints on the table and explained that we could pick up our finished pieces in a few days after they fired them in the kiln in the back room. A moment later, Tiffany, a high school girl who'd worked for Carla before, delivered the decaf coffee cocktails and the scones.

After they'd left, Katie leaned near and spoke low enough the tables beside us couldn't hear. "Number one, I'm younger than Carla, so if I need decaf, so does she. And two"—she jabbed a finger at her partially eaten scone—"I hate to admit it, but this is a little bit of heaven. Not that I'm surprised. I know which bakery she's talking about. They're wonderful, and the owner is a sweetheart."

I nodded my agreement, my mouth full of the pastry. It wasn't even close to the cardboard disasters Carla had served before. After I swallowed, I whispered back, "Please tell me that you're not planning on adding a chocolate scone to the Cozy Corgi Bakery menu."

Katie looked horrified. "Not on your life. In fact, I think I'm going to remove the couple of items I have on there that contain coffee. I want to avoid any chance of Carla thinking we're competing this go-round."

"That's probably for the best." A blood-chilling thought hit me. "You're not going to take actual coffee off the menu, right? I'm not going to be able to live without my dirty chais."

Her horror intensified. "Are you kidding? After the fortune I spent on that espresso machine? Not on your life."

Proving how addicted I was to Katie's dirty chais, genuine relief washed through me. "Wonderful." I gestured toward the icy coffee cocktail. "Maybe we can swing by after we're done painting. This is okay, but it doesn't compare to what you make."

Katie tilted her chin. "Deal. And *I'll* make it *with* caffeine for you."

"Let's not go that far. By the time we're done painting, it really will be late enough caffeine would prove disastrous for someone turning forty in two months."

Katie just chuckled.

We were nearly halfway through painting when Violet and Joan sat down at the table next to ours, each with their own piece of pottery, cocktail, and pastry.

Joan gave a quick squeeze of hands in greeting to both Katie and me before leaning down to pat Watson's head. I hadn't seen her since Valentine's. Violet, on the other hand, had been into the bookshop on a couple of occasions. She held out her pottery for me to inspect. "I have to thank you for special-ordering those books for me, Fred. They've given me several new ideas, not that Simone isn't a wonderful teacher. She is, but I'm discovering I'm rather fond of the abstract."

"You're welcome. I'm so glad I could help." I'd also been glad for the business. Violet had ordered over a thousand dollars in pottery books. "And it looks like it's paying off. That..." I'd started the sentiment before I truly looked at the piece sitting in front of Violet. The clay had been formed into some twisting, curving loops that failed to resemble anything recognizable. "Um... you're leaning toward abstract, you said?"

"Isn't it marvelous?" Joan spoke up from across the table, her tone of affection reminding me of how Carla had been with Simone. "Violet is able to catch such emotion in her work."

Violet pulled a strand of silvery white hair behind her ear that had escaped her loose bun. "Thank you, sweetheart." She angled the piece toward Katie and me. "It represents passion, obsession, and consuming fire."

"Oh." Katie sounded relieved and gestured toward one of the spiraling points. "I can see that. That's like a lick of flame right there."

"No." Violet set the piece back on the table as she shook her head seriously, the tendrils escaping from her loose bun dancing artfully as they framed her face. "It isn't."

Joan shot Katie an annoyed glance, then peered at my bowl, as if trying to distract. "You're painting a dish for Watson. How sweet. You're even putting a... corgi in the middle of it."

I nodded at her in approval. "Impressive. *I'm* not trying to be abstract, but I can't believe you were able to tell I was trying to paint a corgi. It looks more like a hedgehog that rolled in lint. I'm afraid I don't have an artistic bone in my body."

"Not all of us are blessed, dear." Violet patted my shoulder in sympathy. "But keep coming back. The Koffee Kiln will help it seep into your blood. That's what it's done for me. I swear I found a new religion when Joan and I came on Valentine's. I think I fell in love all over again."

Joan reached across the table with a smile and stroked her wife's hand. "It's been a while since I've seen Violet so consumed with such artistic fervor. She even—" She broke off as Simone knelt beside their table.

She gave an apologetic smile for interrupting. "Violet, sorry to say, but I'm afraid I can't stay after closing with you tonight. Something's come up and I have to leave in about half an hour."

Clear disappointment washed over Violet's features, but she regrouped quickly, forcing a smile. "That's okay. I have my key. I can lock up after I leave. We can try again tomorrow."

"Violet," Joan said hesitantly.

She didn't have to finish before Violet shook her head. "No, that won't work, will it, dear? We're going to Denver for the theater tomorrow night. How could I forget?" She refocused on Simone. "I'll use my key after that's over as well, but I won't expect you to meet me that late. It will probably be around midnight by the time we get home. How about the next night? Will that work for you?"

"Sure, that will be fine." For the first time, irritation flashed behind Simone's eyes, but it was so quick I barely caught it. "I hate to ask again, but since you're going to be here two nights in a row, would you mind trying to pick up a little better like we talked about? There was dried clay on the keypad of the kiln this morning."

"Of course. Of course." Violet was already focused on the pottery in front of her. "Look at this section and tell me what you think. I'm planning to use the sgraffito method to—"

"Oh my goodness, I'm sorry I'm running late." A woman rushed up to the table, bumping into Simone as she came to a halt. "My last client *wouldn't* take a hint and leave."

Simone gave a forced smile toward the woman and took the opportunity to escape.

"Violet!" The woman gasped, long and exaggerated. "Oh, Violet, it's stunning. The depth of emotion and angst simply seeps from the movement and artistry." She gestured toward Violet's jumble of clay with one hand and placed her other on Violet's shoulder.

Violet shot Katie a justified smirk, then smiled cordially. "Rachel, meet some of Joan's and my new friends, Winifred and Katie. And Watson of course." She motioned back to the woman. "Ladies, this is Rachel Kerns, a friend and artistic muse of mine."

Rachel stuck out a hand toward Katie and me, ignoring Watson fully. "Lovely to meet you both." Without waiting for a reply she refocused on Violet, adoration in her eyes. "It's really just so moving."

"I agree." Joan nodded, but her tone didn't hold the same worshipful ring Rachel managed.

As Violet began to expound on the piece, I studied Rachel while she was dragging over the nearest empty chair. Though she appeared about twenty years younger than the couple, she easily could've been Violet's twin or younger sister. Her hair was pulled back into a similar loose bun, complete with tendrils framing her face, though on her the style didn't seem quite so effortless. She also wore a feminine suit jacket, but it clearly wasn't the same quality of cut and fabric as Violet's. Instead of getting any clay or pottery of her own, she quickly settled down to simply watch Violet work. "I can't be too angry with my client, at least I can stay as long as I want while you work tomorrow."

Violet didn't miss a beat, but never took her eyes off her swirling clay. "Oh no, I was wrong, dear. I can't do tomorrow after all. Joan and I are going to the city."

"Oh." A look of devastation crossed Rachel's face, but her voice only trembled slightly. "No problem. I completely understand."

"But, you have tonight. I'm sure the two of you will get lots accomplished." Joan directed a quiet smile at Rachel, her tone conciliatory.

"Yes. That's true." Rachel didn't look Joan's way. "We'll have tonight."

"Goodness." Katie made a *Whoa* expression at me, then turned to Violet. "Sounds like you really do love this place. You have a key?"

Violet nodded and finally spared a glance up from her artwork, a small smirk on her lips. "I'm dear friends with Carla's mother-in-law." She shrugged. "I'm sure it's horrible of me, but I'm taking advantage of that fact. I'm certain it annoys Carla. And Simone's been a wonderful teacher, but I know sometimes my messiness can get under her skin." She shrugged again. "But Carla knows it's best to keep her mother-in-law happy, and if indulging one of Ethel's friends is part of that, then so be it." She started to turn back to her own pottery but flinched as her gaze scanned over my dog bowl. She leaned nearer, her voice puzzled. "Are you sure you're *not* going for an abstract corgi, dear?"

Katie snickered.

Such a powerful wave of happiness washed over me as I stepped into the Cozy Corgi that after I locked the dead-bolt, I rested my back against the door and sighed.

Watson, who trotted toward the stairway, paused and looked back in concern. After a moment, clearly deciding his mama was simply being her ridiculous self and beyond help, he continued on his way, scampered up the steps, and disappeared into the bakery.

I chuckled, then sighed again as the scent of yeast and cinnamon wafted down as if stirred by Watson's presence. The clatter of Katie and her assistant, Nick, baking away only added to the sensation.

Happiness wasn't quite right. It was more than that.

I'd woken at dawn to a morning text from Leo as he'd reported for his shift at the national park, and then Watson and I had taken a brisk stroll through the snowy forest that surrounded our little log cabin. It'd been nearly silent, even the birds were still sleeping, the only sound our footsteps and light breathing as the stars gave way to the glowing gold of the sun. That perfection was only increased by walking into the bookshop of my dreams, knowing that after the day's rush of tourist families out on spring break was done, I could curl up with a book in front of the fire in the mystery room.

Contentment—that was closer, accompanied by a sense of gratitude. I knew how few people got to live their dreams.

With a final sigh, I began the morning routine. It was my turn, as my assistant, Ben, wasn't scheduled to come in until noon. I flipped on the lights, ignited the two fireplaces, and chose the piped-in background music for the morning— I settled on a station that played an instrumental selection from the 1930s and '40s. When all was ready to go, it was time to indulge my favorite part. After unlocking the front door, I followed Watson's footsteps to the bakery to retrieve the first of the day's dirty chais.

"Morning, Fred." Nick offered one of his shy smiles as he artfully arranged platters of cinnamon rolls, bear claws, and assorted muffins.

"Hey there." I gestured toward Watson, who sat on the other side of the counter, gazing up at Nick plaintively. "I take it my little beggar has already finished his first treat of the day?"

"His second, actually." Katie called out before emerging from behind the espresso machine, a steaming mug in her hand. "It's a mystery where he learned that the bakery is the source of all joy in this world."

I accepted the dirty chai, the warmth of the ceramic and the smell of the spices only increasing my good mood. "Yes, it is. I've no idea where he'd get such a notion."

Katie disappeared behind the espresso machine once more, eliciting gurgling and dripping noises as a cloud of steam emerged.

I watched the dance of the bakery for a little longer as I sipped my dirty chai. Then, as Katie stepped out from the machine once more and dumped two shots of espresso into a bowlful of chocolaty batter, all contentment flitted away. I blinked a couple of times, hoping I was dreaming. When she leaned closer and took a deep satisfying sniff of the aroma, I decided I wasn't. "Please tell me you're not doing what I think you're doing."

Katie looked up, eyes filled with guilt behind a fall of her brown spirals. "No. I'm not." She cleared her throat. "And I don't know what you're talking about."

I moved closer, peering into the bowl. Watson scurried over and took sentinel by my feet, clearly hoping there was a treat to be had, or I was about to prove I was a klutz once more and knock a trayful of baked goodness all over the floor. The scent reached me, clearing away doubt—not that I'd had any. I refocused on Katie, narrowing my gaze. "I see it, I smell it, and yet I must repeat, *please* tell me you're not doing what I think you're doing."

Katie started to shake her head, then let out an annoyed huff. "I've not been able to get the taste out of my mouth since we had those scones a few days ago. They were delicious and *almost* perfect. It was so close, it created an itch on my tongue, and I have to satiate it. I'm getting closer."

I groaned and leaned on the marble counter. "You swore you wouldn't. No chocolate-and-espresso scones. You know Carla's going to take it as a personal challenge."

"I'm not making scones." Katie brightened. "It's a chocolate espresso torte. It has more of the dense, silky texture I'm craving. I've made one at home the last three nights. Like I said, I'm getting closer." She gestured toward Nick with the wooden spoon she'd been using, a bit of batter flying his direction. Prayers answered, Watson darted off to find wherever it landed. "Nick's more than got things under control. He can handle the breakfast rush. I *had* to try one more time. I think this one's going to be it."

"At least it's not scones, but I thought we weren't going to sell chocolate-and-coffee *anything* in the bakery."

She brightened even further. "I'm not going to sell it. This is for my own personal consumption and artistic expression."

I let out a disbelieving growl. "Really? It has nothing to do with needing to prove you can make better flavors than anything Carla might have to offer, especially from an almost-James Beard-award-winning pastry chef?"

Katie sniffed. "This isn't murder, Fred. No one asked you to solve anything. You're not always right, you know." She dipped the wooden spoon again, then held it out to me. "However, you happen to be right in this case. Taste the batter and tell me if I'm on the right track."

Nick chuckled as he pulled fresh loaves of cinnamon swirl bread out of the oven.

Katie ignored him. "If it makes you feel better, we won't even keep it in the bakery. The three of us will have a piece, and Ben of course, when he arrives." She glanced down at Watson, who'd returned from his hunt, his happily lolling tongue revealing that he'd been successful. "None for you, though, little buddy. Too much chocolate and we'd be out of a mascot." She refocused on me. "The rest I'll take across the street to Paulie and Anna and Carl."

"Oh!" Nick's exclamation drew both of our gazes, and his cheeks blushed under our attention. He pulled a thick envelope from his back pocket. "I forgot. Gerald Jackson dropped this off for Carl this morning. I'd barely unlocked the front door before he started knocking."

"Really?" I walked over and took the outstretched envelope, squeezed around on it, then exchanged knowing glances with Katie. "It feels like a stack of cash."

Nick nodded. "That's what I thought."

Katie responded with a cocked eyebrow. A couple of months before, I'd learned Carl Hanson—who, with his wife, owned the high-end furniture store across the street—was secretly investing money in some scheme dreamed up by Gerald Jackson, a lawyer who I had yet to figure out how he'd managed to pass the bar exam, as common sense and intelligence didn't seem high on his list of attributes. Carl had asked me not to tell his wife. I hadn't, but of course, I *had* told Katie.

I bent the envelope back and forth again, and from the feel, it had to be cash. Why in the world...? A sudden arrow of fear shot through me, and I whipped back toward Nick. "Why did Gerald give this to you? Are you doing business with him?" Nick was sweet and innocent, only a few months out of high school. It wouldn't shock me at all to hear Gerald was trying to take advantage of his naivety.

Nick flushed again but shook his head emphatically. "No. Mr. Jackson said he was heading out of town for the next day or two and needed to get this to Carl. Cabin and Hearth wasn't open yet, but I don't know why he didn't take it to Carl and Anna's house."

I did.

"Are you... upset?" Nick's tone shifted from embarrassment to worry. "Did I do something wrong?"

"No, not at all!" Katie hurried over and rubbed his shoulder, leaving a trail of chocolate batter on his shirt.

At that moment, the faint sound of the front door opening reached us, causing Watson to let out a sharp bark and tear from the bakery.

"I guess that means the day's starting." I tucked the

envelope of cash into the pocket of my broomstick skirt and smiled reassuringly at Nick. "Sorry. I didn't mean to jump down your throat like that. I'm not upset in the slightest, and Katie's right, you didn't do anything wrong. However, do you mind if I hand-deliver this to Carl?"

He shook his head, looking relieved.

I halted as I reached the bottom of the staircase at the sight of Simone kneeling in the center of the bookshop, her hand outstretched to Watson, who stood about a yard away sniffing warily. Maybe Carla had sensed Katie working on her chocolate and espresso combination and sent Simone to spy.

The beautifully open smile she flashed my way when she looked up from her kneeling position swept away the absurd notion. "He doesn't give his affection away freely, does he?"

"Not hardly." I offered a smile of my own and closed the distance between us. "A lot of people would call Watson a curmudgeon, and they wouldn't necessarily be wrong."

Simone shook her head. "Maybe he's just discerning. Personally, I like that quality in a man." At her movement, her long dreadlocks swung, a couple of the metal bands clinking together, causing Watson to growl and back up. She smirked. "It seems he's also a fashion critic."

"No, but there is a huge list of things he doesn't like— unusual objects on heads is one of them." I paused by Watson to give a reassuring pat to his side. "My uncle wears a headband with a spring-loaded mistletoe on top at Christmas. Every time Watson sees it, he acts like there's an alien invasion."

"Spring-loaded mistletoe? Can't say I blame him. Once more, discerning." Using both her hands to move the heavy locks, Simone twisted so her hair fell down her back.

"There. Maybe that'll make it a little less stressful for him."

"That's kind of you." Despite Watson being discerning, as she put it, I liked Simone. A little surprising, considering she was Carla's business partner. I would've predicted her to be more abrasive. "What brings you into the Cozy Corgi so early? You even beat the breakfast rush, though not by much." As I spoke, I attempted to figure out a way to distract her if she started to head to the bakery, or to come up with a way to let Katie know to put her espresso-infused torte away.

"I already had an egg-white omelet this morning. I'm completely stuffed." As she had before, she patted her flat stomach. "I'm here for a book, not breakfast."

"Then we're kindred spirits in one way only." I patted my own stomach, which wasn't flat. "An egg-white-only anything would feel like a punishment to me, which is probably why I prefer skirts with elastic waists. However, I'm clearly with you on the love of books. Looking for something specific or needing a suggestion?"

"Something specific. A book called *Men Explain Things to Me*. I think the author is Rebecca someone or other."

Strangely, a sense that I didn't want to disappoint her flitted through me. "I haven't heard of that. I'm afraid I don't have it in stock."

"From what I understand, it's basically about mansplaining. You know, a man talking to you like you're an idiot, being dismissive, or trying to inform you of things you know much more about than he does." She watched as Watson trotted over to the front room and curled up in his favorite spot of sunlight by the window.

The description of the book made the envelope of cash

in my pocket burn—that was how Gerald Jackson was around me and almost every other woman I'd seen interact with him. Not preachy, necessarily, but definitely dismissive. "I'm certain I can order it for you, if you don't mind waiting a day or two." I always felt silly offering that, knowing the customer could do that on their own without paying the middleman. Even so, I walked toward the computer. "Mansplaining... is that the situation in the world of pottery-making?"

"Isn't it common everywhere?" Simone gave a little snort as she followed, meeting me on the other side of the counter. "But yes, not a week goes by that I don't have at least one guy in my pottery-teaching class, who's never so much as held a ball of clay, try to inform me how I might do it better." A playful glint lit her eyes. "Truth be told, I probably get a little too much enjoyment out of watching their failed attempts, only to rub it in, *in front* of their dates."

Chuckling along, I found the book with the next few keystrokes. "The author's last name is Solnit." I angled the screen so she could see the cover. "Would you like me to order it for you? How soon do you need it?"

"That would be great. Thank you." After inspecting the cover, she leaned back. "No rush. The group I'm in isn't starting our first discussion for another week or so."

No wonder I liked her. "You're in a book club. Whose?"

"Not a book club. But I am the newest member of the Pink Panthers." My expression must've betrayed me, or something, as her eyes narrowed. "I take it you know of it? And don't approve?"

I adjusted my features. The Pink Panthers belonged to Delilah Johnson, and was a sorority, of sorts. And though I'd been offered admittance, like Delilah herself, something about the group triggered every lingering middle-school insecurity I had. "No, I... approve." I forced a smile and then felt it become genuine. "Not that you need my approval. I just... well, it's not exactly a book club." Even as I said it, the book in question made complete sense from Delilah's point of view. And from Simone's beautiful face and her outgoing and direct personality, she, too, made sense for Delilah's group.

"I'm surprised you haven't had more orders for it. Delilah suggested we all order it through you."

"Did she?" That surprised me, though I suppose it shouldn't have. "That's kind of her."

I placed the order and swiped Simone's credit card before handing it back to her. "It should be in the day after tomorrow. If you give me your cell, I'll call you, or I can run it down to the Koffee Kiln, if you'd prefer."

"I'd hate for you to do that." Simone tore off a portion of her receipt and began to scribble her name and number. "However, I'm firing the pottery you and Katie painted the other night. They should be ready for you to pick up later this evening, so come on down whenever you get the chance."

I groaned exaggeratedly. "Do me a favor and accidentally break my piece as you put it in the kiln, would you? The thing's an embarrassment."

"I think you might be surprised, it's amazing how different the paint looks after it's been fired." She winked. "And if not, skip the painting altogether next time and come to one of my pottery classes instead."

"Trust me, you'd regret that. There'd be clay flung all over your shop." I gestured to the craft section where I'd shelved a couple of pottery books I'd selected alongside Violet's order. "I'll stick with reading about it."

Simone grimaced in annoyance. "Trust *me*, you'd

hardly be the messiest person in the Koffee Kiln. I swear I spend a couple hours every morning cleaning up the back room." She shook her head and waved me off. "Never mind. I shouldn't be complaining. But I should get back. I'll have your pieces ready for you shortly." As she sashayed toward the front door, she twinkled her fingers toward Watson's snoring form. "See you later, handsome."

My fingers slipped off the door handle of the Koffee Kiln. I tried again but discovered the door was locked. I leaned closer, peering into the window against the glare of the morning sunlight. Sure enough, the lights were on, but I didn't see anyone. Just as I was about to pull away, Carla appeared from behind the espresso machine. She didn't seem to notice us. I knocked.

With a little hop of surprise, Carla looked up. She relaxed when she saw me at the door, and then proving that recognition came a few seconds later, her eyes narrowed. For a moment I thought she was going to pretend I wasn't there. As she hesitated, apparently she thought the same thing. Finally, with a visible huff, she walked out from behind the counter and headed toward us.

I took a couple of steps back, giving her room.

There was a click of a lock, and then the door swung open. "Fred, I..." Carla halted, looking down at Watson, who panted in expectation. I suspected he still associated Carla with the treat of scones. He never seemed to mind that they were drier than the desert. She looked back up at me, annoyed. "I have a baby and I'm with him less than you're with your pet. Don't you think it's a little strange that you two are attached at the hip?"

I managed to hide my bristle of exasperation. "That would be a little strange. His hips are down by my calves. I'd be falling constantly."

Her eyes narrowed even further to barely there slits. I couldn't blame her; it had been a lackluster attempt at humor. "I hardly walked in here more than two minutes ago. I got a call from Tiffany saying she wasn't feeling well, so I'll be on my own for the first hour or so. I'm running behind."

I opened my mouth to let her know I wasn't going to take much of her time, but she launched in again.

"And really, Winifred, it was a nice gesture for you and Katie to come in the other night, but I'd rather you leave it at that. How about we agree that you stay to your shop and I'll stay to mine. I know Katie's barista skills are subpar, but"—she shrugged—"choices. I'm afraid you'll have to keep getting your Americano with steamed coconut milk from her."

"No, actually I get a—" I barely stopped myself. Carla always got my order wrong, but why did it matter? I switched directions. "I'm not here for coffee. Simone came by yesterday, letting me know that Katie's and my pottery was done. I was hoping to come by last night, but by the time the tourists left the Cozy Corgi and we got it cleaned up, it was too late."

"You can't help bragging, can you?" Carla propped one hand on her hip but stood aside, allowing us to enter.

"I wasn't..." My protest faded away. *This* was the Carla I remembered. However, instead of simply agreeing to her request, one that I found more than satisfactory, as I turned to face her, I slipped into one of my intended spiels I'd practiced for the other night. "Listen, Carla. I should've said this ages ago, but with Black Bear Roaster closed for so long, I didn't get the chance, and I doubted you wanted me to come by your house. But I'm sorry for everything that happened last year." Even as I spoke, as I'd practiced, I still couldn't quite figure out what I was apologizing for. Katie had been right; I *hadn't* done anything wrong. "I don't want you or your family to—"

"You're going to imply *I* had my business closed for too long?" Carla's voice was so sharp I noticed Watson cringed. "How long have your brothers-in-law been designing and redesigning their stupid invention store? And what's their excuse? No one tore *your* family apart."

Yeah... that was pretty much how I thought it would go. It was like Carla had gotten a script to my own rehearsals of our conversations. I started to head back to the door. "You had the right idea. I'll stick to the Cozy Corgi, you stick to the Koffee Kiln, and all will be good." Unable to stop myself, I tossed out one more olive branch. "And Katie and I have already agreed that we're not going to do any bakery items with coffee in them. You'll have the monopoly on—"

She laughed. "You think I'm worried about competition from Little Miss Walking Encyclopedia? *Please.*"

"Carla, I didn't mean—"

"And don't leave without your pottery. Just get it now so you don't have to come back later, or expect me to make a trip to bring it to you." She stormed toward the back of the shop, then paused to glare over her shoulder when Watson and I didn't move. "Well, come on. I don't know which pieces you and Katie painted, and I'm not sure of Simone's labeling system."

Making a mental note to strangle Katie as soon as I saw her for suggesting we ever darken the door of Carla's new shop, I followed.

Watson perked up once more as we headed toward the

back room, visions of scenes doubtlessly flitting through his mind.

Carla was moving so fast that when her fingers slipped from the handle of the back door as mine had moments before from the front one, she crashed into it with a curse. She tried again. "Odd. Simone normally doesn't lock this. Hold on." She hurried away and was back moments later, sorting through a key ring. After unlocking the door, she walked in and flipped on the lights, then stood aside and crossed her arms as she nodded toward the opposite wall. "The finished pieces are over there."

Watson and I walked into a room that was as big as the front of the shop. Following Carla's gesture, I headed toward the row of open shelving filled with pottery. It only took a second to realize why Simone had been irritated. The place was a mess. Clay flung here and there, in various stages of drying out, some on wet sheets of plastic, others simply lying on the concrete floor. Some unrecognizable half-formed something or other sat partially finished near the large potter's wheel. Chances were it was something Violet was working on, judging from its *abstract* form. Beside it, a huge,stainless steel cylinder took up a lot of the space. The kiln, I assumed. It was as tall as I was. A partially filled glass of wine sat on the edge of the potter's wheel, a couple of empty bottles lay on the floor.

Watson sniffed here and there, quizzically inspecting different lumps of clay as I finished the path toward the shelves. Even from a few feet away, I spotted the dog bowl I'd painted, and mentally reprimanded myself for daring to criticize Violet's artistic ability when my own was lacking. It was atrocious. However, I didn't see a mug beside it. I wasn't sure if I'd recognize what Katie had done or not. As I moved closer to inspect, a figure caught my attention from the corner of my eye, and I gave a little jump.

Reacting to me, Watson let out a little yelp and hurried to my side. He noticed the form as well and began to slink toward it, cautiously inspecting.

I laughed and fluttered my hand over my chest. "Good grief, Carla, your sculpture nearly scared me to death. She's so lifelike."

"I swear you can find drama anywhere, Fred. Just grab your..." Carla had spoken from across the room, but after she paused, I heard her come closer. "Wait a minute, what sculpture?"

I pointed to the far side of the kiln. Though the clay clearly wasn't finished drying, suggesting the sculpture was in progress, the work was spectacular. A woman's figure sat on the floor, legs tucked beside her like a mermaid's tail, hands folded in her lap, her back against the wall. The thick ropes of hair hanging over her chest also brought to mind an image of a mermaid on the rocks. "Simone truly is talented. I swear, for a second I really thought—" My words fell away as something struck me as familiar about the sculpture's face.

Just as Watson reached the statue and gave a final sniff before he started to growl, Carla arrived beside me and began to scream.

Officer Susan Green stood with her arms crossed, surveying the scene as the other policeman, Brent Jackson, tried to calm Carla in the main room of the Koffee Kiln. Finally, her head cocked, Susan looked at me. "Seriously, Fred? How do you do it? You find every dead body there possibly is to find in Estes Park. For a while it got old. Now... the pendulum is almost swinging to intriguing. *Almost*."

A few months ago, a statement such as that from Susan would've been followed by either an accusation of me being the one who committed the murder—even though she wouldn't have truly thought so—or laden with so much annoyance, I'd feel like a reprimanded schoolgirl. Instead, there was almost a hint of awe in it.

"I have no idea." I threw up my hands. "I really don't. Trust me, I don't enjoy it."

She smirked. "Come on. Both of us know that isn't true." Before giving me a chance to reply, she turned her attention to Watson. "And you? Have you uncovered the murder weapon yet? Have you found a glove, cell phone"—she pointed toward the body—"whatever tools people who need to get a life use to play in the clay?"

Watson grunted his dislike of Susan but refrained from growling.

"That's what's strange about it. Watson didn't notice anything amiss before I did." I hadn't realized it until after I'd called the police. "I'm guessing the smell of the clay threw him off, and it's not like there's any blood."

Susan didn't answer but trudged toward Violet's body to inspect it again. "Can't really say I blame the fleabag. If it weren't for the fingerprints on her throat showing her skin—which I'm assuming is your fault since you *love* tampering with the murder scene—I'd be fooled into thinking she was a sculpture as well."

I did bristle then. "I wasn't *tampering* with the murder scene. I was checking for Violet's pulse." I lowered my tone. "There wasn't one."

"Clearly." Susan looked back toward the body. "Man, you've got to hate someone to cover them in clay, or at least really enjoy hating someone." She leaned closer, squatting and putting both hands on her knees, bringing her face a few inches from the victim's. "Although... I gotta say, I've never seen Violet look so good."

"Susan!" It was like my mother's voice had just burst from me, a reprimand for inappropriateness.

She spared me a glance. "Well, you have to admit, she looks at least thirty years younger, all her wrinkles are smoothed away. And I never would've guessed her hair was quite so long. She should have taken it out of that prissy bun once in a while, it suits her."

"I never guessed you being one to critique hairstyles."

Susan flinched, and though she didn't address it, her cheeks flushed. "Seriously, though, you and the fleabag didn't find a murder weapon? And don't bother telling me you didn't look around before we got here."

"No. No weapon." We had looked. Watson sniffed all over, but there were no guarantees he was looking for a weapon instead of food. I didn't share that probability with Susan. "I also didn't see any wound marks on the bo—on Violet." I was still adjusting to thinking of the body by Violet's name. Susan wasn't wrong about that either. She looked years younger, so much so that it had been Carla whispering her name, when she'd stopped screaming, before I realized why the sculpture had looked familiar.

"Let's leave cause of death to the coroner, shall we? Though if I had to guess, judging from all the clay in her nose, I'd say suffocation. But I don't see signs of a struggle. It's like she sat there, letting herself be arranged and covered in clay." Susan straightened once more, looking around the back room. "However, this place is a pigsty. Maybe there was a struggle. Though I don't see any places that make me think of a fight or violence at all."

"From what Simone has mentioned, it sounds like Violet used the shop a lot and was rather"—I gestured toward the clay all over the floor—"messy."

Susan didn't respond for a long time, her green gaze flitting from me to Watson to Violet and then around at the mess. Her internal debate was clear, but I wasn't entirely sure what the topic of that debate was. Finally, with a sigh, she folded her muscular arms once more and looked me in the eye. "Okay, how about this—there's no reason to make you hang here all day, and goodness knows I don't need your constant input. So can we agree you go about your day without saying anything until you hear from me? Don't start interrogating people, and above everything, don't contact Joan. Let me swing by their house and let her know her wife has been murdered. It will also give me a chance to see her reaction. Chances are it's the spouse—not always, as you know, but a good percentage of the time."

"I can't see Joan..." The implications of Susan's words finally clicked in my mind, and I gaped at her.

She scowled as if she tasted something sour. "What? Why are you looking at me like that?"

I played through what she'd said once more. "It... sounds like you just gave me permission to investigate."

Susan's eye roll was so exaggerated it looked painful. "Do I look like an idiot to you? When have you ever waited for permission?"

"I..." She had a point.

"Exactly." She smoothed a hand over her tight cap of hair, secured in a short ponytail. "Besides, like I said, I'm not an idiot, and we're past all that. You're as obnoxious as the day I met you, but you're good at this. And since I have nothing to hide, unlike my predecessor, it only makes sense to work with you. *Unless* you get so obnoxious that I murder you myself, and then both of us lose."

I nearly laughed, then glanced toward poor Violet and stopped myself. "Okay then. So… you'll call and fill me in after you talk to Joan?"

"No. That's not how this is going to go. I didn't just make you my partner. You're not a police officer." Susan snarled at Watson. "And that fluffy ball of lard is definitely not a German shepherd. I don't owe you a timeline or schedule so you can go snooping."

I started to point out the contradictory messages she was sending but simply nodded. "Got it."

"Good." She gave an answering nod. "Now get out of here, and go act like the bookworm you are."

I offered an exaggerated salute, nearly earning myself a smirk, and then grabbed Watson's leash and turned to leave.

Susan's mumble was barely audible as we reached the door back into the public portion of the Koffee Kiln. "I'll call you this afternoon."

FIVE

Before returning to the Cozy Corgi, I went back home, showered, and changed clothes. I'd washed my hands free of the remnants of clay from checking for Violet's pulse, but after being in the back room for so long with Susan, I felt like the murder scene was all over me. With the way the clay had been strewn about the space, though the notion hadn't hit me while I was there, it was like bits of Violet had been spread throughout the room. I wasn't sure why it was hitting me so hard. In truth, I'd seen more gruesome killings, but other than knowing Violet was dead and that she probably didn't turn herself into a statue, there were no visible signs of foul play.

Clean and with a huge thermos of freshly brewed coffee, I felt almost like myself again as Watson and I parked downtown. When I'd changed clothes, I discovered Gerald's envelope for Carl on my dresser. I hadn't run it by Cabin and Hearth the night before and had forgotten again when I'd left that morning. It wasn't a priority, not compared to Violet, but I figured I should get it over with before news of the murder spread if I had any hope of squeezing some details out of Carl.

Though he'd already had a treat at home while I showered, Watson perked up the second we headed toward the front door of the high-end home furnishing shop. He didn't particularly care for Anna or Carl, but he would act like it in order to receive one of his favorite all-natural dog-bone treats.

We'd barely set foot in Cabin and Hearth when Anna gave a pleased cry. "You came to us first! And quickly!" She leaned forward, angling her head toward the back and raised her voice. "Carl, get out here. Fred needs us!"

I froze in place as Carl hurried into view. Surely not. *Surely not*. Knowing it was pointless, I played dumb just in case. "Why do you think I need you?"

Confusion flitted over Anna's face, then morphed into offense. "Obviously you require our input around Violet's murder." She shuffled to the other end of the counter while she spoke and pulled out a pad of paper. "I've been preparing. I have a whole list of suspects."

I shouldn't have been surprised, but I was. "How in the world do you know?" I doubted I'd left the Koffee Kiln more than forty-five minutes before. There was no way Susan had wrapped up and already spoken to Joan.

Anna gave me a look like I was an idiot. "*Really*, Fred, you're being insulting. Of course we know. And I feel like I need to point out, I just got off the phone with Percival, and Carl and I knew before him and Gary." She sniffed. "So there." She ripped off the top sheet of paper. "Now hurry over here and I'll explain them one by one."

Watson tugging at the leash finally helped my feet to start moving again, and we joined them at the counter. Watson looked up with pleading eyes. Neither of them noticed.

"I don't agree with Anna on all of these. There's no way

old Ms. Melvin killed Violet. Not only is she as sweet as the day is long, but she's too frail."

Anna swatted at him. "No one asked you. And you're wrong anyway. Anyone can find the strength for murder when they're being evicted." She gave a long-suffering sigh and turned toward me. "Though she's not at the top of my list, not really. Even if she did kill Violet, I don't know why Maud would cover her in clay. Personally, I think the clay has to have some special importance, don't you?"

I was having a hard time catching up, not an unusual sensation with Anna and Carl. "Honestly, I'm still wrapping my brain around seeing it at all. I haven't gotten that far."

Anna reached across the counter and patted my hand in sympathy. "Poor dear. This must be taking a toll. You typically have a much stronger constitution." She pulled her hand back only to slide the list toward me, but instead of releasing it, she pointed down the list with the pen, one by one. "Joan, clearly—she's the wife, so she's first. Ms. Melvin —*see*, I told you she wasn't at the top of my list." She tapped the next name twice. "Ethel Beaker. She's got my vote."

"Me too." Carl nodded enthusiastically, earning himself an approving nod from Anna before she moved on to the last two names.

"Gerald Jackson, and then the Irons family, of course."

Carl nodded once more as he piped up, "Of course."

I felt like I'd stepped into a cold shower. I'd been honest when I said I hadn't gotten as far as the suspect list, but I had pondered a name or two. However, I hadn't even considered the crime syndicate that had been responsible for so much disruption in my life. "The Irons family? Why? Was Violet connected to Branson?"

"Not that I know of." Again Anna looked at me as if this should've been obvious. "But it seems like every death lately has been connected to them one way or another."

There were moments I felt the same, but when I took a step back, that wasn't even close to being reality.

Watson whimpered, giving up on his pleading gaze having any power.

Neither Anna nor Carl noticed, and I pressed onward. Might as well get their input, I'd be back asking for their insight into all the gossip later anyway. "The Irons family is something to consider, I suppose. But why the rest of them?"

Matching expressions of delight lit behind Anna's and Carl's eyes, and as if they were one entity, both leaned forward, placing their weight on their elbows. "We'll start with the most likely. Ethel Beaker."

Again Carl nodded.

She hadn't been on the short list of suspects I'd pondered either. "From what I understand, she and Violet were good friends. Violet told me herself that her relationship with Ethel was the whole reason Carla and Simone were giving her free rein of their shop."

"That woman does nothing for free. You can't have friends when you don't have a heart." Pure hatred dripped from Anna's tongue as she jammed the point of the pen hard enough on Ethel's name that she ripped the paper.

I nearly commented that it sounded like Anna was the one angry enough to commit murder, not Ethel, then I put the pieces together from other conversations we had. "Because of the town council?"

"Yep." Carl jabbed at the name as well, though it wasn't quite as effective only using his fingertip. "Ethel slid onto the town council after her husband died—no vote, no nothing. And then what do you know? Two months later Violet fills up one of the slots too. Again, no votes, no warning, nothing."

"Yet the whole time, Ethel's telling Carl and me that they were going to let the seats stay empty for a season or two. They didn't want to make any *rash* decisions." I'd never heard Anna snarl in such a violent way before. "Nothing more than a pack of lies. She doesn't want the two of us, or *either* of us, to have a chance. She's afraid we'll hold her accountable for the choices she makes in this town. Percival isn't even able to pull any strings."

Clearly the two of them were furious, and though they were both prone to exaggeration, I believed them. From what I'd seen from Ethel Beaker, that sounded exactly like something she would do. Though how she got away with it, I wasn't sure. But still... "I'm not sure how Ethel pulling Violet into the town council would be a motive for her to turn around and kill her."

"Well, clearly Violet proved to be more competition than Ethel counted on." Anna gave another sniff. "Ethel has to be queen bee at all times. Now she is once more."

What was clear was that Carl and Anna had both made up their minds, so I didn't push. "I will definitely add her to the list."

"No need, I have the list for you. You can take it with you. But first, we'll go over the others to be fair." Anna moved on to another name. "Anyhow, back to Joan. I know they say it's always the spouse, but I do think it's Ethel."

I pressed on before she started another anti-Ethel diatribe. "Other than Joan being Violet's wife, do you have any other reason to suspect her?"

"I think Violet and Simone, Carla's new business partner, were having an affair." Anna cocked a scandalous eyebrow.

I was unable to catch myself before I laughed. At their twin annoyed expressions, I cleared my throat. "Oh. You're serious." Not only were there decades between the two women, but Simone hadn't been acting about her annoyance of Violet.

"Serious as a heart attack. Violet has been staying at the Koffee Kiln all hours of the night, nearly every night. For weeks. And..." Anna leaned in again, the enjoyment of gossip slipping back into her tone, though this time it was mixed with disdain. "She's part of that Pink Panther group led by that nasty Delilah woman. Just a bunch of hussies. Every one of them out to steal someone's husband." She glared at Carl, then blinked. "Or... wife, in this case."

Carl blushed and mumbled something under his breath.

I jumped in before a spat could start. "An affair was one of my thoughts as well, but not with Simone. I was considering Rachel Kerns."

Anna looked at the paper, at Carl, then at me. "She's not on the list. Who is Rachel Kerns?" She answered before I had the chance. "Oh! That new art teacher at the school. I've not met her yet." She leaned forward. "Why do you think she's a suspect? Who's she having an affair with? Violet? Joan?" Her eyes widened and she reached toward Carl as if for support. "*Both?*"

I nearly laughed at her expression. "I'm *not* saying there is, or was, an affair at all. I've not heard anything like that."

Anna waved me off. "Clearly you saw something." She added Rachel's name to the list.

"I didn't notice an affair." I tried to choose my words carefully lest the two of them used my name to start an ugly rumor. "It simply seemed that Rachel has... had a lot of...

admiration for Violet." Not to mention the identical style of hair and clothes.

"Hmm..." Anna underlined Rachel's name. "I'll have to look into her."

I wasn't used to having any sort of gossip knowledge, founded or otherwise, in advance of the Hansons. *Strange.*

"Sounds like she's a stronger suspect than the Pink Panthers in any case." Carl sounded a little too relieved by that, and flushed at Anna's glower before hurriedly pointing toward Maud Melvin, though he'd already said he didn't think she was capable. "Ms. Melvin lives in one of the rental properties Violet and Joan own. She's been late on rent the past couple of months and is getting evicted. Though, that's happened to a number of people who've lived in Violet and Joan's properties, so the list of angry tenants would be pretty long there."

"That is true." Anna winced in way of apology. "I'll need a little bit more time to dredge my memory and make some calls to find out who they all are." She moved on to Gerald Jackson, and as she did, Carl gave a wince of his own. "I know that Carl and Gerald are friends, even though I don't approve of Gerald's drug abuse problem. However, I don't think that played into Violet's murder. I can't see her lowering herself to partake in marijuana-infused kombucha, of all the ridiculous things." She shot Carl another glare, then refocused on me. "*However*, I heard that Violet and Gerald had a very public altercation a few weeks ago. I'm embarrassed to say I haven't yet discerned what it was about, but it sounds like she was positively livid."

That was interesting. As Anna spoke, I watched Carl for his reaction. His cheeks only grew redder, but his gaze stayed glued to Anna's list.

She kept going. "Personally I can't see Gerald having

the gumption to murder anyone, but maybe in a drug-fueled haze, he—" A chime from the door opening sounded, causing Anna to look over, annoyed at being interrupted, and then her eyes widened in excitement. "Oh, Rick Meyers. I bet you he has some more details. I'll be right back." She started to rush off, then paused, shaking her finger at Carl and me. "Don't you dare say one important thing without me."

Watson attempted to follow her, but stopped at the end of the leash, casting a glare at me and Carl.

When I turned back around, Carl's gaze was intense, but his voice was barely a whisper. "Gerald did not kill Violet. Or anyone."

Instead of responding, I glanced over my shoulder. Anna and Rick had remained close to the front door. I pulled the envelope from my pocket as I faced Carl again and slid it across the counter. "Gerald stopped by the store yesterday morning, wanted Nick to give this to you. I meant to bring it over yesterday, but things got carried away."

Carl's round cheeks grew so red at that point, his white fluffy beard looked in danger of catching on fire. Moving faster than I'd ever seen him, his hand darted out, snagged the envelope from my grip, and yanked it below the counter —I presumed to stuff into his own pocket. "This has *nothing* to do with Violet."

"No, of course..." I paused, thrown off. "I didn't think it did."

"Oh." He took a step back, and though I couldn't see them, I heard his shoes shuffling on the hardwood floor. "Well. Don't start thinking it." The directive sounded more like a plea than a demand.

Given his retreat, I leaned forward, lowering my voice.

"Why is Gerald making early drop-off of money to you, Carl, especially right before he leaves town?"

"He left..." Understanding seemed to light in his eyes, but he shook his head. "It's a... payment from my investment. Right on schedule, I might add. You know about that."

I did, I also knew he was lying, not that it took much intuition to see through him. "Carl..." I infused as much Anna-like warning into my tone as I could.

I didn't get the chance to see if it would work, though, as Anna bid Rick goodbye from behind me. She spoke as she came closer. "Well, not at all on topic, but that was some delicious gossip. Wait until you—" She let out a horrified screech, causing me to whirl around.

"Watson!" She hurried forward, rushing toward him in a way that made Watson take shelter beneath my skirt. She halted, seeming devastated rather than offended. "He won't even look at me. Not that I blame him. I didn't even say hello when he came in." She looked at her husband. "Carl, go in the back and get—"

"No." Carl's answer was firm, almost a bite, and caused Anna and I both to look at him. I'd never heard him speak in such a tone to Anna.

"Carl, really." And for the first time, I heard a plaintive tone in Anna's voice as she spoke to Carl. "I'm simply asking you to—"

"I know what you're asking." His words softened but stayed firm. "You can go get the treat yourself. You're already closer to the back room than I am."

I prepared to scoop up Watson and run for the door, certain World War III was about to break out.

To my surprise, instead of an explosion, a wounded expression crossed Anna's face, and her gaze flitted toward my feet, where I imagined only Watson's paws were showing under the hem of my skirt, before she walked slowly toward the back room.

Carl didn't waste a second. "This has nothing to do with Violet. I would never hurt anyone, and neither would Gerald." He hadn't softened with me either.

"Carl, I didn't think it did. And I know you would never hurt anyone."

Relief flooded over him, but then he hardened again and swallowed. "Good. And this *does not* get mentioned to Anna. Clear?"

I'd often wished Carl would stand up for himself with his wife. At times I felt she was a little mean to him, but either way, while I was willing to give him an allowance, since he clearly was worried I suspected him of murder, I didn't appreciate him taking that tone with me. I leaned forward, speaking softly, leaving no room for argument. "As a reminder, Carl, I agreed not to mention it to Anna, which I have reservations about since your choices could impact her financial future. But the second I feel I need to tell her, I will. The only accommodation I'm willing to give is that I'll let you know before I speak to her if that day comes."

He blinked a couple of times, clearly debating how far he could push. It was strange, not like Carl at all. "Fine." His voice moved back to normal. "Just please don't—" He looked toward the sound of the fabric of Anna's skirt moving as she arrived from the back room.

She still had a hurt expression, but she used the adoring baby voice she always did when she spoke to Watson. "Here you go, sweet baby. I brought you your favorite treats. I'm so sorry, sweetie."

At the word, Watson dared to stick his head out from

under my skirt, took a sniff, and then darted forward happily.

Proving that even her love for my furry friend couldn't heal her mood, Anna didn't even protest after Watson had gobbled down his two snacks, and I used getting back to the Cozy Corgi as my excuse to leave—without taking their list of suspects.

The next few hours, I was caught up acting like the business owner I was. The breakfast wave to the bakery was beginning to die down when there was a sudden resurgence. Proving that Anna and Carl—and my uncles, for that matter —were ahead of the curve in the gossip chain, news of Violet's death took a bit longer to hit the rest of the town. Once it did, many of the ones who'd just left from filling up on coffee and pastries returned to get the scoop and speculate. The Cozy Corgi Bakery had become the gossip hubbub ever since Black Bear Roaster closed its doors. I hadn't noticed that lessening any with the opening of the Koffee Kiln, though I was willing to bet that once it opened for business again, there would be a resurgence of their early morning business.

Amid it all, the spring-break tourist families began to show up for late breakfasts and shopping. Though Watson was less than ecstatic over all the attention he received from newcomers, I was thankful for the excuse to avoid the locals' questions about me finding Violet's body.

After the lunch rush, things slowed enough that Watson and I left Ben in charge of the bookshop and made our way up to the bakery.

"Finally!" Seeing us approach, Katie pointed to a table

in the far corner, not our usual, but away from where most of the remaining tourists were scattered among the antique tables and overstuffed sofas. "I've been dying to get it straight from the horse's mouth all day. I'll meet you over there in a second."

I'd rewritten Anna and Carl's list between customers downstairs. As Katie hurried over with two steaming mugs, doubtlessly a hot chocolate for her and a dirty chai for me, Nick followed her, two plates in his hands.

"Thank you, sweetie." Katie patted Nick's shoulder as he deposited the slices of torte on the table. Giving Watson and me both a fleeting smile, he headed back behind the counter. As she sat, Katie slipped Watson one of the smaller versions of his favorite treat, and he settled down under the table to enjoy. "Okay, fill me in. You can't imagine all the different versions I've heard this morning." She started to stab her slice of torte with a fork then paused. "Actually, you probably can, but there's no need to go through them."

Instead of responding, I gaped at the tortes in front of us, then to the few groups of tourists and diners left, seeing if they had similar morsels on their plates. "This isn't what I think it is, is it?"

"Yes, it is, but breathe, Fred." Katie popped the bite into her mouth, groaned in pleasure, then chewed for a few moments before continuing. "I still wasn't happy with yesterday's recipe. This one just about has it. I'm close. I can feel it." She pointed her fork at me when I started to sputter. "Breathe, I said. I'm not going to start a war with Carla. These aren't for sale. Nobody has tasted them…" She hesitated. "Actually, no one's *purchased* them. So they're technically not part of the bakery. Although I have asked for flavor opinions. I'm *not* going to start selling it. Carla is *not* going to freak out. Besides, the Koffee Kiln is closed anyway."

"Temporarily."

Katie shrugged one shoulder as she took another bite.

Giving in, I followed her example, and let out a groan of my own and felt myself relax back against the chair as the thick rich chocolate, intensified by the espresso, melted over my tongue and instantly shot through my veins like a drug. "Dear Lord."

Katie grinned vindictively. "It's almost worth the civil war with Carla, isn't it?"

I nodded, then shook my head, realizing what I was saying. Even so, I took another bite so quickly it was like I was afraid she was going to rip it away from me. "You're not satisfied with *this*? It's perfect."

"No. It isn't. But close. I'm betting tomorrow's will be." Katie set down her fork and sipped her hot chocolate. "Enough about my baking brilliance. What's going on?"

Before I could respond, Watson let out an ecstatic yip and shot out from underneath the table, racing across the bakery.

My heart did a happy little jump of its own as Leo rounded the top of the steps, managing not to fall back down them at Watson's collision. After a moment's greeting, which stirred up a cloud of corgi fur, Leo scanned the bakery, and flashed a smile as he headed our way.

From his ranger uniform, he looked like he'd just come from work. He gave me a quick kiss as he sat beside me, and I marveled once more about both the ease and the normalcy of our transition, and how he managed to make my breath catch. "Sorry I couldn't come by earlier. The park was filled with people."

"It's okay, we've been pretty busy here as well. And it's not like it's my first time stumbling on a body." Of its own accord, my hand found his. "But I didn't get a chance to ask when you texted earlier—how did you find out so quickly? You were almost as fast as Anna and Carl."

"Nadiya is part of the Pink Panthers, remember? Simone talked to Delilah first thing." Leo paused at Katie's annoyed grunt from across the table. "What?"

Her brown eyes widened. "Sorry. I didn't mean to make a sound. I just have such a problem with that group. At least I *think* I do. On one hand, it's clearly meant to be like the Pink Ladies from *Grease*, too-cool-for-school beautiful girls with their own exclusive club. Yet..." She winced. "They're not all Barbie dolls or anything, even though most of them are disgustingly attractive. One part of me really respects the camaraderie and support the women give each other. I think it's a good thing. Yet the other part of me, probably what's left over from being in school and longing to be part of the cool club, or part of any club, has a guttural negative reaction to it." With a sigh, she shook it off. "Never mind. It's beside the point."

She'd summed up how I felt about the Pink Panthers almost perfectly. Instead of agreeing with her, I focused on Leo. "Do you know how Simone found out? She wasn't at the Koffee Kiln this morning."

His eyes narrowed, knowingly. "You suspect her." It wasn't a question.

"No. I don't." I shook my head definitively. I didn't get that feeling from Simone at all. Even so, I glanced at my recreated list, and there was her name. "But she wasn't there. It's strange that she found out so quickly, and strange that she'd call and tell Delilah."

"I've admitted that I'm not the biggest fan of that group, but that seems like a little bit of a stretch to me." Katie repositioned as if she didn't want to be overheard gossiping about Delilah and her club. "Simone is Carla's business partner, so it makes sense that she'd be told quickly. And even though Simone is relatively new to town and therefore new to the group as well, if I put myself in her shoes, it only makes sense that she'd call her friends. I'd call you."

As she spoke, Leo reached across the table, snagged Katie's fork, and took a bite of her torte.

"Hey!" She smacked his hand as he tried for another bite. "I'll get you one of your own, you little thief."

Giving her a wink, he snagged the plate and pulled it toward him. "*Or* I can finish this one off and you can get a brand-new one for yourself."

Katie opened her mouth to protest, but then her expression shifted into a grin. "I like the way you think." She cocked an eyebrow playfully. "Pretty spectacular, right?"

"Do you ever make anything that isn't?" Leo took a third bite.

She beamed. "Keep sweet-talking like that, and I'll steal you away from Fred. Make you a permanent taste-tester."

"As long as you keep making me things like this, I'd probably let you." I snagged a bite from Katie's stolen plate, even though I still had some of my own left.

Leo shrugged, unconcerned. "Can't say I blame you. How in the world could I ever compete with Katie's baking?"

"You're both ridiculous. And I'm glad of it." Katie stood and headed toward the bakery. Watson followed, clearly intent on begging.

Leo grew serious as he looked at me. "You're really okay?"

"Yeah, I really am." I warmed under his concern. "It did throw me off for a little bit, but I'm okay."

He inspected a moment longer before he seemed satisfied and glanced down at the list. "Looks like you're already on your way to figuring out who killed Violet."

"Maybe. These are all Anna and Carl's suspects."

Leo studied the list for a second. Thoughts flitted behind his eyes as he took in the different names, and then he grinned up at me once more, an expression like pride over his face. "Huh."

I waited for more, but it didn't come. "Huh? What does *that* mean?"

He grinned again. "I don't know. It's just... you've settled even more into yourself. It's beautiful to see."

I appreciated the sentiment, but I still didn't get it. "Thanks, but once more, what does that mean?"

"You have no connection to Violet, not really. And it's not the first time you came across a body that didn't implicate either family or a close friend, but at least at this point, there's no reason for you to look into it."

His words didn't seem to match his expression, and I tried not to feel stung. It almost sounded like he was telling me to keep my nose out of it. But... I knew better.

As if reading my mind, he rushed forward. "I mean, I don't hear you debating like you have before. If you should get involved or if you shouldn't. No one's having to convince you, and has anyone asked for your help?"

I managed to shake my head.

He gave a sharp nod of confirmation. "Exactly. You're doing it because you're good at it. No more asking for permission, or debate. Winifred Page is many things, one of which is that she helps get justice for those who were killed. It's nice to see you simply doing it like it's second nature, since it is."

I sputtered out a laugh of embarrassment. "That feels

like a little bit of an exaggeration—getting justice. Makes me sound like a superhero."

He lifted a hand and briefly stroked my cheek with his thumb. It was a frequent touch of endearment from him, one that made me feel special and safe. "Then I'd say it sounds about right."

"Good grief, if I didn't love you both so much, I'd find you absolutely disgusting." Katie plopped back down, a fresh slice, larger than the last, accompanying her. "Strangely, seeing you two together makes the world feel a little more right." She reached out and adjusted the piece of paper. "Now, let's see who we've got."

We debated the merits of Carl and Anna's list for a few minutes, not making any huge revelations or insights. The cell in my pocket buzzed before we'd even finished our slices of torte. I pulled it out, expecting to disregard whoever it was, but was surprised to see Susan's name on the display. I considered walking away to have privacy, but then realized I would fill Leo and Katie in on it all anyway. After showing them Susan's name, I clicked Accept and lifted the phone to my ear. "Hey."

"Hey, yourself." Susan's voice was brisk, and irritated—though that didn't seem directed at me. "Just because I'm calling to fill you in, *doesn't* mean you're part of the police force. Got it?"

I blinked, then nodded, a surreal sensation passing over me. Officer Susan Green was actually calling me—*me*—to fill me in on the details of the case. On one hand, that had been building gradually, but I never would've predicted it being so straightforward, not in a million years.

"You still there?" Now her irritation felt directed at me.

"Yes. Sorry."

"Okay then, got it?"

I had to replay the brief conversation, trying to catch up. *Not part of the police force.* "Oh. Yes. Got it."

"Good grief." Susan breathed out an exasperated sigh. "Two things. One, obviously we don't have the cause of death back yet, but from the coroner's initial speculation, we're leaning toward poisoning or some sort of asphyxiation. If poisoned, it's most likely either inhaled or ingested, as we're not finding any puncture wounds, though those can be missed. There's also no bruising around the throat to insinuate strangulation, nothing under her nails that would indicate she fought back. However, they were so full of clay, there wasn't room for anything else. With no signs, I'd almost guess a gas leak or something." She chuckled, an unusual sound from Susan. "Well, except the fact that there was no gas leak. Either way, it will be several days before we have conclusive cause of death. We've already got the blood work moving, and the internal autopsy will start shortly."

Again, I was caught up in how surreal this was. In the matter-of-factness of it all, more than anything. It was like Leo said, this was all like second nature. Even the way Susan was speaking to me, as if it were only natural. Such a far cry from—

"I feel like I'm talking to myself here. What's your problem?"

It was almost a relief to hear the bite in her tone. A little more familiar. "Nothing. Sorry. Just taking it in. That all makes sense."

"Well, I'd hope so, it's hardly rocket science." She sighed again, and the sound seemed hesitant, an abrupt shift. "This next part is where I hope your strengths will do better than mine. I met with Joan. Informed her of Violet's death. Did a little questioning, but not much. She was an absolute wreck. Cried like the world was ending. I didn't know a person had that much snot in their body."

"Susan." I tried to keep the reprimand out of my tone but failed. "Violet was Joan's wife. Of course she cried."

"It wasn't a judgment on my part. Calm down." Susan cleared her throat. "It's just an observation, there were a lot of tears, enough that I have to admit I was thrown off and didn't get a good sense."

"You think Joan might be faking?"

Across the table, Katie's eyes widened.

"No way was she faking the tears. Not a chance. And she was genuinely distraught." Susan was unemotional. "That doesn't mean she's innocent. I'd..." Susan sighed again, and when she spoke, it sounded like her words pained her. "I'd appreciate your take on it, if you get the chance to speak to Joan today or tomorrow—whichever you feel is best."

I nearly dropped the phone. "Absolutely."

"Great. I won't give you any details of her supposed alibi. I'm not taking the chance of you slipping up and her realizing the two of us have spoken. Call me when you have news."

The phone clicked in my ear.

I stared at the cell for a few moments before looking at Katie. "I think we've entered an alternate universe."

SEVEN

The plan was to meet Leo at my house after work. We were going to order in Chinese or something. I'd barely turned onto Elkhorn Avenue and headed that direction when the impulse hit me to visit Joan then and there. I wasn't certain if it was some sort of nudge from the universe or if I simply wanted to get it over with. Either way, I called Leo and told him I'd be late, then checked the address Susan had sent in a text after our phone call.

To my surprise, Joan and Violet were practically my neighbors. There was a newish development of mini-McMansions on the road that led to my grandparents' old cabin. Thankfully, there was a thick enough stretch of untouchable forest between the mess of houses and me that, for all intents and purposes, it still felt like I lived in the middle of the wilderness.

I'd only been in one of the mansions before. The houses were fine, I supposed. Though smaller than something belonging to Daddy Warbucks, they still felt a little pretentious and grandiose, and didn't fit the easy, natural feel of Estes Park and the mountains.

After pulling into the driveway and shifting my Mini Cooper into Park, I turned to Watson. "I need you to work your magic, buddy. Don't be grumpy. Be sweet. She's hurting."

In response, Watson inspected the view outside the windshield and looked thoroughly annoyed. When we'd left the shop, I'd made the mistake of telling him we were about to see Leo.

It was a stupid request on my part anyway. Watson might not be a people person, but he'd demonstrated countless times not only an awareness, but a compassion, for people in emotional distress. I was probably simply trying to calm my own nerves. I supposed it made sense. Joan had lost her wife only a matter of hours before, there was no way this would be pleasant. But still... I'd had plenty of unpleasant conversations in the past, and while I had a tendency to put my foot in my mouth, I didn't think I was any less compassionate than Watson.

I reached for the door handle of my car and then hesitated, long enough that I considered putting it in Reverse and hightailing it out of there. I might have, if I hadn't noticed a curtain being pulled back from the large front window and Joan's face peering out. Caught, I offered a little wave, then bit the bullet. The curtain fell back into place.

Watson hopped out of the Mini Cooper behind me, and masterfully weaved around patches of ice on the sidewalk that led to the porch.

Joan opened the door just as we stepped up to the front porch. She blinked puffy, bloodshot eyes in confusion, and then her gaze landed on Watson. "Oh, Fred." She sniffed, looked like she attempted a smile, but didn't quite make it. "Sorry. Didn't recognize you for a second. I'm a bit of—" She let out a sob and then whimpered.

Not a nudge from the universe, unless it was playing

mean tricks. "I'm sorry, Joan, I shouldn't be intruding. It's too soon. Watson and I will—"

She shook her head frantically but didn't attempt to speak as she moved back and waved us inside.

Watson trotted slowly in. Filled with both guilt and an ever-increasing sense of dread, I followed.

Joan shut the door behind us and motioned toward a large ornate sofa in the massive living room just off the entryway. "Can I get you anything? Water or—"

"No. Nothing. We're fine." I turned and started to reach for her arm, but that felt too familiar. "I should've brought you something. Do you need anything? I'd be happy to go pick you up something for dinner or make a grocery store run."

Again, Joan shook her head. "I don't need anything. Thank you. People have already started dropping off casseroles. Though what in the world I'm going to do with a bunch of casseroles all by my—" Tears burst from her, which left me feeling completely helpless.

As ever, Watson shoved aside his cranky personality, pushed against Joan's shins, and then sat on the toes of her house slippers.

She let out a choked sob, then sank to the floor and wrapped her arms around Watson and cried.

After a few awkward moments, I sat on the floor as well, a couple of feet away, and just waited.

It wasn't a short wait. Susan hadn't been wrong; Joan seemed like she was broken. A glance around the room revealed what looked like boxes' worth of used Kleenex spread over the coffee table, sofa, and floor.

As she shook, Watson gave me a wide-eyed plea from between her arms.

I wasn't sure how to rescue him, so I waited.

It was then that it hit me. Why talking to Joan so soon after her wife's death was hitting me harder than I would've expected, though I supposed it should've been obvious. Things with Leo were new. Very new, but we'd already settled in with each other in many ways. And though neither of us had spoken of it, I had the sense that neither of us questioned where it would be going. I wasn't sure of the time line, but some part of me knew intrinsically that I was done, that he was done. That some page had been turned and the rest of my life looked different.

But someday… hopefully years and decades away, another page would turn and one of us would pass. I might be Joan, on the floor, arms wrapped around a dog, sobbing.

Then the next thought—I might be my mother.

Going through my father's murder had been torture, not only because of losing him, but in watching my mother survive his death.

Being with Joan this soon after Violet's passing was too much. I should've realized much earlier.

After what felt like years, Joan finally quieted, pressed a kiss to Watson's forehead, and released him.

Though he didn't hesitate, Watson managed not to dart away as he sauntered toward me. He didn't stop by my side, however, but continued across the room and settled down by the fireplace, clearly having had his fill of human interaction.

"Oh, Fred. I didn't realize you were sitting on the floor." Joan wiped her eyes with both of her hands as she stood. "I'm so sorry."

"Don't be." I stood as well, one of my feet having gone numb. "I don't want to take your time. I can visit later."

"No. I don't want to be alone." She moved past me, swept a few tissues from the couch and onto the floor, making room for both of us. "I don't even care that you're here because you probably suspect me."

"Suspect you? I—" My objection fell away. I wasn't entirely sure if I suspected Joan or not, but I should've been prepared for that as well. Anytime there was a murder, the people I talked to assumed they were on my suspect list. And rightly so, in most cases. "I'm sorry. I don't mean—"

"I'm not offended. I'm glad you're here." She patted the mostly clear space beside her. "Not only because you're a distraction, but because it means you think Violet is important enough for your time. And she is... was..." Another sob, but she clenched her fists and managed to hold it together. "Do you want to ask me questions? You can ask anything you want. Anything you think will help."

She surprised me. As mild-mannered as my mother was, if anyone had come into our house the day Dad died, or anytime thereafter, and insinuated she could've been responsible, she might've committed a murder there on the spot. Me as well. It seemed Joan saw it as an act of love.

How did I start? As a policeman's daughter, I probably should have been more prepared for that too—how to question someone even in the middle of their grief.

I glanced around the room for help. For the first time really taking in the space. Both from the room and what I could see through the open doorways that led elsewhere, the house practically dripped money. Everything looked expensive, *everything*, but it was also a mess. And not only because of the wadded-up tissues. Clay figures and pottery pieces of all shapes and sizes were strewn as far as the eye could see—on shelves, tables, stacked around the hearth. It felt like a hoarder had moved into a palace. There was no question that they were Violet's—like at the Koffee Kiln, not one of them was identifiable as anything recognizable.

On the coffee table in front of us, between several pieces of pottery, was a photo album. It was open and showed Joan and Violet in their wedding gowns.

"I've gone through it about a thousand times today." Joan reached for the album, clearly aware of me noticing, moving it from the coffee table onto her lap as she scooted closer to me. "This was our wedding day. We got married a couple decades before it was legal, but that didn't stop us. We renewed our vows once the laws changed, but *this* was our real wedding, the one that counted."

I was thankful for the distraction and leapt on it. "The pictures are beautiful. And your gowns are stunning." Like the house, the images of the wedding screamed money. Apparently wealth wasn't a new thing in Violet or Joan's lives.

"They were. And wait till you see this." It was a relief to hear a bit of brightness in her tone. She flipped a few pages and sat back, revealing a wedding cake. "It was lemon, Violet's favorite flavor. I chose to have a lavender curd between the layers, because it was purple, like Violet's name."

I wished Katie could see it. "I think it's the most beautiful wedding cake I've ever seen. It somehow manages to be huge and elaborate, but yet there's an ease and grace about it that makes it timeless."

"I agree." Joan was quiet as a whisper. She turned the next page to show a photo of the two women feeding the cake to each other. The violet hue between the soft yellow layers truly was lovely.

The next image had been caught the exact moment Joan had shoved a piece of cake into Violet's mouth. From the way Joan's lips were parted, I could practically hear the laughter all the years later.

"She was *so* mad." Joan chuckled. "I'd promised her we weren't going to do anything as tactless as smash cake. But the moment was there, and I just couldn't resist." Her voice trembled once more. "She forgave me, of course."

There was such joy in the photograph, even if Violet had been angry about it. Though it was decades before, and the women were so much younger, they were both easily identifiable, and both nearly as beautiful as the cake itself. Joan's hair was brown instead of gray, but still cut in the short, spiky fashion it was currently. Violet's was long, hanging down in thick ash-blonde waves to the small of her back. "Her hair was nearly white, almost silver-like..." I wasn't sure how to finish that sentence.

Joan didn't seem to notice, tracing the flowing locks with her fingertip. "Violet always had the most beautiful hair. When I first met her, I was jealous. Mine barely reaches my shoulders before it starts breaking off. Hers was breathtaking, almost mesmerizing." Fresh tears began to fall. "She was the most beautiful woman I'd ever seen. Somehow she only got more stunning through the years." Joan's hand began to tremble, and she pulled it away from the picture.

A quiet fell between us, the only sound the crackling of the fireplace and Joan blowing her nose. She didn't put the wedding album back but kept it on her lap like she couldn't hold it close enough.

After a while, Watson yawned from his warm spot by the fire.

It was like he nudged me to go forward. "Joan." The moment felt sacred somehow, so I whispered, "Who do you think did this?"

Again she whimpered. While she clutched the photo

album with one hand, she lifted another tissue up and covered her mouth and nose as she shook her head.

I dared to touch her knee. "I'm sorry. I don't want to cause you more pain."

"You're not. *You* didn't do this." She lowered the tissue, but her eyes remained closed as she continued to shake her head. "But, that's it, I have no idea. I can't answer that question. No one would do this. No one. Violet didn't have enemies. She was wonderful. Perfect."

From the way Anna and Carl had spoken about her, I hadn't anticipated that reaction. Though part of my brain screamed for me to leave it there, I couldn't. "Do you think *everyone* thought she was perfect?"

Joan still shook her head, but the motion changed somehow. "No. Not everyone, but anyone who didn't was wrong."

That was quite a statement. I tried to determine if it was simply where Joan was at the moment, having just lost Violet, or if she truly had always seen her wife as perfect. I couldn't tell anything other than that Joan meant what she said completely. "Then... who was wrong? Who didn't realize Violet was perfect?"

She sighed like the thought exhausted her, but opened her eyes finally and met my gaze. "There were disagreements, conflicts. People who would rent some of the properties, or the handyman she'd have do repairs. But that's part of it—Violet wasn't wrong, and they knew that. She simply followed rules. If a tenant didn't pay rent, they couldn't stay. If a contractor didn't do a satisfactory job, he didn't get paid for unsatisfactory work. They couldn't really hold that against her."

I had to take a second to determine if Joan was serious,

and she was. Suddenly, Anna's and Carl's suspicions made a lot more sense. I didn't know if old Ms. Melvin, as Carl had called her, was capable of murder, but with the ease Joan had delivered that statement, it sounded like there was quite a list of people who might have problems with the two of them. The thought brought on a new concern. Maybe Joan was in danger as well. "Were those same people angry at you too?"

She looked at me in confusion, but the crease between her brows smoothed. "Oh, at me because of the renters? And the handyman?" She shook her head in complete dismissal. "No. Violet handled all that. Not me. I've never had a lick of business sense my whole life. My daddy always said so. Luckily, thanks to him I didn't have to."

I wasn't entirely sure what that meant, but it sort of matched what Carl and Anna had said. They hadn't implied Joan would be the target of any tenant's wrath. I put a mental checkmark by Ms. Melvin's name and moved down the list. "Was Violet... er... were the two of you having any financial troubles?"

"Goodness, no." Joan's reply was quick and easy. "We've been very blessed, always. But we've also always given back. Violet handled our finances, thankfully. Like I told you, I'm a complete dunce around such things, but she always kept me informed on whatever I needed to know about. We aren't hurting financially. We could both live to be two hundred and be just fine. In fact..." She whimpered, her words fading away.

Maybe it made me hardhearted, but I couldn't help but continue to press. "Did she have any business dealings with Gerald Jackson?"

Joan's countenance altered instantly, disgust wafting over her features. "Never. That man is an idiot. And a misogynist to boot."

I couldn't disagree.

I didn't have to, Joan kept going. "He was always rude to us. Most of the time dismissive more than anything, but every once in a while, he'd make fun of Violet in social settings. Calling her crazy and such." She shuddered. "I hate that man."

"He'd call her crazy? To her face?" I hadn't seen that side of Gerald.

"To her face!" Self-righteous fury shone in her blue eyes. "Of course he'd say it in a laughing manner, like he was joking or teasing, sometimes even like he was flirting. But he meant it. He really thought she was."

"Why?"

"Violet had her... obsessions." Joan gave a dismissive flick of her wrist around the room. "Pottery is only the most recent. There's been knitting, macramé, stained glassmaking, scrapbooking, wine collecting." A smile played on her lips and her voice sounded faraway. "There was even a period where she got obsessed with diagramming sentences."

"Diagramming sentences?" I couldn't keep the astonishment out of my tone. I remembered doing that in school. I'd been the only one in my class who'd enjoyed it, but never enough to do it in my free time.

"Yes. But it didn't last long. None of them ever do." Joan seemed to come back to the moment and focused on one of the pieces on the coffee table, and the sadness returned. "Typically they lasted about two or three weeks. This one... only seemed to be getting stronger. Ever since Valentine's Day. Honestly, I've never quite seen her like this before." Joan sounded as if she'd forgotten I was there, and she leaned forward, picked up the pottery with her free hand, and pulled it to her, then settled it on top of the wedding album. Tears began to flow again as she stared at the piece. "That's where I thought she was this morning. She's been staying at the Koffee Kiln after I'd go to bed and then be up again and right back at it before I even woke up. I didn't think twice about anything being wrong when..." She started to shake.

That had to be the alibi Susan had alluded to—no alibi at all.

Still, it matched the impression I got from Simone. She'd implied that Violet was at the Koffee Kiln at all hours. Of course, Violet had implied that herself. Most definitely obsessive. I wouldn't have worded it the same as Gerald, but I had to admit, from the way Joan described it, Violet didn't sound exceptionally stable. "Gerald would make fun of her for that?"

She came back to the moment with a flash, practically growling. "Yes. I hate that man. Violet hated him as well, and she *did not* do business with him." From the fury in her tone, if Gerald had been the dead body, his killer would've been sitting across from me holding a wedding album and an unidentifiable piece of clay.

"Did he feel the same? Do you think he held some grudge against Violet?"

"No." Joan didn't even consider. "Violet would never let herself be killed by that imbecile."

A pounding sounded before I could work my way through that logic, causing both of us to jump and Watson to spring from the hearth and tear across the room barking.

"Oh, probably more food." Joan attempted a smile as she stood. "People are kind."

After a second's hesitation, I decided to follow, patting my thigh. "Watson. Come here, buddy."

He paused a few feet from the door, peering at me

before returning to growling at the blurry silhouette on the other side of the front door.

Joan stepped around him and unlocked the deadbolt.

No sooner had she done so than the door whipped open and a sobbing woman lurched through and fell into Joan's arms. "I just got back into town and heard—" Her voice cracked and she took a long snot-filled sniff. "Oh, Joan!"

For a split second, I thought I was seeing Violet, with the loose bun and the business suit. Then I realized the hair color was wrong, the years on the face, and the quality of the clothes. Rachel.

Joan didn't speak as she began to sob harder than ever.

The women were still crying, holding each other and shaking when Watson and I made our escape a few minutes later.

Watson issued a long, undignified sound somewhere between a sigh and snore. From the way his tongue lolled out of his open jaw, I suspected it was the doggy equivalent of *You can kill me now, life can't get any better than this.* He lay, sprawling on his back, on the oversized ottoman in the mystery room. Ben sat cross-legged on the floor beside him, rubbing Watson's belly with one hand, and alternating massaging each of his foxlike ears with his other.

"You keep that up, and you'll take the lead over Barry and Leo as Watson's favorite person." I watched from my spot on the matching antique sofa, enjoying the moment of contentment by the fire. "You know, maybe for Watson's Christmas present this coming year, I'll schedule an hour with the three of you sitting around that ottoman and doing exactly what you're doing. Although he really might die from happiness at that point."

"I think anyone might die from happiness from getting a six-handed massage. It sounds like heaven." Ben stayed focused on Watson.

I started to agree and then gave an involuntary shudder. That sounded horrible. Too many hands, too claustrophobic, too... just too much.

Unlike the day before, the Cozy Corgi had slowed

down after the breakfast rush. There were still a few people in the bakery keeping Katie and Nick busy, but there hadn't been any customers in the bookshop for a while, so Ben and I had retreated to the mystery room, and wherever Ben went, Watson followed.

I thought reading by the fire might shake free some new ideas about Violet's murder, but it seemed like my brain was molasses, or maybe it was my heart. I couldn't free myself from an overall sense of depression after my talk with Joan.

Watson made another one of his happy grunting sounds, accompanied with a less-than-subtle spot of flatulence, not that he was embarrassed by it.

Ben chuckled and kept right on rubbing.

Though he and Nick were identical twins, and I'd struggled to tell them apart at the beginning, save for the scar on Ben's bottom lip and an answering scar on Nick's right eyebrow, over the time that they'd worked the bookshop and bakery, they were changing. Both growing into themselves.

Ben had gotten even more invested in his Ute ancestry and started wearing his black hair in a braid down his back. Every once in a while, he'd weave in some beads or a feather or two. It was good to see him feeling braver. He'd confided about some of the discrimination he and his family had experienced.

As if feeling my thoughts, Ben's beautiful dark eyes glanced up at me, though his fingers never stopped lavishing affection on Watson. "I... um... finished the rough draft of my novel last night."

I hadn't heard him sound that nervous in a while. I sat up straighter. "You did? That's awesome!"

His gaze refocused on Watson, but he nodded. "Yeah. Still don't have a name for it, though."

"That's okay. Half the time, when we'd get manuscripts at the publishing house, we'd often suggest a name change anyway. I bet one will come to you as you read through it and work on your first round of edits."

"I still can't decide if I want to seek a traditional publishing company or do it myself." Ben had been working on the beginning of a detective series, with the main character named Coyote, a thief who solved murders, weaving in a lot of the Ute traditions and folklore. He looked up at me once more, and I could see an unasked question there.

I was tempted to ignore it. It was dangerous. "Do you... want me to take a look at it?"

He froze, even his fingers. Barely a heartbeat passed before Watson shifted and jammed his nose against Ben's hand. With a nervous laugh, Ben relaxed a little and began to pet again. "Yes and no. I want the whole world to read it, but I don't want anyone to see it either."

"I think that's probably a pretty normal reaction." I offered an out, though I wasn't certain if it was for him or me. Ben was smart and creative enough that I imagined his writing would be beautiful, deep, and moving. But there were no guarantees, and I didn't want there to be any glitch in our relationship. "Well, let me know. I'll help in any way I can. Sometimes it's better to get a stranger's opinion anyway. I can easily put you in touch with a couple of options who will give you honest feedback and constructive criticism."

"Thanks... maybe." That time when he looked at me, his gaze was direct. "I might take you up on that, but I'm not going to ask you to pull any strings with your old publishing company. I know things didn't end well for you there. Plus... I want to make it on my own merit."

I'd wondered if he'd ask me to contact my old business

partner and ex-best friend. Part of me wanted to tell him to take advantage of that connection. It was a mystery publishing house, and from what I knew of his book, it would fit perfectly, and if the manuscript was good, could launch him in ways that most writers would only dream of. The other part had dreaded him asking, because I knew that I'd give in. He might be the only person I would be willing to swallow my pride for and ask a favor of the one who'd betrayed me so greatly. "There's no rush. Besides, I'd suggest taking a little time away and then going through it with fresh eyes before anyone else sees it. You'll be amazed at—"

Watson growled and twisted ungracefully to stand on the ottoman.

Ben and I both looked in the direction of his attention and saw a thin, stern-looking woman in the doorway of the mystery room. I couldn't believe we didn't hear her come in.

"It strikes me that your dog may have aggression issues." Ethel Beaker sneered at Watson, not bothering to look at me. "Not to mention, I'm certain I can find some town ordinance against having animals in the same location as a bakery."

Sometimes my temper ignited quicker than a match, and it did so then, but atypically, I channeled it into a cold disdain instead of smarting back. "Good morning, Ms. Beaker. Often when I'm cranky, I find a little caffeine helps. Would you like me to get you something from upstairs?" Okay, maybe I didn't *completely* keep from smarting back.

"Like I'd drink that dog-hair-filled swill." She looked at Ben. "Which one are you again?" She waved her hand. "Never mind. Would you leave us, please?"

The Beakers were one of the families who had given the twins a hard time. Showing more restraint than I possessed,

Ben stood with grace and dignity and looked over at me. "Do you need me to stay?"

"No. Thank you, Ben." I considered, then made a quick decision. "Would you mind taking Watson with you? Maybe a walk by the river out back, or a quick trip to Paulie's to visit Flotsam and Jetsam."

He brightened, like I hoped he would. "Yeah, you bet. Nick and I promised Cinnamon we'd get her a new cat toy anyway." He tapped his thigh as he headed out of the room and passed Ethel. "Come on, buddy."

Proving his love was a true and powerful thing, Watson paused in his excited dash from the room and looked back at me.

Touched, I motioned him onward. "Go on, have fun."

He did, and I swear it was intentional when he darted directly at Ethel, causing her to jump back and bump her shoulder into a bookcase.

"Nasty animal," she hissed after him, and then glared at me.

I didn't respond, and since I had a feeling I knew why she was here, I told myself to play nice. I moved my discarded book from the other side of the sofa. "Feel free to have a seat, Ethel."

She bristled at the use of her first name. "I'd rather not be covered in dog hair for the rest of the day, thank you very much." Tilting her nose in the air, she moved across the small room and leaned elegantly against the mantle of the river rock fireplace. She came directly to the point. "You went to see Joan last night."

Yep, exactly what I'd thought. "I did." I considered standing so we'd be on equal footing, but decided staying my ground somehow managed to hold on to a bit of my power. Even so, I sat straighter. "Don't tell me Joan complained. She wasn't upset and seemed glad for my company. She wanted to talk."

"Joan's an idiot. Wanting to speak to you is only more proof."

That surprised me, and I flinched at the harsh words. "That's quite a thing to say about your best friend's widow."

"Spare me your judgment. I'm not interested." Despite the sentiment, she seemed to attempt to explain herself. "Just because Joan is an idiot doesn't mean she doesn't need protecting. She's a sweet, innocent soul, even if she can be insufferable."

I tried to parse through that but gave up quickly, narrowing in on the meat of it. "Protecting? From me?" That was interesting. "Is Joan guilty of something?"

"The entire town needs protection from you." Ethel closed her eyes and took a deep breath as if calming herself. "This is insane. I didn't come to trade barbs."

"Why did you come?"

Her eyes opened with a flash. "To tell you to mind your own business and let the police do their job. I already knew you were utterly tactless, but the very idea that you went to Joan on the same day her wife was murdered is a new low, even for you. It's time you learned your place."

I'd only had one other conversation, if that's what it could be called, with Ethel, and it had gone pretty much like this. The woman hated me. At first, I assumed it was because she correlated me with the events around her husband's death, or that she saw the Cozy Corgi as competition for her daughter-in-law's coffee shop. But really, I think it was just a matter of hating me. Honestly, that was easier to deal with. Before I spoke, I made certain my voice would be calm, quiet, and not have a waver of weakness. "Ethel, I'm aware we don't know each other very well, but here's something you should know about me. I don't accept being told what to do by anyone, especially by one who has no authority over who they're issuing commands. I'm sorry you don't like that I'm looking into your friend's murder, but I'm not doing anything illegal, therefore you have no say over it."

For a second, I could see her rage, saw her tremble with it, then her smirk grew. "Is that how you spoke to Sergeant Wexler when he'd tell you to keep your nose out of a case? Not that it did any good, clearly. I never understood how a woman like you managed to wrap a man like him around your finger. But *I'm* not so easily thwarted."

I nearly laughed. "Are you actually comparing yourself to a dirty cop? And even if you are, you're on the town council, not a member of the police."

"I have more power than the police." There was no irony in her tone, not even a sense of bravado. Clearly she believed she was stating a fact.

"If you think I'm breaking the law, feel free to contact Officer Green. I'm sure she'll—"

Ethel scoffed, then jumped over that argument entirely. "One of my dearest and oldest friends in the world was murdered yesterday. I want justice for her, and I know you fancy yourself a detective, and even I have to admit you've gotten lucky on occasion, but I don't want you messing this up. Nor do I want you harassing those of us who knew and loved her."

Once more I was tempted to stand, but pride held me in place. Even so, I leaned forward, propping my elbows on my knees as I looked up at her. "Worried what I'll find out about you?"

She laughed then, intentionally loud and hard. "Terrified."

I settled back into the sofa, transitioning my elbow to rest on the dusty gold fabric of the arm. "If we're done here, I have work to do. Unless you want to purchase a book. I'm happy to make suggestions."

"So smug." To my surprise, Ethel crossed the space and perched on the edge of the sofa, lowering her voice to a whisper. "If you bother Joan again, or get it in your craw to give Carla and Simone a hard time, I can promise you the town council will come after you and your second-rate bookshop."

My first instinct was to fight back. I'd heard her make a similar threat to Delilah's old-time photography shop because of the Pink Panthers. I wasn't scared of Ethel Beaker or the town council, and not only because Percival was a member. Not to mention, Barry might not be part of the council, but despite his flighty personality and less than elegant tie-dyed wardrobe, he had as much power and money as any of them. I was untouchable, as was the Cozy Corgi. It was that surety that allowed me to skip over that particular threat and focus on the real matter at hand. "What don't you want me to find out, Ethel? If you were truly Violet's friend, you'd want to utilize any and all resources to find her killer. I wouldn't have thought Carla or Simone had anything to do with it, but maybe they did."

She snorted. "There you go, proving you're as much of a fool as everyone says. I've no concern of anything you'd find out. Joan mentioned you suggested Gerald of all people. Ridiculous. You want to talk about a real moron... that man wouldn't have the gumption or intellect to kill someone if you tied up the victim and handed him a gun."

"Protecting him too?"

Another laugh. "Trust me, sweetheart, if I could take the two of you down together, I would." She cocked her head as if considering, then smiled. "That's actually not a bad idea."

"You know..." Even as I spoke, I knew trying to get deeper under Ethel Beaker's skin wasn't the smartest move, but I couldn't keep from it. "I hear there are a couple open spots on the town council. Maybe I'll give it a go."

All mockery left her smile, leaving it deadly cold. "Oh, Winifred, please try. I'd enjoy that so much. Even your uncle won't be able to pull that for you." Ethel stood. "I must be on my way, but I do hope you'll take my advice and leave well enough alone. You don't want to play around in the big kids' sandbox. Trust me." When she reached the doorway to the main room, she turned back once more. "Oh, and by the way, let me offer my congratulations. I hear that you've snagged yourself another handsome man, and this time taking the route of robbing the cradle, no less. *Figures*. I must say, for a woman who claimed she wasn't trying to get herself a man, you really do work your way through them."

My first inclination was to march directly down to the Koffee Kiln and confront Carla. Well, not really *confront* Carla—I didn't think she had killed Violet—simply to talk to Carla, if for no other reason than to rub it in Ethel's face by speaking to her daughter-in-law. Then my better sense took over, and I realized making such a move out of spite wouldn't help; if anything, it would hinder. Well, not really my *better* sense, more so remembering that the Koffee Kiln was closed for the crime scene inspection. Not to mention, I couldn't think of a legitimate pretense to drive all the way out to Carla's house.

Instead, I went to the bakery and got both a dirty chai and sound advice from my best friend. By the time Watson and Ben returned from their walk, I'd calmed down and Katie had managed to infuse some reason into my brain. I could either take a break and go downstairs and get lost in a mystery novel, go talk to Ms. Melvin to find out who some of the other evicted renters were, or find out what Violet and Gerald Jackson had been arguing about. The smartest option was to take a break. I, instead, chose Gerald Jackson. Still, it was a better choice than driving to Carla's, and since there was still a good chance I'd lose my temper, I figured I might enjoy doing so on Gerald.

I called his office.

A prim voice answered. "G & J Associates."

I hesitated, I didn't think I'd ever heard the name of his practice before. "Is this the office of Gerald Jackson?"

"Yes, it is."

G & J? I had no idea Gerald had a business partner. "May I speak to him please?"

"Mr. Jackson is out of the office. May I take a message?"

"He's—" Then I remembered. I'd been so caught up in the moment, I'd forgotten he was out of town. That was the whole reason he dropped the envelope of cash off with Nick. "No, thank you. Do you know when he'll be back in town?"

There was a brief hesitation on the other end of the line. "If you leave your number, I can have Mr. Jackson call you when he is back in the office."

Evasive... it seemed she wasn't supposed to confirm that he was out of town. At least that's how it felt. Interesting. "May I speak to his associate?"

Another hesitation. "I'm sorry, who?"

It was my turn to hesitate, confusion flitting over me. "G & J Associates. The J is out of town... or out of the office, so could I speak to whoever G is?"

A strange mix of irritation and panic seeped into the woman's tone. "If you leave your number, I'll have Mr. Jackson call you back when he returns."

I nearly laughed at the realization. "There is no associate, is there? The G stands for Gerald and the J stands for Jackson, doesn't it?"

"Ma'am, do you have a message to leave, or a number that I can pass on to Mr. Jackson when he's back?"

I almost left my name to see if Gerald truly would return my call, but then decided it was best not to give him a heads-up. "No, but thank you for your time." I hung up.

I shouldn't have been surprised. That sounded like something Gerald would do, although it was cleverer than I would've given him credit for. I settled for the next best thing.

Watson looked up in irritation from his napping spot in the sunshine when I suggested he come with me, and offered a look that indicated he didn't appreciate being disturbed when he'd *just* returned from an outing and gotten comfortable.

"Fine, you can stay." I ruffled his fur and walked toward the front door. Pushing things to the last second, Watson stayed frozen in place until I'd started to close the door, and then he launched up and hurried after me. I ruffled his fur again. "Always letting me know who's in charge, aren't you?"

Though there were a couple of spots of old snow lined up in the shadowy portions where the buildings and sidewalk met, the beautiful March day was unusually warm yet again. The few embers of anger that Katie hadn't been able to douse started to fade away in the pleasant afternoon as we crossed the street and walked along past the shops of Elkhorn Avenue. Part of me was tempted to dart into Cabin and Hearth and find out if Anna and Carl had heard any more gossip, but things had been so uncomfortable the last time, that I stayed on track.

If there was any more irritation lingering, walking into Knit Witt would've swept it away. I wasn't an extreme type A personality, but the graduated color arrangement of all the yarn covering the walls of the knitting store was both lovely and soothing. The astoundingly intricate and gorgeous knitted decorations didn't hurt either. The last time I'd been in, there'd been a Christmas scene with a life-size knitted fox. Now there was a small knitted baby deer curled up in a meadow of green grass and spring flowers in a far corner—so lifelike it nearly took my breath away. Beside it was a circle of wooden folding chairs, only two of which were occupied. One by Angus Witt, Gerald's good friend and the reason for my visit. The other, to my surprise, was Simone. Both were knitting.

"Dear Winifred." Angus's smile was sweet and genuine, deepening as he looked toward my feet. "And charming Watson. Come, join us. Your timing is perfect. I just finished a demonstration, and Simone and I are comparing techniques." He patted the nearest folding chair. "I take it you're Violet's champion."

I hadn't seen him since January, during a weekend away at a nearby inn. There'd been a murder, and he'd been one of my suspects. I'd always liked Angus, but some of that suspicion lingered, even though he'd been innocent. Seeing him, I realized I continued to like him, despite my feelings while we'd been at Baldpate.

Watson and I crossed the store together, and I sat, one seat down from where he'd motioned so I could see them both face-to-face. I addressed Simone. "You're a potter *and* a knitter?"

She gave a shrug that seemed as if it was meant to be humble. "I like nearly every artistic medium, but pottery is my favorite and the one I'm best at by far." She held up a partially knitted... something... in a fuzzy brown yarn. "This is supposed to be a scarf right now. It'll be lucky if it can pass as a hot-pad holder."

"Don't sell yourself short." Angus gave her a friendly smile as well and then reached his hand down for Watson to sniff.

As every time we'd been around him, Watson was neither excited nor repulsed by Angus. He trotted up to the offered hand, sniffed, gave a lick, and then turned, left the circle and inspected the knitted fawn. After a second, he seemed satisfied, curled up beside it, placed his head on the deer's hip and closed his eyes with a sigh.

"Well, that's the cutest thing I've ever seen in my entire life." Angus twisted in his seat to get a better view. "And I'm not exactly a spring chicken, so that's saying something."

"I can move him. You'll never get the dog hair off that display."

He waved me off. "Not on your life. Does my heart good." He switched the motion to point at Simone. "I take it you know Miss Pryce?"

"We've met." Simone winked. "Watson doesn't care for my hair nearly as much as he likes your baby deer." She looked from Angus to me. "I heard… through the rumor mill, that you were looking into Violet's death."

"Would that rumor mill be your partner's mother-in-law?" I couldn't help myself. "I imagine you heard quite the earful if so."

Her smile confirmed that she had certainly earned an earful, but she didn't indulge. "And from a few other people. The way it sounds, you have quite the reputation."

"For good reason." Angus puffed up his chest as if proud of me. "Ms. Page is smart as a whip, and whatever you've heard, I guarantee you doesn't live up to the reality. I've gotten the pleasure of seeing her in action." Though he left out that it was while he was being interrogated by Susan, Leo, and myself, the twinkle in his eye included me in the joke as he focused on me. "Am I a suspect in Violet's murder? Would you like to speak to me alone, or is this satisfactory?"

As before, he didn't sound the least bit offended at being a murder suspect. I needed to take lessons from the guy on how to stay cool under pressure. "No, you're not. Unless you know something that I don't."

"I was friendly with Violet, but we weren't close, though we ran in the same circles. Well, *some* of the same circles. The ones that involved champagne and cocktails." He met my gaze directly. "I'm sorry to hear of her passing, and I'm sorry for Joan, but I didn't harm Violet."

"I was wondering if you know when Gerald's getting back into town?" I hoped the abrupt switch would offer some telltale sign in his reaction.

"I don't. But I didn't get the impression he'd be gone for long." He offered no reaction. Either he was expecting the question, or had nothing to hide. He cocked his head. "Is *Gerald* a suspect? Really?" I didn't get the chance to respond before he sucked in a breath and nodded. "Oh, of course. You've heard about the altercation between him and Violet. My guess is the Hansons informed you of that, but I suppose it could be anyone. It wasn't exactly a private display."

I blinked, thrown off. And then, since I hadn't done a good job of covering it, was direct. "You're always one step ahead, Angus. And always so calm and collected. I don't know what to make of you."

He only smiled. "Coming from you, Fred, I will take that as the highest praise. You are an intelligent and intuitive woman. I'm flattered you don't find me to be a cardboard cutout caricature of an old white man."

Suddenly I was aware of Simone's intense gaze darting back and forth between the two of us. It seemed like she realized she'd been caught and settled her attention on Angus. "You knitted a baby deer and about ten thousand flower buds over there. I'd hardly say you're a typical old white man." She surprised me by looking at me once more, the humor leaving her tone. "So you suspect Gerald? He's the lawyer, right?" Her gaze flicked toward Angus but didn't stay long enough for confirmation before returning to me. "Who else are you considering? Do you think Violet's murder was somehow connected to the Irons family?"

That time when I flinched, Angus flinched right along with me.

Simone looked between the two of us once more. "I'm sorry. Am I not supposed to say that name?"

Still thrown off, Angus hesitated, then gave a shake of his head. "I don't know why I'm surprised. You've been in town a few months. How would you *not* have heard about the Irons family?" His eyes narrowed on her. "Though you weren't here that long ago. I believe you arrived after members of that crime organization were discovered within our own police department?"

"Yes, from what I understand, I just missed it." She looked at me again. "You were dating one of them, weren't you?"

That time, it was Angus and I who exchanged glances.

Simone laughed good-naturedly, but I couldn't tell if it was real or not. "There I go again. Sorry. I'm sure that feels weird, me being a newcomer and knowing all of that. But you said yourself, it's a small town. And especially considering there's been a murder. I heard speculation about the Irons family." She repositioned the knitting needles and gestured with her thumb toward the pink jacket that hung over the back of her chair. "And whether it's kosher to admit or not, Fred, your love life has been the topic of conversation from time to time. From the pictures I've seen, Branson was movie-star handsome, and the man you're dating now is rather smoking hot as well. Sounds like you have a thing for a guy in uniform."

Having come from my conversation with Ethel, my temper spiked once more, but I managed to hold my tongue long enough for me to realize there was no judgment or insult in her voice or expression. Even so, I had no clue how to reply.

Thankfully, as so often was the case in Estes, a tourist provided a distraction by walking into the knitting shop. Angus stood and headed toward them, but paused by my chair and laid his hand on my shoulder. "In case they're doing more than browsing, don't leave without talking to me first. I have a little something for you. I've been meaning to run it to the bookshop." He gave a gentle squeeze and then went on his way to greet the tourist.

The distraction gave me enough time to realize the truth of Simone's words. Of course she'd heard about the Irons family, and it was only natural she heard about my history with Branson and Leo. Not only because it was a small town and everyone knew everything about everyone else, but she was in Delilah's inner circle. Both Delilah and Nadiya were friends with Leo.

Simone scooted closer. "I really am sorry, Fred. I wasn't trying to overstep." Her apology sounded sincere, and her clear dark eyes were free of shadows.

"It's okay." I forced a smile. "I've lived here for a year and half now, but I'm still a city girl at heart. It throws me off at times, having everyone around me know all the details of my life, sometimes details even I'm not aware of."

"Well, I didn't mean to add to that." Her look altered, growing harder. Not in an unfriendly way, but more direct. "As you may have noticed, I tend to be a little blunt. Does that bother you? Do you mind if I'm blunt again?"

With that, all was forgiven, and I relaxed. "I'm the same way. It's a quality I appreciate, even when it's uncomfortable. I prefer it, as long as you're okay with the same from me."

"Definitely." She nodded, her gaze flicking over my shoulder to where I assumed Angus was still talking to the tourist, and then back to me. "I want you to know, your relationship with Carla and her mother-in-law will have no impact on me. I'm very aware of who my business partner is and what her family is like."

Some of my unease returned. "Did you know that Ethel came and spoke to me?"

She gave what sounded like a sigh of helplessness. "Oh. I thought I was being preemptive. I knew that Ethel was on the warpath this morning, but I didn't realize she'd move quite so quickly. She and Carla were both worked up that you went to see Joan." It looked like Simone was done, but then she continued. "I know this is none of my business..." She stopped, seemed to consider for a second. "Actually, it is completely my business, come to think of it. Literally. Carla and I are friends and business partners. And I know there's a history between her old shop and the Cozy Corgi. As far as I'm concerned, there will be no animosity. This town is big enough for our two businesses, even if both have a bakery and coffee shop. But what I wanted to say is that I do hope you'll also give Carla a fresh start, maybe a couple of them. I'm sure you're clear on how Ethel feels about you, but I can guarantee, she treats Carla a thousand times worse than you could ever imagine. I wasn't quite aware of Carla's temper until we were already in business together, but watching the family dynamics, it makes sense. So..." She shrugged. "If there's conflict you or your partner have with the Koffee Kiln, I'd appreciate it if you come to me. I'll do my best to smooth things over."

"Thank you." I almost added *I think* but managed to bite my tongue in time. I couldn't tell if she was being a proactive business owner or playing some hidden angle. I decided to see if I could figure it out. "Now it's my turn to be direct, if you don't mind?"

"Not at all." She sounded relieved.

I leaned forward slightly. "In talking to a few people, your name has come up more than once as someone who might have wanted Violet dead." A bit of an exaggeration, but whatever.

"I'm not surprised." Simone neither flinched nor missed a beat. "While I do my best to be professional where the business is concerned, I must admit, I was beginning to lose patience with Violet. She was one of Ethel's dearest friends, so I didn't feel like I had a lot of leeway, but her commandeering my business and workspace was getting old, fast. And it was about to come to a head."

She was direct. "Is that a denial?"

She laughed, and her smile widened. "I guess I did work my way around the question, didn't I? So, no, I did *not* murder Violet, even if there were moments I wanted to."

I couldn't hold back a smirk. She was confusing me somewhat, but I still liked her. Still, I pushed on. "Any idea who did?"

She slunk in her chair a bit as she issued a long sigh. "Goodness, I'd say that would be a long list."

"Really?"

She looked at me puzzled, as if my response was a surprise. "From what I understand, and frankly from what I saw first-hand, Violet didn't suffer fools lightly. Her words, not mine. I never got the sense that she was trying to be unkind, but she was very black-and-white. I can't tell you how many different people I heard her air grievances against as she worked. Renters not paying their bills on time. Contractors doing a litany of things wrong and still expecting payment." For the first time, her wince seemed to indicate she almost held back. She didn't. "This sounds horrible, but my impression was growing that if a person was of a certain—" Simone paused, clearly looking for the right word. "—socioeconomic status, let's say, they could get by with just about anything, but if she saw you as beneath her? Her rules were hard, rigid, and swift."

That was basically the same thing I'd been told in a variety of ways, but it clarified things—helped me see below Violet's soft beauty and composure.

Once again, Simone's expression shifted, and I felt like I was being tested again. "I get the sense that you're working closely with Officer Green?" She paused for less than a heartbeat, only long enough to see if I would react. I didn't think I did. "So maybe you already know this, or will be told soon, but I'll tell you what I told Susan, even though she didn't see the importance of it. I went through the crime scene with them yesterday afternoon. A plastic bag was missing."

I waited for more, but nothing came. "A plastic bag?"

She nodded, then gave a self-conscious laugh and rushed ahead. "Sorry, that probably didn't make any sense. The clay that I order comes in five-pound blocks. Each one in an individual bag so it doesn't dry out. Violet used two new blocks of clay on the night of her death. Only one of the bags was accounted for."

I felt like I was trying to play catch-up and failing horribly.

Simone cocked an eyebrow and waited. Once again I got the sense I was being judged or tested.

Then it hit me. "Oh. You're thinking murder weapon."

Proving my instincts had been right, she nodded in approval. "Angus is right. You're quick."

"Suffocated with the plastic bag?"

She nodded. "Maybe."

It could work. "However, if that was the case, I would think there would've been skin under Violet's nails, even with all the clay. She wouldn't have been still and let herself get suffocated without trying to fight back."

"Oh." Another cock of an eyebrow. "I wasn't aware of that. Hmm. Maybe that's not a likely probability, then."

That time, I'd failed the test. Or at least confirmed what she'd already suspected—that I was getting inside information from Susan. I tried not to let that bother me. "How are you certain about the loss of one plastic bag?"

Irritation crossed her features. "Because I cleaned up before I left the night before. Cleaned up, took out the trash, put everything away. The space was spotless." She bugged her eyes at me. "You saw that back room. That mess *wasn't* due to the murder. That was every single time Violet used the workroom. *Every* time. I was about to lose my mind."

I couldn't blame her. "So... since you took out the trash before, if the bag had been thrown away, or were left on the floor, you would've found it."

"Exactly." She nodded. "On the floor is where I found one of them. The other was nowhere to be found."

Angus rejoined us once again. I hadn't even noticed the tourist leaving. He squeezed my shoulder as he had before. "I'll be right back."

Simone and I didn't speak in the few moments he was gone, each lost to our own thoughts. She might be onto something. Maybe Violet had been suffocated with a plastic bag. Horrible thought, though it seemed unlikely if she hadn't fought back, at least as far as we could tell.

"Here we are. I hope you like it." Angus was in front of me, holding something out.

All thoughts of murder and death fled, and tears stung the corner of my eyes instantly. In his hand he held a knitted Watson, about the size of a bagel, curled up napping. I looked from it to where Watson was sleeping by the deer, then reached out and touched it reverently. "It looks just like him. Angus..." I could barely speak. "It's so beautiful. It almost looks alive. I can almost see it breathing."

"Glad you like it." He smiled gently down at me.

Overwhelmed, I stood and acted very un-Winifred-Page-like and threw my arms around him in a hug. "I love it!"

TEN

The phone barely rang twice before Susan's growl filled my ear. "If you tell me you've already figured out who killed Violet, I might murder you myself."

I laughed as I snapped on my seat belt. "Not hardly."

"Really? Not living up to your reputation, are you?" She almost sounded relieved, and laughed as well.

I nearly dropped the phone as I realized what was happening. Susan and I were laughing together. Like we were... friends. That notion made me laugh even harder. Susan truly would kill me if she was aware of that thought.

Feeling an inspecting gaze on me, I glanced at the passenger seat to find Watson giving me his judgmental side-eye.

Reaching over, I bopped his nose. "I think Susan would agree with you."

He huffed in indignation and shifted so his back was to me and he stared out the window.

"Agree with who on what?" Susan brought me back to the moment. "Are you actually calling me while you're interrogating someone?"

"No. I was talking to Watson."

"Good grief, you are so weird." I could practically hear Susan's eye roll.

I chuckled again. "That's pretty much what I was telling Watson you'd agree with him about."

"What?"

"Nothing."

Susan spoke again before I could change the subject. "I don't know if I have the strength for you right now. You *or* your mutt. I just left Rachel. She was as much of a mess as Joan, maybe more. Utter hysterics."

I started to share how distraught the two of them had been the night before, but Susan didn't give me a chance.

"She doesn't have a solid alibi either. At home in bed, by herself, and then left town early that morning to get something from her ex in Longmont. All of which leaves her perfectly open during the possible hours of Violet's death."

"Well, I was asleep by myself during those hours as well, so I'm not sure how compelling that is. But, it for sure opens her up to being a possibility." She was on the list. "I've not come up with a motive for her yet, have you?"

"If I had, I'd have led with that, don't you think?" Though the words indicated irritation, her tone suggested boredom.

Okay... not friends... Maybe frenemies? *Ugh*, what a thought!

With a sigh, I shook my head. "Okay then, moving along. We don't have a motive, but I think I'm going to go see if Maud Melvin is a viable suspect. She would have a motive and is why I called you to begin with, to check and see if you've already spoken to her? And if not, find out if you have her address."

"Number one, you got the wrong number if you're looking for information. And two, no I haven't. But I've met her before. She's frail enough I don't think she can kill a moth."

"A moth?"

"What?"

I was starting to feel like we were going in circles. "The saying is I don't think she can kill a *fly*, not a moth."

"Oh for crying out loud. Who cares about a fly? I hate moths. The freaky little things dart right at your face." Susan was starting to sound exasperated. "Is this really necessary?"

I rather liked the mental image of big, strong Susan Green batting away at a moth darting at her face, but managed not to chuckle. "You're the one who distracted me. And back to the point, again, sounds like you haven't spoken to her about Violet, but that you considered it a waste of time."

"Pretty much." There was a soft crunching in my ear, and as she spoke, Susan's words were garbled. I suspected she was eating potato chips. "But she was on my list to speak to anyway. I'd rather waste your time than mine."

"Well, great. Thanks."

"Don't mention it." There was a hint of laughter in her voice again. "I did speak to Bob Wrigley. He was a construction worker that did some renovations on one of Violet's rental properties, one she stiffed on the payment. He hated her with a fiery passion, but I didn't get the sense that he was stupid enough to murder her over it."

"Oh, perfect. I'm glad you spoke to him, I didn't have a name yet, but he was on my list." I started the car. With the afternoon sun beginning to dip, it was starting to get colder. "Do you have Maud's address?"

"I thought we covered that." The growl seemed a little forced that time. "But yes, hold on."

I started to ask my next question, hesitated, then went ahead with it. "What's your impression of Simone Pryce?"

"Pryce?" Susan's voice lilted in surprise.

"Yeah, Carla's business partner, the potter."

"I'm aware of who Simone is, Fred. You think she'd really kill Violet because she was a pain in her side and a mess to boot? Or is there more?"

"No." I shook my head again, then shrugged, as if Susan could see me. "Well, maybe. I don't know."

Susan snorted. "Wow. I think I miss the days where I told you to keep your nose out of it. Getting to see the inside of your process is a little bit of a let-down, and I didn't have high expectations to begin with."

I ignored her, processing the thoughts to myself as much as asking Susan's opinion. "On the surface, I like her, but I just left her and Angus, and I got a funny feeling a couple times. Although, it's all easily explained away. But... she asked about the Irons family."

"The Irons family?" Susan sounded like she'd sat up straighter. "She thinks they're involved with Violet?"

"No, she was asking if *I* thought the Irons family was involved with Violet. I was surprised for her to bring them up, that's all. But like she said, at this point, everyone in town knows about the Irons family." For some reason I lowered my voice to a whisper even though the only one eavesdropping was Watson, not that he wanted to. "Is there any reason to think Violet *was* involved with the Irons family?"

It was a few moments before Susan answered. "Not that I know of. I wish I could tell you to not be paranoid, but... after everything, maybe we should be."

"Maybe." This didn't feel like the Irons family. And Simone didn't feel like part of that group either, but I didn't trust my judgment around that. At least not enough to bet my life on it, which... could be exactly what it was. But even speaking it out loud to Susan somehow lessened the likelihood instead of giving me a sense of surety about it, so I moved on. "She told me her theory about the bag."

"Oh, right. I forgot to mention that to you, did I?" Susan didn't sound too concerned about the oversight. "We still haven't received the results of the autopsy back, but I ran that theory by the coroner. It's one of the scenarios that fits."

"Even without any signs of a struggle, with nothing but clay under Violet's nails?"

"I said it's *one* of the scenarios that fits, not *the* only. But the assailant could've worn gloves, or maybe Violet was unconscious. It's a possibility that if the clay covered her hands, she might not have been able to get a firm grip on her assailant. We don't know."

Could be. "That makes me think I'm wasting my time visiting Maud as well."

"Why? Because if she's not strong enough to kill a *moth*, how could she suffocate someone? Remember, I just said, Violet might've been unconscious."

"No, not that. This feels too personal. Putting a bag over someone's head and suffocating them is... well, it's very hands-on. It's not removed. And then covering Violet in clay, arranging her body. It seems personal."

Susan considered. "I do think Maud will probably be a waste of time, but not because of that. Getting evicted from your home would seem pretty personal to me."

I couldn't help but think of Violet and Joan's mansion as I pulled up to Ms. Melvin's house. The two couldn't be more different. The little cabin would've been a charming gem of a home fifty years ago. It was in the typical mountainy Estes Park style—flat dark brown logs with white chinking between, pine-green shutters on the windows, and green wooden shingles on the roof. Complete with a river rock chimney billowing out smoke. However, some of the dark brown logs were missing, the chinking was now a spongy-looking gray, dark mold growing over it here and there, and the wood of the shutters and shingles only held the memory of being green and looked like they'd served as insect feasts for the past several years.

As we made our way up onto her porch, I worried I was heavy enough that I'd break through. Beside me, Watson sniffed and gave a whimper as the boards groaned in protest. He couldn't smell anything, but from the rot and decay, I figured he was picking up all sorts of unpleasant scents.

A ghost of a voice answered my knock, but it took well over a minute before I heard the click of a lock and the door wedged open. A weary-looking brown eye peered out at me.

"Hi there." I infused as much gentle pleasantness in my voice as I could. "I hate to bother you."

"Sorry. I'm not buying anything." She started to shut the door.

On instinct, I shot my hand out, holding it in place. After a second of embarrassment I yanked my hand away. "Sorry about that. I'm not selling anything. My name is Winifred Page, and this is—"

"Watson!" Her voice lightened somehow, and the door opened the rest of the way, revealing a small, shriveled woman. Susan had been right. She wouldn't be able to hurt a fly or a moth. "Well, I've heard all about you two. Who hasn't?" Some of the tiredness left her voice. With one hand, she supported her weight on the door handle, and her other hand stretched down toward Watson.

Without hesitation, he tilted his head up, pressing his nose against the palm of her hand and leaving it there.

She sighed happily. "Sweet lamb."

Strangely, I felt like I was intruding on a moment and stayed silent.

A soft, sad smile played on her wrinkled lips. When she spoke, she addressed Watson, not me. "I had a corgi once. Her name was Hera. Fattest, most loveable thing you ever saw. A little grumpy, though."

If I hadn't already known the second I'd seen her, at that moment, I was certain I was wasting my time. Maud Melvin didn't kill anyone.

Finally straightening, she looked up at me. "You're here because of Violet?"

I wanted to lie, but then couldn't think of a good excuse. "I am."

"Such a sad thing. She was young, had a lot of life left."

I nearly did a double take. Violet hadn't been ancient, but as Angus had said only an hour or so before, she wasn't a spring chicken. Although, Maud might have a different perspective. She looked as if she was pushing a hundred. The thought gave me pause. I hadn't quite grasped the implications of Violet evicting the woman. It was a common practice, justifiable. The agreement was to pay rent. If you couldn't pay rent, you couldn't live there. But... the idea of making this woman homeless, when she was already, quite literally, living in a shack, was unfathomable. I wouldn't have guessed it from my impressions of Violet. Before that thought even finished forming, I was taken aback by the sincerity I had heard in her words. There'd been no animosity or righteous indignation at all.

Maud shuffled back a few steps, wobbling as she did so. "Come on in. I'll put on some tea."

"No, I don't want to take your time. This was a... you wouldn't..." Good grief, I had no idea how to finish that without being insulting.

She gave a weak chuckle. "Decided I didn't kill Violet, did ya?"

Why pretend? "Yes."

"Well, I've heard you were good. You just proved it."

"Any idea who might have?" Didn't hurt to ask. I was already here.

"Not a clue." The apologetic expression on her face was genuine. "If I did, I would have called the police."

Not knowing what else to do, I simply nodded. "Well, thank you for your time. So sorry to bother you."

"Not a bother at all, dear." She refocused on Watson, who was sitting at my feet. Her voice became wistful. "You sure you don't have time for tea, though?"

I had family dinner in less than an hour, much more time than I figured I'd need to question the woman. However, I had a feeling tea would be quite the process. Well... whatever. Watson was clearly needed. We could be late. "Tea sounds wonderful. Thank you."

Clearly anticipating me turning her down, Maud looked up in surprise, and twenty years fell off her face as she beamed.

ELEVEN

Mom had gone old-school. The table—actually, the *two* tables shoved together to form one—was laden with a large pork roast, framed on the platter by wedged roasted potatoes and carrots. On either side were bowls of heaping, buttery mashed potatoes, and brown gravy. Closer to the head of the table, near Barry, was a smaller, yet no less impressive, vegetarian seitan "pork" roast. At the other end, closer to Percival and Gary, were two casserole dishes, one of the green bean and crunchy onion topping variety, and another of five-cheese macaroni and cheese, half with crispy pancetta, the other half with *meatless* crispy pancetta.

Leo rubbed his flat stomach even though the meal had barely gotten started. "I feel like I've died and gone to Midwestern heaven."

Verona leaned forward to look down the length of table at him. "With all the butter in this meal, *die* might be exactly what you do."

Zelda tossed a piping-hot homemade dinner roll at her twin. "Oh, lighten up. No need to be so stringent all the time."

Verona tossed it right back, the two of them acting closer to the ages of their children instead of the women pushing fifty that they were. "Just because you soil yourself with soda and ice cream doesn't mean the rest of us have a cancerous wish."

Before Zelda could toss the roll a third time, her husband, Noah, plucked it out of her hand and took a bite, then spoke with his mouth full. "Cancer never tasted so good."

Jonah, *Noah's* twin, smirked from his place at Verona's side.

"Okay, you all. Eat, for goodness' sake." Mom broke in before an all-out food war began, laughter and reprimand in her tone. "I didn't go to all this trouble so it would get cold."

"I wish you hadn't waited on me. I told you not to." Maybe I should've known better, but I really had been surprised when I walked into my parents' house and discovered they hadn't started the meal.

"Nonsense." Barry stood and began carving the meatless pork loin, his fuchsia and red tie-dyed tank top seeming especially garish against a meal from my childhood. "We wouldn't dream of starting without you." Not pausing in the carving, he leaned to peer around the back of chairs. "Or you either. You're the star of the show after all."

Watson had settled in between Leo's and my chairs, but at the attention, waddled over to Barry. He received a hunk of meatless meat for his efforts.

"Don't let your stepfather fool you." Percival brought my attention to the other end. "It's only because he runs a dictatorship around here. I would've voted to begin. I've talked to Maud on a couple of occasions. She's sweet, but *long*-winded." Beside him, his husband barked out a laugh, earning himself a dramatically flared glare. "No comments from the peanut gallery. I'm not long-winded, merely... *expressive.*"

Though barely audible, I heard a contented sigh from

Leo and glanced over. He offered me a soft, happy smile. Though not always able to attend, he'd been included in the weekly family dinners since things had changed between us in January. Of course, like Katie, he'd always had an open invitation to everything the family did anyway, but... it felt different now. I knew it did to him too. Even in that sigh. He wasn't on the outside looking in at my crazy family, but... a part of it.

It was interesting, the little dating Branson and I had done, the idea of him sitting down to dinner with my family had never even crossed my mind. In retrospect, the notion was ludicrous. My family would've driven him nuts. I was sure he would've been polite about it, but was also certain he would've felt like they were beneath him somehow. Not Leo... not Leo. In way of thanks, I shifted my hand to rest on his knee under the table, marveling at the change and how easy it all was.

Apparently, Katie had heard Leo's sigh as well, and interpreted correctly. She leaned in from across the table. "I know. It's like being in a sitcom."

"Yeah. It's exhausting," Verona and Jonah's youngest son, Leaf, muttered under his breath, pure disgust dripping from his tone. Though only nine, with every passing day he seemed to be rushing headlong into the teenaged attitude. He received a glare from his mother.

"So, you said Maud is getting evicted?" Barry had sat back down and looked my way as he helped pass the bowl of potatoes around the table. "I'm ashamed to say I'd forgotten about that poor woman. It's been years since we've spoken."

Mom chimed in before I could reply. "I know. When we got your message, I felt horrible. I'd forgotten about her too. She was always so nice to me when I was a girl. She worked at the taffy shop downtown back then."

"She actually mentioned that. And you." I smiled at Mom, picturing Maud's description of my mother as a kid—long red hair in braids and missing one of her front teeth as she begged for butterscotch taffy. I refocused on Barry. "And as far as eviction, she's not certain now that Violet's dead. She's a little bit in limbo. Maybe it's ugly to say, but Violet's death might've helped her for now, at least buy her a little more time."

"Fred!" Mom looked at me, aghast. "There is no possible way Maud Melvin is a murderer. I refuse to believe it."

"No, I don't think she is. That was obvious the second I met her." My heart ached a little, picturing her wrinkled, age-spotted hand ceaselessly stroking over Watson's face and sides. "And *not* only because she used to have a corgi."

"Oh, right!" Barry sounded faraway suddenly. "I forgot about that. Its name was... some mythological name, I believe. Aphrodite maybe."

"Hera." Percival spoke up, surprising us all. He flinched slightly when the majority of the table turned to gape at him. "Like I could forget. That dog was fatter than Mr. Butterworth over there." He pointed with his fork toward Watson. "I always called her Herapotamus."

Though Mom groaned in embarrassment, the rest of us chuckled. *That* sounded more like Percival.

Barry looked toward me once more, growing serious. "I'm glad you brought it up, Fred. I'll look into it. It might take me a bit. I don't want to bother Joan in the midst of her grief, but Maud will be fine, I promise." He smiled at Mom as she placed a hand over his.

My heart warmed even more. When I first moved to Estes, though Barry and my mother had been married for about six years already, I hadn't felt that close to him. Even struggled at times with how fast Mom had moved on in the midst of her heartbreak over my father's death. But I'd truly grown to love him, and in some ways, he was as heroic as my dad had been. I'd already planned on asking him if there was anything he could do for Maud. He owned a lot of commercial properties, but I thought he had a couple of residential as well. It didn't surprise me I hadn't even had to ask.

"Thank you, Barry. That would mean a lot." I hesitated to switch the subject as the mood was light and happy, but I had a wealth of knowledge at my fingertips and couldn't let it slide by. "While we're close to the topic, what are your thoughts on Violet and Joan? I have to admit I didn't know Violet very well, but my estimation of her is changing. I'm finding it hard to respect someone that would kick a woman like Maud out into the cold."

Though she didn't speak, I got Mom's pointed look toward Barry. She might be flighty and always sees the best in everyone, but she wasn't naïve either. Clearly, she'd had some feelings about Violet and had made them known to Barry.

In response, Barry let out a long sigh, much different than the one Leo had issued only moments before. "It's complicated..."

"Not really." In his blunt way, Percival took over. "We all grew up together. A lot of us old-timers were here together as kids. She wasn't in our inner circle like a few of the others, but still, after all these decades together, a certain bond forms. An alliance."

"Not to mention, for me at least," Gary broke in, "moving here with Percival from the city, especially not having grown up here myself, it was a blessing to find *family* here, you know? It's better nowadays, but when I moved, I felt completely on display. There weren't very many other people of color, and even fewer people who were out. So having Violet and Joan here made it a little more welcoming, made it a little safer. And I know we helped them feel that way too."

Like a tag team, Percival took over again. "That's true. At least for Violet. Joan has always been so head over heels that I don't think she cared two bits about what anyone else thought about her and Violet's marriage, but Violet did. She was always more concerned with status and public acceptance. So, having Gary and I here helped with that too. Normalized it a bit more at a time when we were still seen as unnatural and evil."

One more thing I hadn't thought about. Growing up with my uncles, it seemed normal and natural to me. Even so, though aware of some of their struggles, I forgot about my own privilege. I never had to face anything like that. Once more, I'd overlooked how this might affect them. "I'm sorry for your loss. It sounds like you and Violet and Joan have been through a lot together."

Percival and Gary shrugged as one. But Gary spoke again. "Well, that *is* like Barry said. It's complicated. In a different circumstance, if we were back in the city where there were more of us, I doubt we would've mixed with Joan and Violet very often. We don't exactly have the same outlook on life in a lot of ways."

"You're kind and loving, is what you mean," Katie piped up, looking at Gary and Percival and then twisting to include Mom and Barry. "None of you care about status, or put money above people."

The table was silent for a few moments—sitting in that

truth, clearly none of them could agree as it would indicate that they saw themselves as better.

Well... almost... "Right as always, Ms. Pizzolato!" Percival trilled, intentionally giving into a flourish that cut the mood. "We *are* fabulous. No one can deny it."

"Amen to that." Leo raised a forkful of gravy-covered roast, as if toasting with a champagne glass.

There were a couple rounds of cheers and amens from the rest of us, causing Mom, Barry, and Gary to blush. Percival just tilted his chin and fluttered his eyelashes.

After a few moments, Barry zeroed in on me. "At the end of the day, Violet was a complicated woman. She had... an intense personality. When she focused on something, it was with her whole heart, for however long that focus lasted, nothing else mattered." That matched what her wife had said, but he kept going before I could comment. "She also had a rather childlike view of the world. There was no gray. Take Maud for example. To us, it seems cruel, but that notion wouldn't have entered Violet's psyche. Rules were rules. If you don't pay, you don't get to stay. That was their agreement. The circumstances around it wouldn't matter."

That too matched. Almost to a T.

"It seems a little cruel to call it childlike, but I suppose it's factual, even if it is an insult to children everywhere." Mom truly then surprised me, not sugarcoating at all. She looked at me. "I will admit that I struggled with her... with both of them at times. A lot of us might start out with that sort of thinking, but I can't help but feel staying that way over the years, after seeing so much of life, after going through its hurts and seeing others in pain... as a willful choice. I would think it would take a lot of effort to stay stuck there. And Violet was definitely stuck there."

"And Joan?" It was Leo that time. "She didn't help soften Violet?"

Percival chuckled. "Are you kidding? If anything, it was the opposite. Violet was perfect in Joan's eyes." He twisted to look at Gary. "Say, rather reminds me of you... It's wonderful being in a relationship where the other person knows you're perfect." He patted Gary's hand dramatically. "And you're right, I am. Perfect and flawless."

Instead of responding to his husband, Gary looked toward Barry. "If you find another place for Maud, can you see if it has a second bedroom for Percival?"

After the laughter faded, we got lost to dinner for a little while. To the warmth of family, and friends who were just as good as family, delicious food, and the crackling of the fire across the room. As we ate, Watson cavorted here and there, snagging pieces that fell both accidentally and accidentally on purpose. For a while, I drifted through the comfort of it all, and then the miracle of how beautiful my life was. Some part of me whispered that everything was fleeting, but instead of making me feel melancholy, it only served as a reminder to love each and every moment.

Before too long—my brain being what it was—thoughts went back to the murder, tumbling over the different names and faces that were possibly involved.

It settled on Gerald Jackson. I considered for several moments before I brought him up. He was one of those who'd grown up with the older members of my family. And though I knew Mom had some of the same feelings I did, there seemed to be a blind spot with the men of my family where Gerald was concerned, elements of the good old boys' club that still lingered, surprisingly, even where Percival was concerned.

But it might be worth a try.

"Not to bring down dinner again, but I have another question for you to ponder."

"Do you think it's the Irons family?" Though she cut me off, Zelda's and Noah's oldest daughter was barely audible, her whisper tense.

Zelda's eyes widened as she looked from Britney to me. "They aren't involved, are they, Fred?" Before I could respond, she slipped an arm over her daughter's shoulders. "They're not. They can't be. Not this soon after last time."

I was surprised. Though maybe I shouldn't have been. Clearly my nephews and nieces were having some fear around the Irons family. At least some of them. "No. Although few people have brought that possibility up. I'm sure they're not."

Katie gave me a questioning look but stayed silent.

A few of the adults gave similar expressions. Obviously aware it was impossible for me to know such a thing. I brightened my tone, trying to help soothe further. "I was actually alluding to Gerald Jackson. His name keeps coming up."

"Fred." Though Barry's voice was soft, there was just a touch of reprimand. "I know you don't care for him, nor does your mother, and... I can see why at times. But he's not a killer."

"Is it because of the argument he and Violet had not long ago?" Gary spoke up, as if coming to my defense. I had the feeling that he went back and forth on his feelings about Gerald.

"Partly, yes. It seems like everyone's heard about that. But I have yet to hear what it was about." I looked toward Percival, who was the real gossip queen between the two of them. "Do you know?"

He shook his head. "I'm ashamed to say I don't." Even

so, his eyes twinkled as he leaned forward, preparing to share a juicy tidbit. "But... I've speculated. My guess is that the real conflict is between Gerald and Ethel."

"*Ethel*?" I hadn't expected that.

He nodded sagely, and was clearly pleased to be offering something new. "Ethel and Violet's friendship wasn't simply because of length of years or sharing minority status. They were soul sisters. Same outlook on life, same motivations."

"Maybe." Barry sounded doubtful. "But there were plenty of times when they hated each other. Full-on wars."

Percival simply shook his head at Barry. "Spoken like a stereotypical straight man who hasn't watched enough episodes of the *Real Housewives of Atlanta*. They're the definition of frenemies, my dear brother-in-law." I balked at the word, considering I'd thought it myself less than two hours before. Percival didn't notice my reaction. "They might stab each other in the back, but if anyone dared insult one of them, they'd defend each other to the death. I guarantee you anything, Violet was letting Gerald have it over something he did to Ethel. Probably something with the paper again."

"The paper?" I sat up straighter. I couldn't put my finger on it, but something felt familiar. "The newspaper?"

"Yeah. They're both investors in *The Chipmunk Chronicles*." Percival shrugged a shoulder. "Well... *Eustace* was an investor. But like she did on his spot on the city council, Ethel slid right into his place after he died. And her being on the council has been a nightmare, let me tell you."

"And knowing Gerald, he probably thought he could push Ethel around, though he never would've dreamed of attempting it with her husband."

Barry narrowed his eyes at Mom. "You really think he's

like that? That Gerald would do that simply because she's a woman?"

Every single woman around the table nodded in unison, some of them saying *absolutely* or *yes* or *without a doubt*.

For the first time, I saw realization dawn in Barry's eyes. "Oh. That's... awful."

After a couple of tense moments, Mom stood and motioned toward Katie. "What do you say, dear, dessert?"

Katie popped up, excitement over her face as she looked at me. "I *perfected* the torte this afternoon. Finally. Just wait, you're going to die."

Watson and I had visited Athena enough times at *The Chipmunk Chronicles* that the receptionist didn't pause in her conversation on her headset as she waved us on back.

I paused in the doorway of Athena's office and tapped on the doorframe with my boot since my hands were full.

"Finally! Where did you disappear—" Her perfectly made-up eyes widened as she turned to face me. "Oh, Fred. Watson."

Watson charged in ahead of me, searching.

"Sorry, I probably should've called first. Looks like you're expecting someone." I thrust out the hand that held a drink. "I brought bribes."

"You never need to do that." She twisted the rest of the way around in her rolling chair and took the drink without standing up. "But I love that you do." She took a sniff inside. "Chocolate macchiato. You're a goddess."

"I know what I'm doing." Laughing, I plopped down in the chair beside her desk.

Watson whimpered pitifully.

"Oh, sweet one." Athena bent slightly and caressed his muzzle. "Pearl's getting her hair done this morning. I'm picking her up at noon."

At the name of Athena's white toy poodle, who seemed

to be the object of his affection, Watson whimpered again, made another sniffing trip around the room, and then looked at us in pure heartbreak.

"Sorry, buddy. I should've called first and checked. We'll make a special trip to come see Pearl soon, okay?"

Watson glowered, then moved closer, to nudge the small paper bag I held in my other hand. I pulled away and put the bag in front of Athena with a laugh. "And we've moved on, it seems. This is for you as well. Katie's newest creation. A chocolate espresso torte. It's heaven." I gave her my serious expression. "However, we are *not* selling this at the bakery. This is just between friends."

"Even better. You must really be looking for favors this morning." She took a sip, sighed again, then peered into the bag before glancing down at Watson. "Sorry, pup. I should feel guilty for stealing something so delicious-looking from you, but I don't."

Watson whimpered again.

"Oh, you're good. You're very, very good." Athena twisted and opened the bottom drawer of her file cabinet and came back with four teeny-tiny toy-poodle-sized dog biscuits. "But... here you go. An apology for me thwarting love and chocolate."

He swept them up in one quick slurp of his tongue and curled up under my chair.

"A man who knows what he likes. Always admire that about him." Chuckling, Athena retrieved a wet wipe and cleaned her hands as she straightened once again. "So, with this level of bribery, you must want something really—"

A skinny young man popped in the door, thrusting a handful of papers at Athena. "Here you go."

"Thank you, Tucker." She snagged them and added them to an already tall stack of papers on the corner of her desk. "Next time, put a little get-up-and-go in it, will you? *I'm* the senior citizen around here, not you." Tucker started to stammer, but she waved him away before turning back to me expectantly.

For a second, I lost track of the point of my visit. "I want to be you when I grow up. It's like the whole world bows down to you. And you do it with so much class."

"It's just good makeup, a killer wardrobe, and living long enough that you don't care what anyone else thinks about you." She smiled indulgently, her teeth so straight and white against her dark skin that not for the first time I wondered if they were dentures. I'd never ask. "I do love seeing you, but today is a little bit of a killer. You mind if we cut to the chase?"

"Of course." Even in that, Athena managed to be direct, state her needs, and not feel the slightest bit dismissive. Before I launched in, I glanced out the open door of her office. Neither Tucker nor anyone else was in sight. "I'm looking into Violet's murder."

"Naturally." She floated her fingers, motioning for me to continue.

"When I was talking things over with my family at dinner last night, they reminded me that Gerald and Ethel are both investors in *The Chipmunk Chronicles*. I might've known that already; I don't recall. But part of me is wondering if—"

In the least graceful move I'd ever seen from Athena, she hopped up quick enough that her chair rolled backward as she launched across the small space to shut the door. "Good grief, girl. If we're going to gossip about those two, we *don't* do it where we can be overheard. I barely want to do it in here. Walls have ears, after all."

She'd surprised me. "You think they're dangerous?"

Athena accompanied her exasperated look with a smile. "Not hardly. I think you're a little too much into the cloak-and-dagger mindset. It's that if you make our biggest financial backers angry, Brian, my dear little editor in chief, will change his mind about finally allowing me to be a part-time critic in the food-and-entertainment section. I'll be back to obituaries full-time." She set her chocolate macchiato aside and leaned forward, clearly interested. "You suspect Gerald and Ethel are somehow connected to Violet's death?" She considered, but not long enough for me to even respond. "Ethel *is* a hothead, and she and Violet do go rounds."

"Percival seems to think they're more of a frenemy situation than pure-out nemeses."

She scoffed. "He's right, though I hate that word. Anyone who is over fourteen and can have that quality attributed to them needs to grow up."

"Have you heard about a recent public blowup between Gerald and Violet?"

"I don't have to write the gossip column—" She put her French-tipped fingertips to her plum-colored lips in mock horror. "—excuse me, the *Society Column* to have heard about that."

"Do you also happen to know what it was about?"

"Can't say that I do. Until this moment, I wasn't that interested. But if it somehow ties into murder, well..."

"I'm not sure if it does." I'd played over Percival's theory several times throughout the night, and still wasn't sure how I felt about it. "One possibility is that Violet was arguing with Gerald in Ethel's defense."

To my surprise, Athena nodded and gave an expression suggesting she agreed. Before she spoke, she leaned back and took a sip of her drink while she considered. "That might be. The wars between Gerald and Ethel over the past year have been legendary. A couple of them have occurred within *The Chronicles'* walls. And let me tell you, *everybody* was privy to the show, not just our society reporter."

Maybe Percival's theory held more credence than I'd thought. "What about?"

"Money, power, control." Athena intentionally infused boredom into her tone. "The same things every insecure dictator gets their feathers ruffled over."

I gave in to my bias against Gerald. "I take it that didn't happen between Gerald and Eustace?"

Athena snorted, somehow making *that* sound classy. "Not in the same way. Gerald wasn't up front with Eustace, but he'd go around him, using the law if he needed to. I know some people see him as a fool, and I understand why, but he can be successful at times. He's the only reason I kept my job here when all the drama went down ages ago. I owe him for that."

I'd forgotten, completely. Gerald went up a notch or two. Anyone who had Athena's back wasn't all bad.

She sighed a long breath. "Still... while Gerald wasn't combative with Eustace face-to-face, he doesn't have quite the same deference to Eustace's widow. Though, I guarantee you, Ethel is at least ten times more cutthroat than Eustace ever was, and *he* was no pushover. Gerald doesn't see her that way."

"Ethel seems inconsequential to Gerald. I can see that perfectly." There we were again, the good old boys' club.

Maybe she heard the disdain in my voice. "I hate to poke holes in your theory, Fred, but no matter how much Gerald dislikes Ethel, I can't see him killing *her*, even less killing Violet because of Ethel."

"No, me neither." It was a dead end. Had to be. "Well, I

thought I'd ask your opinion since I assumed you'd seen them close up."

"Sorry it didn't pay off, but thanks for the bribe." She had a dismissive quality in her voice but then brightened. "Oh, actually, I've been working on Violet's obituary. I came across some photos in the archives I think you might enjoy." Without waiting, she faced her computer and her fingers began flying over the keys.

I angled my chair to sit beside her, much to Watson's irritation. Instead of repositioning beneath me, he plodded over and lay down in front of the door, probably deciding that if he was going to be inconvenienced, he'd make himself an obstacle.

Athena didn't notice and had already brought up a file full of pictures. She clicked one, then leaned back, giving me room. "Recognize anyone?"

I leaned closer, studying the black-and-white image. I nearly said no, but then I did. A bunch of someones. "Mom, Barry, and Percival." Mom and Barry looked to be in their late teens, Percival noticeably older. "My goodness, look at them. I don't think I've ever seen this picture."

"That's because it's ancient. It was from a Fourth of July celebration, though the caption doesn't explain why this particular group was together." She singled out a couple more faces from the large crowd and tapped on the screen. "How about these two?"

"Violet." Now that I realized the time frame I was looking at, she was unmistakable due to her waist-length white-blonde hair. "Wow, she really was astonishing-looking. Almost like a mythical creature." I looked toward the other face. "I don't know him."

Athena craned her neck and waggled her eyebrows. "Gerald Jackson."

"No way!" I leaned in even closer. "You are lying. There's no way he was so—" I barely stopped myself in time.

Athena chuckled. "Good-looking?"

I grimaced, embarrassed at getting caught being so shallow. "I didn't say that."

"Mm-hm." Athena hummed, still chuckling. She pointed again. "And here we have Eustace and Ethel." She moved on to a couple of other people I knew from the town, but none were involved in this particular case, as far as I knew.

I had a sudden inspiration. "Would you print me off a copy of that? On photo paper?"

"Of course." Athena clicked a couple of keys. "Think you'll frame it?"

"Actually, I'm going to bribe someone else. Or at least manipulate them somewhat." I sat back in my chair. "I'm willing to bet Joan hasn't seen this either. She'll love it, and seeing Violet, Ethel, and Gerald all in the same photo might trigger something she's forgetting, or that she assumed isn't a big deal. If not, hopefully it will be a comforting gift for her."

"Not letting go of the Gerald theory?"

"I think I am, at least almost. But who knows what that photo will do?"

Athena turned back to the computer and clicked open a few more photos from the file, arranging them to all be seen at once. "I'm trying to decide which ones to use for the obituary. See any others you think might be useful to loosen Joan's tongue, if needed?"

There were around ten photos of Violet, ranging through different periods of her life. The only thing that really changed was the gentle aging she had done. It appeared, after that first photo, she'd chosen a style and stuck with it. Her hair was done exactly as I remembered it in life—a loose bun on top of her head, wispy tendrils around her face. Her clothes, always feminine business attire, a jacket and flowing blouse up top, accompanied by a tight skirt and sky-high heels.

The only exception was a wedding photo, where her hair was down again, and she obviously wasn't wearing a suit. Maybe the photo had been in the album, but I hadn't seen it. That time, I recognized a younger version of the face I knew. "Ethel was Violet's maid of honor?"

Another hum of affirmation, and Athena pointed toward the woman on the other side of the bride. "I believe this is Joan's sister. Or some family member, in any case. She has the same last name." Athena clicked on an image, causing it to stack on top of the others, revealing all of it. "This was on the front page, not a small feat for the early 80s. Even big-city papers weren't featuring lesbian weddings as front-page material, let alone a small town like Estes Park."

"That is progressive."

Before I could take a shot at why, Athena tapped Ethel's face. "It's all in who you know."

It only took me a few seconds to connect the dots. "Violet's best friend was Ethel. Was Eustace already an investor in the paper?"

"Sure was. And a new one at that. I'd been here for a couple of years at that time. The year before this shot, *The Chipmunk Chronicles* nearly folded. Alan Bridges, the founding owner, had to sell off majority shares. Two of them, in fact, at 40 percent each. Any guesses to whom?"

"Eustace and Gerald."

"On the nose." Athena nodded. "That helped Gerald insist I keep my job as well."

What a sacrifice, selling off 80 percent of your business. "Wait a minute. You said Alan was the *original* owner? He is not now?"

"Goodness no. He was old back then. He passed it on to his son, who has also died. Now it belongs to Brody Bridges, Alan's grandson. Although he doesn't care about it in the slightest. Probably enjoys the profits, however, even if it's only 20 percent."

Seemed like everything kept circling around Violet, Gerald, and Eustace... or Ethel, by de facto. "I'll take all of those printed off, if that's okay."

"You bet." She made several more clicks. "I sent them to the printer in reception. There's a photo-quality printer there, and that'll be easiest for you to pick up."

"Thanks, I appreciate it."

"Thank *you*." Athena pointed at the awaiting torte. "And thank Katie for me as well, please."

"You got it." I stood and nudged a sleeping Watson gently with my foot. "Wake up, grumpy pants. Time to go."

Watson made a show of waking slowly, then yawned as he stretched, arching his nub of a tail into the air.

"Your boy's not short on drama, is he?"

"Not hardly." Watson finally moved aside, and I opened the door, but paused before I left, turning toward Athena again. "Actually, I have one more..." I remembered her warning and hurriedly shut the door, earning another irritated glare from Watson. "This might not lead anywhere either, and it might be connected to Violet and it might not, but do you know anything about other financial investments of Gerald's?"

Athena's eyes narrowed. "You mean outside of his law practice?"

I nodded.

"No." She straightened, and I could hear the curiosity grow in her tone. "But apparently *you* do."

"I don't, actually." I considered whether I was betraying Carl's confidence, then decided I wasn't. I'd simply promised not to tell his wife unless I thought I had reason to. "He's got some kind of investment thing going on. He's convinced Carl Hanson to be a part of it and—"

No matter if she was friends with Gerald or not, Athena's groan told me she was instantly on the same page.

"Exactly." I held her gaze for emphasis. "I would ask you to keep this between us. Anna doesn't know, but I've made it very clear to Carl that if I come across something I think she *should* know that I wouldn't hold it back from her."

"You're a good friend, Winifred Page." She smiled sweetly and then morphed, conspiratorial once again. "Want me to dig around? See what I might uncover?"

"I'll make sure Katie showers you with chocolate espresso tortes for life if you will."

Her smile grew wicked. "I would've done it for free. But endless tortes? Who am I to turn down Katie's perfection?"

Instead of going directly to Joan, I opted to be at the Cozy Corgi for the late-morning tourists and the lunch crowd. From what I'd seen of Joan, she was understandably struggling to handle her grief. The last thing I wanted was to wake her up, in case she'd had a hard time sleeping the night before.

Not only did I not have time to play detective, I didn't even have an opportunity to figure out how I was going to present Joan with the photos in a way that might trigger some memory. I couldn't shake the feeling she had to know something that prompted her wife's murder. Even if it was buried deep in her subconscious, or some little passing detail that had seemed inconsequential but was really the key to everything.

Ben and I stayed busy for a couple of hours with tourists. It was almost like summer. I was an actual bookseller.

I directed a man looking for a stellar meatloaf recipe to the Alex Guarnaschelli cookbook.

A woman I judged to be roughly the same age as Maud Melvin, but with better healthcare, bought all five books of the Sara Donati *Wilderness* series—I warned her they could be a little steamy. She informed me they'd better be, or she'd return them.

My breath caught when a high school girl laid *A Monstrous Beauty* on the counter. I'd read the Elizabeth Fama book years ago—gorgeously haunting supernatural mystery and romance. The cover featured a mermaid stretched out over dark, cold-looking rocks. With her long, white-blonde hair surrounding her beautiful face, she could have doubled for the younger picture of Violet. More than that, hadn't I thought something similar when I'd discovered her body? Something about the way she'd been arranged had reminded me of a mermaid. My hands trembled as I rang up the girl's purchase and handed her the book in a Cozy Corgi bag. Part of me didn't want to sell it to her; it was the only one we had in stock. As I watched her leave, I couldn't help but feel like some clue was walking through the front door. Which had to be insanity. Besides, I could upload the book on my Kindle and read by the fire that evening on the off chance it was somehow connected. Which, again, would be insanity.

Watson did his part as well by playing mascot. More than one person purchased a hoodie with the Cozy Corgi logo on the chest and wanted a picture with my little man. He obliged, though every shot revealed his resentment. He'd perk up to receive a treat as payment, but turn grumpy again the second the last crumb disappeared.

I was so busy that when I glanced out the window and noticed Gerald Jackson exiting Cabin and Hearth, I didn't even pause in attempting to explain to a tourist that she'd been misinformed—deer never turned into elk. As she began to lay out her argument, my brain finally clicked, and I did a double take. Sure enough, there he was. Heading in the direction of the Koffee Kiln.

"You're right. Clearly, I've been deceived." Refocusing on the tourist, I forced a smile. "I'm dating a park ranger. I'll make sure to tell him tonight that the elk have been fooling them the whole time."

She sucked in an insulted gasp, but I was already moving around her, searching for Ben. I found him in the children's book section, helping a family of five. "Ben!"

He looked over, pausing midsentence.

"I'm stepping out for a bit. You have everything under control?"

He gave a thumbs-up and refocused on the three children.

Watson scurried over. Maybe he truly wanted to join me, or it could have been a simple escape from yet another tourist attempting to pet him. Either way, the two of us hurried out to the sidewalk.

The day had grown colder than the ones before, and I instantly realized I had both forgotten my jacket and Watson's leash, but there wasn't time to go back. I glanced down at him as we darted across the street and began a slow-paced jog through the crowds of tourists. "Stay right beside me, no shenanigans."

Watson didn't bother to look up, but he kept pace. All bets were off if someone dropped part of a hot dog or funnel cake on the sidewalk.

Though we were closing the distance, Gerald moved out of sight as he turned the corner around the Koffee Kiln. I hollered his name, but he didn't reappear. As we passed the pottery-and-coffee shop, I noticed movement inside. I didn't take the time to determine if it was the police or if Carla and Simone had been allowed to reopen. Gerald was heading to a car parked on the side of the curving street.

"Gerald!"

That time, when I called his name again, he turned around in surprise. Maybe he hadn't heard me before. His expression was so obvious, it was nearly laughable. Within a matter of seconds, his transparent thoughts shifted from a curse, to debating if he could make a run for it, to deflated resignation. He had just enough time before we reached him to work up a forced smile. "Winifred, Watson." There wasn't even an attempted *good to see you* or any such pleasantry.

Since he'd just left Cabin and Hearth, I was willing to bet Carl had informed him I was aware of their dealings. "I've been trying to get hold of you. Your secretary said you were out of town." No, that wasn't right. "Actually, she said you were out of the office, but if I recall, when you gave Nick an envelope full of money, you told him you were heading out of town."

His eyes narrowed. "It's a federal offense to open someone's mail, Winifred."

That was one way to confirm my suspicions. "The envelope was neither stamped, addressed, nor mailed, Gerald. And I didn't open it."

"Then how do you know there was money in it." He gave a little smirk and then tipped the glass bottle to his lips. Doubtlessly his homemade cannabis-infused kombucha.

"Because I'm not an idiot." I gestured to where we stood, and then to the car he'd been heading toward. "Where do you want to talk? We can do it here or in your car."

"I'm sorry, my dear. I have a meeting I have to get to. I simply don't have—"

Without thinking, I grabbed his arm as he began to turn away.

He looked from where I gripped him to my eyes. "Excuse me, I don't appreciate—"

Watson growled.

He glanced down, and when he met my gaze again, he looked afraid.

His expression was so unexpected that I dropped my hand. I think it was the first time in my life either myself or my overly fluffy corgi had struck fear into someone. "Sorry. I didn't mean to grab you. But we really do need to talk."

Gerald took a step back but didn't attempt to leave. "You seem angry." His gaze flicked to Watson again. "You both do. I'm not sure what I did to upset you."

I realized I did indeed seem angry—that I *was* angry. I also realized I wasn't being entirely fair to Gerald. My frustration and distaste of him had grown as I'd spoken about him to different people, hearing of their experiences with him. But he didn't know that. And while he'd been dismissive to me, I knew it hadn't been intentional; it was just who he was. To his way of thinking, he'd never been anything but pleasant to me. Plus, he'd helped Athena ages ago. That counted for something.

I needed to play this better. Either that or be direct with Gerald and air my grievances then and there. But that would hardly help get any information. As was my normal, I decided to be direct, but took the irritation out of my tone as much as I could. "I'm looking into Violet's death. Several people mentioned a public conflict the two of you had recently. No one's really clear on what it was about. Would you mind sharing it with me?"

"You..." He gaped at me, clearly dumbfounded. "You actually think I killed that woman?"

"No. I don't." If I had, his reaction would've changed my mind. Everything I'd seen from Gerald told me that he had a lousy poker face, part of why I couldn't figure out how he managed to be a lawyer. "But any details might help bring her murderer to justice."

He relaxed a little, and as the fear drained away, his smugness returned. "Now see here, Fred, I have a lot of respect for you. And I adore your family. We go back since I was a kid. And I will tolerate quite a bit because of those connections in that respect. But I will not be interrogated. Not by you."

That was the most direct I'd ever heard Gerald. It would have been impressive had it not been for his condescending tone.

"You don't have to, of course. I'm not the police." Though I tried not to, I could hear matching condescension in my voice. "But... speaking of the police, I have been considering if I need to inform them of certain... under-the-table business dealings you have going on."

Indignation flared, quickly overpowered by the return of fear. "I have no idea what you're talking about."

There it was, more proof he'd chosen the wrong career. It almost made me pity him. "Yes, you do. And we both know it."

He sputtered a couple of times, but deflated. "What people choose to do with their money is their business. Not yours, not the police's. I'm not twisting anyone's arm or forcing anyone to do anything."

"Was Violet one of your—" I caught myself before I said *dupes*. "—investors? Like Carl?"

Anger flashed so hot and strong that I nearly took a step back. Clearly feeling it, below us, Watson growled again.

Gerald didn't notice. "No, the stupid woman was too much of an imbecile to see a good thing." I realized his anger wasn't at me, but at Violet. "She called me to ask for a meeting." In what I assumed was an attempt to point at himself, he jabbed his chest with the kombucha bottle, splashing it onto the fabric of his shirt. "She called *me* and then had the audacity to call me a moron. Imagine. *That* crazy loon calling me a moron."

He'd just validated what Joan had said. How he'd seen Violet, how he'd referred to her as crazy. It was the first I'd seen such open hostility from him, and my distaste for him grew. Still, might as well use it. "I have heard she was a little unstable... or at least obsessive about things."

He snorted as if that was an understatement, but relaxed somehow, as if we were finally getting on the same page. "She should've been locked up in the loony bin years ago."

"Why did she want to meet with you? From what I understand, her current obsession was pottery. Do you know anything about pottery?"

He ignored that. "She wanted to buy my shares of the newspaper. And at a ridiculously low price, I might add."

"The Chipmunk Chronicles?" I wasn't really asking for verification, though he nodded at me like I was the moron for needing to do so. I was simply trying to catch up. "Violet wanted to own part of the paper. Do you know why?"

"Because of that nasty Ethel, of course. Violet wanted to play CEO along with her best friend, I'm sure. What a mess that would be. Ethel's even worse than Violet. I never dreamed I'd be an equal partner with her." His anger spiked again. "It was manageable when Eustace was part of it. Then Ethel got her greedy little claws into it and wanted to take over, wanted to micromanage every aspect and boss everybody around. I'm sick to death of it. And that hillbilly paper's not worth it, not anymore."

The breeze was starting to pick up, the chill cutting

through my blouse, making me begin to tremble. I ignored it. "If you're so sick of it, why didn't you sell it to Violet? It seemed that if she wanted it badly enough, she'd pay. It doesn't appear like she was hurting for funds."

"The woman was so cheap she could make a penny squeal. She wouldn't come up, not a dime." He sniffed. "However, I told her I'd sell if she'd—" Gerald's eyes went saucer-wide as his mouth dropped open.

"If she'd what?" When he gave a little shake of his head, I took a step forward, using my height to tower over the shorter man. "Gerald. You told her you'd sell if she'd what?"

"Invest." His whimper was like a surrender.

He had to be kidding. "You told Violet that you'd sell your shares of *The Chipmunk Chronicles* if she *invested* in the same scheme you talked Carl into?"

Gerald bristled. "It's not a scheme. It's a legitimate business opportunity. One with the potential for astounding dividends. She was just too stupid to realize it."

It suddenly hit me, a detail I hadn't asked my family, one that hadn't even occurred to me because I knew them so well. And I was willing to bet Gerald did too. "Barry has quite a bit of money. So do my uncles, come to think of it. Have they invested?"

A blush rose to his cheeks that had nothing to do with the wind chill.

"Have you even asked them?"

He went scarlet. "They're... not the right... sort of people for this investment."

Meaning they weren't gullible, not like Carl, and Gerald knew it. From the way it sounded, Violet hadn't been gullible either. "But *Violet* was the right sort of person... she just didn't realize it?"

"I was wrong. I misjudged how her miserly ways

impacted her vision. She had none." He cleared his throat, took a step away from us, and some of his bluster returned. "She'd have been back. She was desperate for those shares. She would've invested."

His wording caught me. "She struck you as desperate?"

"Pathetically so." His lip curled. "Just another one of her obsessions, I'm sure. Only more reason to believe she would've come back, bought the shares, *and* taken advantage of my investment opportunity."

Though Gerald was easy to read, there was no way of knowing whether Violet truly had been desperate or that was simply Gerald's prejudices and interpretation. But... if her desire to own part of the paper with Ethel had triggered her propensity for obsession, then maybe...

"I think we're done here," Gerald bit out abruptly, cutting off my thoughts. "Like I said, I have an appointment. Thanks to you, I'll be running late."

I nearly let him go, then couldn't help myself. "Gerald."

He'd already started to head toward his car but turned around.

"I'll tell you the same thing I told Carl. If I get the impression that this... *investment*... in any way threatens Anna's financial security without her knowing, I'll inform her."

All the anger he felt at Violet turned on me. "That's none of your business. And I don't appreciate—"

"I don't care whether it's my business or not, Gerald. Nor do I have any concerns about what you appreciate." I decided to offer him an out, a legitimate one. "Here's the deal. I won't poke my nose in it if you present whatever this opportunity is to Barry and my uncles. It doesn't matter if they decide to invest or not. If they judge it to be legitimate, I'll mind my own business, as you say. Or"—why hadn't I thought of this before?—"you can present it to me. Maybe I'll invest."

It looked like Gerald was trying to determine what to say, but finally, he gave up and got in his car.

After I watched him drive away, I turned to Watson. "All right, buddy, let's get back to the fireplace in the mystery room and warm up. We've got some thinking to do."

We were halfway back to the Cozy Corgi and the mystery room fireplace when I changed my mind. Watson gave me a look of betrayal as we walked past the bookshop and headed toward the parking lot.

The notion had come over me, and I feared if I didn't act on it in that instant, I'd lose my nerve. Or that if I built myself up to it at some other point, I wouldn't be able to pull it off.

I didn't have to contact Susan, or information, for that matter, to get the address. I knew it. Everyone in town knew it.

Mom and Barry had a lot of money. Actually, they were rich thanks to Barry's property investments, but it had taken me a long time to realize that. Neither of them were the least bit arrogant. Barry wore his tie-dyed T-shirts and yoga pants till they were threadbare, and their house, other than larger, wasn't any more grand than my own.

The same wasn't true for Ethel Beaker's home. The word *home* barely seemed to fit.

Where Violet and Joan lived in a mini-McMansion surrounded by other mini-McMansions, the Beaker estate sat on a cliff overlooking Mary's Lake. Likewise, the mini-McMansion development stuck out like a sore thumb in

Estes Park, like it'd been built somewhere else and plopped down in the middle of a small mountain town without any regard to aesthetics. Ethel's mansion blended perfectly, not just with Estes Park, but with the mountain itself, almost looking like it'd been crafted out of the rock face. With its wraparound front porch, turrets, gables, steep roofline, and varying surfaces of log and rock, the place was part log cabin, part castle.

My volcanic-orange Mini Cooper felt even smaller than normal as I parked it on the limestone driveway, under the towering peaked shadows. Taking a deep breath, I looked toward Watson, who was scanning the view with apparent curiosity. "Here goes nothing. If you behave, so will I."

For the second time that day, my hand trembled with nerves, causing Watson to peer up at me.

I wasn't intimidated by Ethel's home, her wealth, or status, none of it. I didn't care what she thought of me, that she saw herself as so high above.

I hated that she was able to get under my skin. To poke that childhood scar from Ms. Weser, who'd despised me because of my struggle with spelling and told me through word and action every day of fourth grade how worthless I'd been, worthless I would always be. To twist the knife in the wound that had formed when I'd been served divorce papers out of the blue. I hated that she triggered those parts of me, and that I had yet to figure out how to walk away from Ethel Beaker without feeling sullied somehow. I despised that I allowed her to affect me in ways that caused me to want to respond in manners I didn't respect.

All that heaviness burst from me in a croak of a laugh as an old man in a shiny black tuxedo opened the front door. "May I help you?" Tired blue eyes traveled down the length of me, settled on Watson, and then made the return trip upward before he sniffed.

"I'm here to see Ms. Beaker." Though I didn't laugh again, I couldn't keep a straight face. Ethel lived in an actual mansion, probably the most expensive and ornate home in Estes Park, and she had a butler! *A butler! In a tux!* It was too cliché, and too perfect. For whatever reason, and whether it made me a horrible person or not, it helped me feel superior.

"Is she—" The Butler stopped himself, his eyes closing as if he couldn't believe what he'd been about to say. Then he shifted. "I'm certain she's not expecting you."

"No. I'm certain she isn't." I lifted my chin. Also surprised to realize how tall the lanky man was. There were few people I had to look up at to meet their eyes. When he just stood there, I pushed onward. "I'd like to speak to her, please."

For a second, I thought he was going to refuse. "One moment." He shut the door.

I grinned down at Watson. "I guess we don't even get to wait in the grand entrance hall." Luckily I'd grabbed my extra jacket that I kept in the back of the Mini Cooper, and with Watson's thick, ever shedding layer of fur, and his... plentiful supply of padding, he was as comfortable as a seal on an iceberg.

After several minutes, the butler opened the door and stood aside. I started to walk in, but then Ethel came into view. "Oh, yes, when Mason mentioned a dog, I assumed it would be you. *Lovely.*" She cocked a hand on her hip, clearly debating. "Wait there. I'll not have your mutt inside, and if you're going to accuse me of murder, I might as well be warm." She spun around, and once again, the door shut in my face.

"This is too good to be true." Once again I looked toward Watson. "I wish Katie was here. She'd be getting a kick out of this."

Watson didn't share my sentiment and let me know by collapsing at my feet with an exaggeratedly bored sigh.

Several more minutes passed before Ethel emerged wearing a floor-length black fur. With the silver tips of the coat catching the sunlight, I was willing to bet it wasn't like Percival's boysenberry faux fur, but the real deal. A slice of pain cut through me at the thought of how many silver foxes gave their life for Ethel's dramatic moment. She practically floated to a seating area on the side of the porch and took her place in the center of a cushioned iron-and-log bench as if she was queen.

Only when I sat in the chair across from her, did I notice she held a martini glass in one hand. Once more, I let out a laugh, though I wasn't certain I'd attempted to hold it back. "Are you kidding me with this? Sitting on your throne, wearing a fur, drinking a martini in the early afternoon?" I was no longer that fourth-grade girl. I could say whatever I wanted. "Am I supposed to be impressed, jealous?"

She took a sip. "I don't know what you mean, Winifred. You came to see me. I hardly *prepared* for your arrival. If I had, I can promise you, I would've found some other location to be. But since you're here, please quit wasting my time. Get on with your accusations."

I hadn't come for accusations, not really, only for *reactions*. She had a point, though—might as well get on with it. "I spoke to Gerald. It turns out, his and Violet's disagreement revolved around you, in a manner of speaking. He wouldn't give her what she wanted. To buy his shares of *The Chipmunk Chronicles* so she could—"

"So what's your theory, Winifred? I killed Violet so she

couldn't challenge my leadership of the newspaper? You really are grasping at straws." She took another sip of her martini.

I'd been about to say, so Violet could be part owner of the paper with Ethel. To find out if Ethel had been aware of the reason behind Violet and Gerald's argument. I'd assumed she had been, and I wanted to make sure. This reaction didn't make sense. "Challenge your leadership?"

A puzzled expression crossed Ethel's face, then cleared. "You really aren't as good at this whole thing as everyone claims, are you?" She removed a clear plastic spear from her drink and pulled off one of the skewered olives with her teeth, then chewed as she studied me. "It's rather sad."

I tried to play catch-up, some of that belittled sensation beginning to return.

Violet hadn't wanted to... how had Gerald said it? Wanted to play CEO along with her best friend? It'd been some sort of competition? Some play for power over Ethel?

I managed not to verbalize any of those questions, refusing to give Ethel any more ammunition, and decided to go a different direction. "Clearly none of this is news to you. You were aware of what Violet was attempting to do?"

"Trust me, I'm not as inept or as ill-informed as you." She shifted in her seat, pulling the fur tighter around herself, while managing not to spill her drink—a feat I wouldn't have been able to accomplish—as she sneered at Watson. "I also have higher standards in my furry companions." She leaned slightly forward, addressing him. "You wouldn't even make a quality pair of earmuffs."

Watson peered up at her, twisting his head from side to side, not looking the least bit offended. I suddenly realized he was eyeing the remaining two olives, and I was relieved he didn't understand as much of conversations as I some-times thought he did.

Rage fueled through me at the insult, but I held it at bay. "So you knew and didn't mention it to me when we spoke the other day? If you were concerned about Violet attempting some sort of coup at the newspaper, that seems a little suspicious."

Ethel laughed, soft and cold. "So much arrogance you have. You own a forgettable bookshop, a property acquired by the help of your stepfather instead of your own making, I might add. You do not have a badge. You are not the police. You have no authority. You are absolutely... *nothing*. I owe you no explanations, no insights, no details, personal or otherwise... *nothing*. Not then, not now."

The rage that built began to circle back on myself for being unable to shake her effect on me for more than a few seconds. The flames grew even hotter as I heard a tremor in my voice when I spoke. "I'd think you'd want to do every-thing you could to help your friend find justice, even if she was attempting to be competition at the paper."

"Oh, my dear, dear Winifred. I do want justice for Violet. And she'll have it. But I have no hope of it coming from you." The smirk on her lips gave way to a thin, hard line.

There was something else to ask, some way to twist and return this conversation to get more details, to get more clar-ity, to get something. But I couldn't find it. Couldn't make my brain go where I wanted it to. It was frozen, caught in that old place it had always gotten snagged.

Ethel stood, adjusted her fur once more, and held what remained of her martini aloft, pinky lifted. "We're done now. Although, feel free to enjoy the view from out here for as long as you'd like." She floated toward us, then paused by my shoulder, not leaning down but lowering her voice to barely above a whisper. "The saddest thing, really, is that not only do you consider yourself above your station as a store clerk, but you're trying to be something that you can't be. I'd think you'd have learned from your father's example. *He* clearly wasn't very successful at it either."

I sat, stunned. Didn't even hear the door open, close, and lock behind her.

It was the first time anyone had used my father's death in the line of duty as an insult, as a slight against me, against *him*.

If I'd been in the *Real Housewives* world of Ethel Beaker, like Percival suggested she lived in, I would've done something more than sat frozen. I would've sprung up, knocked the glass from her hand, spilling the olive juice and vodka into her face and over her fur. Let her know in a million ways how despicable she really was.

But I wasn't in that world; that wasn't me. And even if I was, I couldn't make any part of me work, nothing more than demanding my legs stand and my feet slowly carry me to the car.

I slunk away, tail between my legs, as Watson scampered along beside me, *his* nub tail wagging happily, probably hoping we were heading toward food.

Doubtless, I was the only shop owner in all Estes Park who considered it divine intervention when the tourists slowed to a trickle the entire afternoon. I let Ben handle them all, which he was more than capable of, while I curled up on the antique sofa in the mystery room.

There were several aspects to the healing potion I required. Light filtering through the purple portobello shade of the Victorian lamp falling on the pages. The warmth and pleasant crackle of the flames in the river rock fireplace. Watson snoring peacefully away on the oversized ottoman. Katie's dirty chai in one hand, while my other flipped through the pages of a Sherlock Holmes novel. I hadn't cared which installment; I'd simply snagged one off the Sherlock Holmes shelf. In my mind, Sherlock Holmes looked an awful lot like my father. They'd been his favorite novels, and the two detectives had morphed into one being.

It worked, mostly, whether it was a spell or divine intervention. By late afternoon, I almost felt like myself again. Enough so, I began a mental reprimand for allowing Ethel Beaker such power over my emotional state.

I was able to shove that aside quickly enough. Self-flagellation wasn't going to help. Besides, the biggest impact hadn't been about me at all. I could've shaken that off fairly quickly, probably by the time I'd driven back downtown. It was the callous way she'd spoken about my father's murder. The mockery and belittlement in her tone. If anything, I was irritated that I wasn't struggling to sink into anger, resentment, or rage at her. That would've been easier. Instead, it just hurt and ached.

When the sunlight filtering through the window began to soften, announcing the sun would soon begin its colorful descent, my mother called, suggesting that the smart bet would be on divine intervention after all. As soon as I heard her voice on the other end of the line, my throat closed and my eyes stung.

Watson's snore broke off, and he lifted his head, looking at me in concern. I patted the spot beside me, and he made the small leap from ottoman to couch and curled against the side of my leg.

"Fred? Are you okay?"

Why hadn't I thought of her first? She'd been through the pain with me, every second of the way. Throat still clenched, I nodded.

"Fred?"

The concern in her tone forced my words. "Yes." I choked it out, then took a deep breath and found I was able to continue. "Just a rough afternoon. I'm reading Sherlock."

"Oh." She understood instantly. "Sweetheart."

We sat in silence for a few moments, and as if the cell phone was a portal, I could feel her beside me. It was the last injection of strength I needed before I truly became my father's daughter once more.

No more wallowing. The best revenge was to rise above. It was time to get back to it. Figure out who killed Violet, and while I wouldn't rub it in Ethel's face, she'd know, and that would be enough.

And I knew where I wanted to begin again—exactly where I'd planned on starting that morning all along. "Mom, would you come with me to see Joan?"

She didn't hesitate. "Of course. I should swing by there again anyway."

That time, I called first.

When Joan opened the door for Mom, Watson, and me, it was clear the warning hadn't helped. If I thought she looked broken when I'd been there before, it was nothing to the state she was in. I doubted she'd showered. Portions of her short gray hair matted flat against her head while others poked out at odd angles. Her red eyes were so puffy it was amazing she could see through them. Her clothes were a mess, and she smelled.

When she fell sobbing into Mom's arms, Mom held her tight, not concerned about the odor or the river of tears and snot running down Joan's face. She simply wrapped one arm around Joan's back and cradled Joan's head with her other hand. She whispered soothingly, "I know, sweetie. I do. Believe me, I know."

And she did. Mom knew what it was like to wake up one day with everything normal, then by bedtime the entire world had changed, to have that reason be because someone else stole the one you loved from you. As Mom led Joan to the couch, I shut and locked the door, and then Watson and I followed. Unlike the last time, he kept his distance, clearly remembering being trapped in Joan's embrace for entirely too long the other day. From the way he watched Mom cradle Joan from his spot by the fireplace, I thought I saw sympathy in his eyes—for *Mom*.

From what I could see of the house, it had fallen into

shambles in direct correlation to Joan's appearance. There were sections of the table and floor that were not visible underneath the tissues. Photo albums were spread everywhere, though the wedding album was still front and center on the coffee table. A wineglass sat on the mantle. Several bottles littered the room, looking as if Joan had neglected the niceties of a middleman and started drinking directly from the source.

The biggest change, however, was that a majority of the pottery pieces were now shattered, littering the perimeter of the room, dents in the walls here and there, revealing where they'd been thrown. My heart hurt at the sight, knowing Joan would regret such an outburst later. That she'd probably riddle herself with guilt for having destroyed things her wife had made. There were some that still remained intact, at least.

It was a long time before Joan settled, going through several more tissues and a couple of glasses of water. Finally, still sitting close to Mom, Joan looked at each of us in turn. "I'm sorry. I'm such a mess. Such a mess." Her voice was raw, and she peered over at Watson. "I'm probably scaring him to death."

"Don't you worry about that. Watson's tough, and surprisingly understanding when someone's hurting." Mom patted her knee. "Don't worry about Fred or me either. We've suffered loss. I'm sure you remember about my dear Charles."

Confusion flitted over Joan's face, but after a few blinks, she nodded. "Oh, yes. Of course." She smiled, a little. "Maybe it's horrible to say, but that helps some. Knowing that people have gone through this and survived. I... don't think I will."

"You will." Mom nodded assuredly. "Don't think about

the future. Not even tomorrow. Go hour by hour, or minute by minute if you need to. You have my number, you can call anytime." She reached out again, squeezing Joan's knee, and waited until the woman looked her in the face. "I mean it. *Anytime*."

"Thank you." Joan wiped her eyes with the back of her hand and glanced around the room. "Oh my..." She choked out another laugh, though that wasn't quite the right word for it. "Violet would kill me if she could see this. She always demanded the house be kept perfect."

That surprised me, considering the messes she was notorious for at the Koffee Kiln. I latched on to it, though, anxious to feel useful. "Why don't I start picking up? That might help things feel a little more normal."

"That's a great idea." Mom started to stand.

"No." Joan reached out in desperation, grasping Mom's hand. "Please don't. Just... sit with me."

Mom returned to her seat, and after a second, I did as well.

Joan's gaze flitted to the file I held. Her brows creased, and then she looked at me, eyes widening. "You found something, haven't you? You know who—"

"No." I cut her off, wanting to dash her expectations before they could rise too high. "Not yet. This isn't about who..." I shook my head, stopping the train of thought. I debated telling her, but then decided to give her the choice. "These are photos. I saw Athena at the newspaper, and she printed a few off she thought you might like."

Again, Joan's eyes widened. "Of Violet?" For the first time, a grain of hope sounded in her voice.

I nodded. "They're some images they had on file throughout the years." Since it was clear from her reaction Joan wanted to see them, I rose, crossed the room, and sat on her other side, bookending her between Mom and myself. I handed the file to Joan, so that she could decide how to look through them.

She put it on her lap and opened it instantly. The wedding photo with the two maids of honor was on top, and she sighed, which was a relief. I'd feared she'd start crying again instantly. She gestured toward the album on the coffee table. "I already have this photo, but in color. I think I prefer this black-and-white version. A little more timeless somehow." She pointed to the young woman who stood beside her. "This is my sister, Katherine. She passed a few years ago. I've wished she was with me several times over the last few days." She looked over at me, leaning closer as if telling me a secret. "This was on the front page of the newspaper. *Front page*! Quite the scandal, let me tell you, but we didn't care. We were proud—of our love, our marriage, making history." She chuckled a little, clearly seeing back through the years. "I think it made it even more scandalous that we got married the week before Christmas, so this came out in the Christmas Eve edition. We hadn't done that intentionally, but... *goodness*... how some people claimed it was even more blasphemous to have such happenings around the holiday."

Joan flipped through a few more photos, pausing at each one, taking the time to explain whichever event it was shot at, little things she remembered about the evening, the dinner they'd shared, a spat they'd had around the same time, a vacation they'd been getting ready to go on.

When she came to the Fourth of July picture, Joan gasped and covered her mouth, pulling the picture closer with her other hand. "Oh..." She sighed again, and a tear made its way down her cheek. "I've never seen this."

"Me neither." Mom leaned in as well, a reminiscent

smile playing on her lips. "My goodness, look at us. Babies, absolute babies." Chuckling, she pointed at Percival and glanced over at me. "You can't tell here, obviously, but those suspenders he was wearing? Bright pink. He was never subtle."

"Isn't she stunning? The most beautiful woman I've ever seen." Joan didn't seem to notice Mom's words as she traced the young Violet's beautiful face, over her hair, down her legs, and then started again. Though more tears fell, a wistful smile played on her lips. "She wore her hair down. She only did that for me on our wedding day because I begged. She hated it down. Said it made her feel less mature, somehow, less important. She always felt that having it up conveyed power and strength." She traced the hair again. "But look at it, *at her*. She takes your breath away. She—" Joan's voice broke then, and her hand trembled so hard the picture shook.

Mom slipped an arm over her shoulders. "It's okay, sweetie. You can feel whatever you need to feel. We're here. You're not alone."

"I'm never alone, hardly." Joan croaked out a laugh. "People are so kind. Still dropping off more food than I'll ever be able to eat. And, of course Rachel is here several times a day. It both helps and hinders having someone hurting almost as much as me."

"Rachel is still struggling?" Maybe there was a strange sound in my voice, as Mom gave me a quizzical expression.

Joan didn't seem to notice. "Yes. I think she's a little lost, honestly. She thought the world of Violet, looked up to her." She closed her eyes in a painful wince. "Honestly, every time I see her, for a second I think Violet's back. The way Rachel does her hair, it's almost like—" Another wince but her words trailed off.

Though I felt guilty risking causing Joan more pain, I pushed. "Did Violet and Rachel know each other for very long? I had the impression that Rachel was new to town?"

"Hm?" Joan opened her eyes, seemed to struggle then nodded. "Oh, yes. She is. Rachel only moved here recently. Her wife left her late last summer, so Rachel started over here in Estes. She's teaching art at the school." A smile played on her face as she motioned toward the corner of the room. "That's how the two of them met. Art. One of Violet's brief obsessions was macramé. Rachel taught her."

Turning, I found a rather hideous woven web where Joan had pointed. As there was a fern nestled in the center, I assumed it was supposed to be a planter. It looked like all art Violet attempted was of the abstract variety. I stared at the horrid mess, some fuzzy picture trying to clarify in my mind. "Joan... did Rachel always wear her hair in a bun?"

Before she could answer, a knock sounded, causing Watson to leap up and bark, startling all of us out of the moment.

"I can get that." I looked toward the door then back to Joan. "Or... do you want to ignore it?"

Anger flashed in her eyes. "Would you? If it's that Brody Bridges again, tell him that if he comes within so much as a hundred yards of my house, I'm calling the police."

Mom flinched in surprise at the hostility, but gave me a shrug.

"Okay... um..." I stood. "If it's someone else?"

"Please take their name and tell them I'll call them back and that I appreciate them stopping by." Joan's voice still trembled in anger.

Watson followed me to the door, but when I opened it, no one was there. It wasn't till I noticed the van driving away that I peered out onto the porch. A box sat by the door. I picked it up and carried it inside. I'd already rounded the corner within view of the sofa when I saw the return label. I should've checked first, I could've run it to my car, lied and said it had been a flyer or something.

"A delivery?" Some of the anger left Joan's tone. "I haven't ordered anything. That must be..." She shook her head and closed her eyes, tears squeezing free.

"I'll put it in the—"

"No!" Joan nearly sprung up. "Bring it to me. Bring it here."

I did as she asked, once more wishing I'd been a little more careful.

Joan broke again, as her suspicions were confirmed. "I swear, Violet spent a fortune over the last month with this company." As she had the photo before, Joan lovingly traced the Pottery Incorporated label.

Mom gave her a few moments, letting the fresh wave of tears begin to soften, and then attempted to distract her. "Joan, who is Brody Bridges? Someone harassing you?"

I hadn't caught it the first time, but as the man's name left my mother's lips, it clicked. I'd *just* heard about Brody Bridges. "He's the founder of *The Chipmunk Chronicles*' grandson."

"Yes." Joan nearly spit the word. "He dropped by the house yesterday, and I turned him away. Then, he had the audacity to call today."

"Do you know what he wants?" I had a feeling I knew.

Mom looked at me in surprise again, probably hearing an awareness in my voice, but once more didn't say a thing.

"He told me yesterday that Violet approached him about buying his shares to the newspaper, of all ridiculous things. He told me that he'd reconsidered and was willing to accept her offer." Joan punched at the label on the package. "I don't know where he got that idea. Violet wasn't interested in the newspaper. All she could think about was pottery. That was it."

That astounded me. I would've assumed Joan had known about Violet's attempt to own stock in the newspaper. Though, she'd clearly been genuine the other day when she'd claimed not to know why Violet and Gerald had had a disagreement.

I felt bad pushing again, but I had to. "What did he say today when he called?"

Again Mom gave me that look, but it only held curiosity, no reprimand.

Joan didn't notice. "He told me that if I wanted to buy it from him, he'd lower the price even further. Apparently, he needs the cash. I told him to choke on it."

Mom rubbed Joan's back, and though her voice was soothing to Joan, her gaze stayed on me. "It's all right, dear. That wasn't him. I bet he got the message loud and clear when he called today. And if he bothers you again, I think you're right, just call the authorities."

As Mom distracted Joan by returning to the stack of photos, I began to mull over the puzzle pieces in my mind, shifting them around here and there.

Violet hadn't been able to agree to a price with Gerald about his shares in the paper, and had the same result with Brody. But if she'd lived, she would've been able to purchase Brody's 20 percent. I imagined with that accomplished, she would've been more amenable to Gerald's demand. She'd also invest in his scheme in order to purchase his shares. With those together, Violet would've had 60 percent of the holdings of *The Chipmunk Chroni-*

cles, to Ethel's forty. She'd have been majority shareholder and would've held the power.

Had Ethel known Violet approached Brody?

Surely Ethel wouldn't have killed her friend over stock in a small-town newspaper. I'd reached new levels of loathing of Ethel Beaker, but I couldn't imagine her killing *anyone* for such a ridiculous reason.

But... maybe the reason only seemed ridiculous to me. Perhaps there was something more to *The Chipmunk Chronicles* than people knew.

"I didn't realize dating you would turn me into a celebrity." Leo watched Marcus Gonzales walk away from our table, flicking through the photos the server had taken of the three of us. "It's kind of strange, really. How many times have we eaten here with Katie and not had our picture taken?"

"I guess it puts you in a different status or something in Marcus's eyes. Feels like every time my family and I come here, we're subjected to a photo shoot before we're allowed to eat." I scooped a large portion of melted queso onto my tortilla chips. "More than anything, it shows my love of cheese that I'm willing to endure it so frequently."

"You have good taste." Leo helped himself to an equally heaping portion. "If there ever is a murder at Habaneros, it's going to be a real shame if Marcus is the victim and he has to miss all the hoopla."

"You know—" I paused, taking a second to swipe a little of the cheese dip off his chin with my thumb. "—that might be the only way Marcus could get murdered and not be upset by it. I can't help but think he'd be pleased about all the attention somehow."

"You're probably right." Leo snagged my hand and made a show of putting my thumb between his lips and cleaning up the cheese.

I sat there, frozen, wide-eyed.

"Okay. I've seen that on movies and stuff before. They always make it look so romantic." Leo glanced around at the other tables and blushed brighter than I'd ever seen him. "It isn't."

Though I tried not to, I broke out laughing. "No. It really isn't." I grabbed his hand across the table, though, a happy warmth spreading through me. "Thank you, Leo."

Still his blush burned. "For what? Being embarrassingly inept at all of this?"

"Yes." The word burst from me with such heartfelt emotion that I laughed again, and so did Leo. "No, actually, you're not inept, not at all. But you're not smooth and practiced. You're you. That makes it okay for me to be me."

With a smile, he linked his fingers into mine. "Then I'm glad for it. You being you is the only thing I want."

There was such sincerity in his words that I felt my cheeks heat. "See? Not inept at all."

His gaze met mine, held, and I could see something begin to build, but then he blinked and it was gone. When he spoke, his voice trembled slightly, like he was nervous. "What do you think the dog party is up to right now?"

It took me a moment to catch up—the dog party clearly wasn't what he'd actually been thinking. "I imagine Watson is torn, struggling to decide if he's annoyed or beside himself with happiness."

"I'd say you're right." Leo's smile relaxed somewhat, and his voice returned to normal. "We should have asked them to videotape it. Those four could start their own puppy sitcom on YouTube."

"They probably could." Athena and Pearl were getting together with Paulie and his two corgis, Flotsam and Jetsam. They'd invited Watson. He'd grown to care about the two corgis, but they were both like toddlers on speed and tended to wear Watson out quickly. However, I figured he'd be happy enough to be with Pearl that Leo and I were safe to have an extended dinner before I picked him up. "Oh, I forgot. Susan called in between me dropping Watson off and meeting you here."

Leo instantly went serious. "Did she make an arrest?"

"No. Even Marcus's hoopla wouldn't have been able to make me forget that." I took another chip. "They've gotten the main round of results back from Violet's autopsy. There're a few tests that won't come back for another four or five weeks, of course, but the majority are done." I started to dip a chip into the cheese, then discarded it on my plate, realizing I had too much to say. "There wasn't much information. Nothing we hadn't already speculated about anyway. They confirmed Violet died of suffocation, which is what we figured. They did find trace particles of clay in her airway and lungs. That could confirm Simone's plastic bag theory, but it also could just be a buildup from the exorbitant amount of time Violet spent at the pottery studio."

Leo nodded, considering slowly as he chewed. "No other trauma? Nothing to indicate impact or poisoning?"

"No. Although her blood alcohol level was high." I shrugged. "That isn't too surprising either, considering the one glass and the two bottles of wine on scene."

"Well, if she was that inebriated, that would've made suffocation quite a bit easier. She might've put up less of a struggle."

I nodded at his theory. "A thought Susan and I discussed as well. She suggested that Violet was a lightweight, that she might've been passed out at the time. But I don't think so. Judging from the wine bottles scattered around the house when Mom and I went to visit Joan yesterday, I think alcohol was a plentiful commodity with the two of them."

Leo and I paused as a waitress brought out our dinners —pork carnitas for Leo, and cheese enchiladas for me. There was a good chance if my body had to undergo an autopsy anytime soon, they would find that the blood in my veins had been replaced with chocolate, espresso, and cheese.

I waited until the waitress refilled our drinks and wandered away before continuing as we ate. "It really didn't answer much. Although, it didn't raise a lot more questions either, so I suppose that's something. Neither Susan nor I think Gerald is much of a possibility, despite how angry he is—*was* at Violet. Susan's considering Ethel, but..." I took a second, having to twirl my fork to capture the stringy cheese stretching in the air from my enchiladas as I considered. "I don't think I'm in the place to see Ethel clearly right now, and I'm not sure I can fight against how I'm feeling about her so that I don't miss the facts."

"I don't know. I've not been around her very much, but from what I've seen, I wouldn't put it past her." Leo had yet to take a bite of his food, as he was shredding the carnitas with his fork and then building a feast on the homemade corn tortillas. When he spoke next, his voice was hesitant. "You've gone back and forth considering Simone. Where are you falling on her?"

"I hadn't really considered her. Plus, she has you vouching for her. And the rest of the Pink Panthers. I was starting to wonder about Rachel. She's so—" I halted abruptly, realizing what I was doing.

Leo had been about to take a bite but stopped with the taco halfway to his lips. "What's wrong?"

I considered playing it off, then decided to lay it all out

on the table. "We're on a date. And all I'm doing is talking about murder and suspects."

He shrugged, clearly unconcerned. "So what? Just because we're dating doesn't mean we change who we are. That's part of the beauty of it. We don't have to spend time with all that small talk and trying to get to know each other. We already do. We've known each other very well for a long time now, and this"—he gestured back and forth between us with this free hand as if there were tangible clues scattered around the table—"is part of what we've always done. It'd be weird if we didn't, simply because we were on a date, don't you think? A little unauthentic." Finally he took a bite, a big one, then spoke with his mouth full. "This is worth getting our pictures taken every time we come here."

Laughing a little, I relaxed. He was right. This was who we were, and part of what we did. But though I hadn't planned on the change between us, I loved it and wanted to nurture it. "True enough, but"—I motioned sticking it to the wall—"I'm putting a pin in it."

He swallowed. "Works for me."

An unusually awkward silence fell instantly between us, and I was tempted to jerk the pin right back out.

After another bite or so, Leo came to the rescue, and when his gaze met mine, there was a shy expression in his eyes. "So... I ah... mentioned you to my mom when she called a couple of days ago."

I jolted. "You did?"

He nodded, biting his lower lip for a second. "She said you should come meet the family."

I quite literally felt the blood drain from my face. "She did?"

He chuckled. "That might be the most terrified I've ever seen you."

I was willing to bet he was right. Though I wasn't entirely sure why. I hadn't heard all the details of Leo's childhood and family, but I knew that things hadn't been easy, and their relationship remained tense. That there were still some hard feelings and resentments.

"You know, I've met *your* family." He gave a crooked grin. "Once or twice."

"Yeah, but that's different. You've always known my family, way before we started dating. At this point you *are* part of the family."

That crooked grin softened to something tender, as did his voice. "Yeah, I know." He captured my hand again, his gaze intense and sincere. "You are worth everything, all on your own. But your family is a huge bonus. It's amazing to see people who love each other so much."

The hostess came by, seating another couple at the table a few feet from ours, drawing our attention away and causing me to lower my voice when I refocused on Leo. "I'll meet your family whenever you want." It shouldn't feel like that big a deal. It really shouldn't. Everything between Leo and me already felt so settled, but... meeting his family.

"You can breathe." He winked. "I appreciate the offer, but it won't be anytime soon. I saw them at Christmas, remember? Spreading out the visits is the best way to ensure my sanity remains intact."

"Well... say the word whenever you want us to do that." My nerves spiked at the thought. It had been so long since I'd been introduced to anyone's parents. Things hadn't gone well when I'd met Garrett's family. But Leo wasn't Garrett, and I wasn't the same Winifred Page that I was then. Thank goodness!

"The girls were all sharing horror stories about meeting

their significant others' families yesterday." Leo chuckled. "Looks like you might have a few of those yourself."

Garrett and his family fled from my mind. "The girls?"

"Didn't I tell you?" He cocked his head. "The Pink Panthers came to the park yesterday to take a snowshoe tour."

"Oh. No, I don't think you did." I swallowed.

"Fred..." Leo hesitated, unsure. "Does that... bother you?"

"What? Does what bother me?" The words came out a little too quickly, as unconvincing as if Gerald Jackson had tried to play them off before a jury.

Leo met my gaze, completely sincere. "They don't compare to you, Winifred Page. Not one of them."

For the second time in as many days, I battled with the demons of my past. They were so much weaker than they used to be, but... still there. I'd never been the popular girl, the beautiful one. I'd been tall, "big-boned," bookish, and smart. And though I was confident in myself now, some of those insecurities bit at me around women like Delilah and Simone. But it was ridiculous, and a fiction of my own shadows, not reality. That time, I met Leo's gaze and let him see the truth in my words and the vulnerability in my eyes. "It's not a comparison game, Leo. More like stuff from childhood that we try to outgrow and yet still comes back from time to time."

"Trust me, I understand fully." I knew that he did. His expression shifted somewhat, growing hesitant. "If my friendship with—"

"No." I cut him off. "Don't even finish that thought. That's not what we're doing. And that's not the kind of relationship we'll have. Either one of us."

"I only want to make sure you know—"

I shook my head again, and when I spoke, I meant it with every fiber of my being. "I was controlled in my marriage. Garrett wasn't abusive, but I did what I was told in a lot of ways. To this day I still can't figure out why I allowed that to happen. That isn't how I was raised, and it goes against every bit of my real personality, but"—I shrugged—"whatever. I swore I would never be in that situation again, not even a little bit. And I'm not going to turn the tables, where I'm the one controlling either. I might have some issues lingering around the *cool girls* and whatnot, but they're *my* issues. Ones that I work on getting over a little more every day. We are both allowed to be friends with whoever we want to be friends with. I trust you, and you trust me. And that's that."

Leo's grin was so wide and bright it was almost ridiculous, as was how handsome it made him. His beautiful eyes beamed. "You really are spectacular."

I snorted. And really, what else would I do in such an intimate moment?

"You are." He touched my cheek with his thumb in that way of his. "Fred, you're spectacular. You're real, strong, fallible, brave." I saw it in his eyes, knew it was coming, and my heart leapt. "Winifred Page, I—"

"Are you kidding me? You think I'm going to that witch's funeral?"

As one, Leo and I both looked toward the angry voice at the table beside us.

The man glared at his date—I glanced down and adjusted my perception of the two—his *wife*, judging from the wedding ring. His voice was cutting and bitter. "The only reason I'd go is to dance on her grave. Don't tell me we need to do it for appearances either. The whole town knows what a crook that woman was. I didn't listen, and I should've."

"Andrew, she's dead." His wife sounded heated as well. "Let it go. You being stubborn won't bring the money back. In fact, it'll be noticed that you're not there. It will hurt business. You'll get a reputation."

"Then you go." The man, Andrew, apparently, sat back in his chair and folded his arms like a pouting child. "Get all dressed up in black and pretend to grieve. I'll stay home, contact a lawyer, figure out if we can squeeze any dimes from that widow of hers. We had a contract."

Leo and I exchanged glances, and then I couldn't help myself. "Excuse me..."

The couple glanced over, both appearing startled and annoyed at being interrupted.

"Are you talking about Violet Yates?"

The woman blushed, but the man only glared harder. "What of it?"

I scrambled with what to say. Most of the time it was easy; it seemed everyone recognized me. Maybe it was because Watson wasn't with me that the couple didn't instantly know I was looking into Violet's death.

Leo jumped in. "A friend of mine did business with Violet. She stiffed him. Sounds like she did the same to you?"

It took all my effort not to give Leo an impressed smile, instead I stayed focused on the man.

"See?" He turned to his wife, gesturing toward us. "The whole town knows what she was like." He turned back to Leo. "She sure did. I spent the last two weeks getting her blueprints exactly how she wanted them. After she got them, she claimed to find some error, refused to let me adjust them, and then said she wasn't going to pay. Then, just to be an inconvenience, got herself killed that night."

Blueprints? Maybe this was the contractor she'd used to do some things at the house. "What was the project?"

He turned his annoyed eyes on me, but bit out the words. "A pottery studio and coffee shop. It was stupid. And I told her so, though not in so many words. The town already has one of those. It's not like Estes Park is some sprawling metropolis and we can support five of every type of business."

Surely I was hearing him wrong. "She was going to build a new pottery studio and coffee shop? Like the Koffee Kiln?"

"Not exactly like it—three times as big. Fanciest thing I've ever designed." He glared at his wife once more. "And it took me about three times as long to perfect as normal as well, *without* pay. The only way I'm going to that funeral is if I can dig around in her casket for change."

I waited until after the breakfast rush before I called Susan the next day. I meant to do it first thing, but the morning had gotten away from me. As Katie listened, I informed Susan what Leo and I had learned the night before and attempted to share a few of the theories we'd come up with.

"Your timing is perfect, and it fits with what I was told not three hours ago." Susan cut me off. "Alex saw them going into the shop the night of the murder. Took the sniveling little coward this long to tell me, but better late than never."

"Alex?" I was struggling to play catch-up.

"Alex Hines." Susan's annoyance was clear. "The little shrimp that took over Petra's ice cream parlor."

"Oh..." That did add another angle. "He's certain it was *that* night? Do the times match up? Maybe we should—"

"Haven't I told you we're not partners? You're not a cop." Her words were sharper, harder. "You're skilled and you're smart, and I appreciate that. And I will work together with you because I'm not a fool. But I warned you, this isn't a partnership. You don't get a vote. It's a dictatorship, and you get one guess who the big kahuna is."

In some ways the clear-cut ease of our despising each other had been simpler.

She didn't wait for me to confirm or argue. "Meet me at the Koffee Kiln in"—she was probably checking the time —"fifteen... no, twenty-five minutes."

"Susan, wait, I—" That time, I interrupted myself. She'd just said we weren't partners, yet she wanted me there?

"Oh, and bring the fleabag."

That threw me off even more. "Watson?"

"Good grief, you're dense. Yes, Watson. Unless that's your pet name for your new boyfriend."

"Why in the world do you want me to bring Watson?"

"Because"—that time I could hear pleasure in her voice, anticipation—"it'll irritate them. That's how I'll get a confession, or at least enough confirmation. Nothing makes people crack like getting flustered and angry. Well, pain does too, but unfortunately, torture is frowned upon."

"But I really think—"

"Twenty-five minutes. Sharp." She hung up the phone.

Katie grimaced at me from the other side of the bakery counter. "That didn't sound pleasant."

"I can't believe I'm going to say this, but I think I miss the days when Branson was feeding me information one second and then telling me to keep my nose out of it the next."

Her grimace deepened, and then she straightened and pulled something out from under the counter. "It sounds like you're going to need fortification."

I stared at the freshly baked chocolate espresso torte, considered reminding her once more of the issues that raised, then decided pastry was going to be the least of the conflict. "Fine, just make it a big piece. I'm talking large enough to be used as a weapon."

"And that's why I love you." She beamed as she pulled out a huge knife. "Let's make that two."

. . .

At twenty-five minutes on the dot, Watson and I walked up to the front door of the Koffee Kiln at the exact same moment as Susan.

She nodded in approval and reached for the door.

"Susan, slow down. I really—"

Casting me a glare, she threw open the door and strode in.

Feeling like there was no other option, I followed, Watson right beside me.

"All right!" Susan strode to the center of the space and raised both her hands in the air, then gestured toward the door. "Everyone out. Now!"

Silence fell instantly. Every tourist occupying the tables gaped at her, frozen in their seats.

Watson growled nervously.

"I said *now!*" Susan lowered her hand toward the barrel of her holstered weapon. People sprang from their seats and started to move. At the last second, Susan adjusted and hooked her thumb through the belt loop of her pants.

She was slick.

"You listen here!" For the first time, I noticed Ethel as she hurried around the counter. Behind her, Carla and Simone followed. "I agreed to meet you here, Lord knows why, but I did *not* agree to..." As her gaze found me, her words fell away, and her eyes narrowed. "What is this?"

"It's our first day open again. Are you trying to run us out of business?" Carla sounded desperate, and then she too noticed me, though her glare settled on Watson. "Oh... you are." She looked up at me again, then returned to Susan. "When did you two team up?"

"We are *not* a team." Susan bit out the words and

pointed to Simone, then to the door. "You leave too. This has nothing to do with…" She blinked and shook her head. "Actually, it might. Stay where you are." She pointed to the door again. "Fred, lock it."

"Susan, if we could—"

She sent me a cold stare from her pale blue eyes.

I shut my mouth and followed directions, locking the door after the last tourists left. Susan and I were going to have a chat. We might not be partners, but this dictator thing wasn't going to fly.

"Officer Green." Simone approached, her voice cool, calm, strong. "I know I'm new to town, but this isn't protocol. There're such things as rights, and those are being violated. You can't storm in and close up shop."

Susan balked, clearly not expecting to be spoken back to. For a second I thought she was going to argue, but she couldn't. Simone wasn't wrong. Finally, Susan gestured toward the door yet again. "I'm not going to shoot anyone if you open it. No one had to obey. No one is under arrest. Feel free to open it up and invite everyone back in." She refocused on Carla and Ethel. "I have *no* problem making an arrest in public. It'll make a great picture on the front page of the paper, don't you think?"

Simone had already started to walk toward the door, but Ethel called out, stopping her, and then turned toward Susan, pure fury over her features. Susan had said she wanted to make them angry. "What nonsense is this about arresting anyone? None of us have done anything illegal."

Susan didn't play around any longer. "We have a reliable witness who can place you and your daughter-in-law"—her gaze flicked to Carla—"right here on the night of the murder."

At one point, Susan and Carla had seemed like friends,

or at least friendly with each other. I wondered what had happened.

"Utter rubbish." Ethel's nose went imperiously into the air, as was its tendency. But I saw surprise flash across Carla's face, then fear.

Beside her, I realized Simone had noticed as well—her eyes narrowing in confusion before her defensive posture relaxed somewhat.

Proving that though we had different methods, Susan was good at her job, she hadn't missed it either. "You sure it's rubbish, Carla?"

Carla's mouth worked silently as she dragged a trembling hand through her hair, her sharp bangs falling right back into place.

Ethel glared at her. "You really are pathetic."

"I'll take that as a confirmation." Susan grinned, keeping her thumb hooked in the loop, next to her handgun.

"So what?" Ethel whipped back around, sneering at Susan. "It's Carla's shop. We can be here whenever we want."

I was surprised. I hadn't thought the scheme would work, not that I'd fully understood it. Neither was I confident that Alex was a reliable witness. He wouldn't lie—at least my impression of him was that he was honest to a fault —but he was nervous, skittish, and timid. There was a good chance he'd gotten confused or blended nights together after hearing about Violet's murder. Apparently not.

"True. You can." Susan took a step forward, using her much larger frame as an intimidation tactic toward the wispy woman. "But if it was innocent, why did neither of you mention it to me at the time? Or bring it up when you had interactions with Ms. Page as well?"

"Did you deputize little Nancy Drew now?" Ethel

wasn't the least bit intimidated by Susan. She turned hate-filled eyes on me. "I don't know what your game is and what twisted lies you're hoping to pin on us here, but I can promise you, little girl, you don't want to mess with me. I am *so* far out of your league."

Also realizing she wasn't going to intimidate Ethel, Susan stepped around her, trying the same approach on Carla. "Fess up, or we'll take this down to the station. And I'm sure there're still a few tourists lingering outside who will be happily snapping photos of our mini parade."

Carla broke. "We met here. It's true. And Violet was already in the back room as she was almost every night."

"Carla, be still, idiot." The venom in Ethel's tone toward her daughter-in-law brought to mind Simone mentioning how horribly Carla was treated.

Carla hesitated but finally shook her head. "What's the point? We've already been seen. We might as well fess up, or it'll just get worse."

"Then the deal is off."

Carla flinched and stared at Ethel as if she'd been slapped. "But this isn't my fault."

"What deal?" Susan repositioned herself between the two women.

Carla looked utterly defeated, cast an accusing glance toward Watson and me, and then sank down onto one of the seats. "I asked Ethel to meet me here that night because I wanted her to invest in something, or to allow me to borrow money. And I didn't want Jonathan to know. He stayed home with Maverick, and I told him Simone and I were going to be working here at the shop."

Susan moved even closer, though it seemed unnecessary. Carla was already broken. "Invest in what?"

"I can't keep up the note on my grandparents' old

house, so... I want to turn it into an Estes Park museum of sorts." Tears threatened at the corners of her eyes. "I know my grandpa didn't make great choices, but he loves this town, at least used to, and my grandma loved it till her dying breath. I was going to name it after her. Dolana's House." The tears fell then.

Ethel made a disgusted sound.

"That doesn't make any sense. Why would that need to be secret?" For the first time, Susan sounded unsure.

"You think I want my name associated with Dolana and Harold White's property? It's bad enough that my grandchild shares their blood."

I stared in horror at Ethel. She was so much worse than I could fathom.

As if feeling it, she looked at me and then toward Susan and Simone—both were wearing matching expressions to my own, I imagined. Ethel just laughed. "Go ahead and judge. Like I care about your opinions. You're all trash."

I didn't attempt to keep my disgust from showing. "Then why agree to help at all?"

"Because, I—" Carla spoke up, a dawning light of hope —or defiance, I couldn't tell—in her eyes.

"Shut up!" Ethel looked capable of growing fangs.

Carla shut her mouth, but still she glared.

Susan looked between the two, then seemed to skip over the moment as she focused on Carla, her voice a little softer. "So what happened? None of this proves you didn't kill Violet. You admitted you were here at the same time."

Simone started to protest, but Carla was already speaking. "Ethel wanted to see the place before deciding, so we drove out to my grandparents' house, and I showed her what I was thinking. She agreed to it, as long as I told everyone, Jonathan included, that I got the loan from a private investor." Again her eyes flashed at Ethel, a mix of warning and betrayal.

It took everything in me to stay where I was, to not go to Carla and offer comfort. She was so clearly humiliated and in pain. All she ever would've had to do was ask Barry and Mom. They would've been all over that idea. Not that Carla would ever lower herself to ask for help from anyone associated with me. And I hated that I'd added to her embarrassment and pain. I should've made Susan listen to me.

"It's a mostly plausible story, at least for the Beaker family. However, there're still some other glitches." Susan grew hard once again, surprising me.

Before I could protest, Simone beat me to it. "What else could there be? This seems clear enough, and"—she looked at Ethel in disgust—"believable as well, unfortunately."

Though I dropped Watson's leash before I headed toward Susan, he followed at my heels. "Susan, why don't we—"

Cutting me off, Susan wheeled toward Ethel once more. "You also failed to mention that Violet was attempting to own 60 percent of the newspaper. Not only had she approached Gerald, but Brody as well. That would've put her in a position of power over you."

"*Also* none of your business." Ethel was calm and cool once more. "Even if Violet had succeeded, it wasn't a big deal. I've always been able to handle her."

Handle her?

"It looks like you did. Permanently." Susan gestured toward the back room, but didn't let up, this time addressing Carla again as well, the moment of softness gone. "And isn't it funny that Violet had finished her plans to open another pottery and coffee shop, got them the night she died? A bigger and better shop, as if one wasn't too many already."

"She what?" Simone's reaction was pure shock.

Carla didn't protest, nor did she demonstrate even a modicum of Simone's surprise. *So... she had known...*

Susan went in for the kill. "You couldn't have that, could you? You had to close down your first coffee shop in shame because of your grandfather, and because it wasn't half as good as the Cozy Corgi."

Carla and I flinched as one, and her gaze flicked to me in hatred. I hadn't expected Susan to go there, but she wasn't done.

"And you *just* opened this place, and it was about to slip through your fingers in a matter of months." Susan cast a grin toward Ethel. "Your best friend was going to overthrow you at the paper and overthrow your daughter-in-law's business. And while you clearly don't care about Carla in the slightest, she's still a Beaker, whether you like it or not. So you couldn't have that, could you?"

"We... I didn't kill Violet." Pure exhaustion weighted down Carla's words, and she started to look toward Ethel, but her gaze stopped short.

"You knew?" Simone seemed to have found her voice as she stepped closer, the metal coils in her dreads clicking together. For the first time, Watson didn't growl at the sound. "You knew this whole time that Violet was going to try to steal our business from us?"

Carla didn't look at her business partner, but addressed Susan once more. "*I* didn't kill her."

"No, I didn't think you had." Susan's gaze was trained on Ethel. "But you didn't stop it, Carla, and that makes you an accessory to murder."

"You think you're so smart, don't you?" Ethel leered at

Susan, but only for a second before settling on me. "I'll have both your badge and the bookshop. Trust me."

Susan pulled her thumb from the belt loop and moved her hands toward the handcuffs. "Carla and Ethel Beaker, you're under—"

"If you even *think* of touching me with those things, I'll murder you here and now." Ethel stood royally and snapped her fingers at Carla. "Get up and quit sniveling."

"Threatening isn't going to do you much good, Ethel." Susan pulled the handcuffs free. "If you attempt to resist, Officer Jackson is right around the corner."

"You'd love that." Ethel snapped her fingers again, and that time Carla obeyed. "We will walk, *without* handcuffs. So it's up to you, *Officer* Green. We can go easily, or I'll make it where I have a million more reasons to hold against you when I take that badge of yours."

Carla lifted her hands, a pleading in her tired voice. "We'll go, but... let us..." Her words were lost in tears.

To my surprise, that seemed to win Susan over, maybe some lingering remnants of their friendship. "Fine. But if either of you try to make a run for it, I'm not afraid to fire my weapon."

Ethel rolled her eyes. "Insulting *and* boring." Without waiting for Susan, she strode toward the front door, then paused for a split second beside Watson and me. "You will regret this, little girl. And so will your mutt."

"Look how handsome you are, even if you were grumpy." Leo shifted Watson in his left arm so he could use his right hand to angle the framed picture of Watson glaring over his shoulder while wearing a cobalt blue Cozy Corgi sweatshirt.

Most girlfriends in my position would probably have been fixated on the way Leo's T-shirt revealed his arm muscles bunching and flexing at Watson's weight. And I did, but Leo's beauty was secondary to the warring emotions of jealousy and adoration I felt. It was lovely to see how much they idolized each other. However... "I don't know how you get away with it. If I even suggest picking Watson up, he turns homicidal and thrashes around like a walrus stuck on a beach."

"Don't listen to your mama." Leo whispered baby talk in Watson's ear as his eyes twinkled over at me. "You're not a walrus. No, you're not." Leo shifted again, those muscles bunching once more. "Although... you're not too far off."

For Watson's part, he sat in Leo's arms like the world's most gigantic baby, perfectly content, though staring at Leo's face in worship instead of inspecting the items that Leo offered him.

We'd finished washing up from dinner and were going

to watch a movie. I'd changed into pajamas and found Leo giving Watson the tour of the Watson memorabilia on my fireplace mantle.

"And here you are in wood." Leo held up a carved replica of Watson, whittled by Duncan Diamond, who owned the toyshop downtown. "It's a little lighter than you are." He got a lick on the cheek for his insult. Leo refocused on the next framed picture, this time addressing me. "I love this shot, of both of you." Delilah Johnson had taken an old-time photo of Watson and me, having dressed me up in 1920s garb and Watson in a Gatsby-styled tie and a white fedora. "Proof that you're beautiful in any time period."

"Shut up." Though I laughed out a protest, I felt my cheeks flush with pleasure.

Leo merely shrugged. "Simply stating the obvious." He moved to the knitted bagel-sized Watson. "This is new." He held it up for inspection. Watson growled at it. "And spectacular. Must be Angus."

"Yeah. He gave it to us the other day when I went in to question him about Gerald." I was getting quite the collection of Watson items above my fireplace. It was starting to resemble a shrine. "I never knew anything knitted could look so lifelike."

"It really is spectacular." Leo put it back on the mantle, kissed Watson on the top of his head, and deposited him on the hearth. "Angus has items in museums, not that you'd ever sell it, but I bet you that piece will be worth a lot one day, if it's not already."

Watson trailed behind as Leo joined me on the couch, looking as if the world ended now that he was no longer cradled in Leo's arms.

"Sorry, buddy." I leaned forward to ruffle his fur. "My turn." As had become our tradition when we watched television, Leo occupied the corner of the couch, and I settled back against his chest, his arms going around me. I couldn't blame Watson, not in the least. Leo's embrace was the most perfect place I'd ever been.

Snagging the remote from the arm of the sofa, within a couple of presses of buttons, Leo started the movie. He chose a classic, *Turner & Hooch*. I had a feeling he picked it because of the dog, giving Watson something to watch as the two of us always ended up chatting through half the movie.

As it began, with the warmth from the fire, the light fall of snow outside the window, and the pleasant sensation of a full stomach and Leo's arms, I finally began to relax for the first time all day. After the mess at the Koffee Kiln, I'd returned to the Cozy Corgi. As was expected, the onrush of tourists and locals wanting gossip never ebbed. A million different theories were tossed around about Ethel and Carla. Not a single person feigned surprise that Ethel was capable of murdering her best friend. There were mixed reactions to Carla's involvement.

"Mom called late this afternoon." I traced Leo's forearm with my fingertips from where it crossed over my chest. "She and Barry went to Joan's as soon as they heard. Apparently Joan absolutely lost it. Even more than before, which is saying something."

"I'm not surprised." Leo's deep voice rumbled from his chest, coursing through me. "Getting betrayed by someone you've known for decades, someone you count as one of your closest friends. That would be tough for anyone to handle, let alone with the week Joan has had already."

Part of me had wondered if I should go over and visit her. Give my condolences. I couldn't make myself. It was too hard to watch, and I felt rather used up myself. "She told Mom to have me bring Watson to the funeral tomorrow."

"Also not surprising." Leo gave a sober chuckle. "Watson might not want to repeat the experience, but it sounds like he was quite the comfort for her."

Still tracing Leo's forearm, I dropped my other hand and found Watson curled up at the foot of the sofa and rubbed gently at the point of his ears. "He really is a sweetheart. He's grumpy, and I'm not entirely sure if the house was on fire if he would save me or the dog tr... *T.R.E.A.T.S.*, but I do think he's got a little bit of guardian angel in him."

"Without a doubt."

Silence fell between us for a while, just the sound of the movie and the crackling of the fire filling the room. After a bit, Watson stood, plodded over to the hearth, and plopped down in front of the fire, snoozing once again. I couldn't focus on Tom Hanks getting won over by the giant French mastiff, my brain returning to the Koffee Kiln... how cruel Ethel was to Carla. It matched what I knew of the woman, but still, seeing it firsthand was hard to take. I'd replayed several scenes throughout the day and settled on a few things. Clearly Carla had some ace up her sleeve that had gotten Ethel to agree to investing in the museum idea. Not big enough to keep Ethel from making her own demands, but still... I couldn't help but wonder what it was. Not that it could be as big as murdering her best friend, but it had to be sizable.

No matter how many ways I looked at it, I couldn't see Carla knowing about the murder. Maybe she'd suspected, feared, and was too intimidated by Ethel to speak up, but I didn't believe Carla would've witnessed the killing or covered it up if she'd been certain. I tried to understand my own reaction around it, but couldn't. Carla and I had very few exchanges that weren't tense or hostile, but my gut told me that wasn't a line she would cross.

"Do you think Carla knew?"

"Hmm?" Leo rumbled again, confirming I'd spoken out loud, I hadn't really meant to.

"Carla." I shifted, leaving his warm embrace and twisting, facing him on the couch. "Do you think she really knew that Ethel killed Violet?"

Leo sat a little straighter. "Clearly you don't."

"No." I shook my head. "I don't."

A grin crossed Leo's face that didn't match the conversation. He reached out and took a thick lock of my hair that hung down over my shoulder. "When you shake your head, the light from the fire catches your hair. It's mesmerizing." Leo twisted his wrist slowly, his grin spreading, awe in his voice. "Look, so many colors. Different shades of red and orange, blonde, soft browns. Even silver."

"Silver?" Laughing, I pulled my hair away. "That's called *gray*. I'm older than you, you know."

He growled playfully, leaned forward, and pressed his lips to mine.

Proving he was a little bit magic, Leo turned off my brain for a couple of minutes, allowing me to get lost in the feel, the thrill of his lips, and the comfort of his presence.

As he pulled away, he waggled his eyebrows. "Speaking of older..."

I shoved him lightly on the shoulder. "Don't you dare. We agreed not to talk about it."

"No, we didn't." He grabbed my hand before I could pull it back. "You issued a command, but just like our furry little walrus over there, I have a mind of my own." He brushed his lips against my knuckles, quieting my protest. "And we need to talk about it. Turning forty is a big deal. I need to know what you want to do. We've only got a couple of months before—"

"I told you what I want. I want to turn thirty again." I tilted my chin defiantly. "I don't think that's too much to ask."

"Oh, right." He chuckled. "I'll see what I can do."

In truth I had absolutely no desire to be thirty again. In fact, there wasn't enough money in the world to pay me to go backward. However, though age had never bothered me, the closer I was getting to the big four-oh, I had to admit a little nugget of anxiety in my gut had started to grow. A nugget I *didn't* want to think about.

"You didn't answer me, what do you think about Carla?"

"Sweetheart." Leo spoke the word sweetly and plaintively. "You're going to drive yourself crazy. You barely ate dinner because you kept going through scenarios. Let it be done, at least for tonight."

I shook a finger at him. "Like I ever barely eat dinner. Besides, you were doing a rather spectacular job of distracting me, but then you brought up the fortieth birthday, so this is your fault."

"Good point. Let me see if I can fix that." He leaned forward again, angling for a kiss.

I arched out of reach. "Carla isn't the most pleasant person in the world, but she's not a killer."

"Fred..." He growled again. "You're as stubborn as Watson."

"And you wouldn't want me any other way."

"True." Leo settled. "I agree, Carla isn't pleasant, and I don't see her as a killer. But that's not the charge, is it? Only that she knew about Ethel killing Violet."

"But that's just it. Turning in Ethel goes along with

Carla's unpleasantness." I rushed ahead as Leo's brows knitted together. "She's not a killer, but given the relationship she has with Ethel, if she knew about the murder, it would be kind of a win-win for her, wouldn't it? She could finally get her mother-in-law out of the picture. There's no way Carla would've known and not used it to her advantage."

I saw the protest rise to Leo's lips, but then he paused and cocked his head. "Yeah, actually. I can see that." His eyes narrowed. "But you said yourself, you thought Carla had some sort of dirt, outside of murder, on Ethel which was how she got her to agree to help her with her grandparents' house. Maybe Ethel has dirt on Carla."

"Maybe." I shook my head again, and noticed Leo's gaze flicked to my hair, and a smile play on his lips. I ignored it. "But it doesn't feel right. I can't explain it necessarily, but I know Carla wasn't part of this."

As his gaze returned to me, Leo's hand lifted to stroke my hair. "I do trust your gut, always, but it seemed that was how you were feeling about Ethel not long ago as well."

"True." I couldn't argue with that, but I'd already worked through it. "But like I said, I don't think I can trust my gut on Ethel. I *know* I can't. She... does things to me, messes with my head, triggers all my insecurities and anger in a way that makes me not able to see straight. And while Carla isn't pleasant, by any means, she doesn't hold that same level of power, or whatever it is. I see her clearly."

"You're amazing." The gentle smile that crossed Leo's face didn't match our conversation. "I know I've said it before, but that's okay. I'm certain I'll say it a million more times. Because you are. You're absolutely amazing."

"Because I let an elderly woman in a fur coat intimidate me and trigger my issues with sometimes not feeling good enough?" While I loved that Leo felt that way about me, I tried to play it off, make it a joke. Perhaps if he truly did say it a million times, I'd figure out how to accept it with more grace.

"No." He shook his head, not allowing himself to be sidetracked, his hand still stroking my hair. "Because both of these women have been horrible to you, and yet you're wearing yourself out worrying about one of them, wanting to make sure she's treated fairly."

"You'd do the same, don't pretend otherwise."

Leo simply shrugged one shoulder and lifted his other hand to my cheek, running his thumb along my skin in that way that made me melt. "That doesn't stop you from being amazing." He leaned forward once more, kissing me gently. Slow and sweet, and overflowing with emotion. When he pulled back, he halted a couple of inches from my face, his deep eyes meeting mine, his thumb still caressing my cheek as his other hand stroked my hair. "Fred, I lo—"

I sucked in a gasp as his fingertips moved through my hair and over my scalp. "Hair!"

Leo blinked and shook his head as if yanked back to a different dimension. "What?"

"My hair." I pulled away slightly, lifting the same lock of hair between us. "What did you say about my hair a while ago?"

"I..." He shrugged again. "That it was beautiful? It is."

"No." I met his eyes, excitement coursing through me as I felt the puzzle pieces snap together. "You called it *mesmerizing.*" I stood and began to pace.

Watson lifted his head, yawned, and sleepily tracked my movement.

"Mesmerizing. That's why this has felt so off to me the whole time. It's been right in front of my face." I turned once more to look at him. "The way Violet's body was arranged and covered in clay. You should've seen her, Leo. Propped against the wall, her legs curled partly under her, hair sweeping over her. She looked like a mermaid. It was done with love. There was no effort to humiliate or dishonor her. Just the opposite." How had I not seen it the whole time? "Her hair. It was mesmerizing."

NINETEEN

Walking up the cobblestone path, the Estes Valley Church, like the first time I'd seen it, reminded me of a tiny log castle. I was surprised it was the location for Violet's funeral. With her being one of the upper echelon in town, her service would be well attended at any time, but given the drama around her death, attendance would easily be tripled. It would've made more sense to have it at one of the larger, more popular churches. Perhaps Violet and Joan had attended services at this church, but I doubted it. I figured it'd been chosen because of its beauty.

Leo held the squeaky old door open, and Watson and I walked into a long narrow sanctuary, the glowing log walls broken up by stained-glass windows. Sure enough, nearly every line of the wooden benches was filled.

A shiny mahogany casket sat directly in front of the pulpit. Behind it, beneath a round stained-glass window at the base of the peaked ceiling, hung a large cross made from timbers and rusty metal.

Proving that she'd been watching for me, Mom waved her hand frantically in the air from their spot toward the front left side. I turned to Leo and took his hand. "They saved us a spot."

He slipped his fingers through mine. "You sure about this?"

"I am. Totally." With a squeeze, we made our way to our spots. It was the first time I'd lied to Leo. I was sure, but not *totally*. And even less now that I realized it was here, of all places. Though I didn't attend services, I was fond of the little church—it reminded me of my bookshop, had that same warm, cozy feel.

I balked when Mom scooted over, making room for us, and repositioned herself by Joan and Rachel at the far end of the row. I supposed it made sense. From what I knew, Joan and Violet didn't have any family, and Violet's best friend was in jail for her murder.

Joan had cleaned up. Her black dress was crisp and stylish. Her silvery, typically spiky hair had been sculpted down to a sleek, subdued pixie cut. Beside her, Rachel looked like a younger version of Violet. If I wasn't mistaken, she was wearing one of Violet's elegant suits. Possibly I was wrong as fashion was not even close to being on my list of interests or skills, but it appeared of much higher quality than what she normally wore. As she offered a small smile our way, some of the tendrils danced around her face from her loose bun. It seemed rather rude that Rachel had continued to copy Violet's style, even at the funeral. Or creepy. I wasn't sure which.

Joan noticed us enter the row and turned her face our way. She might've cleaned up, but it only helped so much— she looked a hundred years older, gaunt and drawn. Eyes completely bloodshot and exhausted. A faint smile threatened when she saw Watson, and she bent over, sticking both arms out toward him. "Oh, you came! You came, sweet one. How I need you."

Watson froze, hesitating.

Feeling like the worst mama in the world, I nudged his fluffy butt gently with the toe of my boot.

After looking over his shoulder, which was part accusation and part pleading, he slunk toward Joan, who sank to her knees and managed to wrap him in her arms despite the narrowness between the pews.

A motion across the front of the church caught my eye. Under the steep pitch of the roof, on the right side of the stage, if that was the word for it, a hidden door opened, and a short large blueberry emerged. I reprimanded myself at the notion. But that was how Pastor Davis appeared to me, in an endearing way. At around five feet and probably three hundred pounds, he always reminded me of Violet Beauregarde from Willy Wonka when he donned his purple pastor's robes.

A shot of guilt cut through me, but not because of the blueberry comparison. I turned to Leo and the rest of my family. "Sorry, I'll be right back."

Pastor Davis saw me coming, and spread his arms in way of greeting, then pulled me down to a warm embrace. "Dear Fred, so good of you to come. And I noticed you brought your furry friend."

"I hope that's okay. Joan requested."

"All of God's creatures are always welcome." He patted my back and let me go.

I stayed near his ear. "There're still a few minutes before the service is supposed to start. May I speak to you in private?"

He pulled back slightly, meeting my eyes in concern. Instead of asking for clarification, he just nodded, reflections of the stained glass playing colorfully over his shiny bald head. "This way."

Feeling a little bit exposed, I followed him behind the pulpit and back through the hidden door.

Pastor Davis's office matched the rest of the church— tiny, high ceilings, warm, glowing wood everywhere, and even a tall narrow stained-glass window, depicting a dove with an olive branch. He turned to me after he closed the door and took my hands. "Is all well?"

I'd been too impulsive. I shouldn't have said anything to him. If Pastor Davis objected, I didn't have a plan B. But I respected the man, and he'd been good to my uncles. "I... wanted to give you a heads-up. I'm going to use the service to confront Violet's killer. At least... it might be during the service."

His eyes opened so wide they looked in danger of bursting out of his head. "Her killer? But Ms. Beaker..." His eyes narrowed, much to my relief. "Oh... you believe Ms. Beaker isn't the murderer."

"That's correct." I appreciated how sharp the elderly man was. "If I'm correct, and I'm nearly completely certain that I am, I believe her killer is—"

"No, no!" He cut me off with a near bark. "Please don't tell me. I'm not the best of actors. If I'm aware of your suspicions, I'll treat whoever it is differently, or start staring at them in the middle of the service."

I waited for another protest, for him to ask me not to do it during the funeral, but it didn't come. My affection for him grew. "Okay. I won't. Thank you."

"May I have some warning as to when? Do you think toward the beginning of the service, middle, the end?"

"Somewhere in there." I attempted a smile. "I'm not exactly sure. I'm hoping that moment will present itself." As I heard the words out loud, I had to admit that my plan A wasn't all that glorious either.

He squeezed my hands, which he still held. "I'll pray that it does." He began to release his grip, then tightened once more. "Wait a minute, why are *you* telling me? Shouldn't the police have already gone over this with me?"

And here was where it all might end before it even began. "They aren't part of this."

"Really? I saw Officer Green and Officer Jackson come in only minutes ago."

"Well... I guess I should clarify. They don't know of this plan." I couldn't help but wince. "I think this is going to require a little... delicacy."

He cocked an eyebrow and chuckled. "Well... I admire Officer Green for her commitment to the town, but *delicacy* isn't exactly one of her God-given gifts." He squeezed my hands again, then let go. "Thank you for informing me. I'll be praying for the Good Lord to guide you."

To my surprise, that was it, and he opened the door, letting me out. As I made my way back to my family, Susan caught my gaze over the heads of the mourners. Behind her, through the open front door of the chapel, I could see a crowd beginning to form outside. Susan narrowed her eyes, clearly suspicious. I gave her a little wave and hurried back to my seat, shuffling past the knees of my uncles, the newly arrived Katie, and Barry, to take my spot between Leo and my mom.

I did feel a little guilty about not telling Susan, but... she'd said it herself—we weren't partners. And I hadn't appreciated how the day before had gone down. We'd done it her way, now I was going to do it mine.

At a whimper, I looked down and realized Watson was still trapped in Joan's embrace.

Leo leaned into my ear. "I've tried three times to get her to let go of him. She just cried harder every time."

I gave Watson an apologetic grimace and made a mental promise to treat him even more like the royalty he considered himself to be. For at least a week or two.

Within another couple of minutes, Pastor Davis stood behind the pulpit, and the murmuring crowd fell silent. "Welcome, dear loved ones, those of you grieving for our lost sister..."

As he started to speak, I leaned down and stroked Joan's shoulder. "The service is beginning."

Her tear-streaked eyes looked up at me, slowly focused, and with a small nod, she released Watson and sat up.

With a glare, he darted past me, even past Leo, and curled up under the safety of where Barry was seated. I was going to be punished for a long time, I had no doubt.

As Pastor Davis spoke, another member of the clergy, judging from the matching purple robes, approached the casket and opened the top half, revealing Violet's profile.

Beside me, Mom flinched.

An open casket had not been expected. I hadn't attended a service like that since I was a child.

Though it seemed a little morbid, I now realized how the moment was going to present itself, though I still wasn't sure when. I also wasn't completely certain I'd have the nerve to see it through.

The service continued, longer than what I'd expected. Three different songs, each one with an accompanying extensive scripture reading. After about twenty minutes, Pastor Davis gave what he promised would be a small sermon. I'd never heard him speak before, and though long-winded, he was as charming and loving from the pulpit as he was in person.

Finally he motioned toward Joan. "If you'd like to come up and say your goodbyes, my dear." He refocused on the crowd. "After, those of you who wish to follow suit may bid a farewell to Violet until we meet her on the other side, and offer your love, support, and condolences to Joan."

My heart began to race, my pulse pounding in my ears. I looked toward Joan to see her grasp the side of the pew with a trembling hand and stand as if it took great force of will.

To my surprise, Rachel stayed where she was as Joan exited the row and walked the few feet to the edge of the casket. Gripping the edge, she looked in, her shoulders shaking.

This was the moment. Pastor Davis's prayers had been answered, it seemed. A little more publicly than I would've liked.

I stood as well, afraid if I waited any longer, Joan would turn around and the procession would begin.

Feeling a little bit like Judas offering a kiss, I stood next to her and slipped an arm over her shoulder.

She flinched in surprise but offered a trembling smile as she saw it was me. She mouthed a quiet *thanks* and then turned back to Violet.

I could barely believe my eyes as I looked into the casket. Violet appeared thirty years younger and barely waxy at all—she truly could be sleeping. She wore one of her feminine business suits, cranberry in color, and lay amid the dusty pink silk of the casket's interior. Her hair was not as she would've chosen. The long silver tresses cascaded down over her shoulders, under her arms, which were folded over her breasts, and continued to pool around her waist.

Beside me, still trembling, Joan breathed out a shaky breath and reached out, took a strand of hair, and stroked it. "So, so beautiful."

As Joan murmured, I felt another whisper in my ear, a nudge forcing me to finish what I'd started. "She really is beautiful. And her hair... it's mesmerizing."

Joan's gaze flashed to mine in surprise, and she smiled. "That's *exactly* what I always said it was. Mesmerizing."

Before she could look away, I held her gaze and pushed on. "It's nearly as beautiful as the way you did her hair in the pottery studio. How you covered it in clay and arranged it over her, almost like a mermaid on the rocks."

"Yes, I—" Joan gave a half nod, and then her eyes widened in pure shock. She lifted her trembling hand from Violet's hair and covered her mouth. The war that raged behind her eyes was fierce but brief. Her whole body slumped in defeat. If my arm hadn't still been around her, she would've melted to the floor. "Not here." She looked at me once more, pleading. "Please."

I didn't hesitate and tightened my grip over her. Though her feet moved, I nearly carried her past the casket, up the few steps to the stage, and into Pastor Davis's office. As I started to shut the door, Watson darted in, joining us.

At the sight of him, Joan lost her remaining will to stand and crumpled to the ground, wrapping her arms around him again.

Though far from pleased, Watson didn't pull away.

"I didn't mean to. I didn't." Joan sobbed into Watson's fur. "It's like I blacked out, although I remember it. I remember it all. But I didn't mean to. I could never..."

I started to shut the door again, but Pastor Davis pushed slightly against it and entered. He went to Joan, knelt beside her, and put one hand on her back and another on Watson's head.

Susan entered right behind him, slamming the door in

her wake. Before she took another step, it opened once more, and Rachel poked her head in. "What is—"

"Sorry. This is private." Susan literally slammed the door in her face and whipped back to me in a fury. "Fred, what in the—" Her words broke off as she took in the scene, and then she turned narrowed pale blue eyes on me, full of accusation.

I ignored her and knelt on the other side of Joan, touching her shoulder. "Tell us what happened."

Though the sobs nearly made her unintelligible, her words broke loose and tumbled as freely as the tears making their way down her cheeks. "It was our anniversary. Of the night we first met. We celebrate every year." She looked up at me. "Every year."

I nodded encouragingly, unsure what else to do.

"Violet didn't show up. I waited for over an hour, trying her cell, and it went straight to voicemail every time." She unhooked one arm from Watson just long enough to wipe her nose with the back of her sleeve, then captured him again. He didn't fight it. "I *knew* where she was. Where she always was. At that stupid studio. I'd never seen her like this. Her obsessions could be bad, but *never* like this one. She was never home. It was like living with a ghost, a stranger. She looked right through me. All she cared about was making another horrid piece of pottery. I was invisible."

She got lost to sobs again.

After a while, Susan moved closer. I interjected before she could make a demand, afraid it would backfire. "What happened? Did you go to the Koffee Kiln?"

She nodded, then spoke again. "I confronted her, told her how much she'd hurt me. How much I'd been missing her. Violet was drunk and barely acknowledged anything. She just kept working." Anger flashed in Joan's eyes then, and radiated from her voice. "I was standing in front of her, sobbing, heartbroken, and she asked me to get a new bag of clay. *A bag of clay*! Like it was the only thing that mattered. I got the stupid thing, dumped it out beside her, but the bag was still in my hands, and..." She released Watson and scooted backward across the floor until she bumped against Pastor Davis's desk. Pulling her knees to her chest, she hid her head in her arms.

Watson looked to me, and then, shocking me beyond measure, padded over to her and plopped down against her shaking legs.

I didn't know if he was trying to comfort her or if he knew that I needed her to keep speaking.

I moved closer as well and encouraged her onward. "You put the bag over her head?"

She nodded fiercely, still not looking up.

Pastor Davis groaned, and Susan started across the office, reaching for her handcuffs. I motioned for her to stop, and to my surprise, she did.

"You said, by the casket, that you didn't mean to."

She looked up again then, eyes wild. "I didn't. I really didn't. Of course I didn't. I could never! I was just so angry, and..." She sucked in another ragged breath, the sound painful. "Then she was gone. I couldn't believe it. Violet was gone."

I dared to reach out and touch her. "What did you do then, Joan?"

"I broke. Sobbed and sobbed and sobbed until I thought I was going to be sick." As she spoke, both her gaze and her voice made it clear she was no longer in the pastor's office but back in the Koffee Kiln studio. "I'd killed her. I'd taken her away from me, the only thing in the world that ever mattered. I destroyed her. She was lying there, the bag covering her. I ripped it off... She looked so... destroyed. There was... clay in her hair."

I couldn't take it anymore. Though revolted by what she'd done, I hurt for her. "So you made her beautiful again, in the way that she loved the most."

Joan smiled and nodded as if relieved someone understood. "You said yourself. She looked beautiful, like a mermaid." Her smile grew. "I hadn't thought of that, but you're right. She was *that* beautiful. Mesmerizing. I thought... I thought... even though I'd taken her life I could"—she shrugged a shoulder weakly—"make her beautiful again, forever. Immortal. Always so beautiful." Joan came back, eyes locking on mine. "She was, wasn't she? You saw her. You said she was mesmerizing."

I couldn't force out any words, so I simply nodded and then looked toward Susan, letting her take over.

TWENTY

"We've got to stop having this for breakfast." I took another forkful of the huge slice of chocolate espresso torte that Katie and I shared as we leaned on either side of the bakery countertop. "It would be one thing if we weren't also having it for dessert, but it's getting ridiculous."

"But it goes so well with your morning dirty chai." Katie grinned wickedly and took a bite for herself. "I'll stop making them, soon, I promise. I am a little obsessed with them at the moment."

I glared at her for her choice of words. "Really? Obsession?"

Katie cringed. "Good point. Okay... not *obsession*." She lifted a heaping forkful and pretended to consider. "How about... currently in the throes of complete and utter fascination?"

Losing the game quickly, I snorted out a laugh. "That's worse than obsession."

"Just don't kill me and cover me in chocolate torte and I'll be—" Her eyes narrowed as she cocked her head. "Actually, you know what? If you have the desire to do that, go ahead. That sounds like a pretty great way to go."

I laughed again. "I don't even think you're kidding."

"Neither do I." Chuckling along, she peered over the

counter at Watson. "You look like you're ready for another piece."

"No. He's had too much the way it is. Not that I have any room to talk. He needs to—" I halted as sweet chocolate eyes looked up at me, using his puppy pleading power. He didn't need to. "Strike that. Get Watson another piece. He's earned it. I don't know if Joan's confession would've come so easily if it hadn't been for him being such a trooper."

"Exactly." Katie slid over what remained of the dog-friendly peanut butter torte she'd crafted that morning and sliced another large piece for Watson. "Here you go. For our mascot and our little grumpy hero."

His nub tail wagged fiercely as he scarfed it down, making rather disgusting and very ungrumpy noises.

After finishing my last bite, I straightened. "All right, I'm going to head down, otherwise I might dive into a third piece." Though the spring break tourist rush was over, and there were still ten minutes until the Cozy Corgi opened officially, we'd given the twins the day off, and there were a few things I needed to get ready in the bookshop. I pointed at Katie as I started to walk away from the counter. "And no more for Watson either, at least not till after lunch."

"I wouldn't dream of it." From the sound of it, Katie wasn't even attempting to be convincing.

I hadn't even made it to the edge of the bakery counter when I froze in my tracks as Carla rounded the top of the stairs.

She froze as well, the bag in her hand swinging at the abrupt stop. After a second, she gestured down the steps. "The, um, front door was open."

I still couldn't move, still couldn't speak. For one ridiculous moment, I thought she was there to kill me, to get her revenge for the scene in the Koffee Kiln. Then, even more horrific, I remembered the chocolate espresso torte behind me.

Carla moved before I did, striding past me. She lifted the bag and placed it right beside the partially eaten torte on the marble countertop. "You rearranged."

"Yeah." It was Katie who answered, though when I turned around, her face was as pale as mine felt. "We installed an elevator a couple of months ago." She pointed over her shoulder. "It opens up into the kitchen, so we had to widen a few things."

Leaning to get a better view, Carla inspected, then looked around the rest of the shop. "Pretty good. I'd almost forgotten what it looked like before. I haven't been in here since I went into labor with Maverick."

I'd forgotten Carla's water had broken in the bakery, right in the middle of a tirade. Somehow the memory helped me find my voice. At least Carla wasn't screaming this time. "Hard to believe that was a year ago." *That* was all I came up with? Desperately, I pointed toward the display of pastries. "Have you had breakfast? Would you like anything?"

"Not hardly." It was almost a relief to see her sneer return. "I only came by to give you these." She pulled two items from the bag and took off their newspaper wrapping. "In all the chaos, you never picked them up."

I closed the distance and almost laughed, but didn't. Katie's mug and the dog bowl I'd painted.

Katie leaned over to inspect as well and cocked an eyebrow at me. "Wow. I'd forgotten how little like a corgi that thing actually looked."

It was atrocious. "Yours isn't that much better."

"Yes, it is." Katie grinned, but it faded as she noticed Carla's sour expression.

Might as well get it over with. I met Carla's eyes. "I'm sorry about the scene in your shop the other day. I didn't know..." I shook my head, not wanting to blame Susan. "I'm sorry."

The argument was clear at the edge of Carla's lips, but she took a breath and closed her eyes. "I can't believe I have to say this, but Officer Green told us you figured out who truly killed Violet." Her eyes opened. "So... thank you."

I started to wave it off, but then decided that wouldn't be respectful, and I knew this wasn't easy for Carla. "You're welcome. I'm sorry I didn't figure it out sooner."

She shrugged and started to go.

"You should talk to Barry." The words were out before I could pull them back.

Carla halted. "Your stepdad? Why in the world would I do that after what he helped you do to my grandfather?"

If I'd had any thought that maybe we were going to be on friendly terms just because she thanked me and I'd apologized, clearly I'd been wrong. Still, I kept going. "I think he'd be interested in investing in your museum idea. And then you wouldn't have to depend on Ethel's money."

So many emotions raged over Carla's face that I couldn't label a single one. When she spoke, there was no inflection in her tone. "She's not going to stop until she brings you down, you know. She'll never forgive you."

A flicker of fear ignited in me, which only served to make me angry. I straightened, meeting Carla's gaze again, this time firm and hard. "She's horrible. I don't say that about very many people, but your mother-in-law is truly a miserable, mean, awful woman. She can do what she likes. I won't let someone like that ruin my life, not *any* aspect of it."

Carla reared back a touch, almost looking impressed,

but then she shook her head. "Well, good luck with that. I think you've met your match."

"She's not my match, not even close." On impulse I moved near and reached out a hand toward Carla's arm. I stopped halfway and then forced myself to finish the gesture. "I know you and I aren't friends and that we've got a complicated past, but you are *not* like her. Whatever is broken in Ethel isn't broken in you. You don't deserve to have her ruin your life either."

Carla glared down at where my hand gripped her arm, but when she glanced back up, there was a sheen of tears over her eyes, though they didn't fall. She didn't speak until I released her, and when she did, it was in a trembling voice. "I... might call him. We'll see."

I nodded, not knowing what else to say.

As she started to walk away, Carla glanced back toward Katie's mug and my hideous dog bowl and froze. When she stuck out a hand, I realized it wasn't the pottery that had caught her attention. "Is that...?" She stuck her finger into the chocolate espresso torte, scooped out a small portion, took a sniff, her eyes narrowing, and then put it in her mouth. She looked to the torte, to Katie, to me, and then to the torte again. That time when she spoke, her voice trembled for an entirely different reason. "I thought the Cozy Corgi bakery wasn't going to do anything with coffee in it."

"We're... not going to sell it. Fred and I have been..." Katie shot me a panicked, apologetic glance. "Having it for breakfast."

"Chocolate for breakfast." Proving that while she may not be evil like her mother-in-law, she wasn't particularly nice either, Carla's gaze flicked back and forth between Katie and me. "Well, *that* certainly explains a lot."

"Hey!" Katie let out a hurt-sounding protest.

Carla ignored her. "Go ahead, try to compete with the Koffee Kiln. Simone and I will stomp you into the dust." She sneered down at Watson and then at the torte once more before she stormed away, ranting over her shoulder, "At least we don't have nasty dogs in our business, and I would've had the sense to cover that thing in powdered sugar and raspberries. I swear, you two are incompetent."

Suddenly exhausted, I leaned against the counter as Carla disappeared down the steps and looked over at Katie. "Well, I guess we're on exactly the same page we always are with Carla Beaker."

Katie wasn't there. She was already rushing to a shelf on the other side of the kitchen and then to the fridge.

Clearly thinking he was in for a treat, Watson scampered back and forth beside me, pacing in exuberant anticipation.

"What in the world are you doing?"

Katie didn't answer, until she returned, a couple of different items in her hands and her eyes bright. "That was the first time in Carla's life she's ever had a baking idea that wasn't complete rubbish." As she spoke, she cut and plated two more pieces of the torte. "Although, to be fair, the combination of chocolate and raspberries isn't exactly revolutionary. I have no idea why it didn't enter my mind, outside of being too focused on getting the exact right ratio of coffee and chocolate." With a sieve, she dusted the pieces with powdered sugar, then artfully arranged raspberries on the back edge by the crust and on the plate. Then she looked up at me and beamed. "As they say, the third piece of chocolate espresso torte for breakfast is the charm!"

As I lifted a forkful, Katie struck out a hand, stopping me before it reached my lips.

"Hold on!" She whirled and hurried back into the depths of the kitchen once more. "Ice cream!"

Proving that the weeklong tourist rush truly was over, the bookshop and bakery were utterly dead by late afternoon. True, we'd had a higher-than-average attendance for breakfast and lunch, but that was the locals getting the final round of gossip from the funeral the day before.

By the time four o'clock rolled around, I was curled up in the mystery room in front of the fire, with Watson snoring away on his ottoman. Maybe trying to put a bookend on the horrible week, I opened *Monstrous Beauty* on my Kindle and got lost in the beautifully dark tale of a lovely mermaid.

After a while, between the crackle of the fire, Watson's snores, and the perfect coziness of my favorite spot in the bookshop, I dozed off.

When I woke, Watson whimpered happily as Leo, dressed in his park ranger uniform, sat on the edge of the sofa and leaned forward, rubbing Watson's belly as he splayed over the ottoman.

Leo smiled over at me. "Sorry, you looked so beautiful and peaceful sleeping there, I couldn't wake you."

I'd been so sound asleep that it took a heartbeat to catch up. To remember this was real, that I was in my dream bookshop and Leo and I had finally crossed that line, that I was with a man who not only felt that way about me but said it, often.

Sitting up, I straightened my hair and my skirt and joined him petting Watson. "I'm glad I'm awake. This is better than anything I could dream up."

"I couldn't have said it better myself." Smiling, he

twisted toward me, lifting one of his hands to my cheek. "Fred, I..." His smile wavered nervously as he took a breath.

My heart began to race, and for the third time, I realized what he was about to say. And though I couldn't wait to hear it, I also couldn't help myself. "Oh, I'm glad you're here. Katie further perfected her already perfect chocolate espresso torte earlier."

"That's great." Leo flinched, then tried again, meeting and holding my gaze once more. "Fred, I want you to—"

It was all I could do to keep from laughing. "Want me to get you a piece?"

He flinched again, and then his eyes narrowed, the corner of his lips beginning to curl. "You're doing this on purpose."

"Sorry." I laughed then. "I know it's mean, but I couldn't help myself. You're just so adorable."

"Really?" He barked out a laugh. "Me trying and failing time and time again to tell you I love you is adorable?"

My laughter died instantly. I'd known that's what he was going to say. And though it excited me, it was also not big news. Of course he loved me. Of course I loved him. It was weird that, for whatever reason, we hadn't crossed that line yet with how settled we both felt together. I expected him to say *I love you*, and for me to go, *well, of course. I love you too.*

It wasn't like that at all.

The whole world stopped. All of it.

"Say it again. For real this time."

"No." Still he smirked. "You'll interrupt."

That time I lifted my hand to his cheek. "No, I won't."

The humor faded, and his honey-brown eyes grew ocean deep, laying bare the truth of his soul. "I love you, Fred. I love you."

In another turn of events I wouldn't have predicted, I felt my eyes sting. Not only did I not interrupt him, but I couldn't find words. I sank into him, kissing Leo, kissing the man I hadn't realized I'd been waiting for my whole life. Kissing the man who was good, kind, and brave. Kissing my friend who'd become the love of my life.

Finally, I pulled back, breaking the kiss as a couple of tears made their way down my cheeks, and I met his eyes once more. "I love you too, Leo."

"I know." He smiled tenderly.

Watson whimpered beside us, teetering on the edge of the ottoman, clearly offended at being ignored.

Laughing, Leo wrapped his arms around Watson and pulled him onto the couch between us. "Get over here, little man." Leo smashed his face against the side of Watson's muzzle, giving him an exaggeratedly loud kiss.

Putting one arm behind Leo's back, and my other around Watson, I kissed his other cheek. Leo and I carried on like that, kissing the living daylights out of my grumpy little angel until he began to squirm in halfhearted protest. Then we kissed him some more.

A Cozy Corgi Mystery

Ghastly Gadgets

MILDRED ABBOTT

GHASTLY GADGETS

Mildred Abbott

A loud explosion tore through the Cozy Corgi Bookshop and Bakery. Having just reached the top of the staircase, I gripped the banister for support.

At my feet, Watson growled, his fox-like ears flattening against his skull.

I offered him a grimace in solidarity. "It's okay, buddy. We'll be home in a few hours. We can be quiet the whole night. I promise not to make a sound if you don't."

Ignoring me, Watson rounded the corner and trotted toward the pastry counter. He was grumpy at the best of times, but the cacophony over the last three days had turned what was typically a rather charmingly cantankerous disposition into a full-fledged angry canine.

Katie attempted a smile for Watson, but she barely managed to grimace—there'd been a lot of those the past few days. When she looked over at me, Katie was practically unrecognizable. Her brown eyes were bloodshot and sported heavy bags. Even her bouncy chestnut spirals that typically framed her round face, hung limp.

Reaching across the counter, I touched her arm in concern. "Oh, Katie..." My worry grew as I noticed her plain white T-shirt. I didn't think I'd ever seen her wear anything that didn't have some weird, cute, or unexplainable picture over the chest—most often involving hippos. "Are you okay?"

From over her shoulder, I noticed Nick, Katie's baking assistant, look up in a panic from where he was pouring flour into an industrial-size mixer, and shook his head desperately as if in warning.

"Okay?" Katie's voice trembled. "No, I'm not okay. How in the world could I be okay? How can anyone be okay?" Before I could reply, Katie gestured toward the display of sugar cookies on the marble countertop. "Look at those. Tell me what they are."

Again, Nick offered another shake of his head.

I studied the cookies for a second. "Daffodils?" I wasn't certain. "Yes, obviously. They're very pretty daffodils."

At the growl, I looked at Watson, only to realize a few seconds too late that it had come from Katie. "No! They're ducks. At least they're *supposed* to be. Though now that you mention it, they do look more like daffodils, so I'll just lie and tell customers that's what they are." She held up a hand between us. "Look at this. I'm trembling so badly I might as well be a hundred and fifty years old. I can barely function."

The cookies were far from Katie's typical standard of perfection. "Sweetie, whatever they look like, they'll be delicious. People will love them."

"*What* people?" Katie practically screeched. "Tourist season just started, we've been open for five minutes this morning, and we haven't had a single customer yet. Nick and I even had items left over at the end of the day yesterday. That has *never* happened before, at least not to such an extent."

Another bang from next door cut through the air, causing Watson to whimper and Katie to flinch.

Katie pulled her hand away from mine as she spoke,

took the pastry balls off the tray, and began arranging them on the counter. "Loud noises like these trigger the flight-or-fight response, and in those moments a person truly loses all control. Do you know how many times I'm losing control of my functions throughout the day?" Her voice rose and began to pick up speed, as did her hands moving the pastries. "In fact, it's been proven that noise pollution causes high stress, raises a person's blood pressure, and leads to hypertension and cardiovascular problems."

Behind her, Nick sighed and gripped the edge of the mixer bowl. Obviously he'd heard the results of what was clearly Katie's latest Google binge.

"Furthermore," she continued, sounding half-crazed, "it disrupts sleep, even when it's not happening. Just the effects from hearing it all day steals a person's rest. And it increases aggression!" Katie took hold of one of the pastry shells, but grabbed my arm and accidentally smashed it between us. "Do you really think our little mountain town needs *more* aggression, Fred? I know you like solving murders, and you're good at it, but this is ridiculous."

Though Katie was bordering on unhinged, which wasn't like her at all, seeing her in such a state forced me to admit what I'd been trying to ignore. "You're right. I've been dreading coming here, and *this* is my favorite place in the world. It's been bad for a while, but the past three days have been over the top." I dusted the crushed pastry from my arm, and Watson gobbled it up before it hit the floor.

"Tell me about it." That time Katie snarled. "And let me give you a little hint—this *next* murder, you won't have to solve. I'm guilty. By this time tomorrow, I'll have killed those insane twins and turned them into a cake or something." Her eyes brightened in the way they did when she'd stumbled upon a great idea. She looked down at Watson. "Or dog treats. How about that? You're tired of them too, I can tell. I'll beat them to death with my KitchenAid, bake them, and you can eat the evidence. Noah and Jonah dog treats." She clapped her hands as if the decision was final.

Watson did a bunny hop on his front paws at his favorite word before his ears flattened once more when he realized Katie wasn't actually offering him a treat.

I laughed. "You're ridiculous."

"I'm not kidding." Katie leveled a hard stare on me. "I used to worry that being related to murderers would be something that was hereditary. Now... I know it is. But, in my case, it will be justified. I'll get a special hero award from the town council."

I knew she was exaggerating. At least... I thought so. "I'll talk to them. I should've done it before now." I'd arrived late, partly because of dreading coming in due to the noise, and had been coming up for my morning dirty chai, but decided it wasn't worth risking a breakdown if I asked for it. Instead, I tried to distract her and gestured toward the pastry shells that had grown into a virtual pyramid as Katie stacked them. "What are you making?"

"Cream puffs." She barked out the words as if it should've been obvious and gestured toward the trays laddered with them behind her.

"For what? There must be hundreds." A sinking feeling started to settle in my gut, one that had nothing to do with the constant barrage of noise.

"It's a special order, Fred. Don't worry about it. At least they're not supposed to look like ducks. Although at this point—"

The bang that cut through the bakery that time was so loud it made my ears ring and the floor shake. The latter I thought was in my imagination, until the pyramid of cream puff shells shook, and then tumbled, rolling across the marble countertop and bouncing like a bag of marbles released on the hardwood floor.

For the first time in days, Watson perked up into exuberant joy. As if injected with the caffeine from my nonexistent dirty chai, he scurried over the floor, crashing into chair-and-table legs as he snatched up the pastry balls before any could get away.

"Fred." Katie let out a whimper that sounded near tears, and then turned fury-filled eyes on me. "You've got to talk to those idiots right now, or Watson's going to have those special order dog treats within the hour."

With Watson prancing happily beside me, still licking his chops from the puff pastry shells, I used my time storming back down the stairs and across the bookshop to get my temper under control. With that last explosion, the frustration I'd been stuffing away for the past three days came rushing to the surface, threatening to let out an explosion of its own. I waved at Ben, Nick's twin, who was manning the cash register. "I'll be right back. I'm going to go murder my brothers-in-law."

"Sounds like a plan." Ben gave one of his free, easy smiles. "Plus, it'll save you time having to solve who did it."

"Not the first time I've heard that this morning." Close enough anyway.

Watson made a quick detour to accept a fur-ruffle from Ben and then swept out the front door of the Cozy Corgi with me.

I turned to the left, and within five steps, I arrived at the front door of Twinventions. A twist on the handle revealed it to be locked, only causing my temper to spike more. I knocked, and the sound my fist made on the glass should've been enough warning to have Jonah and Noah heading for the hills.

At my feet, Watson whimpered.

Before I could inspect him, another bang reverberated from inside, shaking the door and the store windows. I looked down at him. "You felt that one coming in advance, didn't you?" I knocked again, harder.

After a few seconds, Watson issued a growl at the door as a silhouette approached.

I opened my mouth to let Noah or Jonah have it, I didn't care which of my twin brothers-in-law answered. However, the man who opened the door not only stole my tirade away, but replaced every ounce of anger with utter shock. "Branson." A trickle of fear flitted through me.

He glanced down at Watson, who continued to growl, then back up at me questioningly. "That's some attack dog you've got there."

His cornflower-blue eyes shattered the illusion, even so, he left me shaken. Blue eyes, not green... *not Branson*. Still, I blinked a couple of times, as if trying to get a different view of his face. It didn't change. The man was tall, dark, and movie-star handsome. He could almost pass as a twin for Sergeant Branson Wexler... my... ex and... well, so many other things.

One of his perfectly formed brows arched upward, as did a corner of his full lips. "You okay?"

"Yes. I thought you were..." I blinked again, finally getting control of myself. "Never mind."

"Good, glad you're all right. I'm sorry, though, but the store doesn't open until tomorrow."

Tomorrow? "I'm Noah and Jonah's sister-in-law. Are they here?"

The man's blue eyes lit up along with his smile. "Oh! You're Fred, and this must be Watson." He started to reach down to pet my fluffy corgi's head, but pulled back as Watson continued to growl. The man merely chuckled. "Noah and Jonah said he was grumpy. You own the bookshop next door. Niles and I were going to swing over there later. I hear you've got a great bakery."

I blinked again, feeling like I was doing a horrible job playing catch-up. "Yes. That's... all true. And you are?"

"Miles." He simultaneously offered his hand and used his chiseled jaw to gesture toward the back of the shop. "We're friends with the twins. We go way back."

As my attention caught on "we," one of my brothers-in-law came into view. "Miles, send whoever it is away and get back here quick. Jonah just—" Noah's words fell away when he saw us. "Oh. Hey, Fred. Watson." He grinned, then addressed Miles. "Never mind, don't send them away. This is Fred, my—"

"We've met." Miles stood aside, giving me room to enter. "I don't think I made a very good impression on Watson, though."

Proving this point, Watson made a show of walking the long way around to enter.

Noah eyed Watson, then looked at his friend. "I may have to reevaluate the kind of man I think you are. Watson can spot a murderer a mile away." With a laugh, he reached down to pet Watson, but missed as Watson darted out of reach. Noah simply laughed. Before I could launch into my previously scheduled tirade, Noah grabbed my hand and pulled me through the store. "Come here, you've gotta see this too. Jonah's just outdone himself."

Knowing it was pointless to protest, I allowed myself to be led past massive piles of junk to the back room. Jonah was with another man behind a worktable. Like his twin only moments before, Jonah's eyes lit up as he saw me. "Awesome. Check this out." Without waiting he lifted a little iron man who was roughly six inches tall, twisted a key on his back, and then placed him on the table. The tiny figure spun the opposite direction, wobbled precariously, and then, accompanied with the sound of grinding gears, the middle of his chest opened and a small cannon emerged. With a loud pop, a cannonball shot across the table, sending other iron figures I'd not noticed through the air, only to clatter on the floor.

Watson rushed back into the main room.

Noah and Jonah both beamed as if they'd just cured cancer.

"Whoa!" The awe in Miles's voice suggested that they had, and he pointed toward the wall where one of the iron figures had impaled itself, only its feet visible through the drywall. "That had more force than any of them before."

My rage returned, doubled in fact, at seeing the protruding toy soldier... or whatever it was. "Are you telling me *this* is what has kept exploding all morning?"

"Oh, no. And I'm sorry about the noises. All part of construction and invention." There was actually some humility in Noah's tone, but pride returned when he gestured to the cannon retracting inside the soldier's chest. "This isn't that loud, it's all mechanical. The projectile, the miniature explosion, the movement, all of it. There's not a fuse, gunpowder, nothing like that."

"Amazing, right?" Jonah nodded along. "Completely safe."

The twins had huge success with some of their inventions, to the point that they'd made a fortune on those. But others had nearly cost them a fortune in lawsuits. I pointed at the half-buried soldier in the wall. "I don't know if I'd call that safe. It might as well be a bullet shot from a gun."

"No. Not at all. It's just a toy. These are going to be..." Jonah's words faded away weakly as he looked at the protruding legs of the toy soldier. "Oh. That could hurt someone... maybe..."

Noah gave a matching expression and slumped in defeat.

Miles laughed heartily and slapped Noah on the shoulder. "Back to the drawing board."

Before either of the twins could reply, I jumped in. "While you're at the drawing board, is it possible you guys could remember that you're downtown now? The noises the past several days have been scaring away the customers from the bookshop and bakery. And this morning, you're literally shaking the walls. A whole pile of pastries Katie made were scattered all over the floor from the vibrations."

"Yeah..." Noah sighed, managing to sound both guilty and put upon. "We've had a couple other storeowners start complaining already, but we didn't think you would be one of them."

I gestured again at the protruding feet.

"I am sorry." Noah's apology seemed genuine. "I know the renovations have been... extensive. The last thing we wanted was to wear out our welcome with our shop neighbors."

The man at the table beside Jonah chuckled and nudged him with his shoulder. "Miles and I have the same complaints from our neighbors in Boulder, but I don't think *we've* ruined anyone's pastries yet."

Proving to be loyal and devoted, Watson padded back into the room, but betrayed his nerves by slinking under the hem of my broomstick skirt for protection. I felt the weight of his rump settle on the toe of one of my boots, and his forepaws and head rested on the other.

The fourth man chuckled again. "Cute dog."

"He's Watson, and his nerves are shot from the constant barrage of noise." I hadn't meant to sound so rude. "As are mine, clearly."

"Niles, this is Winifred, the one who owns the bookshop and bakery next door. Noah and Jonah's sister-in-law." Miles motioned between us. "Winifred, this is my twin, Niles."

I nearly did a double take—I wouldn't even have thought the two men were brothers, let alone twins. Niles was short, skinny, and... while not unattractive, wasn't overly captivating either.

He laughed again, good-naturedly. "If I had a nickel for every time a woman gave that reaction when finding out we're twins." Niles gestured toward Miles. "He got the looks. I got the brains."

"No. It's not that. I just..." Not knowing how to finish that gracefully, I did a one-eighty. "I'm just a little overwhelmed by the number of twins in my life. My stepsisters are twins and they own Chakras on the other side of the Cozy Corgi. My business partner and I have twins who work for us in the bookshop and bakery. Jonah and Noah are on this side, and now... you two."

"Don't worry." Miles flashed his charming smile. "The Styles brothers won't be moving up here. We're more the fancy Boulder type than the mountain town of Estes Park type."

The Styles brothers? So... their names were Miles and Niles Styles? Good God. It was nearly enough to make me ask what was wrong with their parents.

"Miles and Niles are inventors as well. We met them at

a convention..." Jonah shot a questioning expression toward Noah.

Noah shrugged. "I don't know, at least twenty years ago."

"We own a similar shop in Boulder." Niles spoke up again, and as his eyes twinkled, I realized they were the exact same shade of blue as his twin's. "Although ours isn't quite as... eclectic as this one."

Jonah narrowed his eyes. "I'm going to pretend you meant that as a compliment." He turned back to me, this time smiling apologetically. "We'll try to keep it down. We really are sorry."

"Please do. Katie's planning to murder you both." Might as well leave out that I'd also made a similar threat.

Noah laughed. "That would almost be funny. You having to solve our murder only to discover it's your best friend."

I sighed. It seemed we'd reached a consensus. "I suppose so."

Jonah came closer, throwing his arm affectionately over my shoulders. Beneath my skirt, Watson growled again. Jonah merely chuckled. "Will you still come over to help us get ready tonight? Prove that there's no hard feelings?"

The Styles twins both nodded, but it was Miles who spoke. "There's a lot to do before the grand opening tomorrow, that's why we came up early. They need as many pairs of hands as we can get." He glanced toward the bottom of my skirt. "And paws, I suppose."

"Oh, shoot!" Jonah released my shoulders. "I forgot to tell you guys. Noah and I scheduled the opening on the wrong day. Fred's turning forty tomorrow, so we pushed back to May thirty-first instead of the thirtieth. Can you hang out an extra day?" Without waiting for a response, he looked back at me. "I can't wait for you to open your present tomorrow. Noah and I have been working on it for months."

I felt the blood drain from my face. "You... *invented* something for me for my birthday?"

The twins nodded enthusiastically, looking more like children than middle-aged men.

I managed both a smile and to not groan, which I felt was impressive. If the iron soldier was a portent, it looked like my fortieth birthday might be my last.

The noise was minimal for the remainder of the day. No walls shook, no books toppled off shelves, and no pastries rolled across the floor, much to Watson's despair—he'd cast off napping in his favorite spot in the afternoon sunshine to wait patiently in the bakery for such an occasion. We even noticed an uptick in tourists. Granted, with it being the very end of May, every day that passed meant more kids were out for summer vacation, so more families arrived to town— but it could only help if they didn't feel like they were in the middle of a war zone while they shopped for books and snacked on almond croissants.

"You sure your family isn't going to be upset if I skip this evening's festivities?" Katie looked at me nervously as she and I finished wrapping up the Cozy Corgi for the day. We'd already sent the twins home. "You all are so important to me, and I don't want to let anyone down."

"They won't even think twice. Plus, there's so many of us, they might not even notice you're not there." The words were already out of my mouth before I realized how that sounded, so I tried to fix my error by squeezing her shoulder. "When they ask about you, I'll tell them you decided to bake at home tonight so that Noah and Jonah would stay alive."

She chuckled. "I think the worst of my anger has passed, Noah and Jonah clearly made an effort. But I truly am going to do some baking. I'm working on a new recipe." She rushed ahead as if that topic was off-limits. "Leo isn't coming either, is he? I figure if the boyfriend can be MIA, the best friend can as well."

"No." I shook my head. "They're putting the finishing touches to the national park's summer youth program. We've barely seen each other more than in passing this week, but that should settle in the next day or so."

As if taking her leave before I changed my mind, Katie tossed her purse over her shoulder, headed toward the door, and wiggled her fingers in farewell at Watson, who only glowered. "I think Watson took it personally that no other pastries were sacrificed to him this afternoon, and apparently he's decided it was my fault."

"See, one more reason you should take the night off. No one deserves to put up with grumpy-corgi attitude." Following her lead, I snagged my purse as well and retrieved Watson's leash, though we wouldn't need it since we were just going next door. "See you tomorrow, don't bake too hard."

Katie was already half out the door, but poked her head back in. "Happy early fortieth birthday!"

She ducked out before I could respond. She'd spent the day reminding me in a billion ways that I only had a few more hours left before I was officially over the hill.

Over the hill. What a phrase that was, as if everything else was sliding toward the grave.

The family was in full swing as Watson and I walked into Twinventions. My mother and stepsisters were arranging things on shelves, my four nephews and nieces had been put to work cleaning, and my stepfather, Barry, and Jonah and Noah were carrying things back and forth from the workroom. There was such chaos, no one even noticed when Watson and I arrived.

For all the constant banging, and over a year of endless remodels of the shop, Twinventions had come together better than I'd predicted. It was unrecognizable from the all-natural, sugar-free candy store that had been there previously. It seemed wider, even though I knew it wasn't, but without the long candy display running through the middle, it gave that illusion. But it was shorter, the main shop just a big square space—they'd cut the length in half, using the front portion for the shop, and the back portion for their workshop, or... *Inventors' Studio*, as they called it. It worried me to no end how thrilled Zelda and Verona were that their husbands were no longer inventing stuff in the large shed in their shared backyard. Clearly the danger had moved right next door to the Cozy Corgi.

They'd designed the walls in exposed brick and aged them beautifully. Everything was steel, copper, iron, bronze, and wood. Nearly every shelf had gears and chains affixed to them. If it had been anyone else besides Jonah and Noah, I would've assumed they were there for decoration, but... they weren't. I was certain even the shelves had some function, practical or not.

Barry noticed me first as he emerged from the back room, abandoning a huge metal contraption right on the floor as he hurried toward us. "Fred, Watson!"

Like two long-lost lovers, my stepfather and my corgi met in gleeful abandon in the middle of the shop, Barry wrapping his long, thin arms around Watson and receiving a face full of puppy kisses. It was a tangle of red-and-purple tie-dye and dog hair.

"Really, Barry..." Though Mom's voice held reprimand, she smiled as she looked at the two of them. "The kids just got done sweeping." She came over and gave me a hug.

Though the majority of the family saw each other nearly every single day, all work stopped for a moment as it was rounds of greetings and hugs and hellos.

After a quick embrace, Jonah stood back and held his arms wide. "Well, what do you think?"

"I think you actually have a shop here. It's beautiful." As I spoke, I realized the truth of my words—the morning felt like weeks ago. "You literally had piles of junk all over the floor. How in the world did you pull this off in such few hours?"

"A little help from our friends." Noah made a similar gesture, encompassing everyone, then shook a finger at me. "And *none* of those piles had a single item of *junk* in them. I can promise you that."

"That's debatable." Zelda ignored the reproachful glance from her husband and turned to her twin. "But we're glad it's *here* now."

Verona nodded enthusiastically. "Amen to that."

"Come on." Jonah took my hand as Noah had earlier in the day. "Let's show you around."

"Everything is in sections," Noah chimed in, and though I was certain everyone had already seen, most of the group followed along. As he spoke, Noah pointed to different parts of the square space. "We've got the family and kids' sections, where you'll find diaper changers, shoelace tiers, and lullaby singers. Over there we have the art section. We have robots that will paint for you, fold origami for you, and write music for you."

I couldn't imagine why anyone would want a robot that folded origami for them—that seemed to negate the point, kind of like if they'd built a machine that read books for a person and simply offered them the CliffsNotes. But I kept my mouth shut as he continued, lest I give them ideas.

"There's the cooking section." Noah leaned in as if it was a secret. "Katie won't like our newest creation. It can make *anything*—it just needs a recipe. Totally replaces chefs. Granted, you have to redesign your kitchen, as the robot arm has to have free rein to get to the shelves and appliances, but once you've made that initial investment, you'll never have to cook again."

"We even have a dog section," Jonah interrupted, grabbing my other hand and leading me toward the opposite wall. He smacked his thigh as he did so. "Come on, Watson. You were the inspiration for all of this."

Watson didn't even glance Jonah's way, and just kept his adoring gaze on Barry.

Jonah didn't notice. "This is a dog robot that does everything a real dog can do. It fetches the paper, wags its tail, barks at squirrels, but you'll never need to walk it or potty train it. There's a ball that your real dog can play with when you're gone—when he hits it against something, your voice comes out of it. Of course, you'll customize it to whatever you want it to say. And over here we've got a treat dispenser, it's attached to a treadmill. For every mile the dog walks, he gets a treat. We thought it might help Watson with his weight issue."

I stared at the tiny treadmill. It was *almost* a good idea. I could predict how Watson would react to just about anything, but I wasn't sure—even with as much as he loved treats—if he'd be willing to do a mile of exercise to get one. Before I could make a comment, my gaze was caught by shifting colors in the next section. I gaped, barely able to believe my eyes. "Is that... it can't be." I turned to look at the twins and noticed my mom behind their shoulders give an exasperated shake of her head.

Not noticing, Noah walked to the glistening garland and scrunched a section in his hand. "It's improved. This one won't cut you. No one's going to be murdered with our garland ever again."

"Although..." Jonah whispered once more, though this time not in excitement. "We're still working out a couple of kinks, so it's not officially for sale yet. Every once in a while, it sends out an electrical charge, but it seems to be killing cell phone batteries more than people."

I couldn't believe my ears. Though *technically* the garland hadn't killed anyone, it had been an accomplice in a murder, and later a piece of it had gotten stuck in Watson's mouth and required a trip to the vet. I decided to let it go. "It seems like you're focusing heavily on robotics for the store. It's all very—" I searched for a pleasant way to say strange without it sounding like I was calling their inventions pointless. "—eccentric."

The twins nodded, apparently pleased with my word choice. Noah jumped in. "It's different from what we sell on the home shopping networks. For one, it's in our contracts that those are exclusively sold through them, so we couldn't have those items here, even if we wanted to."

Jonah took over. "And we didn't want to anyway. Twinventions is cutting edge, and stuff you won't find anywhere else." He pointed to another section. "Take the Manscaper—it's everything a guy needs for grooming in one spot." He patted a six-foot metal cage-like contraption that seemed to be something between a workout device and a torture chamber. It was styled in steampunk fashion, with gears, wheels, and levers of pewter and gold. "We hope to have one for women within the next couple of months. It's a little more complicated and has a few more kinks."

"Plus"—Noah cast an accusing glare toward Zelda and Verona—"we've been unable to find brave volunteers to assist in the finer aspects of its development."

"You know I don't want to doubt either of you, but *dream on*." Verona moved closer and pointed to a couple of different projectiles as she gave me a knowing look. "There's no way this is safe with all these scissors and razor blades."

"Razor blades?" I moved closer and made sense of what I was seeing. Sure enough, one of the robotic arms ended in a pair of scissors, another in an old-fashioned straight razor. Others had tweezers, combs, nail clippers, and several items I wasn't sure what they were for but wouldn't want anywhere near my body. "You're saying this contraption..." I adjusted at the insulted look that passed over the twins' faces. "Er... invention... what? Shaves a man? Cuts his hair?"

They nodded enthusiastically, but it was Jonah who spoke. "Sure does. Plus, *everything* else. Trims eyebrows, plucks nose and ear hair; you name it. And it's not at all dangerous. Noah and I have tried it several times. Granted we've got a couple of nicks in the trial runs, but now it's flawless. There're lasers that catch every plane and curve of a person's face and neck. And it learns quickly—it will know a guy's head and body better than the person himself within a few sessions."

"You actually tried it on yourself?" I couldn't keep the wonder out of my voice, or the horror. Who knew why I was surprised? It sounded like something the twins would do.

Again, Noah nodded. "Yep, we're even going to use it

for the main demonstration during our open house. It'll be the star of the show."

"And *I'm* the guinea pig. That should show you how much faith I have in these two." Miles Styles emerged from the back room. I'd not realized the Styles brothers were there. At the sight of him, my heart rate increased. Miles truly was the spitting image of Branson Wexler. "Doesn't hurt that we"—he motioned to Niles who followed behind —"helped work out some of the kinks. I'm certain this baby is as safe as it can get."

"Here, watch." Niles stepped around his twin and stood in the center of the contraption, then tapped a few buttons on the display pad.

As it came to life, whirling robotic arms moved of their own accord. Gears and cranks and pistons set off a cacophony of commotion.

Watson growled and left Barry to hurry to my side, taking a protective stance. He might get more excited to see Barry, but it was always nice to know, at the end of the day, I was truly his favorite. Keeping my gaze on what surely looked like a deathtrap, I knelt and stroked Watson's side.

Niles continued punching buttons. "I'll show you the haircut. You just put in your preferences, and this baby will get you ready to go to the Oscars."

"Or, better yet, the invention awards." Miles beamed as he looked toward Noah and Jonah. "Which, I think you two might have a shot at it with this. If nothing else, it'll be the talk of this year's convention."

Niles shook his head. "It's not about awards. It's about the love of invention, of creation." He hit a couple more buttons. "Now... watch."

Several of us gasped, me included, as the scissors came rushing toward Niles's head.

It took me a second to realize I'd slammed my eyes shut, expecting to see him stabbed in the forehead. Instead, when I cracked them open, two arms, the one with the scissors and another with a comb worked in unison, trimming Niles's mop of brown hair.

We stood transfixed for the entire three minutes until the robotic arms pulled away and a couple more emerged, one ending with a hairdryer and another with a brush. The hairdryer blew the excess hair from Niles's face while the brush made quick work over his entire body.

Finally, Niles turned to us, beaming. "See, still got both ears and everything. In fact—"

A knock on the door cut him off.

Proving that we were both on edge from the grooming machine, I flinched at the sound, and Watson growled in a more vicious manner than typical.

Turning toward the door, I saw a tall older man illuminated against the night by the lights of the store.

Jonah groaned. "Great... it's Peter. *Perfect* timing."

"I'll take care of him." Noah gestured with his hands around the shop as he walked toward the door. "No need to keep from working, everyone. Shows over."

Most of the family followed the directions, but since I hadn't been given a chore yet, I kept my attention on Noah. Jonah followed shortly behind him.

Though it appeared that the twins tried to block the way by standing shoulder to shoulder when they opened the door, the man, Peter it seemed, stepped around them instantly. "I couldn't wait any longer. Had to come see for myself." He didn't pause at all, but instantly began to walk around the store as if on a mission, casting his gaze over every section without pausing. Neither did he smile at nor greet anyone else.

There was a frantic energy about the man, and I didn't think it was just leftover adrenaline from the witnessing of the whirling scissors and razor blades. As he stormed nearer, both Watson and I took a step back.

He was clearly older, I'd guessed him to be in his seventies, but there was something unusual-looking about the man. It took me a second to place what it was. When overhead lighting hit the planes of his cheeks as he passed by, I understood. Instead of the age lines and wrinkles that accompanied the older members of my family, his skin was smooth and taut over the bones of his face. Almost uncomfortable-looking. I'd bet he'd had extensive plastic surgery.

He made his way through the small store in record time, the twins trailing behind him, looking nervous.

"Where are they?" Peter halted abruptly, turning on them. "I thought we had an agreement."

"We do." Jonah nodded frantically.

Noah took over. "We just haven't set them up yet." He pointed to the far back corner. "That's going to be the Blossom's Beauties section there."

Following the motion, Peter scowled. "In the back? Like an afterthought?"

"No!" Noah sounded a little too enthusiastic. He hurried over toward the corner where they didn't seem to have enough spare wall space for a section of anything. "Actually, it's next to the best spot in the store." He flicked a switch. The bare back wall of the store that separated the shop from the workroom became transparent, like a lightly smoked window. Through it, the workroom was illuminated. With the endless renovations, I'd forgotten about that detail. "It's right next to where people watch us work, where they can see inventions come to life."

To demonstrate, Jonah hurried into the workroom and

went around flipping switches and pushing buttons, setting various contraptions into motion.

When they'd mentioned this idea months ago, I'd thought it sounded interesting, but hadn't quite captured their vision. I had to admit it was impressive. Though the shop part itself seemed filled to overflowing with gadgets and gizmos, wheels and cranks, and things I had no words for, the amount of stuff was nearly tripled in their work-space, and in the abundance of massive clusters of Edison bulbs hanging from the ceilings and various small spotlights here and there on various desks, it was like a modern inter-pretation of Frankenstein's workshop.

Peter took a step back, crossed his arms and considered. "Okay then. This might just work." He glanced toward the corner. "I still don't see a place for the dolls."

"They'll go here." Noah pointed at a corner cabinet filled with what looked like silverware with arms and legs. "We were just... um... filling it up to get an idea of how it would look. We didn't want the dolls to get damaged in the move."

Clearly he was lying, but Jonah didn't give Peter a chance to call him on it as he rushed back in from the work-room, a large box in his hand. "Here you go. You can..." He glanced at the shelf and then his twin. "Noah, clear that junk off of there." Then he turned back to Peter. "You can arrange them yourself, however you like."

At least satiated enough not to argue about it, Peter took the box from Jonah. "Well, it's a good thing I came by tonight, clearly this wouldn't have been done right for tomorrow's opening."

The twins' faces fell again, and Noah spoke as he gath-ered the silverware robots into his arms. "I guess we forgot to tell you as well. We moved the opening to the day after tomorrow. Sorry, we've just been so busy, things are slipping."

"That can't be! You said it was tomorrow. The day after, Blossom and I are heading to Denver. I'm meeting with a potential investor."

"Sorry. It is our fault. We double-booked." Jonah pointed to me. "We forgot that it's our sister-in-law's fortieth birthday tomorrow. We're having a—"

"Having a family dinner to celebrate." Mom jumped in, stepping up beside me. Though her voice was pleasant, there was a *this isn't up for a debate* quality to it. I didn't know if she knew Peter or not, but she clearly didn't care for him, and as my mother tended to see the best in everyone, that was enough for me. "Surely you understand that a person only turns forty once."

Peter turned narrowed eyes on me, then glanced down at Watson, who, though he wasn't growling, had his top lip curled over his teeth as if in warning. "Right... the bookstore woman." He sneered slightly. "Well... still... an agreement is an—"

"You're in plenty of stores already, Mr. Moss." Barry came up to stand on the other side of us. Though I wasn't entirely sure where the tension came from, it felt like we were arranging ourselves for battle. "As you know, Estes tries not to have too many repetitive items throughout the downtown. You're in a couple of shops already. I'd say not to press it."

In his clearly expensive suit and with his arrogant demeanor, it was surprising to see the man give a deferential, albeit begrudging, expression toward my flighty, tie-dye-clad stepfather. After a moment he let out a frustrated sigh. "Fine. Blossom and I can rearrange. The day after tomorrow it is." With that, he turned with his box toward the shelves.

Feeling like I was missing something, I turned toward Barry and opened my mouth.

He shook his head.

"Later, dear." Mom patted my arm as she whispered, "It's not a big deal and really not worth it."

"I don't want my birthday dinner to—"

Barry patted my other arm and smiled lovingly. "Don't even finish that."

As everyone fell back into the roles of getting Twinventions ready, and I helped my mom and stepsisters arrange things on shelves, Watson padded to the dog section and curled up by a robot corgi and napped.

I couldn't keep my attention off Peter Moss as he arranged his dolls on the shelves. To my surprise, I recognized them. I had seen them in a couple of the shops over the past month or so. Typically, they were something I would look over without noticing—I wasn't a huge doll person—but these were... creepy. Clearly they weren't meant to be, even by their name, which Peter affixed with a fancy metal sign at the top of the case that read Blossom's Beauties. They were intended to be pretty. It was also evident in their styling—the wigs they wore were shiny, highly coiffed hair and styles. Their clothes were elaborate and done in clearly expensive material. In a way, they looked like old-time china dolls, but their faces... again, highly detailed and surely meant to be beautiful. Instead of the high gloss of china or the dull sheen of plastic, these looked like they were made from actual skin. I couldn't imagine why the twins wanted them in their store.

Unable to help myself, I moved closer, looking from the

dolls to Peter's face. They shared the same quality. Too tight, too shiny, and triggered goose bumps over my arms.

Feeling my attention, Peter looked over his shoulder. "Beautiful, aren't they?"

I jumped as if caught, which I suppose I was, and took too long in my response. "Yes. Very... lifelike."

Peter nodded his agreement, clearly not hearing the lie, or at least choosing to overlook it. "That's the point. People should be able to see themselves in the dolls. To see both where they are and the beauty they could be."

I was neither sure what he meant by that or how to respond to it, so I went in a different direction. "I've seen a few in some of the other shops, but I don't think we've met. Are you new to town?"

He refocused on arranging the dolls as he spoke. "No. We don't get up here very often. Blossom and I live in Fort Collins. We bought a cabin for the weekends in Estes about a year ago, but we only use it once every couple of months or so."

Blossom's Beauties. "Oh. Is Blossom your—" Suddenly I wasn't sure of the safest guess... Partner? Pet? "—wife?"

He only nodded and continued arranging.

"Does your wife make them?"

Still not looking at me, Peter shook his head. "No, they're my creations. But she allows me to use her name. She's the face of the company. They sell much better as *Blossom's* Beauties than *Peter's* Beauties. Not to mention, all the old biddies who purchase them have old-fashioned notions about a man playing with dolls."

"Oh... I suppose it makes sense." I couldn't fathom *anyone* buying them, regardless of who made them.

Before I could think of anything else to say, or leave him, Peter finally peered over his shoulder and really looked at me, intently studying my face. "You have excellent bone structure, and your skin complexion is lovely. Of course, that tone is common for women with your auburn hair."

I'd never had a compliment make my skin crawl in such a manner, lovely complexion or not—as if he was going to use it to cover some of his dolls. "Um... thank you." I started to turn away.

"Forty is pushing it, but you're not too late to start."

I tried to make sense of his statement, but gave up quickly. "I'm sorry?"

He lifted a finger to the corner of his eyes. "Your crow's feet, less than a lot of forty-year-old women would have." He touched his nose and his chin. "Maybe more of a curve to the bridge of your nose and a little tightening under your jaw. Just a few minor things and you can look a decade younger." His gaze flitted to my waist. "You could be ravishing if—"

"I'm actually okay with turning forty and looking it." That wasn't always entirely true. I did have some nerves around turning forty from time to time, but I had even more nerves occasionally with whatever he was about to say regarding my waistline, and I didn't want to hear it. Not to mention that whatever creepiness his dolls possessed held nothing on how off-putting the man himself was. "I should go help." I started to say good luck with his dolls, but then realized I didn't mean it in the slightest, so I turned away.

"I didn't intend offense." The words sounded like an apology, but his tone didn't. Despite myself I turned back, but found I still had nothing to say. Again he pointed at his own features. "It's just a recommendation, one that I have taken personally. I highly advocate getting work done. As you can see." He smiled, a proud thing. "Take a guess how old I am."

"Ah... no." Why couldn't I just walk away and stop the conversation there? "I've learned it's never good to guess anyone's age, even if they ask."

Peter scowled but answered for me. "Most people think that I'm in my forties or fifties. But I'm sixty-three." He tilted his chin in pride. "As you can see, a little nip and tuck here and there does wonders. I can give you some contacts in the industry if you like."

My dislike of the man was so strong that I nearly confessed I'd thought he was in his seventies when I saw him. If anything, the too-tight, too-plastic-looking skin made him older. I didn't say it, though. Apparently getting ready to turn forty meant that I was learning to keep my mouth shut from time to time. "I'm glad you find satisfaction in it. But I think I'm good as I am." That time, when I turned around, I promised myself I'd keep walking no matter what he said.

"As you wish, but I wouldn't wait too long. You'll be amazed how much elasticity your skin will lose after you turn forty, not to mention if the diet you keep—"

"You don't want to finish that statement. Trust me." I broke my promise and turned back to him, my redheaded temper spiking. "Like you've been told and can tell from my crow's feet, as you kindly pointed out, I am *not* some young, insecure woman you can push around or insult. Regardless of whatever you think your intentions are."

"Now calm down. You're pretty enough, even for forty. I wasn't—"

To my surprise, I realized my fists were clenched. I started to walk away, then felt that gave him the power. "It's time for you to leave, Mr. Moss."

"Now listen here. I'm not done setting up my dolls, and this isn't your shop." He stood.

I took a step forward, knowing he was right, that I was overstepping my bounds, but I didn't care. "I'm helping my family get ready for their grand opening. I don't know why my brothers-in-law want your atrocious dolls here. They definitely don't match the theme." I stopped short of saying I couldn't understand why *anyone* would have the dolls in their store. "But I doubt they're aware of the kind of man you are. You're one of the most insulting, rude, entitled people I've met in ages, and that's saying something."

Only when Barry and Watson arrived beside me did I realize I'd raised my voice. I glanced over to see my entire family staring at us.

Clearly, Barry had heard what I'd said. He took the same tone he had earlier with Peter. "I'm not sure what you said to Winifred, and I'm not interested. But you're aware my brother-in-law, Fred's uncle, is on the town council. I'm not one for conflict, but..." He shook his head, reconsidering. "You have two options. You can take your dolls and leave the shop or—"

"Now listen here. Twinventions isn't yours either, and you have no—"

"Noah. Jonah." For the first time ever, Barry barked words in anger and turned toward his sons-in-law.

Though both of them were sheet-white and nervous, they nodded along as they looked toward Peter. "You heard him. The deal's off."

For a moment it looked like he was going to argue, but then he angrily swept the shelves of dolls into the box once more. "You two will regret this. Mark my words."

Once he left, all eyes turned to the twins.

Jonah raised his hand in defeat.

"Sorry. He..." Noah blushed, and his gaze froze to the

floor. "He convinced us it was a good business decision." Finally, he looked up at me. "Fred, we're so—"

"It's not your fault. No need to be sorry." Some part of me whispered that I needed to apologize for setting my foot down about him leaving. Peter had been right, Twinventions wasn't mine. I couldn't make myself apologize, though. I turned it into a joke. "I think you'll owe me. Those dolls were horrible."

"Even worse than those silverware robots you have," Christina, the youngest of my nieces, muttered, barely loud enough to be heard.

"Hey!" Noah and Jonah exclaimed in unison.

The laughter that followed was needed desperately, and almost made me forget about turning forty in a few hours.

"For a little bit there, I thought you were trying to kill me on my fortieth birthday." I sat down on the double layer of blankets Leo had spread over the rocks, began unfastening my laces, ready to be free of my hiking boots, and looked at the view. "But it was worth the risk."

Watson plopped down between us, tongue hanging out and legs spread wide in imitation of the bearskin rug.

"I think he agrees with you." Leo chuckled and ruffled Watson's fur. "Maybe I should've chosen an easy instead of moderate hike, but this is one of my favorite places around Estes. I couldn't think of anything more beautiful for your birthday, and it's early enough in the season that we have a good chance of having Gem Lake to ourselves."

I wasn't the type who wanted a pampering spa experience for my birthday, but I hadn't predicted a half-day hike either. Although, after the steep first quarter mile or so, things got easier, and with every step, the scenery and views grew more spectacular. Leo had set a calm pace, one that provided a relaxing experience that lent itself to conversation or simply traveling along in comfortable silence.

Stretching out my legs, I took in the view. We sat at the top of the mountain, by a wide but shallow circular lake surrounded on three sides by towering granite walls that looked as if they were made of layers of cake. Tall, twisted evergreens grew from cracks and crevices. At our back, the forest spread out to a view of the entire mountain range and the ant-sized panorama of Estes Park below. The robin's-egg sky, cotton-candy clouds, and bright warm sun saturated the colorful hues in the stones and trees and reflected over the crystalline surface of the lake, making it look like a portal to a mirrored world.

It made me feel small and infinite at the same time.

Leo's hand slipped into mine. Instead of looking at him, I leaned over, letting my shoulder rest against his, the two of us forming an arch over Watson's splayed fluff.

Maybe a hike wasn't what I would've planned, but... with the beauty, the warmth of the sun, the gentle crisp in the breeze, the touch of Watson's weight on my thigh, and the linked connection as Leo's fingers slipped between mine, I realized it was perfect. As if knowing I needed a moment to etch it all into my memory, Leo didn't speak, simply caressed his thumb over the back of my hand.

This wasn't the life I'd envisioned having at forty years old. For a long time, I'd pictured life with my ex-husband, Garrett, the kids I'd assumed we would've had, and rising up the ranks at the university where I'd taught. When that dream crashed, it reformed and grew into a publishing company, and I'd predicted my old best friend and me dominating the world of mystery fiction. Then another crash, another betrayal.

So, I'd rebuilt my life completely on my own terms, for once.

I moved to Estes Park, opened my dream bookshop, and settled down to what I figured the rest of my days would look like. I hadn't thought much about my fortieth birthday, of course, but if I had, it would've simply been just another day working at the Cozy Corgi, then going home to read by the fire with Watson at my feet. In truth, a perfectly lovely existence.

Without pulling away, I turned from the nearly unearthly beauty that surrounded us and studied Leo's profile.

After a moment he looked at me as well, our faces so near it was almost uncomfortable... yet, it wasn't. He grinned, shyly. "What?"

I couldn't answer for a moment, overwhelmed. This... us... hadn't been planned, hadn't even been wanted. In many ways I'd fought against it, pushed against it, right out ignored it and deceived myself at times. Yet, here we were. When I spoke, the words spilled out before I had a chance to think through them. "This isn't going to crash, is it?"

It wasn't really a question, and Leo didn't need any explanation. He shook his head, his honey-brown eyes gentle and clear. "No. It isn't."

It wasn't the first time we'd said something like that. Even though we'd only been dating for a matter of months, we'd known each other well over a year, and things were... settled. Once we'd finally crossed that line I'd refused to acknowledge for so long, everything clicked, and we both knew it. It seemed everyone knew it.

Silence settled over us again, save for the gentle quaking of the newly emerged aspen leaves and the whistle through the pine needles bringing the Colorado scent to us. Birds sang overhead. At our side, a chipmunk scurried, paused to inspect, hoping we would offer him a morsel, then hurried on his way. Next to us, Watson snored.

Not only was it a perfect fortieth birthday, it was a perfect moment, made even more so by the knowledge it was merely one of countless to follow.

The moment was finally broken when Watson's tummy woke up before he did, gurgling loudly. He gave a little jump, startled, and then turned blinking chocolate eyes to me.

"Hungry?"

He whimpered.

"We can solve that." Leo released my hand and twisted to retrieve the picnic basket set behind us.

Within a matter of minutes, Leo had arranged a massive spread between us that would've rivaled any fancy wine bar's charcuterie plate—prosciutto, mortadella sausage, pâté, candied fruit, figs, dried cherries, jam, Parmesan, smoked cheddar, burrata, several varieties of olives, crackers, toasted sourdough slices, and an entire loaf of ciabatta bread.

Watson was nearly beside himself by the time Leo was finished.

"Are we expecting company?" The array was spectacular, and there was enough to feed an army.

Leo pulled two green glass bottles of sparkling water from the picnic basket and handed me one. "Oh please, my guess is the three of us will have this scarfed down in a matter of minutes, and by the time we hike back down this afternoon, our appetites will be raring to go for the family birthday dinner this evening."

He wasn't wrong. "I'm so glad you know that I'm not a salad girl."

He made a disgusted face. "*I'm* so glad you're not a salad girl. In fact..." He twisted around again and retrieved a small Saran-wrapped plate. "All the other stuff I bought, but *this*, I made. I called Mom last night and got the recipe. I'm sure it won't be up to Katie's baking standards, but it's a family favorite."

"Chocolate! You do love me." My mouth watered looking at the small, thick squares. "Fudge?"

He nodded. "Yeah, but maybe a little different than you've had before. It's got cinnamon and cayenne pepper. It's heaven." His eyes widened. "Oh, and another thing." Another twist and he emerged with a huge dog bone. "Paulie said this keeps Flotsam and Jetsam busy for hours. So I figured, with Watson, we might be able to get halfway through dinner before he takes his share."

Watson gave his classic bunny hop with his front paws, followed by a happy spin before snatching the huge dog treat from Leo's grasp and scurrying to the edge of the blanket, as if he feared we expected him to share.

I chuckled, experiencing a warm rush of love for my adorably selfish pup. "I think his food motivation is why he and I connect so well."

We took our time eating, arranging the items in various combinations. Just like everything else, it was perfect. "Thank you for going to all this trouble. It really is—"

"Good grief, Fred." Leo cut me off with a furrowed brow. "This wasn't that much trouble. Not only is it your birthday, it's your *fortieth* birthday. That's a huge deal. It's special. Don't thank your boyfriend for wanting to celebrate it."

I narrowed my eyes. "If you start saying the number forty over and over again, like Katie did yesterday, I'm going to take it as you rubbing it in that you're so much younger than me." I was kidding, at least I thought so.

"I'm not *that* much younger." He winked. "I'll be in my forties as well before you're into your fifties."

I let out a mix of a screech and a laugh, a sound I didn't think I'd ever made before, and smacked Leo on the shoulder. "I'm not having that hard of a time turning forty, but let's never bring up the word fifty again, thank you very much."

He only laughed, and then, after a few moments, grew serious. "You get more beautiful every day. Trust me, at the rate you're going, fifty is going to be astounding."

I narrowed my eyes again. "Just because you're wooing me with piles of cheese, doesn't mean I won't drown you in that gorgeous lake over there. Plus, then I'd have the fudge all to myself."

Another laugh.

I started to tell him about Peter Moss's comment on my forty-year-old skin the day before, but Leo leaned in and gave me a quick kiss on the lips.

As he started to pull back, he pressed in again, making the kiss longer, sweeter, and melting me utterly. "I love you."

"I love you too."

No. This wasn't how I'd ever pictured my fortieth birthday. How could I? I'd never realized life could be so good.

In what surely was only a matter of minutes, Watson's massive dog bone magically disappeared, and he was back at my side, begging to join in the feast. We obliged, tearing off small pieces of meat and spreading them out over longer intervals than he appreciated. "We don't want to give you too much, buddy. The salt content in the prosciutto isn't good for you."

Leo handed him a small slice, then grinned at me. "And it has absolutely nothing to do with the fact that your mom and I want to eat it all ourselves."

"No. It definitely doesn't." At my laugh, Watson stood, walked around the perimeter of the blanket, and took a spot beside Leo instead, clearly judging him to be the weaker link.

After we finished the main course, Leo took out more items from the picnic basket—two champagne flutes and a small gift with a card.

I started to tell him again that he shouldn't have done anything, then stopped myself. He was right. A fortieth birthday was a special deal, and I needed to get better at being loved in such a way.

Leo handed me the present. "Open the card first. It's actually the bigger part of your gift."

I did as he asked, and loved that instead of some sweeping mushy Hallmark card with a poem embossed in glittering calligraphy, it was a picture of a corgi looking over his shoulder, the fuzzy white portion of his nub-tailed bottom forming a heart. As I opened it, a piece of paper fell out. After retrieving it, I unfolded the paper. It took a couple of seconds before I understood. When I did, I looked over at Leo in stunned horror. "No, absolutely not. This is too much. Way, way too much."

He waved me off, laughing. "It doesn't have a price tag on there, so you don't know if it was too much or not. Plus, truth be told, it's selfish. It's a gift I get to enjoy as well."

I was speechless. I looked from him back to the certificate that read Snowy Peaks Travel Agency at the top. It simply stated that it was redeemable for two C-Travel Packages.

"You'll notice"—Leo suddenly sounded embarrassed—"that it's a C package. I couldn't quite afford an A or B experience, but I still think it will be fun."

"A travel package..." I was trying to put the pieces together. "You got a trip?" Actually, more like simply trying to believe he'd done something so lavish.

"Good job, Detective." Some of his nerves faded as he teased.

I turned the certificate over; there was nothing on the back. "To where?"

"There are several options in each package. So, it kinda depends on what you want. There are couple of cruises, a couple of different beach destinations, or some shorter weekend stays in New York City or San Diego." He brightened. "Oh, and I made sure that there's dog-friendly options as well, so Watson can go."

I felt my eyes sting. "You're too much, Leo Lopez. You know that?"

He blushed furiously, making his handsome face turn adorable. As if shoving that away, he continued. "I know it'll be a little bit since tourist season is just getting started, but I thought maybe... this fall, or after Christmas. It could be something to look forward to."

The trip, in and of itself, was wonderful enough. It was that added confirmation that there was no question or wondering about our timeline that took my breath away. That neither of us was going moment to moment to see if it would last. *That* was the best gift of all.

Before I could figure out what to say, Leo motioned toward the package that I'd placed in my lap. "Go ahead."

Feeling embarrassed at receiving so much, I untied the blue ribbon and lifted the lid.

"I know you're not the kind who needs a ton of jewelry," Leo said as I unfolded the tissue paper. "You've got the corgi earrings you wear every day, and the necklace that your mom made, but... I thought maybe you need this too, not that you have to wear it every day, but whenever you want."

I pulled the silver bracelet out, twisting it in the sunshine. The wavy striations glinted as did the jagged edges, but it wasn't until I noticed the thin vein traveling down the center that I realized what it was. "It's a feather."

When I looked up at him, Leo just lifted an eyebrow, as if waiting for me to figure it out.

Inspecting it once more, I turned it over to the gap made for me to slide my wrist into. On one side was the rounded edge of the feather, and on the other the small spike of the quill. Then it clicked, and I felt a huge smile spread over my face as I looked at Leo again. "The owl feather, the one I gave you the day we met."

"Yeah." He beamed, pleased. "Ben told me about an older member of the Ute tribe who lives in the Big Thompson Canyon. She makes jewelry. She modeled it after the tenth primary remix feather of a Mexican Spotted Owl." He shrugged. "It's become my favorite animal. It brought you to me."

Though the sentiment nearly brought tears, I couldn't help but laugh. "The tenth primary remix feather? That's specific."

"It's the feather at the tip of his wing, the ones lower are called secondary..." He rolled his eyes and stopped talking with a shake of his head.

"I love when my park ranger boyfriend geeks out." I leaned in again and kissed him hard, trying to infuse every ounce of love I had for Leo into the kiss. "Thank you, for the trip, the feather, this perfect birthday." I held his gaze. "For wanting to go on this journey with me."

"There's nowhere else I'd rather be." He stroked my cheek softly in that way that made me feel special and loved beyond measure, then grabbed the champagne flutes. "Final bit. And this will probably be your favorite part."

That struck me as odd, though I didn't comment on it. Champagne was all well and good, but it would never be my favorite part of anything. That was okay, Leo had gotten everything else pinpoint perfect.

Instead of retrieving a champagne bottle, he pulled out a huge thermos, unscrewed it, and poured a steaming brown liquid into the champagne flutes. "I swung by the Cozy Corgi this morning. Katie made us enough dirty chai to sustain a normal person for a week." He winked. "I figure it'll last us at least halfway back down the mountain."

Yep. I was truly loved by this man, and known inside and out.

Though Watson was annoyed beyond measure at not being allowed any of the chocolate, Leo and I snuggled up on the blanket and watched the reflection of the clouds dance over the surface of the lake as we savored his Mexican chocolate fudge and toasted my birth with dirty chais.

After a hot shower and cleaning up at my place, I could almost do a second hike up the mountain. The day had been so perfect it was nearly enough to convince me to trade Watson's and my typical morning stroll through the woods surrounding my cabin for a legitimate daily hike. However, I figured the notion would wear off when there wasn't a romantic birthday picnic with the most handsome park ranger in the world at the top of every peak. Even so, I was happier and more content than I could remember, and I had a rather wonderful day-to-day life in Estes Park, so that was saying something.

As Leo finished getting ready, I took a damp towel and cleaned off Watson's paws. He was so worn out he didn't even protest, just lay in his dog bed, his head resting on his stuffed yellow duck and lion, as he allowed me to get in between his toes without even looking annoyed.

The annoyance came soon enough as I requested for him to get up and move. Well, no, not annoyance, more like out-and-out refusal. Of course, when Leo stood by the front door, patted his thighs, and called Watson's name, my Benedict Arnold received a sudden surge of adrenaline and practically fell over himself as he rushed to one of his human forms of corgi catnip. The instant we piled back into Leo's Jeep, however, Watson returned to his snoring.

Leo was oddly quiet as we headed toward my parents' house, and I studied him through narrowed eyes. "What's wrong? You seem nervous."

His mouth moved silently for a few moments as he kept his gaze on the road. "Well... it's not every day a guy has the first birthday dinner with his girlfriend's family."

I flinched. "What? We're together all the—" A heart-stopping thought entered my mind, stealing my words.

At my abrupt silence, Leo finally glanced my way. "What?"

"You're a horrible liar." We were coming to a stop sign, where we'd make a right to go toward my parents' house. I licked my lips. "You're going to take a left up there, aren't you?"

His shoulders slumped. "Do you have to be brilliant and figure everything out?"

My heart sank at the confirmation. "I didn't figure it out soon enough. We're almost to the place where you turn back into town. Kind of a giveaway."

"I was supposed to say that your mom texted and needed us to run by the grocery store." Leo swallowed and looked at me again. "Please don't break up with me." He gave what was probably supposed to be a pitifully charming smile.

"Fine. I won't break up with you. But I will murder you." And it had been such a perfect day. Suddenly I was tempted to crawl in the back seat and curl up with Watson and just hope I wouldn't wake up till morning.

"In my defense, I argued against it. I was outvoted." That time I didn't think the pitiful sound in his voice was there to be charming.

"Still, you could've given me some warning."

"I thought about it." He shrugged as he turned left at the stop sign. "But I wanted today to be as perfect as possible, and if you'd known, you would've just been stressed about it."

I started to argue, then sighed. "You're right." I took his hand, and though part of me didn't want to know, I couldn't keep from asking. "Just tell me there's not that many people coming."

Leo hesitated and then combined his grin and shrug. "You already told me I'm not a good liar."

The yell of "*Surprise!*" rivaled the booming of Twinventions from the day before. Watson whimpered, and if he hadn't been on a leash, he would've darted right back through the open door of the Cozy Corgi. If my hand hadn't been in Leo's, I'd have accompanied him.

My family was large enough that even the planned birthday dinner constituted a sizable party, but from the amount of space filled in the bookshop, it looked like the entire population of Estes Park was in attendance. I had to give them credit—for a town that was so gossip-ridden that a person found out the latest tidbit nearly before it occurred, the fact they'd been able to keep this secret was impressive.

Judging from the amount of decorations, I was willing to bet they'd closed down the bookshop for the day. And decorate they had.

Two gold balloons, each around three feet high, floated in the very middle of the shop. The giant *four* and *zero* driving home my age with dead-on precision. They were the only variation in the color scheme as well. Everything else was black and silver. Twisting streamers alternating in black and silver were draped so thickly from ceiling to book-shelves that the space felt like we'd entered a circus tent designed by spiders. Countless clusters of black and silver balloons were so numerous that it made the already large crowd feel doubled in size. The typically gleaming hard-wood floor was covered in so much sparkling black and silver confetti, I had no doubt we'd be finding pieces for my *next* forty years.

All of this was absorbed in a matter of seconds, right before Leo released my hand and I was swept up in an endless wave of hugs, embraces, and greetings by family and friends, and then more awkwardly by acquaintances and people I was fairly certain were total strangers.

Even the Styles brothers were present. From Leo's reac-tion when he saw Miles, it seemed I wasn't imagining his resemblance to Branson. I shoved that thought away. He was the last person I wanted to think about.

"How many people did you invite?" I tried not to sound too accusing when Katie finally made her way to me. I didn't think I was successful.

"Well..." Katie, wearing a bright pink T-shirt embossed with a fat unicorn wearing a party hat and eating a cupcake, tilted her head from side to side as if considering. "Techni-cally, around thirty." She gestured toward a small group talking to Leo. "People who are truly friends, Paulie, Athena, Anna, Carl, and the like, got formal invitations." She chuckled as Watson pranced happily around Athena's teacup poodle, Pearl—it looked like Paulie's corgis weren't present. Then Katie continued, making a sweeping motion that accompanied the rest of the horde. "For everyone else, I created a Facebook event and made it open to the public, kind of like an open house sort of thing. With as little as you're on social media, I figured it was the safest way to go. Oh..." She smirked. "Your mom also made an announcement on her Instagram account, and she's got quite the following, so you can't just blame me. This was a true group effort."

I sighed in resignation.

Mom arrived, and she gripped my shoulders and met my eyes meaningfully. Clearly she'd overheard. "We know the large crowds and being the center of attention aren't your favorite things, but you only turn forty once, and we have family dinners all the time. We wanted something special." As Katie had only moments before, Mom gestured to the crowd, though she paused here and there, pointing out specific people. "It's also a good time for you to realize what an impact you have in Estes, how much you mean to people, how you make their lives better."

I followed her motion, spotting Myrtle Bantam, who owned the wild-bird store, chatting with Lisa Bloomberg, who ran Baldpate Inn. Then there was Pastor Davis of the Estes Valley Church. The owner of the T-shirt shop, Joe Singer. The Diamond family, who owned the toyshop. Marcus and Hester Gonzales, Angus Witt, and Jared Pitts. Charlene Sweitzer, her wheelchair being pushed by Glenda, who wore fairy wings of black and silver for the evening. Some of the Pink Panthers—Delilah Johnson, Nadiya Hameed, and Simone Pryce, and a few others whose names I couldn't recall. To my shock, even Carla Beaker, who on her worst days hated my guts and on her best wished to never see me again, was present. On and on, people popped out from the crowd. So many that had been impacted by me solving murders. Some of whom started off as suspects and ended up as friends.

It took my breath away.

After a year and a half, I truly had built a life in this little mountain town. And while I didn't relish being the center of attention, I sank into it. Everyone was kind enough to come celebrate my birth. I supposed I should celebrate how wonderful my life had become, and in a way, celebrate all of them.

Katie grabbed my hand, pulling my attention back. "Come on. Let's get this party really started with dessert and then you can open presents."

"No presents!" A fresh wave of embarrassment pummeled over me, but Katie didn't notice.

"All right, everyone!" Katie raised her voice to be heard over the crowd. "Follow us up to the bakery. There's sugar to be had!"

Settling back into the flow quickly enough, I followed Katie and my mother up the stairs. By the time we reached the top, Watson, closely followed by Pearl, was at my feet. I gasped as I turned to look at the bakery and then gaped at Katie. "I can't believe you."

She gave a disgusted grimace. "Let this be proof of just how much I love you. You're the only person in the world I would choose such disgusting colors for."

Instead of the black and silver from below, the streamers and balloons that filled Katie's beautiful bakery were shades of mustard yellow, pea green, rusty orange, and soft gray blue. Ridiculously, the color choice made my eyes sting for what felt like the hundredth time that day. And when we stepped farther in and I saw the spread covering the marble countertop, tears actually fell, and I didn't attempt to stop myself from hugging Katie tightly. "Special order, huh?"

A five-tiered cake sat in the center, the base of the frosting was white, but all the trimmings were done in those same earth tones, as was the filling of the hundreds and hundreds of cream puffs that cascaded in a swirl down the layers of cake and spread out over the counter.

"I didn't say I wasn't the one who placed the special order." She shrugged beneath my embrace. "Just wait until you taste it. The birthday cake is chocolate, but the filling of the cream puffs is your favorite. Dirty chai."

When I released her, Leo had joined us as well, and I grinned over at him. "Just as a warning, your girlfriend is about to gain a hundred pounds this evening."

"Good." He winked "I'd hate to be the only one."

A couple of minutes later, the most uncomfortable part of the evening took place, but it was brief, and by the time the last notes of the "Happy Birthday" song faded, I settled in once more to celebrating with the people I loved. I allowed myself one huge slice of birthday cake, but I wasn't going to put a limit on the spectacular dirty-chai-filled cream puffs.

Thankfully, since my family insisted I open presents directly after the cake—like we'd been transported to a child's birthday party—not everyone had brought gifts. Still, it took an embarrassing length of time to get through.

Katie, once more demonstrating that though she hated my color palette she loved me, got me a box filled with broomstick skirts in my favorite earth-tone hues.

Zelda and Verona gave me a deck of custom-made Corgi tarot. I'd only had my tarot cards read once, less than once, actually, and didn't plan on having it happen again anytime soon. But the artwork was beautiful enough to frame.

Nick and Ben gave me a homemade coupon book that

entitled me to several corgi babysitting sessions. That seemed more like a gift for Watson to be able to spend alone time with Ben, but sweet nonetheless.

In that same manner, Paulie gifted a huge case of jerky made of buffalo meat that he sold at his pet shop. It was the only thing Watson liked from Paws, and one of the few items that took him more than five seconds to devour. It was also incredibly expensive.

Athena had purchased a spa day for Katie, me, and herself.

Carl and Anna, who owned the home-furnishing store across the street, had a huge blanket made from a rather unflattering photo of Watson and me. Well... Watson was adorable, but me? Not so much. Still, I managed a smile and thought I sounded convincingly grateful.

When I opened Mom and Barry's present, I got choked up. It was a framed eight by ten photograph of the previous Fourth of July and had nearly everyone I loved the most in it, even Paulie's corgis. For a second, with everyone pictured, I couldn't recall who'd taken the photo. Then I remembered—Branson, sitting on his police horse, using Barry's camera.

Noah and Jonah shoved Branson from my mind once more as they pushed their package nearer. "Open ours real quick. People are getting bored of presents, and we need to keep their attention."

I hesitated. "I'd rather them not pay attention, to be honest. I feel like I'm on display."

"Come on." Jonah pushed it nearer. "Please."

Noah chimed in, "We really did design it for you, but it won't be bad publicity for us either."

"You designed it?" The memory of the day before came back, them saying they'd invented something for me, and I suddenly felt like I had a bomb in my hands. Glancing past them, I caught Zelda's and Verona's attention, and they nodded reassuringly. With a leap of faith, I unwrapped it and actually sighed with pleasure when I pulled the gift out of the tissue paper. "Oh my goodness, you two! He is adorable. It's like a steampunk Watson."

Leo laughed and rubbed Watson's head. "Well, look at that. You've got a brother!"

The metal corgi was about a fourth the size of the real Watson, and not nearly as fluffy with all its copper, brass, and steel gears, wheels, and springs, but clearly a corgi nonetheless. Enough so, Watson hopped up, balancing his forepaws on my thigh and sniffed at the contraption.

"Put it on the floor." The twins spoke in unison.

At the excitement in their tone, my nerves came back. I placed it gingerly down, and Watson began to sniff it all over. "Are you sure it's safe for him to—"

Watson barked, cutting me off.

"I don't like you." A gruff electronic voice sounded from the steampunk corgi.

Watson and I flinched as one. He cocked his head and gave another tentative sniff.

I looked at the twins questioningly, they were both grinning ear to ear. And sure enough, the contraption had captured the entire room's attention.

Still sniffing, Watson issued a low, warning growl.

"You're suspicious." The robot dog spoke again.

Watson barked once more.

"Danger! Danger!"

At the electronic warning, Watson backed up, bumping into my feet.

I looked toward the twins. "What's it doing?"

"Wally the Corgi is our newest creation. One of the

many inventions you will enjoy at tomorrow's opening, you won't want to miss it." Though Noah answered me, he looked at the crowd, his voice raised to be heard easily. "When an organic dog barks, Wally can input the data and translate to English."

"An *organic* dog." Katie smirked.

The twins ignored her. And Jonah looked toward Watson. "Go ahead, tell Wally something else."

Watson looked to Jonah, to the robotic corgi, considered, took another sniff, and then decided he was utterly unimpressed. Instead, he padded over to Katie and gave a little yip.

"I want a treat," the robot chirped out pleasantly.

At his favorite word, Watson hopped and barked again.

"I'm hungry." When the robot spoke that time, the crowd began to murmur, and I looked at the twins in wonder.

"It's interpreting what Watson's saying?" It felt ridiculous to even suggest, but...

They nodded.

I gaped at them and then stared at the robot dog. I was impressed, to say the least. But I wasn't certain I believed it, though the dog seemed accurate so far. How amazing it would be to be able to hear Watson's thoughts. I knew him well enough. I thought I understood him ninety percent of the time anyway, but... amazing.

"Well, then, a treat you'll have!" Thrilled, Katie clapped her hands and hurried to retrieve one of her freshly made all-natural dog bone snacks. Watson followed at her heels.

I beamed at them. "Thank you. Wally is... amazing."

"My idea." Noah winked and nudged Jonah with his elbow. "Like they say at the twin conventions, one twin gets all the good genes, the other gets the leftovers."

"Oh yeah. Something else that makes noise. That's a *great* use of good genes." My uncle Percival and his husband Gary shoved past the twins and gave me a hug. "Sorry we're more than fashionably late to the party, dear, our flight was delayed." They'd spent the last two weeks in Palm Springs. Before I could reply, Percival grabbed my hand and dragged me through the crowd toward the steps. "The best present is downstairs. Come on."

"It's not about it being the best present." Gary attempted some manners as he followed us.

Percival dismissed him with a *psh* sound. "Doesn't matter if that's what it's about or not. It *is* what it *is*."

Glad to be away from the table of presents, I followed willingly, but when we came to a stop at the counter of the bookshop, I didn't at first see the gift. There wasn't a package anywhere.

Percival rolled his eyes and tapped the counter. "You know, my darling niece, for being so adept at solving murders, sometimes your skills of observation are woefully lacking."

Then I saw it, and breathed out a sigh of wonder as I stepped closer. The plastic cash register that had been there since we'd opened was gone. In its place was one twice its size and made of gleaming polished brass, the edges and keys of nickel. It was like it was designed for the Cozy Corgi. I ran my fingers over the embossed Art Deco patterns that covered its surface. "It's one of the most beautiful things I've ever seen."

Gary let out a happy, satisfied sound, but Percival took the opportunity to gloat. "Well, I'd say so. It's over a hundred years old. We found it at an estate sale several months ago. We've been having it restored for your birthday. It was originally at a bank in downtown Denver."

"It's lovely." Mom arrived at my side, also touching the register, then giving an appreciative nod toward her older brother. "You always have had exquisite taste."

"That's true." Percival nodded his agreement.

Mom chuckled, then started to open her purse as she spoke. "Actually, I have one more gift for you, Fred, but I didn't want to give it to you in front of—"

A smack and a loud curse cut off Mom's words, and the four of us, and the others milling about the bookshop, turned toward the front door.

Delilah Johnson, the gorgeous redhead who owned the old-time photography shop, was pulling her hand back as if she'd just slapped the tall man who stood in front of her. She cursed again and shoved him. Beside her, Simone Pryce, wearing a matching pink jacket, as did the other women in their group, grabbed Delilah's arm, yanking her back and saying something I couldn't hear. In response, Delilah snarled at the man, then seemed to become aware they were the center of attention. To my surprise, when her gaze landed on mine, Delilah almost looked apologetic. Before I could think of how to respond, she turned and hurried toward the door. The rest of the Pink Panthers followed.

I started to head toward them, but halted when the man turned around.

Peter Moss.

At the sight of him, my temper flared. I'd met people with a lot of nerve throughout my life, but after our interaction the night before, I couldn't believe someone would have the audacity to come into my shop after the things he'd said. Let alone crash my birthday party.

He gave a slight tilt of his chin. For a second, I thought

he was actually going to come speak to me, but then he turned and followed the Pink Panthers out.

Beside me, Percival made a disgusted sound. "That man is revolting. Talk about someone without taste or style."

Seizing on the distraction, lest I run after him and take a page out of Delilah's book, I turned to Percival. "You heard what he said last night? That's a new record for Estes Park gossip to travel that quickly and all the way to Palm Springs."

His brows knitted in confusion. "No. What happened last night?"

Gary spoke up, clarifying for me. "He came into the antique shop a few weeks ago, wanting us to sell his collection of dolls."

Percival shuddered.

Gary continued, "We declined, pointing out that we only carry antiques."

"*And* that the dolls are hideous." Percival sniffed.

"Yes, that didn't make things go any smoother." Gary cast a long-suffering sigh toward his husband.

"Well, it's the truth." Percival turned his attention on me. "Fill us in, what happened last night?"

I did, and by the time I finished, rumors and theories around Delilah and Peter's exchange were being passed around the Cozy Corgi like wildfire.

Once they were fully caught up to speed, Gary and Percival spent several minutes showing me the finer details of the cash register. As they walked away, Mom gripped my hand, holding me back. "This might be my only chance to have you to myself for the rest of the night, so I'm going to take it." As she dug in her purse, her long silver hair fell over her shoulder, her remaining lock of auburn practically glowing in the soft light of the bookshop. When she looked back up, her eyes were misty, and she handed me a small item.

I took it, lifting it for inspection. It was a glossy black stone, slender and columnar in shape and about an inch and a half long. What looked like a pewter sheriff's star was affixed to a band around the middle of the stone.

"It's a charm I made for your father." Mom smiled gently at me, with a hint of sadness. "It's black tourmaline, for protection. He carried it in his pocket at all times, unless he was undercover."

I read between the lines easily enough. He'd not had it with him the night he was murdered. At her explanation, the memory of him with it returned. As I fingered the star, I could picture the charm in the same glass bowl by the door where he'd kept his keys. "I'd forgotten about this."

"I found it in a box of your father's..." She closed her eyes and shook her head. "It was in with a bunch of junk stuffed in the back of the closet. I can't imagine how it got there."

My heart leaped. I thought we'd gone through every-thing of my father's. "There's another box of his—"

"I don't mean to bring down your birthday or usher in a dark cloud," Mom interrupted, sounding as if she was regretting her choice.

"No!" I grasped her hand, the pendant between our skin. "I'm so glad to have it."

"I thought you would be." She smiled, some of her brightness returning. "I forgot about it as well. But then it showed up at just the right time, as if your father wanted you to have it on your fortieth birthday."

My throat simultaneously constricted as my heart warmed. "Thanks, Mom."

Before anything else could be said, Paulie and Athena

came over, followed closely by Pearl and Watson. The rest of the time, until nearly midnight, was spent, drama-free, with dearest friends and acquaintances alike, and, as I'd promised myself, I lost count of how many of Katie's cream puffs I devoured. If there was ever a night where calories didn't count, a fortieth birthday was it.

"The glitter was a mistake." Katie flicked a sparkly black fleck off the counter and onto the floor.

Watson leaped up from where he'd been napping and rushed over in excitement. After a tentative sniff, he cast an accusing glare Katie's way and then rumbled back to his favorite spot in the bakery.

"Sorry, buddy," Katie called after him and refocused on me. "You had a good time last night, right? You're not planning on punishing us for surprising you with the party we probably wanted more than you did?"

"Probably?" I cocked an eyebrow and gave an intentionally hard leer.

"Okay..." Katie scrunched up her nose. "No probably about it. But still..." She brightened. "Fun, right?"

Acquiescing, I smiled. "Yes. I wouldn't have wanted a huge party for my fortieth birthday, or for any other occasion for that matter, but it was wonderful. And I'm happy you all didn't do what I would've chosen."

"Good! I'm glad." Katie scowled at another spot of glitter beside where Nick had just placed a tray of cinnamon rolls. She flicked it once more.

Proving that hope springs eternal, Watson tore across the bakery again only to be disappointed and doubly annoyed with Katie, and judging from the side-eye in my direction, with me as well.

Not bothering to apologize, Katie motioned to my mustard-yellow broomstick skirt. "I see you like your gift."

"I didn't realize there was a catch to the skirts when I opened them up last night." Laughing, I ruffled the fabric and took a step back so she could see the bottom hem from her side of the counter. "I should've known better." Though every one was in a hue that I loved and Katie detested, I'd been surprised when I'd hung them up only to discover embroidered silly pictures that matched the style Katie wore on her T-shirts. The mustard-colored one featured a corgi sitting on top of a mountain of doughnuts.

"It's adorable. If you're going to wear hideous colors, I figured we could at least infuse some charm into the equation." Katie nodded her approval. "Joe has finally quit looking at me like I'm crazy when I make special requests from his T-shirt shop."

"That is pretty cute." Nick slid another tray of cinnamon rolls on the counter and cast Katie an apologetic grimace. "I think that's going to be all we have time for before opening. Sorry."

"Don't apologize. I'm the one gabbing with Fred when I should be working." Katie shrugged and addressed me again. "We're running low on product this morning, because we spent a good hour and a half just trying to get rid of *some* of the glitter. We didn't succeed, but I think we managed to keep it out of the pastries. If I'd done a better job planning, we'd have bought edible glitter for the party. Then it wouldn't have mattered. We'll have time later this morning to get enough prepared for the flow over from the grand opening of Twinventions." She shrugged a second time. "For now, we'll send people to the Koffee Kiln when we run out. That should make Carla happy. She was still here when all the drama went down, so I'm sure she'd like the chance to give her increase of customers firsthand gossip.

By the end of the party the night before, speculative theories around why Delilah had slapped the dollmaker were running rampant. Though they all had the same base recipe—an affair. Delilah was notorious for her affairs with men, single and married alike. Since she didn't pretend otherwise, I felt no guilt about joining in. "Maybe we should go to the Koffee Kiln ourselves. Since Carla's business partner is one of the Pink Panthers, she would definitely have the inside scoop. But I can't picture Delilah having any sort of fling with Peter Moss. He's horrible."

Katie waved me off. "*Any* man who would have an affair is horrible. Why should he be any different?"

"I'm not entirely sure. You know that I'm repulsed by some of the choices Delilah makes, but I've come to realize she's not quite as black-and-white as I first thought, though her gray areas definitely make me uncomfortable. And Peter..." Even saying his name made my temper from two nights before rise again. "I think I'm jealous Delilah got to do what I didn't."

Katie bugged her eyes exaggeratedly and made a disgusted face. "Gross! You want to have an affair with the creepy dollmaker?"

"What?" I practically screeched. "No! I meant—" I realized she'd been kidding and leaned across the counter to smack her shoulder. "You're horrible, so I'll slap you instead."

Before she could respond, Watson popped up and scurried toward the steps just as Ben emerged from below.

"Fred, you have a... visitor." Ben greeted Watson with

the same enthusiasm as if they hadn't just seen each other moments before when we arrived at the bookshop.

"Really?" From the way he said it, I grew wary. "Who?"

"Officer Green. And she doesn't seem happy."

Katie and I exchanged glances, and then I headed toward the steps, calling to Katie over my shoulder, "Just as a warning, I'm willing to bet I'll need a quad shot in my dirty chai after whatever this is."

Sure enough, as Ben, Watson, and I reached the bottom of the steps, Susan stood glowering by the new cash register. Large muscled arms were crossed, and one of them had been looped through the handles of a large paper bag. "Imagine that, up in the bakery even though you're supposed to be selling books."

"Good morning to you too." Though we'd nearly hated each other from first sight, over the past many months, Susan and I had built what, for us at least, was nearly a friendship. But I couldn't keep the bite out of my tone, probably seeping in from my leftover feelings of talking about Peter Moss. "And technically we don't open for another five minutes."

"Perfect. Then this will be brief. It's my day off, and I don't want to waste any more time here than I have to." Susan shot a quick glance toward Ben. "Would you mind disappearing for a few minutes? I don't need an audience for what I have to do."

"Sure, I'll—" Ben cast a quizzical look my way and waited for me to give a nod before continuing, "I'll just go upstairs."

Susan scowled at Watson. "Take the fleabag."

"You really are in a mood this morning, aren't you? Are you here to give me a ticket for a noise violation from last night or something?" I looked toward Ben once more.

"Do you mind taking Watson? I do have those gift certificates."

"This one's free." He laughed and motioned toward Watson. "Come on, buddy, let's get you a treat."

As if being with Ben wasn't treat enough. Watson started a happy frolic around Ben's feet and then practically danced beside him all the way up the steps to the bakery.

When I looked back at Susan, I thought I caught the hint of a grin at the corner of her mouth, but it disappeared too quickly to be sure. "All right, what'd I do now?"

Unfolding her arms, she thrust the paper bag in my direction. "This is yours. Take it."

"There hasn't been a murder, so I know I didn't leave any incriminating evidence at a crime scene." I crossed to her and took the bag.

"Like that would stop you." A flush rose to her cheeks. "I didn't wrap it."

"Wrap it?" I paused with my hand halfway inside the bag, thinking I'd misheard. "You got me a—"

"For crying out loud, Fred. Get it over with." She slammed her arms across her chest again.

My fingers closed on the edge of a box, and I pulled it out and just about fell over. I looked from the gift to Susan, then back to the gift. It was a corgi-themed edition of the game Clue. I gaped at her, dumbfounded and touched.

"If you say something sappy, I'll arrest you." She flicked a thick finger toward the game. "Doesn't mean I like you or that nasty mutt of yours. I just happened to see it online. It was too perfect to pass up. Luckily I was working during your party, but..." She shrugged.

"Susan, I don't know—" I was saved from making us both uncomfortable by a loud crash from next door, swiftly followed by three massive explosions in quick succession. It was like a bomb, accompanied by the sound of shattering glass. It made all the explosions before it seem like the popping of Bubble Wrap in comparison. The entire Cozy Corgi shook, books on the side of the wall shared with Twinventions fell from the shelves, and the front windows shattered. From above, I heard Katie scream.

For a heartbeat, everything was perfectly silent, and then the world went into fast motion. Car horns started blaring outside and people began to yell and scream. There was the pounding of feet from above, and then Katie, the twins, and Watson came rushing down the steps. Watson reached me first, his eyes wide with panic.

We all turned toward what remained of the jagged windows that looked out onto the chaos on Elkhorn Avenue. Smoke and dust billowed around the people running.

Susan and I tore off as one, Watson a mere step or two behind us, as we exited the door and stumbled onto the street.

Someone running past bumped into my shoulder, forcing me take a few moments longer to make sense of what I saw. Across the street, the windows of Madame Delilah's Old Tyme Photography, Cabin and Hearth, and Paws were all shattered as well. The screeching of birds from the pet shop added to the cacophony. Though there weren't many cars on the street, being so early, some of those that were there had their windows blown out, and a couple of alarms were blaring.

As if in a dream, I turned toward Twinventions. Not only were the windows gone, but nearly the entire storefront—bricks, shards of glass, and metal wheels, gears, and fragments I couldn't identify—spread out like a fan over the sidewalk and into the street.

Susan rushed toward one of the cars in the middle of the street as a woman got out, blood running down her face.

I ran to Twinventions, Watson at my side, my only thought for Noah and Jonah. As soon as I stepped through, I was greeted with a thicker cloud of dust and debris, making it nearly impossible to see. Glass, or something, crunched beneath my boots. Hesitating for a moment, I realized it would do no good to tell Watson to stay, so I bent and scooped him up to ensure his paws were safe. For once, he didn't protest.

"Noah! Jonah!" I moved farther into the smoke. No... not smoke, just dust. There didn't seem to be a fire. Even so, what I could make out of the store was in complete shambles. I called out for the twins again.

"We're here!" One of their voices, I wasn't sure which, sounded from the back, though I couldn't see them. There was a loud scraping of metal, a curse, and then more scraping. "Fred, stay there. We're okay."

Relief rushed through me, but I didn't listen and made my way, stepping as carefully as possible, toward their back room.

With a screech of metal, they emerged as if from a mist. Something had been blocking the door. "Are you okay?" I thought it was Jonah who asked, but I had a hard time telling them apart at the best of times. I didn't bother with it in the moment.

"Am *I* okay? It's like a bomb went off." Watson started to slip, and I shifted his weight onto my other arm. They were near enough that I could inspect them. "Are *you* okay?" I couldn't see blood or cuts or anything. Not even a scratch. "*How* are you okay?"

"We were in the workroom. The window is safety glass. It—"

One of the twins started to speak, but the other cut him off with another curse. "Peter!"

The first twin gasped, and as one, they turned to look. "Oh no. Peter. I... wasn't thinking." He started to head that way, then froze, cursing again, this time the sound of it chilling my blood.

I took a couple of steps in that direction, then also froze when the scene clarified. The whole area was nothing but shrapnel, more gears, pipes, chains, and glass. Amid it all, mostly buried, was the body. And from the damage seen, even from our distance and muted through the dust, it was clear there was nothing anyone could do to help. In fact, if the twins hadn't said his name, I never would've recognized Peter Moss from the remains that lay before us.

Watson whimpered, shifting as if trying to get down. Before I could tighten my grip on him, another scream sounded, this one louder and more frantic than any that had come before.

"Help! Someone help!" It came from outside the shop. "They're dead! They're both dead!"

Though I wouldn't have imagined it possible, the sick feeling in my gut grew, and I whirled on the spot, rushing toward the voice, clutching the bouncing Watson as tightly as I could.

Katie and the twins were starting to enter Twinventions, but I stopped them as I hurried past. The cloud of dust and debris was already lessening as we stepped outside, and a crowd was gathering as the other storeowners emerged from their shops.

Anna Hanson stood in the shattered window of Cabin and Hearth, screaming for help. Susan was already rushing in through the door.

I shoved Watson toward Ben. "Here, keep him safe."

Without waiting for a response, I darted across the street, following Susan inside, terrified I'd be stumbling across Carl's body.

"Back here! Back here!" Anna was still screaming at the top of her lungs as she joined us, leading us toward the rear of the furniture store. Though the front windows were shattered, most of the shop looked completely fine, night and day compared to Twinventions, just a few things knocked over here and there.

And then we found them. Not Carl. He was nowhere to be seen. My momentary relief flooded through me and then was replaced by a fresh sense of horror.

"Oh Lord. It's Branson." Katie was beside me suddenly, her whisper echoing my own thoughts as I stared at the body skewered against the wall.

"Wexler?" Susan stood like a statue. As if unable to move for the first time since I'd met her.

It was hearing his name out loud that shook sense into me, that and the other body lying on the ground in a growing pool of blood. "No. Not Branson. It's Miles Styles." Even as I spoke, my eyes argued with my logic, insisting that it was indeed Branson Wexler, who was clearly as much past help as Peter Moss who lay across the street. "And his brother, Niles."

As if prompted by his name, Niles groaned from where he lay on the floor, and it triggered Susan into action. She barked orders as she rushed to him and began applying pressure on the wound. "Anna. Call 911. They're probably already on their way, but tell them we need them here, in your shop. That we probably don't even have a matter of minutes. Katie. Check the guy on the wall. I'm sure it's too late, but check anyway." She glanced up at me. "Fred. Help me with this one."

Hours passed, though each one felt like days, as I stared out at the street from the empty windows of the Cozy Corgi. And with every minute, visions continued to flash behind my eyes. The sight of Peter's destroyed body. Miles pinned to the wall of Cabin and Hearth by a metal rod with one of Noah's and Jonah's trademark gears on the end. Niles bleeding out over the hardwood floor. I'd almost lost track of how many murder victims I'd stumbled across by that point, but this was... different. Unlike anything I'd ever seen. Like a war zone. Like a bomb went off. Maybe it had.

Watson sat at my feet, on high alert and in full protection mode. For a long time, he growled at every motion outside the windows, but after a while he settled into silent vigil.

When the ambulance had arrived, Miles was pronounced dead on the scene. Niles was rushed away, and we'd not heard any prognosis or update. There'd been a few minor injuries from people who had been driving or walking on the sidewalk, but nothing that would require a hospital stay from what I'd seen. As soon as the ambulance had left, Susan had all of us wait in the bookshop with Officers Brent Jackson and Amy Lin as our guards. I didn't think she suspected the twins of murder or anything, but she still gave us instructions to not go anywhere. She even allowed a hysterical Verona and Zelda to join us.

When the twins started to tell their versions of what happened to Zelda and Verona, Officer Lin told them to wait, to not discuss it, that Officer Green had given orders. Within minutes, Mom, Barry, Percival, and Gary arrived. Whether they were supposed to or not, Jackson and Lin let them in. So we all waited in a huddle, along with Katie, Ben, and Nick, while the aftermath of the drama unfolded outside.

Paulie, Anna, Carl, and Delilah had been similarly quarantined in another of the undamaged shops. From what I could tell, each of them was unharmed, which helped me breathe a bit easier.

When Susan finally arrived, she was accompanied by recently elected Police Chief Marlon Dunmore, who'd taken the spot of his corrupt predecessor. To my surprise, they were followed by Leo.

He rushed to me and wrapped me almost violently in his arms. "Are you okay?" Without waiting for a response, he released his embrace and gripped my shoulders to inspect me as if in a panic. "You look okay. Are you okay?"

I nodded and forced myself to speak. "I'm okay." For the first time, I realized I felt like I'd been holding my breath. With Leo there, the tension eased a little. "Better now."

"I was leading an early morning hike to Calypso Cascades and didn't hear till we got back down. I just got here." He shook his head, his mouth moving silently for a moment. "I can't believe it. It looks like..."

"I know." I glanced at Susan and the chief. "They let you in here?"

"Yeah. I don't think Chief Dunmore loved the idea, but he listened to Susan."

I never would've imagined that in a million years. I cast her a thankful glance.

Susan gave a little flinch and began to bark, "For crying out loud, Officer Jackson, I never expected you to let the whole family in here. It's not supposed to be a reunion." She waved Brent off before he could reply and stared at our group, the line between her brows deepening. Finally, she looked toward the chief. "There is no reason not to do it here with the whole group. Not like anything is secret"—she gestured toward me—"or that she's not going to shove her nose in anyway."

"Works for me." Marlon Dunmore was a local, and from what I'd gathered, he had been engaged in a private battle with Chief Briggs behind the scenes. On top of that, he ran in the same circles as Barry and my uncles. Though most of the time I chafed against the small town's good old boys' club, in this instance, I was thankful for it. I knew there was no way this would've happened so informally in a large city. He looked at the twins. "All right, Jonah..." He narrowed his eyes, glancing back and forth between them. "Sorry, or Noah, I can never tell you two apart. Not that it matters in the moment. Why don't you both just tell us what happened this morning. See if we can figure out who might have had it in for Twinventions."

The twins looked at each other as if conversing, and then Noah spoke. "No one would have it in for Twinventions. And nothing happened this morning. Nothing unusual anyway. We came in early to do some last-minute preparations to get ready for the grand opening this afternoon. Zelda and Verona stayed home, then dropped the kids off at school and came by to check on us."

Zelda spoke up. "But we didn't stay. When we saw—"

"Just—" Susan cut her off, but paused as she tried to

figure something out, then gave an irritated shake of her head. "Never mind, I can't tell which of you is which either. Just the twins talking at this moment. The *male* twins." She glanced toward Ben and Nick. "Oh, good grief. Just the *Pearson* twins. The *male* Pearson twins." She finished with a glare at me. "Why in the world do you surround yourself with so many twins? How do you keep anything straight?"

Her annoyance was almost a relief. Grounding and familiar.

Chief Dunmore gave a scowl of his own. "Noah and Jonah, please continue."

Jonah took over where Noah had left off. "Well, like Zelda was saying, they didn't stay when they saw that Peter Moss was there."

"He gives us the creeps." Verona shuddered, then winced. "Sorry. We'll be quiet."

Susan rolled her eyes and refocused on the twins. "Why was Peter there?"

"He was trying to convince us to... ah"—Noah glanced at his twin, sounding nervous for some reason—"change our minds about carrying Blossom's Beauties."

"I'm sorry, what now?" Susan looked like she had a sour taste in her mouth. "What in the world is a Blossom's Beauty?"

"You haven't seen them?" Dunmore tilted his head questioningly. "Those creepy dolls that a few of the stores have started carrying lately?"

"As you know, I'm not a big shopper." Susan glared at the chief, then back at the twins. "Why would you ever carry dolls in your... invention or whatever it is... store? And what do you mean he wanted to change your minds?"

"We didn't really ever want to carry them..." It seemed it was Jonah's turn to be nervous. "We were trying to help another local entrepreneur out. But then, after he insulted Fred the other night, we... changed our minds."

Though Susan turned wide eyes on me, it was Leo who spoke. "Peter insulted you?"

I cast him a quick glance and nodded. "Yeah, it wasn't a big deal. And I didn't want to bring it up yesterday. The hike and everything was so perfect, and then—"

"If you two could do a lovers' spat some other time, that'd be great. Thanks." Susan cleared her throat and cocked an eyebrow. "You're telling me you had conflict with one of the victims?"

"Not like that!" Noah practically shouted in a panic, coming to my defense. "Fred wouldn't hurt anyone. She's not a murderer."

Maybe that's why they'd been nervous, afraid they'd implicate me. Something I hadn't even considered.

Susan gave another eye roll, this one huge and exaggerated. "Well, golly gosh darn it, there went my main suspect. You mean to tell me Winifred Page and her fat corgi fleabag didn't plant an explosive device in her brothers-in-law's shop and blow up half the town just because some guy who owns a weird doll business insulted her?"

A rumble gurgled up from Watson, as if he were aware he'd just been insulted. Or possibly, he was just hungry.

"Officer Green..." There was a warning in Chief Dunmore's whisper.

Susan cleared her throat. "We don't suspect Fred of murder. If we did, we wouldn't be doing things this way." It looked like she was done, but then, apparently, she couldn't help herself. "*Nor* do we believe the corgi is a mastermind at bomb making."

"It wasn't a bomb." I hadn't been looking at them, so I wasn't certain which twin spoke.

"That"—Chief Dunmore gestured toward the chaos outside the window—"*wasn't* a bomb?"

"No, of course not." Noah sounded offended. "Why would we make a bomb?"

"We didn't think you—"

"My theory is, something went wrong with the Manscaper," Jonah jumped in before the chief could finish. "Maybe Peter cranked the gear too tight or something, which *shouldn't* be possible. Noah and I have tested every conceivable eventuality, and nothing like that has ever happened before. But, *if* Peter managed to accidentally cause the Manscaper to break in such a way that a piece of it flew off with force, it may have hit one of the tanks of propane or other gasses we use, or even—"

"Oh!" Verona gasped and gripped her husband's arm. "Maybe it wasn't accidental. Maybe Peter did it on purpose, to get back at you for not letting him sell dolls in the shop anymore."

"No." Zelda shook her head. "That man seemed much too in love with himself to basically commit suicide in order to sabotage Noah and Jonah."

"I agree with you. He was." Percival spoke up for the first time, though both Mom and Gary shushed him instantly, which he ignored. "However, I *could* see him sabotaging the opening. Perhaps the reaction was just more violent than he intended. Maybe he just wanted to hurt the"—he cast a quizzical glance at the twins—"*Manscaper* and ended up blowing himself to bits."

Barry sounded skeptical. "But what are the chances of a solitary piece from that machine hitting the exact—"

"If one more of you speaks without raising your hand for permission, I'm putting you all under arrest!" Susan practically yelled.

Other than Percival letting out an offended sniff, no one spoke.

When she was apparently satisfied we were all going to stay that way, she looked at the chief. "Did you understand any of that? What in the world is a Manscaper?"

The chief shrugged and looked toward the twins. "You two, one at a time, and *only* the two of you, explain."

They did, going into detail about what the Manscaper did, and how it had worked flawlessly for the last hundred test runs.

Seeming to understand, the chief nodded slowly and then got back on track. "How could Mr. Moss have had the opportunity to mess with this contraption? Weren't you there?"

Again Noah and Jonah cast nervous glances at each other. Katie seemed to notice as well, and she caught my gaze and lifted a brow as Jonah started to speak. "Well... he'd demonstrated some interest in the Manscaper during previous occasions when he visited, so we're assuming, based on that and how he... how his body was afterward... that he attempted to operate it on his own while we were in the lab—" He rushed to clarify at Susan and Chief Dunmore's confused expressions. "—our workshop in the store. Where we were when the explosion happened. It's only thanks to the strength of our window—"

"Which we invented," Noah interrupted.

Jonah nodded enthusiastically. "Right. It's only thanks to the strength of our window that we're alive. It completely shattered but stayed intact. Not surprising, as we tested it countless times, but never with that much force, obviously."

Noah nodded as well. "Obviously."

"Oh Lord." Susan sighed and began rubbing her temples. "I don't think I have the strength for this."

For once, I couldn't blame her, and felt the same. Though I dreaded what I'd see when I closed my eyes, I wanted nothing more than to go home, crawl into bed, and let the world fade away.

"Let's try this again." Chief Dunmore leveled a stare at Noah and Jonah. "Why were you two in the... lab, or whatever? If Mr. Moss was there to convince you to sell his dolls, why did you leave him unaccompanied?"

The twins' nerves showed once more, and again I could've sworn they were communicating silently. Finally, Jonah's gaze traveled to me, then Noah's followed. There was an apology in Noah's voice as he spoke. "We were debating the... merits of agreeing with his proposition."

"Are you kidding?" Barry's words were rushed and harsh, and very un-Barry-like. At my feet, Watson whimpered in concern, as if he thought something might be wrong with one of his human deities. "You'd let that man back into your shop *after* how he treated Fred? I can't believe that—"

"Hold on!" Susan held up a hand, silencing Barry, a new fire entering behind her eyes. "It only shows how exhausted I am that it's taken me this long to catch on to what you've said. You had *tanks* of propane in your store?" She glared daggers at Noah and Jonah. "And since your nutty lab is still intact, then I can deduce you had them in the actual shop portion, not that it makes that much difference."

"Well, yes." Jonah said it as if it was the most obvious thing ever. "That's what we used to power some of our robots, and some other gases. Of course we also use solar, battery—"

"Enough!" she shouted again and turned toward the

chief. "This isn't at all what we thought it was. No way gas tanks and such passed inspection."

"You're right." Chief Dunmore sighed and cast an apologetic glance toward Barry before addressing the twins. "It changes everything. The two of you will need to come with us, and you'll probably want to contact your lawyer." Finally, he looked toward the other officers. "Jackson, Lin, read them their rights."

With downtown officially closed off, we regrouped at Mom and Barry's house since it was larger than mine. Ben and Nick didn't join us. Barry, Percival, and Gary all went with Noah and Jonah's lawyer, Gerald Jackson, to the police station.

Zelda and Verona had picked up their four children from school, so they joined us as we gathered in Mom's living room. The kids were quiet and sullen, as were their mothers. Katie had brought half the bakery along, so pastries were spread out over the coffee table in front of the couch, while she and Mom took solace in throwing together a quick vegetable soup in the kitchen.

I was on the couch, still feeling stunned, while Leo sat cross-legged on the floor, his back against my legs. Watson snored contentedly, curled in Leo's lap.

The clock on the fireplace mantle, which had belonged to my grandparents, ticked incessantly, every second seeming louder than the last. I narrowed my focus on the jerky, brass second hand, tempted to scream for it to shut up. Gradually, the other hands came into view and brought some grounding through the time of the day. It was barely one in the afternoon. I didn't know why, but it struck me as strange. I'd lost all semblance of time. On the one hand, the events of that early morning felt like moments ago, and on the other seemed interminable. As I stared, some of the chopping sounds from the kitchen reached my ears, helping to lessen the intensity of the clock.

With effort, I shifted my attention to my nieces and nephews on the far side of the room. The older two, Britney and Ocean, tapped away on their phones, while Christina and Leaf sat in front of coloring books, though neither of them touched a crayon. A few feet away, Zelda and Verona looked even more stunned than I felt, both pale and shaky, clearly feeling that their world had crumbled.

That's what it was, I hadn't quite realized until that moment. In addition to the shock and fear of what had happened, and the pure horror of the deaths, I felt a loss. A huge, cutting loss. Every day that had passed since I moved to Estes Park had brought my family closer and closer together, and... there was no coming back from this.

I laid my hand on Leo's shoulder, needing to feel more than just the warm pressure of his back against my legs. I didn't think the morning's events would affect us, but... who knew what was going to happen? He reached up instantly, taking one of his hands from Watson to cover mine and then left it there.

The tension eased somewhat.

"You'll fix it."

It'd been silent for so long and I'd retreated so deeply into my own mind that I barely caught where the words came from, let alone their meaning. With a struggle, I looked toward the twins.

Verona was staring at me intensely, but a little bit of a spark had come into her blue eyes, something that resembled hope. "You'll fix it, Fred."

Zelda looked up, as if she was reaching the surface of

the water, and then pinned her matching blue gaze on me as well, an excited smile beginning to form. "Of course you will. This is just temporary." She grasped her twin's hand. "Just like you did for Verona. She was in jail for a little bit, but we figured it all out. *You* figured it all out."

"Exactly." Verona nodded, that spark of hope blossoming into a full-fledged entity. "Just like you did for Dad. Just like you do for *everyone*."

Leo's fingers curved around my hand and gave a squeeze, offering stability.

I gaped at them, not understanding. "What is there to fix?"

They both gave me an expression that probably matched my own, clearly thinking I was talking nonsense. "You solve murders."

"Exactly," Zelda chimed in. "You'll figure out who murdered Peter and the Styles twins. We know Noah and Jonah didn't do it, obviously."

"Obviously." Verona practically latched on to the word. Across the room, all four of the kids perked up, brightening.

"It sounds like they think Niles will make it. So there's only two deaths." Leo spoke softly. It felt like he was probably trying to find the one sliver of silver lining he could grasp.

"That's horrible, isn't it?" Zelda sniffed. "I'm already counting him as lost. And as much as we care about Miles and Niles, all I can really think about is Noah and Jonah."

"Me too." Verona grimaced her agreement. "But I think that's natural. After Fred clears our husbands' names, and we know our family will be fine, we can grieve our friends."

"Guys, this is different." I tried to keep the desperation out of my voice. "There's no murder, there's nothing to solve. People were killed, yes, but that doesn't make it murder. We're just lucky that more people weren't hurt." I'd called Anna and Paulie shortly after we'd arrived at Mom and Barry's house, needing to assure myself they were okay, despite having seen them before we left downtown. Leo had done the same with Delilah.

"What do you mean there's no murder? Peter and Miles are dead. They were killed." Some of the hope I'd seen in Verona's eyes started to fade. "And possibly Niles."

There'd been no official news from the police station, but being the daughter of a detective, I had a fairly good guess as to what was going to go on. Noah and Jonah would be held while the scene of downtown was investigated. I figured it would take a few days to have them formally charged. "Noah and Jonah aren't being accused of murder, not like that. It'll be involuntary manslaughter, I imagine."

Zelda squinted as if trying to understand. "So... kinda like if they caused a car wreck or something."

Leo nodded. "Yeah. Kind of like that."

I knew he was trying to take some pressure off me, and maybe I should let him, but I didn't want there to be any shred of hope to cause more pain later. "No, not much like that. This will be a little more intense because of the... negligence aspect."

"Negligence?" The twins spoke in unison, both sounding offended, and it was Verona who hardened first. "Jonah wasn't negligent. This wasn't his fault."

Zelda whipped toward her. "Well, it wasn't Noah's either!"

"I wasn't saying—"

"Wait!" I cut Verona off before a war began. "We all know that Noah and Jonah never meant for any of this to happen and would never dream of hurting anyone. It's *unintentional* negligence. Having those explosives in the shop—"

"They weren't explosives!" Again, Zelda and Verona cried out as one.

"Tell that to downtown!" Katie came back into the living room. "It went from charming shopping district to World War III aftermath."

"I think what Fred's trying to say"—Mom followed closely behind Katie, confirming they'd been able to hear the heated conversation in the kitchen, as she picked up where I left off—"is that some of the gasses... or whatever... the boys were using to power some of their inventions, made it an unsafe environment for a public place. No one thinks they intended to cause any harm. Though it doesn't help that they didn't have those power sources present during inspection."

Zelda scowled at Mom and looked near tears. "*They* didn't cause any harm. *Peter* did by messing with the Manscaper without—"

Verona placed a hand on Zelda's knee, cutting her off, though her words had already been fading away. When Verona spoke, it was barely more than a whisper to her twin. "We shouldn't have been so insistent they move their workshop to the store. If it was still in our backyard, then this wouldn't have happened."

"Don't say that." Mom managed that declarative yet caring combination that only a mother possessed. "If it had happened at your house, the kids might've been hurt. This isn't *your* fault." Mom and Katie pulled up a couple of chairs from the dining room and sat. "We're going to let the soup simmer for a while. We'll all feel better with our bellies warm and full."

The room fell silent. I didn't blame Verona and Zelda

for being desperate, for looking for someone else to blame. With the frequency that we discussed murders it was hard to think of a death merely being an accident. But really... it seemed like an eventuality that something bad would happen with Twinventions. Not that anyone would ever have predicted such devastation, but a lot of Noah's and Jonah's inventions were notoriously unsafe. It was part of the reason I'd dreaded them being next door to the Cozy Corgi, though I'd expected commotion and noise, not calamity.

Watson stood from Leo's lap, giving a long, catlike stretch with his rump in the air, and then padded around the coffee table, pausing to sniff the more alluring untouched pastries.

When he came close to her, Mom bent down and scratched his flank. "I've got chicken breast baking in the oven for you, too. Just be patient."

He gave her hand a halfhearted lick, then continued the rest of the way around the table before settling onto Leo's lap once more.

Though I often felt that he was uncannily attuned to the humans around him, and the workings of their lives, I couldn't help but be jealous of how unaware he seemed at the moment. How lovely it would be to only be concerned about your next meal and then fade off into dreams in the embrace of one of the people you loved the most.

"I think it has something to do with Peter Moss." The room had been so silent, that when Zelda finally spoke, all our gazes turned to her. She pushed on, determined. "I know you're saying it was an accident, that something went wrong with the Manscaper, but as much as I hated that thing, they've been working on it for months. It was trust-worthy. And yes, maybe the tanks of"—she waffled her hands in the air—"whatever they were shouldn't have been in the shop, but it wouldn't have mattered if the Manscaper hadn't malfunctioned. And it *wouldn't* have malfunctioned if Peter hadn't done something to it." Her voice grew more excited, as if she was stumbling upon the answer. "I bet you anything he was trying to sabotage the grand opening because Noah and Jonah wouldn't carry his creepy dolls."

"You think Peter was so angry about the dolls that he blew himself up?"

"No, of course not." Zelda shot a glare toward Katie. "I think he was trying to get back at the guys, didn't know what he was doing, and *accidentally* blew himself up."

"Or..." Verona's tone matched Zelda's. "Someone else intentionally messed with the Manscaper to intentionally blow up Peter." She looked at me, eyes filled with hope once more. "That's it, Fred! Figure out who wanted to kill Peter and we have our answer. The list of people who had a grudge against him has to be huge."

"I bet you're right." Katie surprised me by agreeing. "Just the night before, Delilah slapped him. Maybe she—" Katie halted abruptly, and then shook her head in disgust. "Good grief. What am I saying? I must dislike Delilah Johnson more than I realized if I'm willing to go down *that* bunny trail." She adjusted to a more soothing, apologetic nature. "Verona, Noah and Jonah said themselves that no one knew Peter was going to be at the shop that morning, much less mess around on the Manscaper while they were in their lab."

Verona opened her mouth to argue, but Leo spoke up first. "We're also not one hundred percent certain that it was the Manscaper that sparked the explosion. From what you've said, Noah and Jonah had worked out all the kinks, that it was trustworthy. And Katie's right, Peter wasn't supposed to be there. He couldn't have been the target."

"There wasn't a target." I took a moment to adjust, hearing the frustration in my voice. "Not everything is a murder. *This* is an accident, a horrible, horrible accident, but... an accident." I sighed. "And I can't believe I'm saying this, but I wish it was a murder. Then it's something solvable, someone else's fault."

The room was quiet again for a bit before Mom spoke up, surprising me. "I know it doesn't really have anything to do with what happened, probably, and..." She lifted a hand as if stopping an argument before it began. "I'm not trying to cast aspersions on the twins, but from the way Noah and Jonah explained things earlier, it sounded as if they were considering carrying Peter's dolls again. That's why they went to their lab to discuss it. I can't imagine why."

I hadn't gotten that far yet. "That is strange. The dolls didn't fit in with Twinventions in the slightest, and I got the sense that Noah and Jonah didn't want them there to begin with, and that was before my conflict with him." For the first time that day, there seemed an actual mystery, not that it mattered.

"See?" Verona tilted her chin, vindicated. "There is something else going on. *Peter* was up to something. *He* caused this."

Katie opened her mouth, but I shook my head. Like me, I imagined she'd been about to rehash all the reasons why Peter hadn't had some elaborate scheme to blow himself up, but it was pointless. We'd just end up going in circles.

The landline phone rang in the kitchen, startling all of us. Mom rushed toward it instantly, and her side of the conversation was easily overheard.

"Barry." There was a pause. "Oh. Sorry, dear. I must've

left my cell on vibrate." Another pause, I could almost see her looking around the kitchen for it. "It's probably in my purse or the car. But that doesn't matter. Is there news?"

A longer pause that time, but Mom's intermittent sighs, groans, and whimpers told us all we needed to know.

"Okay." The exhaustion in her voice confirmed it all. "Soup's almost ready. Will the three of you be home soon?" Mom hesitated at something Barry said and then sounded both apologetic and tentative. "I... don't think now's the best time for Gerald to join. Maybe we should just keep it family."

We stared at her as Mom hung up the phone and returned to the living room. It was nine-year-old Leaf who spoke. "They're not letting Dad come home, are they?"

"No, dear. Not yet." Mom smiled sweetly but didn't sugarcoat as she turned to the rest of us. "They're not officially charged yet, but they are being held. Barry says it's only a matter of time, but Gerald is confident he'll get them out before the night is over."

Katie let out an ironic snort. We knew if Gerald was claiming that, then there was no possibility at all.

"Please, Fred." Though the kids had been mostly silent the entire time, it was Britney who took away my power to protest any longer. "I know you think it was just an accident, and maybe it was. But... Dad and Uncle Jonah need help right now, and you're the only one I trust to make things better."

"And Watson!" Christina piped up, her wide eyes glistening with tears.

"And Watson." Britney smiled down at her little sister, then cast a glance toward my snoring corgi before looking to me once more. "Please."

Leo still had hold of my hand and gave it a squeeze.

"Well... I guess it can't hurt." I pushed the sinking feeling aside and looked back to the twins. "Let's start at the beginning—help me come up with a list of everyone who might want to harm Peter, Noah, and Jonah, or even Twin-ventions itself." At least the family would have some comfort knowing that I was trying.

As Mom pulled out a notebook and a pen to start taking notes, a measure of ease settled over me. Even if it was a waste of time, doing *something* was better than the alternative.

EIGHT

"I swear, half of the houses in Estes Park look like they fell right out of the pages of *Goldilocks and the Three Bears*." Leo chuckled as I pulled the Mini Cooper into Anna and Carl Hanson's driveway. "Of course, in Estes, it works the other way around. We get a couple of calls a year about a bear wandering into someone's living room, though they don't typically try out the people's beds."

From his happily confined spot on Leo's lap in the front passenger seat, Watson licked across Leo's cheek.

"Thanks, buddy. *You* thought I was funny, huh?" Leo scratched with both hands behind Watson's ears, helping the layer of dog hair in my car grow thicker.

"Sorry. I was barely listening." I smiled a bit as Leo was rewarded with another corgi kiss. "You two are ridiculously cute, though, and make this a lot easier. At least it won't be completely wasting their time if Anna gets to hang out with Watson. However, *you* should be getting home. You have another early morning tomorrow."

"It's not that late, and besides, talking to Anna and Carl is always entertaining. We could use a good laugh."

"Don't let them see you laughing at them. They don't mean to be funny." I unbuckled my seat belt, and as Leo and Watson hopped out the passenger side, I reached behind to snag the box of the remaining pastries. There was never an issue with getting Anna and Carl to talk freely, but I figured sugar couldn't hurt.

We'd spent the remainder of the day, well past dinner, with the family, going over the people Peter Moss had offended in one way or another, and those who'd had problems with Noah's and Jonah's inventions in the past. Both lists were almost endless. Even after we started going in circles, no one seemed in a rush to leave. We needed to simply be together, and hoped to hear that for some reason Noah and Jonah had been released. By the time Gerald Jackson called a little after eight thirty, we'd already given up that notion. Gerald was full of excuses and promises. As per normal.

Even though I felt like agreeing to investigate the situation was a complete waste of time, I realized that I needed to. It gave me something to do. If my brain was busy trying to shove pieces together in a puzzle that didn't exist, I wouldn't have time to worry about how horrible the fallout would be, could focus on something tangible other than the visions of the lives lost flashing through my mind, and the panic that squirmed in my gut at the realization of how close other friends and people I loved had come to losing their lives. It was nearly more than I could take. In that vein, as soon as we started heading back to my cabin, I realized I'd sleep better if I got the ball rolling, so I called the Hansons to see if they minded a late-night visit. Not surprisingly, they sounded eager to talk. Either way, it would be good to see them, both whole and safe.

Sure enough, Anna began to twitter the moment the door opened. She flung her arms around me and pulled me close, nearly smashing the pastry box between us. "Oh, isn't it awful? Just awful!" She released me and then did the same to Leo. "Horrible really. Awful." For once, she wasn't exaggerating. If anything, she hadn't quite captured the severity of it. Neither of us had a chance to reply before she turned on Watson. "And sweet baby, I'm so glad you're okay. I couldn't have handled it if..." Her words trailed off as she looked at me horror-stricken. "I don't have any of his favorite dog treats here. They're all at the shop."

"I can run down and get some for you, dear." Carl, looking like a grim Santa Claus with his round face and belly, bald head, wire-rimmed glasses, fuzzy white beard, and serious expression, spoke softly as he joined us at the door. "I should've thought as soon as you said they were coming."

"Thank you, love." Anna turned toward him, teary-eyed, and stroked his arm. "That's sweet of you. But we can't go downtown, remember? They said it could be days before we could even be in our own shop."

"Oh, right." Carl looked even more crestfallen.

The interaction was so atypical that I stood there, almost as shocked as I'd been hearing the initial blast. I knew Anna and Carl loved each other, but bickering was their normal, *not* pet names. Anna was always bossing Carl around, and if he didn't move quickly enough, she'd swat his arm to make him speed up.

Watson brought me back to the moment by giving his front-legged bunny hop as he whimpered in excitement.

"Dear me." Anna frowned down at him. "I said his favorite word out loud, didn't I? And now I can't follow through."

"That's okay. I have some treats in the glove compartment of my car."

"I'll get them." Leo whirled and headed back toward the Mini Cooper, Watson darting after him.

Anna sighed as she watched them go. "I'm glad you have him, Winifred. Leo is simply a dream."

"Thanks, Anna." She wasn't wrong, but I realized we were still standing on their porch, so I thrust the pastry box at them in hopes of moving it along. "Katie sent some treats, of the human variety."

It worked like a charm. Carl snagged the box, cooing happily, and led us inside, just as Leo and Watson returned. We moved to the kitchen, which was attached to an open-concept dining room. Anna and Carl's house was exactly what I'd expected, like a replica of their store, Cabin and Hearth, which carried high-end, mountain-style home furnishings. Everything was thick pieces of twisted pine, stained glass lamps with images of evergreens and elk, and rustic metal fixtures of copper and brass. Though I knew how expensive such pieces were, the home felt much like the couple themselves—warm, cozy, and just a touch cluttered.

Anna didn't wait before opening the pastry box, and just like at my folks' house, within moments, there were lemon bars, croissants, scones, cream puffs, and cookies spread over the table. But instead of putting them on a dish like Mom had done, Anna simply flattened the box and used it as a platter—apparently, she didn't plan on there being any leftovers.

Carl didn't wait and snagged one of the cream puffs. "I adored these at your birthday party. I even dreamed about them." He popped the entire thing into his mouth, chewed once, and then blinked in surprised confusion before speaking with his mouth full. "That's not chai."

"No, silly. This one had yellow filling. They were at the party too, remember? Lemon and lavender." She stroked his hand. "You only had about a dozen of them at the party."

"Oh, right!" Contentment replaced his confusion as he continued to chew. "Delicious, just not the flavor I expected." He slid the largest lemon bar in front of Anna. "Here you go, my love."

"Thank you, baby." Anna cast him a shy smile, truly making me think I'd entered the twilight zone, and then she looked at me, her tone shifting to business. "So you think it's murder. Carl and I were quite shocked when you called again. We hadn't thought of that."

"No. I don't think it's murder." And if I had, the very fact that the gossip king and queen—an honor they shared with my uncles—hadn't even considered the option, when they typically had a list of suspects a mile long, was proof enough that I was wasting my time. "But Zelda and Verona wanted me to look into things... just in case."

"Oh." Carl had popped in another cream puff, and though I thought it had been one filled with chocolate whipped cream, he didn't seem befuddled by the change in flavors. "That makes sense. I don't see Noah and Jonah faring very well in jail."

"Tragedy, after tragedy." Sorrow laced Anna's expression as she took another bite of lemon bar and then glanced under the table, smiling sadly at the sight of Watson chewing away on his bison jerky. "So glad he's safe."

"I'm so glad *you're* safe, dear." Carl put a heavy arm around Anna's shoulders, pulling her awkwardly into him. "I couldn't face going on if anything happened. I should've been there. If I'd come back to find... if you..." He choked up.

"Don't say it." The emotion was thick in Anna's voice as well. "I'm glad you weren't there. You're safe. We're both safe."

It finally clicked, though I supposed it should've been

obvious. They'd had a close call. It could have just as easily been Anna pinned to the wall, or in the hospital fighting for her life. No wonder they weren't sniping at each other. Suddenly my own emotions spiked. Once more it washed over me how much worse it all could've been.

"You okay?" As ever, Leo proved he was attuned to me, and offered an encouraging smile.

I nodded, taking strength from him and from the weight of Watson's rump resting on the top of my boots, and got down to the matter at hand. "I don't want to upset either of you, but would you mind walking me through what happened from your perspective? Why were the Styles twins at Cabin and Hearth so early?"

To my surprise, Carl and Anna shared a guilty look. With another sigh, Anna leaned forward, whispering though we were in their house. "We didn't want to upset your family. I guess that's silly, since it would've all been public soon enough anyway. But, with Twinventions opening, it seemed like a sensitive time for it to come to light. By the time things were ready, it would be several months from now and things wouldn't have been so fresh."

Carl nodded but didn't offer commentary.

"For what to come to light?" Leo beat me to the question.

Though Anna blushed, her tone took on a slight defensive quality. "Well... you've seen Noah's and Jonah's inventions. They tend to... well, they..." She winced.

"They explode." Carl didn't whisper, and Anna looked at him, shocked. "Well, they do. Clearly."

Typically that was where Anna would've smacked his shoulder. Instead, she considered for a moment and then nodded before looking back and forth between Leo and me. "Have you been to Miles and Niles's store in Boulder?"

We shook our heads.

"We've only been a couple of times, and it's wonderful. Though when we've been in, we've never met either of them. It was always just their employees." Anna darted her hand across the table, touching mine. "But we finally met them at your party and got to talking. Carl had an idea. A new line of inventions. Rather brilliant, actually."

Carl jumped in, and despite how sullen he'd looked when we'd arrived, between the pastries and Anna's praise, he brightened excitedly. "Nowadays the trend is smaller spaces and downsizing. Which doesn't work very well with our type of merchandise."

True to form, Anna took over, though not unkindly. "As we were talking at your party, Carl suggested the twins might be able to come up with a solution. Furniture that looks like what we carry but is multifunctional." She patted the table. "This, for instance—you could dine on it, and then when you're done, flip it over and it becomes an enter-tainment center or something."

"Exactly." Carl removed his arm from Anna's shoulders so he could use both his hands to gesticulate. "A hall tree that turns into an ironing board, a love seat that extends to a four-person sofa. Maybe a log bed you can sleep on during the night and then fold up against the wall during the day to function as a bookcase. That sort of thing."

Part of me wanted to point out that the books would fall off, but I managed to bite my tongue.

"But all high-end, high-quality, and true mountain style. None of that—" She twiddled her fingers while sneering. "—put-it-together-yourself kind of plywood junk."

Beside me, Leo gave an approving grunt. "I can see that going over for the right crowd."

So could I. And I could also see why they didn't want it

to come from Noah and Jonah. "So the Styles twins were meeting you early this morning in hopes of it staying a secret?"

Anna simultaneously nodded, retrieved a couple of cream puffs and a croissant, and managed to look remorseful again. "There really was no offense meant. It's just that—"

"Anna, don't worry about it." That time I reached out to touch her arm. "I wish you hadn't worried about it to begin with. No one would've been upset." That may not have been true. Noah and Jonah might have been, but that didn't need to be said. As I prepared to turn the conversation slightly, I felt silly, knowing I was looking for clues where there was no mystery to solve. "So... when you were meeting with them... at the time of the explosion, you didn't... see anything or notice anything suspicious?"

"I didn't notice anything *at all*. I wasn't in the shop. Carl and I had done a couple of drawings of certain ideas we had, and I'd left them in the car. I'd run out to get them. I was digging through a stack of papers in the passenger seat —I don't keep a very tidy car, I'm ashamed to say—when I heard the explosion. Of course, I didn't think it was nearly as bad as what happened. I walked in through the back door of Cabin and Hearth, expecting to look through the front windows and see a car crash or something. I turned into the main showroom, and..." She shut her eyes and shuddered. "Miles was impaled on the wall, and Niles had a piece of metal..." She shuddered again, lifted the croissant as if needing comfort. She'd just taken a bite when her eyes went wide, and she too spoke with her mouth full. "You think someone was trying to kill Miles and Niles?" She exhaled, sending crumbs flying. "I never would've even considered that."

"Me neither." Carl looked as awestruck as Anna.

"That's why you're brilliant, Fred." Anna finally swallowed. "Although, who would want to hurt either one of them? I don't know them very well, but Niles was so kind, almost shy. And Miles so handsome. I thought he looked just like..." For once, Anna showed some decorum and didn't finish the statement, though her gaze flicked toward Leo.

"I thought the same." Leo confirmed what I'd suspected, though he'd have had to have been blind not to notice.

I pushed past that topic completely. "Anna, Carl, I wasn't saying that anyone was trying to kill the Styles twins. I don't really even believe anyone was trying to kill anyone else at all."

For a second it looked like they were going to argue, try to push the point, but then disappointment crossed Anna's face. "That is a little far-fetched, I suppose."

"Besides, if anyone wanted to kill someone else, it would've been Peter. Though it's horrible to speak ill of the dead, that man won't be missed." Carl gave a sour expression that matched the one his wife made earlier.

Again, Anna leaned forward and whispered, clearly so used to gossiping in the shop while others milled about it was merely habit. "He and that Barbie doll wife of his came in around spring break. They wanted us to have those dolls in our shop. Can you imagine?" She gestured, encompassing the house. "Having those horrible things surrounded by all the beautiful furniture we carry? If anything, it would only highlight just how truly horrible they are." For the first time, anger filtered over her features, accompanied by shame. "He was extremely insulting when we told him no. He suggested that I... that I..." One hand went to her belly, the other to one of the cream puffs.

I winced, certain I was able to imagine exactly what he'd suggested. "He told me that I should get my eyes, nose, and chin fixed... or was it my jaw. I don't remember."

"He did?" Like I hoped, some of the embarrassment left Anna's features.

"*That's* what happened?"

I turned toward Leo at the anger in his voice. I'd forgotten there'd never been a good time to fill him in. I nodded.

"The idiot." Leo reached up and ran the back of his fingers over my cheeks. "You're perfect."

I snorted out a laugh, embarrassed. "Don't be—"

"No, I'm serious." Leo's brown eyes hardened. "You're perfect."

"As are you, dear." Across the table, Carl threw his arm over Anna's shoulders once more and kissed her loudly on the cheek.

She went bright pink.

By the time we left half an hour later, we'd added a few names to the list we already had of people who might have grudges against Peter Moss. Anna and Carl didn't have any theories of who'd want to hurt Noah and Jonah, though they made it clear they weren't familiar with anyone who'd purchased Noah's and Jonah's inventions other than the infamous Christmas garland. They attempted to throw out some ideas of who might have it in for the Styles twins, but as they didn't really know Miles or Niles, they were weak at best. I wrote them down anyway, just to placate them.

Watson and Leo had already gotten into the passenger side of the Mini Cooper and I had the driver's door open when Carl called out from the porch and shuffled my way.

"Anna and I forgot to give you this with your present last night." He spoke loudly as he thrust a card into my hand, then lowered his voice. "There's a little gift from me in there as well. A little token of appreciation for keeping my secret."

"Thank you, but you didn't need to—" His meaning clicked, but before I could protest, he'd patted my shoulder and was hurrying back inside.

With a sinking feeling, I sat behind the wheel, closed the door, and tore open the card. Inside, on a separate sheet of paper, there was a handwritten note.

A five hundred dollar investment has been made in your name.

With a groan, I handed the slip to Leo, who chuckled. "Looks like you have a business connection to Gerald Jackson after all."

I'd discovered that Carl had invested a huge portion of money in some plot Gerald Jackson had come up with. I'd agreed to keep it a secret from Anna as long as I believed it wouldn't affect her or their financial future. I shook my head as I backed out of the driveway and took off. "Let's just hope it's not illegal, and that I somehow now don't have my name attached to some felony Ponzi scheme."

NINE

"Feel up to another late-night interview?" We'd barely made it two blocks from the Hansons' house before Leo looked over with a raised eyebrow.

"Really?" I glanced at the clock. "It's past ten. And, again, you have another early morning tomorrow."

Never ceasing in his stroking of Watson, Leo shrugged. "Not a big deal. Between coffee and crisp mountain air, I'll be wide-awake when the time comes. And Delilah's a night owl, so she won't mind." He gave a little grimace. "As long as she's alone, anyway. Or if she's with her Pink Panthers, which she was when I checked on her earlier."

"Well, if she is with her Pink Panthers, she clearly wouldn't be alone, but..." I didn't finish the thought as I realized his implication. Delilah had no problem with her abundant dating life being public and common knowledge. "Oh." I shook my head, clearing away the possible options that attempted to flip through my mind. "Sure. I'm up for another interview." I glanced toward Leo again, narrowing my eyes. "This is because of what Peter said to me, isn't it?"

Leo didn't even attempt to play ignorant. "Totally. And maybe Delilah won't have any information that helps, but if nothing else, I want to shake her hand for slapping the guy.

I'm kind of upset that he's gone and I can't do something similar."

I flinched in surprise. It was the most aggressive I'd ever heard Leo sound. "I think he's more than paid for his rudeness."

Another shrug. "Not for me he hasn't." His expression softened, and I took my attention from the road for a few more seconds just to see the look in his eyes. "There's nothing about you I'd change, Fred. And not just because I love you. You're beautiful, and he was clearly a..." He didn't finish.

After the unbelievably long, emotional day, the warmth and adoration from Leo was nearly my undoing. Turning back to the road, I put my hand on his leg so I could touch him and Watson at the same time. "Thank you for that, but it's going to be a waste of time. Peter wasn't the target for this. No one else knew he was there, let alone that he would try out the Manscaper." I gave a shrug of my own before Leo could reply. "But... looking into this at all is a waste of time, so we might as well go for broke."

"Great. Give me one second." Leo tilted upward, digging into his pocket for his cell, causing Watson to give a complaining grunt as he had to balance awkwardly on Leo's hips.

Ten minutes later, we pulled into Delilah's driveway. Her house was roughly the same size as mine, but didn't look like it had fallen out of a *Goldilocks and the Three Bears* storybook. It didn't have log walls, wooden shutters, or a river rock chimney billowing smoke over the stars. It was just a normal little house, and with its soft yellow siding—at least I thought that was the color; it was hard to tell given the time of night—it reminded me of a lot of the homes in the Midwest. The fact that it was on a cul-de-sac added to that feeling. The thought made me realize I'd been there before. Sure enough, three doors down was a house Watson and I had been in the previous summer. How strange that it had belonged to a religious fanatic couple who'd been protesting Verona's and Zelda's New Age shop. I did find it humorous that the couple had lived so close to Delilah. You couldn't get much more different in terms of lifestyles.

As soon as we shut the car doors, an outcry of howling filled the night. Watson and I both halted instantly, and he gave a nervous growl.

My first thought was wolves, but the howls were too low, too guttural.

Leo laughed and motioned for us to follow. "Delilah has three Basset hounds, remember?"

"Oh. Right." I hadn't remembered, nor had I ever heard a Basset hound howl. I'd forgotten that Delilah rescued animals, one of the reasons that kept me from being able to put my own moral judgments on her in one category or another, not that I needed to.

Having been alerted to our presence, Delilah opened the door before we'd even reached the porch. Three long, low dogs with ears practically dragging on the ground lumbered out in front of her. Two continued to howl, while one gave a surprisingly deep, ferocious growl.

Watson froze in the face of the three hounds, lowered his ears, and gave a growl of his own.

"Oh, cut back on the testosterone, boys." Clad in a silk pink nightgown, Delilah stepped out from the doorway, moved between the dogs, didn't bother acknowledging Leo or me, and knelt in front of Watson. She cupped his face, rubbing his cheeks with her thumbs. "Nice of you to come visit, handsome."

Watson stopped his growling, and his nubbed tail began to wag. And there was the other aspect that complicated Delilah in my mind. While Watson didn't go crazy for her like he did Barry, Leo, and Ben, he more than tolerated her as he did with most people, even seemed to enjoy her affection.

The two of them barely had a moment together before the three Basset hounds crowded and trundled around their mother, and began sniffing over Watson.

Despite the heaviness of the day, I couldn't help but giggle. As Watson pulled his head free from Delilah's grip, he began to turn in a circle, sniffing each of the Basset hounds in turn and seemed confused like he was seeing things in double, or triplicate in this case. And then I began to giggle some more, a little manically. They made such an adorable, funny sight. The Basset hounds were only slightly taller than Watson, a little longer, and even a little heavier.

Delilah gave a pleased chuckle as she stood. "It's like four really fat, furry hot dogs saying hello."

If Watson could understand he might've been insulted, but it made me laugh harder. It was exactly the right description.

Leo gasped and then nudged my elbow. "Fred, did you just see that?"

My giggling stopped, and I gaped at my grumpy corgi. He'd licked one of the Basset hounds across the face, then the second, and then the third. "Watson... likes them." As if proving my point, he gave one of his bunny hops that normally reserved for the mention of a treat, wiggled through a space between two of the Basset hounds, and galloped over Delilah's front yard. The three Basset hounds gave chase and soon the four of them were in a slow-motion game of tag.

Sighing, I lifted my hand to cover my mouth, completely in awe. And ridiculously, I felt my eyes sting. Watson had a girlfriend of sorts with Athena's little toy poodle, Pearl, but they merely sniffed each other and then curled up to take naps. This was... "I've never seen him play with other dogs, not like this. With Paulie's corgis, Watson's only learned to tolerate them, though I think he actually likes them from time to time, but he never *plays* with them."

"Well, it helps that my dogs aren't insane like Flotsam and Jetsam." Delilah propped a hand on her hip, smiling as she watched the foursome. "Plus, those two are like rabbits on speed. My boys don't care for them either. But Watson's a kindred spirit. Slower, clumsier. Perfect."

Just as she said it, one of the Basset hounds stepped on its own ear, stumbled in front of Watson, who crashed into him, did a small flip over his back and rolled. Another of the Basset hounds did a sort of sluggish pounce at my little man, and then he too tumbled.

We humans stood for several minutes, just watching and giggling at the antics. Leo slipped an arm over my shoulders, and I leaned against him, and for the first time since the explosion, I didn't think about anything and felt at ease.

It didn't take long before all four were worn out and sprawled in the grass. Delilah clapped her hands softly. "Zuko, Kenickie, Putzie, come on, boys. Come in."

At her command, all three popped up at once and shuffled hurriedly toward her, adoration in their eyes. Realizing he was about to be left alone, Watson rolled over and stood awkwardly to follow.

"Did you have a good time, buddy?" I bent, ruffling his

fur. "I didn't even know you could do all of that." He looked up at me, eyes wide and bright, his tongue lolling contentedly, making me even happier.

Leo gave him a quick pat before we followed Delilah and the three Basset hounds inside. "I don't think he knew it either."

I halted a few steps inside the doorway, shocked by Delilah's house. I'd never given a moment of thought to what her home might look like, but it wouldn't have been this, not in a million years. It was clean, neat, and simple, but... if I'd been dropped into the middle of it and asked to depict the owner, I would've chosen an eighty-year-old grandmother. One who knitted gloves, baked apple pies, and more than likely led Bible study.

Delilah smirked, reading my mind. "What did you expect? Did you think you were walking into a brothel?"

"No, of course not. I..." Maybe I had. Something sleek and modern would fit Delilah, or extremely feminine, lacy, and sparkly—more like the shimmery nightgown she wore. "You have a floral couch."

She laughed again and motioned toward the windows. "And matching drapes."

She did. And while it wasn't beautiful, it worked. It was comfortable, relaxing, and cozy. Three descriptors I would never put with Delilah. As I scanned the rest of the room, I narrowed in on a bowl in the center of the coffee table. "Are those... Werther's butterscotch candies?"

Delilah only nodded, her smirk growing. Then she did a come-hither motion with her finger. I complied, and she pointed through the doorway.

My mouth fell open as I stepped in. It was the entertainment room, as the large TV clearly indicated, but the other three walls were lined with bookcases and filled with books.

Delilah stepped so near that I felt her brush against my back as she whispered in my ear, "I'm telling you, you'd make an excellent Pink Panther."

I couldn't come up with a response, but Leo saved me from needing to. "Speaking of, I'm surprised your girls aren't still here after the day you've had."

She stepped away from me and made a dismissive motion. "I sent them away. Seeing my life flash before my eyes made me need the night to myself. Just me and the boys." She gestured toward the Basset hounds, who had commandeered the floral-print couch. Watson was attempting to join them, but it was a little higher set than the one at our house, and he kept slipping off. Chuckling, Delilah went over and helped him. "There you go, stud."

Once on the cushions, Watson hopped over the closest Basset so he could squeeze right in the middle of the herd and then curled up, resting his head on one of the other's hips.

The day just kept getting stranger. I started to comment about the dogs, and then Delilah's words finally sank in. "Your life flashed before your eyes?"

"I didn't go into details when I talked to Leo earlier, I think I was a little too shaken." She motioned for Leo and me to take the love seat nearby. "I had just opened and was arranging some of the outfits I'd gotten mended, when the window shattered and something smashed into the metal trough I use for the bathtub shoots, ricocheted, and stuck into the wall less than five inches from my head. It was some wheel gear-type thingy. Almost like a ninja star, but with ten times the points on it. Scared me so bad I couldn't even scream. I think I was frozen there for a solid minute. I didn't move until the chaos outside on the street registered."

Once more it washed over me just how much worse the day's events could have been. "I had no idea. I'm so sorry."

She shook her head as she absentmindedly stroked one of the dogs. "Not your fault."

"Have you seen Paulie? I spoke to him, but—"

She didn't even wait for me to finish. "He's shaken but fine. He was in the back room of the shop, so he was safe. Two of his fish tanks got hit. He was able to get every single fish in time, so he was happy. None of the other animals were hurt." A soft smile played on her full lips. "Of course, with how fast Flotsam and Jetsam are constantly moving, neither of those corgis were in danger of getting hit with anything. Athena showed up before I left with my girls, so Paulie is well taken care of." She chuckled again. "He's a weird little man, but he grows on you."

"I'm glad you're okay." Leo spoke warmly, but his tone grew businesslike. "But... can you fill us in on Peter? What happened between the two of you at Fred's birthday party?"

Though she'd known why we were coming, Delilah still stiffened, and visibly cooled. She looked toward me. "You really think this was a murder? Am I one of your suspects?"

"No on both. I don't think it's a murder." Even saying it made me feel embarrassed for going to all the trouble. "But my family wants me to look into it, so I am. And even if I did think it was a murder, Noah and Jonah would have to be the intended victims. It doesn't make sense for Peter to be the target. No one knew he was there."

Her gorgeous face twisted into a sneer, but she didn't lose an ounce of her beauty. "Oh, it makes complete sense for Peter to be the target. Maybe not for this particular explosion, but if anyone could make someone murderous, it was that creep."

That sounded like the Delilah I knew. She never pulled any punches.

Before I could continue, Watson let out a happy sigh in his sleep. Two of the Basset hounds answered with grunts of their own.

I smiled at them before I refocused on Delilah. "What happened at my party? Why did you slap him?"

She bristled, her nostrils flaring. "He was just... acting like his creepy self."

To my surprise, I realized she was being evasive. I hadn't expected that. Both because she clearly wasn't the suspect and it wasn't her nature. Unless she wanted to play games around it, but that wasn't what it seemed she was doing. "Did..." I wasn't sure how to ask the question politely. "Did... the two of you... have a past?"

She blushed, but seemingly more in anger than embarrassment. "Did I help him cheat on his wife? Is that what you mean?"

My mouth moved before I could make it form words. "That's... not exactly how I'd put it."

"Delilah." Leo sounded surprised. "We're not here to accuse you of anything. And you won't find any judgment from us."

Her deep blue eyes flashed my way, knowing that Leo's statement wasn't true, at least for one of us. "People may not approve of the choices I make or the way I live my life, but I *do* have standards. And I can and *frequently* say no. And I wouldn't give Peter Moss the time of day if he was the last man on earth."

"Why? What made him so horrible to you?"

That time Delilah's lips moved silently and then closed.

Maybe she needed a little help, needed to feel like I wasn't going to sit in judgment on her. "I can't say I think he deserved what he got, but after only meeting him once, I couldn't stand the man either. Minutes after meeting me, he gave me a whole list of physical features that I needed to change in order to be prettier."

She relaxed instantly. "Of course he did. That was his thing... one of them."

"Really? He did that?" I couldn't believe it. Though Delilah was my exact same height, probably my same weight, and we had similar features with her long auburn hair and pale complexion, she was the pinup manifestation of the sum total of our parts, where mine clearly indicated that I owned a bookstore with the bakery up top. I couldn't imagine any straight male having a solitary complaint about Delilah's appearance. "To *you*?"

She paused, for just a little too long, then began to rattle off things that she listed with her fingers. "Let's see, Botox for my forehead and eyes, some skin tightening under my jaw, a fuller, higher bustline, and a couple of inches off my waist, for starters."

"Really?" Leo sounded as shocked as I had. "*That's* what he said to you? *That's* why you slapped him?"

With a scowl, Delilah nodded. Her gaze flicked from Leo, skipping me, and landed on the dogs.

She was lying. And I was willing to bet she was aware I knew it.

Maybe she *had* been having an affair with Peter.

I cast that notion aside almost instantly. Part of the reason I'd despised her so much at the beginning was how cavalierly she'd admitted her other affairs to me. Why would this one be different?

Before I could formulate a question, she finally met my

gaze again. "I'm sorry about Noah and Jonah, Fred. Really. Even if they are..." She shrugged a shoulder, proving to have more grace than to finish the thought. "For your family's sake, I hope there's a way to prove they're not responsible."

"Thanks." I couldn't come up with anything else to say. I could go over the list of people who hated Peter with her, but it seemed pointless. It was already too long the way it was, and I wasn't convinced anything else she'd say about the man would be true. I stood. "Well, it's late, and we should probably get going. Thanks for talking to us."

"Of course." She stood as well, followed by Leo.

At the commotion, all four dogs lifted their heads, and Watson let out a long, contented yawn. The Basset nearest Delilah slid off the couch like a seal, stepped on its ear, and did a clumsy stumble, bumping into the coffee table but managing to stay upright.

"Putzie, you're such a klutz," Delilah cooed affectionately as she patted the dog's head, and then turned to kiss Watson, who'd stood on the cushion. "I'm so glad you get along with Putzie, Zuko, and Kenickie. We'll have to have a play date if your mama doesn't think I'm too bad of an influence." The teasing was back in her tone, thankfully.

"I'd normally say no to a play date, as they tend to stress Watson out more than anything, but I think that would be a lot of fun. And watching Putzie do battles with his ears is something I don't want to miss." I bent to say goodbye to her three dogs. "Those names. They sound familiar, like..." I paused, looking up at Delilah. It was her pink nightgown that made it click, and I laughed. "Of course, the guys from *Grease*."

Grinning, she shimmed her shoulders. "Naturally. It's only the best movie ever made. I've got my version of the Pink Ladies. We need our T-Birds."

Though her cozy grandmother-like house didn't fit Delilah Johnson, her three well-named Basset hounds certainly did.

After much coaxing, Watson finally followed us to the car, and then, as if punishing both of us for making him leave his friends, he bypassed Leo's lap and curled up with a disgusted huff in the back seat.

"I know, buddy. You've got it really rough, don't you?" I attempted to pat his head as I backed out of the driveway, but he pulled back evasively. "Drama." I stretched farther, petting him anyway.

When I put the car in Drive and headed out of the cul-de-sac, Leo looked over at me. "Delilah was lying."

"I know." I braked at the stop sign and cast a look his way before hitting the gas once more. "But why? There's no way Peter was murdered, and as much as I may not approve of a lot of Delilah's choices, she's not a murderer."

"No, she's not." Leo glanced over his shoulder as Delilah's house disappeared from view, as if it might hold some answers. "Maybe there's more to this whole thing than we think."

"Maybe." Perhaps we were digging into a can of worms that had nothing to do with the explosion and wouldn't help Noah and Jonah at all.

"I feel like I'm living in the lap of luxury, having someone cooking for me for a change." Katie grinned as I set down the fresh grilled cheese sandwich in front of her. She lifted her mug. "The coffee is pretty good too."

"Not when you compare it to your dirty chais, but"—I shrugged—"caffeine is caffeine." I placed a large wooden bowl filled with arugula, cranberries, blue cheese, and bacon chunks between us.

Katie rose slightly off her chair to peer into the bowl. "I'm sorry... you appear to have me confused with a rabbit. There're green things in here." She plopped back down and gave a conspiratorial stage whisper to Watson. "Do you feel personally attacked? Because I do. I feel attacked. And affronted."

Watson, who'd been pacing the perimeter of the table side to side, hoping we'd drop something, paused and looked at her hopefully.

"Sorry, buddy." She shook her head. "You don't want this, trust me."

Laughing, I sat down across from her. "So much drama over a salad. For crying out loud, it's got blue cheese and bacon in it. It's only marginally healthier than your pastries."

She sucked in a Broadway-worthy gasp. "If you *ever* compare my baking to a *salad* again, I'm never making you another dirty chai."

I mimicked her gasp, though not quite successfully. "My life would be over. Actually... *other* people's lives would be over—your perfect combination of caffeine and spicy sweetness is the only thing keeping me from committing murder some days."

"I'll forgive you this once, as this looks delicious." She chuckled and lifted her grilled cheese. "And as far as the green stuff, I'll happily pick out the bacon and blue cheese. Maybe even the cranberries—I'll save them for scone batter or something."

"You're ridiculous." I tore off a corner of my sandwich and tossed it to Watson, who swallowed it in a gulp that looked like a great white inhaling a sardine.

Since downtown was closed, and the windows needed replacing, Katie had come over for breakfast and to brainstorm around the case... or whatever it was. As I was used to having breakfast at the Cozy Corgi most of the time, I didn't have eggs or oatmeal or anything else traditionally served for the first meal of the day, so grilled cheese and an impromptu salad it was. Oh, and coffee.

By the time we each finished half of our sandwiches, I'd filled her in on Leo's and my conversations with the Hansons and Delilah.

"I'm glad I never met that man." Katie sniffed as if the thought of Peter Moss was accompanied by an unpleasant odor. "I'd like to believe I'm secure enough that having an arrogant, misogynist jerk critique my appearance and tell me how I should alter it wouldn't affect my confidence. But honestly, I'd rather not test that theory. Either way, he would've gotten a pop on the nose." She took another bite of the other half of her grilled cheese—a large one—and then spoke with her mouth full. "Actually, I'm really, *really* glad I didn't meet him. If he was critiquing Delilah's looks, I can't even imagine what he'd say about me."

"I'm not convinced he did critique Delilah's looks. Leo and I both got the sense that she was lying."

Katie's brown eyes widened slightly. "Oh... you're thinking an affair."

I scrunched up my nose. "I was, but she adamantly denied it, and not because she wouldn't do such a thing, but because she found him repulsive."

"Oh, come on. Who wouldn't Delilah—" She halted, and I could see her mentally reprimanding herself. "Sometimes I'm not certain if I'm more irritated at Delilah or me. When the conversation turns to her, I have to come to terms with the fact that I have some internalized misogynistic thoughts. And I don't like that she makes me feel that way."

"Don't be too hard on yourself." I gave her a supportive smile. "I have similar thoughts when I'm with her, though not as strongly as you do, at least not anymore. I bet it's kind of like how Susan and I used to be. I'd get so angry with her that I'd end up acting like a twelve-year-old when I'd like to think I was above such things, and that just made me even more irritated with her."

"I suppose. But that doesn't help too much. I like to believe I'm superior to you as well. This just proves I'm not." She gave me a teasing wink, then grew serious once more. "If I'm being open-minded about it, I guess I don't see any reason she would lie. She's honest about other affairs. A little too much, if you ask me."

"That's what I came to as well. But there's something, and whatever it is was enough to cause her to make a scene in the middle of the Cozy Corgi."

"Delilah doesn't mind making a scene." Katie considered as she chewed for a few seconds, focusing on the pink flamingo tie-dye curtains over my shoulder. "Perhaps, if she really finds him as repulsive as she says, and why wouldn't she, then maybe he propositioned her in front of her friends and struck a nerve."

I hadn't thought of that and attempted to play out the possibility. "Maybe, but if that was the case, I think she would've told us. There's nothing to be ashamed about there."

After we finished up the meal, Katie even eating her salad, we moved into the living room to settle side by side on the couch, each of us with our computers on our laps. Watson retrieved his stuffed yellow duck from the bedroom and curled up with it on the hearth, even though the pleasant June morning made it where there was no fire.

We opted to divide and conquer. I began researching Peter Moss the man, and Katie was looking into Blossom's Beauties.

"You said he used his wife as the face of his doll business, right?" We'd barely begun before she tapped her screen, getting my attention. "Look at her! How did a man like Peter get a wife like that?"

I peered over. "Wow! She's not the type of woman I envisioned making dolls either. She looks more like the kind to be selling makeup or jewelry."

"She doesn't make them, remember? He did." Katie leaned closer to the screen as if looking for imperfections. "Well, if that's his wife, and Peter's the cheating kind, that lends credence to him having the nerve to hit on Delilah. Blossom is literal perfection."

She was, at least by the typical American beauty standards—long blonde hair, bright blue eyes, thick lashes, flawless skin, model figure. "I for sure didn't see her at my party."

"Me neither." Katie continued, "But if Peter was hitting on Delilah at your birthday party and Blossom found out, maybe it was revenge."

"By blowing up half of downtown?" I didn't try to keep the skepticism out of my voice.

"Valid point." She narrowed her eyes. "It wasn't *half* of downtown."

Even so, I switched directions and typed in Blossom's name while Katie continued looking into the business.

"These dolls are creepy. Can't even put my finger on why." Katie shivered. "Something about their skin."

I reread the facts twice before I accepted I wasn't *mis*reading them. "Speaking of skin, look at this. Blossom is actually forty-seven years old. Peter is… was, sixty-two. They've been married for over twenty years."

"*She's* forty-seven. She looks younger than I do!" Katie was clearly affronted. "Probably because she eats salads. *Without* bacon and cheese."

"Or…" I craned over, looking at the photo of her on Katie's computer again. "Peter probably had some physical critiques for his wife through the years as well. Maybe she listened—a nip and tuck here and there. Peter definitely had work done."

The answer came quickly enough. After not finding anything interesting on Blossom, I went back to Peter. In the old days, I might not have found the sites, as they were buried deeply enough, but after being best friends with Katie for the past year and a half and having learned her tricks around navigating the internet, I discovered Peter Moss's past. "Oh."

"You found it, didn't you?" Katie instantly shoved her

laptop aside and twisted toward me when I made some noise at the discovery. "What is it? Is he shrinking real human heads and using them for his dolls?"

"Gross, and no." I grimaced at her. "But it's not good. Not as bad as murder, but not good. And it explains a lot." I angled the laptop so she could see the photo of Peter from fifteen years before, standing in a courtroom, and I read the caption. "Celebrated plastic surgeon, Peter Moss, was accused of nine counts of sexual assault." I summarized as I skimmed the remainder of the article. "There were more accusations, but he only faced charges of those nine. They were all former patients." It was my turn to shiver. "No wonder I thought he was creepy."

"And no wonder he was handing out plastic surgery advice." Katie tossed it out before my brain had a chance to catch up, and she read ahead irritably, her voice growing more disgusted with every word. "He pled down to lesser charges, lost his license and his business, but he didn't spend even a day in jail. Paid some of the accusers recompense, or whatever, and a slew of charges and fees, but that was it."

We sat there in silence for a few moments, both disgusted and taken aback. My thoughts returned to the lists I'd made of people who'd been offended by Peter. Not one of the names had anything to do with something so vile. "The possibilities of who would want to hurt this monster are endless. Not even just the victims, but their families and loved ones."

"You're right. But I'd say that takes Blossom off the list. She stayed married to him through all of this. Clearly she is not concerned about cheating." Katie sighed. "These are some of the best reasons I've ever seen to kill someone. Not that I'm saying it makes it right, but..."

I nodded in agreement, then paused, looking at her again. "Wait a minute. We're sitting here actually contemplating that someone blew up Twinventions, accidentally killed Miles and possibly Niles, if he doesn't improve, to kill this man? This all happened years and years ago. Why now? Why here? And why in such an inefficient manner?"

Katie considered and then surprised me with an answer. "I don't think there's a time limit on these things. Don't forget how long it took my parents' victims to come hunt me down. And maybe the inefficient manner is... well... more efficient than we could imagine for the simple fact of it being so random out there. Who would suspect?"

"That's all true, but even if it was plotted out to kill Peter, nobody knew he was going to be on that machine, or even in Twinventions that morning." Though I knew it wasn't a possibility, my heart sank once more. "The only people this implicates in the slightest are Noah and Jonah. They were there. They could've rigged the machine somehow when he demanded getting on it, and then sequestered themselves in the lab where they knew they were safe."

Katie turned horror-stricken eyes on me. "Fred, you don't really think the twins would—"

"No, of course I don't, but if we're going to go with Peter being murdered, I don't see another option." I looked back to the photo of him in the courtroom, only then noticing Blossom sitting in the front row of the crowd behind him, looking even younger and more beautiful. How could she have sat there and heard the things her husband had done and stayed with him? "But you're right, if there was ever a motive for murder, there were plenty for him."

Katie took a deep breath and grabbed my hand. "What if..." She paused as if still working through it before she began again. "What if one of the victims was a family member of the twins. And that's why they agreed to have those horrible dolls in their shop. They were biding their time, waiting for the perfect moment, and then—" She clapped her hands in a loud bang. "—there it was!"

Watson leaped up with a startled bark at Katie's clap. He searched the room for attackers, then turned accusing eyes on us when it was clear we were alone.

"Sorry, buddy." Katie gave him an apologetic wince. "I'll give you an extra T.R.E.A.T. to make up for it."

Though from the look on his face, Watson was nowhere near pacified, and he waddled over and plopped down at my feet.

I laid a comforting hand on his head but was still thinking through Katie's theory. "The twins don't have any family. They lost them early. They cut off ties with their mom ages ago, pretty much like Zelda and Verona. And I can't picture them killing anyone, at least not on purpose."

Katie laughed darkly. "That is an important distinction with those two." She seemed to consider again. "However... given their propensity for... not-well-thought-out inventions, let's say, if they did plan on killing someone, it kinda makes sense that they would go about it in a rather calamitous manner, accidentally, of course."

I cocked an eyebrow. "So our theory is that Noah and Jonah accidentally committed an intentional murder?"

"No... more like an intentional murder but an accidental *mass* murder." She scrunched up her eyes. "Does two and a half killings count as a mass murder?"

I didn't offer commentary on her referring to Niles Styles's life hanging in the balance as a half murder. "No. No matter how we look at it, I don't believe they would kill anyone. I just don't. And not just because they're family and I love them. They're not capable of it. But..." I motioned toward Katie's discarded laptop, where the dolls of Blossom's Beauties stared eerily from the screen. "There's some reason Noah and Jonah were allowing those hideous things in their shop. Even if it doesn't have anything to do with murder."

ELEVEN

"Where's the fleabag?" Officer Green met me at the front desk of the police station, the old poster of a cat hanging from the limb of a tree staring at me over her shoulder. Susan leaned to look behind me, clearly expecting to see Watson.

I gaped at her. "You said not to bring him. Your exact words were, and I quote, 'Leave the annoying fleabag at home.'"

Susan straightened, but cocked her head. "I didn't know you were capable of listening or following directions. I'm almost impressed."

I mentally reprimanded myself for that. From the affronted look Watson gave me as I tossed a treat on the floor and then hurried from the cabin before he could follow, I'd be paying for it for days. However, I'd been surprised I was able to talk Susan into letting me speak with the twins at all and hadn't wanted to push my luck.

Susan motioned me back without waiting for my response, and I followed her past the front desk and down a long hallway. "I don't know whether to think this is a confirmation of your insanity or be impressed that you're looking into this." Susan stopped at a door beside a large one-way mirror, and to my surprise, she almost looked concerned and sounded apologetic. "Even you're not going to be able to turn this into a murder investigation, Fred. And no, no one believes that Noah and Jonah intended to kill anyone. But they did, accidentally, but... still."

"I know that." I bit the words out and then caught myself and adjusted. This wasn't Susan's fault. She was doing me a favor, one she didn't have to do. "I don't think it is either, but the family wants me to look into it, and on the off chance..." I finished with a lame shrug.

"Can't blame you. I would do the same if it was my brother." Susan rolled her eyes and muttered to herself. "Lord knows he's almost stupid enough to do something like this. Just waltzing through his life and unintentionally kill multiple people without knowing it was a possibility."

Her words made me realize I hadn't checked since the night before. "Is there news on Niles? Did he...?"

"No. He's still alive. The bleeding isn't the problem. The doctors fixed that quickly enough and made it clear you and I saved his life. But they thought they'd gotten him clean enough from where the metal punctured his intestines, but now there's an infection, so it's touch and go. He's still in the ICU." Her eyes narrowed knowingly. "And no, you *cannot* go talk to him, so don't even think about it."

"I wasn't." I hadn't been, but it wasn't a half-bad idea, at least no more of a waste of time than anything else. And on that thought, I reached for the door handle. "I should get started." Without waiting, I opened it and walked through.

The twins were seated side by side at the secured metal table in the center of the room. It suddenly hit me that I'd now seen over half my family in this very location. The only ones left were Mom, Percival, and Gary. And... the way things were going, it was probably just a matter of time. Who knew, maybe even one day Watson would be sitting there. Actually, more likely, *I'd* be the one sitting there, and Watson would be the one doing interviews, looking for clues.

At that thought, I groaned. Clearly I'd not had enough coffee that morning, or maybe it was the lack of dirty chais. I was getting loopy.

I started to greet the twins and then realized Susan was right behind me, shutting the door. "What are you doing? I thought you said I could speak to them?"

"You can. I won't stop you. But I didn't say you could do it without me." She grinned wickedly. "Read the fine print, Fred. I know Branson always let you in here by yourself, but I'm not harboring any secret longings for you. So..." Her grin morphed into a smirk. "Take it or leave it."

Reminding myself of the conversation Katie and I'd had that morning, I told myself to *not* regress to a snotty twelve-year-old. "Fine."

If I was reading her correctly, Susan was disappointed at the lack of argument.

"Hey—" I sat across from the twins, getting ready to address them individually. But in their matching prison jumpsuits and without Zelda and Verona by their sides to help me differentiate, I had no idea which one was which. "—you guys. How are you doing?"

It was a silly question. Typically, Noah and Jonah were ageless, not because either was especially good-looking—in fact, they were both average in a nondescript way—but more because they felt like overgrown children. However, at the moment, they looked every second of their fifty-some years. From the bags under their eyes, I doubted they'd slept at all the night before, not that I blamed them.

"The girls called last night." The twin on my left spoke. "They said you were looking into it." The faintest spark of hope lit behind his eyes. "You really think someone else did this? That it was planned?"

I wanted to lie to him, offer something, but I couldn't. "I'm going to turn over every stone I can, see if there's any possibility of... something."

He deflated.

The other one spoke. "Gerald Jackson says that it's all circumstantial. Even if the accident did cause our energy sources to explode, there's no proof that we're the ones who put them there to begin with."

I flinched, and Susan beat me to speaking. "Are you kidding? You're going to go that route? You're going to lie and pretend someone *else* put tanks of propane and"—she fluttered a large hand in the air—"I don't know, hydrogen, chlorine, whatever else, in your store, and hooked them up to your inventions without your knowing?"

The other twin deflated as well. "No. We're not going to lie, but—"

"Hold on—" Again I started to say his name, then stopped myself as I wasn't sure, but grabbed his arm anyway. I looked at Susan. "This changes things, with you present. If you're going to be in here, we need..." Good grief, I couldn't believe what I was about to say. "We need the twins' lawyer present."

She smirked, but not in a mocking way, more like she'd been able to read my thoughts. She even went so far as to angle her face toward me and lower her voice. "Really? You think *Gerald Jackson* can help these two?"

One of the twins solved the problem for me. "Don't worry about it, Fred. We trust you. And we're not going to lie. Even if our lawyer thinks we should. We have no problem speaking in front of Officer Green."

Susan's eyes widened, and she looked at them as if she'd

discovered some modicum of respect for the two of them. After a moment, she addressed me. "That good enough for you, Winifred?"

"Sure." It probably shouldn't have been, I probably should've insisted they have legal representation, but it was their choice, and really, having Gerald Jackson there would only be a hindrance to everyone, the twins included—especially if he was going to try to talk them into lying. I refocused on Noah and Jonah. "I've spoken to a few people and did some research into Peter Moss." I decided to cut out my concerns, to not list all the reasons why he wasn't really a likely candidate, since he'd arrived at their store unannounced. I didn't want to hinder anything the twins had to say, as maybe they knew a clue and weren't aware of it, if there were any clues to find. I also wanted to assess how much the twins might or might not know. "From what I've gathered, the list of people who either disliked or hated Peter is nearly endless."

One of them grimaced, and the other said, "Yeah, he wasn't very nice."

That was putting it mildly. I leaned forward, studying both their faces. "Tell me again why you agreed to have his dolls in your shop to begin with. He wasn't very nice, the dolls were creepy, and they in no way fit with what Twinventions was all about."

They exchanged a look, seemingly unaware that they needed to mask their reactions. "Like we told you before, we were trying to be nice."

The twin on the right took over. "As brand-new shop owners, we needed to make friends, and a few of the other stores were carrying the dolls. We didn't want to get a reputation of being difficult before we'd even opened."

Maybe some of it was true, but they were so transparent it was almost painful.

Susan cast me a look, clearly asking if I was going to press or wimp out.

I pressed. "Why else? I can tell there's another reason."

"No, there isn't." They flinched and spoke in unison.

"I thought you said you weren't going to lie." Apparently Susan couldn't help herself.

They flinched again, and the twin on the right spoke. "We're not."

"Oh, come on, Noah, er..." Susan glanced at me, then back at the twins. "Or are you Jonah? I can't tell the two of you apart. Which one's which?"

The twin on the left raised his hand. "I'm Noah."

"I'm Jonah." The one on the right raised his hand as well, just in case there was more clarification needed.

Relief cut through me that I wouldn't have to be the one to ask and admit that I wasn't sure, and I repeated their location a couple of times mentally, lest I forget. *Noah on the left. Noah on the left. Jonah on the right.*

"Fine. Then, *Jonah*," Susan leered, "you said you weren't going to lie, and then you do so on the very first question."

"No, we didn't," Noah piped in, the truth written across his face as well.

I went another direction, trying to rescue them, though maybe I should've pushed more. "When did you meet Peter?"

Noah shrugged, but then Jonah spoke. "Not sure. He wandered into the store a couple months ago while we were remodeling. He wanted us to carry his dolls. I think he was making his way up and down Elkhorn."

That matched what I'd heard about other stores, and

what Anna had said. I tried again. "And why did you say yes?"

And again, they took too long. "It was the nice thing to do." As he spoke, Noah's eyes begged me to not ask any more questions.

Though I felt bad, I couldn't oblige, and instead, doubled down. "Did you know that he used to be a plastic surgeon and he lost his license because of assaulting several of his patients?"

"What?" Susan wheeled on me. "He *what*?"

I hadn't expected that. "You didn't know?"

An atypical blush rose to her cheeks, but her temper rose hotter than her embarrassment. "We've kind of been busy with an exploded downtown, and two insane inventor twins who thought it was a good idea to keep explosives in the middle of a tourist trap. Forgive me if I haven't been concerned about the past life of a dead dollmaker. I've been focused on getting him justice, not digging up dirt on him."

"I wasn't criticizing." I waited for a moment to see if she was going to go off again, and when she didn't, continued, "In addition, he had a habit of telling random women he met, me included, and Delilah Johnson, apparently, all the ways we needed to improve our looks. Not that him being insulting matches what he did to his patients, but it's providing a very extensive pool of people who have grievances against him."

"So you *do* think it was planned." Jonah sounded excited and genuinely hopeful. "That it wasn't an accident. It was murder."

Susan scoffed but remained silent.

I answered Jonah with a question. "Run me through it again, yesterday morning. When did Peter arrive at Twin-ventions, and why?"

Noah took over. "We told you. He showed up shortly after we did. He was still there when the girls came down. He was trying to get us to agree to carry his dolls again."

There was a flicker of disappointment that their story didn't change, but I kept pushing. "And you went into the lab to consider it?"

They nodded.

"Why?"

"Because," Noah again, "like we said, we didn't want to make waves. And you met him. Peter was... aggressive. Bullyish."

"He threatened you?" Susan perked up.

"Not physically." The twins once more exchanged glances, and Jonah continued, "But... he did make it clear things would go easier for our store if we carried the dolls."

That was new, but it still didn't feel right. "What was he going to do to Twinventions if you didn't?"

"Didn't say." Noah shrugged again.

Maybe it wasn't murder, but there was something. They were lying. Just like Delilah had the night before. "And you didn't know he was going to drop by? He didn't call ahead?"

They shook their heads.

"Is there any reason to think he told anyone else he'd be there?"

Jonah scrunched up his face, considering. "I don't think so. Maybe his wife. But if he did tell someone, he didn't inform us. How would we know?"

"Then it doesn't matter how big your suspect list is of people who might want Peter Moss dead." Susan looked at me. "It's not like he was shot or stabbed in the heat of the moment. If this thing wasn't an accident, then the machine or something else in that shop would've had to have been timed to explode at just the right moment to kill him. That's impossible. The only way the theory of Peter being the intended target of murder flows is if the Wonder Twins here did it, as they were the only ones there."

"We didn't!" They both squeaked in panic.

I met Susan's gaze. "I agree."

"Fred!" One of the twins gasped as if betrayed, but I didn't look at them.

Instead I replayed what Susan said, a couple of new ideas coming to mind, or at least ones that hadn't fully taken root yet but were starting to. Maybe it hadn't been the Manscaper that had exploded. I wasn't sure if that would make a difference or not, so I started with the other possibility—even though it was nearly as crazy as what we were already discussing. Slowly, I turned toward the twins again. "Niles was scheduled to be on the Manscaper during the open house, to do the demonstration, wasn't he?" I caught myself before they had a chance. "No. *Miles* was going to do it, right?"

"Yeah." They both nodded.

"Oh, come on." Susan looked at me in disbelief, catching on quickly. "So now, *Miles* was the intended victim?"

"You're the one that said the Manscaper would have to be timed at just the right moment to kill." I offered her an embarrassed smile for coming up with such a ludicrous theory. "It was kind of your idea."

"Not hardly." She snorted again. "So now, this stupid machine was timed to kill Miles, and just happened to explode early, yet *still* managed to kill the intended victim?"

I offered Susan one of her shrugs. "Stranger things have happened?"

"Have they?" She cocked her eyebrow, and then it settled into a scowl. "All right, let's pretend that actually could happen. Why? Did Miles have some secret life as well? What, he used to be a rodeo clown and secretly abused the animals before he was an inventor?"

Instead of answering, I looked toward the twins. "Maybe? You guys have known the Styles twins for a long time, right? Did he have any enemies?"

"No." Neither of them even had to consider. "Everyone loved Miles. He was the most popular at all the invention and twin conventions. He and Niles."

Susan nearly choked and held up her hand. "Wait a minute. I've heard about the inventor conventions, but there are *twin* conventions?"

They nodded, and Noah spoke. "Yeah. More often they're more like meet-ups. We've done them for years. That's how we all met. We've known Miles and Niles even longer than the girls. Actually, that's where we met Zelda and Verona. At one of the twin meet-ups in Boulder. Miles and Niles were there too."

Susan didn't speak and looked as if she'd been struck dumb.

I knew it was a crazy theory but thought I might as well ask. "Was Peter Moss or his wife ever at the conventions or meet-ups? Either the inventor ones or the ones for twins?"

They both shook their heads.

That would've been too much of a coincidence, probably.

We talked over things for another five or ten minutes, but nothing really emerged. As Susan and I walked out, I couldn't help but be a little encouraged.

Susan gave me a knowing look. "You're going to start digging into the Styles twins, aren't you?"

I nodded. "Are you going to tell me not to?"

She cocked her head at me once more. "Do I *look* like your ex?"

"No, thankfully." I couldn't help but laugh. "And yes, that's where I'll look next. At this point they're a better lead than Peter, at least in terms of accessibility."

"Marginally." Susan looked doubtful, but when she spoke next, her words were sincere. "It doesn't look good, Fred. I know you don't want this to fall in the laps of your brothers-in-law, but every other option is about as far-fetched as... well... about as far-fetched as Noah and Jonah are themselves."

"You're not wrong." I glanced through the one-way mirror at the twins who were deep in a panicked discussion. "But that might actually be why it ends up making sense in the long run." And maybe, just maybe, I was starting to buy into looking into this as a murder after all.

Susan walked me out, and I turned to her once more, unable to refrain myself. "Oh, by the way, just so you know. There's all kinds of corgi meet-ups, kinda like what the twins were talking about, but for corgis. I've never been, but if you'd like to go, Watson and I will accompany you. You could be surrounded by hundreds and hundreds of corgis."

Her eyes narrowed to slits. "I have an extra cell. And I've got no problem throwing away the key."

Nearly twenty minutes passed before I was able to take in the beauty around the Mini Cooper as Katie, Watson, and I traveled down the winding road away from Estes Park. I lifted off the gas slightly as we came upon a meadow near the base of the mountains. Every once in a while, though not very often, the Colorado splendor became just a normal part of life, easy to slip by. But with the azure sky above the rugged mountains that were covered in newly leafed aspens acting as the backdrop for a huge herd of elk grazing by a meandering stream, the scene managed to slice through the heavy cloud of stress that had fallen.

Katie sighed as she pressed her nose against the passenger window. "Look at all the babies. There's probably fifty of them, and those two are playing in the water." She giggled. "I think I'm getting a new T-shirt idea."

"Here." I tapped the window button, lowering it. "Before you flatten your nose."

As soon as the warm June air rushed through the window, bringing with it the scent of pine, I wondered why I hadn't done it sooner. Deciding we could all use a moment, I pulled off a little way ahead, where the road widened, and then leaned over the console to watch the calves frolic.

After a few seconds, at either the sounds or the scent, Watson woke from where he'd been curled in the back seat and propped his forelegs up on the side to observe as well. His barely there tail wagged in excitement as he whimpered.

"I wish we had that robot dog with us to interpret what he's saying." Katie spared Watson a quick glance. "Maybe he wants us to let him out so he can go chase and play."

"If that's what that little robot would tell us, then we'd know it doesn't work. Now, if it said he wanted us to see if the elk had any snacks to spare, then maybe." Although, Watson had surprised me the night before with Delilah's pack of Basset hounds. Maybe he would enjoy chasing the elk.

We watched for a few more minutes. I could literally feel my blood pressure slowing, some of the tension beginning to slip away. However, all too soon, my stationary Mini Cooper alerted the tourists driving by that there was something to see. They began to park, get out of their cars, and trudge toward the herd, their cell phones and cameras snapping away.

"Well, that was that. But it was nice while it lasted." Katie dusted off her hands and faced the front once more.

Watson had already returned to his nap.

Another car took my spot the moment I pulled out onto the road. "Thanks for coming to Boulder with me." The idea had struck as soon as I'd left the police station. "Not exactly sure what I'll be looking for at Miles and Niles's shop, so you might pick up on something I miss."

"It's kind of fun. I feel like I'm playing hooky from work." She smiled brightly and then forced it to dim a bit. "That's probably horrible to say, given the situation."

"Nah. If anything, I think it drives home that we should

enjoy every moment of life that we have, just like those baby elk out there." I glanced at my cell to see if any messages had come through, but we were still out of service range, then refocused on the road. "Besides, the entire theory that the Styles twins were the target is probably a complete waste of time, so we might as well simply enjoy the journey."

"I don't know, I like that you're thinking outside the box. If anything, it sort of makes sense with the situation. With Noah and Jonah involved, it's only natural this thing would take some weird, unexpected turns."

"I think this goes a little bit above and beyond unexpected turns." I'd already thought through the tentative new theory multiple times in the last hour, and discarded the likelihood every time, but... it was the only possibility we had at the moment, so why not? "If somebody did want to hurt Miles or Niles specifically, I can fully accept that they tampered with the Manscaper to do so. But it's simply not possible that it would explode half a day early and still manage to kill an intended victim who was in another shop all the way across the street. That kind of thing doesn't happen."

"But it does." Katie didn't even hesitate. "It's the kind of thing that you hear on the news and on podcasts all the time —some weird random unbelievable twist of fate that sounds like fiction, but happens in real life all around us. It's where the saying 'stranger things have happened' comes from."

I spared her a quick glance. "That's exactly what I said to Susan, but I don't think I really meant it."

"Just goes to show that you're smarter than you think you are." She repositioned her seat belt, which had gotten twisted while we looked at the elk. "And even if we don't find a new suspect in Boulder, by being around their inventions, I bet we'll understand the Styles twins that much more. That can't hurt."

I agreed with her on that. "I'm also curious to see what another invention store looks like. The only inventors I've ever been around are the twins. Surely, they're not all like Noah and Jonah."

"I don't know, I think they might be."

I snorted out a laugh. "Really? You think there's that many people who would build a machine filled with razor blades and scissors and are willing to stand in the middle of it and trust it with their lives? That's got to be a Noah and Jonah Pearson peculiarity."

"But it isn't!" Katie grabbed my leg in excitement as she angled toward me. "Turns out, the Manscaper isn't that original of an idea, after all. There was one in the 1800s that shaved twelve men at once. They all sat in a row and this iron bar with twelve razors attached went to work." She grimaced. "Unfortunately, unlike what Noah and Jonah came up with, it didn't vary its strokes to accommodate for each man's individual face shape."

I cast her a quick side eye. "You're making that up."

She shook her head, brown spirals flying. "I'm not. I went on one of my Google binges, as you like to call them, last night. I swear, history is filled with various versions of Noah and Jonah. If I was a believer in such things, I'd say those two have been reincarnated over and over again just to provide the world with insane inventions." As she spoke, her excitement grew, and her hands became more emphatic. "The 1800s were a particularly good century for inventions. There was this mousetrap that had a fifty-caliber revolver attached. They actually loaded the thing. So if a mouse tried to take the cheese—" She clapped her hands together. "—bam!"

Watson woke up with a startled bark.

"Sorry, buddy." Katie twisted back to attempt an apologetic scratch on his head. He evaded her touch. "That's the second time I've done that to you today. I'm going to owe you so many doggy carbs you're going to be a thousand pounds in a week."

Reaching over, I opened the glove compartment and pulled out one of the buffalo jerkies. "Here, start the reparations early."

Proving how offended he was, Watson studied the dried strip of meat warily from her outstretched hand, as if he was too good to accept gifts from her.

"Oh, come on," I chided him in the rearview mirror. "You're not fooling anybody."

He chuffed, snatched the treat with a flourish, and then turned around to face the back of the car.

Giggling, Katie faced the front once more and continued as if nothing happened. "Another one, again in the 1800s, was this big treadmill-looking thing they put on the railroads. Three or four horses would walk on it at the same time to provide the energy for it to move."

Katie's onslaught of trivia brought a sense of happiness and contentment as much as the gorgeous scenery and the elk. It was a reminder that some things never changed, and though there were no guarantees on how this would end, life would continue. She and I would be back in our bookshop and bakery, and there would always be more laughter, grumpy corgis, and pastries. Katie listed invention after invention as we drove through Lyons, then along the highway at the base of the foothills with the sun highlighting the mountains to our right, and was forced to finish only when we got a prime parking spot right in front of Miles and Niles's shop on Pearl Street in Boulder.

Pearl Street was a twin to Estes Park's downtown, but unlike Zelda and Verona and Noah and Jonah, it wasn't even close to being identical. Whereas Estes Park retained its 1960s mountain style and was charming and cozy—and in certain spots in desperate need of updating—Pearl Street had used its river rock and log motifs to craft a chic outdoor shopping district for the people who could drop a hundred dollars for dinner and drinks, spend a fortune at by-the-ounce tea shops and New Age stores, then turn around and buy designer high-heeled shoes half a block over. The Cozy Corgi was charming enough it would've fit in on Pearl Street, though probably been seen more as quaint. Twin-ventions, with its clutter of wheels and gears, no matter how well arranged, wouldn't have lasted half a day, or even been allowed to open at all. And... considering the explosion, maybe Boulder was on the right track.

"Wow!" Katie gaped at the storefront of Geek Out as I affixed Watson's leash. "This wasn't what I expected at all. And it definitely doesn't match any of the invention shops I saw online last night. This is like... I don't know... Fifth Avenue meets Restoration Hardware meets NASA or something."

It was an apt description. The interior could be seen from the wall of windows under the sleek, steel-cut sign of Geek Out. The entire store was a soft white—the ceiling, the walls, even the hardwood floors. Everything else within gleamed. Its various shiny metals, polished woods, and jewel-toned surfaces sparkled under the endless track and spotlighting.

"I'm a little nervous to go in." Katie looked at me, wide-eyed. "What if I accidentally knock something over and break it? That stuff looks expensive. I might not be able to ever retire."

"As long as nothing explodes, I think we'll be okay." I sounded more confident than I felt. Proving it, I cracked open the door and paused halfway, looking toward a smartly dressed salesclerk, before I motioned down to Watson. "Are dogs welcome?" I hadn't thought twice about bringing Watson with us. Boulder might be fancier than Estes Park, but it was still Colorado, and nothing came between Coloradans and their dogs. But still...

"Absolutely. We have a whole dog section, in fact." The salesclerk-slash-model beamed and hurried over, motioning at the far wall with one hand while reaching toward Watson with the other. "Oh, a corgi! I love corgis! They're all the rage right now!"

Watson evaded her outstretched hand by darting beneath my skirt.

"He's shy." The girl cooed, standing again. "What a sweetie."

"Yeah..." Katie chuckled to herself as she pushed the door wide and stepped around us. "Shy."

"Is this your first time in the store?" Undaunted, the clerk's perma-smile gleamed. "Would you like a tour?"

"Absolutely!" Katie decided for us.

Watson stuck his head out from under my broomstick skirt—a pea-green one *without* one of Katie's custom embroideries, as the cute characters seemed disrespectful given the circumstances. When he saw Katie and the clerk, who'd introduced herself as Alicia, were a few steps ahead of us, he emerged fully, deciding the coast was clear, but stuck close to my side as we began to follow.

Geek Out was at least three times the size of Twinventions, and had, probably, half the amount of inventory. The extra space accentuated the individual inventions, making them seem more special than the ones in Estes. It was easy to see that Noah and Jonah had been in the shop, despite the differences, as a lot of their sections were the same. Home improvement, grooming, cooking, and the like, and as the clerk had said, even a section for pets. Here and there were more unusual inventions that were clearly more art than function, but nothing as wild as the Manscaper.

One of those caught Katie's attention. "Oh, look at this! I'm pink and yellow!"

I thought it just a mirror in a gilded frame, but as I came closer, I noticed what she meant. Instead of Katie's genuine reflection, there was—I wasn't sure how to describe it—the essence of her, I supposed. Katie's features could almost be made out, but was more like a smooth, modern interpretation of them. Instead of flesh-tone and pretty chestnut hair, the curves and edges of her silhouette were lemon yellow and then morphed into a vibrant, nearly neon pink in the center.

Alicia turned and saw where Katie had paused. "The inventors call that the Soul Gazer." Though her smile didn't waver, a slight crease formed between her brows. "They've explained it to me several times, but I struggle with the concept. The closest I can come up with is that it reads your aura, though Niles would describe it in a better, deeper way."

"That's *exactly* the colors I would've guessed my aura to be, if asked." Clearly pleased, Katie grabbed my hand and pulled me forward, forcing me to take her spot. Peering over my shoulder, she groaned. "You've *got* to be kidding me."

It was a strange sensation to look at my reflection and see a different version of myself. Like Katie, my edges were a yellow, but a soft, warm mustard hue that gave way to a warm brown, nearly the shade of Katie's hair. I turned to taunt her. "You can't ever make fun of my earth-tone color palette choice in clothing again. What more proof do you need?"

Instead of answering me, Katie looked to Alicia. "She's going to be insufferable from this point on."

I laughed, started to walk away, and then had another thought. I apologized in advance. "I know you're going to hate me for this, but I have to know." Before he could protest, I bent, swooped my chunky corgi into my arms, and hoisted him so that his head was nearly even with mine.

Though his reflection thrashed about just as he did, a third color joined my yellow and brown. Watson was a deep, nearly glowing rusty orange. Beautiful.

"Good grief, Watson too!" Katie let out a long-suffering sigh. "I bet if Leo was here, he'd be a horrible shade of green, probably like your skirt. The three of you would be quite the splotchy mess."

"Probably." Still laughing, I deposited a thoroughly offended Watson back to the floor. Instead of taking shelter under my skirt, he went to the end of his leash and glared. Katie might've been right about Leo, but my bet would be a soft dusty green, like the color of the pine trees when they were surrounded by morning mist.

Alicia finished the tour, and two things were apparent. One, Noah and Jonah had definitely modeled their store after Geek Out. If you weren't looking for the comparison, it would be easily missed, given that they were so different in aesthetic, but it was there, clear as day. Two, I completely understood why Anna and Carl had wanted to team up with Miles and Niles. Though the furniture pieces they had in their shop were modern and didn't match the aesthetic of Cabin and Hearth, they were beautiful, innovative, and of the highest quality.

We ended the tour at the counter. The wall behind it

was made up with framed awards, articles, and photos. Just as I started to thank Alicia for the tour, one of the photos stood out to me, causing me to gasp. "Katie, look!" Without thinking, I stepped around the edge and moved behind the counter. "Look how young they all are."

Katie joined me and gave a soft sigh, as if she were looking at puppies. "They're babies, absolute babies."

The framed photo showed a much, much younger Verona, Zelda, Jonah, and Noah. Beside them were Miles and Niles, each of their arms over another set of twins—two beautiful, identical African-American women. "This must be at one of the twin meet-ups."

"Oh, are you friends of Miles and Niles?" Though her tone was cheerful, there was a slight edge to it, making it clear she felt that should have been disclosed early on.

"We've met them. Can't say we're friends." I pointed to the picture. "But these are my stepsisters and their husbands."

"How fun!" Alicia brightened again, then her face fell instantly. "Oh, then... you've heard?"

I nodded. "Yes. We have."

"We were there," Katie chimed in, and then instantly looked as if she regretted giving that much away.

Alicia sucked in a breath, partially covering her mouth. "How terrifying. Are you both okay?" She didn't wait for a reply, and tears glistened in her eyes. "I just can't believe it about Miles and Niles. Although it sounds like they think Niles should be okay." She glanced around, as if we might be overheard. "I thought we should close down, but Brooke, the store manager, felt like they would want us to keep it open."

As I so often did, I decided to be direct and blunt. It seemed the simplest way to judge a person's genuine reaction. "The accident is why we're here, actually. Trying to get a better picture of Miles and Niles. Have you worked for them long?"

She nodded, wiping at her eyes. "Almost ten years."

She didn't look old enough to have worked anywhere for nearly ten years, but her reaction felt genuine. "They must be good employers if you've been here that long."

"Oh, they are." That time, a tear escaped before she could wipe it away. "They're both so kind and brilliant."

"Would everyone feel that way?" Katie chimed in again, apparently taking my cue to be direct.

Alicia cocked her head, not understanding. "What do you mean?" She gestured around the store. "I can't imagine anyone arguing that they're not brilliant."

"No," Katie clarified. "I mean, would everyone feel that they're kind? Would some of the neighboring storeowners have a problem with Geek Out, or are other inventors jealous of their success. Looks like they've received a ton of awards."

"Oh, they have. Loads. But no, everyone loves—" Her words fell away as her eyes widened. "Wait a minute." Her green gaze flicked back and forth between Katie and me. "Do you mean... you think..." She took a step back. "It *wasn't* an accident? Someone hurt them on purpose?"

"We don't know," I clarified in a rush. "Probably not. We're just curious." Before she could ask another question, or decide she shouldn't be talking to us, I drew her attention back to the picture. "Who are these women with Miles and Niles? Do you know?"

She shook her head. "No, that was before me. I think they were twins they were dating, but I've never met them." She pointed at Noah and Jonah. "I've met them, though. They've been in here loads of times. They're twins and inventors just like—" She let out a breath and shook her head again. "You know that already."

I expected her to make some comments about Noah and Jonah being responsible for the accident, or to get angry that we'd shown up when I was related to them. Either that wasn't her disposition, or she didn't make that connection, so I decided to push my luck. "You really can't think of anyone the twins had conflict with. Maybe not even someone local, but someone from the invention conventions"—that was a tongue twister—"or the twin... conventions." Not only hard to say, but felt a little ridiculous as well.

"Nobody." Alicia was emphatic. "I'm telling you, everyone loved both of them. And everyone loves the store. Not only is it a great addition to Pearl Street, but Miles and Niles donate a huge portion of the profits to charity. They split it between scholarships for colleges, and funding for science labs in elementary schools."

"Wow." Katie sounded impressed, as was I, but she pushed too. "Anybody think they were *too* good, maybe *too* perfect? Maybe annoyingly so?"

Alicia shook her head again. "I'm sorry, if I could think of anyone, I'd tell you. The thought that I'll never see Miles again and that we might lose Niles..." She shuddered. "Or even worse, if he has some sort of brain damage, or can't work on his inventions, he'd rather not be alive. Although maybe that's true anyway. I don't think he'll be able to function without Miles."

Though I could feel that there was nothing else Geek Out had to offer, Katie and I spent a few more minutes reading over the awards and articles. All of them glowing. Niles was often quoted about his passion around the purity of invention and ingenuity, and Miles talking about creativity and using science to better the world through beauty and creation. I hadn't realized, but I'd cast them in the same light in which I looked at Noah and Jonah. Not insulting, necessarily, but more like their inventions were silly, fun, and rather indulgent hobbies. But it was clear to see that wasn't at all how the Styles twins thought about their work. Though, if I was being fair, Noah and Jonah would be deeply insulted if they knew that's how I thought about them.

After leaving Geek Out, we ate dinner on Pearl Street at a Mexican restaurant that had an open patio and allowed dogs. Though Watson was nowhere close to forgiving me for the humiliation of picking him up, he grudgingly accepted small strips of my tortilla shells when I offered them under the table.

While we ate, Katie and I went into research mode again, using the free Wi-Fi on our cell phones to research the Styles twins. Just as Alicia had said, there wasn't one negative comment to be found, not anywhere.

As we drove back to Estes, I couldn't help but feel that we were back to square one, and that Noah and Jonah were in such deep trouble there was no way I could help them.

After dropping Katie off, I snatched up my cell to text Leo to see if he wanted to meet Watson and me at the house. Before I could tap his name on speed dial, the phone rang. Though not in my contacts, the number was local, so I answered.

"Fred?" A tense, possibly angry, female voice sounded before I could even say hello.

"Yes. How can I—"

"Can you come over?" There was a murmur of someone else in the background. "Right now?"

"Uhm... Who—" A bark, followed by two howls cut me off, but answered my question. "Delilah?"

"Oh, right. I didn't say that, did I?" She sounded off, a little slurred.

"Delilah, are you okay? Have you been drinking?"

"Yes, I've been drinking. The girls were over. We've... been drinking." Definitely angry. "What? Does that make me guilty of murder now?" There was another murmur, of the human variety, not one of the Basset hounds.

"No. I never thought—" I felt my defenses rise at her tone but managed to keep my voice neutral. This wasn't typical for Delilah at all. Neither to call, nor lose her cool. "Of course I'll come over."

. . .

Watson perked up the second we turned onto the cul-de-sac, going so far as to prop his front paws on the passenger door and press his nose against the window, managing to smear his tongue across it as well.

"Wow, you really did like Delilah's dogs. You even know where we are."

Watson whimpered in excitement, his whole body trembling.

That tiny mystery was solved the second we parked, and I opened the door to the sound of the three Basset hounds baying. Watson had probably been able to hear them from inside the Mini Cooper and hadn't memorized Delilah's location.

I barely managed to get my left boot out of the car before Watson tore across me, one of his back legs accidentally giving me a good sucker punch in the stomach as he leaped onto her lawn and tore off for her porch. Gingerly rubbing my stomach, I finished getting out of the car and followed. It was nice to see him so excited about other dogs, but I thought I preferred his reaction to Flotsam and Jetsam. I was at less risk of bodily harm with him hiding below my skirt, at least mostly.

Watson yipped as he reached her door, inciting the barking and howling inside to reach epic proportions.

Delilah arrived before I'd made it to the porch. Zuko, Kenickie, and Putzie rushed past her in a blur of long bodies, short legs, and long floppy ears. They hit Watson at full force, causing him to tumble and roll, and then the four of them rushed out in frantic exuberance onto the lawn. It was late enough I was surprised neighbors didn't start complaining at the noise.

My slight offense at being nailed in the stomach evaporated, watching Watson frolic with his new friends. Even getting whipped across the face multiple times with their long tails didn't seem to diminish his enjoyment.

Most of the time, I thought I knew Watson nearly as well as I knew myself, sometimes better. But then... there were moments like these, where he was a complete enigma. If Flotsam and Jetsam had greeted him in such a manner, Watson would've growled, snapped at them, and brought them to submission... and *they* were other corgis. I had no clue what magic the T-Bird gang of Basset hounds had over him.

When I finally turned to greet Delilah, her smile was tight as she observed the dogs, but when her blue gaze looked toward me, even in the dim moonlight I could see the strain in their depths. "Thanks for coming." Despite the words themselves, there was still a sound of accusal in them.

I started to respond, then noticed another figure in the doorway. Simone, the potter, who was part owner of the Coffee Kiln with Carla Beaker. I gave her a little wave. "Hey, Simone. Haven't seen you in a bit."

She gave a tight nod. "It has been."

Maybe I'd made a mistake in agreeing to come over. Simone and I hadn't had very many interactions, but she'd always been friendly and seemed easygoing, for the most part. But like Delilah, she gave me a feeling like I'd done something wrong.

"Come on, boys." Delilah gave a solitary sharp clap, and her voice left no room for argument.

The three Basset hounds responded instantly, tearing back across the lawn, over the porch, and into the house. Watson stood, perplexed, in the pool of moonlight, clearly wondering why the fun and games had ended so abruptly.

"Come on, buddy." I patted my thigh, calling him over.

Proving that he hadn't been possessed by doggy aliens and that he was still fully Watson Charles Page, he meandered over languidly, taking an exorbitant amount of time to walk up the two steps, and passing between Delilah, Simone, and myself as if he was a visiting dignitary.

Despite whatever mood Delilah was in, she snorted out a soft chuckle. "He's my kind of man."

I followed Watson inside. The night had clearly been a gathering of the Pink Panthers, and although Delilah had assured me—the times when she invited me to be part of the group—that it wasn't just about partying, this occasion had apparently been an exception, judging from several empty wine bottles on the coffee table.

Despite her coldness toward me, Simone bent and offered a hand for Watson to sniff in way of greeting. As she did so, a few of the decorative metal coils in her long dreads clinked together. Though Watson didn't growl as he had the first few times that had occurred, he avoided her hand and went the long way around to join his friends, who'd commandeered the couch.

Delilah chuckled again. "Definitely my kind of man—so much attitude."

With an unoffended smirk, Simone stood, but her dark gaze still seemed hard when she looked at me.

Motioning for me to take the love seat that Leo and I had occupied the night before, Delilah sat on the couch, one of her hounds, though I wasn't sure which, rested its head on her leg, and she began to pet them absentmindedly. She jumped right in. "Thanks again for coming over. And I'll admit up front that I'm doing this under duress... or coercion." She flicked a narrowed gaze toward Simone.

In response, Simone lifted her hands as if in surrender,

and instead of taking the available spot next to me, sat on the far arm of the sofa above the dogs. "I agree that it's annoying to do so, but better to be upfront."

Though he'd settled, at Simone's nearness, Watson stood, hopped over one of the Basset hounds, then nested among them, ignoring that there wasn't enough room for his girth.

"I get the feeling that you're both angry at me, and I'm not sure what I did." I met Delilah's gaze directly. "Like I've told you, I don't suspect you of anything."

"I know that." She bit out the words and closed her eyes, then gave a slight shake of her head before sighing and looking at me again. "I'm sorry. I'm not mad at you. I'm just angry that I'm in this situation at all." I could still hear a slight slur, but she wasn't as drunk as I'd assumed on the phone. "Simone thought it was better to tell you face-to-face, so that when you find it, you won't make any assumptions. Who knows, knowing you, you've probably already found it."

I shook my head. "I've not found anything, not about anyone." For some reason, embarrassment flittered through me at my lack of success, followed by a flash of irritation. Delilah wasn't the only one put in a situation she hadn't asked for.

"Well, you will. You're good, so I know it's only a matter of time." Leaning forward, Delilah lifted a laptop from the middle of the wine bottles on the coffee table and then held it in her lap, the blue light of the screen washing out her beautiful features, highlighting shadows under her eyes. She stared at it in silence for several moments, her internal debate almost painful.

While I didn't agree with a lot of things about Delilah, I'd decided I liked her, for the most part, and was suddenly overcome with the impulse to protect her. "If it doesn't have to do with the murder, you don't have to show me anything, Delilah."

"Simone says it's crazy to think that Peter was murdered, but since you're looking into it that way, this would be a motive." Delilah turned the laptop around and held it out toward me. "I wasn't entirely honest with you and Leo last night."

Settling back against the love seat, I readjusted the screen of the laptop and was surprised to see the Blossom's Beauties website—twelve dolls spread out over three rows stared creepily up at me, their too-human faces combined with the odd baby-doll bodies bringing to mind Katie's joke about him using actual shrunken heads.

"It really is preposterous to think this was a murder." Simone pulled my attention away from the laptop. "I've heard good things about you, like I told you before. And I was impressed on how you handled everything with the murder at the Koffee Kiln, but this is a stretch, and it's honestly an insult to all three victims, and the affected storeowners."

An insult? I gaped at her. "I'm sorry?"

"I get that you're trying to clear your family's name, and on one hand I don't blame you, but *they* are the ones responsible for the deaths. And using this situation to play detective..." Her upper lip curled, matching the slight snarl in her tone. She seemed at a loss for words.

From his spot amid the Bassets, Watson lifted his head.

"You sell books, Fred." There was some other emotion amid Simone's anger, but I couldn't place it. "People's deaths aren't there for you to make yourself feel special." Before I could say anything in my defense, she gestured toward the laptop. "Other people's secrets aren't playthings. You can ruin lives and reputations."

"Simone..." Delilah leaned over the dogs and placed a restraining hand on Simone's leg. "It was *your* idea to ask Fred here."

"I know that." She bit the words out at Delilah as well. "But it shouldn't have to happen."

For a second, it looked like Delilah was going to agree, but she turned back to me and nodded toward the computer. "I trust that you'll keep this to yourself. I know you'll see it as a motive, but I promise it isn't." She grimaced, and when she spoke next, it sounded like the words were being pulled from her. "And I know if you *have* to tell Leo and Katie when you're looking into things, that you'll ask them to keep it secret too. I know Leo will." She shook her head again and spoke to herself. "Why didn't I just call him?"

I looked back and forth from the screen to Delilah. She was acting as if whatever this motive was should be obvious. But it wasn't, not even close. Thinking maybe the screen had moved when she'd handed me the laptop, I started to scroll down the page, and then saw it, or at least I thought I did.

Narrowing my eyes, I looked at one of the dolls. It had long auburn hair and was the final face at the end of the second row. It looked familiar.

Once more I looked back and forth from the screen to Delilah. If I'd realized what I was looking for, I would've seen it instantly, but without it, I never would've noticed. "This doll looks like you." I peered closer. "Almost. But... Peter got some details wrong." The nose had a gentle bump and was slightly turned down, and the chin was a touch softer and less defined. "The motive is that I'm supposed to think you might've killed Peter because he made a doll that resembles you?"

Delilah cocked her head as if surprised. "Maybe I didn't need to bring you in on this after all. We just assumed you'd—"

It clicked, and I couldn't hold back a gasp as I recalled what Peter did before starting up his creepy doll business. "This is you." Another back-and-forth between the doll and Delilah. "Or... it's the old you."

Though she clearly hadn't wanted me to know, Delilah looked pleased that I'd figured it out, as if I'd been on the verge of losing her respect but had just managed to keep hold of it. "Yeah."

I was certain I understood, but clarified anyway. "Peter changed your nose and chin when he was a plastic surgeon."

"And a couple of other things." She tilted that perfect chin a little higher in the air. "It didn't change who I was, just improved on the perfection I already had going."

"Were you..." I didn't know how to ask the question without prying. "Did he..."

"No." Delilah saved me from having to ask. "He worked on me ages and ages ago. I'd barely turned eighteen. He didn't start abusing his patients until later, from what I understand."

Relief flooded through me that Delilah hadn't had to endure that experience. Although that truly would've been an understandable motive. "Thank goodness. But even if I had seen this, I don't think I would've believed you killed Peter just because he made a doll that looked like you before you changed some features." Another option rose to the surface. "Was he blackmailing you? Threatening to tell people you'd had plastic surgery, if you didn't pay him or carry his dolls in your shop?"

"Almost." For maybe the first time ever, Delilah Johnson blushed. "That night at your party"—her hand flicked toward Simone—"right there in front of my panthers, he suggested we invite him to one of our parties. That we could... entertain him, was how he put it... or he'd tell people." She hardened suddenly, and the blush vanished. "I *do not* get threatened or coerced into who I take into my bed. Ever."

"Delilah." Simone gave a warning whisper, probably thinking that Delilah's anger made it sound like more of a motive.

Maybe it should have, but it didn't. Delilah lived life differently from me, but she wasn't a killer. "That's why you slapped him."

She nodded, unapologetic. "And I'd do it again." After a moment, her shoulders slumped. "Even though him trying to force himself on me that way would be more of a motive for me than the doll, or the threat of people knowing I've had some work done—I mean really, who cares in this day and age—I wouldn't kill him for it."

"I believe you." I looked back at the doll of Delilah's old face, I noticed at the bottom of the screen that it said it was page seventy-three of ninety. With a couple of quick calculations... if each page had twelve dolls, then Peter had made over a thousand of them. "So... who knows how many of his other patients he's done this to. And maybe tried to extort them for money, favors, or sex."

"I'm sure he did." Simone's voice was filled with disgust, but not at me this time. "The man was scum, but again, it's ludicrous to think this was murder, and if it was just Peter that died and was hurt by it, honestly I wouldn't care, but it wasn't. I know your brothers-in-law didn't mean to cause the harm that they did, but I do believe justice needs to be served, and I find it the height of arrogance and privilege for you to try to find a loophole for them."

"I'm not looking for a loophole, and, if I'm being honest, I agree with you, I didn't really believe this was a murder." I looked back at the computer. "Although... I've always said I don't believe in coincidence, and there was already a huge number of people who would have it in for Peter Moss, and that's just doubled... more than." I looked back up at Simone, returning her hard stare. "What do you think? Do *you* believe in that sort of coincidence, or would you call it karma? Because that would also be an insult to the other victims."

She opened her mouth to argue but closed it once more.

I turned my attention to Delilah. "Do you know of anyone else in town who was in your situation? Who were patients of his and had dolls crafted after them?"

She shook her head. "I didn't even know I had a doll until that night. Though if you look at its details, Peter made that horrid thing years ago, he just hadn't used it against me yet. I guess it was just my turn."

I still couldn't fathom how anyone could have planned it so well for Peter to be on the Manscaper at that exact moment, but neither could I look past Peter's nearly count-less victims who'd want revenge.

"Fred." Delilah pulled my attention away from my thoughts. "If you decide you have to tell people, or you don't think Katie will keep it a secret, I'd appreciate you letting me know." There was that blush again. "I hate to admit it, because I truly believe that whatever a person decides to do with their body is *their* business and nothing to be ashamed of, I really do. But..." She finished with a shrug.

"I probably will tell Katie and Leo, as I'm sure they'll help me look through the hundreds of these things to see if we recognize anyone else, but I won't say anything." I held her gaze, hoping she could see my sincerity. "And I know Katie. She's just as trustworthy as Leo and me."

FOURTEEN

Dolls filled my dreams.

Instead of novels, they occupied every inch of the book-shelves in the Cozy Corgi. When I ran up the stairs to escape, their heads took the place of the filling in the thou-sands of cream puffs that covered the thick marble coun-tertop of Katie's bakery. A *ding* sounded, and as I watched in horror, the wood panel doors of the elevator slid open and a horde of zombie-like dolls tumbled out. Then, inexplica-bly, I was transported to Delilah's front yard, but it had been transformed into a ball pit. Watson was there with the Basset hounds, the four of them frolicking among the balls—only they weren't the brightly colored plastic things, of course, but more doll heads, each with a distorted face of someone I knew. My family, friends, my ex-husband, even past victims whose murders I'd helped solve. Watson made another running leap into the ball pit, sending them flying. One of the doll heads rolled to a stop at my boots. I glanced down to inspect it and found my own slightly altered face staring up at me.

I sat straight up in bed, gasping for breath. At a concerned whimper, I looked over to find Watson lying in his bed, with his stuffed lion and duck, peering at me with a cocked head. I tried to assure him I was okay, but I couldn't get any words out. I hadn't had a phobia of dolls before, but was willing to bet from this point on, I would.

Glancing around the room, I attempted to ground myself, trying to shake off the effects of the dream. My computer lay over the bedspread. I'd fallen asleep looking at the Blossom's Beauties website. The screen was partially visible, and I smacked it closed before I could see one more horrid doll's face.

I'd made it through a few hundred of them the night before. At first the entire thing felt like a waste of time, none of them looking even remotely familiar, but then, the later it became, the more my vision blurred, and each started to resemble someone. If I squinted just right, that doll looked like Anna Hanson. With the different jawline, one that could have been Percival. I could even see Leo's features in a couple. And by the end, right before sleep overtook me, I found one that might be Branson... or Miles Styles.

Miles... that memory had me reaching for the laptop. Maybe I *had* seen one that truly looked like Miles. Could there be a connection between Miles and Peter?

Before I reached it, my cell rang, saving me from having to look. I answered instantly after a glance at the screen. "Susan. What's wrong? You never call this early in the morning." Not that she made a habit of calling at all.

"Wow, I knew you were a lot of things, but I hadn't realized you were lazy." Her abrasive tone further helped burn through the fog of dreams. "Since when is nine in the morning early?"

Nine in the morning? Must not have set my alarm, though it typically wasn't needed as Watson's demand for breakfast was as reliable as any clock. He must've been truly worn out from playing with Delilah's dogs.

Susan didn't bother waiting for me to reply. "I still think it's a waste of time, but Niles is out of critical care, got out last night. I've already spoken to him but thought you might want to talk to him this morning. I've tried calling you twice already, so you've about missed your chance."

"He's stable?"

"That's what out of critical care means, Fred." Her eye-roll was almost audible. "Meet me at the hospital in twenty minutes. Get some caffeine, or this will be more of a waste of time than it promises to be."

I was already sliding out of bed. "Be right there."

Watson gave a great yawn and then began his breakfast dance by prancing around my feet. The sleep had done him good it seemed; the breakfast dance was rare, most of the time it was a demanding glare that said *Feed me, peasant*.

"Oh, and Fred?" Again Susan didn't wait for me to reply. "Don't bring the fleabag. It's a hospital, not a dog park." With a click, she was gone.

I could've argued that point. Well... *not* that the hospital was a dog park, but Watson had been there on many occasions. Instead of pushing my luck, I decided to ignore her. He'd come anyway.

However, as I fetched him breakfast and me coffee, I changed my mind as I realized what just happened. Susan Green had called me, of her own volition, so that I could question Niles for a case that she saw as a complete waste of time. How times had changed. Maybe I wouldn't strain the thin ice.

As a preemptive reparation, I snagged one of the buffalo jerkies. Not fooled, Watson glowered at me as he gnawed when I slipped out the front door. At this point, we were going to work through the entire case we'd been given in a matter of days.

. . .

Niles was pale and looked exhausted. Around him, connected by wires fanning out from his arms, machines beeped, flashed, and hummed. He didn't smile when Susan and I entered, not that I blamed him. Not with the trauma he'd been through and the loss of his twin.

I wasn't sure what to say. *I'm sorry for your loss* seemed utterly inadequate. Even starting off with *I'm here to help get justice for you and Miles* felt wrong, since the motivation had been to help Noah and Jonah.

Susan managed for me. "Good morning, Niles. I hope you were able to get some rest last night after we spoke."

He shrugged, then winced.

She motioned to me. "This is Winifred Page. She owns the bookshop next door to Twinventions. I believe you two have met."

That caught me off guard. I'd expected her to have cleared my visit with him, or at least told him I was coming. Niles stared at me for a second, clearly not making the connection, then seemed to remember. "Right. You're Noah and Jonah's sister-in-law, or something?"

"I am." I joined Susan at the side of his bed and couldn't keep from giving the platitude, though I knew it didn't help. "I'm so sorry about Miles, and for what you're going through."

"Thanks." His voice was dull, emotionless. "They think, as long as my temperature doesn't spike again, the infection should be gone in another day or so. The recovery will be slow. But... without..." He blinked, in a way that suggested he was battling the haze of medication or memory, I wasn't sure which, then his gaze locked on me and flicked to Susan.

"Oh, right. You said she was the one who helped save my life?"

Susan nodded. "Yes. Fred kept you from bleeding out."

"Thank you." He gave a partial smile then.

I couldn't imagine what he was feeling. Maybe grateful that Susan and I had saved him, but maybe also angry too. Why had we been able to save him and not his twin as well? Maybe if we'd tried harder, gotten there a few seconds earlier, had been smarter and more capable.

If he did think or feel any of those things, he was kind enough not to say them.

Susan helped again by guiding the conversation. "I know you and I spoke last night of your memories that morning. That you don't recall much, just being in Cabin and Hearth, looking at the furniture as Anna got some sketches out of the car, and then the explosion." I got the sense that she was catching me up to speed more than Niles. "Fred's helping me look into different possibilities of what happened that day. She has some questions of her own, if you feel up to it."

Niles didn't respond for a bit, then gave the smallest combo of a shrug and nod.

It had been sprung on me so quickly and the caffeine hadn't had quite enough time to kick in that I hadn't come up with a game plan. "My best friend and I went to Geek Out yesterday. Your store is amazing, as are all your inventions."

There was a flicker of brightness at the mention of the shop in Boulder. "Thanks."

"It was spectacular, really. And judging from the awards on the wall, you and Miles made quite the team." What was I doing? It was the equivalent of talking about the weather. "We met Alicia. She couldn't stop bragging on the two of you."

"She's been with us for years." Another ghost of a smile. "I always expected her to make a play for Miles, but she never did." The smile broadened. "It was typically part of the gig. Went along with him being the looks of the operation."

The meaning didn't seem to match his expression or tone. The words sounded envious, but I didn't get that vibe from Niles. "I think I remember someone saying that before. Miles was the looks, you were the brains?"

Susan flashed me a *You're seriously being that rude to someone who is in a hospital bed* expression, but didn't redirect me.

"Yep." Niles nodded, and again, I got the sense that he was proud, if I was reading him correctly.

"Did that bother you? Miles getting the attention for his looks?"

That time, there was also a spark of admiration in Susan's expression as she gaped at me.

It wasn't until Niles spoke that I realized I'd accidentally just accused him. "So... your theory is I made that thing explode to kill my brother across the street for being better-looking?" There wasn't anger in his voice, simply disbelief, either at the audacity or the suggestion in and of itself.

"No, sorry. I was just..." I shook my head, trying to explain in a way that wasn't insulting. But there wasn't one. Asking a man if he was jealous of his much better-looking dead twin.

Niles rescued me. "We both liked our lot in life. Don't get me wrong, Miles was smart and creative, but he very much enjoyed having the face and body that made women drop to the ground. *I* love being able to create the things that filled the shop that you enjoyed yesterday. We were a team, the best kind. The yin and the yang." He finished with a derisive snort. "Not like..." That time he shook his head as the words faded away.

I'd known where he'd been going. "Not like Noah and Jonah."

Niles hesitated, and then nodded. "Sorry. They're good guys. Just... a lot like each other. Maybe too much."

It was easy to read between the lines. "Meaning... neither one of them have the looks *or* the brains?"

Susan smirked.

"Sorry again." Niles truly sounded it. "I wouldn't verbalize that most of the time. They've been good friends of ours for a long time." His brows creased, and emotion flooded his face as quickly as if a light had been switched on, and when he glanced back up, anger was there. "I hadn't quite put that together. *They* did this. *Their* stupidity is why..." He sucked in a shaky breath and didn't finish.

Though I hated to push him, and hated even more the risk of asking that out loud, I had to. "Do you think Noah and Jonah had a problem with you two?"

"No." His answer was instant, and then he gave me a look that suggested that I'd gone down in his estimation, though I wasn't sure where I'd started to begin with. "They didn't do this on purpose. For one, even if they had, it wouldn't have been meant for Miles or me. We weren't even there. And two, if it'd been for... the other guy, they wouldn't have been able to pull it off anyway. They can do some cute party tricks, but that's about it. They're like a lot of people at the conventions, guys that tinker with things, but aren't real inventors."

Despite not always having the highest faith in Noah

and Jonah, I couldn't help but want to defend them, however I managed to keep the defensiveness out of my tone as I spoke. "They have had a lot of commercial success on the shopping networks, and at least when it worked, the Manscaper was kind of impressive."

Again there was the spark of anger, and Niles's lips moved in silence for a second, the debate clear in his eyes. Then, he spoke. "Miles and I have helped Noah and Jonah for years. All those practical inventions that they sell on the shopping networks? They started off just as pointless as the other junk in their shop. That's thanks to Miles and me nudging them in a more sensible way. And as far as their inventions working? Miles and I went back to Twinvention after your party till well after midnight to help fix some last-minute glitches and things that Jonah had messed up earlier in the day."

Susan flinched. "Wait a minute, you didn't tell me that. The night before the accident, the four of you were at Twin-ventions?"

"No. Noah and Jonah went home after the party." He shrugged like it was no big deal. "They thought it was working well enough, but we didn't. Considering it was a blender that used lasers instead of blades, we felt it was rather important for it to work impeccably, considering they were going to demonstrate it during the grand opening." He flicked his wrist. "Just like that, they're never careful enough."

Susan blazed right on by that. "You were in the store the night before the explosion, just the two of you, alone?" She leaned closer. "Did you make any changes to the Manscaper thingy?"

"Of course not." Anger bit again in his words, and he motioned toward me. "It was working fine. Fred saw it in action. On *me*. And Miles was going to do it for the demo portion of the opening. Do you think Miles and I would've gotten on there if we weren't two hundred percent certain? We checked that thing out from head to toe."

"Then how did it explode?" That time there was no hiding the accusation in Susan's voice.

Once more, Niles opened his mouth, started to speak, but stopped, glancing at me. Guilt flickered over his face, and even though anger joined in once again, he stayed silent.

"It's okay. Say what you're thinking." I nudged him on, certain what was coming.

"I have no proof. And while I know they didn't do it intentionally, I'm willing to bet anything that Noah and Jonah decided to do some last-minute *improvements*." He refocused on Susan. "They're not malicious, and they're friends, but... it took a long time for that to be a genuine feeling. We first met at a twin convention. It was... they were... awkward. Forever made a show of finishing each other's thoughts and stuff. But it was always a little off. Awkward, like I said. Probably just nervous around us. We were more successful, even back then, and lots of guys get insecure around Miles's looks."

I hated where this was going. Hated the thoughts about Noah and Jonah I could practically see whirling around in Susan's mind—not that I could blame her. Truth be told, I couldn't keep them from whirling around in my own. Nevertheless, the reason I was there was to find other leads that pointed away from the twins. "Do you know of anyone who would want to hurt Miles or yourself?"

Niles looked at me once more, brows furrowed. "You really think Miles was *murdered*? That someone tried to kill us? From across the street? How would that even work?" He sounded more exhausted by the second. "Listen, I admit I'm angry at Noah and Jonah for this, and I don't know if I'll ever forgive them, but no part of me thinks they did it on purpose. They weren't trying to hurt us."

Since I couldn't argue against anything he said, and I had no idea how it would've worked if someone *had* been trying to kill them from across the street, I switched directions. "What about Peter Moss? Did you and Miles know him?"

Confusion flickered briefly and then cleared again. "Oh, right, the other guy. The dollmaker." He shook his head. "We met him the same night that he was rude to you at Twinventions. So you tell me. Do *you* know anyone that might want to hurt that guy? He seemed the type. Though, again, no matter how rude and creepy the man was, Noah and Jonah didn't blow up their machine on purpose to kill him. Or anyone. They're... stupid and incompetent, not evil."

One more try. "Did you or Miles ever have plastic surgery?"

"What?" At that one exhausted, exasperated word, I heard the truth. Not only had neither of them had plastic surgery, Niles had absolutely no clue why I'd be asking such a thing. They weren't connected to Peter Moss in any way.

"Never mind. Sorry." There was no other bunny trail to try. "Thank you for your time. I'll let you rest. And again, I'm so, so sorry for your loss. If I or any of my family can do anything, just say the word."

He merely nodded.

Susan followed me out of the room and whirled on me instantly. "What in the world was that about plastic surgery? Have you lost your mind?"

I filled her in on the dolls, but stayed generic, leaving out Delilah's name.

She started to wave me off, then considered. "Huh... that would be a pretty good motive." She punched me on the shoulder with her huge fist, no doubt intentionally doing it harder than a teasing love tap. "Look at you, not being useless."

"All right, the ham-and-cheese croissants are in the oven. What do we want for dessert?" Katie dusted off her hands as she crossed the kitchen to lean on the marble countertop. "Lemon bars, brownies, or cream puffs? It feels so good to be back in here, *with new* windows, I could do all three."

"Not cream puffs." The words burst from me before I could even consider holding them back.

Genuine hurt crossed Katie's face.

"Sorry!" I rushed ahead, trying to fix my error. "They were delicious, but I had a disturbing dream this morning about them."

Across the table from me, Zelda chuckled as Verona gave me a quizzical expression. "You have nightmares about pastries?"

I motioned toward the three laptops that occupied the table. "It combined the cream puffs with the stupid doll heads."

They both grimaced.

"Don't tell us about it." Katie raised a hand, stopping me. "I have a new flavor of cream puffs I want to try next week, and I don't want you ruining it."

"Could you do the lemon bars?" Zelda leaned over, her long brunette hair falling on the computer as she peered around her twin to see Katie. "I love the powdered sugar on top of them."

Verona cast Zelda a judgmental glance but didn't make a comment about the evils of sugar as she would have in the past.

"Lemon bars it is!" Katie clapped her hands, then looked at Watson. "And some fresh dog treats for you."

Watson didn't even notice the use of his favorite word, though he lay curled under his preferred table in the bakery. He was too busy glaring at Wally, the robotic corgi. Zelda had placed it beside him before we gathered around the table to research the Blossom's Beauties website. Even if he had heard Katie, I was willing to bet he would've stayed silent. It was clear he didn't approve of the robot corgi talking back every time he made a noise.

When Susan and I had parted ways after the hospital, she'd let me know that the downtown had been cleared to reopen. Katie and I had decided to keep the bookshop and bakery closed for the time being, but she'd wanted to get back into the kitchen, and I called the twins—who also hadn't wanted to open their shop—to see if they wanted to lend their eyes to the countless doll faces. They'd jumped at the chance and left Ocean and Britney at home in charge of their younger brother and sister.

Even as I peered out the bakery window toward Elkhorn Avenue below, tourists were milling about once more. The glass company had already replaced the pet shop windows as well and were working on Cabin and Hearth's.

Though we'd only been inspecting the dolls less than an hour, faces were already beginning to blend once more. As Katie baked, the three of us had split the pages of dolls into sections. Verona tackled the beginning, Zelda the middle, and I was starting at the end, so at least I wouldn't be repeating ones I'd already seen. It didn't seem to be helping.

"It really is beyond disrespectful that a plastic surgeon would make dolls of his clients' old faces." Zelda had refocused on her laptop. "I mean, I've not had any work done, but you know it's not cheap, and then he goes and recreates the very thing they wanted to get rid of. The least he could have done was use their new appearance."

"I don't think disrespectful quite captures it." As was so frequently the case, Verona disagreed with her twin. "Creepy, and evil, especially when put together with why he lost his medical license. Not to mention, speaking from experience, it's hard to blackmail someone with something they're proud of. Why would he make the improved face if that was the point?"

"I'm not sure if blackmail was the point." Though I'd barely scrolled to the next page, I looked up once more, thankful for the distraction. "At least not in the pure sense of the word. I get the feeling that was more... I don't know, a type of perceived power or control over someone, even if the victim wasn't aware. The person I already spoke to said that the doll had been made of her years ago, and she only recently found out about it." I'd explained in vague detail to the twins, not mentioning Delilah specifically. Though I knew it was a risk they might recognize her doll, I figured it was worth it for the help.

"That makes sense with what he did to lose his license to practice." Katie spoke up from across the bakery. "What he did to his clients was probably more about power than anything else. That kind of victimization normally is."

"To think that type of person was around us, that he was going to have these horrid things in Twinventions."

Zelda shuddered. "They're like really messed-up voodoo dolls."

"Voodoo dolls? That's an interesting thought." I looked up again at her words. "That would go more with Chakras. Did Peter ever come to either of you to carry the line?"

"Fred! Our shop does not carry anything even remotely resembling voodoo dolls. They aren't part of the new age practices." Verona sounded thoroughly offended. "And no, Peter never asked."

"Which is kind of insulting, if you think about it." Zelda scowled. "Sounds like he asked nearly everyone else in town."

That was a little strange, though he hadn't asked the Cozy Corgi either. "Did he have some other connection to Noah and Jonah? Did he attend any of the conventions? Not the twin ones, obviously, but the ones for inventors?"

The twins exchanged glances and then gave identical shrugs. "We never went to the invention conventions."

Verona finished her sister's thought. "Only the twin ones."

"Which is where you met Noah and Jonah." I thought back to the picture Katie and I had seen the day before. "And Miles and Niles." They both nodded. "Do you remember some pretty African-American twins? There's a picture of the eight of you together. It looked like they might've been dating Miles and Niles."

"Oh, right!" Zelda smiled. "Bethany and Sicily. They haven't been to the conventions in forever. They only dated the boys for a matter of weeks. Miles and Niles were too preoccupied with inventing to ever settle down."

"And being with an inventor isn't for the faint of heart." Verona sighed. "Clearly."

I started to go back to the doll website, then decided to

follow through on Niles's sentiment from earlier that morning. "Were you there when Noah and Jonah met Miles and Niles?"

"No, the guys already knew each other, but not for very long, I don't think. But *we* met them on the same day." The twins exchanged knowing glances, but it was Zelda who spoke in a hushed tone. "Honestly, we were more interested in Miles and Niles. Well..." Another glance, another smile. "More Miles, obviously."

"Obviously." Verona smiled as well. "But we had a rule. If we were both interested in the same guy, it was a no-go, so we cut off *that* train of thought after two seconds. Then we ran into Noah and Jonah that very afternoon."

Zelda snorted. "But we weren't interested in them in the slightest. Not until we bumped into them again at the next twin convention."

"Really?" I didn't think I'd ever heard that detail before. "Why didn't you all click the first time?"

"You've met them, right?" Verona chuckled and rolled her eyes. "They're a little weird, in case you haven't noticed."

Chuckling, Zelda nodded along.

It took all my willpower not to point out that many considered Verona and Zelda a little weird as well, with their new age lifestyle. Though, I supposed, those were very different things. "Niles said something similar. That he and Miles found them to be a little awkward. It took a while for them to become friends."

Neither of them looked offended by that. "Awkward is a good way to put it. Noah and Jonah just..." Zelda scrunched up her nose, considering.

"Tried too hard," Verona finished for her.

"Exactly." Zelda gave a definitive nod. "I mean, we've

all enjoyed feeling special being twins, having a connection with someone that most people in the world don't get to experience. But when you're at a twin convention, no one's really impressed by that. When you're all special, no one's special."

My gut buzzed. Though it didn't make sense, there was something there. I could feel it. "Do..." I stopped myself, realizing how offensive my question was going to be. But then... it needed to be explored. After attempting to think about a better way to ask, I gave up and decided to go for it. "Do you think Noah and Jonah were jealous of Miles and Niles?"

"Oh, definitely." The twins spoke at the same time, laughing. And that time, Verona took over. "Miles was so good-looking, and Niles so devoted to experimentation and science, but in a cooler way than our guys that—" Her face darkened the second she caught on.

"Fred, don't even think that." Zelda was plaintive. "Noah and Jonah would never hurt the Styles twins, ever. Or anyone else for that matter."

"They've not been jealous of them in ages. Miles and Niles were good friends to all of us." Verona still looked on the verge of anger.

"You don't really think it's possible that Noah and Jonah were able to intentionally hurt them from across the street, do you?" Katie poured a bright yellow batter into a pan. "I mean, we've all seen their inventions, they're good, but they're not—" Her eyes widened, and her mouth moved silently for a couple of seconds before she finished ungracefully, "I mean, they wouldn't hurt anyone."

"No, I don't think they would." I jumped in before the twins had a chance to respond to Katie's real thoughts about Noah's and Jonah's inventions. I focused back and forth on the twins, trying to convey my sincerity. "I really don't. Sometimes we have to go through every angle to find the right one." If there was a right angle. Even though my gut felt like there was something there, it didn't mean it would clear Noah and Jonah of negligence. I kept that thought to myself. "Let's keep looking. I'd like to get through the whole website. Every time I do this on my own, all the dolls start to blend together."

Though Verona and Zelda both looked like they were close to saying something, after a moment, they simultaneously nodded and went back to their computers.

The next twenty minutes or so passed in relative silence, only broken by Katie's baking, Watson snoring, and the occasional tap on the laptops.

I went through at least a hundred dolls or more, each of them continuing to blend together. Annoyance at them was beginning to replace their creepy factor.

"All right, buddy," Katie called out to Watson, startling the three of us at the table. "The batter is done, so before too long, we'll have freshly baked treats."

Watson let out an excited yip.

"I'm tired!"

At the robot corgi's chirp, Watson skittered away and growled.

"I'm hungry."

Watson growled again, looking murderous.

"I don't care for any physical affection today, thank you very much."

At that, Watson not only took refuge at our table, but crawled underneath my skirt.

"Well, that definitely wasn't right." Katie paused with the tray of bone-shaped dog treats in her hands. "Watson definitely wasn't announcing that he was tired when I said there were going to be treats."

There was a conflicted whimper from underneath my skirt. Clearly Watson was torn between rushing out at the sound of his word again and annoyance at the corgi robot.

I had to admit, I was a little disappointed as I stared at the metal dog. It had been silly, perhaps, but I liked the notion of having an interpreter for everything Watson might say. Not only that, but it highlighted, at a very inopportune moment, how unsuccessful Noah and Jonah's inventions often were.

Probably thinking the same thing, Verona wordlessly stood, walked over to the robot, and turned it off.

Following her lead, I returned silently to the computer screen, then froze.

Had those faces been there a second ago? Maybe things were blurring together even more. I blinked, trying to clear my vision, then leaned forward. Maybe it was because they were on my mind and I was simply seeing things. Had to be.

"I know that look, Fred," Katie called out from behind the counter again. "You just found something."

Verona was near the table once more and came to stand behind me instead of taking her seat. "What is it?"

I wasn't seeing things. Was I? Instead of explaining, I simply pointed, using my index and second finger to touch two of the dolls side by side.

Verona leaned closer, her long blonde hair falling over my shoulder. "I don't see—" She flinched and straightened.

"What?" Zelda jumped up and hurried around. "What is it? What did you see?"

Verona pointed a shaky finger where mine had been only a second before.

Zelda leaned from the other side, then suddenly

grabbed my arm. "I don't..." Her fingers dug in as if for support. "I don't understand."

From the horror in her tone, it was clear that she did understand, even if she didn't want to believe it.

On the screen were two nearly identical dolls. Both of them had Noah's and Jonah's eyes. The one on the left had Noah's chin. The one on the right had Jonah's nose.

SIXTEEN

Identical smiles brightened Noah's and Jonah's faces as I walked into the interrogation room with Zelda and Verona. At any other time, their matching expressions morphing at the exact same moments as they realized their wives weren't there simply to offer their support would have been humorous.

I'd begged Verona and Zelda not to do this, or at least to wait until their emotions were settled. When I hadn't been able to convince them, I put up an argument against joining them. But at the end of the day, they were my sisters, and they got the ultimate call as to what happened with their families.

As the three of us crossed the room to join Noah and Jonah at the table, I could feel Susan's gaze on us from the one-way mirror. I'd been surprised I was able to get her to agree to give us even that much privacy.

I sat between Verona and Zelda, the three of us crammed together at the small table. I took a breath, getting ready to launch in as I opened the laptop we'd brought along. Verona and Zelda were allowing me to start, which had been my request when I agreed to join them. I figured I'd stay calmer than either of them. "Jonah, Noah, we have some—"

"Explain this!" Verona snatched the laptop from my hands, whirled it so the screen faced the boys, and shoved it toward Jonah.

Zelda reached across me and pulled the computer in front of her husband. "Do we even *know* you?"

So much for me hoping to gradually go into things.

Flinching as one, Noah and Jonah looked from their wives to the computer screen, twin expressions of confusion creasing their brows. "What is this?"

I answered Noah before either of my sisters could. "It's Peter's Blossom's Beauties website." That much should have been obvious, since they'd already agreed to carry the line in their shop, but who knew... maybe they were being intentionally obtuse, though I didn't get that impression.

"Oh," Jonah started in. "Like we said, Fred. We're sorry we were considering..." As he spoke, he looked from me to the screen again, then flinched, eyes going wide as he leaned closer to the screen, and then whispered in horror. "Noah... look."

Noah had an identical reaction a second later. The two of them exchanged confused, horrified looks. Then utterly ashen-faced, they turned toward their wives but remained silent.

"Well?" Verona practically hissed.

Jonah licked his lips.

"Don't bother lying." Zelda sounded more hurt than angry.

Again, Noah and Jonah exchanged looks, and not for the first time, I had a strange desire to protect them—to explain that we already knew about Peter Moss using the original faces of his plastic surgery patients, to keep them from lying. I didn't.

Finally, Jonah sighed, and his shoulders slumped. "We're not completely identical."

"Peter... *adjusted* some things... years and years ago." Noah's hand seemed to lift of its own accord and touched his nose. Beside him, Jonah gave a similar reaction, but stopped at his chin.

That much had been obvious. Zelda, Verona, and I waited.

At least they weren't attempting to lie about it.

Noah and Jonah cast each other a quizzical look and then focused on the computer, not saying anything else and looking utterly sick.

"Is that why you agreed to carry Peter's dolls in your shop?"

When they both looked at me in confusion, their reaction was once more clearly genuine. "Why would we do that?" Jonah's voice was edged with anger. "If we'd known he'd done something like this, we wouldn't even speak to him again, let alone carry his stupid dolls."

"Oh, come on." Verona practically spat the words. "Did you forget who you're talking to? *I* know what it's like to be blackmailed."

"Blackmailed? We didn't know about these dolls." Jonah gaped at his wife, then motioned toward his twin. "We weren't blackmailed."

"Not exactly." Noah winced. "Peter never threatened us at all. And we didn't know about... these." He motioned toward the screen.

"What do you mean, *not exactly*?" Zelda leaned toward her husband, clearly hoping for a lifeline.

Noah shrugged. "Well... Jonah and I didn't even discuss it. But I imagine he was thinking the same as I was when Peter asked us to carry the line."

Jonah nodded, confirming even though Noah hadn't fully explained. "We hadn't seen Peter in... I don't know... a couple of decades, until he and Blossom bought their weekend home in Estes a few months ago. When he asked us to carry the dolls in the shop, I didn't even consider saying no. Not when... he knew what he knew. He didn't suggest that he would tell, but..." He gave a matching shrug to Noah's.

"So you caved without him even *hinting* that he might threaten to reveal your secret?" Disgust dripped from Verona.

When Noah and Jonah hesitated, I jumped in, trying to keep the peace. If things devolved into an all-out meltdown, it wouldn't look good with Susan watching. "Judging from those dolls, the two of you look so much alike, hardly anyone would have noticed the difference." Though the screen wasn't facing my way, I gestured toward the computer. "Was it really that big of a deal if you two weren't completely identical?"

Both sets of twins gaped at me like I'd lost my mind.

"Okay." I lifted my hands in surrender. "Apparently that is a big deal." Miles and Niles didn't seem to care that they weren't identical, but I figured it was wise for me to keep that thought to myself.

"I'm not upset that you did it." Zelda refocused on her husband. "I think Verona and I might have done something similar if we had minor differences between us." She lifted a lock of her long brunette hair. "I mean, I dye my hair so people can tell us apart, but we're still identical."

It was the first time I'd had confirmation about their hair, though I'd suspected that Verona was the one who dyed her hair blonde and not Zelda dying hers brunette. I still had the impression they were lying, even then, but wasn't sure.

"But we told you about it. *We* didn't pretend." None of her twin's understanding sounded in Verona's words. "You've lied to us since the day we met."

I couldn't grasp it, not really. I was sure the bond between twins, especially identical ones, was a powerful thing, but to make such a big deal out of subtle differences was beyond me. And again, Susan didn't need to be a witness to the family conflict, even if she couldn't hear what was being said. "Guys, the bottom line is this is a motive. Peter was blackmailing other patients of his. Well... a form of blackmail." I got the sense that my words weren't sinking in to them. "If somebody tampered with the—"

"We need to tell them." Noah looked toward Jonah, cutting me off, confirming that I might as well have been shouting into the wind.

Anger flashed in Jonah's eyes, but after a moment, his shoulders slumped once more. He nodded in defeat, reached out a hand, and took Verona's. "I'm sorry. I'm so, so sorry."

"For what?" Verona pulled her hand away, fear filling her voice. "There's more?"

"You didn't hurt Peter? You couldn't." Zelda was adamant.

"Not that." Noah shook his head, his gaze rising to meet Zelda's, his voice barely audible. "It's just that... we're... we're not twins."

"What?" Zelda whispered as well.

"Noah and me." Jonah kept his gaze razor-sharp on Verona, tears filling his eyes. "We're not actually twins at all."

I nearly laughed, expecting there to be some punch line. After a couple of heartbeats, I realized there wasn't one.

Verona and Zelda sat in stunned silence.

"Maybe you should explain." A part of me felt like I should get up and leave, that this was a private moment between the married couples, but there was a better chance of it not going into utter chaos if I was present. Plus, though I'd like to pretend otherwise, I simply wanted to know.

Though he hadn't been the one to suggest it, Noah launched into the explanation. He no longer looked at his wife, but stared at the image of the dolls on the screen. "Jonah and I *are* brothers."

Jonah nodded emphatically beside him.

"*Half*-brothers." Noah winced again. "We have the same dad."

Zelda whimpered.

As one, each of my sisters grabbed my hands under the table and gripped tightly.

"The same *dad*?" Verona's nails dug into the back of my hand as she spoke. "We met your mother. *Your mother*."

"She was one woman!" Zelda sounded slightly unhinged.

"Our mothers were twins, identical twins," Jonah hurried to explain. "Who you both met was my birth mom, *Noah's* aunt, technically, but she was *Mom* to both of us."

I thought my brain was going to explode. I couldn't imagine how Verona and Zelda were feeling. "That doesn't make any sense."

"Let me." Noah cast a glance toward Jonah and then focused on me, probably easier than looking at either of the twins. "Like we said, our mothers were identical twins. My mom was Peggy, Jonah's was Pamela. Mom was dating a man named Jack and got pregnant with me. Turns out, Jack was also having an affair with Pamela. She got pregnant with Jonah a couple months after Peggy got pregnant with me."

Nope, I was wrong. I didn't *think* my brain was going to explode. It was an inevitability—I could feel the aneurysm beginning.

"There was a big blowup, as you can imagine, and Jack, our dad, left the picture. We've never even met him." Noah kept going. "Peggy died in childbirth. Pamela took me, of course, and a couple of months later, gave birth to Jonah. So, she *was* both our mom."

"She says that we both look like our dad." Jonah took over once more, finally meeting Verona's gaze again, and as he did so, her grip tightened on my hand. "Everything else we've told you has been true. *Everything*. She loved us as much as she could, but as you can imagine, was a bit of a mess. Always. Noah and I pretty much raised ourselves. Mom drank a lot and was in and out of rehab. Then she met Jason our sophomore year in high school. He was a minister who volunteered at one of the rehab facilities. They started another family, one that didn't really include us."

I'd known not only being twins had been part of what had bonded Jonah and Noah to Verona and Zelda, but also their shared difficult childhoods... maybe even more so. In a lot of ways, they were mirror images of each other. Only Verona and Zelda had met their father, Barry, who hadn't even known about them, and changed their lives. The same hadn't been true for Noah and Jonah. After they'd married, Barry had filled the father role for them as well.

"We were always alone. It wasn't even Mom's fault all the time." Noah, like his brother, was focused on his wife, practically pleading for Zelda to understand. "We were always the weird ones, the science geeks. So even in school, the only ones we had were each other. I don't even remember the first time we claimed to be twins. Really, we might as well have been. After we graduated high school, we decided to take the last few steps and... make it official."

"Oh, baby," Zelda cooed in sympathy and released my hand, reached over, and took Noah's. "I'm so sorry you went—"

"Are you insane?" Verona also let go of my hand as she looked around, glaring across me toward her twin. "*You're* sorry? *You're* sorry that our husbands lied to us since the very first day we met? Are you that much of a pushover?"

Zelda stiffened and glared around. "Do I need to remind you that *you* haven't always been honest with me either?"

Verona flinched but didn't pull back. "That's different. That was something I did, not who I was." She turned to Jonah. "How could you?"

"I'm sorry." He sounded it, utterly. "And I don't mean this as an excuse, but... to us, it didn't feel like a lie." He hurried on as Verona began to sputter. "Technically it was a lie. But... Noah and I have always felt like twins. It's how we lived our lives, well before we met and fell in love with you two."

Some of what Niles had said earlier that morning in the hospital came back to me. How Noah and Jonah felt as if they were trying too hard when they'd first met at the conventions. Even Verona and Zelda had referenced something similar. I decided not to point that out. It wouldn't help, and I believed that Noah and Jonah meant everything they were saying. Even if it wasn't the genuine truth, to them... it was.

Verona stood. "I can't do this."

"No, Verona, please." Tears fell down Jonah's cheeks.

"Please don't. Our lives together aren't a lie. My love for you isn't. Please don't leave me."

"I'm not saying that I'm leaving you." Verona tilted her chin in that way she had, and almost managed to conceal the quiver. "But... I don't know."

"Verona, come on," Zelda whispered soothingly. "You know how it was for us growing up. Surely you can understand—"

"I can't understand anything right now. It's... too much. Maybe I'm over-reacting, maybe I'm not. Miles is dead, Niles..." She closed her eyes, suddenly sounding utterly exhausted. "And now, this. Everything I thought was real... I need time." Verona headed toward the door and paused, holding out her hand toward her sister.

Zelda looked from Verona to Noah.

He too had tears streaming, but gave a little nod. "It's okay. Take whatever time you need. Together."

Though he didn't speak again, Jonah nodded his agreement.

The twins left, and the door slammed. I turned to face my brothers-in-law and met their gazes as directly as I could. "Surely you realize that this takes the motive that was already there beforehand and multiplies it by a billion."

They both nodded.

"I need to know, was any of this intentional? You had plenty of reasons to kill Peter."

"We would never do that." Jonah's voice was solid, despite the tears.

"Like we've said, maybe everyone else will see it as a lie, and obviously we kept it a secret, but..." Noah looked toward his brother, then back at me. "It doesn't feel like that to us. We are twins. If we didn't truly believe that, maybe then we would've had reason to kill Peter, so that we wouldn't have to look that fully in the face, but we do... so we didn't."

I didn't follow that logic in the slightest, but that wasn't unusual where Noah and Jonah were concerned. And ultimately, it didn't matter. I was one hundred percent certain they were being honest—none of this was intentional, they'd not set out to hurt anyone.

"You know this will be enough cause to have them officially charged, right?" Susan almost sounded apologetic after I explained what happened.

"Yeah. I know." I felt more hopeless about it than I had even at the very beginning, which was saying something.

To my surprise, Susan patted my hand in support. And she smirked. "Tell you what, I thought my brother was nuts, galloping over the meadows with a broom stuck between his legs like he's some stupid Harry Potter wizard." She chuckled. "Compared to *your* family, he's almost normal."

"I swear I thought the world was ending." Paulie bugged out his brown eyes across the table at Katie, Leo, and me. "I screamed, the boys—" He motioned over to Flotsam and Jetsam, who were secured to a nearby tree and appeared to currently be attempting to climb it. "—were howling like mad. The parrots and birds were going insane, and the poor fish were flopping on the floor."

With the exception of the fish flopping on the floor, that sounded like a normal day in the pet shop. Every time Watson and I went into Paws, it felt like a zoo gone wild.

"I can only imagine." Katie paused with a chip full of melted queso in midair. "Nick and I both thought the world was ending as the bakery windows exploded, and we didn't have a bunch of animals panicking on top of it all."

The four of us had scheduled dinner at Habanero's over a week before and decided to keep the date. Typically on such occasions, Paulie left his two corgis at his house, but he'd come directly from the pet shop, so they'd tagged along.

Watson peered at them from his place under my chair, and I couldn't tell if his expression was more smug or taunting, that he was allowed to be on the outdoor patio. Either way, though Flotsam and Jetsam had greeted him in their typical frantic fashion, they weren't acting as if they felt neglected.

"So..." Paulie pulled my attention away from the dogs. "Who are your suspects, Fred? I was talking to Anna and Carl today. They think it's Peter's wife. Anna said she's certain that Peter and Delilah were having an affair and Blossom found a way to get even." Paulie scratched his thinning hair, then reached for a chip. "I don't know Delilah all that well, but I can't see Peter being her type."

"He's not." Leo was definitive. "Delilah wasn't having an affair with Peter." He glanced at me. "Is what you told Katie and me on the way over shareable?"

I considered for a moment. "I guess so. It's Estes Park, after all. Nothing will stay quiet for very long." I met Paulie's gaze. At this point, he was a trusted friend. "I would ask that you not share it with anyone. Chances are it will be all around town by tomorrow, but if not, I'd like to give my sisters as much privacy as they can get."

"No problem." Paulie nodded sincerely. "I won't even tell Flotsam and Jetsam."

By the time we finished the appetizer and our meals had arrived, I'd finished filling Paulie in on the developments with Noah, Jonah, and the dolls... though I once more left out the details involving Delilah.

To my surprise, Paulie didn't seem that shocked. "I guess we all have secrets in our backgrounds." He glanced toward Katie. "Don't we?"

"That we do. I won't be one to cast the first stone." She clucked her tongue. "I do hope Verona and Zelda can forgive them."

"I think they will. Noah and Jonah's reveal would've been a shock enough on its own, but with the trauma and loss of the past couple of days, I think it drove things over the top. Even so, they're meeting with the rest of the family and the twins'—" I paused, realizing my mistake. "—with Noah and Jonah's lawyer. Verona and Zelda don't have much more faith in Gerald Jackson than I do, so if they're willing to do that, I'd say that's a good sign."

Paulie cocked his head at me, surprised. "Shouldn't you be there? You didn't have to follow through on dinner tonight. I would've understood."

"No. I needed this." I smiled at him and Katie, while I touched Leo's arm. "Time with friends and those I love, just a dinner to turn off my brain. Maybe that will give me some clarity, as I can't seem to find a solitary viable option."

"Plus, you get scrumptious Mexican food, while avoiding Gerald Jackson." Katie giggled. "You're no fool."

"So, you *don't* have any suspects?" Paulie gaped at me.

"No. Not a one." I'd gone over and over the list since Noah and Jonah's confession, and crossed out every name. Couldn't find a motive or opportunity for anyone. And poring over the rest of the Blossom's Beauties website confirmed that there were no other plastic-surgery clients in Estes Park who had been made into dolls, at least that we could see.

"That doesn't make any sense." Paulie was insistent. "You solve murders, it's what you do. Well, and sell books, but really... you solve murders."

"I can't solve a murder if there wasn't one." I sighed, feeling tired, wanting to attempt to curl up beside Watson under the chair, if I could fit. "The only ones with a decent motive are Noah and Jonah, and I know they didn't kill Peter, not intentionally."

"Hey." Leo spoke softly and nudged my shoulder with his, letting the connection linger. "You said it yourself. You need time to have dinner and turn off your brain. So let's do that."

At that moment, a large group of women wearing pink silk jackets was led by Marcus Gonzales onto the patio, and gathered around a long table.

"I swear the Pink Panthers scare me to death." Paulie stared at them as they got seated, partially in longing and, as he'd stated, in fear. "I nearly thought I'd die when we had to play the Cougars at softball—the Pink Panthers make up half that team."

Katie patted his arm. "That's okay, I'd say a good amount of fear of the Panthers is probably healthy."

"You'd like them if you hung out with them, Katie." Leo somehow managed to avoid making the reprimand condescending. "You actually have quite a bit in common with a lot of them."

I was distracted from Katie's bickering answer as Delilah caught my gaze from across the patio and offered a tentative smile. She still looked stressed and worn-out. Beside her, Simone glared. I looked away, refocusing on my chimichanga.

"I still say any grown woman who needs her own private sorority isn't as enlightened as she claims." Katie nodded toward Leo, daring him to contradict her.

At that moment, Marcus Gonzales arrived at our table, bending down to greet Watson first. "Hello there, Mr. Detective, sir." Smooth as butter, Marcus pulled a cell phone out of his pocket and held it out in front of him as he angled it downward.

Watson attempted to slink farther under the chair.

Marcus merely lowered himself with his elbow on the ground and snapped a selfie. From my position above, I was able to see the image. Marcus flashing a bright, wide smile and Watson glowering as if he was on the edge of committing murder.

"Perfect!" Marcus stood, slipping the cell back into his pocket, then dusting off the sleeve of his shirt as he focused on us. "Sorry that I've not had a chance to come speak to you this evening. The tourists are flowing in, even with the downtown being a war zone." As ever, Marcus's view that drama, no matter how deadly, equated to better business, was evident in his cheerful tone. He pointed at me. "Don't you leave before dessert. You're getting a birthday tres leches cake and a song."

"Oh no, Marcus. Please don't do that." Realizing how desperate I sounded, I adjusted. "My birthday is over and done. There's no need for any special treatment."

"Nonsense. You'll look beautiful in our birthday sombrero." He winked. "Plus, I want a picture." He started to point at Leo, narrowed his eyes, and then pivoted to Katie. "I'm putting you in charge of making sure she stays put until that happens. Yes?"

Katie beamed. "You got it!"

Marcus practically skipped away.

"You're a Benedict Arnold, you know that?"

"Anything to get you in jewel tones. I'm willing to bet the sombrero isn't mustard and pea green." Katie simply shimmied and smirked at me. "You'll be lovely."

I turned toward Leo for help, but he simply raised his hands. "Do I look stupid enough to get in between best friends?" With his brown eyes twinkling, he angled down toward Watson. "I can save you, buddy. You and I can watch your mom rock a sombrero from out of range."

At one of his hero's attention, Watson forgot all about his mortified self-involvement, popped up, propping his paws on Leo's leg, and grinning in adoration. He received a tortilla chip for the effort.

Paulie sighed as if it was the cutest thing he'd ever seen.

"I'm surrounded by traitors." Despite myself, I couldn't quite keep my growing grin at bay. This had been exactly what I needed. Even if I didn't figure out any more suspects, it was good to simply breathe.

As I started to take another bite of the green-chili-covered chimichanga, I noticed Simone stand and walk away from the table of Pink Panthers and head back inside, probably to the restroom. To my surprise, she went alone.

"Excuse me." On a whim, I stood. "I'll be right back." Watson started to follow, but I turned to pat his head and motioned back toward the table. "Stay here, this time. With Leo."

His internal debate was clear. Watson hated following directions, but the word *Leo* was just as magical as the word *treat*. It won, and he happily trotted back when Leo called his name.

Sure enough, the bathroom was exactly where Simone was headed. I lingered outside the door a sufficient amount of time, so I looked awkward to anyone who might've been watching, but also enough to not make Simone feel like I was pouncing on her.

By the time I went in, she was washing her hands at the sink, and her gaze met mine in the mirror and narrowed instantly. "Cornering people in the ladies' room is one of your tactics?"

Clearly, I'd failed in any pretense, so I went with it. "Not typically, but I'm pretty good at operating on the fly, so I decided to go with it."

After rinsing her hands, Simone turned off the water and used the towel to dry her hands. She turned toward me, crossing her arms and propping a hip on the sink. "Am I suddenly a suspect now?"

"No." I continued with the no-pretense route. "I don't have any suspects at all."

Simone seemed to deflate a bit at that, or at least relax. "Glad you're not forcing it. Maybe you're as smart as I thought at first."

"That's why I followed you in here." I started across the room then hesitated, considering locking the door so we'd have privacy, but discarded that notion, and took a mirroring position on the adjacent sink. "You seem personally offended that I'm looking into this. It was clear when we spoke at Delilah's last night, and even today you were glaring at me."

She didn't deny it. "Typically I'm better at guarding my facial expressions than that. Sorry."

"Why? What am I doing that's making you so mad about all of this?"

"I told you last night. I believe in justice." She flicked her hand toward me. "Miles *died*, and you're trying to get your brothers-in-law off without paying the price."

I studied her, attempting to judge her sincerity, and it was clear. But the why of it wasn't. "I'm not trying to get them out of anything they didn't do. I'm sure they'll pay a price for having—" Before I could finish my thought, *the why* of it clicked. "You said *Miles* died. Peter did as well, but justice for him doesn't seem to matter to you. Is that simply because of what he did to Delilah, or is there more?"

She opened her mouth, the denial clear, but it faded, and she gave a reluctant grin. "You are good. Better than me at the moment, in any case. I hadn't meant to be that transparent."

"You're connected to the Styles twins?"

As I had with Watson only moments before, I could see the debate behind her eyes. Finally she shook her head. "No, just with Miles."

"Romantic?"

Her smile broadened. "I am annoyed with you, but I do like your bluntness." The smile faded almost instantly into something sadder. "The beginning of one, maybe."

So she'd had feelings for Miles and lost him. "I'm sorry."

"It was just one night. Not even a full one, truth be told." She shrugged, though it was clearly defensive, not uncaring. "But there was *something* there, or at least... it felt like there could be."

Unsure how to respond, I waited.

Simone kept going, though her tone shifted, speaking more to herself. "I keep thinking that if Miles had stayed the full night, hadn't gotten up so early to meet his brother to go to Cabin and Hearth... maybe..."

"Oh." I realized what she meant and couldn't keep myself from gasping. "You were with him... *that* night."

She nodded again. "Yeah. We hit it off at your party. After Peter... tried what he did with Delilah and we left, Miles followed shortly after, reaching me before I got to my car." That time, though still sad, there was a sweetness to her smile, clearly picturing him. "We had a wonderful night together. And it didn't feel like a one-night kind of thing. But... who knows."

It all made sense. One night or not, the possibility that she'd stumbled onto something meaningful and long-lasting only to have it ripped away was horrendous. And if Simone thought I was trying to defend the very ones who'd helped steal that from her, I couldn't blame her.

In a moment where I channeled my mother more than

myself, I moved toward Simone, paused, and then pulled her into an embrace. "I'm so sorry. So, so sorry."

Though my impression of Simone was that she was tough as nails, her arms wrapped around me and she gave in to tears.

I arrived back at the table the exact moment as Marcus, a nearly four-foot-wide sombrero clutched in his hands. And much to Katie's delight, there wasn't an earth tone to be found. It was sparkly red, blue, green, and yellow.

Marcus jammed it onto my head and began taking photos. Katie practically howled her pleasure. From their spot by the tree outside the patio's reach, Flotsam and Jetsam began to bark along, and Marcus and three servers sang to celebrate my birthday.

It wasn't until I sat back down, my hair a flattened, ratted mess from the sombrero, that I realized I suddenly had a suspect.

"Good grief, didn't know you were bringing the entourage with you." Susan glared at Watson as she approached us at the front desk, but finished with a friendly nod toward Leo —even when she and I had been at odds, Susan had been one of the only members of the police force to take Leo's poaching concerns seriously. She motioned down the hall toward the interrogation room. "Well, whatever, come on. Maybe one day I'll have my own office, but until then, we'll have some privacy in here."

Leo and I followed, Watson trotting along happily at Leo's side like we were going on an adventure where there were destined to be treats at the end.

Susan had been about to leave the station at the end of her shift when I'd called. She'd said to come over.

As Leo and I took our seats around the metal table, Watson peered up at Leo, and then me in clear disappointment. Not only were there no treats, but there was no cozy place to nap. Clearly dejected, he turned and padded away. He'd barely taken two steps when his ears perked up, and he lowered his nose to the ground and began zigzagging across the floor until he reached the far corner. He gave his excited whimper.

I didn't need the robot dog to interpret the *food is close, I can tell* meaning.

Still sniffing, he turned in a circle and then refocused his attention on the corner, sniffing from the floor, then up higher. After a second, with an awkward thrust, he propped his forepaws on the wall, stretching and straining with all his might to reach higher than his nose could make it. He chuffed in frustration.

"Wow." Susan managed to make the word sound both impressed and bored. "I'm still not convinced that dog of yours helps solve crime, but he's got a killer sniffer on him, I'll give him that." She pulled out the metal chair, causing it to squeak across the floor, and plopped down. "We had a family visit in here earlier that didn't go very well. They were eating dinner, and the mother got angry and threw fried chicken. It hit the wall about a foot above where the fleabag can reach."

Still straining, Watson gave a pitiful look over his shoulder.

"Sorry, buddy." I patted my thigh. "Come back over here. The smells are lying to you."

Ignoring me, he redoubled his efforts by hopping and licking the wall as high as he could reach.

"I like his determination." Susan chuckled. "And I'll have to talk to our cleaning crew. Apparently they're not doing a good enough job."

I felt my mouth fall open, amazed at Watson's atypical exertion as he continued his jumping and licking. "It's kind of like a Jazzercise video gone bad."

"Or really, really right." Leo looked as if he'd just been given a Christmas present.

"Valid point. Although I'm afraid he's going to strain his

tongue." I stood. "Actually, I can't take it anymore. I'm going to go get one of the jerkies from the car."

"I'll get it." Leo held out his hands for the keys. "You fill Susan in on your theory."

Though Watson spared Leo a glance as he left the room, he never stopped his hopping and licking.

"It must've been really, really good chicken." I considered trying to get him to come back over, but knew it would be pointless, so I sat down again and refocused on Susan. "Niles lied to us about being at Twinventions after my birthday party."

Susan's brows shot up. "Really? Where was he?"

"*He* was at Twinventions, but Miles wasn't." I debated for a second how upfront to be, but decided it was different than what Delilah had shared in confidence. "Miles spent the night with Simone Pryce. According to her, they left together directly from my party at the Cozy Corgi. Well, a couple minutes between, but close enough."

Susan cocked her head, and I waited, seeing if she'd come up with the same conclusion that had hit me. "So... *Niles* wanted to kill Peter. But why?" Before I could answer, she shook her head. "No. Not Peter. He wanted to kill the twins." Again she shook her head, accompanying it with one of her eye rolls. "*Not* twins, but... whatever the Pearson weirdos are now." Once more I started to respond, but Susan interrupted, a smirk playing over her lips. "You know... I hadn't taken a moment to put that together. Jonah and Noah may not be twins, but they're both half-brothers *and* first cousins." She let out a loud laugh and made a show of peering over my shoulder at Watson, whose nails could still be heard hitting the concrete floor as he hopped. "I swear your family is a circus sideshow."

"Huh." For a second, all thoughts of Miles and Niles

and murder were swept from my mind. I'd not put that together, or even considered it. "I honestly have no idea what to say to that."

She sighed. "This is going to have me in a good mood for about a month."

Honestly, I couldn't blame her, but brought us back to the moment. "Glad you're enjoying yourself. Should we maybe talk about murder?"

"You and your one-track mind. But yes. We should." Susan sobered. "So what's the theory? We're supposed to believe that Niles was jealous of *Jonah's and Noah's* skills? Because no one's going to buy that."

"No, not exactly." I'd discarded that possibility as soon as it flipped through my mind as well. Feeling a bit ashamed, I looked toward the closed door, almost expecting to see Noah and Jonah there. "I think maybe the opposite. You heard how he spoke about them earlier, at least if you read between the lines. He found them beneath him and Miles. Almost like they were an insult to the... invention field, if that's what it's called."

The door opened right then, causing me to jump. But instead of my brothers-in-law, Leo entered with Watson's snack. He closed the door behind him and took his seat beside me before holding out the buffalo jerky. "Come on over. We've got a nice big treat for you."

Watson looked over in excitement at the word, spied the jerky, and then considered. He even went so far as to look up at the wall that was now slick from his tongue. Finally, he plopped back down on all fours and trudged begrudgingly back to Leo, accepted the jerky, and collapsed between us to gnaw at it in defeat.

"Wow. That *really* must've been some good fried chicken." I bent to scratch his head. "You're a mess."

"Circus sideshow, I'm telling ya." Susan was downright cheerful, but got back to the task in the next heartbeat. "It's kind of a far-fetched theory, but I'm not sure why else Niles would lie about Miles being with him that night. And I checked with Jonah and Noah this afternoon. They confirmed that the Styles twins had a key to Twinventions, so it would work."

"It does make sense." Leo dove into one of the theories we'd discussed on the way over. "Niles could've rigged the Manscaper, or something else in the store, to explode at just the right time. Late enough that he'd be guaranteed Noah and Jonah were in the shop, but early enough that no one else should have been in there."

"If he really hated Noah and Jonah enough to kill them," I jumped in, "since his and Miles's meeting at Cabin and Hearth was already scheduled, Niles could be across the street to see it happen. It just had bigger consequences than he imagined."

"That doesn't work." Susan folded her arms, her muscles flexing beneath the police uniform as she rested her elbows on the tabletop. "There were no explosives found on site, other than what your idiot brothers-in-law were using for power sources. Nothing that indicates a bomb—no timer, nothing."

Leo and I both froze at that, the sound of Watson chewing away on the buffalo jerky the only sound in the room.

"Maybe..." I'd been so sure, it had felt right. As soon as I sat back down at the table at Habaneros and realized Niles had lied, everything clicked into place, mostly. "Maybe they just haven't found it. There's a lot of rubble in that shop to go through."

She shook her head. "No, they're finished. The situation

was big enough that we outsourced, had experts from Denver come in. Explosives are a little above our pay grade here. They were quick and thorough. It's done. There was no bomb."

I never dreamed there'd be a circumstance where I'd *not* be relieved at hearing there *wasn't* a bomb, but disappointment coursed through me. I'd been so certain I'd found what would exonerate Noah and Jonah. "But... Niles lied."

Susan's eyes narrowed. "Or Simone lied. Something's not right about her. I can feel it."

"You can..." I thought that was the first time I'd heard Susan say something like that. She was always the first to scoff when I mentioned my gut or puzzle pieces clicking. I jumped over it, though. "Simone wasn't lying. Trust me. Plus, there'd be no way of her knowing what Niles told us about that night. And what motive would Simone have to try to kill Noah and Jonah. She doesn't—" A different thought entered. She would have a motive to kill *Peter*. To protect her friend, to protect Delilah's reputation. But surely—

"And again, I repeat for those of you in the back of the room..." Susan spoke intentionally slow. "There was *no* evidence of bombs or other explosive devices, other than the ones your moronic family had there for the fun of it."

Leo sighed. "Susan, there's no need—"

"Fred!" The door burst open, and Jonah walked in, followed by Noah. Or the other way around, I couldn't tell. "They just let us out, we were walking by and saw you through the wind—" He pointed toward the one-way mirror. "Oh, right. Forgot about that."

"Really, gentlemen, you can't go bursting into places in a police station." Gerald Jackson, their lawyer, hurried in after them and tried to shoo them back out the door. "We really need to get out of here."

Susan sprang to her feet. "What is this?"

Watson jumped up as well and issued a growl that resembled Susan's voice, but instead of going on the offensive, he snagged up his buffalo jerky and retreated over to the corner under the unreachable fried-chicken stain.

For my part, I sat frozen, shocked to see the two of them, but even more so that Gerald Jackson had managed to do something quickly. In truth, I'd not expected him to be able to do anything at all.

Susan whirled on me. "Was this just a distraction? You've joined forces with this idiot now?"

"*Officer Green!*" Chief Dunmore entered the room behind Gerald. "Watch how you speak of respected members of the community."

Susan paled and turned to face the chief. "This is under your authorization?"

"Of course." He motioned toward Gerald. "I received a call at home about the change in circumstance, that new evidence had come to light."

"You... left your house and..." Susan shook her head, cutting herself off. "I'm afraid you haven't been told the entire outcome, chief. There is some evidence that Niles Styles lied, but it doesn't clear anything. As stated in the report earlier today, there were no explosives. There's nothing to indicate Niles was responsible for—"

"As Gerald pointed out to me, there is now more than one possibility." As the chief spoke, both Jonah and Noah beamed at me, as if I'd worked magic and set them free. "The twins here have..." Chief Dunmore's brows creased as he glanced at Noah and Jonah. "Er... the... uh... Pearson brothers have agreed not to leave town, or Glen Haven, in this case. There's nothing to be gained by keeping them here until things are sorted."

"But—" Susan stopped short again at the glare from Chief Dunmore, and once more she turned an accusing glare toward me. "That will teach me." With that she stormed away, intentionally walking between Noah and Jonah, so her broad shoulders banged against both of them.

I nearly called after her but didn't. I couldn't blame her. It was clear what this was. Their release. The chief going so far as to leave his home to come in personally. Just one more example of the good old boys' club. The privilege of friendship, connection, and maybe even money. I couldn't blame Susan for thinking that *I'd* had a part in it.

"Come on." Still beaming, one of the brothers motioned toward Leo and me. "Let's get out of here."

We drove nearly twenty minutes down the canyon to Glen Haven, where Verona's and Zelda's homes were side by side. Gerald Jackson was a neighbor as well.

I'd dropped Leo off at his apartment since he had to work early the next morning. He and Katie were the only ones missing as the rest of the family gathered in the living room of Verona and Jonah's, bringing to mind when we'd done something similar roughly a year before when Verona had been arrested, only Gerald hadn't been present. He leered at me from his spot on the recliner and glanced around, checking to make sure we weren't overheard. "You didn't think I could do it, did ya?" I'd recently made it all too clear to Gerald what I'd thought of him.

I bristled but managed to bite my tongue. There was no guarantee that would actually work, but luckily, at that moment, Barry raised a champagne flute—his filled with some of Gerald's homemade kombucha—in the air. "To Fred! Who saved the day yet again." His free hand continued scratching Watson's belly, who was sprawled on his back, pressed against Barry's kneeled knee.

From the corner of my eye, I noticed Gerald flinch, and as much as some small part of me wanted to revel in that, I didn't. "I don't think I deserve all of that. Things aren't really figured out yet. There's no proof and no motive."

Barry took a sip anyway and winked. "You'll figure that out too, darling. You always do."

"Here, here!" Noah and Jonah called out together, clinking their glasses—theirs with actual champagne.

Percival and Gary joined in, and after a moment, Gerald shifted his weight, struggling to get up from the recliner, and plodded over to where the kids and the rest of the men gathered around the snacks spread over the table. "Don't forget the Master of Law, I still had strings to pull, you know."

Noah spoke up once more, raising his glass again, his tone somber. "And to Miles. A good friend, brilliant inventor, and one of the best humans to ever walk the earth."

After murmured agreements and another drink to Miles's memory, Mom deposited a fresh tray of sliced cheeses and meats and then joined me on the couch. "You look troubled."

"Sorry." I forced a smile. "I don't mean to be a wet blanket. I'm glad Noah and Jonah are out of jail, obviously."

"But things don't make sense." It wasn't a question. Mom patted my knee. "Like Barry said, you'll figure it out."

Noah, or possibly Jonah, let out a big whoop, and set off another cacophony of cheers and laughter.

Scowling, Verona emerged from the master bedroom and joined Mom and me.

Seeing her twin, Zelda hurried over as well. "If Noah and Jonah were the intended victims, do you think we should be worried? I know Niles is in the hospital now, but that doesn't mean he'll stay there. Maybe he'll try again."

"Then he'd better hurry up, or he won't beat me to it," Verona snarled.

Following her glare, I was able to figure out which one was Jonah. He was in red. Noah in blue.

Zelda swatted at Verona. "Don't say that. Think how close we came to losing our husbands."

"We don't even know our husbands." Though venom practically dripped from her words, Verona's lower lip quivered, just for a moment, showing that she was hurt more than angry. "I'm sorry. I know I sound unhinged. But I can't wrap my mind around it. Them lying all these years. And being so... stupid to have those tanks in the store. I know they didn't mean harm, but..."

Mom reached out to pat Verona's hand.

"I think it's human nature to assume something bad won't happen. I know they shouldn't have brought in the propane and such..." Zelda sighed, shook her head, then switched directions. "And as far as their lies? Quite honestly, I think by the time we met them, they believed it. I bet they feel as much like twins as we do. I mean, come on, they were going to the twin conventions before we were and had been living that way since they were kids."

I could see a retort rise to Verona's lips, so I jumped in. "What are your theories? If I recall, you met Miles and Niles even before Noah and Jonah. Why would Niles try to hurt them?"

Mom leaned a little closer. "You really think Niles was trying to hurt Noah and Jonah, not Peter?"

"It doesn't make any sense he would try to hurt Peter. There was no doll that represented him, and we've not found anything to link Niles, or Miles for that matter, to plastic surgery. Peter wasn't going around Boulder asking people to carry Blossom's Beauties, so there wasn't that conflict either." It was the same circular logic I'd been around a billion times since the explosion. "And no one knew Peter was going to be there. The only way he's a target is if Noah and Jonah singled him out."

Mom narrowed her eyes, studying me. "I'm a little surprised. I know you don't believe in coincidence. You think Peter just happened to be there when the explosion occurred?"

Across the room, the men grew louder once more. Watson, having had enough, waddled toward us, casting a forlorn look over his shoulder toward Barry as he settled in at my feet.

"Wow. That's saying something when you abandon one of your heroes." I scratched behind his ears while I addressed Mom. "I don't know if that qualifies as a coincidence or not. Maybe. If we're looking at it that a despicable man ended up getting what was planned for Noah and Jonah, then..." I shrugged. "I guess so."

"Plus the coincidence of Niles trying to kill Noah and Jonah and then accidentally killing his twin, and almost himself." Zelda didn't sound bothered by that at all. "But I believe in coincidence, so I don't see why that couldn't happen."

"I don't think you know what coincidence means." Continuing her rotten mood, Verona offered another scowl, that time at Zelda. But she was serious when she looked at me. "As angry as I am at the guys, I can't think of a single reason why Niles would want to hurt either of them."

"He wouldn't." I looked over my shoulder to see... I checked the blue shirt, so... Noah came to a stop behind the couch. "Niles would never try to hurt us. We've been friends for ages."

Jonah was a few steps behind him. "Nope, never would."

"What are you two talking about?" I gaped at them, and

maybe Verona's temper was contagious as I felt mine rise. "In the middle of mourning Miles, you're over there celebrating because Niles is the new suspect for the murder."

"No, we're not." Jonah's tone suggested that should've been obvious.

"We're celebrating that *we're* not suspects anymore," Noah clarified. "And like everyone said, we trust you to figure out what really happened. And it won't be Niles."

"Well now, I wouldn't be too sure of that." Gerald sauntered over with the rest of the men. "That's the argument I used with Chief Dunmore. Convinced him they had the wrong guy... or guys in this case."

They shrugged as one, unconcerned, reminding me of Zelda's theory that they truly did believe they were twins at this point. Maybe she was right. "Fred will figure it out." Noah repeated the sentiment.

"While I appreciate your faith, I don't just make things up. I can't pull something out of thin air." I leveled my gaze on both of them. "If Niles isn't the suspect, then it falls back to you two. There are no other options."

The twins... the... whatever they were... I mentally shook myself. I couldn't have that correction every time I thought about them. In my brain, just like in theirs, they were going to stay twins. They sobered, and it was Noah who finally spoke. "Niles wouldn't do that."

Jonah nodded. "He wouldn't."

"You'd be surprised what people will do. And the secrets friends will keep." Percival sat down in the recliner Gerald had occupied before. "There was a drag queen we knew, Harper BraSir, back in the day..." He looked toward his husband. "How long ago was that?" He waved the answer away before Gary could reply. "Doesn't matter. Point is, we'd seen her in and out of drag for a long time. She was a big, beautiful drag queen. And a big old bear of a man out of drag, but... come to find out..." He leaned forward, clearly gearing up for the big reveal. "She was a *woman* the *whole* time. The only time she was actually in drag was when she was a man."

"I don't think this is quite the same thing, dear." Gary patted Percival on the shoulder, earning himself a grimace.

"Plus, that's more of an issue of gender identity than—"

Percival cut Zelda off with another wave of his hand. "No, it wasn't like that. She didn't think she was a man or even wanted to be a man. She just wanted to be a drag queen and didn't think the drag bars would accept her if they knew she was a woman."

We all stared at him.

"Oh! I think I remember her." Mom sucked in a breath. "Was she the one who officiated your wedding?"

Percival nodded proudly. "Right in one, little sis. See what I mean? We had no idea."

"Well, no wonder, she really did make a beautiful woman." Mom paused, scrunching up her nose. "Although... I guess, she was a woman."

Barry giggled. "Dear Lord, I love you people."

At his laugh, Watson popped up and scurried over to him, happy as a clam once more.

Leave it to Percival to break the tension, and though part of me hated to make it heavy again, it couldn't be helped. "Well, unless Harper BraSir also had a double life as a murderer, I don't know if she helps us too much right now." I angled toward Noah and Jonah once more. "Take a minute. You said yourselves, you have been friends with the Styles twins for decades. Is there anything that's occurred, in all that time, that Niles might be carrying a grudge against? Something that happened at a twin convention? Or maybe the one for inventors? Did something you created beat one of their inventions?"

"As if," Verona snorted, and then at the hurt look that crossed Jonah's face, she grimaced. "Sorry. That was... uncalled for."

Despite the insult, at the apology a little hope flickered in Jonah's eyes.

For his part, Noah still sounded offended when he spoke. "No, Fred. We never beat the Styles twins in any competitions. Niles wouldn't have any reason to hold jealous grudges."

"Well, it could be—" I halted, shocked at what I was about to say, how much it could hurt them.

Jonah narrowed his eyes knowingly at me. "What is it, Fred?"

Maybe I didn't have a choice, maybe it was worth it. "You won't like it, and it will probably hurt your feelings."

"Then it's a good time to get it out." Noah crossed his arms and cast a quick glare at his sister-in-law. "Might as well get all the insults over with at once."

He had a point. "Well... when Susan and I were speaking to Niles in the hospital, he... insinuated that he and Miles were light-years ahead of you two. That they were the real inventors and you guys were... wannabes."

Twin expressions of hurt crossed their faces again, and Noah shook his head. "No, Niles wouldn't say that."

"He did." I hurried to clarify, hoping it would soften the blow somewhat. "It wasn't in those exact words, but that was definitely the gist."

"Maybe because he's angry." Noah softened a little bit at his own argument. "If he thinks we're responsible for Miles's death, he can't be held accountable for anything he might say about us."

Jonah let out a disgusted snort. "That's pretty rich coming from *him*."

Noah wheeled on his brother. "Jonah, don't go down that road. He deserves our loyalty. And kindness. Especially now."

When Jonah's expression suggested he was faltering, I pushed on, whether it was kind or not. "Finish the thought, Jonah. Why is the insult rich coming from Niles?"

Noah and Jonah exchanged looks, and though Noah shook his head warningly, Jonah sighed and explained, "You know how everyone said Miles was the looks and Niles was the brains behind the Styles's success?"

I nodded, and noticed most of the family around us doing the same.

"Well... that wasn't entirely true." Jonah winced. "Or at all."

With a resigned sigh of his own, Noah shook his head, then clarified, "Miles was the looks *and* the brains. Niles just didn't know it."

Silence fell as the entire family waited for the punch line, but it was Mom who caved first. "What do you mean Niles didn't know it? From what I understand, you're saying Miles was smarter, the better inventor. How could his twin not be aware of that?"

"Okay, fine, but this can't leave this room." Noah shot a plaintive look around the space, but luckily didn't pause for commitment to such a ridiculous request before continuing. "Anytime Niles invented something, Miles would go behind his back whenever Niles was distracted and fix whatever he was doing wrong."

"And anytime they were helping us figure things out, it was always Miles who came up with the solution." Jonah tilted his head slightly. "Although, he'd often sort of lay the groundwork, you know? Throw out clues or hints that would help Niles think he got to the answer first." A soft smile played on his lips. "He did the same for us, too, truth be told."

"You really think Miles could do that for his twin all these years and Niles not catch on?" When they nodded emphatically at my question, I threw another one at them. "Then how do *you* know it? Did Miles tell you?"

"No!" Noah was emphatic. "Well... not on purpose. We only found out about it the other night."

Jonah jumped in, as they so often did with each other's stories. "Niles finished making some modifications on the Manscaper and then went to pick up our to-go order from Penelope's. While he was gone, we came out of the lab and found Miles making adjustments. Fixing what Niles had done wrong. It was the same night Miles demonstrated it for you all."

"He made us promise not to tell." Noah took over again. "Said it would devastate Niles."

"Are you kidding me?" Verona stood, eyes blazing. "Are you idiots kidding me?" She lunged at Jonah, her hand raised.

She would've slapped him if Zelda hadn't been quicker and grabbed her arm. "Don't! Verona, don't."

To everyone's surprise, instead of trying again, Verona broke down in tears and sank back on the couch. "I can't, I just can't..."

"What?" Jonah rushed toward her, falling in front of her on his knees. "What's wrong? What'd we do?"

"Don't you see? You've had the motive the whole time." Zelda answered for her twin, though her tone was more disgustedly sad than angry. "The *whole* time."

"We did?" Noah looked at his wife in confusion. "Why

would any of that make Niles want to kill us? We didn't tell him."

"He wasn't trying to kill you." It finally clicked. Though I didn't quite understand how, the who and the why finally clicked. "Or Peter for that matter. He was trying to kill Miles."

Everyone considered that in silence, and once more it was Mom who broke it. "You know I don't doubt you, Fred. And I'm aware I'm the one who believes in coincidence and not you, but that's quite a leap of faith, even for me. Miles was the intended victim of the Manscaper, but Peter somehow sets it off instead and it *still* manages to kill Miles?"

"Well... when you put it like that, I guess..." An image of that fated morning flashed in my mind. The entire wall of Twinventions gone, the debris spread across Elkhorn Avenue, the shattered windows of the shops across the street, Miles and Niles inside Cabin and Hearth. And suddenly I thought I understood the *how*. I yanked out my cell, pulled Susan up in my contacts, and tapped her name, then lifted my phone to my ear. "Actually, there was a coincidence, but a small one, at least by comparison."

When the phone began a weird beeping, I stared at the screen. I'd forgotten where I was. There was no cell service in Glen Haven. "May I use your phone?" I spared a glance toward Verona but didn't wait for a reply as I crossed the room.

At my movement, Watson left Barry and trotted along beside me, then plopped down when I reached the phone.

Retrieving the numbers from my cell, I punched the buttons on the keypad. Susan answered on the second ring. "Gerald Jackson, I swore if you ever called me again, I'd—"

"It's not Gerald." My gaze flicked to the man, who stiffened at his name. "It's Fred."

"Fred? My phone said Glen Haven, why... Oh, your sisters." Though confusion had clouded her voice for a second, it grew hard again. "You know what, how dare you call me as well. After what you—"

"Hold on." I cut her off again. "Have you gotten the autopsy results on Miles back yet?"

"No, it's only been a couple of days." She spat the words out, letting me know I'd insulted her again. "They've been kinda busy with Peter Moss. He was only in about a thousand pieces, in case you didn't notice."

"Have them switch to Miles. If I'm right, I bet they'll have an answer within minutes." Before she could protest, I explained my theory.

"I'm sorry about yesterday." I held Watson's leash close as I stopped in front of Susan. "I promise it wasn't a setup, and I didn't know—"

"Do you think I'd go along with this asinine plan of yours if I hadn't figured that out already?" Susan didn't bother uncrossing her arms from where she leaned against one of the brick pillars outside the front doors of the hospital, but spared a sneer down at Watson. "Or let the fleabag join in on this charade?"

For his part, Watson plopped down beside me and peered up at Susan. He didn't even growl. If I didn't know better, I'd think he was starting to like her.

She looked back at me. "This really is one of your crazier schemes, you know. No chance it's going to work."

I cocked an eyebrow. "You think there's a chance, or you wouldn't have said yes."

"No, I simply need entertainment, and what better way than watching you make a fool out of yourself?" She shrugged one of her broad shoulders. "Plus, there's no way you can mess it up. They already have more than enough to charge him, so what's the harm?"

"But a confession will make it a more solid case." My phone buzzed, and I pulled it from the pocket of my broomstick skirt and checked the display. "Paulie is running a bit behind. He thinks he'll be here in about seven minutes."

Susan snorted. "That's specific." With a shake of her head, she straightened and uncrossed her arms. "I'll go on up to Niles's room. Need to go over the plan again?"

"It was *my* plan." I didn't bother holding back a smirk. "I think I got it."

"I was talking to the fleabag." Susan smirked right back before turning and heading into the hospital.

Watson positively glared at me as the elevator doors shut us inside and our newly acquired, hyperactive corgi began to frolic. Or panic, I couldn't tell.

Risking a limb, I knelt and stroked his head. "It's okay, Jetsam. You're safe. You'll see your daddy again soon."

He launched up, dragging his wet tongue over my face, then did a partial twist in midair and offered Watson the same affection.

Watson bared his fangs, causing Jetsam to cower. Once he had Jetsam in line, Watson narrowed his gaze up to me again. He'd already been offended by the gaudy bejeweled collar and leash I'd put on him that morning, but Jetsam was clearly one step too far. He'd been doing better with Paulie's dogs. To the point that I thought they were friends, or at least friendly acquaintances. Nothing compared to how he reacted to Delilah's Basset hounds, but still.

In Watson's defense, in the few minutes since we'd picked him up from Paulie, Jetsam was proving himself to be in rare form. That was okay. It might work better for what I had planned anyway.

Jetsam went into another frenzy as the elevator chimed and the doors opened. He darted like a rocket dragging me out behind him. Watson meandered onto the second floor, twice as slow as normal, overcompensating for our furry companion.

I wrapped Jetsam's plain gray vinyl leash a few times around my wrist so he stayed closer to my body, and had less chance of causing havoc.

Niles's room was only a few doors down, and I could hear Susan's voice drift into the hallway as we approached. "The city will be holding the Pearson twins responsible for everything that happened, even though it wasn't malicious intent. However, you can also bring charges against them for the loss of Miles and your own pain and suffering. I know you had some reservations about that, some... *misplaced* loyalty to your friends, some twin-inventor code or something." That confirmed that Niles hadn't heard about Noah and Jonah not being biological twins.

"No, I think you're right. It's really a matter of public safety. Noah and Jonah shouldn't be allowed to be part of the inventors' community anymore." Niles truly sounded regretful. "I'll do my civic duty where they're concerned. It's for the greater good."

Whether Jetsam knew what we were doing, recognized Susan's voice, or just happened to fling himself into the right doorway, he pulled us into Niles's room right on cue.

Niles looked up from the bed, startled.

"Winifred, *really*." Susan stood. "I must insist you keep your animals outside. This is a hospital. Show some common sense for once." She was already enjoying this too much.

"We were just finishing up with our weekly visit to the children's ward, and I thought we'd pop in and check on Mr. Styles. We won't stay long." It was only a partial lie. Well... *mostly* a lie. Paulie did take Flotsam and Jetsam every week to the nursing home, not that it mattered—I had no problem lying to Niles. It was going to be far from the last one I told. I turned what I hoped was a concerned expression on Niles. "How are you doing? Any better?"

"Yeah... quite a bit. They think I'll be released sometime this evening, tomorrow at the latest." Niles leaned up in the bed, peering over to where Jetsam was demonstrating a death wish by licking Susan's boot. "You have two corgis? I only remember meeting the one... Watson, wasn't it?"

"Oh yes." I knelt slightly to stroke Watson's head and was surprised when he didn't pull away, given how irritated he was with me. "Watson is my pride and joy." I forced a grimace and gave a stage whisper. "Dawson over here... Watson's twin... well... he doesn't quite measure up. He stays at home most of the time."

The flash of a glare Susan sent my way indicated she clearly thought I was overselling it, and maybe I was.

Niles looked between the two dogs. "They're twins?"

"Yep. Quite literally twins. They were the only two in the litter, and identical." I'd specifically chosen the red-and-white Jetsam over his tricolored brother, Flotsam, as his markings more closely matched Watson's. "As you can see, Dawson is a little... fluffier than Watson." Another stage whisper, "And not as bright."

Feeling Niles's attention, the newly named Dawson abandoned Susan's boot and launched himself up at the bed, trying to lick Niles.

"I can see that." Niles reared back.

"Je—" I barely got myself. "*Dawson*, stop that. Come here."

Not minding what he was called, Jetsam twisted once more and shot back toward me, tongue lolling and eyes wide with frantic joy. Attempting to stop, he slid over the linoleum and crashed into Watson.

"Fred, either control your dogs or—"

Watson growled, drowning out Susan's words and causing Jetsam to cower once more.

Jetsam darted under my skirt, with a whimper, as he'd seen Watson do countless times.

Watson's growl grew more menacing at the sight of another dog claiming his safe space.

Poor Jetsam emerged quickly, clearly understanding the warning, and sat calmly a few feet away.

Really, they couldn't have played it any better if I'd had them rehearse. I chuckled and looked at Susan. "It's just like they say, in twins, one gets all the good genes and the other..." I shrugged as if saying *what can you do*?

"I've noticed that." Susan didn't miss a beat, but added a line of her own. "It's pretty clear with your sisters which one is which, but honestly, I can't tell with Noah and Jonah. Which one do you think got all the good genes?"

"I..." My mouth moved wordlessly, thrown off, knowing that I couldn't pick one. as Susan would doubtlessly hold that over my head indefinitely. "I honestly couldn't say."

"My theory—" Susan angled more toward me so Niles couldn't see her face, as she was fighting to hold back a grin, clearly enjoying this. "—is that they were triplets and there's a missing brother out there somewhere. Judging from how the other two are lacking, *he's* probably a genius."

Unsure how to respond without having to insult my family, I moved to the chair beside the bed and sat down. Jetsam followed Watson, remaining calm and a few feet behind before settling back down once more. Susan and I had gone down this particular road sooner than antici-pated, but I decided to go with it, and turned my gaze back on Niles. "Noah says it's a joke twins often tease their siblings about at the twin conferences, that one of them got all the good genes. At least, that's how he portrays it when Jonah is around. When he's not, Noah says it's actually a fact." I gestured toward the dogs—Watson sitting regally with his bejeweled collar glittering, while Jetsam lay sprawled, his gray collar looking drab against the glossy orange of his coat—and lowered my voice once more. "Weird how it seems to be true, isn't it? One twin getting all the looks, intelligence, and poise, and the other... well..."

Though I didn't think my voice or face showed it, I started to feel embarrassed. Susan was right, the whole thing really was over the top and utterly, utterly ridiculous. How in the world had I thought using an inside joke against Niles would work?

However, there was a tightness to Niles's lips that hadn't been there moments before, and dark shadows behind his eyes as he stared at the dogs.

"I know you said that you got the brains and Miles got the looks." Susan apparently noticed it as well, as she decided to push just a touch more, ridiculous or not. "But it wasn't quite so evenly split, was it?"

His eyes flashed toward Susan.

"I can't imagine how you felt." Susan managed to infuse more sympathy in her tone than I'd ever heard from her. "Spending every day of your life with someone better look-ing, more dynamic, and more popular. Then... once you're grown, to have to begin your career alongside that same person and discover not only were they all that, but they were smarter than you as well."

"What do you mean?" Niles spoke through clenched teeth. "That's not how it was. Not at all." He cleared his throat. "Miles said it himself, a million times. He was the face. I was the brains."

"Noah and Jonah told me last night about how Miles had to fix all your inventions." Matching Susan's tone, I leaned forward, making sure to use the hand that gripped the gray leash, and patted Niles's arm. "Believe me, it doesn't make you less valuable, or less important."

He jerked his arm away. "That isn't true."

"Oh no. I'm sorry. Maybe I shouldn't have said anything." I shared a panicked look with Susan. "After Noah and Jonah talked about the way Miles spoke about you, I just thought... I thought you knew."

"Miles didn't keep it a secret from you, did he?" Susan didn't manage quite the same level of concern that time.

"What did they tell you?" His attention was fixed solely on me. "What would Miles say?"

I moved my mouth wordlessly as if debating, then shook my head. "Nothing. Forget I said it. Miles loved you. And had the utmost respect for you. It doesn't matter what he said to friends. Publicly he made it very clear, just like you said. He was the looks, and he claimed you were the brains. No one else will ever know."

"I *was* the brains." Niles clenched the top sheet in his fists. "*I* had the vision, the passion, the purity."

"Right. You had the passion and the vision." I gave what I hoped was a reassuring smile.

"Just not the brains." Susan reverted back to her typical mocking tone. "Just like the Pearson twins, your passion and vision simply needed Miles to come along and inject some smarts into your inventions to make them actually function correctly. Don't pretend you didn't know."

"I didn't." Niles began to tremble. "I thought... I didn't know until..." He shook his head, shutting his mouth.

This was it. I knew the chances were low to get a confession, but it was now or never. "When you adjusted the Manscaper to malfunction when Miles demonstrated it on the evening of the open house, were you planning on it killing him, or just disfiguring him?"

"I—" When Niles's lips moved silently, it wasn't for show. "That wasn't—"

I pushed on again. "And even though Peter Moss got on there early, you still lucked out, didn't you? The explosion reached all the way across the street, shooting shrapnel and debris right into Cabin and Hearth. You were alone with Miles, and he was probably distracted and shaken from the impact, so you took your chance and shoved him into a metal bar that had lodged in the wall."

"No." He shook his head again, and his voice became firm. I'd pushed too hard. "You're crazy. None of that happened."

"Oh come on." Susan sneered, pulling his attention toward her. "If you expect us to believe that, you really did get the short end of the stick on brains compared to Miles, didn't you? You're busted, Niles. The coroner has all the proof we need. The exit wounds on Miles were on his chest, not his back."

"They..." His brows knitted. "What?"

That time, Susan laughed. "That thing about twins really is true, isn't it? You can't even understand *that*? We have proof you shoved your twin onto that metal bar, basically stabbed him through the heart." She leaned closer, her voice dipping to a growl. "The only thing I don't know is if you were struck by shrapnel, or if you were such an idiot that *you* did it, trying to make it look like an accident but nearly killed yourself in the process."

Below us, Watson gave an answering growl, sounding like Susan. A second later, Jetsam joined in.

Taking the only shot I had, I tried to sound like the one person who was on his side, the one who might understand. "You didn't mean for the explosion to be as big as it was, did you? You had no way of knowing. You didn't mean to kill Peter Blossom."

"It wasn't supposed to combust like that." He latched on to my gaze, pleading for me to understand. "I wasn't trying to kill my brother." Even in his panic, the lie was clear. "I... just... wanted to make us a little more even. I merely adjusted the laser so they wouldn't read his facial contours correctly and the shave would go wrong."

Susan snorted again. "And you couldn't even do that right, could you?"

"It wasn't supposed to explode. And how was I to know that creepy Peter guy would..." Niles's eyes widened, realizing how much he was admitting, then he twisted, attempting to fling himself from the other side of the bed as if he was going to run away.

He didn't make it two inches before Susan's large hand smacked against his chest and held him against the mattress. "Please don't embarrass yourself anymore. I can't take it."

As Niles continued to resist, for all the good it did, Watson added his part by positioning himself in front of me and growling a warning.

Dawson, or Jetsam, seemed to think it was all a game and once more began to frolic at Susan's feet, barking joyfully.

Watson didn't even redirect him.

"I thought this day would never come." Katie sighed as she joined Watson and me on the sidewalk and locked the front door of the Cozy Corgi. "I don't think Nick and I will remember how to bake without constant banging, but I'm sure looking forward to trying."

"I'm just thankful there haven't been any more explosions." I started to take a step but paused at her reprimanding expression. "What?"

"I don't think you should say that out loud. You'll jinx it and kill us all." Katie sounded deadly serious. She even made an audible gulp as she looked up over the sign reading Ark & Whale that hung over the new storefront next door. "I don't care if they say the most dangerous thing in there is cotton fluff, I don't trust it."

Truth be told, I didn't either. "Well, hope springs eternal." I laughed at her withering expression, grabbed her hand, and took a step, leading her and Watson at the same time. "Come on. What's the saying? Lightning doesn't strike the same place twice? I bet we'll survive."

Katie continued to grumble as we joined the crowd filtering in the newly refurbished shop. Nearly four weeks had passed between the grand opening of Twinventions that had ended before it began and the grand opening of

Ark & Whale. On the one hand, following the ins and outs of the legal drama that swirled around Noah and Jonah made it seem like only minutes had passed, but on the other, as Katie had referenced, given the constant noises of remodeling, it felt like centuries had dragged by.

And what a remodel it was. Unlike before, Noah and Jonah hadn't relied on any help from family, and had contracted it all out, so it was the first time I'd seen it. From Katie's awed gasp beside me, it sounded like she was as equally impressed as me. The walls on either side were done in thin, slightly curved wood planks, giving the feel that we were stepping into the hull of a ship, or... an ark, as it were. There were even roughed-in round windows with painted scenes of ocean views to complete the illusion. Just like before, there were sections, but instead of wheels, gears, and random inventions, the shop was filled with stuffed animals of every variety. Wooden walls made to look like what might've separated animals on the biblical ark designated sections for teddy bears, monkeys, birds, amphibians, reptiles, fish, and even mythical creatures.

Without a doubt, the most astounding part was the back wall—right where the window had been looking into the laboratory, there was a gaping mouth, giving the impression that a whale was taking a huge bite out of the ark. Jonah and Noah had kept the details of the shop secret, and it was a good thing. If they'd asked my opinion about making it look like the equivalent of a sea monster attacking a stuffed animal shop, I would've said that would have been too scary for kids. But I would've been wrong. Somehow, through lighting, and a slightly cartoonish exaggeration, it felt whimsical and fun.

Katie nudged me with her elbow and pointed to a spot a

little ways in front of the whale's mouth. "You'd never know Peter Moss was blown to bits right about there would you?"

"Katie!" Hissing, I elbowed her back, looking around to see if she'd been overheard. Probably silly, even though the place was practically filled with tourists, there was no doubt they'd all heard of what happened on the last day of May, but still.

"Pretty wonderful, isn't it?" Verona appeared from out of the crowd of tourists.

"Noah and Jonah not being allowed to invent anything anymore has made our lives so much better." Zelda was right behind her and greeted Watson with a friendly scratch between his ears.

Verona nodded. "Not to mention our marriages." She smiled at me. "We didn't expect to see you yet. The rest of the family isn't coming till later."

"We closed a little early." Katie waggled her eyebrows. "We thought we should get in and out quickly, you know... just in case..." She clapped her hands and then spread out her fingers, mimicking an explosion.

"Oh, stop it!" I elbowed Katie again. "You're horrible."

"We all work through trauma in our own special ways." She tilted her chin, brown eyes twinkling. "I do mine through dark humor and pastries."

Verona leveled a serious stare at Katie, but paused while one of the tourists slipped between us before replying. "Trust me, there's not a single thing here that can explode. I've checked."

"And that's not really why we're early anyway," I clarified, "Leo is leading a moonlit hike for the Feathered Friends Brigade and Katie's tagging along."

"You're not going?" Zelda sounded concerned. "Is everything okay?"

I nodded. "Oh yes. Watson and I have big plans of our own tonight, though."

"Fred, Katie!" Jonah called out with a wave, emerging from the whale's mouth. "And Watson, of course. Thanks for coming. What do you think?" He spun with his arms outstretched.

"It's perfect," I jumped in before Katie could demonstrate some more dark humor, as she called it. "Are you pleased how it came out?"

"I am." Though his smile was sincere, there was a wistful quality to his eyes. "I can't say this is what Noah and I dreamed about, but..." He shrugged and took Verona's hand. "We have what's important and what we love most. We could've easily lost it all. And in a weird way, this kinda fits us."

As a result of everything that had happened, Jonah and Noah had lost their lives' work. They'd been kicked out of every inventors' association that they'd belonged to. And the state had forbidden them from having any hazardous material—for business or personal reasons, which took away most of their energy sources. I'd expected them to shrug it off and simply use mechanical or solar power, but they hadn't even suggested it. I was willing to bet they knew their wives had reached the threshold of what they were willing to put up with. And it proved their remorse over Miles, Peter, and the damage to the town had been deep and genuine.

Compared to Peter Moss and Miles Styles, however, they hadn't lost all that much. In truth, I'd expected them to lose a lot more. But between the confession and irrefutable proof that Niles was behind the tragedy, Gerald Jackson had been able to keep the consequences for Noah and Jonah relegated to the confines issued by the state, and a relative fortune in reparations to the town.

Since all their inventions had been pulled from the market, no matter how benign, Noah and Jonah would never have the money they used to enjoy. But that had never been a motivator for them, or for Verona and Zelda either. Between Chakras and Ark & Whale, I figured they'd be just fine.

Noah joined the group and took my hand. "Come on." He glared at his brother. "What are you waiting for? I thought you were bringing them right back." Without waiting for a reply, he led us through the store, and into the mouth of the whale.

I halted as soon as he let go of my hand, staring at the room, dumbstruck.

"Well... that's..." Katie looked around, gaping, apparently experiencing a similar sensation to me. "Unexpected."

I must've dropped Watson's leash as he wandered across the room and growled at a large barrel filled with what appeared to be severed teddy bear arms and legs.

The room was painted bubblegum pink on the ceiling and walls with the faint impression of ribs, as if we were inside the whale. The entire space was filled with barrels and shelves containing an endless assortment of stuffed-animal parts. Various heads here and there, tails, and bodies of all sorts of animal species.

The brothers laughed. Beside them, Zelda and Verona joined in.

"I wish you two could see your faces." Noah looked over at Watson. "Well... all *three* of your faces."

Jonah grinned. "We couldn't quite give up our passion for invention, so we're passing it along to the next generation." He pointed to the large empty table in the center of the room. "This is our Imagination Station."

Before I could figure out what to say, the four of them

gathered various body parts from around the room and spread them on the table... or... *imagination station* it seemed.

"Oh!" Katie brightened as she walked toward the body parts. "I get it! That's pretty cool."

"Is this supposed to resemble the explosion?" I gaped at the spread, not believing my eyes.

"*What?*" Noah sounded shocked. "Absolutely not."

Jonah winced. "Oh, I can kinda see how you thought that, but no." He motioned toward the child of a small family that had just walked through the mouth of the whale. "Come here, build yourself the stuffed animal of your dreams. Any kind you want."

Though hesitant at first, as the kid picked up the fat body of a panda and snapped on the head of a penguin, I finally caught on. I couldn't help but laugh. "Okay, that's a pretty fun idea."

It should've been obvious, but I cut myself some slack, considering who owned the shop.

Grinning again, Noah hurried to another barrel, dug around, and pulled up another head. "We even have Corgi parts. You can make another friend for Watson." He held it close to the floor for inspection.

Watson waddled over, sniffed, and growled once more.

Katie snatched the stuffed corgi head and shoved it back into the barrel. "What are you trying to do? Give our mascot nightmares?"

"He's tougher than that." Noah waved her off and refocused on me. "I know we're not allowed to do inventions anymore. But if you bring in the corgi robot we gave you for your birthday, we can transfer the internal workings into one of these. Something fuzzy and cute that will interpret what Watson's saying."

Jonah sucked in an excited breath. "That's a great idea. Since we already invented it, that's not *technically* breaking any rules."

I could see Verona getting ready to launch in, but I saved her the trouble. "I think I'll pass. Watson's annoyed enough with Wally the way it is." I'd planned on sparing Noah and Jonah's feelings, but changed my mind. "Besides, it's not actually interpreting what Watson's saying. You preprogrammed it to say things about being hungry or grumpy."

Noah shrugged. "Well, come on. You've met him." He gestured toward Watson. "That's going to be spot on a good ninety-nine percent of the time, when *isn't* Watson grumpy or hungry?"

Watson scowled.

"See?" Jonah joined in. "Grumpy."

Half an hour later, Watson and I commenced our big plans for the evening as we snuck back into the Cozy Corgi. I left all the lights off, so no tourists would think we were open, and we made our way back to the mystery room.

Though it was the first day of July, I put the river rock fireplace to use, and by the time a blaze was crackling I'd opened the window to let in the cool night breeze, which caused a couple of sparkling black and silver confetti pieces left over from my birthday party to swirl across the floor. Letting them be, I settled down on the antique sofa.

I patted the matching ottoman my uncles had given Watson for Christmas, and he hopped up. Anticipating the moment, I'd gathered an assortment from the bakery and left them on a covered plate before we headed to the grand opening. I pulled out Watson's favorite all-natural dog treat bone, and he curled up and began chewing away with a contented grunt.

Snatching up one of the plain whip-cream-filled cream puffs I'd chosen from the bakery, I popped it in my mouth—not thinking of creepy doll heads for even a second, thank you very much—and then settled back into the crook of the sofa and let the light from the dusty purple portobello lampshade filter on to the first page of the newest JD Robb mystery. It had come out a couple of months before, but I'd been saving it for this moment. Well... actually for a moment that I'd thought would arrive several weeks before. At least it was finally there.

Before I read a word, I closed my eyes. I wasn't certain if I was savoring or making sure that the moment truly had arrived.

And it had. The gentle breeze rustled outside the window, the wood in the fireplace crackled and popped, Watson smacked and chomped happily. And that was all. No more bangs, hammers, crashes, or explosions from next door. My charming little bookshop was finally cozy once more.

Recipes provided by:

2716 Welton St Denver, CO 80205
(720) 708-3026

Click the links for more Rolling Pin deliciousness:

RollingPinBakeshop.com

Rolling Pin Facebook Page

KATIE'S CHOCOLATE ESPRESSO TORTE RECIPE

Ingredients:
- 1 pound and 2.25 oz dark chocolate
- 6 oz bittersweet chocolate
- 1 pound and 8.25 oz butter
- 12.25 oz granulated sugar
- 12.25 oz coffee, strong brewed
- 8 eggs, whole

Directions:

1. Grease 8" cake pan with shortening and line bottom with parchment paper.

2. Melt first 5 ingredients over double boiler.

3. Whisk eggs until they are smooth.

4. Whisk all ingredients together.

5. Pour into prepared cake pan.

6. Place into larger baking pan and add water until it reaches halfway up the side of 8" pan.

7. Bake for 30-40 minutes at 350 degrees (bake time will vary depending on oven). You should see mixture start to bubble.

8. Remove from oven and cool completely.

9. Refrigerate overnight

10. To remove from pan, place pan in shallow hot water for a minute. Invert onto serving plate.

11. Dust with powdered sugar and garnish with raspberries and serve. Great with ice cream on the side.

KATIE'S CREAM PUFF (PÂTE À CHOUX) RECIPE

Ingredients:
- 1 1/2 cups water
- 1 stick plus 1 tablespoon unsalted butter, cut into cubes
- 1 teaspoon sugar
- 1/2 teaspoon salt
- 200 grams all-purpose flour (about 1 1/2 cups)
- 8 large eggs

Directions:

1. Preheat the oven to 400°.

Line 2 large baking sheets with parchment paper.

2. In a large saucepan, combine the water, butter, sugar and salt and bring to a boil. Reduce the heat to moderate. Add the flour all at once and stir vigorously with a wooden spoon until a tight dough forms and pulls away from the side of the pan. Cook for 2 minutes until you get a nutty smell. Remove the pan from the heat. Place in electric mixing bowl. With paddle attachment, beat until cool.

3. In a bowl, beat 7 eggs and add to the dough in four batches, stirring vigorously between additions until the eggs

are completely incorporated and the pastry is smooth. The dough should be glossy and very slowly hang, stretch between two fingers. If necessary, beat in the remaining egg.

4. Transfer the dough to a piping bag fitted with a 1/2-inch plain tip. Pipe 1 1/2-inch mounds onto the baking sheets, leaving 1 inch between them.

5. Bake for 30-35 minutes without opening the oven. Check for doneness by lifting a puff. They should feel dry and lighter than they look.

6. Let cool and fill with whip cream, chocolate mousse or whatever filling you desire.

Cornbread recipe provided by:

The Baldpate Inn

1917   2017

Estes Park, Colorado

4900 South Hwy. 7, Estes Park, Co. 80517
(970) 586-6151

Click the links for details on Baldpate Inn. Fred and Watson highly recommend booking a room or stopping by for a scrumptious buffet:

Baldpate Inn

BALDPATE INN'S CORNBREAD RECIPE

Ingredients:
- 1 Cup Butter
- 1 Cup White Sugar
- 4 Eggs
- 2 Cups Creamed Corn
- ½ Cup Monterey Jack Cheese, grated
- ½ Cup Medium Cheddar Cheese, grated
- 1 Cup all-purpose White Flour
- 1 Cup yellow Cornmeal
- 4 teaspoons Baking Powder
- ¼ teaspoon Salt

Directions:

Preheat oven to 350 degrees. Using an electric mixer, cream butter and sugar, then add eggs one at a time. Gradually, mix in corn and cheeses. Stir in the remaining ingredients. Spread evenly in a greased 9 x 13 inch cake pan. Place in oven, close door and IMMEDIATELY reduce oven temperature to 300 degrees. Bake for 1 hour. Top will still seem

678   BALDPATE INN'S CORNBREAD RECIPE

moist-looking, not dry as with a cake. Center should be set, not gooey. Serve warm.

Although the Baldpate Inn is at the very high altitude of 9000 ft. this recipe works equally well at lower elevations. Just plan to make extra, because even folks that say they don't like cornbread, seem to love this recipe!! It does keep delicious and moist for hours – if hidden!

AUTHOR NOTE

Dear Reader:

Thank you so much for reading the forth collection of the Cozy Corgi Cozy Mystery series. If you enjoyed Fred and Watson's adventures, I would greatly appreciate a review on Amazon and Goodreads. You can review the collection, each book individually, or, even more wonderfully, both! Please drop me a note on Facebook or on my website (MildredAbbott.com) whenever you'd like. I'd love to hear from you. If you're interested in receiving advanced reader copies of upcoming installments, please join Mildred Abbott's Cozy Mystery Club on Facebook.

I also wanted to mention the elephant in the room... or the over-sugared corgi, as it were. Watson's personality is based around one of my own corgis, Alastair. He's the sweetest little guy in the world, and, like Watson, is a bit of a grump. Also, like Watson (and every other corgi to grace the world with their presence), he lives for food. In the Cozy Corgi series, I'm giving Alastair the life of his dreams through Watson. Just like I don't spend my weekends solving murders, neither does he spend his days snacking on scones and unending dog treats. But in the books? Well, we both get to live out our fantasies. If you are a corgi parent, you already know your little angel shouldn't truly have free rein of the pastry case, but you can read them snippets of Watson's life for a pleasant bedtime fantasy.

Much love, Mildred

PS: I'd also love it if you signed up for my newsletter. That way you'll never miss a new release. You won't hear from me more than once a month, nobody needs that many newsletters!

Newsletter link: Mildred Abbott Newsletter Signup

ACKNOWLEDGMENTS

A special thanks to Agatha Frost, who gave her blessing and her wisdom. If you haven't already, you simply MUST read Agatha's Peridale Cafe Cozy Mystery series. They are absolute perfection.

The biggest and most heartfelt gratitude to Katie Pizzolato, for her belief in my writing career and being the inspiration for the character of the same name in this series. Thanks to you, Katie, our beloved baker, has completely stolen both mine and Fred's heart!

Desi, I couldn't imagine an adventure without you by my side. A.J. Corza, you have given me the corgi covers of my dreams. A huge, huge thank you to all of the lovely souls who proofread the ARC versions and helped me look somewhat literate (in completely random order): Melissa Brus, Cinnamon, Ron Perry, Rob Andresen-Tenace, Anita Ford, TL Travis, Victoria Smiser, Lucy Campbell, Sue Paulsen, Bernadette Ould, Lisa Jackson, Kelly Miller, Gloria Lakritz, and Reg Franchi. Thank you all, so very, very much!

It is with all gratitude that I thank Lois Smith and Baldpate for allowing me to set a mystery in their historic inn for the book Killer Keys. I have such wonderful memories visiting it as a child and appreciate the food, views, and history even more when I visit now as an adult. It is such a treasured part of Estes Park's story. I'm beyond humbled that Fred and Watson were allowed to solve a murder while feasting on cornbread.

Janice Colomb, thank you for helping name Carla's shop, the Koffee Kiln—a stroke of brilliant (and probably caffeinated) genius.

Erica Chaillot, you came up with the PERFECT names for Delilah's Basset hounds. You're brilliant. Thank you!

Robyn Vyner-smith, thank you for naming Miles and Niles's store, Geek Out.

Nann Pollock-Tucker, your brilliance of the name Ark & Whale helped change the downtown of Estes Park! Thank you!

Brandi M. Nolan, Robin Powers, Donna Keevers-Driver, and the rest of the Mildred Abbott's Cozy Mystery Club on Facebook for such wonderful invention ideas to help fill up Twinventions!

A further and special thanks to some of my dear readers and friends who support my passion: Andrea Johnson, Fiona Wilson, Katie Pizzolato, Maggie Johnson, Marcia Gleason, Rob Andresen- Tenace, Robert Winter, Jason R., Victoria Smiser, Kristi Browning, and those of you who wanted to remain anonymous. You make a huge, huge, huge difference in my life and in my ability to continue to write. I'm humbled and grateful beyond belief! So much love to you all!

ALSO BY MILDRED ABBOTT

-the Cozy Corgi Cozy Mystery Series-

Cruel Candy

Traitorous Toys

Bickering Birds

Savage Sourdough

Scornful Scones

Chaotic Corgis

Quarrelsome Quartz

Wicked Wildlife

Malevolent Magic

Killer Keys

Perilous Pottery

Ghastly Gadgets

Meddlesome Money (Coming July 2019)

Made in the USA
Coppell, TX
20 September 2020

38482922R10404